Richard Woodman was born in London in 1944 and crewed in a Tall Ships race before becoming an indentured midshipman in cargo-liners at the age of sixteen. He has sailed in a variety of ships, including weather ships, lighthouse traders and trawlers, serving from apprentice to captain. He is the author of over twenty works of fiction and non-fiction, a member of the Royal Historical Society, the Society for Nautical Research, the Navy Records Society and the Square Rigger Club. In his spare time he sails an elderly gaff cutter with his wife and two children.

'This author has quietly stolen the weather-gauge from most of his rivals in the Hornblower stakes' *Observer*

'Packed with exciting incident, worthy of wide appeal to those who love thrilling nautical encounters and the sea' *Nautical Magazine*

The First Nathaniel Drinkwater Omnibus

An Eye of the Fleet
A King's Cutter
A Brig of War

RICHARD WOODMAN

timewarner
paperbacks

A *Time Warner* Paperback

This edition first published in Great Britain by Warner Books in 2000
Reprinted by Time Warner Paperbacks in 2003

Previously published separately:

An Eye of the Fleet
first published in Great Britain in 1981 by John Murray (Publishers) Ltd
Published by Sphere Books Ltd 1984
Reprinted 1987, 1989, 1990
Reprinted by Warner Books 1993
Reprinted 1995 (twice), 1996

A King's Cutter
first published in Great Britain in 1982 by John Murray (Publishers) Ltd
Published by Sphere Books Ltd 1984
Reprinted 1987, 1989, 1990
Reprinted by Warner Books 1993
Reprinted 1995 (twice), 1997

A Brig of War
first published in Great Britain in 1983 by John Murray (Publishers) Ltd
Published by Sphere Books Ltd 1984
Reprinted 1987, 1988, 1990
Reprinted by Warner Books 1995

The moral right of the author has been asserted.

A CIP catalogue record for this book is available from the British Library.

ISBN 0 7515 2979 6

Typeset in Palatino by M Rules
Printed and bound in Great Britain by Clays Ltd, St Ives plc

Time Warner Paperbacks
An imprint of
Time Warner Books UK
Brettenham House
Lancaster Place
London WC2E 7EN

www.TimeWarnerBooks.co.uk

An Eye of the Fleet

I am taking all Frigates about me I possibly can; for if I . . . let the Enemy escape for want of 'the eyes of the Fleet', I should consider myself as most highly reprehensible.

NELSON

Contents

Author's Note

The major incidents in this novel are matters of historical fact. Some of the peripheral characters, such as Admirals Kempenfelt and Arbuthnot, Captain Calvert, Jonathan Poulter and Wilfred Collingwood are also factual and the personalities, as depicted, tally with the images they have left later generations.

The exploits of *Cyclops*, though fictional, are both nautically and politically within the bounds of possibility. The continental currency of Congress was indeed worthless to the extent of almost ruining the Revolution. Fighting in the Carolinas and Georgia was characterised by atrocities, though the Galuda River does not exist.

No nautical claim has been made which was impossible. The details of the Moonlight Battle, for instance, can be verified from other sources, though the actual capture of *Santa Teresa* is *Cyclops*'s own 'part' in the action.

Pains have been taken over the accuracy of facts concerning the life on board men-of-war during the American War of Independence and pedants may like to note that at the time Drinkwater went to sea commissioned officers messed in the gunroom, midshipmen and master's mates in the cockpit. By the beginning of the next century the latter occupied the gunroom with the warrant officer gunner exercising a sort of parental authority and schoolmasters appointed to attempt the education of the 'young gentlemen'. By this time the officers had a grander 'wardroom'.

Chapter One

The Greenhorn

A baleful sun broke through the overcast to shed a patch of pale light on the frigate. The fresh westerly wind and the opposing flood tide combined to throw up a vicious sea as the ship, under topsails and staysails, drove east down the Prince's Channel clear of the Thames.

Upon her quarterdeck the sailing master ordered the helm eased to prevent her driving too close to the Pansand, the four helmsmen struggling to hold the ship as the wheelspokes flickered through their fingers.

'Mr Drinkwater!' The old master, his white hair streaming in the wind, addressed a lean youth of medium height with fine, almost feminine features and an unhealthily pallid complexion. The mid-shipman stepped forward, nervously eager.

'Sir?'

'My compliments to the Captain. Please inform him we are abeam of the Pansand Beacon.'

'Yes, sir.' He turned to go.

'Mr Drinkwater!'

'Sir?'

'Please repeat my message and answer correctly.'

The youth flushed deeply, his Adam's apple bobbing with embarrassment.

'Y . . . your compliments to the Captain and we're abeam the Pansand Beacon, aye, aye, sir.'

'Very good.'

Drinkwater darted away beneath the quarterdeck to where the red-coated marine sentinel indicated the holy presence of the Captain of His Britannic Majesty's 36-gun frigate *Cyclops*.

1

Captain Hope was shaving when the midshipman knocked on the door. He nodded as the message was delivered.

Drinkwater hovered uncertainly, not knowing whether he was dismissed. After what seemed an age the Captain appeared satisfied with his chin, wiped off the lather and began to tie his stock. He fixed the young midshipman with a pair of watery blue eyes set in a deeply lined and cadaverous face.

'And you are . . .?' He left the question unfinished.

'M . . . Mister Drinkwater, sir, midshipman . . .'

'Ah yes, it was the Rector of Monken Hadley requested your place, I recollect it well . . .' The Captain reached for his coat. 'Do your duty, cully, and you have nothing to fear, but make damned sure you know what your duty is . . .'

'Yes . . . I mean aye, aye, sir.'

'Very well. Tell the Master I'll be up shortly when I've finished my breakfast.'

Captain Hope smoothed the coat down and turned to look out through the stern windows as the door closed behind the retreating Drinkwater.

He sighed. He judged the boy to be old for a new entrant and yet he could not escape the thought that it might have been himself nearly forty years ago.

The Captain was fifty-six years of age. He had only held his post rank for three years. Devoid of patronage he would have died a half-pay commander had not an unpopular war with the rebellious American Colonies forced the Admiralty to employ him. Many competent naval officers had refused to serve against the colonists, particularly those with Whig sympathies and independent means. As the rebels acquired powerful allies the Royal Navy was stretched to the limit, watching the cautiously hostile Dutch, the partisan 'neutrals' of the Baltic and the actively hostile French and Spanish. In their plight their Lordships had scraped the barrel and in the lees at the bottom had discovered the able person of Henry Hope.

Hope was more than a competent seaman. He had served as lieutenant at Quiberon Bay and distinguished himself several times during the Seven Years' War. Command of a sloop had come at the end of the war, but by then he was forty with little hope of further advancement. He had a widowed mother, tended by a sister whose husband had fallen before Ticonderoga in Abercrombie's bungled attack, but no family of his own. He was a man used to care and tribulation, a man well suited to command of a ship.

But as he stared out of the stern windows at the yeasty, bubbling wake that cut a smooth through the choppy waters of the outer estuary, he remembered a more youthful Hope. Now his name silently taunted him. He idly wondered about the young man who had just left the cabin. Then he dismissed the thought as his servant brought in breakfast.

Cyclops anchored in the Downs for three days while she gathered a small convoy of merchantmen about her and waited for a favourable wind to proceed west. When she and her covey of charges weighed they thought they would carry a pleasant easterly down Channel. In the event the wind veered and for a week *Cyclops* beat to windward against the last of the equinoctial gales.

Nathaniel Drinkwater was forced to endure a brief, hard schooling. He lay aloft with the topmen, shivering with cold and terror as the recalcitrant topgallants billowed and thundered about his ears. There was no redress when an over-zealous bosun's mate accidentally sliced his buttocks with a starter. Cruelty was a fact of life and its evils were only augmented between the stinking decks of an overcrowded British man o'war. Worn out by a week's incessant labour in conditions of unaccustomed cold; forced by necessity to eat indifferent food washed down by small beer of incomparable badness; bullied and shouted at, Drinkwater had broken down one night.

He wept into his hammock with bitter loneliness. His dreams of glory and service to a grateful country melted into the desperate release of tears and in his misery he took refuge in thoughts of home.

He remembered his careworn mother, desperate to see her sons maintain their station in life; her delight when the Rector had called with a letter from the relative of a friend, a Captain Henry Hope, accepting Nathaniel as midshipman aboard *Cyclops*, and how jubilant she had been that her elder son at last had reached the respectability of a King's officer.

He wept too for his brother, the carefree, irrepressible Ned, who was always in trouble and whom the Rector himself had flogged for

3

scrumping apples: Ned with whom he used to practice single stick on Barnet common, of whom his mother used to say despairingly that only a father's firmness would make of him a gentleman. Ned had laughed at that, tossed his head and laughed, while across the room Nathaniel had caught his mother's eyes and been ashamed for his brother's callousness.

Nathaniel had only one recollection of his father, a dim, shadowy being who had tossed him in the air, smelled of wine and tobacco, and laughed wildly before dashing his own brains out in a riding accident. Ned had all his father's reckless passion and love of horses, while Nathaniel inherited the mother's quieter fortitude.

But upon that miserable night when fatigue, hunger, sickness, cold and hopelessness lay siege to his spirit, Nathaniel was exposed to the vicissitudes of fate and in the surrounding darkness his sobbing was overheard by his neighbour, the senior midshipman.

At dinner the following day as eight or nine of *Cyclops*'s dozen midshipmen struggled through their pease pudding, the president of the cockpit, Mr Midshipman Augustus Morris rose solemnly from his place at the head of the filthy table.

'We have a coward amongst us, gentlemen,' he announced, a peculiarly malevolent gleam in his hooded eyes. The midshipmen, whose ages varied between twelve and twenty-four, looked from one to another wondering on whom the wrath of Mr Morris was about to descend.

Drinkwater was already cringing under the onslaught he instinctively felt was destined for him. As Morris's eyes raked over the upturned faces they fell, one by one, to dumb regard of the pewter plates and tankards sliding about before them. None of them would encourage Morris neither would they interfere with whatever malice he had planned.

'*Mister* Drinkwater,' Morris sarcastically emphasised the title, 'I shall endeavour to correct your predilection for tears by compelling your arse to weep a little – get over that chest!'

Drinkwater knew it was pointless to resist. At the mention of his name he had risen unsteadily to his feet. He looked dumbly round at the indicated sea chest, his legs shaking but refusing to move. Then a cruel fate made *Cyclops* lurch and the tableau dissolved, Drinkwater was thrown across the chest by the forces of nature.

4

With an unnatural eagerness Morris flung himself on Drinkwater, threw aside the blue cloth coat-tails and, inserting his fingers in the waistband of Drinkwater's trousers, bared his victim's buttocks to an accompaniment of tearing calico. It was this act more than the six brutal stripes that Morris laid on his posterior that burnt itself into Drinkwater's memory. For his mother had laboured on those trousers, her arthritic fingers carefully passing the needle, the tears filling her eyes at the prospect of parting with her elder son. Somehow, with the resilience of youth, Drinkwater survived that passage to Spithead. Despite the pain in his buttocks he had been forced to learn much about the details of handling a ship under sail, for the westerly gale compelled the frigate to wear and wear again in a hard, ruthless fight to windward and it was the second week in October 1779 before she brought to her anchor in St Helen's Roads under the lee of Bembridge.

Hardly had *Cyclops* gathered sternway, her main topsail aback, and the cable gone rumbling through the hawse than the third lieutenant was calling away the captain's gig. Morris acted as the gig's coxswain. He ordered Drinkwater to the bow where a grinning seaman handed the youth a boat-hook. The gig bobbed alongside the wooden wales of the frigate's side, the hook lodged in the mainchains. Above him, but unseen, Drinkwater could hear the thumping of the marines' boots as they fell in at the entry port. Then came the twittering of the pipes. He looked up. At the entry port, fingers to his hat, stood Captain Hope. It was only the second time Drinkwater had seen him face to face since their brief interview. Their eyes met, the boy's full of awe, the man's blank with indifference. Hope turned around, grasped the manropes and leaned outboard. He descended the side until a foot above the gunwale of the boat he paused waiting for the boat to rise. As it did so he jumped aboard, landing with little dignity between stroke and second stroke. He clambered over the intervening thwart from which the seamen deferentially drew aside and sat himself down.

'Toss oars!' yelled Morris.

'Bear off forrard!' Drinkwater pushed mightily against his boat-hook. It caught in the iron work of the chains; he tried to disengage it as the boat's head fell off but it refused to move, its shaft drawing through his hand and sticking incongruously outwards from the ship's side. He leaned further outboard and grabbed the end of the handle, the sweat of exertion and humiliation poured off him. He lunged again and nearly fell overboard.

'Sit down forrard!' roared Morris, and Drinkwater subsided in the bows, his cup of agony overflowing.

'Give way together!'

The oars bit the water and groaned in the thole pins. In minutes the men's backs were dark with perspiration. Drinkwater darted a glance aft. Morris was staring ahead, his hand on the tiller. The captain was gazing abstractedly at the green shores of the Isle of Wight away to larboard.

Then a thought struck Drinkwater. He had left the boat-hook protruding from the frigate's side. What in God's name was he going to use when they reached the flagship? His mind was overcome by sudden panic as he cast about the bow sheets for another boat-hook. There was none.

For nearly twenty minutes as the gig danced over the sparkling sea and the westerly breeze dashed spray off the wavecaps, Drinkwater cast about him in an agony of indecision. He knew their destination was the flagship, *HMS Sandwich* of 90 guns, where even the seamen would look haughtily on the frigate's unremarkable gig. Any irregularities in the boat-handling would be commented upon to the disservice of *Cyclops*. Then a second thought struck him. Any such display of poor seamanship would reflect equally upon Mr Midshipman Morris and he was unlikely to let Drinkwater discredit him unscathed. The prospect of another beating further terrified the boy.

Drinkwater stared ahead of the boat. The low shore of Hampshire lay before him, the sun shining on the dun blocks of the forts at Gosport and Southsea, guarding the entrance to Portsmouth Harbour. Between the gig and the shoreline a long row of ships of the line lay at anchor, their hulls massive beneath the masts and crossed yards. Large ensigns snapped briskly at their sterns and the gaudy flutter of the union flags over their fo'c's'les gave the vista a festive air. Here and there the square flag of a rear or vice-admiral flew at a masthead. Sunlight glittered on gilded figureheads and quarter galleries as the battleships swung head to wind at the

6

slackwater. The sea surrounding them was dotted with small craft. Coastal vessels crowded on sail to avoid pulling boats of every conceivable size. Small launches and gigs conveyed officers and commanders; larger long boats and cutters under pint-size midshipmen or grizzled master's mates brought stores, powder or shot off from the dockyard. Water hoys and shallops, their civilian crews abusive under their protection from the press gangs, bucked alongside the battleships. A verbal duel between their masters and anxious naval lieutenants who waved requisition orders at them, seemed endless. The sheer energy and scale of activity was like nothing Drinkwater had ever witnessed before. They passed a small cutter aboard which half a dozen painted doxies sat, pallid with the boat's motion. Two of them waved saucily at the gig's crew amongst whom a ripple of lust passed at the unaccustomed sight of swelling bodices.

'Eyes in the boat!' yelled Morris self-importantly, himself glancing at the lushness exhibited by over-tight stays.

The *Sandwich* was nearer now and a cold sweat broke out again on Drinkwater's forehead. Then, by accident, he solved his problem. Wriggling round to view the prospect before him his hand encountered something sharp. He looked down. Beneath the grating he caught sight of something hook-like. He shifted his weight and lifted the slatted wood. In the bilge lay a small grapnel. It had an eye at the end of the shank. It was this that saved his backside another tanning. Fishing it out he bent on the end of the gig's painter and coiled the bight in his hand. He now possessed a substitute boat-hook and relaxed. Once again he looked about him.

It was a splendid sight. Beyond the line of battleships several frigates lay at anchor. They had already passed one lying as guardship at the Warner and had Drinkwater been less perturbed by the loss of his boat-hook he might have been more attentive. But now he could feast his eyes on a sight that his provincial breeding had previously denied him. Beyond Fort Gilkicker more masts rose from hulls grey blue with distance. Drinkwater's inexperienced eyes did not recognise the lines of transports.

It was a powerful fleet; a great effort by Britain to avert the threat to her West Indian possessions and succour the ailing ships on the North American station. For two years since the surrender of

Burgoyne's army Britain had been trying to bring the wily Washington to battle while simultaneously holding off the increasing combination of European enemies from snapping up distant colonies when her attention was occupied elsewhere.

That this effort had been further strained by the corruption, peculation and plain jobbery that infected public life in general and Lord Sandwich's navy in particular was not a matter to concern Drinkwater for grander spectacles were before him. As the gig drew close to the massive side of *Sandwich* Captain Hope drew the attention of Morris to something. The midshipman turned the boat head to sea.

'Oars!' he ordered and the blades rose dripping to the horizontal.

Drinkwater looked round for some reason for this cessation of activity. There was none as far as he could see. Looking again at *Sandwich* he noted a flurry about her decks.

Glittering officers in blue and white, pointed polished telescopes astern, in the direction of Portsmouth. Drinkwater could just see the crowns of the marines' black hats as they fell in. Then a drum rolled and the black specks were topped by a line of silver bayonets as the marines shouldered arms. A pipe shrilled out and all activity aboard *Sandwich* ceased. The great ship seemed to wait expectantly as a small black ball rose to the truck of her mainmast.

Then round her stern and into view from *Cyclops*'s gig swept an admiral's barge. At its bow fluttered the red cross of St George. The oarsmen bent to their task with unanimous precision, their red and white striped shirts moving in unison, their heads crowned by black beavers. A small dapper midshipman stood upright in the stern, hand on tiller. His uniform was immaculate, his hat set at a rakish angle. Drinkwater stared down at his own crumpled coat and badly cobbled trousers; he felt distinctly uncomfortable.

Also in the stem of the barge sat an old-looking man wrapped in a boat cloak. The lasting impression made on Drinkwater was a thin, hard mouth, then the barge was alongside *Sandwich* and Admiral Sir George Brydges Rodney was ascending the side of his flagship. A squeal of pipes, a roll of drums and a twinkle of light as the bayonets flashed to the present; at the main masthead the black ball broke out and revealed itself as the red cross of St George. At this sight the guns of the fleet roared out in salute.

8

Admiral Rodney had arrived to take command of the fleet.

A few minutes later Drinkwater hurled his grapnel at *Sandwich*'s mainchains. By good fortune it held first time and, to indifferent ceremonial, Captain Hope reported to his superior.

Chapter Two

January 1780

The Danish Brig

On New Year's Day, 1780, Rodney's armada was at sea. In addition to the scouting frigates and twenty-one line of battleships no less than three hundred merchantmen cleared the Channel that chill morning. In accordance with her instructions *Cyclops* was part of the escort attending the transports and so took no part in the action of 8th January.

A Spanish squadron of four frigates, two corvettes and the 64-gun ship *Guipuscoaño* was encountered off Cape Finisterre with a convoy of fifteen merchantmen. The entire force was surrounded and taken. Prize crews were put on board and the captured vessels escorted back to England by the *Guipuscoaño*, renamed *Prince William* in honour of the Duke of Clarence then a midshipman with the fleet. The captured vessels which contained victuals were retained to augment the supplies destined for Gibraltar.

As the concourse of ships plodded its slow way down the Iberian coast on the afternoon of the 15th, Drinkwater sat in the foretop of the *Cyclops*. It was his action station and he had come to regard it as something of his own domain, guarded as it was by its musket rests and a small swivel gun. Here he was free of the rank taint between decks, the bullying senselessness of Morris and here too, in the dog watches, he was able to learn some of the finer points of the seaman's art from an able seaman named Tregembo.

Young Nathaniel was quick to learn and impressed most of his superiors with his eager enthusiasm to attempt any task. But on this afternoon he was enjoying a rest, soaking up the unaccustomed luxury of January sunshine. It seemed impossible that only a couple of months previously he had known nothing of this life. So packed with events and impressions had the period been that it seemed another lifetime in which he had bid his widowed mother and younger brother farewell. Now, he reflected with the beginnings of pride, he was part of the complex organisation that made *Cyclops* a man o'war.

Drinkwater gazed over the ship which creaked below him. He saw Captain Hope as an old, remote figure in stark contrast to his first lieutenant. The Honourable John Devaux was the third son of an earl, an aristocrat to his fingertips, albeit an impoverished one, and a Whig to boot. He and Hope were political opponents and Devaux's haughty youth annoyed the captain. Henry Hope had been too long in the service to let it show too frequently since Devaux, with influence, was not to be antagonised. In truth, the younger man's competence was never in doubt. Unlike many of his class he had taken an interest in the business of naval war which was motivated by more than an instinct for survival. Had his politics been different or the government Whig he might have been in Hope's shoes and Hope in his. It was a fact both had the intelligence to acknowledge and though friction was never far from the surface it was always veiled.

As for *Cyclops* herself she had shaken down as well as any ship manned under the system of the press. Her crew had exercised at the great guns under their divisional officers and her signalling system had been sorely strained trying to maintain order amongst the unruly merchantmen but, by and large both captain and first lieutenant agreed, she would do. Hope had no illusions about glory so fanaticism was absent from his character. If his officers were able and his crew willing, he asked no more of them.

To Nathaniel Drinkwater dozing in his top *Cyclops* had become his only real world. His doubts had begun to evaporate under the influence of a change in the weather and youthful adaptability. He was slowly learning that the midshipmen's berth was an environment in which it was just possible to exist. Although he loathed Morris and disliked several of the older members of his mess, the majority were pleasant enough boys. They got on well together bearing Morris's bullying with fortitude and commiserating in their hatred of him.

Drinkwater regarded Lieutenant Devaux with awe and the old sailing master, Blackmore, whose duties included the instruction of the midshipmen in the rudiments of navigation, with the respect he might have felt for his father had the latter been living. The nearest he came to friendship was with the topman Tregembo who handled the foretop swivel gun in action. He proved an endless source of wisdom and information about the frigate and her minutiae. A Cornishman of uncertain age he had been caught with a dubious cargo in the fish-well of his father's lugger off the Lizard by a revenue cutter. His father had offered the officers armed resistance and been hanged for his pains. As an act of clemency his son was given a lighter sentence which, the justices assured the court, would mitigate the grief felt by the wife of the dastardly smuggler: impressment. Tregembo had hardly stepped ashore since.

Drinkwater smiled to himself feeling, up here in his little kingdom, the self-satisfaction of youth seeping through him. Below on deck one bell rang through the ship. He was on watch in fifteen minutes. He rose and looked up.

Above him the topmast met the topgallant and at the upper hounds sat the lookout. A mood of devilment seized him; he would ascend to the hounds and from there slide down the backstay to the deck. The long descent would be an impressive demonstration of his proficiency as a seaman. He began to climb.

Casting his leg over the topgallant yard he joined the man on lookout. Far below him *Cyclops* rolled gently. His view of the deck was broken by the bellying sails and lent perspective by the diminishing rigging, each rope leading down to its respective belaying pin or eyebolt.

The seaman made shift for him and Drinkwater looked around. The blue circle of the sea was broken by some two hundred odd white specks as the armada sailed south. In that direction, below the horizon, the advanced frigates reconnoitred. Behind them in three divisions came the dark hulls of the ships of the line, a few of them wearing the yellow gunstrakes that would soon become uniform. In the centre of the middle column *Sandwich* carried Admiral Rodney, the man responsible for all this puissance. Behind the battleships a couple of cutters and a schooner, tenders to the fleet, followed like dogs in the wake of their master. Then in a great mass came the convoy of troopships, storeships, cargo vessels with an escort of four frigates and two sloops of war. *Cyclops*'s station on the inshore bow of the convoy made her the nearest frigate to the rear division of battleships and the most advanced ship of the convoy itself.

From his elevated position Drinkwater looked out to larboard. Eight or nine leagues distant, slightly dun coloured in the westering sun, the coast of Portugal was clearly visible. His eyes raked over the horizon casually and he was about to descend to the deck when his attention was caught by an irregularity. A small speck of white almost abeam of them was set against the backdrop of the coast. He nudged the seaman and pointed.

'Sail, sir,' the man responded matter-of-factly.

'Yes – I'll hail,' then in as manly a voice as he could muster: 'Deck there!'

Faintly the voice of Keene, the third lieutenant came back, 'Aye, aye?'

'Sail eight points to larboard!' Drinkwater reached for the back-stay and began his spectacular hand over hand descent. In the excitement of the strange sail nobody noticed him.

'Signal from flag, sir,' said Lieutenant Keene to Captain Hope as Drinkwater came aft.

'Well?'

'Our number. Chase.'

'Acknowledge,' said the Captain, 'Mr Keene put the ship before the wind.'

Drinkwater assisted making up the answering signal as the lieutenant turned to bellow orders through his speaking trumpet. Bosun's mates chivvied the people and the helm was put up. *Cyclops* swung to the east, the braces rattling through the sheaves as the yards swung round.

'All sail if you please Mr Keene.'

'Aye, aye, sir!' There was enthusiasm in the lieutenant's voice and a ripple of excitement ran through the ship. Free of the con-strictions necessary in keeping station the frigate spread her wings. Clew and bunt-lines were cast off the pins as the topmen spread out along the footropes loosening the canvas. As the master's mates sta-tioned at the bunt of each sail waved to the deck the order was given to sheet home. The topgallants billowed, collapsed and billowed

13

again as the waisters tallied on to the halliards and the yards rose from the caps. *Cyclops* leaned to the increase of power, the hempen rigging drew tight and the vessel began to tremble gently as she gathered speed. The frigate surged through the dark Atlantic, the white vee of her wake creaming out from under her transom.

On deck the watch changed and the waist cleared as men, drawn on deck by the excitement, went below again.

Drinkwater found the captain staring at him. 'Sir?' he ventured.

'Mr, er . . .'

'Drinkwater, sir.'

'Ahh. Mr Drinkwater take a glass to the foremasthead and see what you make of her. D'you think you can do that?'

'Aye, aye, sir.' Drinkwater took from a rack an exceedingly battered telescope which was provided by a generous Navy Board for the exclusive use of the ship's 'young gentlemen'. He started for the foremast rigging.

It was nearly a quarter of an hour before he returned to the deck. Aware that Hope was testing his ability he had waited until he had something positive to report.

He touched his hat to the captain.

'She's a brig, sir. Not flying colours, sir.'

'Very well, Mr Drinkwater.'

'See her from the deck now, sir,' drawled Devaux who had come up on deck.

The captain nodded. 'Clear away the bow chasers, Mr Devaux . . .'

Drinkwater too could see the two masted vessel they were bearing down upon. He watched for the bright spot of colour that must surely appear soon to denote her nationality. A dozen other telescopes were endeavouring to glean the same information. A red speck rose to her peak, red with a white cross.

'Danish!' A dozen people snapped out simultaneously.

Cyclops tore down on her quarry and on a nod from Hope a gun barked from forward, its smoke rolling slowly ahead of the onrushing frigate.

A white spout rose ahead of the Danish ship. It was a cable short but it had the desired effect as the Dane backed his main topsail and hove to.

14

'Mr Devaux, you'll board.'

Orders flew. Where previously every idler in the ship had been intently watching the chase, chaos erupted. Out of this apparent disorder the main and forecourses rose in their bunt-lines and groups of organised men appeared to lower the lee quarter boat as *Cyclops* turned to back her main topsail.

Devaux shouted more orders and Drinkwater heard his own name in the confusion.

'Get in that boat, cully!' roared the first lieutenant and Nathaniel ran to the waist where a net had been flung over the side. The boat's crew were aboard but extra seamen armed with cutlasses were swarming down into her. Drinkwater cocked a foot over the rail, caught the leg of his trousers on a belaying pin and heard the fabric rip. But this time it did not seem to matter.

He scrambled down into the boat. To his surprise Devaux was already there, still shouting.

'Where in God's name is Wheeler?' he roared at nobody in particular. Then as the red-coated marine lieutenant and six of his men clumsily descended the netting, their Tower muskets tangling in the cordage, 'Come on you bloody lobsters!' Devaux yelled to the appreciative grins of the seamen. Lieutenant Wheeler resented the insult to his service, but he was unable to retaliate due to his preoccupation with getting himself and his hanger into the boat without a total loss of dignity.

'Shove off! Out oars! Give way together and put your backs into it!'

The big boat drove forward and Devaux pushed the tiller into Drinkwater's hand.

'Take her alongside his lee side and keep her there.' He turned to Wheeler, 'She's a neutral so don't board unless you hear me shout.' He raised his voice, 'Bosun's mate!' The petty officer with the armed seamen stood up in the bow.

'Sir?'

'Make no attempt to board unless I need help – if I shout I want the whole bloody lot of you!'

The seamen grinned and fingered their blades. Minutes later Drinkwater's cracking voice was bellowing 'Oars! . . . Toss Oars! . . . Hook on!' Lieutenant Devaux leapt for the Dane's chains. For a second or two his elegant legs dangled incongruously, then he had hoisted himself to the deck of the brig.

The boat bounced up and down the side of the strange ship. Occasionally a towheaded face looked curiously overside at them. All in the boat were nervous. A few cannon balls dropped from the rail would plummet through the boat's planking. It seemed to Drinkwater that the first lieutenant had been gone hours. He watched the rail advance and recede as the Atlantic shoved the boat up the Dane's side then dropped her down again. He looked anxiously at Wheeler. The marine officer just smiled, 'Don't worry, cully. When the Hon John is in trouble he'll squeal.'

At last, to his infinite relief, Drinkwater saw Devaux's legs swing over the rail. He heard the lieutenant's suave voice, all trace of coarseness gone,

'Yer servant ma'am,' and the next instant he had tumbled into the boat. He grabbed the tiller from Drinkwater without ceremony.

'Shove off! . . . Oars! . . . Give way together and pull you buggers!' Devaux crouched in the stern, his body bent with urgency.

'Pull! Pull! Pull like you'd pull a Frenchman off Yer mother!' The men grinned at the obscenity. Devaux knew his business and the seamen bent their oar looms with effort, the blades sprang from the water and flew forward for the next stroke. Astern of them the Dane made sail. Once Devaux looked back and, following his gaze, Drinkwater made out a flash of colour where a woman waved.

'Wheeler,' said Devaux, 'we've work to do.' Quite deliberately Devaux told Wheeler the news. He knew the men within hearing would pass it on to the lower deck. Equally he knew Hope would not bother to do so, only a garbled version might reach the innermost recesses of Cyclops unless Devaux disseminated the information himself. These men could shortly be called upon to die and the first lieutenant sought to infect them with blood lust. He had seen what a fighting madness such enthusiasm could induce in British seamen and he knew Cyclops might need just such an infection in the coming hours.

'That Dane has just sailed from Cadiz. The Dons are at sea, a fleet of 'em. Bit of luck he was pro-British.' He paused reflectively. 'Married to an English girl. Damned handsome woman too . . .'

he grinned, the marines grinned too – the message was going home.

It was dark when *Cyclops* rejoined the fleet. A full moon enabled Hope to take her in amongst the concourse of ships to where the three horizontal lanterns in *Sandwich*'s rigging marked the presence of the Admiral.

Shortening sail the frigate sent a boat across and Devaux had reported to Rodney. The outcome of this momentous news was that *Cyclops* had been ordered to make sail and warn the advance frigates. The fleet had shortened sail at sunset to avoid dispersal and aid station keeping so that *Cyclops* soon drew ahead of the battleships, passing down the regular lines of massive sides which dwarfed the swifter frigate as they lumbered along, creaking in the moonlight.

At dawn Cyclops was in sight of the frigates. Astern of her the fleet's topsails were just visible with one ship, the two decked seventy-four-gun *Bedford*, crowding on sail to come up with the cruisers.

Hampered by the poor signalling code in use Hope had difficulty in conveying the meaning of his message to the more distant frigates. By a happy coincidence, however, he chose 'Clear for action' and two hours later *Bedford* came up flying the same signal, her two lines of gun muzzles already visible, for Rodney had thrown out the order to his fleet at dawn.

At the first beat of the marine drummer's sticks Drinkwater had sensed the tension in *Cyclops*. He raced for his station in the foretop where the swivel was loaded and primed. But there was no occasion for haste. All morning the British stood at action stations without any sign of the enemy. During the forenoon division after division of the fleet had altered course to the south east, rounding the pink cliffs of Cape Saint Vincent and heading for the Straits of Gibraltar. At noon half of *Cyclops*'s company stood down for a meal of beer, flip and biscuit.

After a hasty meal Drinkwater, eager not to miss a moment of what popular comment was saying would be a fleet action, returned to the foretop. He looked around him. The frigates had drawn back on the main body and *Bedford* had come up to occupy the inshore station.

In the foretop his men had loaded their muskets. Tregembo was musingly caressing the toy swivel gun. Astern in the main top Morris's blue coat could clearly be seen. He was bending over a young Devon seaman whose good looks had excited some crude jibes from his messmates. Drinkwater could not quite identify the feeling engendered by the sight of Morris thus engaged beyond the fact that it was vaguely disquieting. He was still a comparative innocent to the perversions of humanity.

Astern of Morris Sergeant Hagan commanded the mizzen top and its marine sharpshooters. Their scarlet coats were a splash of vivid colour against the black hemp rigging that almost obscured the view. Looking down Nathaniel had an unimpeded view of the quarterdeck as, cleared for action, the maincourse and cross-jack were clewed up.

He saw Captain Hope and Lieutenant Devaux there with the old sailing master standing by the quartermaster and helmsmen. A gaggle of midshipmen and master's mates were also in attendance to run messages and transmit signals. But as well as blue there was scarlet aft. Wheeler, resplendent in his brilliant coat, crimson sash and the glittering gorget of a military officer had his hanger drawn. He carried it negligently in the crook of his arm but the flash of its blade was a wicked reminder of death. It was very different from the ash single stick Drinkwater had thrust and parried with at home. He had not much considered death or the possibility of dying. Falling from the rigging had at first terrified him but he had overcome that. But supposing a mast, the foremast perhaps, was shot away? He looked down again to where nets were stretched above the deck to keep falling spars and rigging off the guns' crews toiling below. At the moment those gun crews were lazing around their pieces. Just visible to Nathaniel, below him on the main deck, beneath the gratings the second and third lieutenants conferred with one another on the frigate's centreline. Their demeanour was studiously casual as they waited to command their batteries.

Apart from the creaking of the ship's fabric, the passage of the wind and the noise of her bow wave, *Cyclops* was a silent thing. Upwards of two hundred and fifty men waited expectantly, as did the crews of all the fleet.

At one o'clock in the afternoon *Bedford* fired a gun, signalled

18

Sandwich and let fly her topsail sheets. For those too distant to see the signal the flutter of her topsails was a time honoured indication of the presence of an enemy fleet in sight.

'Wind's getting up,' said Tregembo to no one in particular but breaking the silence in the foretop.

The Moonlight Battle

The battle that followed was one of the most dramatic ever fought by the Royal Navy. The waters over which the opposing fleets contended were to be immortalised twenty-five years later when Nelson was to conquer and die off Cape Trafalgar, but the night action of the 16th/17th January 1780 was to be known by no geographical name.

In an age when admirals were absolutely bound, upon pain of death, to the tactical concept of the unbroken line ranged against that of the enemy, Rodney's unleasing of his ships was an innovation of the utmost importance, and the manner of its doing in that wild Moonlight Battle was an act of daring unsurpassed by sailing warships in such large numbers.

Tregembo had been right. An hour after *Bedford*'s sighting of eleven Spanish battleships and two frigates the sky had clouded over. The wind backed westerly and began to freshen.

At *Bedford*'s signal Rodney had thrown out the 'General Chase' to his warships. Each captain now sought to out-do the rest and the vessels fitted with the new copper bottoms forged ahead. The two-deckers *Defence*, *Resolution* and *Edgar* began taking the lead. Officers anxiously checked their gear as captains, reckless as schoolboys, held on to sail. Still the wind rose. Telescopes trained with equal anxiety on the Spaniards who, faced with such overwhelming odds, turned away to leeward and the shelter of Cadiz.

Seeing the retrograde movement Rodney signalled his ships to engage from leeward, thereby conveying to his captains the tactical concept of overhauling the enemy and interposing themselves between the Spanish and safety.

It had become a race.

As the British ships tore forward dead before the wind, puffs of smoke appeared from their fo'c's'les as gunners tried ranging shots. At first the plumes of water, difficult to see among breaking wave crests, were a long way astern of the Spaniards. But slowly, as the minutes ran into an hour, they got nearer.

Aboard *Cyclops* Devaux stood poised on the fo'c's'le glass to eye as the frigate's long nine-pounders barked at the enemy as she lifted her bow. Almost directly above Drinkwater watched eagerly. His inexperienced eyes missed the fall of shot but the excitement of the scene riveted his attention. *Cyclops* trembled with the thrill of the chase and giving expression to the corporate feeling of the ship, O'Malley, the mad Irish cook, sat cross-legged on the capstan top scraping his fiddle. The insane jig was mixed with the hiss and splash of the sea around them and the moan of the gale as it strummed the hempen rigging.

Captain Hope had taken *Cyclops* across the slower *Bedford*'s bows and was heading for the northernmost Spaniard, a frigate of almost equal size. To the south of their quarry the high stern of the Spanish line of battleships stretched in a ragged line, the second frigate hidden behind them to the east.

A sudden column of white rose close to the *Cyclops*'s plunging bowsprit. Drinkwater looked up. Held under the galleries of a Spanish two-decker by the following wind a puff of white smoke lingered.

Tregembo swore. 'That's good shooting for Dagoes,' he said. It was only then that Drinkwater realised he was under fire.

As *Cyclops* crossed the stern of the two-decker in chase of the frigate the battleships had tried a ranging shot. Suddenly there was a rush of air and the sound of two corks being drawn from bottles. Looking up Drinkwater saw a hole in the fore-topsail and another in the main. It was uncomfortably close. As their sterns rose to the following seas the Spaniards were firing at the oncoming British silhouetted against the setting sun.

Drinkwater shivered. The brief winter warmth was gone and the fresh breeze had become a gale. He looked again at the Spanish fleet. They were appreciably nearer. Then he saw two plumes of white rise under the Spaniard's quarter. Their own guns were silent. He looked interrogatively at Tregembo.

'What the . . .?' Then the seaman pointed.

21

To starboard, hidden from the huddling midshipman by the mast, *Resolution*, a newly coppered seventy-four, was passing the frigate. Conditions now favoured the heavier ships. *Resolution* was overhauling the Spaniards rapidly and beyond her *Edgar* and *Defence* were bearing down on the enemy. Before the sun set behind a bank of cloud its final rays picked out the *Resolution*.

The almost horizontal light accentuated every detail of the scene. The sea, piling up from the west, its shadowed surfaces a deep indigo, constantly moving and flashing golden where it caught the sun, seemed to render the warship on it a thing of stillness. The *Resolution*'s hull was dark with the menace of her larboard batteries as she passed scarcely two cables from *Cyclops*. Her sails drew out, pulling the great vessel along, transmitting their power down through the masts and rigging until the giant oak hull with its weight of artillery and 750 men made ten knots through the water.

Drinkwater could see the heads of her upper-deck gunners and a line of red and silver marines on the poop. At her stern and peak battle ensigns stood out, pointing accusingly at the enemy ahead. Her bow chasers barked again. This time there was no white column. Devaux's glass swung round. 'She's hit 'em, by God!' he shouted.

Somebody on the fo'c's'le cheered. He was joined by another as *Cyclops*'s crew roared their approval at the sight of *Resolution* sailing into battle. Drinkwater found himself cheering wildly with the other men in the top. Tears poured down Tregembo's cheeks. 'The bastards, the fucking bastards . . .' he sobbed. Drinkwater was not sure who the bastards were, nor, at the time, did it seem to matter. It is doubtful if Tregembo himself knew. What he was expressing was his helplessness. The feeling of magnificent anger that overcame these men: the impressed, the drunkards, the gaol birds and the petty thieves. All the dregs of eighteenth-century society forced into a tiny hull and kept in order by a ruthless discipline, sailed into a storm of lead and iron death cheering. Stirring to their souls by emotions they could not understand or control, the sight of puissant *Resolution* had torn from their breasts the cheers of desperation. It is with such spontaneous inspiration that the makers of war have always gulled their warriors and transformed them into heroes. Thus did the

22

glamour of action infect these men with the fighting anger that served their political masters supremely well.

Perhaps it was to the latter that the barely articulate Tregembo alluded.

'Silence! Silence there!' Hope was roaring from the quarterdeck and the cheering died as men grinned at one another, suddenly sheepish after the outburst of emotion.

Faintly across the intervening sea a cheer echoed from *Resolution* and Drinkwater realised *Cyclops* must appear similarly magnificent from the seventy-four. A shudder of pride and cold rippled his back.

Before darkness isolated the admiral from his ships Rodney threw out a final command to his captains: 'Engage the enemy more closely.' He thus encouraged them to press the enemy to the utmost degree. Both fleets were tearing down upon a lee shore with off-lying shoals. By five o'clock it was nearly dark. The wind had risen to a gale and gloomy clouds raced across the sky. But the moon was rising, a full yellow moon that shone forth from between the racing scud, shedding a fitful light upon the baleful scene.

At sunset *Resolution*, *Edgar* and *Defence* had drawn level with the rearmost Spanish ships. Exchanging broadsides as they passed they kept on, heading the leeward enemy off from Cadiz.

'Larboard battery make ready!' The order rang out. Drinkwater transferred his attention to port as *Cyclops* was instantly transformed. The waiting was over, tension was released as gunners leapt to their pieces and the British frigate rode down the Spanish.

The enemy was close on *Cyclops*'s larboard bow. Below Drinkwater a chaser rang out and a hole appeared in the Spaniard's main topsail.

Devaux ran aft along the larboard gangboard. He was yelling orders to the lieutenants on the gun-deck below. He joined Hope on the quarterdeck where the two men studied their enemy. At last the captain called one of the midshipmen over.

'M'compliments to Lieutenant Keene, when his battery engages he is to cripple the rigging . . .'

The boy scrambled below. Hope wanted the Spaniard immobilised before both ships, distracted by the fury of battle, ran down to leeward where the low Spanish coast lay. Offshore the shoal of San Lucar waited for the oncoming ships of both nations.

'Mr Blackmore,' Hope called over the sailing master.

'Sir?'

'The San Lucar shoal, how far distant?'

'Three or four leagues, sir,' answered the old man after a moment's consideration.

'Very well. Post a mate forward on the fore t'gallant yard. I want to know the instant that shoal is sighted.'

A master's mate went forward. On his way aloft he passed Drinkwater who stopped him with a question.

'Old man's worried about the shoals to looard,' the mate informed him.

'Oh!' said Drinkwater looking ahead of the frigate. But all he could see was a tumbling waste of black and silver water as clouds crossed the moon, the spume smoking off the wave crests as they tumbled down wind.

A squealing of gun trucks told where the men of the larboard gun battery were hand-spiking their carriages round to bear on the enemy. The Spanish frigate was ahead of *Cyclops* but when the British ship drew abeam they would be about two cables distant.

'Make ready!'

The order was passed along the dark gun-deck. In his foretop Drinkwater checked the swivel. Under the foot of the topsail he could see the high Spanish poop. Tregembo swung the swivel gun round and pointed it at where he judged the Spanish officers would be. The other seamen cocked their muskets and drew beads on the enemy's mizen top where they knew Spanish soldiers would be aiming at their own officers.

The Spanish frigate was only two points forward of *Cyclops*'s beam. In the darkness of the gun-deck Lieutenant Keene, commanding the larboard battery of twelve-pounders, looked along the barrel of his aftermost gun. When it bore on the enemy's stern his entire broadside would be aimed at the frigate.

A midshipman dodged up to him touching his hat. 'Captain's compliments, sir, and you may open fire when your guns bear.' Keene acknowledged and looked along the deck. Accustomed to the gloom he could see the long line of cannon, lit here and there by lanterns. The men were crouched round their pieces tensely awaiting the order to open fire. The gun captains looked his way

24

expectantly, each grasping his linstock. Every gun was shotted canister on ball . . .

A ragged flash of fire flickered along the Spaniard's side. The noise of the broadside was muted by the gale. Several balls thumped home into the hull, tearing off long oak splinters and sending them lancing down the crowded decks. A man screamed, another was lifted bodily from the deck and his bloodily pulped corpse smashed against a cannon breech.

Aloft holes appeared in the topgallant sails and the master's mate astride the fore topgallant yard had his shoes ripped off by the passage of a ball. With a twang several ropes parted, the main royal yard, its sail furled, came down with a rush.

Orders were shouted at the topmen to secure the loose gear.

Meanwhile Keene still watched from his after gun-port. He could see nothing but sea and sky, the night filled with the raging of the gale and the responsive hiss of the sea.

Then the stern of the Spanish frigate plunged into view, dark and menacing; another ragged broadside rippled along her side. He stepped back and waited for the upward roll:

'Fire!'

Chapter Four

The Spanish Frigate

Frigates varied in size and design but basically they comprised a single gun-deck running the full length of the ship. In battle the temporary bulkheads providing the captain and officers' accommodation were removed when the ship cleared for action. Above the gun-deck and running forward almost to the main mast was the quarterdeck from where the ship was conned. A few light cannon and anti-personnel weapons were situated here. At the bow a similar raised deck, or fo'c's'le, extended aft round the base of the foremast. The fo'c's'le and quarterdeck were connected along the ship's side by wooden gangways which extended over that part of the gun-deck otherwise exposed and known as 'the waist'. However the open space between the gangways was beamed in and supported chocks for the ship's boats so that the ventilation that the opening was supposed to provide the gun-deck was, at best, poor.

When the larboard battery opened fire the confined space of the gun-deck became a cacophonous hell. The flashes of the guns alternately plunged the scene from brilliance to blackness. Despite the season of the year the seamen were soon running in sweat as they sponged, rammed and fired their brutish artillery. The concussion of the guns and rumbling of the trucks as they recoiled and were hauled forward again was deafening. The tight knots of men laboured round each gun, the lieutenants and master's mates controlling their aim as they broke from broadsides to firing at will. Dashing about the sanded deck the little powder monkeys, scraps of under-nourished urchins, scrambled from the gloomier orlop deck below to where the gunner had retired in his felt slippers to preside over the alchemical mysteries of cartridge preparation.

At the companionways the marine sentries stood, bayonets fixed to their loaded muskets. They had orders to shoot any but approved messengers or stretcher parties on their way to the orlop. Panic and cowardice were thus nicely discouraged. The only way for a man to pass below was to be carried to Mr Surgeon Appleby and his mates who, like the gunner, held their own esoteric court in the frigate's cockpit. Here the midshipmen's chests became the ship's operating theatre and covered with canvas provided Appleby with the table upon which he was free to butcher His Majesty's subjects. A few feet above the septic stink of rat-infested bilges, in a foetid atmosphere lit by a few guttering oil lamps, the men of Sandwich's navy came for succour and often breathed their last.

Cyclops fired seven broadsides before the two ships drew abeam. The Spaniards fired back with increasing irregularity as the dreadful precision of the British cannon smashed into their vessel's fabric.

Even so they carried away *Cyclops*'s mizen mast above the upper hounds. More rigging parted and the main topsail, shot through in a dozen places, suddenly dissolved into a flapping, cracking mess of torn canvas as the gale finished the work the cannon balls had started.

Suddenly the two frigates were abeam, the sea rushing black between them. The moon appeared from behind the obscurity of a cloud. Details of the enemy stood out and etched themselves into Drinkwater's brain. He could see men in the tops, officers on her quarterdeck and the activity of gun crews on the upper deck. A musket ball smacked into the mast above him, then another and another.

'Fire!' he yelled unnecessarily loudly at his topmen. Astern of him the main top loosed off, then Tregembo fired the swivel. Drinkwater saw the scatter of the langridge tearing up the Spaniard's decks. He watched fascinated as a man, puppet-like in the bizarre light, fell jerking to the deck with a dark stain spreading round him. Someone lurched against Drinkwater and sat down against the mast. A black hole existed where the man's right eye had been. Drinkwater caught his musket and sighted along it. He focussed on a shadowy figure reloading in the enemy's main top. He did it as coolly as shooting at Barnet fair, squeezing the trigger. The flint sparked and the musket jerked against his shoulder. The man fell.

27

Tregembo had reloaded the swivel and the moon disappeared behind a cloud as it roared.

The concussion wave of a terrific explosion swept the two vessels, momentarily stopping the combatants. Away to the south six hundred men had ceased to exist as the seventy-gun *San Domingo* blew up, fire reaching her magazine and causing her disintegration.

The interruption of the explosion reminded them all of the other ships engaged to the southward. Drinkwater reloaded the musket. Enemy balls no longer whizzed round him. He looked up levelling the barrel. The Spanish frigate's mainmast leaned drunkenly forward. Stays snapped and the great spars collapsed dragging the mizen topmast with it. *Cyclops* drew ahead.

Hope and Blackmore stared anxiously astern where the crippled Spaniard wallowed. Wreckage hung over her side as she swung to starboard. If the Spanish captain was quick he could rake *Cyclops*, his whole broadside pouring in through the latter's wide stern and the shot travelling the length of the crowded decks.

It was every commander's nightmare to be raked, especially from astern where the comparative fragility of the stern windows offered little resistance to the enemy shot. The wreckage over her side was drawing the Spaniard round. One of her larboard guns fired and splinters shot up from *Cyclops*'s quarter. Certainly someone appreciated the opportunity.

Cyclops's helm was put down in an attempt to bring *Cyclops* on a parallel course but the spanker burst as the Spaniard fired, then the mizen topmast went and *Cyclops* lost the necessary leverage to force her stern round.

It was a ragged broadside compared with that of the British but its effects were no less lethal. Although nearly a quarter of a mile distant, the damaged enemy had fought back with devastating success. As Captain Hope surveyed the damage with Devaux a voice hailed them:

'Deck there! Breakers on the lee bow!'

Although the British frigate had started her turn the loss of her after sails deprived her of manoeuvrability. There were anxious faces on the quarterdeck.

The officers looked aloft. The lower mizen mast still stood, broken off some six feet above the top. The wreckage was hanging over the larboard side, dragging the frigate back that way while the gale in the forward sails still drove the ship inexorably downwind to where the San Lucar shoal awaited them. Axes were already at work clearing the raffle.

Hope saw a chance and ordered the helm hard over to continue the swing to port. Devaux looked forward and then at the captain.

'Set the cro'jack, bend on a new spanker and get the fore tops'l clewed up!' The captain snapped at him. The first lieutenant ran forward screaming for topmen, anyone, pulling the upperdeck gun crews from their pieces, thrusting bosun's mates here and there . . .

Men raced for the rigging . . . disappeared below, hurrying and scurrying under the first lieutenant's hysterical direction.

'Wheeler, get your lobsters to brace the cro'jack yard!'

'Aye, aye, sir!'

Wheeler's booted men stomped away with the mizen braces as the topmen shook out the sail. A master's mate unmade the weather sheet, he was joined by another, they both hauled as two or three seamen under a bosun's mate loosed the clew and bunt-lines. The great sail exploded white in the moonlight, flogging in the gale; then it drew taut and *Cyclops* began to swing.

Still in his top Drinkwater could see the shoal now, a line of grey ahead of them perhaps four or five miles away. He became aware of a voice hailing him.

'Foretop there!'

'Aye sir?' he looked over the edge at the first lieutenant staring up at him.

'Aloft and furl that tops'l!'

Drinkwater started up. The fore topsail was already losing its power as the sheets slackened and the clew and bunt-lines drew it up to the yard. It was flogging madly, the trembling mast attesting to the fact that many of its stays must have been shot away.

Tregembo was already in the rigging as Drinkwater forsook the familiar top. He was lightheaded with the insane excitement of the night. When they had finished battling with the sail Drinkwater lay over the yard exhausted with hunger and cold. He looked to starboard. The white line on the bank seemed very near now and *Cyclops* was rolling as the swell built up in the shoaling water. But she was reaching now, sailing across the wind and roughly parallel with the shoal. She would still make leeway but she was no longer running directly on to the bank.

To the south and west dark shapes and flashes told of where the two fleets did battle. Nearer, and to larboard now, the Spanish frigate wallowed, beam on to wind and sea and rolling down on to the shoal.

Drawn from the gun-deck a party of powder-blackened and exhausted men toiled to get the spare spanker on deck. The long sausage of hard canvas snaked out of the tiers and on to the deck. Thirteen minutes later the new sail rose on the undamaged spars.

Cyclops was once more under control. The cross-jack was furled and the headsail sheets slackened. Again her bowsprit turned towards the shoal as Hope anxiously wore ship to bring her on to the starboard tack, heading where the Spanish frigate still wallowed helplessly.

The British frigate paid off before the wind. Then her bowsprit swung away from the shoal. The wind came over the starboard quarter . . . then the beam. The yards were hauled round, the head-sail sheets hardened in. The wind howled over the starboard bow, stronger now they were heading into it. *Cyclops* plunged into a sea and a shower of stinging spray swept aft. Half naked gunners scurried away below to tend their cannon.

Hope gave orders to re-engage as *Cyclops* bore down on her adversary, slowly drawing the crippled Spaniard under her lee.

Cyclops's guns rolled again and the Spaniard fired back.

Devaux was shouting at Blackmore above the crash of the guns. 'Why don't he anchor, Master?'

'And have us reach up and down ahead of him raking him?' scoffed the older man.

'What else can he do? Besides there's a limit to how long we can hang on here. What we want is offing . . .'

Hope heard him. Released from the tension of immediate danger now his command was again under control, the conversation irritated him.

'I'll trouble you to fight the ship, Mr Devaux, and leave the tactical decisions to me.'

Devaux was silent. He looked sullenly at the Spanish ship and was astonished at Hope's next order: 'Get a hawser through an after port, quickly man, quickly!' At first Devaux was uncomprehending then the moon broke forth again and the lieutenant followed Hope's pointing arm, 'Look man, look!'

The red and gold of Castile was absent from the stern. The Spanish frigate had struck.

'Cease fire! Cease fire!'

Cyclops's guns fell silent as she plunged past the enemy, the exhausted gunners collapsing with their exertions. But Devaux, all thoughts of arguing dispelled by the turn of events, was once more amongst them, rousing them to further efforts. Devaux shouted orders, bosun's mates swung their starters and the realisation of the Spanish surrender swept the ship in a flash. Fatigue vanished in a trice for she was a war prize if they could save her from going ashore on the San Lucar shoal.

Even the aristocratic Devaux did not despise his captain's avarice. The chance of augmenting his paltry patrimony would be eagerly seized upon. He found himself hoping *Cyclops* had not done too much damage . . .

On the quarterdeck Captain Hope was enduring the master's objections. The only person on board who could legitimately contest the captain's decisions, from the navigational point of view, Blackmore vigorously protested the inadvisability of taking *Cyclops* to leeward again to tow off a frigate no more than half a league from a dangerous shoal.

But the exertions of the night affected men differently. As Blackmore turned away in defeat Hope saw his last opportunity. Shedding years at the prospect of such a prize his caution fell a prey to temptation. After a life spent in a Service which had consistently robbed him of a reputation for dash or glamour, fate was holding out a fiscal prize of enormous magnitude. All he had to do was apply some of the expertise that his years of seagoing had given him.

'Wear ship, Mr Blackmore.'

The captain turned and bumped into a slim figure hurrying aft.

'B . . . Beg pardon sir.'

Drinkwater had descended from the foretop. He touched his hat to the captain.

'Well?'

'Shoal's a mile to leeward, sir.' For a minute Hope studied the young face: he showed promise.

'Thank you, Mr, er . . .'

'Drinkwater, sir.'

'Quite so. Remain with me; my messenger's gone . . .' The captain indicated the remains of his twelve-year-old midshipman messenger. The sight of the small, broken body made Drinkwater feel very light headed. He was cold and very hungry. He was aware that the frigate was manoeuvring close to the crippled Spaniard, paying off downwind . . .

'First lieutenant's on the gun-deck, see how long he'll be.' Uncomprehending the midshipman hurried off. Below the shadowy scene in the gun-deck was ordered. A hundred gunners lugged a huge rope aft. Drinkwater discovered the first lieutenant right aft and passed the message. Devaux grunted and then, over his shoulder ordered, 'Follow me.' They both ran back to the quarterdeck.

'Nearly ready, sir,' said Devaux striding past the captain to the taffrail. He lugged out his hanger and cut the log ship from its line and called Drinkwater.

'Coil that for heaving, young shaver.' He indicated the long log line coiled in its basket. For an instant the boy stood uncertainly then, recollecting the way Tregembo had taught him he began to coil the line.

Devaux was bustling round a party of sailors bringing a coil of four-inch rope aft. He hung over the taffrail, dangling one end and shouting at someone below. Eventually the end was caught; drawn inboard and secured to the heavy cable. Devaux stood upright and one of the seamen took the log line and secured it to the four-inch rope.

Devaux seemed satisfied. 'Banyard,' he said to the seaman. 'Heave that at the Spaniard when I give the word.'

Cyclops was closing the crippled frigate. She seemed impossibly large as the two ships closed, the rise and fall between them fifteen to twenty feet.

The two ships were very close now. The Spaniard's bowsprit rose and fell, raking aft along *Cyclops*'s side. Figures were visible on her fo'c's'le as the bowsprit jutted menacingly over the knot of figures at the after end of *Cyclops*. If it ripped the spanker *Cyclops* was doomed since she would again become unmanageable, falling off before the gale. The spar rose again then fell as the frigate wallowed in a trough. It hit *Cyclops*'s taffrail, caught for an instant then tore free with a splintering of wood. At a signal from Devaux Banyard's line snaked dextrously out to tangle at the gammoning of the bowsprit dipping towards the British stern.

'Come on, boy!' shouted Devaux. In an instant he had leapt up and caught the spar, heaving himself over it, legs kicking out behind him. Without thinking, impelled by the force of the first lieutenant's determination Drinkwater had followed. Below them *Cyclops* dropped away and was past.

The wind tore at Drinkwater's coat tails as he cautiously followed Devaux aft along the spar. The dangling raffle of gear afforded plenty of handholds and it was not long before he stood with his superior on the Spanish forecastle.

A resplendently attired officer was footing a bow at Devaux and proferring his sword. Devaux, impatient at the inactivity of the Spaniards, ignored him. He made signs at the officer who had first secured the heaving line and a party of seamen were soon heaving in the four-inch rope. The moon emerged again and Devaux turned to Drinkwater. He nodded at the insistently bobbing Spaniard.

'For God's sake take it. Then return it – we need their help.'

Nathaniel Drinkwater thus received the surrender of the thirty-eight gun frigate *Santa Teresa*. He managed a clumsy bow on the plunging deck and as graciously as he knew how, aware of his own gawkiness, he handed the weapon back. The moonlight shone keenly on the straight Toledo blade.

Devaux was shouting again: 'Men! Men! Hombres! Hombres!' The four-inch had arrived on board and the weight of the big hawser was already on it. Gesticulating wildly and miming with his body Devaux urged the defeated Spaniards to strenuous activity. He pointed to leeward. 'Muerto! Muerto!'

They understood.

To windward Hope was tacking *Cyclops*. It was vital that Devaux secured the tow in seconds. The four-inch snaked in. Then it snagged. The big ten-inch rope coming out of the water had caught on something under *Santa Teresa*'s bow.

'Heave!' screamed Devaux, beside himself with excitement. *Cyclops* would feel the drag of that rope. She might fail to pay off on the starboard tack . . .

Suddenly it came aboard with a rush. The floating hemp rose on a wave and swept aboard as *Santa Teresa's* bow fell into a steep trough.

Drinkwater was astonished. Where she had been rolling wildly the seas had been breaking harmlessly alongside. He sensed something was wrong. That sea had broken over them. He looked around. The sea was white in the moonlight and breaking as on a beach. They were in the breakers of the San Lucar shoal. Above the howl of the wind and the screaming of the Spanish officers the thunder of the Atlantic flinging itself on to the bank was a deep and terrifying rumble.

Devaux sweated over the end of the ten-inch rope. 'Get a gun fired quick!'

Drinkwater pointed to a cannon and mimed a ramming motion. 'Bang!' he shouted.

The sailors understood and a charge was quickly rammed home. Drinkwater grabbed the linstock and jerked it. It fired. He looked anxiously at *Cyclops*. Several Spaniards were staring fearfully to leeward. '*Dios!*' said one, crossing himself. Others did the same.

Slowly Devaux breathed out. *Cyclops* had tacked successfully. The hemp rose from the water and took the strain. It creaked and Drinkwater looked to where Devaux had passed a turn round *Santa Teresa's* fore mast and wracked lashings on it. More were being passed by the sailors. The *Santa Teresa* trembled. Men looked fearfully at each other. Was it the effect of the tow or had she struck the bottom?

Cyclops's stern rose then plunged downwards. The rope was invisible in the darkness which had again engulfed them but it was secured and *Santa Teresa* began to turn into the wind. Very slowly *Cyclops* hauled her late adversary to the south-west, clawing a foot to windward for every yard she made to the south.

Devaux turned to the midshipman and clapped him on the back. His face broke into a boyish grin.

'We've done it, cully, by God, we've done it!'

Drinkwater slid slowly to the deck, the complete oblivion of fatigue enveloping him.

Chapter Five   *February–April 1780*

The Evil that Men do . . .

Rodney's fleet lay at anchor in Gibraltar Bay licking its wounds with a sense of satisfaction. The evidence of their victory was all about them, the Spanish warships wearing British colours over their own.

The battle had annihilated Don Juan de Langara's squadron. Four battleships had struck by midnight. The Admiral in *Fenix* surrendered to Rodney but *Sandwich* had pressed on. At about 2 a.m. on the 17th she overhauled the smaller *Monarcha* and compelled her to strike her colours with one terrible broadside. By this time, as *Cyclops* struggled to secure *Santa Teresa* in tow, both fleets were in shoaling water. Two seventy-gun ships, the *San Julian* and *San Eugenio*, ran helplessly aground with terrible loss of life. The remainder, Spanish and British, managed to claw off to windward.

In the confusion of securing the prizes one Spanish battleship escaped as did the other frigate. With the exception of the *San Domingo* and the escapees, De Langara's squadron had fallen into Rodney's hands. It was a bitter blow to Spanish naval pride, pride that had already suffered humiliation when late the previous year the treasure flota from the Indies had fallen to marauding British cruisers.

Now the great ships lay at anchor. *Fenix* was to become *Gibraltar* and others were to be bought into the British service. Their presence boosted the morale of General Elliott's hard pressed garrison and forced the besiegers to stop and think. Behind the fleet the convoy had arrived safely and the military dined their naval colleagues. Midshipmen, however, at least those of *Cyclops* dined aboard, on hard tack, pease pudding and salt pork.

During her stay at Gibraltar *Cyclops* became a happy ship. She had come through a fleet action with distinction and the experience had united her crew into a true ship's company. Her casualties had been light, four dead and twenty-one wounded, mostly by splinters or falling wreckage. Every morning as the hands turned up there was not a man among them who did not cast his eyes in the direction of the *Santa Teresa*. The Spanish frigate was their own, special badge of honour.

The men worked enthusiastically repairing the damage to *Cyclops*. It was a task that fascinated Drinkwater. The elements of seamanship he already knew were augmented by the higher technicalities of masting and rigging and when Lieutenant Devaux turned his attention to the *Santa Teresa* his knowledge was further increased. The first lieutenant had taken a liking to Drinkwater after their sojourn together on the captured frigate. Revived from his faint Devaux had found him an eager and intelligent pupil once his stomach had been filled.

Cyclops's crew spared no effort to efface as much of the damage their own cannon had done to the *Santa Teresa* so that the frigate presented as good an appearance as possible to the prize court. Presided over by Adam Duncan, Rodney's Vice-Admiral, this august body was holding preliminary hearings into the condition of the fleet's prizes before despatching those suitable back to England. Once this intelligence had been passed to the hands they worked with a ferocious energy.

The intensive employment of *Cyclops*'s crew meant that the midshipmen were often absent and rarely all on board at the same time. For the first time Drinkwater felt comparatively free of the influence of Morris. Occupied as they all were there was little opportunity for the senior midshipman to bully his hapless juniors. The anticipation of vast sums of prize money induced a euphoria in all minds and even the twisted Morris felt something of this corporate elevation.

Then, for Drinkwater, all this contentment ended.

Cyclops had lain in Gibraltar Bay for eleven days. The repairs were completed and work was almost finished aboard the *Santa Teresa*. Her spars were all prepared and it was time to send up her new topmasts. Devaux had taken almost the entire crews of *Cyclops* over to the Spaniard to make light of the hauling and heaving. Topmen and waisters, marines, gunners, fo'c's'le men were all set to man the carefully arranged tackles and set up the rigging.

Captain Hope was ashore with Lieutenant Keene and only a handful of men under the master kept the deck. The remainder, off-duty men, slept or idled below. A drowsy atmosphere had settled over the frigate exemplified by Mr Blackmore and the surgeon, Appleby, who lounged on the quarterdeck, their energies spent by recent exertions.

Drinkwater had been sent with the launch to pass the convoy orders to a dozen transports in the outer bay. These ships were bound for Port Mahon and *Cyclops* would be escorting them.

As he returned to *Cyclops* he passed *Santa Teresa*. The sound of O'Malley's fiddle floated over the calm water. Signs of activity were visible, the creak of tackles lifting heavy weights clearly audible as two spars rose up the newly erected masts. Drinkwater waved to Midshipman Beale as the launch swept round the frigate's stern. The yellow and red of her superimposed ensign almost brushed the oarsmen as it drooped disconsolately under the British colour. Drinkwater brought the launch alongside the mainchains of *Cyclops*.

Mr Blackmore languidly acknowledged his report. Drinkwater went below. He had half expected to find Morris on deck, not wishing to encounter him in the cockpit. So intense was Drinkwater's loathing of Morris that he would return to the deck rather than remain in his company below. There was something, something indefinable, about him that Nathaniel found distasteful without knowing what it was.

Between decks *Cyclops* was dim and almost silent. The creaking of her fabric went unnoticed by Drinkwater. A few men sat at the mess tables slung between the guns, lounging and talking. Some swung in hammocks and several watched Drinkwater with idle curiosity. Then one, a fox-faced man named Humphries, nudged his neighbour. A large topman turned round. Drinkwater scarcely noticed the malice that appeared in Threddle's eyes.

He descended to the orlop and turned aft to where, screened off with canvas, the frigate's 'young gentlemen' lived. Drinkwater was happily oblivious of the menace in the air. The foetid atmosphere of the orlop was dark; a darkness punctured by swinging lanterns suspended at intervals from the low deckhead which glowed dimly in the poor air. Drinkwater approached the canvas flap which answered the midshipmen for a door.

He was stopped in his tracks.

At first he was completely uncomprehending. Then the memory of similar, half-glimpsed, actions, and a pang of instinctive recognition in his own loins brought the realisation slamming home to him.

He felt sick.

Morris was naked from the waist down. The handsome young seaman from the main top was bent over a midshipman's chest. There was little doubt what was happening.

For a few seconds Drinkwater was rooted to the spot, helplessly watching Morris's breathless exertions. Then Drinkwater noticed the initials on the chest: 'N.D.' He turned and ran, stumbling along the orlop, desperate for the cool freshness of the upper deck.

He ran full-tilt into Threddle who hurled him back. Drinkwater staggered and, before he could recover, Threddle and Humphries were lugging him aft. Drinkwater struggled in pure terror at re-entering his dismal quarters.

Threddle threw him forward and he fell on his back. For a minute he closed his eyes then a kick in the kidneys forced them open. A fully dressed Morris stood looking down at him. Threddle and Humphries were behind the midshipman. The handsome seaman had shrunk into a corner. He was crying.

'What are we goin' to do wiv 'im, Mr Morris?' asked Humphries his eyes glittering with possibilities. Morris looked at Drinkwater his own eyes veiled. He licked his lips considering the physical possibilities himself. Perhaps he read something in Drinkwater's expression, perhaps his lusts were temporarily slaked or perhaps he feared the consequences of discovery. At last he came to his decision and bent over Nathaniel.

'If,' Morris laboured the word, 'if you mention a word of this to anyone we will kill you. It will be easy – an accident. Do you understand that? Or perhaps you'd like friend Threddle here . . .' the seaman shuffled forward eagerly, a hand passing to his belt, '. . . to show you what a buggering is?'

Drinkwater's mouth was quite dry. He swallowed with difficulty.

'I . . . I understand.'

'Then get on deck where you belong, lickspittle.'

Drinkwater fled. The normality of the scene on deck shocked him profoundly. As he arrived in the waist Tregembo came up and gave him an odd look, but the midshipman was too terrified to notice.

'Mr Blackmore wants you, sir,' called Tregembo as he rushed past. Drinkwater went aft his heart thumping, doing his best to master his shaking limbs.

A week later Gibraltar was once more closely invested by the besieging Spanish. Rodney had sent the transports on to Minorca and the units of the Channel fleet back to home waters under Rear Admiral Digby. The empty transports had gone with them. His task fulfilled the Admiral sailed for the West Indies with reinforcements for that station.

It is 500 miles from Gibraltar to Port Mahon. The brief respite in the weather was over. A Lleventades blew in their teeth as *Cyclops* and her consort *Meteor* struggled to keep the transports and storeships in order. The convoy beat to windward, tack upon weary tack. At first they kept well south avoiding the unfavourable current along the Spanish coast and the flyspeck island of Alboran but, having made sufficient easting, they held to a more northerly course until they raised the high, snow-capped peaks of the Sierra Nevadas and could weather Cape da Gata. With more sea room the convoy spread out and the escorts had even more trouble shepherding their charges.

The weather worsened. *Cyclops* was a misery. Damp permeated every corner of the ship. Fungi grew in wet places. The companionways were battened down and the closed gunports leaked water so that the bilges required constant pumping. The lack of ventilation between decks filled the living spaces with a foul miasma that made men gasp as they came below. Watch relieved watch, four hours on, four off. The galley fire went out and only the daily grog ration kept the men going, that and fear of the lash. Even so tempers flared, fights occurred and men's names were listed in the punishment book.

Things did not improve when *Meteor* signalled that she would keep the convoy company in Port Mahon while *Cyclops* cruised offshore and waited for the ships to discharge. *Meteor*'s captain, though half the age of Hope, was the senior. He was known to have a weakness for good wine, dark-haired women and the tables. It was *Meteor* therefore that secured to a buoy in the Lazaretto Reach and *Cyclops* that stood on and off the coast, hard-reefed and half-hearted in her lookout for Spanish cruisers.

The fourth day after they had seen the convoy safe into Mahon Humphries went overboard. No one saw it happen, he just failed to answer the muster and a search of the ship revealed nothing. When he heard the news Drinkwater was suddenly afraid. Morris shot him a malignant glance.

On the seventh day the weather began to moderate, but the ocean with typical perversity, sent one misery to succeed the last. Towards evening the wind fell away altogether and left *Cyclops* rolling viciously in a cross sea, a swell rolling up from the south east.

So chaos remained to plague the frigate and filled Midshipman Drinkwater's cup of misery to overflowing. Somehow the happiness he had felt in Gibraltar seemed unreal, a false emotion with no substance. He felt his own ingenuous naivety had betrayed him. The ugliness of Morris and his perverted circle of lower deck cronies seemed to infect the ship like the dampness and the rank stink. Indeed it so associated itself in his mind with the smell of malodorous bodies in cramped, unventilated spaces that he could never afterwards sense the taint in his nostrils without the image of Morris swimming into his mind. It had a name this thing; Morris had used it with pride. The very recollection made Drinkwater sweat. He began to see signs of it everywhere though in truth there were about a dozen men in *Cyclops*'s crew of over two hundred and sixty who were homosexual. But to Drinkwater, himself in the fever of adolescence, they posed a threat that was lent substance by the continuing tyranny of Morris and the knowledge that Morris possessed henchmen in the form of the physically heavyweight Threddle and his cronies.

Drinkwater began to live in a cocoon of fear. He wrestled unresolvedly with the possession of knowledge he longed to share.

Free of the disturbances of bad weather at last *Cyclops* cruised a week in pleasant circumstances. Light to fresh breezes and warmer winds took March into April. The frigate smelt sweeter between decks as fresh air blew through the living spaces. Vinegar wash was applied liberally and Devaux had the waisters and landsmen painting and varnishing until the waterways gleamed crimson, the quarterdeck panelling glistened and the brasswork sparkled in the spring sunshine.

On the last Sunday in March, instead of the Anglican service, Captain Hope had read the Articles of War. Drinkwater stood with the other midshipmen as Hope intoned the grim catechism of Admiralty. He felt himself flush, ashamed at his own weakness as Hope read the 29th Article: 'If any person in the Fleet shall commit the unnatural and detestable crime of buggery or sodomy with man or beast he shall be punished with death . . .'

He bit his lip and with an effort mastered the visceral fear he felt, but he still avoided the eyes of those he knew were staring at him.

After the solemnly oppressive reminder of the Captain's power the hands had been made to witness punishment. In the recent bad weather two men had been persistent offenders. Hope was not a vicious commander and Devaux, with a simple aristocratic faith in being obeyed, never pressed for strict action, infinitely preferring the indolence of inaction. He was content that the bosun's mates kept *Cyclops*'s people at their duty. But these two men had developed a vendetta and neither captain nor first lieutenant could afford to stand for that.

A drum rolled and the marines stamped to attention as a grating was triced up in the main rigging. A man was called out. Before passing sentence Hope had endeavoured to discover the source of the trouble but to no avail. The lower deck kept its own counsel and guarded its own secrets. The man came forward to where two bosun's mates grabbed him and lashed his wrists to the grating. A piece of leather was jammed into his mouth to prevent him from biting through his own tongue. It was Tregembo.

The drum rolled and a third bosun's mate wielded the supple cat o'nine tails and laid on the first dozen. He was relieved for the second and his relief for the third. After a bucket of water had been thrown over the wretched prisoner's body he was cut down.

With difficulty Tregembo staggered back to his place among the sullen hands. The second man was led out. Threddle's powerful back testified to previous punishment but he bore his three dozen as bravely as Tregembo. When he too was cut down he stood unsupported, his eyes glittering with tears and fierce hatred. He looked directly at Drinkwater.

The midshipman had become inured to the brutality of these public floggings; in some curious way the spectacle affected him far less than the sonorous intonation of that 29th Article of War.

Like many of the officers and men he managed to think of something else, to concentrate on the way the row of fire buckets, each with its elaborately painted royal cipher, swung to the motion of the ship. He found the device reassuring, helping him to master himself after the disquiet of that uncompromising sentence. It was thus disarmed that Threddle caught his eye.

Drinkwater felt the occult force of loathing hit him with near physical impact. The midshipman was certain that he was in some strange way connected with the animosity that existed between these two men that had broken out in persistent and disruptive fighting. It was only with difficulty that Drinkwater prevented himself from fainting. One seaman did. It was the handsome young topman who had been Morris's pathic.

Later in the day Drinkwater passed close to Tregembo as the man worked painfully at a splice.

'I am sorry you were flogged, Tregembo,' he said quietly.

The man looked up. Beads of sweat stood out on his brow, evidence of the agony of working with a back lashed to a bloody ruin.

'You don' have to worry, zur,' he replied. Then he added as an afterthought, 'It shouldn't have to come to that . . .' Drinkwater passed on, musing on the man's last, incomprehensible remark.

Later that night the wind freshened. At 4 a.m. Drinkwater was called to go on watch. Stumbling forward to the companionway he was aware that once more *Cyclops* was pitching and tossing. 'They'll shorten sail soon,' he muttered to himself struggling into his tarpaulin as he emerged on deck. The night was black and chilly. A patter of spray came aboard, stinging his face. He relieved Beale who gave him a friendly grin.

At a quarter after four the order came to double reef the topsails. Drinkwater went aloft. He thought little of it now, nimbly working his way out to the place of honour at the yardarm. After ten minutes the huge sail was reduced and the men were making their way to the backstays, disappearing into the darkness as they returned to the deck. As he came in from the yardarm and transferred his weight to a backstay a hand gripped his wrist.

'What the hell . . .?' He nearly fell. Then a face appeared out of the windtorn blackness. It was the good-looking topman from the main top and there was a wild appeal in his eyes.

'Sir! For Christ's sake help me!' Drinkwater, swaying a hundred feet above *Cyclops*'s heaving deck, yet felt revulsion at the man's touch. But even in the gloom he saw the tears in the other's eyes. He tried to withdraw his hand but his precarious situation prevented it.

'I'm not one of them, sir, honest. They make me do it . . . they force me into it, sir. If I don't they . . . kick me, sir . . .'

Drinkwater felt the nausea subside. 'Kick you? What d'ye mean?' he could hardly hear the man now as the wind whipped the shouted confidences away to leeward.

'The bollocks, sir . . .' he sobbed, 'For Christ's sake help me . . .'

The grip relaxed. Drinkwater tore himself away and descended to the deck. For the remainder of the watch as dawn lit the east and daylight spread over the sea he pondered the problem. He could see no solution. If he told an officer about Morris would he be believed? And it was a serious allegation. Had he not heard Captain Hope read the 29th Article of War? For the crime of sodomy the punishment was death . . . it was a serious, a terrible allegation to make against a man and Drinkwater quailed from the possibility of being instrumental in having a man hanged . . . and Morris was evil, of that he was certain, evil beyond his own perversion, for Morris was allied to the huge physical bulk of Able-Seaman Threddle and what would Threddle not stop at?

Drinkwater remained in an agony of fear for himself and helplessness at his inability to aid the topman. He felt he was failing his first test as an officer . . . Who could he turn to?

Then he remembered Tregembo's remark. What was it he had said? He dredged the sentence out of the recesses of his memory: 'It shouldn't have to come to that.' To what? What had Tregembo said before his final remark . . .

'You don't have to worry.' That was it.

Meaning that he, Drinkwater, did not have to worry. But another doubt seized him. He had only expressed regret that the seaman had been flogged for fighting. Then he realised the truth. Tregembo had been flogged for fighting Threddle and had said the midshipman did not have to worry. Tregembo must therefore know something of what had gone on. 'It' should not have to come to Drinkwater himself worrying? Would the lower deck carry out its own rough justice? Had it already passed sentence on and executed Humphries?

Then Drinkwater realised that he had known all along. Threddle's eyes had blamed his flogging on Nathaniel and subconsciously Drinkwater had acknowledged his responsibility for Tregembo's pain.

He resolved that he would consult Tregembo . . .

It was the second dog watch before he got Tregembo to one side on the pretext of overhauling the log for Mr Blackmore.

'Tregembo,' he began cautiously, 'why did you fight Threddle?' Tregembo was silent for a while. Then he sighed and said, 'Now why would you'm be axing that, zur?'

Drinkwater took a deep breath. 'Because if it was over what I believe it to have been then it touches the midshipmen as well as the lower deck . . .' He watched Tregembo's puzzled frown smooth out in comprehension.

'I know, zur,' he said quietly and, looking directly at Drinkwater, added 'I saw what they'm did to you in Gib, zur . . .' It was Tregembo's turn to be embarrassed.

'I kind of took to 'ee, zur,' he flushed, then resumed with a candid simplicity, 'that's why I did fur 'Umphries.'

Drinkwater was shocked. 'You murdered Humphries?'

''E slipped and I 'elped 'im a bit.' Tregembo shrugged. 'Off'n the jibboom, zur. 'E ent the fust,' he said to alleviate Drinkwater's obvious horror. The midshipman absorbed the knowledge slowly. The burden he had borne was doubled, not halved as he had hoped. The respect for the law engendered by his upbringing was suffering a further assault. Tregembo's lawless, smuggling, devil-may-care attitude was a phenomenon new to him. His face betrayed his concern.

'Doan ye worry yerself, Mr Drinkwater. We're used to buggers and their ways. Most ships 'ave 'em but we doan like it when they doan keep it to 'emselves . . .' He indicated the handsome seaman

44

coiling a rope amidships. He looked up at them. There was appeal and desperation in his eyes, as though he knew the substance of a conversation taking place sixty feet away.

'Yon Sharples is a good topm'n but 'e's scared of 'em, see. I doan wonder if ye'd seen what they done to 'im . . .' Tregembo reached into a pocket and slipped a quid of tobacco into his mouth.

"E won't 'ave owerlong to wait,' he concluded ruminatively.

Drinkwater stared sharply at Tregembo. 'The lower deck'll look after its own, zur, but Mr Morris 'as a cockpit problem. Cockpits usually 'ave their own justice, zur.' Tregembo paused sensing Drinkwater's sense of physical inadequacy.

'You'd easy outnumber 'im, zur, wouldn't 'e?'

The log line was neatly coiled in its basket and Tregembo rose. He walked forward knuckling his forehead to the first lieutenant as he passed. Drinkwater remained aft at the taffrail staring astern unseeing. He felt no shame at the suggestion that he was alone unable to thrash Morris . . . yet it saddened him to think that Morris could terrorise not just him and his fellow midshipmen but the less fortunate Sharples . . . There was so much in the world that he did not comprehend, that was at variance with what the picture books and learning had given to his mind's eye . . . perhaps . . . but no it was not possible . . .

He turned to walk forward. The whole of *Cyclops* lay before him. Devaux and Blackmore were at the foot of the mizen mast. The boom and spanker overhead. She was a thing of great beauty, this ship, this product of man's ingenuity and resolve to conquer. For mankind went onwards, following an undirected destiny at no matter what cost to himself. And in the echo of that resolve, exemplified by the frigate, he cast about for the will to do what he thought was right.

Chapter Six   *May 1780*

Prize Money

His Britannic Majesty's frigates *Meteor* and *Cyclops* saw their charges into Spithead in the last week of May 1780. News had just come in from the West Indies that Admiral Rodney had fought a fleet action with De Guichen off Martinique on 17th April. But the battle had not been decisive and there were disturbing rumours that Rodney was courtmartialling his captains for disobedience.

The news, though vital to the progress of the war, was of second-ary importance to the ship's company of *Cyclops*. All the weary voyage from the Mediterranean the ship had buzzed as every mess speculated on the likely value of the prize.

There was not a man in the entire crew who did not imagine him-self in some state of luxury or gross debauch as a result of the purchase of *Santa Teresa* into the Royal Navy. For Henry Hope it meant security in old age; for Devaux the means of re-entering society and, hopefully, contracting an advantageous marriage. To men like Morris, Tregembo and O'Malley fantasies of splendid pro-portions rose in their imaginations as they prepared to make obeisance at the temples of Bacchus and Aphrodite.

But as the two frigates and their empty convoy sailed northward the initial excitement passed. Arguments broke out as to how much hard money was involved and, more important, how much each man would receive. Rumour, speculation and conjecture rippled through the ship like wind through standing corn. A chance remark made by an officer, overheard by a quartermaster and passed along the lower deck, sparked off fresh waves of debate based on no single thread of fact but by mountains of wishful thinking. Only the previous year frigates like *Cyclops* had taken the annual treasure fleet from the Spanish Indies. It had made their captains fabulously wealthy; even able-seamen had received the sum of £182. But it was not always visions of untold wealth that occupied the imaginations of her people. As the frigate drew north other rumours gained currency. Perhaps *Santa Teresa* had been retaken by the Spaniards who were once again besieging Gibraltar. Or sunk by shell-fire, or burned by fireships . . .

If the Spanish could not take her would they not have made an attempt to redress their honour by destroying at least some of the prizes in Gibraltar Bay?

Gloom spread throughout *Cyclops* and as the days passed the talk of prize money occurred less and less frequently. By the time *Cyclops* sighted the Lizard all discussions on the subject had become taboo. A strange superstition had seized the hands, including the officers. A feeling that if the subject were mentioned their greed would raise the ire of the fate that ruled their lives with such arbitrary harshness. No seaman, irrespective of his class or station, could admit the philosophical contention that Atropos, Lachesis or Clotho and their elemental agents acted with impartiality. His own experience continually proved the contrary.

Gales, battles, leaks, dismastings, disease and death; Acts of God, Acts of My Lords Commissioners of the Admiralty and all the other factors which combined to cause maritime discomfort, seemed to direct the whole weight of their malice at Jack Tar. Hardship was a necessary function of existence and the brief appearance of a golden ladder to a haven of wealth and ease became regarded with the deepest suspicion.

When *Cyclops*'s cable rumbled through the hawse and she brought up to her bower at Spithead no man dared mention *Santa Teresa*. But when the first lieutenant called away the captain's gig there was not a soul on board whose heartbeat did not quicken.

Hope was absent from the ship for three hours.

Even when he returned to the boat lying at King's Stairs the gig's crew were unable to read anything from his facial expression. Drinkwater was coxswain of the gig and set himself the task of conning her through the maze of small craft that thronged Portsmouth Harbour. In fact Drinkwater had thought less than most about the prize money. Money was something he had no experience of. There had been enough, barely enough, in his home and his interest in his new profession had both prevented him from dwelling on the subject of poverty or from realising how little he had. As yet the disturbance of lust had been a confused experience in which the romantic concepts imparted by a rudimentary education were at sharp variance with the world he found around him. He had not yet realised the power of money to purchase pleasure and his adolescent view of the opposite sex was one of total ambivalence. Besides, whilst there were no other distractions, he found the business of a sea-officer vastly more interesting and he had changed significantly since his first boat trip on the waters of Spithead. Although he had added little to his girth and height his body had hardened. His muscles were lean and strong, his formerly delicate hands sinewy with hard labour. His features remained fine drawn but there was now a touch of firmness, of authority about the mouth that had banished the feminine cast to his face. A dark shadow was forcing him to shave occasionally and his former pallor was replaced by a weathered complexion.

There remained, however, the bright eagerness that had attracted Devaux's notice so that he used Drinkwater when he wanted a difficult task undertaken by one of the 'young gentlemen'. The first lieutenant had placed Drinkwater in a post of honour as coxswain of the captain's gig. If he could afford no fancy ribbons about his boat's crew at least Hope could have a keen young middy to swagger, dirk at his side, in the stern sheets.

Blackmore too considered the youth the aptest of his pupils and, had it not been for the spectre of Nemesis in the form of Morris, the approbation of his seniors would have brought the keenest pleasure to Nathaniel.

The gig danced over the water. Next to Drinkwater Hope sat in stony silence, digesting the facts that the admiral's secretary had told him. *Santa Teresa* had been purchased as a prize. The court had been assembled under the authority of Rear-Admiral Kempenfelt whose purpose it was to examine the findings of Duncan's preliminary hearing at Gibraltar. Kempenfelt and his prize court had decided that she was a very fine frigate indeed and had purchased her into the Service for the sum of £15,750. Captain Hope's share would amount to £3,937. 10 shillings. After years of grinding service with little glory and no material rewards beyond a meagre and delayed salary, fate had smiled upon him. He could hardly believe his luck and regarded it with a seaman's cynicism which accounted for his stony visage.

Drinkwater brought the gig alongside. Hope reached the deck and the pipes twittered in salute. Every man upon the upper deck ceased work to look at the captain for some sign of news of the *Santa Teresa*. All they perceived was a stony face.

So, they concluded, their worst fears were realised. Hope walked directly aft and disappeared. The eyes of the ship's company followed the captain's retreating back. One hundred and seventy-six men, just then occupied upon the upper deck of *Cyclops* were united in a moment of immobile, silent, bitter disappointment.

Some half-hour later Drinkwater was dispatched again in the gig. Instead of the captain the midshipman had orders to convey Mr Copping, the purser, ashore. Mr Copping imparted the intelligence that he was entrusted to buy some special provisions for the captain's table that evening and that the captain was holding a dinner for his officers. He also handed Drinkwater a letter written in the old captain's crabbed hand. The superscription was to 'His Excellency Richard Kempenfelt, Rear-Admiral'. Drinkwater was to deliver it while the purser attended to his purchases.

Hope had invited all his officers, the master, gunner and the midshipmen. Appleby, the surgeon, was also present. They gathered noisily aft at three bells in the second dog watch with only the first lieutenant and Wheeler absent forming an honour guard to greet the Admiral.

When Hope had impulsively dashed off his invitation to Kempenfelt he was in boyish high spirits. He had suppressed his mirth as he snapped orders at Copping so that that individual had left his commander with the positive belief that the worst fears of the ship's company were realised and had lost no time in sending word forward that further optimism was futile.

Hope saw the Admiral as the true author of his good fortune and in some way wished to acknowledge his gratitude. For Kempenfelt was a popular sea officer whose brilliance shone in an age when brains were not the qualification for flag rank. His innovations were admired throughout the fleet where thinking men discussed the handling of fleets under sail more than jobbery or place seeking. Kempenfelt was, perhaps, more than that to Hope. To the captain, whose post rank he owed to the political faction he despised, the Rear-Admiral was a respected figure, and in an age when lip service of the greatest extravagance disguised base motives, Hope wished to demonstrate honest, simple admiration.

But as his officers collected on the deck above, the captain had his private doubts. Midshipman Drinkwater had brought back the Admiral's acceptance and he was beset by second thoughts. The prank he was playing on his own ship's company was childish – but captains could indulge themselves to some extent with their own people; admirals were rather different. He was not sure now what Kempenfelt would think . . .

Above his head the buzz of speculative conversation came down the skylight. The officers might have got wind of the prize court's decision; it was unlikely that they had not heard by now and were doubtless writing him off as old fool. Hope flushed but re-collected himself when he heard the note of resignation in the babble above. He listened more attentively. He heard the second lieutenant, Mr Price, his lilting Welsh voice vaguely angry, say 'I told you so, eh Blackmore?' Hope could imagine the old sailing master, called in as an ally in disappointment, a man so like himself that the captain could imagine the years of experience formulating a reply to Price.

'That's right, Mr Price, you'll never see Jolly Jack make a brass far-thing out of his business,' the remark was made dully, authoritatively, an oft-uttered and oft-heard contention. Hope suddenly grinned – to hell with admirals! He had a surprise for Blackmore, a good surprise too, and of all his ship's company he would be most pleased to see the white-haired master receive his share.

A knock came at the door. 'Enter,' Devaux stepped inside.

'All ready sir, and the Admiral's barge is in sight.' The first lieu-tenant hesitated, wanting to say more. 'Sir . . .?'

Hope enjoyed Devaux's discomfort. So often the easy-mannered savoir faire of the man had irritated him. Assuredly this was Henry Hope's day.

'Yes, Mr Devaux?'

'The . . . prize, sir?'

Hope looked up sharply – perhaps his little drama made him overreact but it had its effect on Devaux. The first lieutenant

50

jumped for the captain's threshold like a chastened midshipman.

'The prize, Mr Devaux, the prize . . .' Hope managed a tone of outraged propriety, 'don't talk to me of prizes when there's an Admiral to meet.'

Rear-Admiral Richard Kempenfelt greeted Captain Hope with a smile. He doffed his tricorne to Wheeler and his guard and nodded to Devaux. His eye rove over *Cyclops* and her company as Hope conducted him aft to where the now silent group of officers waited. Those who noticed such details watched their captain earnestly addressing the admiral. They might also have noticed the admiral's smile broaden and crack open in a brief laugh. At the laugh Hope relaxed. It *was* going to be his day after all.

Hope introduced his officers, the warrant officers and midshipmen. Then Kempenfelt asked to be conducted round the ship.

'I merely want to see something of *Cyclops* and the brave fellows who took that Spaniard.'

Someone in the waist raised a formal cheer for the Admiral. To Devaux's ears its very half-heartedness was shameful. He did not notice Kempenfelt's eyes twinkle with amusement.

After his brief tour of the frigate the admiral turned to Hope.

'You've a damned taut ship, Captain Hope. We shall find work for you to do. In the mean time . . .' he lowered his voice. Hope nodded and turned to Devaux. 'Call all hands aft, Mr Devaux.'

There was a vast shuffling and scurrying to a twitter of pipes and a bellowing of orders. Red-coated marines stamped aft and gradually a sort of order fell on the ship. Kempenfelt stepped forward and addressed them.

'D'you hear now my lads, Captain Hope has asked that I give ye all the news of your prize, the frigate *Santa Teresa*.' He paused to watch the shuffle throughout the assembly. Expectancy, kindled in their faces by the presence of the admiral, now became a restless eagerness. The ragged line wavered.

'You'll be pleased to know she's been purchased for . . .' He tailed off as a buzz that swiftly became a hum broke out.

'Silence there!' yelled Devaux.

'. . . she's been purchased for 15,000 guineas sterling and you'll all receive your due according to usage and custom.' The admiral stepped back.

Devaux looked at Hope; he was smiling cherubically. Then, sensing the moment was right he called out:

'Three cheers for the Admiral . . .'

It was no longer half-hearted. They heard the noise on *Cerberus* a mile away. As the cheering died down Hope announced to Devaux, 'Mr Devaux, you may allow wives and sweethearts tomorrow, apparently the admiral's office announced us a few days ago . . .'

Captain Hope was having his day. As he ushered the Admiral and his flag lieutenant into the cabin there were more cheers for the captain himself.

The dinner in Captain Hope's cabin that evening was, as naval dinners went, unremarkable. But the setting sun laid a path of glittering gold from the horizon to the very stern windows of *Cyclops* and invested the scene with some of its magic. The excited babble of talk amongst the juniors present and the natural elation due to the unaccustomed wine and natural headiness of the occasion nevertheless lent to the proceedings a degree of memorability.

Copping had provided a banquet within the limits of his materials. If Kempenfelt was unimpressed by the cookery he did not show it and to the short-rationed midshipmen any meal of more than one course automatically assumed the dignity of *haute cuisine*.

Fortunately the *Santa Teresa*'s loot had yielded a sufficiency of both Oporto and Jerez wines which made up for the indifference of Hope's claret. Some Havana cigars were also salved which, after the duff and capons had been consumed, filled the air with the aromatic luxury of their blue smoke.

A bare hour after they had sat down Drinkwater's body was enjoying the pleasant sensations of a mild drugging. His stomach was distended to unusual proportions and his head just beginning to assume that lucid detachment from his limbs that is the pleasantest but also the briefest stage of drunkenness. As for his forgotten legs, they reclined as he had negligently left them before the increase in his cerebral concentration had drawn all the energy from them. He heard without fully comprehending the senior officers discussing Kempenfelt's new code of signals. The admiral's explanation of Rodney's action off Martinique passed through his aural organs and left his brain to seize on and amplify certain graphic phrases that his overwrought imagination dwelt on.

Hope, Price, Keene, Devaux and Blackmore listened to the rear-admiral with professional deference, but to Drinkwater the splendid figure of Kempenfelt poured forth the very stuff of dreams.

After the loyal toast Kempenfelt proposed one to the *Cyclops*'s gallantry in the night action off Cadiz. In turn Hope toasted an admiral 'without whose ratification their fortunes would have remained uncertain'. The admiral prodded his flag lieutenant and that worthy rose unsteadily and read a prepared statement toasting Lieutenant John Devaux and Midshipman Nathaniel Drinkwater for their bold action in boarding the prize and earning a special place in Hope's report. Devaux rose and bowed to the flag lieutenant and the admiral. Recalling that the midshipman had the post of honour in receiving the Spaniard's surrender he called upon the young gentleman to reply.

Drinkwater was barely aware of what was required of him, but he was suddenly aware of Morris staring at him from the far side of the table with an evil grin upon his face. The face seemed to grow larger, terrifying in its size, oppressive with malice. Conversation died as all turned to stare at him. He was confused. He remembered a succession of his seniors standing in turn and he rose unsteadily to his feet. For a moment or two he stood there swaying slightly. The bored expression of the flag lieutenant changed to one of sudden interest at the prospect of a neat gaffe with which to entertain his fashionable friends.

Drinkwater stared out through the stern windows to where the last shreds of daylight flared above the horizon. Morris's face faded and that of his mother swam before him. He remembered her preparing his sea-kit, sewing a table cloth for her son to use at sea. It lay hidden and unused at the bottom of his chest. It bore a motto. That motto sprang into his midshipman's mind now and he uttered it in a loud, commanding voice:

'Confusion to the king's enemies!' He said it all in one breath and without a slur. He sat down abruptly as a roar of assent went round the table. The flag lieutenant resumed his bored expression.

He vaguely heard Kempenfelt's approbatory comment: 'Damme Captain, a real fire eater!'

53

The Duel

On awakening next morning Drinkwater had only the haziest notions of turning in the previous night. He was not sure at what hour the Admiral had left for after his toast the evening had become a blur. The blue and white uniforms, the gold braid and pink faces seemed shrouded in more than tobacco smoke. Wheeler's scarlet coat and glittering gorget had glowed like a surrogate sun in the candlelight as they joked and laughed and became serious again. The conversation had turned on a variety of topics; had been general, then particular; bawdy then technical as the portions of the table concentrated, divided then joined again in a verbal tide.

The event had been a triumph for Henry Hope. As a crowning to the evening Blackmore had suggested a little music and word was passed for O'Malley. The diminutive Irish cook entered, stealing sidelong glances at the ruins of the meal and the empty bottles. He produced some sweet and melancholic airs after the fashion of the time which brought an appreciative silence to the table. He concluded to loud applause with a frantic jig from his native land which, drawn from the wild turbulence of his people, seemed to Drinkwater to summarise the exhilaration of that Moonlight Battle in which these genial fellows had taken such a part.

Little O'Malley had gone forward two guineas better off with a farewell whose obsequiousness was not that of sobriety but suggested that, in the course of roasting the very capons whose ruins he had so enviously regarded, he had partaken of 'pusser's dips'.

Despite the vague recollections of a successful evening Drinkwater woke to the disturbing sensation that all was not well. He had a headache due to the quite unaccustomed quantity of wine he had consumed but it was more than that. He groped in his mind for some memory that would give him a clue to his disquiet. At first he thought he hàd committed some impropriety. His stomach contracted at the thought of an indiscretion in front of the admiral. But the approach of a figure traversing the darkened orlop brought the memory back.

It was Morris coming to call him at one bell to stand the morning anchor watch. Morris's face was lit demoniacally by the lantern. The rest of his body was invisible in the blackness of the cockpit. This apparition finding Drinkwater awake was a very mask of malice which spat out a torrent of invective in a sibilant whisper. Nathaniel was transfixed with horror, a feeling made worse by his prone position. Jealousy and hate burned within Morris, contesting with the fear of Drinkwater's knowledge of himself. The resulting conflict of powerful emotion burned within him in a terrible, bullying anger.

'Come on admiral's lickspittle, get out of your hammock and convey your greasy arse on deck, damn you for a crawling get!'

Drinkwater made no reply, vulnerably shrinking within his blanket. For a second Morris's face hung over him, the malevolence in his eyes an almost physical force. In a sudden, swift movement Morris had a knife out, the lantern catching the dull glint of its blade. It was a micro second of suspense wherein Drinkwater suddenly, inexplicably, found himself drained of all fear. He simply tensed and awaited the inevitable . . .

Morris slashed with the knife. The hammock lashing parted and with a jarring crash Drinkwater landed on the deck. Fighting out of his blanket he found himself alone in the creaking darkness.

On deck a squall of rain skittered across Spithead and the wind behind it was cutting. Drinkwater shivered and drew his cloak closer around him. Dawn was not yet visible and Morris's figure was barely discernible, huddled in the paltry shelter of the mizen rigging.

The figure detached itself and approached Drinkwater. Morris's face, dark now, came close. The older midshipman gripped the arm of the younger. Spittle flecked offensively on to Drinkwater's cheek.

'Now listen,' hissed Morris, 'just because you are a crawling little bastard don't get any God-damned ideas about anything. Threddle hasn't forgotten his flogging and neither of us have forgotten Humphries. So don't forget what I'm saying. I mean it.' Morris's vehemence was irresistible. Drinkwater shrunk from the voice, from the spittle and the vicious grip upon his arm. Morris's knee came up into his groin. He gasped with pain. 'D'ye understand, God-damn you?' queried Morris, an undetected doubt in his voice.

'Y . . . yes,' whispered Drinkwater doubling with agony and nausea, his head swimming. Another figure loomed out of the rain-swept darkness. For a terrifying moment Drinkwater thought it was Threddle but the voice of Tregembo asked, 'Everything all right, Mr Drinkwater?' He felt Morris freeze then relax as he straightened up. Tears flowed down his cheeks but he managed to steady his nerve enough to mutter, 'Yes thank you.'

In a clipped tone Morris handed over the watch. 'The lieutenants are excused watches tonight. Call all hands at three bells.' A quarter-master approached, the half-hour glass in his hand. The lower half was almost full.

'Eight bells, Mr Morris.'

'Make it so then.'

'Aye, aye, sir.'

Four o'clock in the morning.

When Morris had gone below Drinkwater went to the weather side. The rain stung and wet his face. He felt it with relief. The pain in his groin eased and his head felt less thick. Then a wave of nausea swept over him. The pain, the wine and the self-disgust caused him to vomit into the inky, hissing waters of Spithead. After that he felt better. He still stared to windward, his hands gripping the rail. His self-disgust rankled. Why had he not hit Morris back? Just once. He had to face the fact that he was scared, forgetful of the bold resolutions he had formulated and continually put off, pending a more propitious opportunity. He had one now. Morris had assaulted him. Hitherto he had lain low in the hope that by effacing himself Morris would leave him alone. But Morris could not do that . . .

The thing that he knew about Morris he devoutly wished he did not know. It was so disgusting that the very image of it, so vivid in his impressionable mind, was abominable to him.

Drinkwater was terrified of what he had seen almost more than of those who had been doing it. In that terror was submerged the real-isation of the power he had over Morris. In Morris's aggression all Drinkwater saw was brutality. He failed to perceive the brutality masked fear. He saw nothing of the source, only the source's mani-festation.

He was suddenly aware of someone alongside of him.

'H-h'm.' A voice coughed apologetically.

Drinkwater nervously began to move away. 'Beg pardon, zur . . .'

'Yes?'

'I saw what 'appened, zur. I saw 'im 'it 'ee . . . if you'm be wantin' a witness, zur.'

'No, Tregembo, thank you,' Drinkwater paused. He remembered that conversation with Tregembo in the Mediterranean. A brief memory of Humphries flashed in his brain, of Sharples and Threddle, and of the flogging Tregembo had received. Drinkwater looked hard at Tregembo . . . the seaman expected Drinkwater to thrash Morris, Tregembo would otherwise see Drinkwater as a coward . . .

Drinkwater suddenly recalled the moment when fear had left him not an hour earlier. A bold feeling swept over him. He could no longer suffer Morris's tyranny and determined to challenge his senior. It was a desperate throw but in such circumstances resolves are easily made, though less easily carried out. He forced a grim note into his voice. 'No Tregembo, this is a cockpit matter, as you said. I'll thank you to hold your tongue . . .'

The man backed away disappointed. He had mistimed his assistance to the young gentleman. Having conceived a respect for the midshipman, Tregembo had assumed that he sought a legitimate means to encompass the destruction of Morris. Tregembo remembered the Twenty-Ninth Article of War, if ever one man held the other in the palm of his hand Drinkwater held sway over Morris. Tregembo was puzzled. He had 'taken' to the youth and could not understand why some attack had not been made on Morris as he had seen many of the youngsters carry out from time to time on various ships. Tregembo was too blunt to be aware of Drinkwater's sensibilities just as Drinkwater was unaware that Morris's bullying concealed a pusillanimous soul, a fact that was very plain to Tregembo.

In the first glimmer of dawn Drinkwater saw the topman's crest-fallen retreat.

'Tregembo!'

'Zur?' The man hesitated.

'Quietly have a word with one of the carpenter's mates to get two ash single sticks made up. Each thirty inches long, d'you under-stand?'

'Aye zur. And thank'ee.'

Drinkwater had not the slightest idea why Tregembo had thanked him but suddenly the rain fell sweet upon his upturned face.

The news of *Cyclops*'s prize and the promise of allowing visitors on board made her the happiest vessel in the anchorage. Before the morning watch was over the hands, uncommonly cheerful, had swabbed her decks and flaked and coiled all the ropes. When Devaux appeared the brasswork already gleamed in a watery sun-shine that promised a fair day after the dawn's wet beginning.

The men were already staring across the leaden water to Fort Gilkicker and Portsmouth Harbour. For days past hired punts and galleys had brought out women and children. Many were full of whores but there had been some with wives of both the churched and common law variety. They had made a forlorn sight, lying just clear of the ship's sides, exchanging unhappy waves or little snatches of conversation with the sailors until the bosun's mates or the officers had driven the men back to their work. The boats too were driven off either by the abuse of the ship's officers and marine sentries, or by the efforts of the guard-boats provided by the units of fleet themselves. This was an especial joy to the seamen who manned them for, if you are denied the pursuit of pleasure yourself there is a certain gratification in denying it to others.

Although *Cyclops* had commissioned at Chatham some of her company, volunteers mainly, had wives in the Portsmouth area. Occasionally a young wife would travel, at God knows what cost and on the chance that leave would be given to meet her man. But it was the other variety of female that most interested *Cyclops*'s hands that pale morning. Today no guard-boat could interrupt them as they took their pleasure, a fact that was doubly appreciated by the messes as they broke their fast to the news that *Meteor* was rowing guard. It was a sweet revenge for their consort's debauch at Port Mahon.

In the gunroom Lieutenant Devaux presided over fresh coffee and toast in evident good humour. 'Well Appleby,' he said addressing the chubby surgeon, 'Why are you looking so damned glum?'

'The reason for my glumness is occasioned by my contemplation of the follies of mankind, Mr Devaux. Ah, yes, a cup of coffee would be most welcome, I thank you for your courtesy.' He sat in the chair indicated by the first lieutenant.

Devaux poured. 'The women, Mr Appleby?' enquired Devaux with a smile.

'The women, Mr Devaux,' replied the surgeon resignedly. 'And, of course – the men.'

Devaux laughed outright. 'Poor Appleby, we win or lose in action but you can never win, poor devil.'

'But you've plenty of mercury, I don't doubt, to cope with the inevitable problems?' interjected Lieutenant Price with a sense of nicety in which his sensibility fought a losing action with his curiosity.

Appleby drew a deep breath and Devaux knew he was about to deliver a lengthy peroration, for which he was notorious.

'Mr Price, the provision of mercury by My Lords Commissioners for the execution of the office of Lord High Admiral, I say the provision of mercury to ships of war is insufficient to combat the outbreak of a chronic dose of syphilis in all but the smallest vessels, since their Lordships have failed to take cognisance of the fact that vessels of the various rates have an increasing number in their complement in inverse proportion to the number of their rating.

'Now – by syphilis I mean that corrupting infection of the blood known colloquially as 'pox' (which euphemism scarcely moderates its effect upon the human body, but only serves to render its acquisition a little easier to the witless sailor who foolishly considers it no worse than the common cold, having been misapprehended by the employment of the common vernacular). Unfortunately he continues in this mind until, with unsteady tread and wandering mind, disfigured beyond his fellow's toleration, he is led raving to an asylum, to the inevitable shame of his family and the everlasting damnation of his immortal soul.' Devaux had heard it before.

'Furthermore,' Appleby continued as Devaux groaned. 'Furthermore, the administration of mercury, in my opinion, only serves to suppress the symptoms rendering the individual's life more agreeable, but enabling him to pass the contagion on to other partners undetected. In time, however, the bacilli attack essential organs and precipitate death by a stroke or other cessations of essential bodily functions.'

'Don't you consider the expression of lust an "essential bodily function"?' asked Devaux, winking at Price. The latter was exhibiting a distinct pallor.

'The Honourable John Devaux asks me a question to which a man of his erudition surely knows the answer.'

'The expression of lust is a natural manifestation of procreational urges which holy ordinances proclaim sanctified under the matrimonial coverlet. Nature did not intend its indiscriminate proliferation . . .'

'But it *is*, Bones,' interrupted Price again, rallying now the discussion was of a less medical nature.

'Aye, Mr Price, and so is the proliferation of the disease so lately under discussion. Surely a punishment from God.'

'Pah!' exploded Devaux at last exasperated by the doctor.

'Not "Pah!", sirrah,' droned on Appleby, undeterred. 'Consider the evidence. The appearance of Christ on this earth was followed by an expansion of the church under the divine felicity and a thousand years in which the Christian religion gained ground against paganism. Only when the Church of Rome reached a state of corruption offensive to God did the devil descend to tempt men's hearts with temporal arts, and produce what educated people are pleased to call the "renaissance". Off men went in search of "knowledge". And what did Columbus bring back from his fabulous Americas? Syphilis!'

'*Bravo medico!*' laughed Devaux sardonically. 'Such a simple deduction scarcely becomes a man of science whose profession descends from such self-same intellectual quest; who would be an indigent fellow without it and whose mind has such a high regard for its own opinions.'

'I cannot escape my time,' replied the good surgeon whose tragic tones were not ennobled by his pudgy frame.

'You sound like a God-damned Wesleyan, Appleby.'

'Maybe I have some sympathy with the man.'

'Hah! Then I'm damned if ye'll get any more coffee at my table. Yes, Drinkwater?' This last was addressed to the midshipman who had appeared at the gunroom door.

'Beg pardon, sir, but boats approaching.' The gleam in Devaux's eye was an eloquent endorsement of the accuracy of Appleby's forebodings.

'Thank you, Drinkwater.' The midshipman turned away. 'Oh, Drinkwater!'

'Sir?'

'Sit down, cully, and listen to some good advice,' said the first lieutenant indicating a vacant chair. Drinkwater sat and looked at the two lieutenants with a bewildered expression on his face. 'Mr Appleby has something to say to you, haven't you Appleby?'

Appleby nodded, marshalled his facts and began cannonading the midshipman.

'Now young man, the first lieutenant is alluding to a contagion which is best and successfully avoided by total abstinence . . .'

For a second Devaux watched the look of horror cross Drinkwater's face, then, clapping the tricorne on his head and waving Price out behind him, the two lieutenants quit the gunroom.

'. . . total . . . abstinence to which end I do earnestly implore you to bend and address your best endeavours . . .'

The arrival of the women brought all hands on deck. Men craned over the hammock nettings, leaned from gunports and ascended the lower rigging to leer at the wherries bobbing alongside.

The hands gave no thought to the fact that what was to follow was no substitute for proper shore leave, something they could not have for fear they might desert. The immediate preoccupation was a debauch.

Women and gin were aboard.

Whilst Wheeler and his marines made a token effort to maintain order the usage of the service permitted all classes of women to board and all offences of drunkenness and fornication to be ignored. It was inevitable therefore that the greater part of the women were whores and that the mess-deck deteriorated instantly into an inferno of desperate debauchery. The women were of various ages: tired, painted and blowsy doxies in worn and soiled dresses whose vernacular was as explicit as 'Jolly Jacks', and younger molls, their youth blown on the winds of experience, their eyes dull with the desperate business of survival.

Some few were bona fide wives. The older among them used to their sisters in trade, the two or three younger astonished and shocked at the dim squalor of the gun-deck. Where, perhaps, a poor counting-house clerk had been pressed into the service his wife, possessing some slender claim to gentility, found her husband living in the vilest conditions. Such women instantly became a butt for the others to vent their coarse wit upon, which was a double tragedy since their husbands had probably just managed to live down their genteel origins. Legitimate wives were quickly recognised by their demeanour at the entry port, for they waved chits and passes at the marine sentries.

These genuine spouses looked earnestly for their husbands and avoided the leering and grasping propositions of others. For several such wives their journey ended in battle royal. Not expecting their spouses, men were engaged in coupling with whores. One enormous creature, the churched wife of a yeoman of sheets, found her man thus occupied between two twelve pounders. She belaboured his heaving buttocks with the tattered remnants of a parasol. A stream of filthy invective poured from her and she was quickly surrounded by a mass of cheering seamen and harlots who egged the trio on. The wife ceased her beating and took a long pull at a gin bottle someone held out to her. In the interval her husband finished his business and, to a cheer, the girl wriggled out from beneath him, hastily covering herself. She held out her hand for money but changed her mind when she saw the expression in the wife's eyes. She dodged under the barrel of the adjacent cannon as the offended lady screeched at her, 'Try and take the money that's mine ye painted trollop, why, ye don't know y're business well enough to axe fur it fust!'

At this remark the yeoman caught his wife's arm and slapped her across the mouth with 'And how in hell's name ud youm be knowin' that, my Polly?'

The crowd melted away for this was now a domestic matter and not the common property of the gun-deck.

All day the ebb and flow of liaisons took place. What little money the men had soon found its way into the pockets of the women. Mr Copping, the purser, in the manner of his race, set up a desk at which the eager men could sign a docket relinquishing a portion of their pay or prize money for an advance of cash. Many thus exceeded the dictates of prudence, the favours of a woman being a most urgent requirement. Thus were pursers a hated breed, though rarely a poor one.

Meteor rowed a dismal guard around *Cyclops*. Occasionally a bottle or a woman's drawers would be thrown out of an open gunport to an accompaniment of cheers and shrieks. The cutter's crew visibly smouldered and at one point she ran in and hailed the quarterdeck. The master's mate in charge of the boat was livid.

'Sir,' he yelled at Lieutenant Keene. 'Yer men show no respect. There are three of them baring their arses at me from yer gunports . . .'

Appleby joined the chuckling lieutenant who disdained to reply.

'Sure you did not bare yours at Mahon, mister?' enquired the surgeon.

There was no reply. 'That found its mark, eh lieutenant?' said Appleby as the man looked sulkily away.

'If the ship offends ye, sirrah, row guard round the rest of the fleet. Ye'll get little pickings from this lot!'

The master's mate spat overside and snarled at his boat's crew, 'Give way you damned lubbers.'

During the forenoon the wife of the man Sharples made her appearance at the entry port. She was very young and, though few knew it, had made the journey from Chatham purely on the chance of seeing her husband. The journey had taken a week and her expectant condition had made of it a nightmare.

But Sharples had seen her board and embraced her at the entry port amid the sentimental cheers of his messmates. No one had seen the sour look on the face of Mr Midshipman Morris who happened to be passing at the time. No one, that is, except Tregembo who, by another coincidence, was in search of Morris.

As Sharples and his wife, clasped together, stepped over the prostrate, active bodies, oblivious of the parodies of love enacted all about them, Tregembo stepped up to Morris and touched his forelock.

'Beg pardon, Mr Morris,' said Tregembo with exaggerated politeness, 'Lieutenant Keene's orders and will ye take the launch over to flag for orders.'

Morris snarled at Tregembo then a gleam of viciousness showed in his eyes. Calling a bosun's mate known for 'starting' he strode forward. As he went he called men's names. They were the least desirable of *Cyclops*'s company. A few, otherwise engaged, told him to go to the devil, one or two he let off, the rest he left to the bosun's mate.

At the forward end of the gun-deck Morris ran his quarry to earth. Sharples and his wife lay on the deck. Her head was pillowed on his hammock and her face wore a look of unbelieving horror. Her man, father of her unborn child whose image she had cherished, lay sobbing in her arms. The whole foul story of Morris had poured out of him for there was no way he could be a man to her until he had unburdened himself. Sharples was unaware of the presence of Morris until the author of his misfortune had been standing over the pair for a whole minute.

'Sharples!' called Morris in a voice which cut through the unhappy man's monologue. 'You are required for duty.'

The girl knew instinctively the identity of the intruder and struggled to her knees. 'No! No!' she protested.

Morris grinned. 'Are you questioning my orders?'

The girl faced Morris, biting her lip.

'I can report you for obstructing an officer in the execution of his duty. The punishment is a flogging . . . your husband is already guilty of disobeying orders in having a hammock out of the nettings . . .' He spat the words in her face. This threat to his wife revived Sharples who pulled his wife gently aside.

'W-what orders, Mr Morris?'

'Man the launch.'

The topman hesitated. He was not in the boat's crew. 'Aye, aye;' then turning to his wife he whispered 'I'll be back.'

The girl collapsed sobbing on the deck and one of the older women, to whom midshipmen were small fry, put an arm around her. A stream of filth followed Morris down the deck.

The launch was absent three hours. After a while the girl, disgusted with the scenes on the gun-deck, sought fresh air and light on deck. Finding her way to the forward companionway she groped her way to the starboard side where she made a little bright patch against the coils of black hemp belayed and hung upon the pinrail.

Staring out over the bright waters of Spithead she touched the life quickening within her. Her heart was full to bursting with her misery. The horrors of her week-long journey rose again before her at a time when she had thought to be burying them in happiness. Shame for her man and for herself, shame for the unborn child and for the depths of degradation to which one human could subject another welled up within her. Tears rolled down her cheeks.

Her eyes stared out unseeing at the ships lying to the tide. She was a small, broken piece of the price Britain paid for its naval puissance.

It was some time before old Blackmore noticed the lonely figure forward. He had relieved Keene of the deck and soon sent Drinkwater to turn the woman below again. Blackmore, trained in the merchant service, retained his civilian prejudice for refusing women leave to come on board. He sighed. In the merchant service a master gave his crew shore leave. If they wished to visit a brothel that was their affair, but they could be relied upon to return to their ship. The navy's fear of desertion prevented any liberty and resulted in the drunken orgy at present in progress between decks. If the old sailing master could do nothing to alter the crazy logic of Admiralty he was damned if he would have the upper deck marred by the presence of a whore.

Drinkwater approached the girl. In her preoccupation she did not hear him. He coughed and she turned, only to blench at his uniform. She drew back against the coils of hemp imagining Morris's threat of a flogging about to be carried out.

'Excuse me ma'am,' began Drinkwater, unsure of himself. The woman was obviously distressed. 'The Master's compliments and would you please to go below . . .'

She looked at him uncomprehending.

'Please ma'am,' the midshipman pleaded, 'None of you, er, ladies are permitted above decks.' She began to perceive his meaning and his embarrassment. Her courage rallied. Here was one she could answer back.

'D'you think I'm one of them 'arlots?' she asked indignantly. Drinkwater stepped back and the girl gained more spirit from his discomfiture.

'I'm a proper wife, *Mrs* Sharples to the likes o'you, and I journeyed a week to see my 'usband Tom . . .' she hesitated and Drinkwater tried to placate her.

'Then, please ma'am, will ye go to Sharples and bide with him.'

She rose in scorn. 'Aye willingly, Mister Officer, if ye'd return him to me but he's out there . . .,' she waved over the side, 'off in a boat, an' me with child and a week on the road only to find 'im beat and, and . . .' here she could not bring herself to say more and her courage failed her. She stepped forward and fainted into the arms of a confused Drinkwater. Then in an intuitive flash he realised she knew of her husband's humiliation.

He called aft for Appleby and the surgeon puffed up along the gangway. A glance took in the lady's condition and her nervous state. Appleby chafed her wrists and sent Drinkwater off for sal volatile from his chest. A few minutes later the girl recovered consciousness. Blackmore had come up and demanded an explanation. Having made an enquiry on passing through the gun-deck en route to the surgeon's chest, Drinkwater was able to tell the master that Sharples had gone off in the launch with Morris. 'But the man's not in the launch crew.'

'I know, Mr Blackmore,' replied Drinkwater.

'Did Morris single him out?'

'It appears so, sir.' Drinkwater shrugged and bit his lip.

'D'ye have any idea why?' asked Blackmore, shrewdly noticing the midshipman's face shadowed by doubtful knowledge. Drinkwater hesitated. It was more eloquent than words.

'Come on now, young shaver, if ye know, let's have it out.'

The midshipman swallowed hard. He looked at the distressed girl, golden curls fell about a comely face and she looked like a damsel in distress. Drinkwater burnt his boats.

'Morris has been buggering her husband,' he said in a low voice.

'And Sharples?' enquired Blackmore.

'He was forced, sir . . .'

Blackmore gave Drinkwater another hard look. He did not have to ask more. Long experience had taught him what had occurred. Morris would have bullied Drinkwater, may even have offered him physical violence or worse. The old man was filled with a loathing for this navy that ran on brutality.

'Let the lady get some air,' said Blackmore abruptly and turned aft for the quarterdeck.

When the launch returned Sharples was reunited with his wife. He had endured three hours of abuse and ridicule from Morris and his boat's crew.

Having delivered the Admiral's orders Morris made his way to the cockpit.

Drinkwater had also been relieved and going below he met Tregembo. The Cornishman was grinning. He held in his hand two ash sticks, each three feet long, with a guard of rattan work obviously untwisted from one of the blacksmith's withy chisels. 'Here, zur,' said Tregembo. Drinkwater took the sticks.

Drinkwater looked at Tregembo. He had better let the man know what had happened on the upper deck before it became known below.

'The Master knows Morris has been buggering Sharples, Tregembo. You'd better watch Threddle . . .'

A cloud crossed the Cornishman's face and then he brightened again. The midshipman was not such a disappointment after all.

'Ye'll thrash him easy, zur. Good luck . . .' Drinkwater continued below. He had uttered words that could hang a man, words that he would never have dared to utter at home. And now he felt ice cold, apprehensive but determined . . .

In the cockpit Morris and the other midshipmen were eating, mugs of ale at their places. The messman produced a plate for Drinkwater. He waved it aside, went to his place and, standing, cleared his throat.

'H'hmm.' Nobody took any notice. The blood pounded in his throat and adrenaline poured into his blood stream. But still he was cool. 'Mr Morris!' he shouted. He had their attention now.

'Mr Morris. This morning you threatened me and struck me . . .' A master's mate put his head in through the canvas door. The tableau was lit by two lanterns even at 2 p.m. here in the orlop. The air crackled with tension. Two master's mates were now looking on.

Morris rose slowly to his feet. Drinkwater did not see the apprehension turning to fear in his eyes. He was too busy remaining cool.

'You struck me, sir,' he repeated. He threw a single stick on the table, it knocked over a mug of ale and in the ensuing pause the air was filled with the gurgle of beer running on to the deck.

'Perhaps, gentlemen, you would be kind enough after dinner to give me room to thrash Mr Morris at single stick. Now, steward, my dinner if you please . . .'

He sat down grateful that his own mug remained full. The meal was completed in total silence. The two master's mates disappeared.

It was afterwards agreed that Drinkwater had been extremely *sporting* in allowing notice of the forthcoming match to be circulated. It was quite a crowd that eagerly cleared a space for the protagonists while Drinkwater removed his coat and stock. Both combatants were in their shirt-sleeves and Drinkwater took up his stick and tested it for balance. He had chosen the weapon for its familiarity. In Barnet it had been a favourite with the lads, imitating the gentleman's short sword, it combined the finesse of that weapon with some of the blunt brutality of the quarterstaff. The carpenter's mate had done well.

Drinkwater watched Beale push the last sea-chest back against the ship's side.

'Mr Beale, will 'ee stand second to me?'

'With pleasure, Mr Drinkwater,' said the other youngster shooting a sidelong glance at Morris.

The latter looked desperately around him. At last one of the master's mates stood second to Morris rather than spoil the match.

As duelling was illegal on board ship Drinkwater's choice of weapons was fortuitously apt. Although he had been guided by his own proficiency with the weapon and chose the single stick in ignorance, any action by the lieutenants could be circumvented by an explanation that it was a sporting occasion. To this end the seconds conferred and decided to send the messman in search of Wheeler who, despite his commissioned status, could be relied upon for his vanity in presiding over such a match.

It was a tiny space in which they had to fight, about five feet four inches high and some fifteen feet by ten in area. The spectators backed up against the ship's side further restricted it. Someone offered odds and the babble of excited voices attracted more attention. Into this babel, calling for order strode the resplendent figure of Lieutenant Wheeler. His arrival was accompanied by a rending of canvas as the forward screen was demolished, thus augmenting the spectators by some two score. Wheeler looked about him.

'Damn my eyes, what an evil coven have we here. For the love of God bring more lanterns, a fencing master has to *see*, d'ye hear . . .'

The protagonists faced each other and Wheeler issued his instructions.

'Now gentlemen, the rules of foil, hits with the point, on the trunk only. You are unmasked, which I do not like, but as this is only a sporting match,' this with a heavy emphasis, 'I should not have to caution you.' He paused.

'*En garde!*'

'*Êtes vous prêts?*'

'Aye,' 'Aye,' Wheeler grimaced at the common response.

'*Allez.*'

Drinkwater's legs were bent ready for the lunge and his left hand was on his hip as there was no room for it in equipoise. Morris had adopted a similar position. Beads of sweat stood out on his forehead.

Drinkwater beat Morris's stick; it gave. He beat again and lunged. The point hit Morris on the breastbone but he side swiped and would have hit Drinkwater's head but the latter parried on the lunge and recovered.

'*Halte!*' yelled Wheeler, then, '*En garde!*'

This time Drinkwater extended, drew Morris's stick and disengaged, pressing the lunge. His point, blunt though it was, scraped and bruised Morris's upper arm, ripping his shirt away.

'*Halte!*' cried Wheeler but as Drinkwater returned to guard Morris, with a yell of rage, cut at his opponent's flank. The blow stung Drinkwater's sword arm and bruised his ribs so that tears started in his eyes and his arm dropped. But it was only for a second. He lost his temper and jabbed forward. Wheeler was yelling for them to stop but Drinkwater's stick drove savagely into Morris's stomach muscles. Morris stumbled and bent forward. Drinkwater recovered and raised his smarting arm. He beat the length of his stick down upon Morris's back.

'*Halte! Halte!*' screamed Wheeler jumping up and down with the excitement.

'Leave 'em! Leave 'em!' yelled the cheering onlookers.

Drinkwater hit Morris again as he went down. His arm was filled now with the pent-up venom in his soul. He struck Morris for himself, for Sharples and for Kate Sharples until someone pinioned him from behind. Morris lay prone. Someone passed a bucket along. A woman shouted it was full of 'lady's pee' and the crowd roared its approval as it was emptied over Morris's back.

Lieutenant Devaux, disturbed from the quiet consumption of a third bottle of looted Madeira by the yelling and stamping, elbowed his way through the crowd. He was blear-eyed and dishevelled. He regarded the scene with a jaundiced eye.

'Our bloody little fire eater, eh?'

Silence fell. Punters melted away into the darkness. 'Send this rabble forward. Wheeler! What in God's name are you doing here? Who's in charge? Wheeler, what's the meaning of all this tomfoolery?'

But as Wheeler began to explain an astonished Lieutenant Price came in. Looking at the tableau in ill-disguised regret that he had missed the rout, he addressed the first lieutenant.

'Captain's compliments, Mr Devaux, and will you attend him in the cabin immediately.'

For answer Devaux swore horribly and left the company. A few moments later, hair clubbed, hatted and coated he made his way aft.

'Orders to sail, I believe,' Price said quietly to Wheeler by way of explanation.

Drinkwater overheard. He drew a deep, deep breath and turned his back on the shakily standing Morris. They could sail to hell and back now, thought Nathaniel, for he no longer felt oppressed by his boyhood.

Chapter Eight   *July–August 1780*

The Capture of the *Algonquin*

Cyclops was under easy canvas standing southward. At noon the ship was hove to and soundings tried for the Labadie Bank. As the yards swung round there was a sudden cry from the masthead: 'Sail Ho!'

Devaux ordered Drinkwater up with a glass. When he returned Hope was on deck.

'Schooner, sir,' the midshipman reported.

'Raked masts?'

'Aye, sir.'

'Yankee,' snapped Hope. 'Belay that nonsense, Mr Blackmore. Mr Devaux all sail, steer south.'

Blackmore looked crestfallen, holding the lead and examining the arming, but around him the ship burst into activity. The top-gallant sails were cast loose in their slack buntlines and the yards hoisted. Within minutes, braced round to catch the wind, the canvas tautened. *Cyclops* drove forward.

'Royals, sir?' queried Devaux as he and Hope gauged the wind strength.

'Royals, sir,' assented the captain. 'Royal halliards . . . hoist away!'

The light yards were set flying, sent aloft at the run to the bare poles above the straining topgallants. As the frigate spread her kites Hope walked forward and carefully ascended the foremast. Behind him Devaux, already querying the wisdom of setting royals in the prevailing breeze, expressed his opinion of captains who could not trust their officers to make reports. Ten minutes later the captain descended. Approaching the knot of officers on the quarterdeck he said, 'She's Yankee all right. Small, light and stuffed full of men. Luckily for us she's to loo'ard and the wind's inclined to freshen.'

'Should catch him then,' said Devaux, looking pointedly aloft.

'Aye,' ruminated Blackmore, still peeved at the captain's disregard for his navigational technicalities, 'but if he once gets to windward he'll stand closer than us . . .'

'Quite!' snapped Hope, 'and now Mr Devaux we will clear for action.'

Since sailing from Spithead on a cruise against enemy privateers and commerce raiders, the mood in *Cyclops*'s cockpit had changed. The affair of Morris and Drinkwater had been the ship's own *cause célèbre* since many, particularly on the lower deck, knew the background to the quarrel. The immediate consequences for the protagonists had been a mastheading each after which Morris lost all credibility in the mess and, aware of the thinness of the ice upon which he now skated, assumed an attitude of almost total self-effacement. The change in his attitude was quite incredible and while he nursed a venomous hatred for Drinkwater he was himself now haunted by the noose.

Drinkwater, on the other hand, had become overnight a popular hero. His own stature increased with the hands and his self-confidence grew daily. Wheeler had made of him a sort of friend and had undertaken to school him in the smallsword. Drinkwater rapidly became adept at fencing and was once or twice invited to dine in the gunroom. Tregembo and Sharples attached themselves firmly to the midshipman and formed a sort of bodyguard.

After the scrap Blackmore had taken Drinkwater aside and quizzed him further about Morris. Drinkwater had not wanted to press charges and Blackmore saw to it that Morris knew this. The old man was confident that Morris would give no more trouble on the present cruise.

The sighting of the Yankee schooner was the first opportunity *Cyclops* had had of intercepting all but merchant ships and the crew were in high spirits as she bore down on her quarry.

The chase had seen *Cyclops* but failed to recognise the danger until too late. Approaching end-on the Americans had taken the frigate for a merchantman and a potential prize. The appearance of *Cyclops*'s gun muzzles however, urged the rebels to flee. The schooner's helm was put up and she made off before the wind.

She was a small, low vessel, a fast soft-wood craft built in the shipyards of Rhode Island. But *Cyclops*, now carrying her studding sails in the freshening breeze, was tearing down on her. The American held his canvas but his smaller vessel laboured with its huge gaff sails threatening to bury her bow and broach her. The British frigate came on with a great white bone in her teeth. On her fo'c's'le Devaux waited for her bow to rise. The bow chaser barked.

'Short by God!' The gun's crew loaded again. Smoke belched a second time from the muzzle as the frigate ascended.

A dozen glasses were pointed at the schooner fine to larboard. The knot of officers on the quarterdeck muttered their opinions to each other. Drinkwater lingered, retained as messenger to the captain.

'We're closing all right.'

'He still hasn't hoisted colours.'

'There they are.' The American ensign rose to the peak and snapped out in the wind. The schooner was driving forward under too great a press of canvas. White water surged beneath her bow and along her side. A brief puff of smoke appeared, instantly dissipated by the wind. A hole opened in the frigate's forecourse.

'Good shooting by heaven!'

'Aye, and Hon Johnny will be bloody cross . . .'

Devaux's long nine-pounder barked again. A hole was visible in the schooner's mainsail.

'*Quid pro quo*,' said Keene.

'What'd you do now?' asked Wheeler of no one in particular.

'I'd stand to windward as fast as I could, once up wind of us he'll get away,' said Lieutenant Price. Everyone knew the schooner, with her fore and aft rig, could haul a bowline faster than a square-rigged frigate, but Price's opinion was contested by Drinkwater who could no longer hold himself silent.

'Beg pardon, Mr Price, but he's his booms to larboard with the wind aft. To stand to wind'ard he has to gybe on to the larboard tack. To do so on the starboard he must needs cross our bow . . .'

'He'll have to do something,' said Price irritably . . .

'Look!' said several voices at once.

The American commander knew his business. Aware that his desperate gamble of overcarrying canvas had failed, he decided to stand to windward on the larboard tack. But the risk of a gybe that would carry away gear was unacceptable if he was to escape, and he had to think of something to reduce this risk. Hope had been intently studying the Yankee, had reasoned along the lines that Drinkwater had followed and was anticipating some move by the rebel ship.

What the officers had seen was the scandalising of the two big gaff sails. The wooden gaffs began to hang down on their peak halyards, taking the power out of the canvas. But Hope had already noticed the topping lifts tighten to take the weight of the booms even before the peak halyards were started. He began roaring orders.

'Hands to braces! Move damn you!'

'Foretack! Maintack!'

The officers and men were galvanised to action. Hope looked again at the schooner, her speed had slackened. As Devaux's gun barked again the shot went over. The schooner began to turn. Now her stern was towards *Cyclops*. Through the glass Drinkwater read her name: *Algonquin, Newport*. He reported it to Hope. The schooner rolled to starboard as she came round, then her booms whipped over as she gybed. But the Americans were skilful. The main and foresheets were overhauled and the wind spilled from the scandalised sails.

'Down helm!'

'Lee braces!'

'Mainsail haul!'

'Let go an' haul!'

Even as *Algonquin*'s gaffs rose again and her sails were hauled flat, *Cyclops* was turning. Hope's task was to traverse the base of a triangle the hypotenuse of which formed *Algonquin*'s track. The schooner pointed to windward better than the frigate and if she reached the angle of the triangle before *Cyclops*, without damage, her escape was almost certain.

On the fo'c's'le Devaux was transferring his attention to the starboard bow chaser as *Cyclops* steadied on her new course, heeling over under her press of canvas.

A crack came from aloft. The main royal had dissolved into tattered strips.

'Aloft and secure that raffle!'

The *Algonquin* was pointing well up but still carrying too much canvas. Nevertheless she was head-reaching on the British frigate. For a few minutes the two ships raced on, the wind in the rigging and the hiss of water along their hulls the only significant sounds accompanying their grim contest. Then Devaux fired the starboard bow chaser. The shot passed through *Algonquin*'s mainsail close to the first hole. A seam opened up and the sail flogged in two . . . three pieces.

Cyclops came up with her victim and hove-to just to windward. The Yankee ensign remained at the gaff.

Hope turned to Drinkwater. 'My compliments to Mr Devaux and he may fire the first division at that fellow.' Drinkwater hurried forward and delivered his message. The first lieutenant descended to the gun-deck and the six leading twelve-pounders in the starboard battery roared their command. The American struck.

'Mr Price, take a midshipman, two quartermasters, two bosun's mates and twenty men. Plymouth or Falmouth, Mr Price. Mr Wheeler, a file of your marines!'

'Aye, aye, sir!'

The long boat was swayed up from the waist and over the side, the yardarms blocks clicking with the efforts of the seamen. Once in the water men tumbled down into it. Drinkwater heard his own name called out by Price.

'Mr Drinkwater, see the Master for our position and a chart.'

'Aye, aye, sir!' The midshipman went in search of Blackmore. The old master was still grumbling about interruptions to his soundings on the Labadie Bank, but he wrote out the estimated latitude and longitude quickly enough. As Drinkwater turned away the old man grabbed his arm.

'Be careful, lad,' he said, full of concern, 'Yon's not like the Don.'

Drinkwater swallowed. In the excitement he had not realised the implications of boarding the prize. He went off to join the longboat. In minutes it was pulling across the water between the two ships.

Once clear of the ship's lee the force of the wind tore off the wave-caps, dashing the spray into the boat. Sergeant Hagan reminded his men to cover their primings and the marines moved as one man to place their hands over the pans. Halfway between *Cyclops* and *Algonquin* the longboat swooped into the wave troughs so that only the mastheads of the two ships were visible. Then those of *Cyclops* receded as those of the rebel ship loomed over them.

Drinkwater had a peculiarly empty feeling in the pit of his stomach. He was aware of the collective tension of the prize crew as they sat, stony-faced, each man wrapped in his own apprehension. Drinkwater felt vulnerably small, sitting alongside Price, as they took the frail boat over this turbulent circle of the vast ocean. Astern of them *Cyclops*, the mighty home of thirteen score of men dwindled into insignificance.

Hope had deliberately detailed a large body of men for taking the privateer. He knew she would have a numerous and aggressive crew capable of manning her own prizes. As the longboat neared the privateer Drinkwater realised Blackmore's predictions would be right. This was no comparison with the boarding of the *Santa Teresa*. There, wrapped in the powerful protection of a victorious fleet, he had felt no qualms. The dramatic circumstances of the Moonlight Battle and the rapid succession of events that had resulted in him accepting a surrendered sword, had combined into an experience of almost sublime exhilaration. The remnants of chivalric war were absent now. The bayonets of the marines glittered cruelly. With a dreadful pang of nauseous fear Drinkwater imagined what it would be like to be pierced by so ghastly a weapon. He shrank from the thought.

The next moment they were alongside the schooner.

The twenty seamen followed Price up the side, Hagan and his marines brought up the rear. Lieutenant Price addressed a blue-coated man who appeared to be the commander.

'I must ask you for your vessel's papers, sir.' The blue-coated one turned away.

Sergeant Hagan swept his men through the ship. She had a crew of forty-seven seamen. Having ascertained the large fo'c's'le was secured by one hatch he herded them below. Under the guns of *Cyclops* three cables distant they went resentfully but without resistance.

Price, having possessed himself of the ship had a man run up British colours and set his men to securing and repairing the main-sail. The privateer's officers were confined in the cabin aft and a marine sentry put on guard. Next the lieutenant turned two of the quarter guns inboard to sweep the deck and had them loaded with grapeshot. The keys of the magazine were secured and the vessel's details passed down into the waiting longboat for return to *Cyclops*.

With a damaged mainsail Price was limited to the gaff foresail and a staysail but he set course and trimmed the sheets. In twenty-three minutes the privateer *Algonquin* of Newport, Rhode Island, operating under letters of marque from the Continental Congress was seized by His Britannic Majesty's Navy.

The blue-coated man remained on deck. He was staring at the frigate that had taken his ship from him. The distance between the two vessels was increasing. He banged his fist on the rail then turned to find the British Lieutenant at his elbow.

'I am sorry, sir, to be the agent of your distress, but you are oper-ating illegally under the authority of a rebel organisation which does not possess that authority. Will you give me your parole not to attempt to retake this ship or must I confine you like a felon?' Price's courteously modulated Welsh voice could not disguise his mistrust of the silent American.

At last the man spoke in the colonial drawl.

'You, sir, are the practitioners of piracy. You and all your country's perfidious acts and tyrannous oppressions be damned! I shall give you no parole and I shall take back my ship. You are outnumbered and may rest assured that my men will not take kindly to you con-fining them forward. You will get little sleep lootenant, so you think on that and be damned to 'ee!'

Blue coat turned away. Price nodded to Hagan who, with two marines, roughly urged the commander below.

Price looked about him. The sail repair was progressing. Midship-man Drinkwater and the two quartermasters had organised the deck, the tiller was manned and the course set for the Channel. Lieutenant Price looked astern. *Cyclops* was already only a speck on the horizon, resuming her cruise. He felt lonely. During his eight years at sea he had been prizemaster on several occasions but the prizes had invariably been docile, undermanned merchantmen. True their masters and crews had resented capture but they had given little trouble in the face of armed might.

In the dreary years of the war with the Americans the British had learned their opponents possessed an almost unfair capacity for seizing opportunities. True their generalissimo, Washington, continually faced mutiny in his own army, but when the British might be caught at a disadvantage the damned Yankees would appear like magic. Burgoyne had found that out. So had St Leger. Even when the greatest American tactician, Benedict Arnold, changed sides, the laconic British High Command learned too late the value of such talents.

The fate of Lieutenant Price was sealed in that same restless energy. He was surprised, even in death, that men of his own race could treat his humanity with such contempt.

For two days *Algonquin* steered south east to pass south of the Scillies before hauling up Channel. The big mainsail had been repaired and hoisted. Drinkwater took a keen interest in the sailing of the schooner. Unfamiliar with the qualities of fore and aft rig he was fascinated by her performance. He had no idea a vessel could move so fast with a beam wind and listened with interest when the two quartermasters fell to arguing as to whether it was possible to sail faster than the wind itself. Indeed the fears planted by Blackmore were withering as Nathaniel experienced the joys of independence.

The weather remained sunny and pleasant, the wind light but favourable. The Americans appeared in small groups on deck forward for daily exercise and Sergeant Hagan and his marines saw to the policing of the schooner.

The American mates gave little trouble, remaining confined in one cabin whilst the privateer's commander was locked in the other. They were allowed on deck at different times so that one or other of them was usually to be seen standing close to the mainmast shrouds during daylight.

The principal stern cabin had been seized by Price and the midshipmen whilst the seamen and marines used the hold tween decks for accommodation. This space had been intended to house the crew of prizes taken by the *Algonquin.*

By the evening of the second day Price had relaxed a little. An hour earlier one of the American sailors had asked to see him. Price had gone forward. A man had stepped out and asked if they could provide a cook since the food they were receiving was making them ill. If the 'lootenant' would agree to this they would promise to behave.

Price considered the matter and agreed they could supply a cook but that no further relaxation of their regimen could be allowed. He estimated his position to be some ten leagues south of the Lizard and hoped to stand north the following day and make Falmouth.

But that night the wind fell light and then died away altogether. As dawn filtered through it revealed a misty morning. The schooner lay rolling in the water as a lazy swell caused her blocks to rattle and her gear to chafe.

When Price was called he was in a passion at the change of weather. By noon there was still no sign of wind and he had the big gaff sails lowered to reduce chafe. The hands were engaged with this work as the American cook went forward, a pot of stew in his hands.

Drinkwater was standing right aft. As the big mainsail was lowered he hove in the slack of the sheet and coiled it down.

There was a sudden scream from forward.

The marine sentry, bending down to open the companionway for the prisoners' cook had had the boiling contents of the pot dashed into his face.

In a trice the American had picked up the marine's musket and threatened the four seamen lowering the foresail. For a split-second every man on *Algonquin*'s deck was motionless then, with a whoop, the Americans were pouring aft. They hurled themselves at the unarmed seamen as the latter let go the halyards, they pulled belaying pins from the rail and rolled aft, a screaming human tide. The foresail came down in a rush, adding to the confusion.

The seamen forward were quickly overpowered but further aft Hagan had got several marines to present. The muskets cracked and three Americans went down. Lieutenant Price lugged out his hanger and leapt for the lanyard of the starboard quarter gun. He tugged it. A flash and roar emanated through the fog as the grape cut a swathe through friend and foe. Momentarily the human tide was stemmed. Then it rolled aft again.

Drinkwater remained rooted to the spot. This was all a dream. In a moment the fog would clear and *Algonquin* become her ordered self again. A pistol ball smacked into the rail beside him. He saw Price, mouth drawn back into a snarl, whirling the slender hanger. One, two rebels received its needle point in their bodies then, with a sickening thud, a handspike whirled by a giant half-caste Indian split the lieutenant's skull.

Drinkwater suddenly felt inexplicably angry. Nothing could withstand the furious onslaught of the Americans. He was dimly aware of struggling British seamen and marines being held by three or four of the privateersmen. He knew he was about to die and felt furious at the knowledge. He choked on his rage, tears leaping into his eyes. Suddenly his dirk was in his hand and he was lunging forward. The big half-caste saw him coming too late. The man had picked up Price's hanger out of curiosity. Suddenly aware of the midshipman rushing towards him he bent and held it outwards like a hunting knife.

Drinkwater remembered his fencing. As the Indian jabbed the sword upwards Drinkwater's dirk took the hanger's foible in a semi-circular parry. Taking the blade he exerted a *prise-de-fer*, raised his point and his own momentum forced his toy weapon into the stomach of the Indian.

The man howled with pain and surprise as they collided. Then he collapsed on top of him. For a moment Drinkwater's anger evaporated into sudden, chilling fear, a fear mingled with an overwhelming sense of relief. Then he received a blow on the head and was plunged into a whirlpool of oblivion.

When Drinkwater recovered consciousness it was several minutes before he realised what had happened. He was confused by total darkness and a regular creaking sound that terminated in a number of almost simultaneous dull knocks before starting again.

'Wh . . . where the hell am I?' he asked out loud.

A groan came from alongside him. Then a hand grasped his knee.

'Mister Drinkwater?' A strained voice enquired, pain and anxiety in the tone of it.

'Yes.'

'Grattan, sir, marine.'

'Eh . . . Oh, yes.'

'We're in the fo'c's'le . . . just the wounded, sir . . .'

'Wounded?'

'Aye, sir, you were unconscious. My arm's broken . . .'

'Oh, I'm sorry . . .'

'Thank you, sir.' Drinkwater's brain was beginning to grasp the situation and an enormous and painful bump on the crown of his head testified to the accuracy of the marine's report. Recollection came back to him. He sat up and took stock.

'What's that noise then?'

'Sweepin', sir . . . that's what the others are doin'.'

Before he could ask more the hatch flew open. A few cold drops of moisture dripped into Drinkwater's upturned face, then the shape of a man lowering himself down blotted out the foggy daylight.

The man bent over each of the prisoners in turn. When he got to Drinkwater he grunted: 'You're fit. Get on deck!' He grabbed Drinkwater's arm and dragged him to his feet.

A few moments later Drinkwater stood unsteadily on the deck of *Algonquin* and looked aft. The source of the strange noise revealed itself. Still shrouded in fog, *Algonquin* was making slow but steady headway over the calm, grey sea. Between the gunports oak thole pins had been driven into the caprail. At each set of pins a long oar, or sweep, was shipped. Two men were stationed at each sweep, heaving it back and forth so that the schooner made way to the southward. The men at the sweeps were nearly all British. One of the American mates walked up and down the deck with a rope's end. Every now and again he brought it down on the bare back of a seaman or the sweat-darkened red coat of a marine.

Drinkwater was pushed along the deck, given a pannikin of green water from the scuttle butt and shoved alongside a marine pulling the aftermost larboard sweep. The man was Hagan. He was running with sweat as the rigging dripped with foggy dew.

Hagan grunted a welcome and Drinkwater grasped the loom of the sweep. It was slippery with the blood and plasma of the man he had relieved. Within a quarter of an hour Drinkwater knew why the privateer was under sweeps. The progress through the fog was an advantage to the American commander but it was also the most efficient way of exhausting the British. An exhausted prize crew would not attempt further resistance.

After an hour Drinkwater had reached a state of physical numbness that utterly overpowered him. He had ceased to feel the mate's starter. His head throbbed but his brain had ceased to function. It was Hagan who roused him from his torpor. The marine sergeant hissed between clenched teeth, 'Breeze comin'.'

Drinkwater raised his head and wiped the sweat out of his eyes.

81

A catspaw rippled the greasy surface of the sea. The sun was brighter now, warmer. He had no idea of the time nor of how long he had been semi-conscious. The fog began to disperse. Imperceptibly at first, wind and sunshine broke through the murk.

An hour later there was a breeze. Light and fitful, it steadied to become a north westerly air. From a zephyr it graduated to a breeze and the American commander ordered the sweeps inboard and the sails hoisted. Before they were herded below into the fo'c's'le Drinkwater was aware that *Algonquin* was headed south-east for he had heard the helm order. As the hatch closed over the British the schooner heeled and the water of the Channel hissed past her washboards with increasing speed.

A Turning of Tables

The British prize crew aboard the *Algonquin* were in a pathetic state. It had been evening when the Americans had retaken their ship. All that night the British had swept the craft south, away from the Cornish coast. It was the following dawn when the midshipman, recovering consciousness, had been forced on deck. By the time the breeze sprang up the day was far advanced.

In the stinking fo'c's'le the British sprawled in all attitudes of exhausted abandon. After a while the eyes adjusted to the darkness and Drinkwater could see the men asleep. He looked for Grattan. The man tossed restlessly, his eyes staring. He was the only other man awake. Another, whose name Drinkwater did not know, was dead. His head had been injured and dried blood blackened his face. He lay stiff, his mouth open, emitting a silent cry that would echo forever. Drinkwater shivered.

Grattan was muttering incoherently for the pain of his arm had brought on a fever.

At noon the hatch was shoved open. A pan of thin soup, some biscuit and water were lowered down. The hatch was being closed again when Drinkwater roused himself and called, 'We've a dead man down here.'

The hatch stopped and the silhouette of a man's head and shoulders was visible against the sky.

'So?' he drawled.

'Will you permit him to be taken on deck?' There was a pause.

'He's one of yours. You brought him: you keep him.' A gobbet of spittle flew down and the hatch slammed shut.

The exchange had woken the men. They made for the food,

improvising means of eating it, dunking the biscuit and sucking it greedily.

After a while Sergeant Hagan crawled over to the midshipman.

'Beg pardon, Mr Drinkwater, but 'ave you any orders?'

'Eh? What's that?' Drinkwater was uncomprehending.

'Mr Price is dead. You're in charge, sir.'

Drinkwater looked at the quartermasters and the marines. They were all older than him. They had all been at sea longer than he had. Surely they were not expecting him to . . .? He looked at Hagan. Hagan with twenty-odd years of sea-soldiering to his credit, Hagan with his bragging stories of service under Hawke and Boscawen, Hagan with his resource and courage . . .

But Hagan was looking at *him*. Drinkwater's mouth opened to protest his unsuitability. He had not the slightest idea what to do. He closed it again.

Hagan came to his rescue.

'Right lads, Mr Drinkwater wants a roll-call,' he said, 'so let's see how many of us there are . . . Right . . .' Hagan coughed, 'Marines speak up!' Apart from the sergeant there were five marines left.

'Quartermasters?' The two quartermasters were both still alive and unwounded.

'Bosun's mates?' There was silence.

'Seamen?' Eleven voices were eventually identified, one of whom complained of a sprained ankle.

Hagan turned to Drinkwater. 'That's . . . er, counting yerself, sir, that's exactly a score, though one is unfit, sir . . .' Hagan seemed to think that this round figure represented some triumph for the British.

'Thank you, Sergeant,' Drinkwater managed, unconsciously aping Devaux in his diction. He wondered what was next expected of him. Hagan asked:

'Where d'ye think they mean to take us, sir?'

Drinkwater was about to snap that he had not the faintest idea when he remembered the helm orders as he left the deck.

'South-east,' he said. Recalling the chart he repeated their course and added their destination. 'South-east, to France . . .'

'Aye,' said one of the quartermasters, 'The bloody rebels have found some fine friends with the frog-eating Johnny Crapos. They'll be takin' us to Morlaix or St Malo . . .'

Hagan spoke again. His simple words came like a cold douche to Drinkwater. Hagan was the fighter, Hagan the expediter of plans. Hagan would not shrink from a physical task once that task had been assigned to him. But he looked to the quality to provide the ideas. To him Drinkwater, in his half-fledged manhood, represented the quality. In the general scheme of things it was assumed a person of Drinkwater's rank automatically had the answer. He was what was known on a King's ship as a 'young gentleman'.

'What do we do, sir?'

Drinkwater's mouth flapped open again. Then he collected himself and spoke, realising their plight was hourly more desperate.

'We retake the ship!'

A pathetically feeble, yet strangely gratifying, cheer went round the men.

Drinkwater went on, gaining confidence as he strung his thoughts together.

'Every mile this ship covers takes her nearer to France and you all know what that means . . .' There was a morose grumble that indicated they knew only too well. '. . . There are nineteen fit men here against what? . . . about three dozen Americans? Does anyone know approximately how many were killed on deck?'

A speculative buzz arose, indicative of rising morale.

'Lots went down when the lieutenant fired the gun, sir . . .' Drinkwater recognised Sharples's voice. In the bustle of events he had forgotten all about Sharples and his being in the prize crew. He was oddly comforted by the man's presence. '. . . and we fixed a few, you did for one, sir . . .' admiration was clear in the man's voice.

Hagan interrupted. It was a sergeant's business to estimate casualties. 'I'd say we did for a dozen, Mr Drinkwater . . . say three dozen left.' Grunts of agreement came from the men.

'Right, three dozen it is,' Drinkwater continued. An idea had germinated in his brain. 'They're armed, we're not. We're in the fo'c's'le which is sealed from the rest of the ship. It was the one place *we* chose to put *them*.' He paused.

'They got out because they made a plan long before we took them. As a . . . er . . . contingency . . . I heard the American captain tell Lieutenant Price he would retake his ship. It was almost like a boast. I've heard Americans have a reputation for boasting . . .' A desperate cackle that passed for a laugh emanated from the gloomy darkness.

Hagan interrupted again. 'But I don't see how this helps us, sir. They got out.'

'Yes, Mr Hagan. They got out by using their plan. They were model prisoners until they had made their arrangements. They lulled us until the last possible moment then they took back their ship. If we hadn't run into fog we might have been under the lee of the Lizard by now . . .' he paused again, collecting his thoughts, his heart thumping at the possibility . . .

'Someone told me these Yankee ships were mostly made of soft-wood and liable to rot.' A murmur of agreement came from one or two of the older hands.

'Perhaps we could break through the bulkhead or deck into the hold, and work our way aft. Then we could turn the tables on them . . .'

There was an immediate buzz of interest. Hagan, however was unconvinced and adopted an avuncular attitude. 'But, Nat lad, if we can do that why didn't the Yankees?'

'Aye, aye,' said several voices.

But Drinkwater was convinced it was their only hope. 'Well I'm not sure,' he replied, 'but I think they didn't want to raise our suspicions by any noise. It is going to be difficult for us . . . Anyway, if I am right they already had a plan worked out which relied on us behaving in a predictable manner. Now we've got to better them. Let's start searching for somewhere to begin.'

In the darkness it took them an hour to find a weak, spongy plank in the deck of the fo'c's'le. Hagan produced the answer to their lack of tools by employing his boots. The joke this produced raised morale still further, for the booted marines, the unpopular policemen of a man o'war, were the butt of many a barefoot sailor's wit.

Hagan smashed in enough to get a hand through, timing his kicks to coincide with the plunging of the *Algonquin*'s bow into the short Channel seas. For the wind veered and the schooner was laid well over, going to windward like a thoroughbred. Regularly and rhyth-mically she thumped into each wave and as she did so she disguised the noise of demolition.

The deck lifted easily once an aperture had been made. Access was swiftly gained to the cable tier below. Drinkwater descended himself.

The schooner's cable lay on a platform of wooden slats. Beneath these the swirl and rush of bilge water revealed a passage aft. It was totally dark below but, doing his best to ignore the stench, he pressed on driven by desperation. He wriggled over the coils of rope and in one corner, unencumbered by cable he found the athwartships bulkhead that divided the forepart of the ship from the hold. Here he found the slatting broken and ill-fitting.

He had to get aft of the bulkhead. He struggled down in the corner, worming his way beneath the cable tier platform where they failed to meet the ship's side properly. Something ran over his foot. He shuddered in cold terror, never having mastered a fear of rats. Fighting back his nausea he lowered himself into the bilge water. Its cold stink rose up on his legs and lapped at his genitals. For a long moment he hung poised, the malodorously filthy water clammily disgusting him. Then a strange, detached feeling came over him: as if he watched himself. In that moment he gained strength to go on. Continuing his immersion Nathaniel Drinkwater finally forsook adolescence.

Algonquin was on the larboard tack, leaning to starboard. By sheer good fortune Drinkwater's descent was on the larboard side. There was therefore a greater amount of water to starboard and a 'dry' space for him to cling to. Even so it was slippery with stinking slime. He could see nothing, and yet his eyes stared apprehensively into darkness. All his senses were alert, that of smell almost overpowered by the stench of the bilge. But although he gagged several times he was possessed now by an access of power that drove him relentlessly on, ignoring his bodily weaknesses, impelled by his will.

He moved aft over each of *Algonquin*'s timbers. Eventually he found what he hardly dared hope he would discover. The schooner's builders had not constructed the pine planking of the bulkhead down to the timbers. It extended to cross 'floors' which supported the 'ceiling' that formed the bottom of the hold. Between that and the ship's skin a small bilge space ran the length of the vessel.

Drinkwater continued aft. Having eventually completed his reconnaissance he began to return to his fellow prisoners. He was excited so that twice he slipped, once going into the foul water up to his chest, but at last he wriggled back into the fo'c's'le. The men were expectantly awaiting his return. They offered him a pull at the water pannikin which he accepted gratefully. Then he looked round the barely discernible circle of faces.

'Now my lads,' he said with new-found authority, 'this is what we'll do . . .'

Captain Josiah King, commander of the privateer *Algonquin*, sat in the neat stern cabin of his schooner drinking a looted bottle of Malmsey. He would be in Morlaix by morning if the wind did not veer again. There he could disencumber himself of these British prisoners. He shuddered at the recollection of losing his ship, but as quickly consoled himself with his own forethought. The contingency plan had worked well – the British lieutenant had been a fool. The British always were. King had been with Whipple when the Rhode Islanders burnt the Government schooner *Gapée*, back in '72. He remembered her captain, Lieutenant Duddingstone, acting the hero waving a sword about. A thrust in the groin soon incapacitated him. They had cast the unfortunate lieutenant adrift in a small boat. King smiled at the memory. When the magistrates eventually examined the cause of the burning the entire population of the town protested ignorance. King knew every spirited man in Newport had answered Whipple's summons. The American smiled again.

Burgoyne had been a fool too with his clap-trap about honourable terms of surrender. Never mind that Gates had promised his army a safe-conduct to the coast. The British had surrendered and then been locked up for their pains. That was what war was about: winning. Simply that and nothing else.

Warmed by recollection and wine he did not hear the slight scuffle of feet in the alleyway outside . . .

Drinkwater's plan worked perfectly. They had waited until well after dark. By this time such food as the Americans allowed them had been consumed. Each fit man was detailed off to follow in order and keep in contact with the man ahead.

The midshipman led the way. The wind had eased and *Algonquin* heeled less. The passage of the bilge was foul. Rats scrabbled out of their way, squealing a protest into the darkness, but no one complained. The filthy fo'c's'le was stinking with the corpse's corruption and their own excrement. Activity, even in a malodorous bilge, was preferable to the miasma of death prevailing in their cramped quarters.

When he reached the after end of the hold Drinkwater moved out to the side. Here there were gratings that ran round the schooner's lazarette. The wooden powder magazine was set in the centre of the ship with the catwalk all around. This was decked with the gratings that now barred their passage. Upon these the gunner's mates walked round tending the lanterns that, shining through glass, safely illuminated the gunner within and enabled him to make up his cartridges.

Sergeant Hagan followed Drinkwater. Between them they lifted a grating and got through. Men followed silently. They were still in darkness but a faint current of air told where a small hatch led on deck at the top of a panelled trunking. It was locked. Drinkwater and Hagan felt round the space. Behind the ladder they found a door that led into the after quarters. It too was locked.

Hagan swore. They knew that once they were through that door they had a fair chance of success. In there were the officers' quarters. On either side of the alleyway beyond there were a couple of cabins and at the end, athwart the ship, the stern cabin. If they failed to capture the deck possession of the after quarters would probably result in the capture of an officer who might be useful as a hostage. But the door was secured against them.

Drinkwater dared not rattle the lock. In the darkness he could hear his men breathing. They all relied on him; what could he do now? He felt the hot tears of frustrated anger begin to collect and he was for the first time thankful for the darkness.

'Beg pardon, sir . . .?' A voice whispered.

'Yes?'

'Locked door, sir?'

'Yes.' He replied without hope.

'Let me have a look, sir.'

There was a pushing and a shoving. A man came past. There was a silence as eighteen men held their breath, the creaking of the schooner and hiss of the sea seemed inaudible. Then a faint click was heard.

A man shoved back into the queue.

'Try it now, sir.'

Drinkwater found the handle and turned it very slowly. The door gave. He pulled it to again. 'What's your name?'

'Best you don't know it sir.'

There was a muffled snigger. The man was doubtless one of *Cyclops*'s many thieves. With the scum of London pressed in her crew it was not surprising. Nevertheless the man's nefarious skill had saved the situation.

'Are you ready?' Drinkwater enquired generally in a loud whisper.

'Aye! Aye! . . .' The replies were muffled but nothing could disguise their eagerness.

Drinkwater opened the door. He made directly for the companionway. Hagan and the marine behind him made for the arms chest outside the stern cabin. Alternately a marine and a seaman emerged blinking into the dimly lit alleyway. The marines armed themselves with the cutlasses Hagan thrust at them; then in pairs they burst into the cabins. They took Josiah King before the Rhode Islander's feet hit the deck. His flimsy cabin door was dashed to matchwood and Hagan, his face contorted into a furious grimace presented the point of a cutlass to King's chest.

Drinkwater dashed on deck. His heart was pounding and fear leant a ferocity to him. The companionway emerged on deck abaft a skylight that let on to the passageway. Fortunately for the British a canvas cover was pulled over this to prevent the light disturbing the helmsman. But the helmsman stood immediately aft of the hatch, behind the binnacle. He leant against the huge tiller, straining with the effort of maintaining weather helm.

The mate on deck was a little further forward but he turned at the helmsman's exclamation. Drinkwater ran full tilt at the mate, knocking him over. The two men behind him secured the helmsman. He was tossed howling over the stern while the next man grabbed the tiller so that *Algonquin* scarcely faltered on her course.

The American officer rolled breathless on the deck. He attempted to rise and summon the assistance of the watch but Drinkwater, recovering from his butting charge, had whipped a belaying pin from the rail. The hardwood cracked on the man's head and laid him unconscious on his own deck.

Drinkwater stood panting with effort. The noise of blood and energy roared in his ears. It was impossible that the *Algonquin*'s crew had not been awakened by the din. Around him the British, several armed by Hagan's marines gathered like black shadows As one man they rolled forward. Too late the Americans on deck realised something was amiss. They went down howling and fighting. One attempted to wake those below. But resistance was useless. Men threatened with imprisonment in a French hulk or the benches of a galley are desperate. Five Americans perished through drowning, hurled over *Algonquin*'s side. Several were concussed into insanity. Eight were killed by their own edged weapons, weapons intended to intimidate unarmed merchantmen. The remainder were penned into the hold so lately reserved for their victims.

In ten minutes the ship was retaken.

Half an hour later she was put about, the sheets eased and, on a broad reach, steadied on course for England.

Chapter Ten   *August 1780*

Elizabeth

Drinkwater leaned over the chart. Beside him a quartermaster named Stewart was pointing out the navigational dangers. Stewart had served as mate of a merchant ship and Drinkwater was thankful for his advice.

'I think Falmouth, Mr Drinkwater,' the man said. 'You'll find the distance less and you'll not need to fear the Eddystone. The lighthouse is fine but the light feeble. Nay I'd say the twin cressets of the Lizard will be a better mark.'

Drinkwater heeded Stewart. The former mate was a tough and experienced mariner which the incongruous paradoxes of human social order placed under his orders.

'Very well. Falmouth it is. But I fear them retaking the ship. We have at least twenty leagues to run before sighting the Lizard . . .'

'I do not think they will attempt it. Hagan's guard won't let them trick us again. The boys'll spit them with their baynits before asking any questions. Just you refuse them all requests and favours, Mr Drinkwater.'

Rolling the charts up they went on deck.

Algonquin raced along, her canvas straining under the force of the wind. On either side of her the white water hissed urgently as her keel tramped down the waters of the Channel underfoot.

The breeze was fresh but steady, allowing them to keep sail on the schooner and reel off a steady seven knots. At eight bells the next morning the sun caught the twin white towers of the Lizard and at noon *Algonquin* ran into Falmouth Harbour, under the guns of St Mawes and Pendennis castles. At her peak she flew British over American colours. Drinkwater brought her to an anchor under the guns of a frigate lying in Carrick Roads.

Drinkwater was reluctant to leave *Algonquin* and report to the frigate, but the warship sent her own boat. Amidst a crowd of unfamiliar faces he was rowed across to her. She proved to be the *Galatea*.

Reporting to the third lieutenant he was informed the Captain was in lodgings ashore but that the first lieutenant would receive his report.

Drinkwater was conducted aft to where a tall, thin officer was bent almost double under the deck beams. He was coughing violently.

'Beg pardon, sir, this is Midshipman Drinkwater of the *Cyclops*. Prizemaster of the schooner yonder . . .' Drinkwater was suddenly a boy again, the responsibility of command lifted from him in the presence of this intimidating stranger. He felt very tired, tired and dirty.

The tall man looked at him and smiled. Then in an unmistakably Northumbrian accent he said, 'Watched you anchor mister. Well done. You'll have prisoners, no doubt?'

'Aye, sir, about twenty.'

The lieutenant frowned. 'About?' He fell to coughing again.

'I haven't allowed them on deck, sir. I'm not sure how many were killed last night.'

The officer's frown deepened. 'You say you're from *Cyclops*, lad?'

'Aye, sir, that's correct.'

'She's off Ireland or thereaboots, so how were you fighting last night?'

Drinkwater explained how the Americans had retaken the ship, how Lieutenant Price had been killed and briefly related the prize crew's desperate attempt to retrieve the situation. The first lieutenant's frown was replaced by a wry grin.

'You'll be wantin' to be rid of such troublesome fellars then.'

'Yes, sir.'

'I'll send some men and our longboat over. You'll have to take them to Pendennis. After that report to Captain Edgecumbe at the Crown.' The tall man indicated first the squat tower of Pendennis on its headland above the harbour and then the huddle of houses and cottages that constituted the market town of Falmouth. He broke into another fit of coughing.

'Thank you, sir.'

'My pleasure, lad,' said the tall man moving away.

'Beg pardon, sir?' The man turned, a bloody handkerchief to his mouth.

'May I ask your name?'

'Collingwood,' coughed the tall lieutenant.

Lieutenant Wilfred Collingwood was as good as his word. Half an hour later *Galatea*'s longboat was alongside and a file of marines came aboard. Hagan had done his best to smarten the crew up but they did not compare with *Galatea*'s men.

The Americans were herded into the boat. Drinkwater ordered *Algonquin*'s boat into the water and was rowed ashore with Stewart. On the stone pier of Falmouth's inner harbour the marines were lining the American prisoners up. Josiah King was paraded scowling at the head of his men and the scarlet coats were lined along either side of the downcast little column. Drinkwater, his trousers still damp and smelling of bilge, swaggered at their head while Stewart and six seamen followed with cutlasses.

Hagan, also stinking of bilge, marched beside Drinkwater. The column moved off. It was market day and Falmouth was crowded. The people cheered the little procession as it tramped through the narrow streets. Drinkwater was conscious of the eyes of girls and women, and found the sensation thus produced arousing. But such is the vanity of humanity that Sergeant Hagan threw out his chest and received the same glances with the same assurance that they were for him. Whereas in truth they were intended for the handsome, sulking American commander who, in the romantic hour of his defeat appealed to the perverse preference of the women.

Josiah King burned with a furious rage that seemed to roar in his skull like a fire. He burned with shame at losing his ship a second time. He burned with impotent anger that fate had wrested the laurels of victory from him, Josiah King of Newport, Rhode Island, and conferred them on the skinny young midshipman whose wet and smelly ducks stuck to his legs with every swaggering stride he took. He burned too with the knowledge that he had been outwitted at the very moment he had been congratulating himself on his forethought. That was perhaps the bitterest, most private, part of the affair. Behind him his men trooped disconsolately as the column moved out of the town and began to climb the headland.

The road passed the end of the hornworks ascending through low undergrowth. It was hot and the sun beat down upon them. Suddenly the ramparts rose on their left and they swung over the fosse, under the Italianate guard-house inside which the huge expanse of the castle enclosure revealed itself.

The guard had called the sergeant and the sergeant called his captain. The captain despatched an ensign to attend to the matter and continued his post-prandial doze. The ensign was insufferably pompous, having discovered that the escort was commanded by a none too clean midshipman. His condescending manner annoyed the exhausted Drinkwater who was compelled to endure the tedium of the unfamiliar and bewildering paperwork without which even the business of war could not be expedited. Each individual American had to be identified and signed for both by the ensign and the midshipman. All the while the sun beat down and Drinkwater felt the fatigue of a sleepless night merge with the euphoric relief from responsibility. At last the disdainful officer was satisfied.

The marines had fallen in again and the little party began to descend to the town.

With Stewart, Drinkwater repaired to the Crown Inn.

Captain Edgecumbe of His Britannic Majesty's frigate *Galatea* was an officer of the old school. When a ragamuffin midshipman appeared before him in filthy ducks the Captain was rightly wrathful. When that same scruffy midshipman attempted to report the arrival of the captured privateer *Algonquin* the captain refused to be side-tracked by incidentals. He also disliked interruptions.

The diatribe to which he subjected Drinkwater was as lengthy as it was unnecessary. In the end the midshipman stood silent, discovering, after some minutes had elapsed, that he was not even listening. Outside the hot sun shone and he had an odd longing to be doing nothing but lounging in that sunshine and perhaps have his arm about the waist of one of those pretty girls he had seen earlier. The sweet scent of Cornwall wafted in through the open window distracting his senses from the path of duty. Only when the Captain ceased his tirade did the sudden silence break into his reverie and drag his conscious mind back to the inn room. He looked at the Captain.

Sitting in his shirt-sleeves Edgecumbe looked what he was, a dissipated and incompetent officer, living out of his ship and indulging his sexual appetites with local ladies. Drinkwater felt a sudden surge of contempt for him.

He touched his forehead. 'Aye, aye, sir. Thank you, sir.' He turned and marched smartly from the room.

Downstairs he found Stewart in the taproom. He was chaffing with a red-cheeked girl. Drinkwater noticed with a flutter in his stomach the girl had bright eyes and apple breasts.

Stewart, slightly abashed, bought the midshipman a pot of beer.

'Be 'e yer Cap'n?' the girl asked Stewart, giggling incredulously and setting the tankard down in front of Drinkwater.

The quartermaster nodded flushing a little.

Drinkwater was confused by the unaccustomed proximity of the girl, but he felt Stewart's deference to his apparent importance as a spur to his manhood. She leaned over him boldly.

'Does y're honour need anything,' she enquired solicitously.

The heaving bosom no longer embarrassed him in his newfound confidence. He sucked greedily at the tankard, staring at the girl over its rim and enjoying her discomfiture as the beer warmed his belly. He was, after all, prize-master of the *Algonquin*, who had strutted through Falmouth under the admiring glances of scores of women . . .

He finished the beer. 'To tell the truth ma'am, I have not the means to purchase more than a pot or two of beer . . .'

The girl plumped herself on the bench next to Stewart. She knew the quartermaster had a guinea or half sovereign about him, for she had seen the glint of gold in his hand. Stewart's experience ensured he never ventured ashore without the price of a little dalliance or a good bottle about his person. The girl smiled at Drinkwater. It was a pity, she thought, he looked a nice young man, handsome in a pale sort of way. She felt Stewart's arm encircle her. Ah, well a girl had to live . . .

'Yer honour'll have matters of great importance to deal with,' she said pointedly. She began to nestle up to Stewart who was staring at him. Drinkwater was aware of the pressure of Stewart's arm on a large breast. The white flesh swelled up, threatening to eject itself from the ineffectively grubby confines of the girl's bodice.

Drinkwater smiled lightheartedly. Rising, he tossed a few coppers on to the table.

'Be on board by sunset, Mr Stewart.'

On his return to *Algonquin* Drinkwater found the schooner being washed down. Upon the deck lay a bundle. It was a dead man. The other wounded were up and about, Grattan had had his arm splinted by the surgeon of *Galatea*. In the absence of the midshipman Collingwood had been aboard the schooner and arranged for *Cyclops*'s injured to attend *Galatea* for medical attention. He had also ordered the remainder into cleaning their prize.

Collingwood took an interest in the *Algonquin* for he was shortly to be posted to the West Indies where such vessels abounded. Besides he had liked the look of the young midshipman, who had done well by all accounts. A little discreet questioning among *Algonquin*'s prize crew told how well. The lieutenant left a message that Drinkwater should report to him on his return aboard.

The quarterdeck of *Galatea* reminded Drinkwater of *Cyclops* and he experienced a pang of nostalgia for his own frigate. Collingwood took him to one side and questioned him.

'Did you see Captain Edgecumbe?'

'Yes, sir.' The lieutenant broke into a fit of coughing. 'What orders did he give you?' he asked at last.

'None, sir.'

'None?' queried the lieutenant, a mock frown creasing his forehead.

'Well, sir . . .' Drinkwater faltered. What did one say to a first lieutenant whose captain had filled you with contempt?

'He told me to change my uniform, sir, and to . . . and to . . .'

'To report to the Flag Officer, Plymouth, I don't doubt. Ain't that so, lad?'

Drinkwater looked at Collingwood and through his fatigue the light slowly dawned on him.

'Oh! Yes . . . yes, sir, that's correct.' He paused.

'Very well. I'd get under way tomorrow if I were you.'

'Aye, aye, sir.' The midshipman knuckled his forehead and turned away.

'Oh, and Mr Drinkwater!'

'Sir?'

'You cannot bury that man in the harbour. My carpenter is making a coffin. I have taken the liberty of arranging a burial service later this afternoon. You will attend the church of St Charles the Martyr at four o'clock. Do you give thanks to the Lord for your deliverance . . .' The tall lieutenant turned away in another paroxysm of coughing.

Drinkwater slept briefly and at five bells was called to find his ducks cleaned and pressed. Hagan had spruced up his marines and the little party that solemnly marched to the parish church with their dismal burden carried with them a kind of rough dignity. The organisation of a church burial for one of their number was a touch that Drinkwater did not really appreciate at the time.

Called upon to squander their life's blood in the service of an ungrateful country, the British seaman was inured to being treated worse than a beast. When gestures such as that made by Wilfred Collingwood touched their hearts they became an emotional breed. While Edgecumbe pursued the libertine path of the insensitive autocrat, Collingwood and others were learning the true trade of leadership. No-one was to play upon the sailor's heart-strings as well as Horatio Nelson, but he was not the only one to learn.

The church was marvellously cool after the heat of the afternoon. The little congregation shuffled awkwardly, sensing the incongruity of the occasion. Afterwards under the yew trees, the heat wrapped itself around the party again. Three men wept as the plain coffin was laid to rest, worn out with exertion and over-strung nerves.

The brief burial over, the seamen and marines prepared to march into town. The priest, a thin shrivelled man who wore his hair to the shoulder in the old fashioned manner, came over to the midshipman.

'I would be honoured, sir, if you would take a dish of tea with me at the vicarage yonder.'

'Thank you, sir,' Drinkwater bowed.

The two men entered the house which contained something of the cool of the church. It reminded Drinkwater abruptly and painfully of his own home. A table was set for three. It seemed that the priest had some knowledge of the prize crew's exploits for he addressed Drinkwater in enthusiastic tones.

'I am but the interregnum here, but I am sure that the incumbent would wish me to welcome the opportunity of entertaining a naval hero in his home . . .'

He motioned Drinkwater to a chair.

'You are most kind, sir,' Drinkwater replied, 'but I do not think my actions were those of an hero . . .'

'Come, come . . .'

'No, sir. I fear the threat of a French prison revived our spirits . . .' He rose as a woman came in bearing a tea kettle.

'Ahh, my dear, the tea . . .' The old man bobbed up and down wringing his hands.

'Mr Drinkwater, I'd like to present my daughter Elizabeth. Elizabeth, my dear, this is Mr Drinkwater . . . I fear I do not know the gentleman's Christian name though it would be an honour to do so . . .' He made little introductory gestures with his hands, opening and closing them like an inexpertly-managed glove puppet.

'Nathaniel, sir,' volunteered Drinkwater. The woman turned and Drinkwater looked into the eyes of a striking girl of about his own age. He took her hand and managed a clumsy little bow as he flushed with surprise and discomfiture. Her fingers were cool like the church. He mumbled:

'Y'r servant ma'am.'

'Honoured, sir.' Her voice was low and clear.

The trio sat. Drinkwater felt immediately oppressed by the quality of the crockery. The delicacy of the china after months of shipboard life made him feel clumsy.

The appearance of a plate of bread and cucumber, however, soon dispelled his misgivings.

'Nathaniel, eh,' muttered the old man. 'Well, well . . . "a gift of God"', he chuckled softly to himself, '. . . most appropriate . . . really most appropriate . . .'

Drinkwater felt a sudden surge of pure joy. The little parlour bright with chintzes and painted porcelain reminded him poignantly of home. There was even the air of threadbare gentility, of a pride that sometimes served as a substitute for more tangible sustenance.

As she poured the tea Drinkwater looked at the girl. He could see now that she was indeed his own age, though her old fashioned dress had conveyed an initial impression of greater maturity. She bit her lower lip as she concentrated on pouring the tea, revealing a row of even and near perfect teeth. Her dark hair was drawn back behind her head in an unpretentious tress and it combined with her eyes, eyes of a deep and understanding brown, to give her face the inescapable impression of sadness.

So struck was he with this melancholy that when she looked up to pass him his cup he held her gaze. She smiled and then he was surprised at the sudden vivacity in her face, a liveliness free of any reproach that his directness deserved. He felt contentment change into happiness absent from his life for many months. He felt a keen desire to please this girl, not out of mere gratuitous bravado, but because she had about her the soothing aura of calm and tranquillity. In the turmoil of his recent life he felt a powerful longing for spiritual peace.

Occupied with such thoughts he was unaware that he had consumed the greater part of the sandwiches single handed.

Isaac Bower and his daughter showed some surprise.

'Pardon me for the liberty, sir, but you have not eaten for some time?'

'I have not eaten like this for near a twelvemonth, sir . . .' smiled Drinkwater unabashed.

'But on board ship you eat like gentlemen and keep a good table?'

Drinkwater gave a short laugh. He told them of what his diet consisted. When the parson showed a shocked surprise he learned himself how ignorant the people of Britain were as to the condition of their seamen. The old man was genuinely upset and questioned the midshipman closely on the food, daily routines and duties of the respective persons aboard a man o'war, punctuating Drinkwater's replies with 'Pon my soul' and 'Well, well, well' and copious sighs and shakings of his venerable head. As for Drinkwater he discoursed with the enthusiastic and encyclopaedic knowledge of the professional proselyte who had done nothing but imbibe the details of his employment. His picture of life on a frigate, though slightly lurid and excusably self-important, was, once sifted by the old man's shrewdness, not far from the truth.

While the men talked Elizabeth refilled their cups and studied her guest. Ignoring the soiled state of the linen about his neck and wrists she found him presentable enough. His mop of dark hair was drawn carelessly back into a queue and framed a face that had weathered to

100

a pale tan, a tan that accentuated the premature creases around his eyes. These were of a cloudy grey, like the sky over the Lizard in a sou' westerly gale, and they were shadowed by the blue bruises of fatigue and worry.

As he talked his face blazed with infectious enthusiasm and a growing self-confidence that, if it was not apparent to its owner, was clear to Elizabeth.

For she was more than the sheltered daughter of a country parson. She had experienced near poverty since her father had lost his living some two years previously. He had unwisely attacked the profligacy of his patron's heir and suffered the heir's revenge when that worthy succeeded suddenly to the estate. The death of his wife shortly afterwards had left Bower with the child of their declining years to bring up unaided.

In the event the girl had matured quickly and assumed the burden of housekeeping without demur. Although brought up in the shadow of her father's profession, the hardships and rigours of life had not left her untouched. In his younger days Bower had been an active man, committed to his flock. Within the circumscribed world of a country parish events had served to temper Elizabeth's growing character. Much of her adolescence had been spent nursing her consumptive mother and during the last weeks of her life Elizabeth had come face to face with the concomitants of sickness and death.

As she contemplated the ruins of a fruit cake that would have lasted the parson and herself a week, she found herself smiling. She too felt grateful for the tea-party. Drinkwater had blown in with some of the freshness of youth absent from her life until that moment. It was a refreshing change from the overbearing bombast of the red-faced squireens, or the languid indolence of the garrison infantry officers who had been until then almost the only eligible members of the male sex that she had met. She detected a sympathy about the young man sitting opposite, a sensitivity in him; something contained in his expression and given emphasis by the early lines appearing on his face, the umbra of nervous strain about his eyes.

At last the discussion ceased. Both men were, by now, firm friends. Drinkwater apologised for monopolising the conversation and ignoring his hostess.

'It is quite unnecessary to apologise, Mr Drinkwater, since my father has too little of such stimulating talk.' She smiled again. 'Indeed I am glad that you have come, albeit in such circumstances.' With a little pang of conscience Drinkwater remembered he had that afternoon attended a funeral.

'Thank you, Miss Bower.'

'But tell me, Mr Drinkwater, in all these comings and goings did you not feel afraid?'

Drinkwater answered without hesitation. 'Aye greatly . . . as I told your father earlier . . . but I think fear may be the mainspring of courage . . .' he paused. It was suddenly imperative that he convey exactly what he meant. He did not wish the young woman opposite to misunderstand, to misjudge him.

'Not that I wish to boast of courage, but I found the more I feared the consequences of inactivity, the more I found the . . . the resolve to do my utmost to alter our circumstances. In this I was most ably supported by the other members of the prize crew.'

She smiled without coquetry.

Nathaniel basked in the radiance of that smile. It seemed to illuminate the whole room.

The cake consumed, the tea drunk and the conversation lapsing into the silences of companionable surfeit Drinkwater rose. The sun was westering and the room already full of shadows. He took his leave of the parson. The old man pressed his hand.

'Goodbye my boy. Please feel free to call upon us any time you are in Falmouth, though I do not yet know how much longer we shall be here.' His face clouded briefly with uncertainty then brightened again as he took the young man's hand. 'May God bless you, Nathaniel . . .'

Drinkwater turned away strangely moved. He bowed towards Elizabeth.

'Y'r servant, Miss Bower . . .'

She did not answer but turned to her father. 'I shall see Mr Drinkwater to the gate, father, do you sit and rest for you look tired after your long talk.' The old man nodded and wearily resumed his seat.

Elated at thus receiving a moment or two alone with the girl Drinkwater followed Elizabeth as she moved ahead of him, flinging a shawl about her shoulders as she left the house.

She opened the gate and stepped down into the lane. He stood beside her, looking down into her face and fumbling with his hat, suddenly miserable with the knowledge that he had enjoyed his simple tea with all its reminders of home and English domesticity. But it was more than that. It had been the presence of this girl that had made the afternoon and evening so memorable. He swallowed hard.

'Thank you for your hospitality, Miss Bower . . .'

The air was heavy with the scent of foliage. In the gathering gloom of the Cornish lane fern fronds curled like fingers of pale green fire in the crevices of rocks that marked the boundary of the glebe. Overhead swifts screamed and swooped.

'Thank you for your very kind hospitality, Miss Bower . . .' She smiled and held out her hand. He grasped it eagerly, holding her eyes with an exhilarating boldness.

'Elizabeth . . .' she said defying the bounds of propriety yet leaving her hand intensely passive in his firm grip, 'please call me Elizabeth . . .'

'Then call me Nathaniel . . .' They paused, uncertainly. For a second the spectre of awkwardness hovered between them. Then they smiled and laughed simultaneously.

'I thought . . .' she began.

'Yes . . .?'

'I thought . . . I hoped you would not disappear completely . . . it would be pleasant to see you again . . .'

In answer Nathaniel raised her hand to his lips. He felt again the coolness of her flesh, not the coolness of rejection but the balm of serenity.

'I am,' he said with absolute conviction, 'your very devoted servant, Elizabeth . . .' He held her hand a moment longer and turned away.

He looked back once before the lane bent away in descent. He could see her face pale in the twilight, and the flutter of her hand raised in farewell.

That night *Algonquin* seemed to him a prison . . .

Chapter Eleven   *August–October 1780*

Interlude

It was autumn before Drinkwater rejoined *Cyclops*. News had arrived in England of the defection of Benedict Arnold to the King's cause and the consequent shameful hanging of Major John André. To Drinkwater, however, languishing at Plymouth, it scarcely seemed possible that a ferocious war was taking place at all.

Arriving in that port with *Algonquin* he had been swiftly dispossessed of the schooner which passed to the port admiral's hands. He found himself with Stewart, Sharples and the rest, kicking his heels on the guardship. This vessel, an obsolete 64-gun battleship, was overcrowded and stinking, filled with newly-pressed seamen awaiting ships and young officers like himself daily expecting the return of their own vessels or the arrival of new posting. The conditions on board necessitated the vessel being run like a prison and the consequent corruption found in those institutions therefore prevailed. Gambling, rat-baiting and cockfighting were clandestinely practised. Drunken and sexual orgies took place almost nightly and the enforced idleness of twelve hundred and seventy men gave the devil's agents excessive scope for improvisation.

From command of his own ship Drinkwater became less than nothing, one of many midshipmen and master's mates with sufficient time to reflect on the paradoxes of a sea officer's career.

It was a dismal time for him. The thought of Elizabeth Bower plagued him. Falmouth was not too far away. He panicked at the thought of her father's interregnum ending and the pair being sent God knew where. He had never been in love before and submitted to the self-centred lassitude of the besotted in an atmosphere utterly conducive to the nurturing of such unsociable emotions.

Week succeeded week and the period was one of utter misery.

Yet in its way the amorous depression that accompanied the congested privation served to keep him away from other more immediate amusements. His romantic preoccupations encouraged him to read, or at least to daydream over, such books as the guardship possessed.

As time passed the memory of Elizabeth faded a little and he read more diligently. He spent some of his small stock of gold on books purchased from messmates needing ready cash for betting. In this way he acquired a copy of Robertson's 'Elements of Navigation' and one of Falconer, reflecting that the money, some loose Spanish coin he had found on *Algonquin* and rightly the property of the crown, was being correctly spent on the training of a King's officer and not lining the pockets of an Admiralty lackey.

After ten weeks of ennui Drinkwater had a stroke of luck. One morning an elaborately decorated cutter anchored in Jennycliff Bay. A boat pulled over to the guardship with a request to the commanding officer for the loan of one master's mate or midshipman. It so happened that the second mate of the cutter had been taken ill and her master required a replacement for a few days.

By chance Drinkwater happened to be on deck and the first person the lieutenant dispatched to find a 'volunteer' clapped eyes on. Within minutes he was in the cutter's gig and being rowed across the steely waters of the Sound. A sprinkling rain began to patter on the water.

The boat rounded the cutter's stern and Drinkwater looked up to see the state cabin windows richly ornamented with gilt work and a coat of arms consisting of four ships quartered by St George's Cross. The ensign at the vessel's stern was red and bore a similar device in the fly. The officer in charge of the boat, who happened to be the mate of the cutter, explained that she was the Trinity House Yacht, bound to the Scillies to attend St Agnes lighthouse.

Drinkwater had heard of the Elder Brethren of the Trinity House who maintained buoys in the Thames estuary and some lighthouses around the coast. However his main source of information had been Blackmore. As a sailing master in the Royal Navy Blackmore had had to suffer examination by the Brethren, who passed the navy's navigators, before he could obtain his warrant. Blackmore, the former master of a Baltic trader had resented the fact and commented somewhat acidly on the practice.

However Drinkwater was immediately impressed by the immaculate appearance of the Trinity Yacht. The crew, all volunteers exempt from the press-gang, were smart and well fed when compared with the Royal Navy's raggamuffins. The master, one John Poulter, seemed a pleasant man and welcomed Drinkwater cordially. On explaining his lack of clothing (since his chest remained on *Cyclops*) the master offered him fresh ducks, a tarpaulin and a pea jacket.

A great sensation of relief flooded over Drinkwater as he settled into his tiny cabin. He luxuriated in the privacy which, although he had partaken of it aboard *Algonquin*, had not been without the worrying responsibility of command. Until that moment he had not realised the extent of the guardship's oppression upon his spirit.

Later he went on deck. It was now raining steadily. The Cawsand shore was blurred into grey mist but the rain fell with the hiss of freedom. Pulling the tarpaulin round him he examined the vessel. She was sturdily built and mounted a few swivel guns on either side. Her mainsail was clearly larger than *Algonquin*'s and she had a solider, more permanent feel about her. This was due to her oak construction and opulent appointments, for she fairly dripped with gilt gingerbread-work. Her spars gleamed even in the dreary weather and Drinkwater examined the details of her rigging with great interest.

Captain Poulter had come on deck and walked over to him.

'Well, cully, had much experience with this kind of vessel?' His accent was unmistakably that of the capital.

'Not a cutter, sir, but I was lately prize-master of a schooner.'

'Good. I hope I shall not detain you long from the King's business but I am bound for the Scilly Islands with Captain Calvert to examine the lighthouse there. Perhaps a King's officer may find that interesting.' Drinkwater detected the flicker of insinuation in Poulter's voice. He recognised it as a device used by old Blackmore and other merchant masters who resented the navy's social superiority. To his credit he coloured.

'To tell the truth, sir, I am greatly obliged to you for removing me from yonder guardship. Methought I might die of boredom before I saw action again.'

'That's well,' said Poulter turning to windward and sniffing the air. 'Plague on this damn coast. It's always raining.'

The Trinity Yacht left Plymouth two days later. August had passed into September. The rain had given way to windy, mist-laden days. But the weather had no power to depress the young midshipman's spirits. After the claustrophobic atmosphere of the guardship, service on the Trinity Yacht was stimulating in the extreme. Here was a fine little ship run as efficiently as a first-rate without the lash and human degradation prevalent in His Majesty's service.

Captain Poulter and his mate proved generous instructors and Drinkwater quickly learned more of the subtleties of handling the fore and aft rig of the big cutter than he had mastered aboard *Algonquin*.

He found Captain Anthony Calvert willing to discourse with him, even interested to hear how Drinkwater would undertake certain navigational problems. He joined the Elder Brother and Poulter at dinner one evening. Calvert was treated with as much deference as Drinkwater had seen accorded to Admiral Kempenfelt. Indeed the captain flew his own flag at the cutter's masthead, although his privileges and responsibilities were considered to be exterior to the management of the yacht. Nevertheless he proved to be an interesting and interested man. As the cutter bucked her way to the west Drinkwater found himself recounting the story of the recapture of the *Algonquin*. At midnight Drinkwater left Poulter and Calvert to relieve the mate. It was still blowing hard, the night black, wet and inhospitable.

The mate had to bellow in Drinkwater's ear as he passed over the position and course.

'Keep her off on the starboard tack another hour. You're well off the Wolf Rock now but keep a sharp lookout when you stand north. We should be well west of it by now but the flood's away and will be fierce as the devil's eyebrows with this wind behind it. Ye'll be well advised to use caution.'

'Aye, aye,' replied Drinkwater, shouting back to the black figure whose tarpaulin ran with rain and spray. He was left to the night ruminating on the dangers of the unmarked Wolf. This totally isolated pinnacle of rock was, with the Eddystone, the most feared danger to mariners on the south coast of England. Continually swept by swells on even the calmest days it was to be 1795 before an abortive attempt was made to erect a beacon on it. This structure collapsed at the first gale and it was to be a generation before a permanent seamark was finally grouted into that formidable outcrop.

It was claimed by some that in certain sea conditions a subterraneous cavern produced a howling noise and this had given the rock its name, but, howling noise or not, nothing could have been heard that night above the roar of the gale and the creak and crash of the Trinity Yacht as she drove to the south-south-west.

Poulter had put four reefs into the enormous mainsail before dark. He was in no hurry since he wished to heave to off the Scillies to observe the light at St Agnes. It was for this purpose Calvert had journeyed from London.

At two bells Drinkwater prepared to put about on to the port tack. Before doing so he went forward to inspect the headsails. The staysail was reefed down but out on the long bowsprit a small spitfire jib stood against the gale. Drinkwater had learned that to balance the huge mainsail a jib had to be kept as near the end of the bowsprit as conditions permitted. He watched the big spar stab at a wavecrest even as the bow he stood on pitched down off its predecessor. Beneath him the figurehead of a lion guardant disappeared in a welter of white water that rolled hissing away from the cutter's steadily advancing stem.

He returned aft, calling the watch to their stations, glanced at the compass then up at Calvert's flag standing out from the masthead like a board. Two men leaned against the big tiller. He shouted at them:

'Down helm!' They grunted with exertion.

The yacht's heel reduced, she came upright, her canvas slatting madly, cracking like thunder. The hull swooped and ducked as she met the seas head on.

Drinkwater bit his lip. She took her time passing through the eye of the wind but her crew clearly knew their business. His orders were as much for his own satisfaction as the vessel's management. As she paid slowly off to starboard the little spitfire jib was held aback. The wind caught it and suddenly it exerted its tremendous leverage at the extremity of the bowsprit. The cutter spun on her heel, the mainsail filled, then the staysail was hauled over. Finally the weather jib sheet was started and the canvas cracked like a gun before it was tamed by the lee sheet. The yacht sped away to the north west and Drinkwater breathed a sigh of relief.

There was no opportunity to study the chart in the prevailing conditions. The deck was continually sluiced by seas coming aboard so that the two boats on chocks amidships appeared to be afloat of their own accord.

After a further hour of this the sails suddenly slatted. At once several men perceived the veering of the wind.

'Keep her full and bye,' roared Drinkwater to the helmsmen, to which a slightly reproachful voice answered, 'Aye, aye, but that's north, sir.'

Drinkwater checked himself reflecting that this was no king's ship and the helmsman's reply was not insubordinate but informative.

North.

He shook his head to clear away fatigue and too much of Calvert's port. With leeway and a roaring flood tide to set them east he might be setting on to the Wolf Rock! A knot of panic gripped his stomach until he mastered it with the thought that the total area of the rock was less than that of the cutter's deck. Surely the odds were impossibly against them striking that isolated spot?

A figure loomed up beside him. It was Poulter.

'Heard her luff, cully. You'll be concerned about the Wolf.' It was not a question but a statement simply made. Drinkwater felt the load lifted from his shoulders. His brain cleared and he was able to think.

'D'ye wish me to put about again Captain Poulter, with the shift of wind she'll hold a more westerly course, sir . . .?'

Poulter was glancing at the dimly lit compass. Drinkwater thought he caught a glimpse of a smile in the wet darkness.

'That will do very well, Mr Drinkwater. See to it if ye please.'

'Aye, aye, sir . . .'

The Trinity Yacht arrived off Hugh Town later that day and remained there for several days. Calvert and Poulter had themselves pulled across to St Agnes and the crew discharged several cauldrons of coal into their boats to feed the light's chauffer-fires.

Ten days after leaving Plymouth Calvert pronounced himself satisfied with the lighthouse and on coming aboard from a final visit Drinkwater overheard him talking to Poulter.

'Well Jonathan, we'll make passage tomorrow at first light observing the cresset again tonight. I'll post to London from Falmouth and you may then proceed to the east'ard.' Calvert's words fell dully on Drinkwater's ears until he mentioned Falmouth.

Falmouth meant Elizabeth.

On arrival at Falmouth it was discovered that the yacht's second mate had recovered sufficiently to rejoin the ship. Drinkwater was therefore discharged by Poulter with a letter explaining his absence and a certificate as to his proficiency. Greatly delighted with his luck he was even more astonished when Calvert sent for him and presented him with four guineas for his services and another certificate testifying that as an Elder Brother of the Trinity House he had examined Mr Drinkwater and found him to be competent in navigation and seamanship. The document he presented to Drinkwater certified that he had passed the examination for master's mate.

'There, Mr Drinkwater. Under the latest regulations you are now permitted to board prizes as prize-master in your own right. Good luck to ye.'

Stammering his delighted surprise Drinkwater shook hands with Calvert and was pulled ashore with the Elder Brother. Having seen Calvert off in the post chaise Drinkwater turned his steps to the vicarage.

Autumn was in the air but he strode along without a care in the world, his heart thumping at the prospect of seeing Elizabeth again.

He swung back the gate. At the door he hesitated, his hand actually in the act of drawing back the knocker. Changing his mind he moved to a side window. It was the parson's study. Peering in he saw the bald dome of the old man's head, the white locks from the sides and nape of his head falling sideways in the relaxation of sleep.

Drinkwater crept round to the rear of the house. He found Elizabeth in the garden. She was unaware of his presence and for a moment he stood watching her.

She was picking fruit from a tree whose gnarled boughs were

bent under a load of russet apples. As she stretched out to pluck the fruit her face was in profile. The lower lip was caught in her teeth in an expression he recognised as one of concentration. There was something sweetly pastoral in the scene to one whose eyes had become accustomed to the monotony of the sea.

He coughed and she started, losing hold of her apron. A cascade of apples ran out on to the grass. 'Oh! . . . Nathaniel!'

He laughed, running over to help pick them up. 'I'm sorry to have startled you.'

She smiled at him. Kneeling, their faces were very close. He felt her breath on his cheek and was about to throw caution to the winds when she stood, brushing a wisp of hair behind her neck.

'I am glad that you have come. How long can you stay?'

Drinkwater had not given the matter much thought. He shrugged.

'How long would you have me stay . . .?' he smilingly asked.

It was her turn to shrug. She laughed, refusing to be drawn, but he could tell she was pleased.

'I ought to return to Plymouth tomorrow . . . well I *ought* to return today but . . .' he shrugged again, 'well let us say I am recuperating.'

'The New York packet is due and there'll be a post leaving soon, stay till then?'

'Well, er, I, er . . .'

'Father will be delighted, please stay . . .'

She uttered the last words pleadingly, so that Nathaniel had little choice and less inclination to choose. He looked into her brown eyes. They waited for his reply anxiously . . .

'Would you wish it that I stayed?'

She smiled. She had given away too much already. She gathered the last of the apples and moved towards the house.

'Do you like apple pie, Nathaniel?' she called over her shoulder.

The day passed delightfully. *Cyclops*, Morris and the anxieties and fears of the past months might have been the experience of another person, a callow frightened youth compared with the vibrantly energetic young man Drinkwater had become.

As his daughter had said the old parson was delighted to entertain the midshipman. He took great pride in showing Drinkwater his library and it was clear that the collection of books constituted

111

practically the whole of Bower's possessions, since the artefacts of the house were the property of the absent clergyman. Closer acquaintance with Isaac Bower revealed him to be a man of considerable learning who had not only brought his daughter up but educated her himself. She was, he told Nathaniel with an air of confidentiality, the equal to most men and the superior of many in her knowledge of mathematics, astronomy, Greek and Latin, while her literary tastes encompassed those French authors who did not abjure the existence of God. Had there been any doubts about Elizabeth's talents in other directions these were swiftly dispelled at dinner when a roasted chicken was followed by an apple pie of generous proportions.

After dinner Drinkwater found himself alone in a darkening room with a bottle of port that Bower had unearthed in his host's cellar. He had drunk two glasses when the old man came into the room. He threw some logs on to the fire and poured himself a glass.

'I, er, had a little news the other day . . . after you had left. My Lord Bishop of Winchester had appointed me to a parish near Portsmouth. It is a poor parish, I believe, but . . .' the old man shrugged resignedly, '. . . that is of no matter. At least,' he continued on a brighter note, '. . . it will bring us nearer you brave naval fellows and, I trust,' he looked pointedly at Nathaniel, 'I trust you will continue to visit us there.'

Warmed by the wine Nathaniel replied enthusiastically. 'I shall be delighted, sir, absolutely delighted . . . After my last visit I found the prospect of reacquainting myself with you and Eliz . . . Miss Bower most comforting.'

Bower asked him something of his own circumstances and he told the parson of his widowed mother. Elizabeth joined them for a while before she announced she was retiring and the conversation was relaxed and informal. After she had left Nathaniel said, 'I am, sir, very grateful for your kindness to me . . . it has meant a great deal to me . . .'

The two men drained the bottle. Nathaniel's remark unsprung the older man's greatest fear. 'My boy, I do not expect to remain much longer in this world. I have no fortune to leave after me but my daughter and on her account I am oppressed in spirit . . .' he coughed a little self-consciously.

'I would have her left with one friend, for I fear she has had no opportunity to establish herself anywhere whilst following me upon my travels . . .' he paused diffidently, then, with a note of firmness in his voice he said, 'D'ye take my meaning?'

'I am sure, sir,' said Nathaniel, 'that I shall do all in my power to assist your daughter should she need my protection.'

The old man smiled into the darkness. He had known it the instant the boy told them his name . . . Nathaniel . . . in the Hebrew tongue it meant a gift from God. He sighed with contentment.

The unusual sound of birdsong woke Drinkwater next morning. Realisation that he lay under the same roof as Elizabeth woke him to full consciousness. He was quite unable to sleep so rose and dressed.

Quietly descending the stairs he moved through the kitchen and unlatched the door. The invigorating chill of early morning made him shiver as he strode out on the dew-wet grass.

Without thinking he began pacing up and down the lawn, head down, hands behind his back, plunged in thoughts of last night's conversation with the old parson.

He felt a surge of excitement and relief at Bower's approval and smiled inwardly with self-congratulation. He stopped midway between the apple trees and the house. 'You're a lucky dog, Nathaniel,' he muttered to himself.

The creak of an opening window and the ring of laughter brought him back to reality.

From the kitchen window Elizabeth, her hair about her shoulders, was smiling at him.

'Are you pacing your quarterdeck, sir,' she mocked.

Nathaniel was suddenly struck by the ridiculousness of his actions. With the whole of Cornwall at his feet he had paced over an area roughly equal to a frigate's quarterdeck.

'Why . . .' he raised his hands in a shrug, '. . . I never gave it a thought.' Elizabeth was laughing at him, the sound of her laughter coming out of the window borne on the scent of frying eggs.

The haunting paradoxes of *Cyclops* and the malice of Morris seemed no longer important. All that mattered now was the laughter and the smiling face . . . and the sizzling freshness of fried eggs.

'Y're a lucky dog, Nathaniel,' he muttered again as he crossed the

113

grass to the kitchen door.

The London mail left Falmouth later that day with Nathaniel perched on its exterior bound for Plymouth. By the time it reached Truro Nathaniel, riding on the crest of growing confidence, had ascertained he possessed sufficient funds for the fare to London and back.

The weather remained fair and the experience of hurtling through towns and villages so agreeable and in harmony with his spirits that he decided the Plymouth guardship could do without him for a further three or four days. The idea had come to him while pacing the lawn that morning. Discussion of his family had filled him with a longing to return home, no matter how briefly. There had been no news of *Cyclops* when he had left Plymouth in the Trinity Yacht and Poulter, he knew, would not put into Plymouth to inform the authorities that he had landed him at Falmouth. It was, therefore probable that a few days of additional absence would go unnoticed.

He came to an arrangement for a half price fare riding on the 'conveniency' and settled down to enjoy the unprecedented pleasure of a journey through the green of southern England on an uncommonly fine day.

It was late in the afternoon following when, stiff from the long journey and tired from the trudge up the Great North Road, Drinkwater reached Barnet. He pressed on to Monken Hadley reaching the small house at last.

His desire to see his mother and brother had increased with the growing love he felt for Elizabeth. The strong attraction of her home had reminded him of his own and Bower's infirmity had emphasised the effect of passing time upon his remaining parent. His stay in Falmouth was limited by propriety yet he did not wish to kick his heels aboard that festering guardship.

Nathaniel, despite his fatigue, was pleased with himself. The freedom and independence he had experienced on *Algonquin* and the Trinity Yacht had served to mature him, the responsibility of the prize had stamped its imprint upon his character. His growing relationship with Elizabeth, certain in at least its foundation, lent him both hope and stability, banishing many of the uncertainties of the past.

His altered outlook had found expression and practical reward.

He had looted King's small hoard of gold from the *Algonquin* somewhat shamefacedly, aware that his morality was questionable despite the usages of war. When this had been supplemented by Calvert's respectably acquired guineas and, most important of all his certificate of examination as master's mate, he had a degree of autonomy for the first time in his life. It lent a jauntiness to the final steps to his mother's front door.

He knocked and lifted the latch.

Afterwards, when there was time to think, he realised he was right to come. His mother's pleasure in his visit was only clouded by its brevity. To him, however, her failing health and increasingly obvious penury were distressing and oppressive. He had not stayed long. He had talked and read to his mother and, when she dozed, slipped out to ask the Rector to engage someone from Barnet to attend to some of her needs. Calvert's guineas had gone there, and from the Rector he had learned that Ned was rarely seen in Monken Hadley. Nathaniel's brother had found employment as a groom at West Lodge with his beloved horses, had taken a common-law wife from among the maids there and come near to breaking his poor mother's heart. The Rector had shaken his head and muttered 'Like father, like son . . .', but he promised to do what he could for Mrs Drinkwater, closing his hand over the gold.

Nathaniel sat in the quiet of the room watching motes of dust in the oblique shaft of sunlight that streamed in through the little window. He would return to Plymouth on the morrow; he felt the inactivity, the strange silence, discomposing. His mother dozed and, recalling the reason for his visit, he quietly resumed his letter to Ned. It was badly phrased, awkward in admonition but it spoke with the new-found authority of the young man. 'What are you doing?' the old lady's voice startled him.

'Oh! Mother! . . . You are awake . . . just a note to Ned, to tell him to take more care of you.'

He saw her smile.

'Dear Nathaniel,' she said simply. 'You cannot stay longer?'

'Mother, I must return to duty, already I . . .'

'Of course my dear . . . you are a King's officer now . . . I understand . . .'

She held out her hand and Nathaniel knelt by her chair. He felt

115

her frail arthritic hand brush his hair. He could think of no words adequate to the moment and had lost the means to say them.

'Do not be too hard on Edward,' she said quietly. 'He has his own life to lead and is very like his father . . .'

Nathaniel rose and bent over his mother, kissing her forehead, turning away to hide the tears in his eyes.

When he left next morning it was still dark. He did not know it but his mother heard him leave. It was only then she wept.

A Change of Orders

Drinkwater joined *Cyclops* again on the last day of October 1780. She had been in Plymouth Sound some days recruiting her prize crews and taking in fresh water and the tale of the retaking of *Algonquin* had preceeded him, borne on board by Hagan and the others. Drinkwater therefore found himself something of a hero to the lower deck with whom he was already popular after his beating of Morris.

The latter, however, had re-established something of his former ascendancy in the cockpit. Drinkwater's absence had helped, but a few new appointees to the frigate in the form of very young midshipmen had given Augustus Morris more victims. There was, though, one new member of the mess whom Drinkwater was quick to realise was a potential ally. Midshipman Cranston, a silent man of about thirty, had little liking for Morris's bombast or bullying. A former seaman, Cranston had fought his way up from the lower deck by sheer ability. He was clever and tough, and utterly unscrupulous. Drinkwater liked him instantly. He also liked another, though much younger addition to the mess. Mr White was a pale, diminutive boy of thirteen. White was the obvious choice for victimisation by Morris.

In the course of the succeeding weeks the now overpopulated cockpit, whose members varied in age and pursuits was to become a bedlam of noise and quarrels.

Towards the end of November Captain Hope expressed himself ready once more to cruise against the enemy and the frigate left Plymouth beating west and south to resume her station. The weather was now uniformly foul. Depression succeeded depression and a cycle was established of misery below decks and unremitted labour above. The outbreaks of petty thieving, fighting, insubordination and drunkenness that were the natural consequences of the environment broke out again. When a man was flogged for petty theft Drinkwater wondered if it was the same man who had been instrumental in the retaking of the *Algonquin*. At all events he no longer baulked at such a spectacle, inured now to it, though he knew other methods existed to keep men at unpleasant labour. But they had no part here, in the overcrowded decks of *Cyclops* and he felt no anger with Captain Hope for maintaining discipline with the iron hand that enabled the Royal Navy to sustain its ceaseless vigilance.

To the ship's company of *Cyclops* it was the dull, monotonous routine of normality. A fight with the enemy would have come as a blessed relief to both officers and men.

Captain Hope appeared on deck as little as possible, nursing a grievance that he had not yet received his share of the prize money for the capture of the *Santa Teresa*. Lieutenant Devaux showed signs of strain from similar motives, his usual bantering tones giving way to an uncharacteristic harassment of his subordinate lieutenants, especially Mr Skelton, a young and inexperienced substitute for the late Lieutenant Price.

Old Blackmore, the sailing master, observed all and said little. He found these peevish King's Officers, deprived of their twopence prize money and behaving like old maids, distasteful ship-mates. Bred in a hard school he expected to be uncomfortable at sea and was rarely disappointed.

Mr Surgeon Appleby, ever the philosopher, shook his head sadly over his blackstrap. He ruminated on the condition of the ship to anyone who cared to listen.

'You see, gentlemen, about you the natural fruits of man's own particular genius: Corruption.' He enunciated the word with a professional relish as if sniffing an amputated stump, seeking gangrene. 'Corruption is a process arrived at after a period of growing and maturation. Medically speaking it occurs after death, whether in the case of an apple which had fallen from the bough and no longer receives sustenance from the tree, or, in the case of the human body which corrupts irrevocably after the heart has ceased to function. In both cases the span of time may be seen as a complete cycle.

'But in the case of spiritual corruption, I assure you, the process is faster and independent of the heart. Observe our noble ship's company. A pride of lions in battle . . .' Appleby paused to fortify his monologue with blackstrap. '. . . They are corrupted by the foetid atmosphere of a frigate.

'Sit down, Mr Drinkwater, sit down and remember this when you are an Admiral. As a consequence all manner of evils appear; drunkenness, quarrelling, insubordination, sodomy, theft, and worst of all, for it is a crime against God and not merely man, discontent. And what nurtures that discontent?'

'Why prize money!'

'*What* damned prize money, Bones?' interrupted Lieutenant Keene.

'*Exactly* my friend. *What* prize money? *You* won it. *You* were awarded it, but where the deuce is it? Why, lining the pockets of Milor' Sandwich and his Tory toadies. *Someone* is growing fat on merely the interest. God's blood they too are as corrupted as this stinking ship. I tell you, gentlemen, this will rebound upon them one day. One day it will not only be the damned Yankees that defy their Lordships but Tom Bowline and Jack Rattlin . . .'

'Aye and Harry Appleby!' shouted a voice.

A bored laugh drifted round the gloom of the gunroom. *Cyclops* plunged into a sea and expletives exploded in short, exasperated grunts from several voices.

'Who'd be a god-damned sailor?'

To Drinkwater these weeks were less painful than to most. It is true he dreamed of Elizabeth but his love did not oppress him. Rather it sustained him. Blackmore was delighted that he had acquired his certificate from Calvert and tutored him in some of the more abstruse mysteries of celestial navigation. He also struck up a firm friendship with Lieutenant Wheeler of the Marines. Whenever the weather moderated sufficiently to allow it Wheeler and Drinkwater engaged in fencing practice. The frequent sight of his 'enemy' thus engaged was a painful reminder of his humiliation to Morris; and the longer Drinkwater seemed immune from Morris the more the latter wished to revenge himself upon the younger man. Morris began to form his earlier alliances with like-minded men amongst the least desirable elements of *Cyclops*'s company.

Only this time there was more purpose to the cabal. Morris was degenerating into a psychopathic creature to whom reality was blurred, and in whom hatred burned with a flame as potent as love.

Christmas and New Year came and went almost unnoticed as they can only at sea. It was a dull day in the middle of January before any event occurred to break the monotony of life aboard the frigate.

'Sail Ho!'

'Where away?'

'Lee beam, sir!' Lieutenant Skelton sprung into the mizen rigging and levelled his glass. Jumping down he turned to Drinkwater. 'Mr Drinkwater!'

'M'compliments to the Captain and there's a sail to starboard, might be a frigate.'

Drinkwater went below. Hope was asleep, dozing in his cot when the midshipman's knock woke him. He hurried on deck.

'Call all hands, Mr Skelton, and bear away to investigate.'

A topsail was clearly visible now, white as a gull's wing against a squall, for a grey overcast obscured what sun there was. Occasionally a fleeting glimpse of a pale lemon orb appeared which Blackmore patiently strove to capture in the horizon glass of his quadrant. The two ships closed rapidly and after an hour came up with one another.

Recognition signals revealed the other to be friendly and she turned out to be *Galatea*. The newcomer hove to under *Cyclops*'s lee and a string of bright bunting appeared at her foremasthead.

'Signal, sir,' said Drinkwater flicking the pages of the codebook, 'Repair on board.'

Hope bridled. 'Who does Edgecumbe think he is, damn him!'

Devaux suppressed a smile as Wheeler muttered *sotto voce*: 'A Tory Member of Parliament, perhaps . . .'

After a little delay, just long enough for it to be impertinent, Hope snapped, 'Very well, acknowledge!'

'Your gig, sir?' asked the solicitous Devaux.

'Don't smirk, sir!' rasped Hope irritably.

'Beg pardon, sir,' replied Devaux still smiling.

'Huh!' Hope turned away furious. Edgecumbe was a damned, worthless time-server half Hope's age. Hope had as much time as lieutenant to his credit as Edgecumbe had time at sea.

'Gig's ready, sir.'

Drinkwater laid the gig alongside *Galatea*. He watched his captain's spindly legs disappear to a twittering of pipes. A face looked down at him.

'Moornin' lad.' It was Lieutenant Collingwood.

'Morning sir.'

'I see you have clean ducks on today,' the officer smiled before bursting into a violent and debilitating fit of coughing. When he had caught his breath he held out a bundle wrapped in oiled paper.

'I have some mail for *Cyclops*,' he called, 'I believe there's an epistle from a Miss Bower . . .'

Elizabeth!

'Thank you, sir . . .' answered the delighted and surprised Drinkwater as the bundle was tossed into the boat. Collingwood began coughing again. It was the tuberculosis that a posting to the West Indies would shortly aggravate and which eventually killed Wilfred Collingwood. It was his brother Cuthbert who became Nelson's famous second-in-command.

Elizabeth!

Strange how the mention of her name out here on the heaving grey Atlantic had the power to cause his heart to thump in his breast. The man at stroke oar was grinning at him. He smiled back self-consciously. Then he realised the man was Threddle.

In *Galatea*'s stern cabin Hope was sipping a glass of excellent claret. But he was not enjoying it.

Sir James Edgecumbe, his prematurely florid face and pop-eyes a contrast to Hope's thin, leathery countenance, was trying to be pleasantly superior and only succeeded in being offensive.

'I shall overlook the slackness in acknowledging my signal as due to the quality of your midshipmen, Captain. I had the experience of meeting one of 'em. A snotty boy with filthy garments. Clearly no gentleman, eh Captain?' He snorted a contemptuous laugh that was intended to imply that as captains they had problems only appreciated by other commanders. Hope bridled at the insult to *Cyclops*, wondering who the offending middy had been. He said nothing beyond a grunt, which Edgecumbe took for agreement.

'Yes, well, m'dear fella, the problem of rank, don't you know.'

Hope said nothing. He was beginning to suspect Sir James of having an ulterior motive in summoning him.

'Well, as I say, Captain, problems of rank and exigencies of the Service. I'm not helped by m'parliamentary duties either, b'God. Makes m'life in the public service a most arduous task I do assure ye.

'This leads me to a question, m'dear fella. How much food and water have ye?'

'About two months' provisions I suppose, but if you're relieving me I don't see . . .'

Edgecumbe held up his hand.

'Ah, there's the rub, m'dear fella. I'm not you see . . .' Edgecumbe interrupted.

'More wine? At least,' he said slowly in a harder voice, an edge of malice in it, '. . . at least I don't intend to.' Hope swallowed.

'Are you trying to tell me something unpalatable, Sir James?'

Edgecumbe relaxed and smiled again. 'Yes m'dear Captain. I would deem it a great favour if you would relieve me of a rather odious and fruitless task. In fact m'dear fella,' he lowered his voice confidentially, 'I have to be in Parliament shortly to support the Naval vote and one or two other measures. In these times every patriot should do his utmost. Don't you agree Captain. And I'm best serving my country, and you brave fellas, by strengthening the navy.' He dropped the sham and the note of menace was again detectable. 'It wouldn't do *either* of us any good if I missed it, now would it?' Hope did not like the inflections in Edgecumbe's speech.

He had the feeling he was being boxed into a corner.

'I trust Sir James that you will do your utmost to ensure that ships like *Foudroyant*, *Emerald* and *Royal George* are properly dry-docked . . .' Edgecumbe waved his hands inconsequentially.

'Those are mere details, Captain Hope, there are competent authorities in the dockyards to deal with such matters . . .'

Hope bit off an acidic reply as, from nowhere, the servant of Sir James appeared with a new bottle of claret. Edgecumbe avoided Hope's eyes and sorted through some papers. He looked up with a smile and held out a sealed envelope.

'Life's full of coincidences, eh Captain? This,' he tapped the envelope, 'is a draft, I believe, on Tavistock's Banking House. Had a bit of

122

luck with prizes I hear, well, well, my wife's a daughter of old Tavistock. He's a mean old devil but I expect he'll honour an Admiralty draft for £4,000.'

Hope swallowed the contents of his glass. He swore mentally. Righteous indignation was no weapon to use against this sort of thing. He wondered how many people had connived to get this little scene to run its prescribed course? So that he, Henry Hope, should do something unpleasant on behalf of Sir James in order that the latter should occupy his seat in Parliament. Or worse, perhaps Sir James had other reasons for not carrying out his orders. Hope felt sick and swallowed another glass of claret.

'I presume you have my change of orders in writing, Sir James,' Hope asked suspiciously although he already knew he would be compelled to accept the inevitable.

'Of course! Did you suspect that I was acting unofficially, m'dear sir?' Edgecumbe's eyebrows were raised in outrage.

'Not at all, Sir James,' replied Hope with perfect honesty. 'Only there are occasions when one doubts the wisdom of their Lordships . . .'

Edgecumbe looked up sharply. Hope found the suspicion of treason vastly amusing. Edgecumbe held out another envelope.

'Your orders, Captain Hope,' he said with asperity.

'And the odious and fruitless task, Sir James?'

'Ah!' breathed Edgecumbe, reaching for a strong box that had all the while been lurking by his chair.

In the cockpit the single lantern swayed with *Cyclops*'s violent motion. Its guttering flame cast fitful and fantastic shadows that made reading difficult. Drinkwater had waited until it was Morris's watch on deck. He had a vague feeling that if he attempted to read Elizabeth's letter in his presence it would somehow sully his image of her. For, although Morris had made no attempt to reassert himself as Drinkwater's superior, Nathaniel knew instinctively that Morris was playing a waiting game, covertly watching his fellow midshipman, probing for an opening that he could exploit. Reading Elizabeth's letter in his presence would almost certainly afford him some such opportunity.

Drinkwater opened the little package. Inside was a second packet and a letter. The letter was dated a few days after his departure from Falmouth.

My Dear Nathaniel,

Lieutenant Collingwood had just come to say that he believes his frigate will be meeting Cyclops *early in the New Year. He came to settle the account for your (sic) funeral and when father said that it should be borne by your own ship he said he would reimburse himself when he met your Captain.*

Drinkwater bit his lip, annoyed that he had not thought of that himself. He read on,

All of which is a poor way of wishing you well. I hope you like the enclosure, father tells me you sea officers are inordinately vain of your first commands. It was done the morning after your first visit, but I did not think it good enough to give you before.

We have news that we shall move to Portsmouth in April and I pray that you will visit us there. Please God that you are unscathed by battle or disease, for I fear your Service uses men barbarously as poor Lieutenant Collingwood's cough testifies.

The weather had turned now and we expect a miserable winter. Father says prayers regularly now for the Navy. Now I must conclude in haste for L. Collingwood is just leaving.

God bless you,
Ever yours,
Elizabeth.

Drinkwater read the letter four times before opening the packet.

Inside, set in a small frame was a tiny water colour. It showed a sheet of water set round by green shores and the grey bastion of a castle. In the foreground was a ship, a little dark schooner with British over Yankee colours.

'*Algonquin,*' he muttered aloud, holding the picture to the lantern. '*Algonquin* off St Mawes . . .'

He tucked the picture safely in the bottom of his sea-chest, scrambled into his hammock and re-read Elizabeth's letter.

Elizabeth wished him safe and well. Perhaps Elizabeth loved him.

He lay basking in the inner warmth the news gave him. A kind of bursting laughter exploded somewhere inside his chest. A feeling of superhuman triumph and tenderness welled up within him, so that he chuckled softly to himself as *Cyclops* creaked to windward in the gale.

The month of January 1781 was one of almost continuous bad weather in the North Atlantic. The 'families' of depressions that tracked obliquely across that great expanse of water dashed a French fleet to pieces on the rock-girt coasts of the Channel Islands. Two thousand French soldiers had embarked to capture the islands but hundreds perished as their troopships were smashed to bits. Eight hundred who got ashore at St Helier almost succeeded in taking the town until twenty-six year old Major Pearson led a desperate bayonet charge in which the French were routed but the young man lost his life.

But it was not only the French fleet that had suffered. Earlier, in October of 1780, Rodney's West Indies Fleet had been virtually destroyed in a hurricane. Most of Hotham's squadron had been dismasted and six ships lost. Although Sir Samuel Hood was even then proceeding to Rodney's aid, things were going ill for British arms. The situation in North America, handled in a dilatory fashion by Lord North and Lord George Germaine, had become critical. None of the principals were to know it at the time but the combination of the Franco-American armies around an obscure peninsula on the James River in Virginia was to prove decisive. As Lord Cornwallis fought his way through the swamps and barrens of Carolina with a pathetically small army, Nathaniel Greene opposing him, 'fought and ran, fought and ran again', slowly exhausting the British who staggered from one Pyrrhic victory after another in ever diminishing numbers.

In Gibraltar Augustus Elliot and his little garrison held out whilst *Cyclops* suffered the battering of the elements, herself like a half-tide rock.

Topgallant masts were struck and twice the frigate drove off before the wind heading back towards the Europe that Hope strove to leave astern, bound as he was for the coast of Carolina.

Life between decks had resumed its dismal round so familiar to the ship's company. Damp permeated every corner until fungi grew freely and men sickened with lassitude and discomfort. Once again the lash was employed with nauseating regularity. The men became surly and the atmosphere thick with discontent.

In this climate it was not only the spores of floral parasites that flourished. Such conditions seemed to release the latent energies of Midshipman Morris, perhaps because the ship was less efficiently policed, perhaps because in the prevailing environment men were less interested in reminding him of previous humiliation.

Morris's position as the senior midshipman was a puissant one, and young White was the chief recipient of Morris's unpleasantness. No sarcasm was too trifling but the opportunity must be taken to hurt the hapless child, for his voice had not yet broken and as yet no hair grew upon his upper lip. He was made to 'fag' for Morris, although the latter was careful not to make this too obvious in either Drinkwater's or Cranston's presence. This treatment served chiefly to terrorise the weak into a cringing obsequiousness that may possibly have served them well if they entered public life, but was no training for the officers of a man o'war.

One night, black and blue from a beating by Morris, the unfortunate White had lain unable to sleep. Tears had come to him and he lay quietly sobbing in the subterranean blackness of the cockpit.

On deck it had come on to rain. Drinkwater slipped below for his tarpaulin and found the boy weeping. For a moment he stood listening in the darkness, then, remembering Morris discovering him in identical circumstances, he went over to the boy.

'What's the matter, Chalky?' be enquired softly. 'Are you sick?'

'N-no, sir.'

'Don't "sir" me, Chalky . . . it's me, Nat . . . what's the matter?'

'Nnn . . . nothing, Nnn . . . Nat . . . it's nothing.'

It was not very difficult for Nathaniel to guess the person responsible for the boy's misery, but it was a measure of his worldliness that he assumed the crime fouler than mere bullying.

'Is it Morris, Chalky?'

The silence from the hammock had an eloquence of its own.

'It is isn't it?'

A barely perceptible 'Yes' came out of the gloom.

Drinkwater patted a thin and shaking shoulder. 'Don't worry, Chalky, I'll fix him.'

'Thanks . . . N . . . Nat,' the boy choked and as Drinkwater crept away he heard a barely audible whisper: 'Oh mmm . . . mother . . .'

Returning to duty Nathaniel Drinkwater received a rebuke from Lieutenant Skelton for leaving the deck.

The following day was Sunday and after divine service the watch below were piped to dinner. Drinkwater found himself at mess with Morris. Several other midshipmen were in the cockpit struggling with their salt pork. One of them was Cranston.

Drinkwater swallowed the remains of his blackstrap and then addressed Morris in tones of deliberate formality.

'Mr Morris, as you are senior midshipman in this mess I have a request to make.'

Morris looked up. A warning sounded in his brain as he recalled the last time Drinkwater had uttered such formal words to him. Although he had scarcely exchanged any word with his enemy beyond the minimum necessary to the conduct of the vessel he regarded Drinkwater with suspicion.

'Well what is it?'

'Simply that you cease your abominable tyranny over young White.'

Morris stared at Drinkwater. He flushed, then began casting angrily about.

'Why the damned little tell-tale, wait till I get hold of him . . .' he rose, but Drinkwater objected.

'He told me nothing Morris, but I'm warning you: leave him alone . . .'

'Ah, so you fancy him do you . . . like that fancy tart you've got at Falmouth . . .'

Drinkwater hadn't expected that. Then he remembered Threddle in the boat and the letter lying in his sea-chest . . . for a second he was silent. It was too long. He had lost the initiative.

'And what will you do, Mister bloody Drinkwater?' Morris was threatening him now.

'Thrash you as I did before . . .' maintained Drinkwater stoutly.

'Thrash me, be damned you had a cudgel . . .'

'We both had single st . . .' Drinkwater never finished the sentence. Morris's fist cracked into his jaw and he fell backwards. His head hit the deck. Morris leapt on him but he was already unconscious.

Morris stood up. Revenge was sweet indeed but he had not yet finished with Drinkwater. No, a more private and infinitely more malevolent fate would be visited on him, but for the present Morris was content . . . he had at least re-established his superiority over the bastard.

Morris dusted himself off and turned to the other midshipmen.

'Now you other bastards. Remember ye'll get the same treatment if you cross me.'

Cranston had not moved but remained seated, his grog in his hand. He brought the patient wisdom of the lower deck to confound Morris.

'Are you threatening me, Mr Morris?' he asked in level tones, 'because if you are I shall report you to the first lieutenant. Your attack on Mr Drinkwater was unprovoked and constituted an offence for which you would flog a common seaman. I sincerely hope you have not fatally injured our young friend, for if you have I shall ensure you pay the utmost penalty the Articles of War permit.'

Morris grew as pallid as *Cyclops*'s topsail. Such a long speech from a normally silent man delivered with such sonorous gravity gripped him with visceral fear. He looked anxiously at the prostrate Drinkwater.

Cranston turned to one of the other occupants of the mess. 'Mr Bennett, be so good as to cut along for the surgeon!'

'Yes, yes, of course . . .' The boy dashed out.

Morris stepped towards Drinkwater but Cranston forestalled him. 'Get out!' he snapped with unfeigned anger.

Appleby entered the midshipmen's berth with a worried Bennett behind him. Cranston was already chafing the unconscious midshipman's wrists.

Appleby felt the pulse, 'What occurred?' he enquired.

Cranston outlined the circumstances. Appleby lifted the eyelid.

'Mmmmmm . . . lend a hand . . .' Between them they got Drinkwater propped up and the latter held some smelling salts under the patient's nose.

Drinkwater groaned and Appleby felt around the base of the skull. 'He'll have a headache but he'll mend.' Another groan escaped Drinkwater's lips and his eyelids fluttered open, closed and opened again.

'Oh God, what the . . .'

'Easy, lad, easy. You've received a crack on the skull and another on the jaw but you'll live. You midshipmen get him into his hammock for a little while. You'll bear witness to this?' The last remark was addressed to Cranston.

'Aye if it's necessary,' answered Cranston.

'I shall have to inform the first lieutenant. It will remain to be seen whether the matter goes further.' Appleby picked up his bag and left.

Devaux regarded the matter seriously. He was already aware of some doubt as to the exact nature of Midshipman Morris's sexual proclivities and, though he was ignorant as to the extent Morris exerted an influence over certain elements of the ship's company, he realised the man was a danger. With the prevalent sullen atmosphere on board it only needed some stupid incident like this to provoke more trouble. With the rapidity of a bush fire one such outbreak led to another and it was impossible to hush such things up. The unpunished breach of discipline in the midshipman's mess might lead to God knew what horrors. He sought an interview with Captain Hope.

He found Hope more concerned with their landfall on the coast of the Carolinas than with the future of Mr Midshipman Augustus Morris.

'Do as you think fit, Mr Devaux,' he said without looking up from the chart, 'now I pray your attention on this chart . . .'

For a few moments the two men studied the soundings and coastline.

'What exactly is our purpose in making a landfall here, sir?' asked Devaux at last.

Hope looked up at him. 'I suppose you had better be aware of the details of this mission since any mishap to myself necessitates the duty devolving upon yourself . . . we are to make a landing here . . .' Hope pointed to the chart.

'We will rendezvous with a detachment of troops at Fort Frederic, probably the British Legion, a provincial corps under Colonel Tarleton. An accredited officer will accept the package in my strong box. In the package are several millions of Continental dollars . . .'

Devaux whistled.

'The Continental Congress,' Hope continued, 'has already debased the credit of its own currency to such a state that the flooding of the markets of rebel areas will ruin all credibility in its own ability to govern, and bring large numbers of the Yankees over to the Loyalist cause. I believe large raids are planned on the Virginny tobacco lands to further ruin the rebel economy.'

'I see, sir,' mused Devaux. The two men considered the matter, then the younger said, 'It does seem a deucedly odd way of suppressing rebellion, sir.'

'It does indeed, Mr Devaux, decidedly odd. But my Lord George Germaine, His Majesty's Secretary for the Colonies, seems to be of the opinion that it is infallible.'

'Ha Germaine!' snorted the indignant Devaux. 'Let's hope he exercises better judgement than at Minden.'

Hope said nothing. At his age youthful contempt was an expenditure of energy that was entirely fruitless. He took refuge in silent cynicism. Germaine, North, Sandwich, Arbuthnot and Clinton, the naval and military commanders in North America, they were all God's appointed . . .

'Thank you Mr Devaux.'

'Thank you, sir,' replied Devaux picking up his hat and leaving the cabin.

Morris was below when the first lieutenant summoned him. Ironically it was White who brought the message. Sensing no threat from the boy Morris swaggered out.

'Sir?'

'Ah, Mr Morris,' began Devaux considerately, 'I understand there has been some difference of opinion between you and your messmates, is this so, sir?'

'Well, er, yes as a matter of fact that is so, sir. But the matter is settled, sir.'

'To your satisfaction I presume,' asked the first lieutenant, scarcely able to disguise the sarcasm in his voice.

'Yes, sir.'

'But not to mine.' Devaux looked hard at Morris. 'Did you strike first?'

'Well, sir, I, er . . .'

'Did you, sir, did you?'

'Yes, sir,' whispered Morris scarcely audible.

'Were you provoked?'

Morris sensed a trap. He could not claim to have been provoked since Cranston would testify against him and that would further militate in his disfavour.

He contented himself with a sullen shrug.

'Mr Morris you are a source of trouble on this ship and I ought to break you, never mind stretching your neck under the Twenty-Ninth Article of War . . .' Morris's face paled and his breath drew in sharply. 'But I shall arrange to transfer you to another ship when we rejoin the fleet. Do not attempt to obtain a berth aboard any ship of which I am first lieutenant or by God I'll have you thrown overboard. In the meantime you will exert no influence in the cockpit, d'ye understand?'

Morris nodded.

'Very well, and for now you will ascend the foretopgallant and remain there until I consider your presence on deck is again required.'

131

Chapter Thirteen   *February 1781*

The Action with *La Creole*

His Britannic Majesty's 36-gun frigate *Cyclops* was cleared for action, leaning to a stiff south westerly breeze, close hauled on the port tack. To windward the chase was desperately trying to escape. As yet no colours had broken out at her peak but the opinion current aboard *Cyclops* was that she was American.

She had the appearance of an Indiaman but cynics reminded their fellows that Captain Pearson had been compelled to surrender to Paul Jones in the *Bonhomme Richard*. She had been an Indiaman.

On his quarterdeck Hope silently prayed she would be a merchant ship. If so she would prove an easy prey. If she operated under letters of marque she might prove a tougher nut to crack. What was more important was that Hope wished his arrival on the coast to be secret. Whatever the chase turned out to be Hope wanted to secure her.

Devaux urged him to hoist French colours but Hope demurred. He had little liking for such deceptions and ordered British colours hoisted. After a while the chase brailed up his courses and broke out the American flag.

'Ah there! He's going to accept battle. To your posts, gentlemen, this will be warm work. Do you likewise with the courses Mr Blackmore and take the topgallants off her . . .'

Shortened down for the ponderous manoeuvres of formal battle, *Cyclops* closed with her enemy. In the fore-top Drinkwater peered under the leech of the fore-topsail.

There was something odd about the ship they were approaching.

'Tregembo . . . clap your eyes on yon ship . . . do you notice anything peculiar . . .?'

The Cornishman left his swivel and peered to where the enemy vessel lay to, seemingly awaiting the British frigate.

'No zur . . . but wait there's siller at her rail no . . . it's gone now . . .' He straightened up scratching his head.

'Did you see flashes of silver?'

'Aye, zur, leastways I thought I did . . .'

Drinkwater looked aft. Cranston in the main-top waved at him and he waved back suddenly making his mind up. He swung himself over into the futtock shrouds.

On the quarterdeck he bumped into Morris who was now signal midshipman.

'What the hell are you doing aft?' hissed Morris, 'Get forrard to your station pig!' Drinkwater dodged round him and hovered at Hope's coat tails.

'Sir! Sir!'

'What the devil?' Hope and Devaux turned at the intrusion of their vigilant watch on the closing American.

'Sir, I believe I saw the sun on bayonets from the fore-top . . .'

'Bayonets, by God . . .' Wheeler too whirled at the military word. Then he turned again and clapped his glass to his eye. Briefly visible the sun caught the flash of steel again.

'Aye bayonets by God, sir! He's a company or two there sir, damned if he hasn't . . .' exclaimed the marine officer.

'You'll be damned if he has, sir,' retorted Hope, 'so he wants to grapple and board with infantry . . . Mr Devaux, lay her off a little and aim for his top hamper.'

'Aye, aye, sir.' Devaux went off roaring orders.

'Thank you, Mr Drinkwater, you may return to your station.'

'Aye, aye, sir . . .'

'Lickspittle!' hissed Morris as he passed.

Hope's assessment had been correct. The enemy ship had indeed been a French Indiaman but was then operating under a commission signed by George Washington himself. Despite her American authority she was commanded by a Frenchman of great daring who had been cruising under the rebel flag since the Americans first appealed for help from the adventurous youth of Europe.

This officer had on board a part battalion of American militia who, though recently driven out of Georgia by their Loyalist countrymen, had recovered their bravado after receiving a stirring harangue from their ally and were now eager to fire their muskets again.

Although Hope had correctly assessed his opponent's tactics he was too late to avoid them. As the two vessels opened fire on one another the enemy freed off a little and bore down towards the British ship. As they closed her name was visible across her transom: *La Creole*.

La Creole's main yard fouled *Cyclops*'s cro'jack yard and the two vessels came together with a jarring crash. The pounding match already started continued unabated, despite the fact that the gun muzzles almost touched. Already the adjacent bulwarks of the two ships were reduced to a shambles and the deadly splinters were lancing through the smoke laden air. *Cyclops*'s shot had destroyed the enemy's two boats on the gratings and the stray balls and resultant splinters were unnerving the militia. The French commander, knowing delay was fatal, leapt on to the rail and waved the Americans on. His own polyglot crew followed him.

The tide of boarders swirled downwards over the upper deck gunners and Wheeler brought his after guard of marines forward in a line.

'Forward! Present! Fire!' They let off a volley and reloaded with the ease of practice, spitting the balls into their muzzles and banging the musket stocks on the deck to avoid the time consuming ritual of the ramrod.

Back in the foretop Drinkwater discharged the swivel into the throng as it poured aboard. He reloaded then turned to find Tregembo wrestling with a sallow desperado who had appeared from nowhere. Looking up Drinkwater saw more men running like monkeys along the enemy's yards and into *Cyclops*'s rigging. In the main top Cranston was coolly picking off any who attempted to lash the yards of the two ships, but men were coming aboard via the topsail yards and sliding down the forestays in a kind of hellish circus act.

On the maindeck the gun crews continued to serve their pieces. Occasionally the rammer working at the exposed muzzle would receive a jab from an enemy boarding pike until Devaux ordered the ports closed when reloading. It slowed the rate of fire but made the men attentive and reduced the risk of premature explosions through skimpy sponging. Small arms fire crackled above their heads and a small face appeared at Lieutenant Keene's elbow. It was little White.

'Sir! Sir! Please allow the starboard gun crews on deck, sir, we are hard pressed . . .'

Keene turned. 'Starbowlines!' he roared, 'Boarding pikes and cutlasses!' The order was picked up by the bosun's mates and the men, assisting their mates at the larboard guns, ran for the small arms racks around the masts.

'Skelton, do you take command here!'

Keene adjusted the martingale of his hanger on his wrist. Turning to White he managed a lopsided smile, 'Come on young shaver . . .'

White pulled out his toy dirk.

'Starbowlines! Forrard Companionway! Follow me!'

A ragged cheer broke out, barely audible amid the thunder of the adjacent guns. But it broke into a furious yell as the men emerged onto the sunlit deck where the mêlée was now desperate. Although the attempts of the rebels to enter *Cyclops* through the main deck ports had been repulsed, on the upper deck it was a different story. The initial shock of the boarding party had carried them well on to the British frigate's quarterdeck. At the extreme after end Wheeler and his marines were drawn into a line loading and firing behind a precise hedge of bayonets. After a few sallies the boarders drew back and turned their attention to the forward end where the resistance, led by Lieutenant Devaux, was fierce but piecemeal, the seamen and officers defending themselves as best they might.

Although the American militia were unsteady troops they fought well enough against the seamen and gradually began to overwhelm the defenders. Once the Americans reached the waist in force they could drop down into the gun-deck and their possession of the British frigate was only a matter of time. The fighting was fierce, a confusion of musketry, pistol flashes and slashing blades. Men screamed with rage or pain, officers shouted orders, their voices hoarse with exhaustion or shrill with fear and all the while the two ships discharged their main batteries at each other at point blank range in a continuous cacophony of rumbling concussions, the smoke of which rolled over the frightful business above.

Poor Bennett, forced over a gun, died of a bayonet wound.

135

Stewart, the master's mate, weakened by the consequences of his amorous adventure at Falmouth, parried the French commander's sword but failed to riposte. The Frenchman was quicker and Stewart too fell in his own gore on the bloody deck.

From the fore-top Drinkwater was uncertain of the progress of the fight below since it was obscured by powder smoke. Between the fore- and main-tops the threat of aerial invasion via the rigging seemed to have been stemmed when Drinkwater heard the yells of Keene's counter attack. He saw them on the American ship where more men were assembling to attack. They sent a case of langridge into the Rebel waist: men fell, dispersed and reassembled. Drinkwater's gun fired again.

'Two rounds left, zur!' Tregembo shouted in his ear.

'Blast it!' he shouted back. 'What the hell do we do then?'

'Dunno zur.' The man looked below. 'Join in down there, zur?' Drinkwater looked down. The gunfire seemed to have eased and the wind cleared some of the smoke. He saw White, his dirk flashing, shoved aside by an American who lunged at a British warrant officer. The master's mate took the thrust on the thigh and the American grimaced as the spurned White stabbed him in the side. Devaux, with his hanger whirling in one hand and a clubbed pistol in the other, was laying about himself like a maniac urging on Keene's men and the remnants of the upper deck gun crews.

Aft of him Drinkwater saw Cranston out on the main yardarm cutting away any gear that bound the two ships together.

Of course, they must prise *Cyclops* away from the rebel ship.

'We must separate the two ships, Tregembo!'

'Aye zur, but she'm to wind'ard.'

It was true. The wind's pressure was holding *La Creole*'s hull alongside *Cyclops* as efficiently as if they were lashed together. Drinkwater looked below again and his eyes rested on the anchors. Earlier in the day Devaux had had the hands bending a cable to the sheet anchor as they closed the American coast. All they had to do was to let it go.

'The sheet anchor, Tregembo!' he shouted excitedly, pointing downwards.

Tregembo instantly grasped the idea. They both leapt for the forestay. The anchor was secured to the starboard fore channels by

136

chain. The chains terminated in pear links through which many turns of hemp lashing were passed, securing the anchor to the ship.

Snatching out his knife Tregembo attacked the stock lashing whilst Drinkwater went for that at the crown.

The shouting, screaming mass of struggling men were only feet away from them yet, because *La Creole* had come aboard on *Cyclops*'s port quarter, the fo'c's'le was a comparative haven. Then someone in the privateer's tops opened fire with a musket. The ball struck the anchor fluke and whined away in ricochet. Sweat rolled off the two men and Drinkwater began to curse his fine idea, thinking the seizing would never part. His head throbbed with the din of battle and the bruise that Morris had given him. Another ball smacked into the deck between his feet. His back felt immensely huge, a target the marksman could not fail to hit at the next shot.

Tregembo grunted, his seizing parted and the sudden jerk snapped the remaining strands of Drinkwater's. The anchor dropped with a splash.

'I hope to God the cable runs . . .'

It did, enough at least to permit the anchor to reach the bottom where it bit, broke loose and bit again, snubbing the two ships round head to the current that runs inexorably north east up the coast of Florida and Carolina. The current pulled each hull, but *Cyclops* held, her anchor bringing her up against the force of it. Drinkwater moved aft. He was the first to detect a grinding between the ships that told where *La Creole* slowly disengaged herself from her foe.

'She's off lads, we've got 'em!' One head turned, then another, then all at once the British rallied, seeing over their heads the movement in the enemy's ship.

They took up the cry and with renewed vigour carried on the work of stabbing and cutting their adversaries. Looking over their shoulders the Franco-Americans began to realise what was going on. The militia were the first to break, running and scrambling over friend and foe alike.

La Creole scraped slowly aft, catching frequently and only tearing herself finally clear of *Cyclops* after a minute or two. Sufficient time elapsed for most of her men to return to her, for the exhausted British let them go. The final scenes of the action would have been comic if they had not occurred in such grim circumstances with the dead and dying of three nations scattered about the bloody deck.

Several men leapt overboard and swam to where their comrades were lowering ropes over the side. One of these was the French commander who gesticulated fiercely from the dramatic eminence of the frigate's rail before plunging overboard and swimming strongly for his own ship.

On *Cyclops*'s gangway a negro was on his knees, rolling his eyes, his hands clasped in an unmistakable gesture of submission. Seeing Drinkwater almost alone in the forepart of the ship the negro flung himself down at his feet. Behind him Devaux seemed bent on running him through, a Devaux with blood lust in his eyes . . .

'No, no massa, Ah *do* surrenda sah! Jus' like that Gen'ral Burgoyne, sah, Ah do surrenda!' It was Wheeler who eventually overcame the first lieutenant and brought him to his senses by telling him the captain wanted him aft. The negro, thankfully ignored, attached himself to Drinkwater.

The two ships were now two cables apart. Neither of them was in a fit condition to re-engage immediately.

'That,' said Captain Hope to Mr Blackmore as they emerged from the defensive hedge made for them by Wheeler and his marines, 'That was a damned close thing!'

The sailing master nodded with unspoken relief. Hope barked a short, nervous laugh.

'The devil'll have to wait a little longer for us, eh Blackmore?'

La Creole drifted astern.

'Cut that cable, mister,' ordered Hope when Devaux eventually reached him, 'and find out who let the anchor go.'

'Might I suggest we weigh it, sir . . .'

'Cut it, dammit, I want to re-engage before he spreads the news of our arrival on the coast.'

Devaux shrugged and turned forward.

Hope turned to the sailing master. 'We're in soundings then.'

'Aye, sir,' said the old man recollecting himself.

'Make sail, we'll finish that rebel first.'

But *La Creole* was already shaking out her canvas. She was to lee-ward and soon under way. Fifteen minutes later *Cyclops* was before the wind, two and three-quarter miles astern of the privateer.

That was still the position when darkness set in.

Below, in the cockpit Drinkwater sat having his shoes polished by the negro. He was unable to rid himself of the encumbrance and in the aftermath of action no one seemed to bother about the addition to *Cyclops*'s complement.

'What's your name?' he asked fascinated by the ebony features of the man.

'Mah name, sah, is Ach'lles and Ah am your serbant . . .'

'My servant?' said Drinkwater astonished.

'Yes sah! You sabe ma life. Ach'lles your best fre'nd.'

The Best Laid Plans of Mice and Men . . .

Daylight revealed *Cyclops* alone within the circle of her visible horizon. *La Creole* had given her the slip and Captain Hope was furious that her arrival on the coast would now be broadcast. He now had no alternative but to execute his orders as speedily as possible.

He waited impatiently for noon and Blackmore's meridian altitude. When the master had made his calculations he brought the answer to Hope. 'Our latitude is thirty-four degrees twelve minutes north, sir. That is,' he glanced at his slate, 'That is forty-three miles to the north of our landfall although we shall have to weather Frying Pan shoals.'

Hope nodded. 'Very well, make the necessary arrangements and be kind enough to attend me with the first lieutenant . . . and, er, Mr Blackmore, have young Drinkwater bring your charts down here.'

When the master reappeared with Devaux, Hope cordially invited them to sit. Drinkwater spread the charts out on the table between them.

'Ah hhmmm, Mr Drinkwater,' began Hope. 'The first lieutenant has informed me that it was you that let go the sheet anchor during the late action with *La Creole*?'

'Er, yes, sir. I was assisted by Tregembo, fore-topman, but I take full responsibility for the loss of the anchor . . .'

'Quite so, quite so . . .'

'If you'll permit me to observe, sir,' broke in Devaux, 'it may well have saved the ship.'

Hope looked up sharply. There was the smallest hint of reproach in Devaux's voice. But Hope had not the energy for anger, his glance caught Blackmore's. Barely perceptibly the old master shrugged his shoulders. Hope smiled to himself. Old men saw things differently . . .

'Quite so, Mr Devaux. Mr Drinkwater I wish to congratulate you on your initiative. It is a quality which you appear to possess in abundance. I shall do what I can for you and if I fail I am sure Mr Devaux will prompt me . . . in the meantime I would be delighted if you and Mr Cranston together with Lieutenant Wheeler, Mr Devaux and yourself, Master, would join me at dinner. Who will have the watch, Mr Devaux?'

'Lieutenant Skelton, sir.'

'Very well, we had better have Keene and of course no dinner aboard *Cyclops* would be complete without an after-dinner speaker in the shape of the surgeon. Please see to it . . . Now Mr Drinkwater, the charts . . .'

The men bent over the table, their bodies moving automatically to the motion of the frigate.

'Our destination,' began the captain, 'is the mouth of the Galuda River here, in Long Bay. As you observe there is a bar but within the river mouth there is a small fort: Fort Frederic. Our task is to enter the river, pass to the garrison such stores and munitions as they require and to hand a certain package to some sort of agent. The details of this are known to Mr Devaux and need not concern us here . . .' Hope paused and wiped his forehead. He resumed. 'When we close the coast we will send boats in ahead to sound the channel into the anchorage.'

Devaux and Blackmore nodded.

'To be on the safe side we will clear for action as we enter the river and put a spring on the cable when we anchor. I do not intend being here a moment longer than is absolutely necessary for I fear our late adversary will come looking for us with reinforcements.' Hope tapped the chart with the dividers.

'Any questions, gentlemen?'

Devaux cleared his throat. 'If I am not mistaken, sir, you are as apprehensive of this operation as I am . . .?' Hope said nothing, merely stared at the lieutenant.

'I mislike the whole thing, sir. It has a smell about it, I . . .'

'Mr Devaux,' bristled Hope, 'it is not part of your duties to question orders, I imagine their Lordships know their business.' Hope spoke with a conviction he was far from feeling, his own misgivings lending his voice an asperity that was over-severe.

But Devaux knew nothing of the circumstances of Hope's reception of his orders. To him Hope was no longer the man who had towed the *Santa Teresa* off the San Lucar shoal. The tedious weeks of patrol had wearied him, the worry over prize-money had worn him and he had learned from Wheeler how Hope and Blackmore had taken an abject refuge behind a steel hedge of bayonets in the recent fight. Devaux's reaction was jaundiced for he, too, had been subject to the same strains for similar reasons. But he saw Hope now as a timid old man, blindly obeying the orders dished up by a hated Tory cabal . . . he mastered his impatience with difficulty; events had conspired against him . . .

'With respect, sir, why send us to this remote spot to cripple the rebel economy with counterfeit bills?' Blackmore looked up with sudden interest and Drinkwater had the sense to remain absolutely motionless. Hope opened his mouth to protest but Devaux ploughed on. 'Why not get them through New York where Clinton's agents must have a clearing house? Or Virginny where the rebel wealth really comes from? Even New England is better than the Carolinas . . .'

'Mr Devaux! I must remind you that what I told you was in confidence . . . but since you lack the self control I had thought to be an attribute of your class I will explain, as much for your benefit as for these other gentlemen here . . . And I must ask you to treat the matter with confidence . . . The Carolinas are in Lord Cornwallis's hands, Mr Devaux. I assume the notes are for him. He is, I believe, extending operations under Major Ferguson into the back country where, I presume, the money is required. That is all gentlemen . . .'

Drinkwater left the captain with a profound sense of disquiet. He knew his presence had been an embarrassment to Captain Hope who might have dealt more sharply with the first lieutenant had the midshipman not been there. But there was more than the rift between captain and first lieutenant to set his mind working. The negro Achilles had been telling odd stories in the cockpit. Stories that did not tally with Hope's pat summary of the military situation in the Carolinas.

After some thought Drinkwater sought out Wheeler and

consulted him. It was a breach of the captain's confidence in him but, under the circumstances that appeared to prevail ashore, he felt confident in so doing.

'Well, young shaver, we'd better go and have a word with your friend . . . what d'ye say he is . . . your servant?'

'He claims the right. Says I saved his life . . .'.

'Get him to come up to the gunroom . . .'

They found Achilles to be an intelligent man who had been a plantation slave. When the British Military authorities offered freedom to any negroes who took up arms against the rebels, Achilles had forthwith escaped and promptly obtained his release from bondage. Soon obtaining a post as officer's servant to a lieutenant in the 23rd Foot he had been separated from his master at the battle of Camden and, by an evil fate, captured by the son of his former owner who was then a captain in the militia battalion that later embarked in *La Creole*.

His unique position, ready wit and intelligent powers of observation had made him a favourite with the officers of the 23rd and made him privy to many of their conversations. This had given him a reasonably accurate idea of the real military state of South Carolina. Wheeler set about extracting as much information as possible. He had little trouble since Achilles had a great love of the splendid scarlet soldiers and enjoyed their attention and amusement, contrasting their indolent disinterest with his former owner's ferocity.

'Yes, sah, dis war is no good, sah. Dere is not enuff ob de reg'lar sojers in de Carolinas, sah. Dat Major Ferguson, he dam' fine sojer, sah, but dey Tory milisha all dam' trash an' no more join afta Maj' Ferguson get kill up on dat ole King's Mount'n.'

Wheeler whistled. So the brilliant Patrick Ferguson was dead. The best shot in the British Army who had invented a breech loading rifle, who fenced with his left hand when he lost the use of his right at the Brandywine, had been killed. The negro rolled his eyes dolorously.

'What about Lord Cornwallis then, Achilles?'

'He dam' fine sojer too, sah! He lick dat Yankee rebel Gates and whip him proper at Camden. Gates he ride sixty mile after de battle, yeees sah! But poor Ach'lles, sah, Ah get the wrong side o' sum trees

143

an' Ah run smack inta mah old boss's son who is mighty mad, cos he'm running from dey redcoats . . .'

'Yes, yes, Achilles, you've told us all that but what about his Lordship . . .?'

'He keep marchin',' replied the negro sitting bolt upright and making little swinging gestures with his arms, 'an' he keep fi'tin' but he nebber stop, so de officers ob the Twenty Third, they say he nebber win nuffin'.'

'What do you mean?'

'Well, sah. Afta Gen'ral Gates gone back to dam' Congress wiv his lil' old tail hangin' 'tween his legs they send Gen'ral Greene down an' Gen'ral Greene he wun dam' fine sojer too, eben s'posin' he a rebel 'cos all de officers of de Twenty Third say so, sah!' Achilles was defensive, as if in admiring Greene he be thought to sympathise with the rebels. Then a puzzled look came over his face.

'Ah don' rightly unnerstand but dat Genr'l Greene he jus' don' know when he' beat. He fight, then he run, then he fight an' run agen . . . but he jus' don' get beat . . .' Achilles shook his head in incomprehension, his eyes rolling expressively.

'Ma Lord Cornwallis he send dat Lord Rawdon here an' dere, an' he send dat Co'nel Tarleton here and dere and dem two fine sojers dey charge up an' down the swamp lands tryin' for to catch de Swamp Fox an' de Gamecock . . .'

'The *what*?' queried Wheeler grinning in spite of himself.

'Dey de names of de rebel raiders, sah. Dam' clebber men. Dey say dey look jus' like trees all de time. Dey nearly get caught by Tarleton one, two time but always dey 'scape. Maybe dey nobody,' Achilles hinted darkly, '. . . Maybe dey voodoo . . .' Again Achilles shook his head and rolled his eyes.

'De war no good for us Loy'lists, sah. De reg'lar loy'lists fight like wild cats, sah. De reg'lar redcoat sojers dey fight better'n any dam' Yankees but dere jus' ain't enuff, sah. Dat's all, sah. Ach'lles tell you truth, sah. Ebbery word. I hear all de officers say dis, plenty times, sah, and de Twenty Third one dam' fine corp' of fine fuzileer, sah.'

Despite the seriousness of his news Wheeler could not stifle his laughter at the negro. At the end of his monologue Achilles had risen to his feet and come stiffly to attention to give due importance to the mention of His Majesty's Royal Welch Fusileers. Regrettably this zealous action had ended in sharp contact with the overhead deckbeams which were too low to accommodate the negro at full height. His swift reduction to a crouching position caused Wheeler and Drinkwater to burst out laughing.

'Very well, Achilles. And what about you . . . you may volunteer for service in the navy . . .'

'Don' know nuffin' 'bout no navy, sah,' said Achilles with feeling rubbing his bruised head . . . 'Achilles dam' fine servant, sah . . .'

'Well in that case I think you had better attend to me . . .'

'Ach'lles dis gennelman's servant, sah.' He indicated Drinkwater loyally.

Wheeler looked at Drinkwater. 'I don't know what the Hon. John will say to that, cully . . . I should get him appointed a messman . . .'

Wheeler took the news to Devaux who snorted with exasperation when he heard it.

'Young Nat was pretty perceptive to realise the significance of the nigger's intelligence.'

'Not really,' said the first lieutenant, still angry with Hope. He tossed off a tankard of flip and wiped the back of his hand across his mouth. 'He was in the cabin when the Old Man re . . . oh, dammit, when *I* blew up and revealed all . . . still perhaps it's an ill wind. At least my suspicions are confirmed . . .'

'What'll we do?' Devaux thought for a bit then poured another tankard of flip.

'Listen, Wheeler, I'll raise it conversationally at dinner tonight. Do you back me up . . .'

It was inconceivable that the mission should not come up during the meal as the prime subject of conversation. The poor quality of the food served to remind them all that they had been pitched across the North Atlantic with insufficient provisions for a prolonged stay on the coast. Indeed it was Hope who broached the subject in general terms, explaining their presence off the Carolinas.

'I still don't see why they had to send a frigate to this desolate destination of ours. It doesn't make military, naval or any other kind of sense to me,' opined Devaux cautiously, seeking to channel the drift of talk. But Appleby sensing an opening for more expansive dialogue beat Hope to the breach. Drinkwater sat open mouthed at the pedagogic delivery of the surgeon.

'If you will permit me, gentlemen, to offer an opinion on your preoccupation . . .' Devaux sighed resignedly and Hope could scarcely suppress a smile. 'Your naivety does you great credit, Mr Devaux . . .' Devaux protested. 'Nay, hear me out, I beg. It seems to me, and with all due respect to Captain Hope, that this operation of ours is a political expedient not a military or naval exercise and therefore, if I may say so, not so readily comprehensible to you gallant gentlemen of the sword . . .'

Well, well, thought Hope. Either Appleby was psychic or omniscient.

'Imagine, messieurs, it was obviously conceived by a politician, who else has been passing Coercive Acts and playing at warfare with Parliamentary statutes? Why politicians! Milords North and Germaine hatched this one up! Germaine probably told North this was the very thing to do. Wouldn't cost much. Print a few million notes, ruin the rebel economy, bring Congress to its knees. No need for more troops, no credit to general officers or admirals but . . . and here's the beauty of it . . . brilliant stroke by Milordships!'

There was a rumble of appreciation from the officers assembled round the table and lounging back in their chairs.

'You perceive the outline, gentlemen. The idea hatched by a man cashiered for cowardice after Minden but with a skin as thick as hide . . . and a changed name to hide under.'

'Sackville by God!' exclaimed Wheeler, ignoring Appleby's pun. 'I had clean forgot. Didn't the King himself strike Sackville off the Army list with an injunction that he was never to serve again in a military capacity?'

'Exactly so, my dear sir, the late king certainly did. And what is this creature now? Why none other than the virtual director of military operations in the Americas, a continent of which he knows nothing. Barré does, but the Government ignores the good colonel. Burke and Foc and Chatham realised, but nobody took any heed of them. So here *we* are!' Appleby expelled his breath contentedly looking round as if expecting applause.

'You are not quite right about Germaine, Mr Appleby.' Appleby frowned and looked round to see who dared to contradict him. It was Cranston.

'I beg your pardon?' he said archly.

146

'Lord George Germaine might well be exactly what you say but he has as his Secretary an American Loyalist who is reckoned to be an expert in several fields. His name is Benjamin Thompson.'

'Pah!' retorted Appleby. 'Thompson is his catamite!' Drinkwater had not the slightest notion what a catamite was except that it was clearly something suspect for sniggers and grins appeared on several faces.

'I think, Mr Appleby, that Cranston has a point,' Hope spoke with quiet authority but Appleby was not to be gainsaid.

'I disagree sir.'

'So do I sir. The facts alone speak for themselves. Surely Thompson, if he is the genius he claims to be, knows far more damage can be done the rebels by us arriving off Charleston or New York?' Devaux tried again to manipulate the conversation's direction.

'Ah! There's the rub don't you see,' plunged in Appleby once again. 'Germaine turns to Thompson. "Damme Benjamin,"' he mimicked Germaine's reputedly haughty tones, '"I don't like Clinton, irresolute little fella and that damned traitor Arnold's in his suite, probably playing a double game. Best not send the cash there." Germaine turns to map: "Where shall we send it then Benjamin? To Cornwallis, damme never liked his wall-eyes, or his second, young Rawdon, or that dammed know-all Ferguson . . ."'

'Ferguson's dead,' Wheeler intoned flatly.

Appleby raised his eyebrows imploringly heaven-ward at the interruption.

'". . . no, no that won't do at all, Benjamin. Bring that map nearer; now which bit is Carolina? Ah yes, well how about there!"' Eyes closed Appleby stabbed the damask table cloth with his finger, then opened them and looked down at the imaginary map. '"That will do fine, Benjamin, see to it for it is now five of the clock and I must to the tables for an hour or two's relaxation . . ." Picks up hat, exeunt.' Appleby sat back at last, smirked and folded his hands across his stomach.

Several officers clapped languidly. They all smiled smugly with the generous contempt sailors reserve for politicians . . . after all, the smiles seemed to say, what does one expect . . .

Hope clearly had to dispel such thoughts from the minds of his men. It was an attitude that begot carelessness.

147

'I find your assessment amusing Mr Appleby, but inaccurate. That *Cyclops* had been ordered to carry out a part which to us seems incomprehensible is scarcely a new situation in naval war. The whole essence of the naval service is an adherence to orders without which nothing can be achieved . . .'

'Sir,' said Devaux slowly and deliberately, 'Lieutenant Wheeler has interrogated the negro who surrendered from *La Creole*. The blackamoor informs us that the Carolinas are in a state of utter confusion with no man knowing who has the upper hand. Lord Cornwallis has insufficient troops to do more than hold a few posts and chase the rebels.'

It was enough for Hope. 'Mr Devaux,' he almost shouted, 'what do you expect a damn nigger to say – he's a rebel. D'ye think he's going to tell us we're winning . . .?'

But Devaux was equally flushed. 'For God's sake hear me out, sir,' he altercated, 'in the first place he's Loyalist with papers to prove it, and that's no mean achievement considering he's been with the rebels, in the second he's a slave freed by ourselves so hardly likely to sympathise with the rebels and voluntarily submit to slavery, and in the third he's been batman to a lieutenant in the 23rd Foot.'

'And I suppose,' replied Hope sarcastically, 'that you consider all that cast iron proof that every word is true . . .?' He was really, deeply angry now. Angry with Devaux and Appleby for voicing the doubts in his own heart, angry with himself for submitting so tamely to the blandishments of Edgecumbe and the £4,000 prize money which was not one whit the more use to him on this side of the ocean, and angry with the whole system that had created this ridiculous situation.

'Time will tell, sir, which of us is right . . .'

'That's as maybe, mister, but it will not stop us all doing our duty,' the captain looked meaningfully round the assembled officers. Their averted gazes and embarrassed complexions further angered him.

He rose and the officers scrambled to their feet. 'You, Mr Devaux, may take such measures as you see fit in the way of precaution. Good night, gentlemen!'

A screech of chairs and buzz of retreat accompanied the departure of the officers. Devaux's words rang in his ears:

'Time will tell, sir, which of us is right . . .'

The trouble was Hope already knew . . .

Drinkwater left the dinner with the uncomfortable feeling that he had witnessed something he should not have done. He had hitherto considered Hope's position as unassailable and was shocked by Devaux's outspoken attack. In addition he was surprised at the giggling of some of the dinner guests, particularly Devaux and Wheeler, who seemed in some curious way pleased with what they had achieved. But perhaps it was the face of Blackmore that he remembered most. The old man's white hair was drawn severely back and his face passed the midshipman like a kind of fixed figurehead. The expression it bore as it passed Wheeler and Devaux was one of utter contempt.

Drinkwater followed Cranston below. In the shadows of the orlop an arm reached out and grabbed his elbow. His exclamation was silenced by a face with a commanding finger held to its barely visible lips. It was Sharples.

'What do you want?' whispered Drinkwater, unable to shake off the foreboding engendered by the recent conversation. Somehow the appearance of Sharples, whom he had ignored for months now, came as no surprise.

'Beg pardon, sir. You ought to know I believe Threddle and Mr Morris are hatching something up, sir. Thought you ought to know, sir . . .' Drinkwater felt his arm released and Sharples melted away in the shadows . . .

Drinkwater entered the cockpit.

'So you are back from your dinner at the captain's table, eh?'

Morris's voice was loaded with venom. At first Drinkwater did not reply. Then, aware that Cranston was still in the mess he decided to bait his enemy.

'Tell me Morris, why do you hate me?'

'Because, lickspittle, you are less than a dog's turd, yet you have been a source of trouble for me ever since you came aboard this ship. You are an insufferable little bastard . . .'

Drinkwater's fists clenched and he shot a look at Cranston. The older man was disinterestedly climbing into his hammock. 'I'll call on you for satisfaction when we get to New York for that remark . . .'

'Ah! But not now, eh? Not so bloody bold without a cudgel are you? Bit more careful of our pretty face since we got that little whore in Falmouth aren't we, or is it because you're keeping company with the officers now, Wheeler's quite a dandy-boy now isn't he . . .' Drinkwater paled at the allusion to Elizabeth but he held his rage. He saw Cranston, sitting up in his hammock, making negative motions with his hands. Morris was working himself up into a violent rage, a torrent of invective streaming from him in which he worked through every obscenity known to his fertile and warped imagination. Drinkwater grabbed his boat cloak and went on deck . . .

'Why don't you shut your filthy mouth, Morris?' asked Cranston from the shadows.

But Morris did not hear Cranston. Hatred, blind and unreasoning hatred, burned in his heart with the intensity of fever. There could be no justification for such bitter emotion any more than there was explanation for love. Morris only knew that from thwarted purpose Drinkwater had come to represent all that had dogged Morris's career: ability, charm, affability and a way of inspiring loyalty in others, qualities in which he was lacking.

Morris was a victim of himself: of his own jealousy, of his sexuality and its concomitants. Perhaps it was the onset of disease that upset his mental balance or perhaps the bitter fruits of a warped and twisted passion; a frustrated love that suffered already the convolutions of self-torture by its very perversity.

... Oft Times go Astray ...

If the ship's company of HMS *Cyclops* expected a dramatic coastline for their landfall they were disappointed. The Carolinian shore was low and wooded. Blackmore, the navigator, had the greatest difficulty in locating the least conspicuous feature with any confidence. In the end the estuary of the Galuda River was found by the longboat scouting inshore.

It was afternoon before the onshore breeze enabled Hope to take the frigate into the shoaling waters with confidence.

Leadsmen hove their lines from the forechains on either bow and the longboat, a loaded four-pounder in her bow, proceeded ahead under Lieutenant Skelton, sounding the channel. Behind her under topsails, spanker and staysails the frigate stood cautiously inshore.

The Galuda River ran into the Atlantic between two small headlands which terminated in sandspits. These twin extensions of the land swung north at their extremity where the river flow was diverted north by the Gulf Stream. Here a bar existed over which the frigate had to be carefully worked.

Once into the estuary the river banks were densely wooded, seamed by creeks and swamps as the Galuda wound inland. Just within the river mouth itself the land was a little higher, reaching an elevation some thirty feet above high water. Here the trees had been removed and Fort Frederic erected.

It was towards the fort that attention aboard *Cyclops* was directed once the dangers of the bar had been negotiated. The serrated stockade rampart was just visible over the surrounding trees. No Union Flag was visible from its conspicuously naked flagpole.

'Shall I fire a gun, sir?' enquired Devaux.

'No,' replied Hope. The tension in the situation blotted out the memory of their former disagreement. *Cyclops* crept slowly onwards, the leadsmen's chants droning on. The frigate was abeam of the headlands into the main river; slowly the fort drew abeam. There was not a soul in sight and the very air was pregnant with the desolation of withdrawal.

'Abandoned, by God!'

'We will bring the ship to her bower, Mr Devaux,' said the captain, ignoring Devaux's outburst, 'kindly see to it.'

The longboat was brought alongside and a party of seamen and marines detailed into it. Drinkwater watched the boat pull away from the ship.

A small wooden jetty, obviously for use by the garrison, facilitated disembarkation. His hanger drawn Wheeler advanced his men in open order. Drinkwater watched as they ran forward in a crouching lope. The seamen followed in a ragged phalanx. At the boat the four-pounder covered the assault.

The occupation of Fort Frederic was carried out without a shot. The fort was empty of men, ammunition or provisions of any kind. There was not the slightest clue as to where or when the garrison had gone. But it had a weird, sinister atmosphere about it as some deserted places do. It made the stoutest hearts shiver.

Devaux, who had commanded the landing party turned to Wheeler. 'If he's going to stop here we'd better occupy the place.' Wheeler agreed. 'We can put swivels here and . . : er, over there. My marines can manage. Will you row a guard-boat all the time?' Devaux smiled at the scarlet-coated figure, gorget glinting in the sunshine. Wheeler was nervous. Devaux looked around him. 'This *is* a bloody business, Wheeler, and I like none of it, I'll report to Hope. Yes of course we'll row a guard. I wouldn't leave a dog in a place like this . . .' Wheeler shivered despite the sun's heat. He was not given to premonitions but he was put in mind of another American river. Wheeler had lost his father on the Monongahela . . .

He shook off the oppressive feeling. He began shouting orders to Hagan and the seamen to put Fort Frederic into a state of defence . . .

Cyclops was a ferment of activity. As 'a precautionary measure' Devaux had her topgallant masts struck down so that they might not appear above the surrounding trees. Three boat guns and a few swivel guns were mounted in Fort Frederic of which Wheeler, losing his earlier misgivings, was appointed commandant. He embraced the post with enthusiasm and it was not long before properly-appointed sentinels were mounted and patrols were sent out into the surrounding woods. Wheeler's only regret was that Hope forbade him to hoist British colours over the fort.

'It is conceivable that we may have to abandon the post in haste, I have no wish to appear to surrender a British fort,' Hope explained, and with that Wheeler had to be content.

As a precaution against attack from seaward the longboat was sent to cruise on the bar commanded by a midshipman or a master's mate. The other boats were variously employed ferrying men and stores ashore.

After twenty-four hours no contact had been made with friend or foe and Hope decided to despatch an expedition inland to recon-noitre. A spring had been secured to the frigate's cable so that her broadsides might bear on either bank, up, or down stream. But it was from seawards that the captain expected trouble and a lookout was kept at the main-topmast cap. From here the longboat was assiduously watched.

That second evening *Cyclops* had been placed in a defensive position and the final preparations were made by rigging boarding nettings. These extended from the ship's rails to lines set up between the lower yardarms. As the sun set and the red ensign fluttered down from *Cyclops*'s stern the sick, brought on deck for some air, were taken below as the bites of the mosquitoes ren-dered their position on deck untenable. But the insects that infested the forested banks of the Galuda River boarded unper-turbed. The restless moans of the sick and hale as they endured the torment of the biting parasites floated away from the frigate over the twilit water, punctuating the sinister stillness of the surround-ing foliage.

Thus did *Cyclops* pass two nights waiting for some news of British or Loyalist forces.

The following morning Wheeler was relieved of his command to take over the entire marine detachment in support of Lieutenant Devaux and a party of seamen who were to undertake a probe inland. It was a desperate attempt by Hope to fulfil his orders; if the prophet would not go to the mountain then some attempt must be made to bring the mountain to Mahomet . . .

Thus reasoned the captain as he wiped his perspiring forehead. He poured himself a glass of rum grog and walked aft. The slick waters of the Galuda bubbled under *Cyclops*'s stern, chuckling round the rudder which moved slightly with a faint creak and soft grind of tiller chains.

In the corner of his vision he could just see the landing party forming up after disembarking. He saw Wheeler throw out an advanced picket under Hagan and lead off with the rest of the marines. In a less precise column he saw Midshipman Morris follow with a squad of seamen. Midshipman Drinkwater brought up the rear followed by a file of marines under their corporal. The head of the column had already disappeared in the trees when he saw Devaux, after addressing a few final words to Keene left as fort-commander, look back at the ship then take to his heels in chase of his independent command . . .

Hope tossed off the rum and looked seawards. The longboat was down there under Cranston. Skelton was the only other commis-sioned officer left on board. With a surprising pang of affection he thought anxiously of Devaux and the gaudy but competent Wheeler . . . he thought idly of young Drinkwater . . . so very like himself all those years ago . . . he sighed again and watched the Galuda run seawards . . . out to the open sea . . . 'From whence cometh our help' he muttered in silent cynicism to himself . . .

Drinkwater had little taste for the inland expedition. Once they had lost sight of the frigate it seemed to him that the whole party was instantly endangered. The sea was their element and as if to confirm his worries seamen ahead of him, men as nimble as monkeys in the rigging, were tripping and stumbling over tree roots and cursing at the squelching morasses that they began immediately to encounter. He was also over-shadowed by the earnest entreaties of Achilles who had refused to come with Drinkwater but who impressed upon the midshipman the folly of going inland. Drinkwater therefore plunged into the forest with his nerves already highly strung, with every fibre of his being suspicious of the least faltering of the head of the column, of the least exclamation no matter how innocent the cause . . .

Despite the nature of the terrain the landing party made good progress along the track that led inland from Fort Frederic. About five miles from the fort they came across a cleared area with a saw pit and indications of some sort of logging post. There was also evidence that its occupants had made a hurried departure. A few miles further on they came across a small plantation with a clapboard house and outbuildings. The house had been partially burned and the outbuildings were a mass of flies. Carrion eaters were feeding on the decomposing corpses of cattle.

The stink of that burnt out farm seemed to linger with the little column as it made its way through the oppressively empty pine barrens. They crossed a creek that drained north into the Galuda and set up a bivouac for the night. The men were now grumbling in a murmur that soon became an uproar as the mosquitoes began biting. Devaux had no zeal for this kind of service but Wheeler, able to assume the unofficial leadership through his military training, was revelling in his own element. Watches were posted and the party settled down to eat what they had brought with them.

About sunset, having ascertained his watch duties for the night, Drinkwater went off into the surrounding forest to answer a call of nature. After the sweaty progress of the day, the incessant grumbling of the men and the struggle to keep them going towards the end, he was feeling very tired. Squatting over a tree root he became light-headed, convinced that this was not really him, Nathaniel Drinkwater, who squatted thus, emptying his bowels God knows how many thousand miles from home. He looked down. Was this soggy, mossy undergrowth really the fabulous Americas? It seemed so illogical as to be impossible. As so often happened at such private moments he found his thoughts drifting to Elizabeth. Somehow the image of her was more real than this ludicrous actuality . . .

So strongly was he able to fantasise that he seemed to see himself telling Elizabeth of how, once, many years ago, he had sat across the roots of a pine tree in somewhat indelicate circumstances in far away Carolina thinking of her. So disembodied were his instincts that he failed to hear the crack of a dead branch behind him.

Even when Morris pitched him forward on his face he did not react immediately. Only when it dawned on him that he had his face pressed in a mossy hummock and his naked backside revealed to the world did he come to.

'Well, well, what a pretty sight . . . and how very appropriate, eh, Threddle?'

At the sound of that voice and the mention of the name he tried to turn, putting an arm out to push himself up. But he was too late. Even as he took his weight a foot came down on his elbow and his arm collapsed. Almost instinctively he drew his knees up, twisting his head round.

Threddle stood on his arm, a cutlass in his hand. There was a cruel glitter in his eyes and the corners of his mouth smirked.

'What *shall* we do with him, eh, Threddle?' Morris remained behind him, out of sight but Drinkwater felt horribly exposed, like a mare being steadied for the stallion. As if reading his own fear Morris kicked him. The wave of nausea that spread upwards from his genitals was overwhelming, he fought for breath as the vomit emptied from him. Suddenly he felt Threddle's hand in his hair, twisting his face round so that he faced his own excrement . . .

'What a very good idea, Threddle . . . and then we will bugger him, eh? That'll cut him down to his proper size . . .' Drinkwater had no power to resist, all he could do was clamp his mouth and eyes shut. But even as the smell of his own ordure grew stronger in his nostrils the pressure of Threddle's hand ceased and pulled sideways. The big man fell with a squelchy thud.

'What the . . .?' Morris half turned to see in the gathering twilight the figure of a man holding a boarding pike. Its end gleamed wetly as it was pointed at Morris.

'Sharples!'

Sharples said nothing to Morris. 'Are you all right Mr Drinkwater?' The midshipman rose unsteadily to his feet. He leaned against the tree and, with trembling fingers, buttoned his ducks. Still not trusting his voice he nodded dumbly.

Morris made a move but ceased as Sharples jabbed the point at his chest.

'Now *Mister* Morris take the pistol out of your belt and no tricks . . .' Drinkwater lifted his head to watch. It was getting quite dark but there was still light enough to see the furious gleam in Sharples's eyes.

'No tricks now, *Mister* Morris I want you to place that pistol at Threddle's head and blow his brains out . . .' the voice was vehemently insistent. Drinkwater looked down at Threddle. The pike had pierced his abdomen, entering below the rib cage and ripping through the digestive organs. He was not dead but lay with blood flowing across his belly and gobbets of gore trickling from his mouth. Occasionally his legs twitched weakly and the only thing about him that seemed not to be already half dead were the eyes that screamed a silent protest and cry for mercy . . .

'Cock it!' ordered Sharples. 'Cock it!' He jabbed the pike into Morris's buttocks, forcing the midshipman round to face Threddle. The click of the hammer coming back sounded in Drinkwater's ears. He roused himself. 'No,' he whispered, 'for God's sake Sharples, no!' His voice gathered strength but before he could say more Sharples shouted 'Fire!'

For perhaps a split second Morris hesitated, then the boarding pike made his muscles involuntarily contract. The pistol cracked and Threddle's face disintegrated.

No one moved for perhaps thirty seconds.

'Oh, my God!' managed Drinkwater at last. 'What the hell have you done, Sharples?'

The man turned. A soft, childish smile played around his mouth. His eyes were deep pools in the near-night, pools of tears. His voice when it came caught on breathless sobs.

'It came in the mail, Mr Drinkwater, the mail we got from *Gal'tea* . . . the letter that tol' me my Kate was dead . . . they *said* she died in chil'birth but I know better'n that, sir . . . I know better'n that . . .'

Drinkwater mastered himself at last. 'I'm sorry, Sharples really sorry . . . and thank you for your help . . . But why did you kill Threddle?'

'Because he's shit, sir,' he said simply.

Morris looked up. His face was deathly white. He began to walk unsteadily back towards the encampment. With a final look at Threddle Sharples followed, then, sensing Drinkwater lagged behind, he turned back.

'It ain't no good crying over spilt milk, Mr Drinkwater . . .'

'Shouldn't we bury him?'

Sharples snorted contemptuously. 'No.'

'But what am I to tell the first lieutenant . . .?' Sharples was already tugging him away from the darkening clearing. There was the sound of branches breaking underfoot. Ahead of them they saw Wheeler and two marines, their white cross-belts glowing in the gathering night, close round Morris.

Sharples let go of the boarding pike.

They came up with the others. 'What's going on?' demanded Wheeler looking pointedly at Morris's hand which still held the pistol. Morris's face remained an impassive mask, he looked through, rather than at, Wheeler.

Drinkwater came up. 'Just a stupid mistake, Mr Wheeler. I was emptying my bladder when Morris thought I was a rebel . . . Sharples was doing the same thing about ten yards away . . .' he managed a smile. 'That's right isn't it Morris?'

Morris looked up and Drinkwater felt ice-cold fingers of apprehension round his heart. For Morris smiled. A ghastly, complicit smile . . .

'If you say so, Drinkwater . . .'

And it was only then that Drinkwater realised that by explaining their actions with lies he had become a party to the crime . . .

At dawn the next morning the camp was astir early with discontent. Unable to comprehend the seemingly pointless purpose of the march, employed outside their own environment and stung into a half-crazy state, the men were now openly mutinous. Devaux did his best to placate them but lacked conviction for he shared their belief, with more justification, that their mission was an ill-conceived waste of time.

'Well Wheeler,' he said, 'we may be marching along a fine "military road" but I see few of the fine military upon it, barring your good self, of course. For my money we may as well retrace our steps before being utterly consumed by these damned bugs.' Here he slapped his face, missing the offending insect and presenting a ludicrous spectacle to those near him.

Wheeler considered the matter and a compromise was reached. They would march until noon then, if they still found nothing, they would turn back.

An hour later they set off . . .

*

Out on the bar of the Galuda River Midshipman Cranston served biscuit and water to the longboat's crew. Despite their cramped and aching bodies after a night in the boat the seamen were cheerful. Cruising offshore there was either a land or sea breeze and the insect life was negligible. They looked forward to a pleasant day, a yachting excursion comparable with that enjoyed by the wealthy members of the Duke of Cumberland's fleet. It all seemed to have little to do with the rigorous duties of a man o'war. Fitted with a lugsail the longboat cruised with little exertion necessary from her crew. Lulled into such complaisance it was a rude shock to discern the topgallants of a large vessel offshore.

Cranston put the longboat off before the wind and headed for the Galuda estuary. He was certain the stranger was *La Creole* . . .

The sun had almost reached its zenith when they came upon the mill. It was another weatherboard edifice and indicated the presence of human habitation since the farther trail was better cleared and recently trod. Nevertheless it was deserted despite a partially-filled sack of flour and a dumped cartload of Indian corn.

'That's been left in a deuced hurry,' said Wheeler pointing to the pile.

'Very perceptive,' said Devaux annoyed that, just as it seemed he would have his way and return, they were going to find people.

'D'ye think they fled at our approach?'

'I don't know . . .' said Devaux flatly.

'Shall we feed the men before proceeding further, for I don't like this.' Wheeler's confidence was shaken for the first time. Devaux noted this and pulled himself together. He was in command of the party. First they'd eat and then decide what was to be done.

'D'ye attend to it, Wheeler, and a couple of men at the top of the mill will set our minds at ease, eh?'

'Aye, aye,' answered the marine officer, biting his lip with chagrin that he had overlooked such a very elementary precaution.

The men settled to another meal of dried biscuit and water. They lay in languid poses scratching themselves and grumbling irritably. Having posted his sentinels Wheeler flung himself down in the shade.

All morning Drinkwater had toiled on in the heat trying

desperately to forget the events of the night before. But his testicles ached and from time to time the gorge rose in his throat. He choked it manfully down and avoided all contact with Morris. Sharples swung along with the seamen, a benign smile on his face. Drinkwater was filled with the overwhelming sense of relief when they lay down in the shade of the mill. He closed his eyes and drifted into semi-consciousness.

Then the rebel horse were on them.

The raiders swept into the clearing in a sudden thunder of hooves and dust and the sparkle of sabres. Most of the British were caught lying prone. Surprised in the open the seamen were terrified at the appearance of horses. The flying hooves and flaring nostrils were unfamiliar and horrifying to these men who gave their lives without protest in the claustrophobic darkness of a gun-deck. They defended themselves as best they might, stark terror adding to their confusion.

Wheeler and Devaux came to their feet blaspheming.

'To me, sergeant! Oh, Christ Jesus! To *me* sergeant, damn you!' The marines began to fight their way through to the base of the mill, coalescing in little groups to commence a methodical discharge of musketry.

The general mêlée lasted ten long minutes in which a third of the seamen had been cut down and there was scarce a man in the entire force who had not received a cut or graze.

Drinkwater leaped up with the rest. He had brought a cutlass with him and lugged it out, its clumsy unbalanced blade awkward to his hand. A man on a bay plunged towards him. Drinkwater parried the blow but the impetus of the horse threw him over and he rolled to one side to avoid the hooves. A pistol ball raised dust by his head as he struggled to his feet again. Weakness overcame him and he was filled with the overwhelming desire simply to lie down. He rolled on to his back, half submitting to the impulse. A man ran past him with a musket. He dropped to one knee and fired at the horseman, now turning to make another pass. It was Sharples. He discharged the musket and half dragged Drinkwater closer to the mill. The horseman swerved and rode off to attack four seamen fighting back to back and already going down before the slashing sabres.

Drinkwater got to his feet. He saw Devaux and Wheeler with a group of men forming a defensive group. He pointed and Sharples nodded. Suddenly another man had joined them. It was Morris. He pushed Drinkwater who staggered back against the mill. Sharples turned and thrust the barrel of his musket between them. Morris fired his pistol and Sharples doubled over, a great hole in his chest. Drinkwater was dazed, his vision blurred. He comprehended nothing.

Another horseman rode up and slashed at them. Morris turned away, running round the corner of the mill. The horseman followed. Drinkwater took one brief look at Sharples. He was dead.

He looked up again, the little group round the two lieutenants had grown. In a blind panic he put down his head and ran, dodging among the whirling sabres and stamping horses' legs with animal instinct.

The rebel cavalry had played out their advantage of surprise. Used as they were to attacking lonely farms or ambushing parties of raw Tory militia the horsemen were used to speedy and uncontested victory. Having fought the intruders for some minutes the surviving seamen steadied. Devaux was among them his teeth bared in a snarl of rage. They began to rally, their cutlasses slashing back at the horses or the riders' thighs, concentrating on the bright red spot which, through the swirling dust, marked where the marines were forming a disciplined centre of resistance.

The American officer felt his squadron's will to fight was on the ebb. Seeking to rally his force he yelled out: 'Tarleton's quarter, my lads! Give the bastards Tarleton's quarter!' This reference to the leader of the British Legion, a force of Loyalist Americans under British officers, who let not a rebel escape them if they could help it, had its effect and they renewed their attack. But the resistance of the British was now established and the Americans gradually drew off, reining in their steaming horses just out of short musket range.

Slowly the dust subsided and the two contending parties glared at each other across a no-man's-land of broken bodies and hamstrung horses. Then the enemy wheeled their mounts and vanished into the trees as swiftly and silently as they had come.

The news of the arrival of *La Creole* off the Galuda came as no surprise to Hope. On receiving Cranston's intelligence the captain ordered Skelton to the mainmast cap to watch the enemy privateer. It was with some relief that the lieutenant reported that *La Creole* had stood offshore towards the late afternoon thus buying valuable time for the British. Why she had done so Hope could only guess, possibly the enemy commander wanted time to make preparations, perhaps he did not think he had been observed and wished to make his attack the following day. Perhaps, and Hope hardly dare believe this, perhaps *Cyclops* had not been spotted and *La Creole* was working her patient way southward still searching. At all events the captain was too old a campaigner to worry when fate had dealt him a card he did not expect.

The appearance of *La Creole* enabled him to make up his mind in one direction. He would recall Devaux and the landing party immediately. The indecision that had manifested itself earlier and annoyed Devaux was gone now for it had been caused, not by senility, but lack of faith in his orders. Hope ordered the garrison of Fort Frederic to be withdrawn and the frigate's defences strengthened against a night boat attack.

At a conference of officers he called for a volunteer to take the message of recall to Devaux. The pitifully small group of officers regarded the silent forest visible through the stern windows with misgiving.

'I'll go,' said Cranston at last.

'Well done, Mr Cranston. I shall endeavour to do everything possible for you for such a service. Will no one else support Mr Cranston . . .?'

'There's no need, sir. I'll take the blackamoor.'

'Very well, you may draw what you require from the purser and small arms from Lieutenant Keene. Good luck to you.'

The officers shuffled with relief at Cranston filling such a dangerous office. When they had gone Hope poured himself a glass of rum and wiped his forehead for the thousandth time that day.

'I'll be bloody glad when Devaux and Wheeler get back . . . I pray heaven they're all right . . .' he muttered to himself . . .

The landing party reached their bivouac of the previous night dragging with them the remnants of their expedition. The men collapsed on the banks of the creek to bathe their wounds or drink the bloody water. The badly injured groaned horribly as the mosquitoes

162

renewed their assaults and several became delirious during the night.

Drinkwater slept badly. Although unwounded beyond a bruised shoulder from the flat of a sabre and the endemic scratches collected on the way, the heat, fatigue and events of the preceding hours had taken their toll. He had marched from the mill in a daze, his mind constantly fastening unbidden on images of Threddle lying dead in the gloaming and Sharples stiff with blackened blood in the heat of noon. Between these two corpses floated Morris, Morris with a pistol still smoking in his hand, Morris with the smile of triumph on his face and, worst of all, the superimposition of Morris over his image of Elizabeth.

He fought hard to retain her face in his mind's eye but it faded, faded beyond recall so that he thought he might go mad in this forested nightmare through which they trudged.

And when night came there was no rest, for the mosquitoes reactivated the exhausted nervous system, constantly recalling to wakefulness the mind and the body that only wished to sleep. Death, thought Nathaniel at that midnight moment, would be a blessed relief.

Wheeler, too, slept little. He constantly patrolled his outposts, apprehensive lest the enemy renew their attack on the sleeping men. He shook his head sadly as a grey dawn revealed the encampment. The men were tattered, their limbs scarred and gashed by briars and branches, dried blood blackening improvised bandages and flies settling on open wounds.

Several of the wounded were delirious and Devaux ordered litters improvised and an hour after dawn the party moved off, resuming its painful march.

At mid-morning they found Cranston and Achilles.

The negro had been tied to a tree and flayed alive. His back was a mass of flies. Hagan, himself badly wounded limped forward and cut the body down. Achilles was still alive, his breath coming in shallow gasps.

Cranston had evidently put up a fight. He had been hanged from a tree but it was obvious he had been dead before the rebels strung him up. Or at least Devaux hoped so. Scarce a man there refrained from vomiting at the sight of the mutilation inflicted on Cranston's body. Devaux found himself wondering if the man had a wife or a mistress . . . and then he turned away.

Wheeler and Hagan laid the negro gently on the ground, brushing the flies from his face. Devaux stood beside him and touched his shoulder. Wheeler stood up. 'Bastards,' he choked.

Achilles opened his eyes. Above him he saw the scarlet coat and gold gorget. His hand moved slightly in salutation before dropping back in death.

The two officers had the midshipman cut down and crudely buried with the negro, then the column pressed on.

In the evening they emerged from the forest and staggered down to the landing jetty. Wheeler could raise no protest when he saw no men in the little fort and Devaux felt relief flood through him. Relief from the tension of independent command, and relief that very soon he would see the comfortable old face of Henry Hope.

All Nathaniel Drinkwater saw was the frigate, dark and strangely welcoming in the twilight and he waited impatiently for the boat to ferry him off.

'Are you all right, Nat?'

It was little White, sunburned and bright from new responsibility.

Drinkwater looked at him. It did not seem possible that they belonged to the same generation.

'Where's Cranston?' asked White.

Drinkwater raised a tired arm and pointed at the surrounding forest. 'Dead in the defence of His Majesty's dominions,' he said, aware that cynicism was a great relief, 'with his bollocks in his mouth . . .'

Somehow he found White's shocked look amusing . . .

Chapter Sixteen   *April 1781*

The Cutting Out

If the remnants of the landing party expected rest after their labours they were to be disappointed. After a bare three hours exhausted sleep several found themselves rowing a guard-boat cautiously down stream to prevent a surprise attack by *La Creole* or her boats. Hope was especially concerned since he had seen the enemy stand southwards.

Although he could not know it *La Creole had* missed *Cyclops* in her search, but the last of the onshore breeze the next afternoon brought her back. An hour before sunset she had anchored on the bar. There was no longer any doubt that she had found her quarry.

The twenty-four hours that had elapsed since the return of the landing party had proved tiring and trying for all. Without exception the members of the expedition had about them the smell of defeat and their low morale affected the remaining men. The immediate failure of the mission was forgotten in the urgent necessity of allevi-ating the sufferings of the wounded and preparing the frigate for sea. The topgallant masts were re-hoisted and the upper yards crossed. It may well have been this that discovered her to *La Creole* but no one now cared. Action was infinitely preferable to lying supinely in the stinking jungle-surrounded Galuda a moment more than was necessary. Appleby and his mates worked harder than anyone else, patching up the walking wounded so that they might man their guns again, or easing the sufferings of the badly wounded with laudanum.

The time passed for Drinkwater in a daze. Outwardly he carried out his duties with his customary efficiency. When the roll was called he answered for Sharples having been killed at the mill.

When Threddle's name was called his mouth clamped shut. His

eyes swivelled to Morris. The enigmatic smile still played around the mouth of his adversary but Morris said nothing.

Strain and fatigue continued to play havoc with Drinkwater's nerves as the day wore on until, when the news of the arrival of *La Creole* on the bar spread rapidly through the ship, he seemed to emerge from a tunnel. He had found his second wind. Morris was just Morris, an evil to be endured, Achilles had been a brief and colourful intrusion into his life and was so no more; Cranston was dead, just that, dead; and Threddle . . . Threddle was discharged dead too, killed in action at the mill . . . or so the ship's books said . . .

It was only when he received the summons to attend the Captain, however, that his mind received the final jerk that returned him to sanity. As he entered the cabin in company with all the other officers he found himself standing next to Morris. It came to him then, the awful truth, the fact that his numbed mind had automatically excluded in its pain . . .

Sharples had not died in action. Sharples had been shot down in cold blood under the cover of action. And the man next to him had done it . . .

'Well, gentlemen . . .' Hope looked round the ring of tired yet expectant faces. They were all here. The welcome features of Devaux and Wheeler, the careworn, lined face of old Blackmore, the younger Keene and youthful Skelton. Behind the commissioned officers the mature warrant officers; the gunner, the bosun and the carpenter, and the eager yet apprehensive faces of his midshipmen and master's mates.

'Well gentlemen, it seems our friend has returned, I suspect with reinforcements. I imagine he will attempt a cutting out so I am not intending to warp the ship round. If we see *La Creole* approaching then we shall have to do so and for that eventuality the spring is already rigged, but I do not foresee this. The wind during the night will be offshore and therefore favour an attack by boats. I have a mind to bait a trap and for that purpose have summoned you all here . . . Moonset is about two o'clock. We may, therefore, expect his boats soon after in order that, having taken us,' here Hope looked round and swept what he believed to be a sardonically inspiring grin around the company, '. . . he may carry the *terral* to sea . . .'

A little shuffle among the officers indicated a stirring of interest.

Hope breathed a silent sigh of relief. 'Now, gentlemen, this is what I intend that we should do . . .'

Cyclops settled down to await the expected attack. The hands had been fed and the galley fire extinguished. The men had been told off to their stations and the most elaborate dispositions made. Apart from a watch the hands were, for the time being, ordered to rest on their arms.

Anxious to stimulate the morale of his crew Hope had accepted several suggestions for improvisation in the frigate's defence. Of these the best had been suggested by Wheeler. *Cyclops*'s two largest boats were hoisted by the yardarm tackles fitted to the extremities of the fore and main yards. By this means the boats were slung outboard of, and higher than, the frigate's sides. In each boat a party of the ship's best marksmen lay hidden, awaiting the order to open fire upon the anticipated boarders as they scrambled up *Cyclops*'s sides.

The lower deck gunports were all secured and the hands issued with small arms.

An hour after moonset the faint chuckle of water under a boat's bow was heard from downstream. Peering intently from the stern cabin windows Devaux touched Hope's arm.

'Here they come, sir,' he whispered. He turned to pass word forward but Hope held him back. 'Good luck Mr Devaux . . .' Hope's voice cracked with age and emotion. Devaux smiled in the darkness. 'Good luck to you, sir,' he replied warmly.

The first lieutenant slipped through into the gun-deck, passing a whispered warning to the men stationed there. Emerging on to the upper deck he ordered the men to lie down. In a crouching position he moved up one side and down the other. At each post he found the men waiting eagerly.

Drinkwater was one of the party waiting in the forward gun-deck. Commanded by Lieutenant Skelton their task was to counter attack once the enemy had boarded in the manner that had been so successfully used in the previous action. Up on the fo'c's'le O'Malley, the Irish cook, scraped a melancholy air on his fiddle and several men sang quietly or chatted in low voices as might be expected from a casually maintained anchor watch . . .

The boats came alongside at several points. Faint

bumps told where they secured. Devaux waited. A hand reached over the rail and grasped the hammock netting, another followed. One groped upwards and a moment later a knife was sawing through the boarding netting, another followed. Another hand came over the opposite rail. It was followed by a head.

'Now!' bellowed Devaux, expelling his pent up breath in one mighty roar that was taken up by the waiting seamen. The tension burst from them in smoke, flame and destruction. Fifty or sixty twelve-pound cannon balls were dropped overside to plummet down through the bottoms of *La Creole*'s boats. From her own boats, suspended high above, *Cyclops*'s marksmen opened a lethal fire on the invaders. This desperate refinement quickly cleared the frigate's sides.

From the deck too a withering fire was poured down at the hapless privateersmen now struggling in the river . . .

Aft the attacks had been driven off with similar success. Hope looked round. He was suddenly aware that his ship was swinging, her head falling off from pointing up river. Someone forward had cut *Cyclops*'s cable and instinct prompted Hope to stare over the stern, searching in the darkness for the spring. Shouting anxiously for Blackmore to get sail on the ship he sprung himself for the wheel in case the spring parted and the ship was in danger of going aground.

Forward the rebels had had more success than the mere severing of the frigate's cable. Having driven a boat in under *Cyclops*'s figurehead where access was comparatively easy via the bowsprit rigging and the foretack bumpkins, twenty or thirty men had gained access to the deck under an enterprising officer and a fierce hand to hand engagement now took place. Several of the privateersmen were engaged in turning one of the bow chasers inboard along the length of *Cyclops*.

The situation became critical and Devaux shouted for Skelton's reserve.

Hearing the shouts and screams from above Lieutenant Skelton was already on his way, leading the counter attackers out of the Stygian gloom of the gun-deck. Behind him Drinkwater drew his dirk and followed.

On the fo'c's'le the French privateer officer was achieving a measure of success. His men had swung the starboard bow chaser round and were preparing to fire it. He was determined to destroy the British frigate if he could not take her. If he could force her aground and fire her . . . already she was head downstream . . . it occurred to him that she should be broadside on . . .

He turned to shout orders to two men remaining in the boat to bring combustibles on board, then he swung round to rally his men for a final attempt to secure the upper deck in the wake of the bow chaser's discharge.

A British lieutenant appeared in front of him leading a fresh body of men that had appeared from nowhere. The lieutenant slashed at the Frenchman but before Skelton's blade even started its downward path the latter executed a swift and fatal lunge.

'*Hélas!*' he shouted. Skelton reeled backwards carrying with him two seamen coming up behind. The French officer's eyes gleamed in triumph and he turned to order his men to discharge the cannon.

'*Tirez!*' A thin youth confronted him. The Frenchman grinned maliciously at the dirk his opponent held. He extended his sword arm. Drinkwater waited for the lunge but the other recovered and the two stood for a second eyeing each other. The Frenchman's experience weighed the midshipman . . . he lunged.

Skelton's blood flowed freely across the deck. The French officer slipped as Drinkwater half turned to avoid the blade. The sword point, raised involuntarily by his opponent's loss of balance, caught his cheek and ripped upwards, deflected out of the flesh by the cheekbone. Drinkwater had gone icy cold in that heart-beat of suspension, he already knew he had his man as his fencer's instinct told him the other was losing his balance. Now the sting of the wound unleashed a sudden fury in him. He stabbed blindly and savagely, giving the thrust impetus by the full weight of his body. The dirk passed under the man's biceps and buried itself in his shoulder, piercing the right lung. The Frenchman staggered back, recovering his balance too late, dropping his sword, blood pouring from his wound.

Drinkwater flung away the dirk and grabbed the fallen sword. It leapt in his hand, balanced exquisitely on the lower phalange of his forefinger. He threw himself into the fight screaming encouragement to the seamen struggling for possession of the deck.

In twenty minutes it was over. By then *Cyclops* had brought up to her spring and Drinkwater, the only officer left standing forward was joined by Devaux and they began securing the prisoners . . .

Instead of travelling slowly downstream beam on, the frigate's spring had the effect of re-anchoring her by the stern since it was led out of an after gunport and secured to the anchor cable below the cut. This fortuitous circumstance permitted Hope to set the topsails so that the vessel strained at her anchor as the sails bellied out to the *terral*.

Drinkwater hurried aft touching his forehead.

'All the boarders secured, sir, what orders?'

Hope looked astern. He could make out the splashes of men struggling in the water and the taut spring rising dripping with water from the tension on it.

Devaux hurried up. 'Get those boats cut down and you, Drinkwater, get the spring cut . . .'

The two ran off. 'Mr Blackmore!'

'Sir?'

'Take the conn, have a man in the chains and a quartermaster back at the wheel. Pass word to the leadsman that I want the soundings *quietly*.' Hope emphasised the last word as Keene came up. 'Work round the deck Mr Keene, not a word from anyone . . . anyone, do you understand?'

'Aye, aye, sir.'

Drinkwater ran up again. 'Spring cut, sir,' he reported.

'Well done, Mister.' Hope rubbed his hands gleefully, like a schoolboy contemplating a prank. 'I'm going out after that fella, Mister Drinkwater,' he confided, pointing ahead to somewhere in the darkness where *La Creole* awaited them. 'She'll be expecting us under her cutting out party – we'll give 'em a surprise, eh cully?' Hope grinned.

'Aye, aye, sir!'

'Now run off and find Devaux and tell him to man the starboard battery and have topmen aloft . . . oh, and men at the braces . . .' Drinkwater ran off with his message.

Blackmore was letting the wind and current take the frigate downstream, trusting that the run of water would serve her best. As the ship cleared the wooded headlands he adjusted the course and trimmed the yards. Drinkwater was ordered forward to keep a look-out for *La Creole*.

He strained his eyes into the night. Small circles danced in his vision. He elevated his glance a little from the horizon and immediately, on the periphery of his retina a darker spot appeared to starboard. He clapped the battered glass to this eye.

It was *La Creole* and at anchor too!

He raced aft: 'She's two points to starboard, sir, and at anchor!'

'Very well, Mr Drinkwater:' then to Blackmore, 'starboard a point.'

Blackmore's voice answered, 'Starboard a point, sir. By my reckoning you are just clear of the bar . . .'

'Very well. Mr Drinkwater, get a cable on the second bower!'

Cyclops slipped seawards. *La Creole* was just visible against the false dawn. Hope intended to cross *La Creole*'s stern, rake her and put his helm down. As he turned to starboard and ran alongside the enemy ship he would anchor. It was his last anchor, except for the light kedge and it was a gamble. He explained to his principal officers what he intended . . .

Drinkwater found two bosun's mates and a party of tired seamen hauling an eight-inch rope up to the ring on the second bower. The two ships were closing fast.

'Hurry it up there,' he hissed between clenched teeth. The men looked up at him sullenly. After what seemed an interminable delay the cable was secured.

Returning to report the anchor ready Drinkwater passed the prisoners. In the haste they had been trussed up to the foremast bitts and a sudden thought occurred to him. If these men shouted a warning, *Cyclops*'s advantage would be lost. Then another idea came to him.

He ordered the marine sentries to herd them below, all of them except the French officer who lay groaning on the deck. Drinkwater still had the man's sword in his hand. He cut the rope securing the man to the bitts.

'Up mister!' he ordered.

'*Merde*,' growled the man.

Drinkwater pointed the sword at his throat: 'Up!'

The man rose reluctantly to his feet, swaying with dizziness. The midshipman prodded him aft, he ordered the last marine to go below to slit the throat of the first man that so much as squealed. Afterwards his own ruthless barbarity surprised him but at the time it seemed the only logical thing to do under the uncompromising prompting of a desire to survive.

He arrived on the quarterdeck. 'What the devil?' queried a startled Hope, to be reassured by a sight of his own midshipman, a drawn sword in his hand, behind the Frenchman.

'Anchor's ready, sir. I thought this fella would help allay any suspicions, sir. Shout to the enemy, sir, tell 'em the ship's his . . .'

'An excellent idea Drinkwater. Speaks English, eh? Must do with that polyglot rebel crew. Probably uses French with his commander. Prick him a little, sir,' said the captain.

The man jerked. Hope addressed him in English, his voice uncharacteristically sinister and brutal:

'Now you dog. I have an old score to settle with your race. My brother and my sister's husband died in Canada and I've an un-Christian hankering for revenge. You tell your commander that this ship is yours and you'll anchor under his lee. No tricks now, I've the best surgeon in the fleet and he'll see to you, you've my word on that but,' here Hope looked significantly at Drinkwater and paused, 'but one false word and it's your last. D'ye understand, *canaille*?'

The man winced again. '*Oui*,' he nodded, breathing through clenched teeth. Drinkwater shoved him to the main chains. Hope turned away.

'Pass the word to Mr Devaux to have the gun crews stand by. On the command I want the ports opened and the guns run straight out and fired.'

'Aye, aye, sir,' a messenger ran off.

Cyclops was less than one hundred yards off *La Creole* now, crossing her stern from starboard to larboard. A hail came from the big privateer.

'Very well, Mr Drinkwater, prompt our friend.'

The Frenchman drew a breath.

'*Ça va bien! Je suis blessé, mais la frégate est prise!*'

A voice replied across the diminishing gap between the two ships. '*Bravo mon ami! Mais votre blessure?*'

The French officer shot a glance at Drinkwater and took a deep breath.

'*Affreuse! A la gorge!*' There was a moment's silence then a puzzled voice:

'*La gorge? . . . Mon Dieu!*' A shout of realisation came from *La Creole*.

Hope swore and the Frenchman, his left hand to his chest where his punctured lung gave him great pain, turned triumphantly to Drinkwater. But the midshipman could not kill him in cold blood, indeed he only half comprehended what had transpired . . .

But events now moved in rapid succession so that Drinkwater's dilemma was short lived. The French officer slumped to the deck in a faint as *La Creole*'s people ran to their guns. A gust of wind filled *Cyclops*'s topsails so that she accelerated a little and suddenly the privateer's stern was drawing abeam.

'Now Devaux! Now by God!'

The ports opened, there was a terrible squealing rumble as the starboard battery of twelve-pounders were run out. Then the concussion of the broadside overwhelmed them all, rocking the frigate. In the darkness of the gun-deck Keene and Devaux were leaping up and down with excitement and a fighting madness. They had double shotted the guns and topped off the charges with canister. The devastation thus inflicted upon *La Creole* almost destroyed her resistance at a blow. As the guns recoiled inboard *Cyclops* swung to starboard. Her impetus carried her alongside *La Creole* and a further broadside smashed into the ex-Indiaman's hull. A few bold souls aboard the American fired back and the engagement became general, though all the advantage lay with the British.

Drawing a little ahead *Cyclops* lost way. Her anchor was let go and her sails clewed up. Veering the cable *Cyclops* settled back and brought up on *La Creole*'s larboard quarter.

For twenty dreadful minutes the British poured shot after shot into her. Aboard the American ship men died bravely. They got eight guns into action and inflicted some damage on their opponent but in the end, lying in his own gore, his ship and crew a shambles around him, the French commander ordered his ensign struck and an American officer complied.

The pale light of dawn revealed to Hope the limp bunting lying across the jagged remnants of what had once been a handsome carved taffrail and he ordered his cannon to cease fire . . .

Later in the morning Drinkwater accompanied his commander aboard the enemy's ship. Captain Hope did not consider her worth taking as a prize. His depleted crew were barely enough to guard the prisoners and work *Cyclops*. The rebel ship had been old when the Americans commissioned her and the damage that she suffered at the hands of *Cyclops*'s gun crews had been frightful.

Drinkwater gaped at the desolation caused by the frigate's broadsides. The planking of her decks was ripped up, furrowed by ball and canister into jagged lines of splinters reminiscent of a field of petrified grass. Several beams sagged down into the spaces below and cannon were knocked clean off their carriages. Trunnions had been sheered and three had had their cascabels cut off as if with a knife. Scattered about all this destruction were petty items of personal gear. A man's stocking hat, a shoe, a crucifix and rosary beads, a clasp knife and a beautifully painted chest split to fragments . . .

Grimmer remains of what had once been men lay in unseemly attitudes and splashes of vivid colour. Dried blood was dark beside the ochreous pools of vomit, the stark white of exposed bone, the blue of bled flesh and the greens and browns of intestines. It was a vile sight and the hollow eyes of the surviving members of the crew regarded the British captain with a dull hatred as the author of their fate. But Hope, with the simple faith of the dedicated warrior, returned their gaze with scorn. For these men were nothing but legalised pirates, plundering for profit, destroying merchant ships for gain, and visiting upon innocent seamen a callous indifference to their fates.

The captain ordered out of her such stores as might serve the frigate and had combustibles prepared to fire her. Lieutenant Keene boarded *La Creole* at sunset to ignite her. As the offshore *terral* began to blow seawards *Cyclops* weighed her anchor. *La Creole* burned furiously, a black pall rolling seawards away from the coast of that benighted land.

Cyclops was standing well off shore when *La Creole*'s magazine exploded. An hour later she altered course for Cape Hatteras and New York.

Decision at the Virginia Capes

The weather was once more against them. Off the dreaded Cape they met a gale of unbelievable ferocity which tried the gear severely. The main topgallant mast went by the board and took with it the fore and mizen topgallants. During this blow the wounded were, of course, confined below. The cockpit was a scene of utter degradation. The filth in the bilge was augmented by the water made by the straining frigate as she laboured in the seaway and the whole slopped about the bottom of the ship, driving the rodent population higher. The rats ran almost unchecked over the bodies of the dying who retched and urinated without relief. For die they did. Scarce a man who received anything more trivial than a scratch escaped gangrene or blood poisoning of one kind or another.

Drinkwater was one of the fortunate few. His cut, a superficial one, was disfiguring rather than dangerous. Appleby sutured it for him, an Appleby who had lost much rotundity and whose pitifully few medicines were exhausted as he fought disease and sepsis with his own diminishing energies. At last, utterly worn with fatigue and exasperation he wept angry and frustrated tears in the darkness of his hellish kingdom.

Hope buried the bundles in their hammocks. Six one day, nine another as the wind howled, the frigate bucked and the spray drove inboard in hissing sheets. The burial service became curtailed into the briefest formality.

Although the weather was poor it allowed *Cyclops* to limp north undetected. For she was in no condition to fight. In addition to the heavy losses incurred at the Galuda River the ship's company now had to subsist on rotten stores. Opening the last casks of salt provisions Copping, the purser, had discovered the usually tainted pork was uneatably putrid and the misery of *Cyclops*'s company immeasurably increased.

At last she made her number to the guardship at Sandy Hook and, in company with the members of the North American Squadron, let go her anchor in the Hudson River.

For the last months of effective British rule in any part of her thirteen colonies, His Britannic Majesty's frigate *Cyclops* lay passive. Arriving at New York on the last day of April 1781 she lay in the mouth of the Hudson without positive orders beyond the general directive to effect repairs to her fabric.

Admiral Arbuthnot did not appear to take a great interest in her arrival as she was not on the establishment of the North American Station. Indeed he seemed rather offended that she should make her appearance anywhere in his command without his receiving prior notice, and visited his displeasure on Captain Hope whom he greeted with icy politeness.

Secretly angry that he had ended up between two stools, Hope claimed his mission had been confidential but, when challenged as to its success, was compelled to report failure. His explanation was received with disbelief, the Admiral firmly maintaining the Carolinas were in British hands. Hope also wished to rid himself of the Continental currency but this was too much for Admiral Arbuthnot who studied the captain through rheumy eyes.

'You arrive on my station, sir, occupy a British post without authority, fail in a mission you claim is secret yet was given you by the captain of a frigate and now you wish *me* to rid *you* of an embarrassing sum of rebel currency.' The admiral rose. 'You may retain the stuff until you report to y'r own flag officer, Admiral . . . Admiral . . .'

'Kempenfelt, sir.'

'Exactly.' Arbuthnot appeared to consider the matter closed.

'But sir, I have to refit my to'gallants . . .'

'Your topgallants, sir, are your topgallants and not mine . . . I suggest you contact Admiral Kempenfelt on the matter. Good day, sir.'

Hope left.

Eventually Arbuthnot's secretary received instructions from London to render such assistance as might be necessary to the frigate *Galatea*. A note was appended to the effect that due to political circumstances of the greatest importance, *Galatea* had been retained in home waters and her mission undertaken by *Cyclops*, Captain Henry Hope, R.N.

The secretary therefore prepared an order for her to come in and draw such stores as she required and refit her gear. Arbuthnot signed the order without comment since he was at that time prone to sign almost anything, being nearly blind. On receipt of these orders *Cyclops* moved to a berth at the Manhattan Dockyard to commence her repairs. On that evening Hope and Devaux dined together. Over their port, several cases of which had been removed from *La Creole*, Hope drew Devaux's attention to a decision that the weather and the frigate's cranky tophamper had deferred.

'Assuming that we eventually receive definite orders, Devaux, we have to consider the matter of a replacement for Skelton. Cranston was a loss to us and the Service as a whole . . .'

'Yes,' agreed Devaux nodding. His mind slid back to the dense forest and the sight of Cranston's mutilated body . . . He tore his mind away from the grisly memory.

'D'ye have any opinions?' asked the Captain.

The first lieutenant recollected himself. 'Well sir, the next senior is Morris. His journals are poorly kept, though he's served the six years . . . I consider him quite unsuitable and I would appreciate his removal from the ship . . . indeed I threatened him with it I seem to remember . . . I am of the opinion that young Drinkwater is a likely candidate for an acting lieutenancy.' He paused. 'But surely, sir, there's a junior in the fleet hereabouts . . .' Devaux indicated the riding lights of several warships visible through the stern windows.

'An Admiral's favourite d'ye mean, Mr Devaux?' asked Hope archly.

'Just so, sir.'

'But Admiral Arbuthnot informed me that the ship is under Kempenfelt's flag. Who am I to question his decision?' he enquired with mock humility, and then in a harder tone, 'besides I am not disposed to question him on the matter of my midshipmen.' He sipped his port. 'Furthermore I submitted a list of casualties that clearly indicated the state of our complement of officers. If he does not see fit to appoint someone he can go to the devil.' He paused. 'Besides I rather suspect Kempenfelt would approve our choice . . .' Hope smiled benignly and tossed off the glass.

Devaux raised an eyebrow. 'Old Blackmore will be pleased, he's had Drinkwater under his wing since we left Sheerness.' The two officers refilled their glasses.

'Which,' said Devaux choosing his moment, 'brings me to the matter of Morris sir. I'd be obliged if a transfer could be arranged . . .'

'That is a little drastic, is it not, Mr Devaux. What's behind this request?'

Devaux outlined the problem and added the remark that in any case Morris would resent serving under Drinkwater. Hope snorted.

'Resent! Why I've resented serving under half the officers I've submitted to. But Morris is fortunate, Mr Devaux. Had I known earlier I'd have broken him. Another time I'll trouble you to tell me as soon as you have any inkling of this kind of thing . . . it's the bane of the Service and produces officers like that loathsome Edgecumbe . . .' Hope added expansively.

'Yes, sir,' Devaux changed the subject hastily. 'What are the Admiral's intentions, sir?'

Again Hope snorted. 'Intentions! I wish he had some. Why he and General Clinton sit here in New York waving the Union Flag with enough soldiers to wipe Washington off the face of the earth. Clinton shits himself with indecision at the prospect of losing New York and saves face by sending General Philips into Virginny.

'However I hear that Arbuthnot's to be relieved . . .'

'Who by, sir?'

'Graves . . .'

'Good God, not Graves . . .'

'He's a pleasant enough man which is more than I found Arbuthnot.'

'He's an amiable incompetent, sir. Wasn't he court-martialled for refusing battle with an Indiaman?'

'Yes, back in 'fifty-seven . . . no 'fifty-six. He was acquitted of cowardice but publicly reprimanded for an error of judgement under the 36th Article of War . . . you must admit *some* Indiamen pack a punch . . .' Both officers smiled ruefully at memories of *La Creole*.

'D'ye know, John, it's one of the great ironies that on the very day the court at Plymouth sentenced Tommy Graves, a court at Portsmouth got John Byng for a similar offence which was far more strategically justifiable. You know what happened to Byng. They sentenced him under the 12th Article . . . he was shot on his own quarterdeck . . .' Hope's voice trailed off.

'*Pour encourager les autres* . . .,' muttered Devaux. 'Voltaire, sir,' he said in explanation as Hope looked up.

'Ah, that Godless French bastard . . .'

'Does anyone know what's happened to Cornwallis, sir?'

Hope stirred. 'No! I don't believe any of 'em know anything, John. Now what about my main to'gallant . . .?'

The next morning Devaux sent for Drinkwater. The lieutenant was staring north up the Hudson River to where the New Jersey Palisades could be seen, catching the early sunlight.

'Sir?'

Devaux turned and regarded the young man. The face had matured now. The ragged line of the wound, rapidly scarring, would hardly alter the flesh over the cheekbones though it might contrast the weathered tan. The figure beneath the worn and patched uniform was spare but fit. Devaux snapped his glass shut.

'That hanger you had off *La Creole*'s lieutenant . . . D'ye still have it?'

Drinkwater coloured. At the end of the action he had found himself still clasping the small sword. It was a fine weapon and its owner had not survived long after the capture of his ship. Drinkwater had regarded the thing as his own part of the spoil. After all the gunroom officers wallowed in the captured wine for weeks afterwards and he felt the weight of a dirk too useless for real fighting. The sword had found its way to the bottom of his sea-chest where it lay wrapped in bunting. He did not know how Devaux knew this but assumed that omniscience was a natural attribute of first lieutenants.

'Well, sir?' queried Devaux, a note of asperity in his voice.

'Er, yes, sir . . .I, er, do have it . . .'

'Then ye'd better clap it on y're larboard hip!'

'Beg pardon, sir?' The young man frowned uncomprehendingly.

Devaux laughed at Drinkwater's puzzled expression. 'The captain is promoting you acting third lieutenant as of now. You may move your chest and effects up on to the gun-deck . . .' He watched the effect of the news on Drinkwater's face. The lad's mouth

179

dropped open, then closed. He blinked, then smiled back. At last he stammered his thanks.

Cyclops lay at her anchor with Arbuthnot's squadron through May and June. During this time Drinkwater's prime task was to get a new broadcloth coat from a New York tailor. The ship had recruited its complement from the guardships but there was little for the men to do. Then, on 12th July, things began to happen. Admiral Graves arrived, a kind, generous but simple incompetent who was to be instrumental in losing the war. Then Rodney's tender *Swallow* arrived with the intelligence that Admiral De Grasse had left the West Indies with a French fleet bound for the Chesapeake. Graves chose to ignore the warning despite its significance. Since May Lord Cornwallis had abandoned the Carolinas and was combining his force with General Philips's in Virginia. If Cornwallis had De Grasse sitting on his communications with New York he would be cut off. Captains and officers had themselves rowed about the fleet while they grumbled about their admiral's failure to grasp the simplest strategic facts. Cornwallis was retreating to the sea for the navy to support him . . . but the navy was in New York . . .

Once again the opinion was expressed that in executing Byng their Lordships had taken more leave of their senses than was usual; they had shot the wrong man.

Another message arrived via *Pegasus* that urged Graves to sail south and join Sir Samuel Hood, to whom Rodney had relinquished command through ill health. But the fleet remained supinely at anchor.

At the beginning of August Clinton decided to act, not against Virginia, but against Rhode Island where French troops and men o'war were based. Admiral Graves ordered a number of ships down to Sandy Hook in preparation. One of these was *Cyclops*.

It was at this time that Midshipman Morris left the frigate.

When *Cyclops* left the Galuda her ship's company were hard put to fight the elements, guard their prisoners and simply survive. The remaining lieutenants were on watch and watch, with the mates and midshipmen equally hard pressed. Drinkwater and Morris were in opposite watches and the preoccupations of working and sleeping

180

allowed no-one the luxury of contemplating the events of past weeks objectively. It would not be true, however, to say that the events and circumstances that had occurred were forgotten. Rather they sat at a level just above the sub-conscious, so that they influenced conduct but did not dominate it. Drinkwater was particularly affected. The horrors he had seen and the guilt he felt over his involvement in the death of Threddle impinged on his self-esteem. And his knowledge of the manner of Sharples's death lay like a weight upon his soul.

Although Sharples had been the true murderer of Threddle, Drinkwater knew that he had been driven to it. Morris's cold-blooded execution of the seaman at the mill, however, was another matter.

To Drinkwater's mind it was a matter for the law or, and he shuddered at the thought, a matter for vengeance.

When *Cyclops* arrived at New York there was time, too much time, for the mind to wander over possible causes and effects and the consequences of action.

In the midshipmen's mess some contact with Morris was unavoidable and there had been potentially disruptive scenes. Drinkwater had always avoided them by walking out, but this action had given Morris the impression of an ascendancy over Nathaniel.

Morris had entered the mess some time after, but on the day that Drinkwater had been told of his promotion.

'And what's our brave Nathaniel up to now?' There was silence. Then White came in. 'I've taken your boat-cloak and tarpaulin to your cabin, Nat . . . er, sir . . .'

Nathaniel smiled at his friend. 'Thanks, Chalky . . .'

'Cabin? Sir? What bloody tomfoolery is this . . .?' Morris was colouring with comprehension. Nathaniel said nothing but continued to pack things in his chest. White could not resist the chance of aggravating the bully at whose hands he had suffered, particularly when he had a powerful ally in the person of the acting third lieutenant.

'Mr Drinkwater,' he said with gravity, 'is promoted to acting third lieutenant.'

Morris glared as he assimilated the news. He turned to Nathaniel in a fury.

'The devil you are. Why you jumped-up little bastard you don't have time in for lieutenant . . . I suppose you've been arse-licking the first lieutenant again . . . I'll see about this . . .' He ran on for some minutes in similar vein.

Drinkwater felt himself seized again by the cold rage that had made him so brutal with the wounded French lieutenant of *La Creole*. It was a permanent legacy of that horrendous march inland and was to stamp his conduct in moments of physical confrontation. As the influence of his widowed mother had made him soft clay for Morris's viciousness, the events of the Galuda had tempered the latent iron in his soul.

'Have a care, sir,' he said, his voice low and menacing, 'have a care in what you say . . . you forget I have passed for master's mate which is more than you have ever managed . . . you also forget I have evidence to have you hanged under two Articles of War . . .'

Morris paled and Drinkwater thought for a moment he was going to faint. At last he spoke.

'And what if I tell of your conduct over Threddle?'

Drinkwater felt his own heart thump with recollection but he retained his head. He turned to little White who was staring wide-eyed between one and the other of the older midshipmen.

'Chalky, if you had to choose between evidence I gave and evidence Morris gave whose would you favour?'

The boy smiled, pleased at the dividend his revenge was receiving, 'Yours, Nat, of course . . .'

'Thank you. Now perhaps you and Morris would be kind enough to carry my chest to my cabin.'

Drinkwater luxuriated in the privacy of his little cabin. Situated between two twelve-pounders on the gun-deck it dismantled when the frigate cleared for action. He no longer had to endure the constant comings and goings of the cockpit and was able to read in privacy and quiet. Perhaps the greatest benefit his acting rank conferred upon him was the right to mess in the gunroom and enjoy the society of Wheeler and Devaux. Appleby, though not at that time technically a member of the commissioned officers' mess was a frequent, indeed a usual, visitor. In New York Drinkwater obtained new clothes and cocked hat without braid so that his appearance befitted his new dignity without ostentation, though he was rarely on deck without his captured sword swinging, as Devaux put it, 'upon his larboard hip'.

His acquaintance with the multifarious duties of a naval officer increased daily as there was a constant stream of boats between the ships and town of New York but his social life was limited to an occasional dinner in the gunroom of another vessel. Unlike Wheeler or Devaux he eschewed the delights of the frequent entertainments given by New York society for the garrison and naval officers. This was partly out of shyness, partly out of deference to Elizabeth, but mostly due to the fact that the other occupants of the gunroom now had a junior in their midst sufficiently subordinate not to protest at their abuses of rank.

Drinkwater's chief delight at this time was reading. In the bookshops of New York and from the surgeon's small travelling library he had discovered Smollett and made the consequential acquaintance of Humphry Clinker, Commodore Trunnion and Roderick Random.

It was the latter that led his thoughts so often to Elizabeth. The romantic concept of the waiting woman obsessed him so that the uncertainty of Elizabeth's exact whereabouts worried him. That he loved her was now beyond a doubt. Her image had sustained him in the dreary swamps of Carolina and he had come to think of her as a talisman against all evil, mostly that of Morris.

There was more to his enmity with Morris than a poisonous dislike. He was convinced that the man was an evil influence over his life. Buried deep in the natural fear of the green young midshipman of two years earlier this idea had grown as successive events had seemed to establish a pattern in his imagination. That they had served to strengthen him and his resolution seemed inconsequential. Had he not been made aware of Morris's depravity and the fate of Sharples? Could not someone else have come in from the yard arm that night the topman had begged for help? Could not another midshipman have been sent forward to ask Kate Sharples to leave the deck that day in Spithead?

But now there was a more vivid reason for attributing something supernatural to Morris's malevolence. For Drinkwater was subject to a recurring dream, a nightmare that had its origins in the swamps of Carolina and haunted him with an occasional but persistent terror.

It had come first to him in the exhausted sleep after the taking of *La Creole* and occurred again in the gales off Cape Hatteras. Twice while *Cyclops* lay in New York he had suffered from it.

There was always a white lady who seemed to rear over him, pale as death and inexorable in her advance as she came ever nearer, yet never passed over him entirely. Sometimes she bore the face of Cranston, sometimes of Morris, most horribly of Elizabeth, but an Elizabeth of Medusa-like visage before which he quailed, drowning in a vast noise like the clanking of chains, rhythmically jerking . . . or of *Cyclops*'s pumps . . .

It was therefore with relief that Drinkwater learned of Morris's transfer. Since his promotion he had not sought to impose his new-found authority upon Morris and simply heard that he was joining a ship in Rear Admiral Drake's division with an inner and secret lightening of the heart.

Perhaps, after all, his fears were the groundless suppositions of an overtaxed nervous system . . .

But on the morning of Morris's departure Drinkwater was again in doubt.

He was reading in the confined privacy of his tiny cabin when the door was flung unceremoniously open. Morris stood on the threshold. He was drunk and held in his hand a piece of crumpled paper.

'I've come to shay good-bye, Mishter Fucking Drinkwater . . .' he slurred, his hooded lids half closed, '. . . I want to tell you that you and I have unfinished businesh to attend to . . .' he managed a mirthless chuckle, spittle bubbling round his mouth.

'Ish funny really . . . you and I could've become friends . . .' Tears were visible in the corners of his eyes and Drinkwater slowly realised the awful, odious implication in the man's words. Morris sniffed, drawing his cuff across his nose. Then he began chuckling again.

'I've a letter from my shishter here . . . she knows a man or two at the Admiralty. She promises me to use her four-poshter to make me a posht Captain . . . now don't you think thatsh bloody funny Mishter Drinkwater? Don't you think thatsh about the funniesht thing you've ever heard . . .?' he paused to chuckle at the ribald pun, then his smile vanished and with it his drunken laxity. The threat he had come to utter reinforced by rum was from his heart:

'And if as a consequence I can ever destroy you or your Miss Bower I will . . . by God I will . . .'

At the mention of Elizabeth's name Nathaniel felt the terrible icy rage that had despatched the French privateer officer flood his veins. Morris fell back abruptly and stumbling, sprawled on the deck. Drinkwater had the captured sword half out of its scabbard when the abject spectacle of his adversary quailing before him brought him to his senses. He slammed the fragile door of his cabin and snapped the sword down in its sheath. Outside he heard Morris's feet scrape on the deck as he staggered upright.

Drinkwater stood stock still in the centre of the room, his breathing slowly returning to normal. He began shaking like an aspen leaf in a breeze and found himself looking at the little picture of the *Algonquin* that Elizabeth had given him and that his new-found privacy had allowed him to hang.

He reached out a shaking hand to reassure himself of its reality . . .

On August 16th, 1781, the ships at Sandy Hook sighted sails to the southward. Sir Samuel Hood arrived in a lather, furious to find Admiral Graves still in New York. The Rear Admiral had himself rowed up the harbour to harangue Graves when he found the latter ashore in his comfortable house. Though junior to Graves, Hood impressed his superior of the size of the French fleet in North American waters. In view of Graves's apparent pusillanimity he suppressed details of the unseaworthiness of his own squadron, one ship of which was actually in a sinking condition.

Graves was suddenly infected with the panic of rapid action and ordered his fleet to sea.

But it was still the end of the month before the twenty-one line of battleships were proceeding south. De Barras at Rhode Island with eight of the line had already sailed and the previous day Admiral De Grasse had anchored his own twenty-eight of the line, numerous frigates and transports in the Chesapeake. He had also landed 3,000 troops to surround an obscure peninsula called Yorktown.

Lord Cornwallis was cut off, for Washington and Rochambeau were marching south from the Hudson Highlands, across New Jersey their flank exposed to the inactive Clinton at New York, to join up with La Fayette and close the iron ring round the hapless Earl.

What happened to Cornwallis is history. The British fleets sailed south too late. Graves flung out his frigates and *Cyclops* stood to the eastward, thus taking no part in the forthcoming battle.

The fleet fought an action with De Grasse which was indecisive in itself. But it was enough for Graves. De Grasse retained possession of the Bay of the Chesapeake. At the time De Barras had not arrived but when Graves, realising the enormity of his blunder tried a second time to draw out De Grasse, the British Admiral found De Barras had reinforced the Comte and drew off.

Cornwallis was abandoned.

A gallant effort was made to cross the James River under cover of darkness to where Tarleton held a bridgehead at Gloucester, but after the first boats had got over a violent storm got up and the breakout to New York was abandoned. A few weeks later Lord Cornwallis surrendered and the war with America was effectively, if not officially, over.

Cyclops, scouting eastward, missed both the action off the Virginia Capes and a sight of De Barras's squadron. She eventually returned to New York to receive belated recognition from the new Commander in Chief that she belonged to the Channel Fleet. After despatching the fast tender *Rattlesnake* with the news of the loss of Cornwallis's Army at the end of October, Admiral Graves recollected that although fast she was lightly armed and a vulnerable prey to a French cruiser or a marauding Yankee privateer. In typical fashion he vacillated, fretting about the fate of *Rattlesnake*, worrying that his report might fall into enemy hands. Eventually he decided to send a frigate with a duplicate set of despatches.

It seemed a good idea, his secretary advised, to take the opportunity of sending *Cyclops* back to Kempenfelt.

Acting Lieutenant Nathaniel Drinkwater stopped pacing to stare up at the main topgallant. His body balanced effortlessly as the ship moved beneath him, a near south-westerly gale thrumming in the rigging and sending a patter of spray over the starboard quarter rail.

He studied the sail for a moment. There was no mistaking the

186

strain on the weather sheet or the vibration transmitted to the yard below. It was time to shorten sail.

'Mr White!' The boy was immediately attentive: 'My compliments to the captain and the wind's freshening. With his approval I intend furling the t'gallants.'

'Aye, aye, sir.'

Drinkwater stared into the binnacle. The two helmsmen grunted and sweated as they fought to hold *Cyclops* on course. He watched the gently oscillating compass card. Advancing daylight already rendered the oil lamp superfluous. The heavy grey Atlantic lifted the frigate's quarter, sent her scudding forward until it passed under her and she dragged into the trough, stabbing her bowsprit at the sky. Then her stern lifted again and the cycle repeated itself, over and over, all the three thousand miles from New York to the chops of the Channel . . .

Drinkwater felt none of the shame being experienced by Captain Hope shaving in the cabin below. For Hope already knew the heady wine of victory, having fought through the glorious period of the Seven Years War. To end his career in defeat was a bitter blow, a condemnation of the years of labour and a justification of his cynicism that was only alleviated by the draft on Tavistock's for four thousand sterling.

To Drinkwater the events of the last few weeks had been a culmination. In their fruitless search for De Barras they had boxed the compass off Long Island and the New England coast. To Nathaniel, free of the oppressive presence of Morris, it had been a glorious time, a fruitful splendid time in which, cautiously at first, but with growing confidence, he had handled the ship.

He looked up at the now furled topgallants. His judgement was vindicated for *Cyclops* had not slackened her pace.

He saw Captain Hope ascend the companionway. He vacated the windward side, touching his hat as the captain passed.

''Morning, sir.'

'G'morning, Mr Drinkwater.' Hope glanced aloft. 'Anything in sight?'

'Nothing reported, sir.'

'Very well.' Hope looked at the log slate.

'Should raise the Lizard before dark, sir, by my reckoning,' volunteered Drinkwater. Hope grunted and began pacing the weather quarterdeck. Drinkwater moved over to the lee side where young Chalky White was shivering in the down-draught of the main topsail.

'Mr Drinkwater!' The captain called sharply.

'Sir?' Drinkwater hurried over to where the captain was regarding him with a frown. His heart sank.

'Sir?' he repeated.

'You are not wearing your sword.'

'Sir?' repeated Drinkwater yet again, his forehead wrinkling in a frown.

'It is the first morning you have had your present appointment that you have not worn it.'

'Is it, sir?' Drinkwater blushed. Behind him White giggled.

'You must be paying the correct attention to your duties and less to your personal appearance. I am pleased to see it.'

Drinkwater swallowed.

'Y-yes, sir. Thank you, sir.'

Hope resumed his pacing. White was in stitches, the subject of Mr Drinkwater's sword having caused much amusement between decks. Drinkwater turned on him.

'Mr White! Take a glass to the foremasthead and look for England!'

'England, Nat . . . Mr Drinkwater, sir?'

'Yes, Mr White! England!'

England, he thought, England and Elizabeth . . .

A King's Cutter

For the crew of the cutter KESTREL

Contents

Author's Note

The exploits of Nathaniel Drinkwater during the period 1792 to 1797 are based on fact. The services of cutters for all manner of purposes were, in the words of the contemporary historian William James, 'very effectually performed by British cruisers even of that insignificant class.'

A man named Barrallier did escape from France to build ships for the Royal Navy while, shortly before the collapse of the Nore mutiny, eight men disappeared in a ship's boat. Until now their destination was a mystery. During the mutiny scare wild tales circulated about mysterious strangers traversing the lanes of Kent and French subversion was popularly supposed to lie behind the trouble at the Nore.

Many of the characters that appear actually existed. Apart from the admirals, Warren and the famous frigate captains and the commanders of Duncan's ships, Captain Schank was inventively employed at this time. Captain Anthony Calvert and Jonathan Poulter did indeed destroy the Thames buoyage to prevent the mutineers escaping.

The precise reason why De Winter sailed is still open to question. Both his fleet and the considerable number of troop and storeships that lay with him in the Texel were clearly intended to form part of a grand expedition and Ireland seems the likely destination. Wolfe Tone was with De Winter during part of 1797 as he had been with De Galles at Bantry the year before. It has also been suggested that the Dutch sailed to destroy Duncan who was supposed to command an unreliable force, or that they sallied to restore Dutch prestige. In fact De Winter retired before contacting Duncan. Yet, when the battle was inevitable, his fleet fought with great ferocity. Perhaps the parts played by Drinkwater and Eduoard Santhonax in a campaign disastrous to the Dutch fleet explains some of the tension of that desperate year.

PART ONE

The English Channel

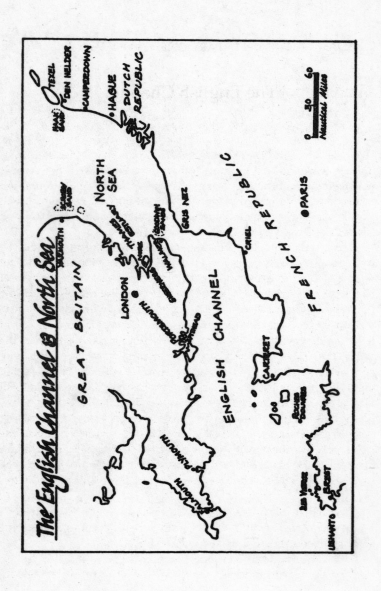

The English Channel & North Sea

Chapter One October–November 1792

The Puppet's Hand

'You will be,' said Lord Dungarth, lifting his hands for emphasis, 'merely the hand of a puppet. You will not know what the puppet master intends, how the strings are manipulated or why you are commanded to do the things that you will do. Like hands you will simply execute your instructions efficiently. You were recommended for your efficiency, Nathaniel . . .'

Drinkwater blinked against the reflected sunlight silhouetting the two earls. Beyond the windows the dark shapes of the Channel Fleet were anchored in the sparkling waters of Spithead. Beneath his feet he felt the massive bulk of the *Queen Charlotte* trim herself to the tide. For a second or two he revolved the proposition in his head. After six years as second mate in the buoy yachts of Trinity House he was at least familiar with the Channel, even if the precise purpose of the armed cutter *Kestrel* was obscured from him. He had held an acting commission as lieutenant eleven years earlier when he had expected great things from it, but he was more experienced now, married and almost too old to consider probable the dazzling career the Royal Navy had once seemed to offer him. He had found a satisfying employment with the Trinity House but he could not deny the quickened heartbeat as Dungarth explained he had been selected for special service aboard a cutter under direct Admiralty orders. The implications of that were given heavy emphasis by his second interviewer.

'Well, Mr Drinkwater?' Earl Howe's rich voice drew Drinkwater's attention to the heavy features of the admiral commanding the Channel Fleet. He must make his mind up.

'I would be honoured to accept, my lords.'

Lord Dungarth nodded with satisfaction. 'I am much pleased,

Nathaniel, much pleased. I was sorry that you lost your promotion when Hope died.'

'Thank you my lord, I have to admit to it being a bitter blow.' He smiled back trying to bridge the years since he and Dungarth had last met. He wondered if he had changed as much as John Devaux, former first lieutenant of the frigate *Cyclops*. It was more than the succession to a title that had affected the earl; that alone could not have swamped the ebullient dash of the man. It might have produced his lordship's new introspection but not the hint of implacability that coloured his remarks. That seemed to stem from his mysterious new duties.

A month later Drinkwater had received his orders and the acting commission. His farewell to his wife had affected him deeply. Whatever her own misgivings in respect of his transfer from buoy yachts to an armed cutter, Elizabeth kept them to herself. It was not in her nature to divert his purpose, for she had loved him for his exuberance and watched it wither with regret when the navy had failed him. But she could not disguise the tears that accompanied their parting.

His arrival on board the cutter had been as secret as anyone could have wished. A late October fog had shrouded the Tilbury marshes as he searched for a boat, stumbling among the black stakes that rose out of the mud oozing along the high water mark. Patches of bladder wrack and straw, pieces of rotten wood and the detritus of civilisation ran along the edge of the unseen Thames. Somewhere in the region of Hope he had found a man and a boat and they had pushed out over the glass-smooth grey river, passing a mooring buoy that sheered and gurgled in the tide. A cormorant had started from the white stained staves and overhead a pale sun had broken through slowly to consume the nacreous vapour.

The cutter's transom had leapt out of the fog, boat falls trailing in the tide from her stern davits. He had caught a brief glimpse of a carved taffrail, oak leaves and her name: *Kestrel*. Then he had scrambled aboard, aware of a number of idlers about the deck, a huge mast, boom and gaff and a white St George's ensign drooping disconsolately aft. A short, active looking man bustled up. About forty, with beetling eyebrows and a brusque though not impolite manner. He conveyed an impression of efficiency.

196

'Can I help you, sir?' The blue eyes darted perceptively.

'Good morning to you. My name's Drinkwater, acting lieutenant. D'you have a boat down?' he nodded aft to the vacant davits.

'Aye, sir. Jolly boat's gone to Gravesend. We was expecting you.'

'My chest is at Tilbury fort, please to have it aboard as soon as possible.'

The man nodded. 'I'm Jessup, sir, bosun. I'll show you to your cabin.' He rolled aft and hopped over the sea-step of a companion-way. At the bottom of the ladder Drinkwater found himself in a tiny lobby. Behind the ladder a rack of Tower muskets and cutlasses gleamed dully. Leading off the space were five flimsy doors. Jessup indicated the forward one. 'Main cabin, cap'n's quarters . . . he's ashore just now. This 'ere's your'n sir.' He opened a door to star-board and Drinkwater stepped inside.

The after-quarters of *Kestrel* were situated between the hold and the rudder trunking. The companionway down which they had come left the deck immediately forward of the tiller. Facing the bottom of the ladder was the door to the main cabin extending the full width of the ship. The four other doors opened on to tiny cabins intended by a gracious Admiralty to house the officers of the cutter. The after two were tapering spaces filled with odds and ends and clearly unoccupied. The others were in use. His own was to star-board. Jessup told him the larboard one was 'for passengers . . .' and evaded further questioning.

Drinkwater entered his cabin and closed the door. The space was bare of a chair. A small bookshelf was secured to the pine bulkhead. A tiny folding table was fitted beneath the shelf, ingeniously dou-bling as the lid of a cabinet containing a bucket for night soil. A rack for a carafe and glass, both of which articles were missing, and three pegs behind the door completed the cabin's fittings. He went on deck.

The visibility had improved and he could see the low line of the Kent coast. He walked forward to enquire of Jessup whether the boat had returned.

'Aye, sir, been and gone. I sent it to Tilbury for your dunnage.'

Drinkwater thanked him, ignoring the scrutiny of the hands for-ward. He coughed and said, 'Perhaps you would be kind enough to show me round the deck.' Jessup nodded and went forward.

The huge bowsprit came inboard through the stemhead gammon iron and was housed in massive timbers that incorporated the windlass barrel. Abaft this was a companionway to the fo'c's'le, a large dark space extending beyond the mast which rose from the deck surrounded by its fiferails, belaying pins, lead blocks and coils of cordage.

'How many men do we bear, Mr Jessup?'

'Forty-eight full complement, forty-two at present . . . here's the hatch, sir, fitted with a platform, it ain't a proper 'tween deck . . . used as 'ammock space, sail room an' 'old.' Jessup ran his hand along the gunwale of the larboard gig chocked on the hatch as they continued aft. Drinkwater noted the plank lands were scuffed and worn.

'The boats see hard service, then?'

Jessup gave a short laugh. 'Aye, sir. That they do.'

Abaft the hatch were the galley funnel, the cabin skylight and the companionway surmounted by a brass binnacle. Finally the huge curved tiller dominated the after-deck, its heel secured in the brass-bound top of the rudder stock, its end terminating in the carved head of the falcon from which the cutter took her name.

Jessup ran his hand possessively over the proud curve of the beak and nodded to a small padlocked hatch let into the stem cant and surrounded by gratings.

'Magazine 'atch.' He turned forward pointing at the guns. 'Mounts twelve guns, sir. Ten three-pounders and two long brass fours forrard, throws a broadside of nineteen pounds. She's seventy-two feet on the gun deck, nigh on one 'undred and twenty-five tons . . .' he trailed off, still suspicious, weighing up the newcomer.

'You been in cutters before, sir?'

Drinkwater looked at him. It did not do to give too much away, he thought. Jessup would know soon enough. He thought of the buoy-yacht *Argus*. It was his turn to look enigmatic.

'Good heavens yes, Mr Jessup. I've served extensively in cutters. You'll not find me wanting there.'

Jessup sniffed. Somehow that indrawn air allowed him the last word, as if it indicated a secret knowledge that Drinkwater could not be a party to. Yet.

'Here's the boat, sir, with your traps.' Jessup walked over to the side to hail it. To seal the advantage he had over the newcomer he spat forcefully into the gliding waters of the Thames.

Shortly before noon the following day the captain had come on board. Lieutenant Griffiths removed his hat, ran a searching eye over the ship and sniffed the wind. He acknowledged Drinkwater's salute with a nod. The lieutenant was tall and stoop-shouldered, his sad features crowned by a mane of white hair that lent his sixty-odd years a patriarchal quality. A Welshman of untypical silences he seemed to personify an ancient purpose that might have been Celtic, Cymric or perhaps faerie. Born in Caernarfon he had served as mate in Liverpool slavers before being pressed into the navy. He had risen in the King's service by sheer ability and escaped that degree of intolerance of his former messmates that disfigured many of his type. Lord Howe had given him his commission, declaring that there was no man fitter to rise in the navy than Madoc Griffiths who was, his lordship asserted in his curious idiom, an ornament to his profession. Whatever the idiosyncracies of his self-expression 'Black Dick' was right. As Drinkwater subsequently learnt there was no facet of the cutter's activities of which Griffiths was not master. A first, superficial impression that his new commander might be a superannuated relic was almost instantly dispelled.

Drinkwater's reception had been guarded. In a silence that was disconcerting Griffiths examined Drinkwater's papers. Then he leaned back and coolly studied the man in front of him.

A week short of twenty-nine, Drinkwater was lean and of medium height. A weathered complexion told of continuous sea service. The grey eyes were alert and intelligent, capable of concentration and determination. There were hints of these qualities in the crowsfeet about the eyes and the pale thread of a scar that puckered down from the left eye. But the furrows that ran down from the straight nose to the corners of a well-shaped mouth were prematurely deep and seemed to constrain more than a hint of passion.

Was there a weakness there? Griffiths pondered, appraising the high forehead, the mop of brown hair drawn back into a black ribboned queue. There was a degree of sensitivity, he thought, but not sensuousness, the face was too open. Then he had it; the passion of temper lurked in the clamped corners of that mouth, a temper born of disappointment and disillusion, belied by the level eyes but recognisable to a Welshman. There was something suppressed about the man before him, a latent energy that Griffiths, in isolating, found reassuring. '*Duw* but this man's a terrible fighter,' he muttered to himself and relaxed.

'Sit you down, Mr Drinkwater.' Griffiths's voice was deep and quiet, adding to the impression of otherworldliness. He enunciated his words with that clarity of diction peculiar to some of his race. 'Your papers do you credit. I see that your substantive rank is that of master's mate and that you held an acting commission at the end of the American War . . . it was not confirmed?'

'No sir. I was given to understand the matters had been laid before Sir Richard Kempenfelt but . . .' He shrugged, remembering Captain Hope's promise as he left for the careening battleship. Griffiths looked up.

'The *Royal George* was it?'

'Yes sir. It didn't seem important at the time . . .'

'But ten years is a long while to keep a sense of proportion.' Griffiths finished the sentence for him. The two men smiled and it seemed to both that a hurdle had been crossed. 'Still, you have gained excellent experience in the Trinity Yachts, have you not?'

'I believe so, sir.' Drinkwater sensed his commander's approval.

'For my personal satisfaction, *bach*, I require your oath that no matter discussed between us is repeated beyond these bulkheads.' Griffiths's tone was soft yet uncompromising and his eyes were briefly cold. Drinkwater closed his imagination to a sudden vision of appalling facts. He remembered another secret learned long ago, knowledge of which had culminated in death in the swamps of Carolina. He sighed.

'You have my word, as a King's officer.' Drinkwater stared back. The shadow had not gone unnoticed by Griffiths. The lieutenant relaxed. So, he thought, there was experience too. '*Da iawn*,' he muttered.

'This cutter is under the direct orders of the Admiralty. I, er, execute an unusual office, do you see. We attend to certain government business on the French coast at certain times and at certain locations.'

'I see, sir.' But he did not. In an attempt to expand his knowledge he said, 'And your orders come from Lord Dungarth, sir?'

Griffiths regarded him again and Drinkwater feared he had been importunate. He felt the colour rising to his cheeks but Griffiths said, 'Ah, I had forgotten, you knew him from *Cyclops*.'

'Yes, sir. He seems much changed, although it is some years since I last spoke to him.'

Griffiths nodded. 'Aye, and you found the change intimidating, did you?'

Drinkwater nodded, aware that again Griffiths had exactly expressed his own feelings. 'He lost his wife, you know, in child-bed.'

Drinkwater did not keep pace with society gossip but he had been aware of Dungarth's marriage with Charlotte Dixon, an India merchant's daughter of fabled wealth and outstanding beauty. He had also heard how even Romney had failed to do her likeness justice. He began to see how the loss of his countess had shrivelled that once high-spirited soul and left a ruthless bitterness. As if confirming his thoughts Griffiths said, 'I think if he had not taken on the French republic he would have gone mad . . .'

The old man rose and opened a locker. Taking two glasses and a decanter he poured the sercial and deftly changed the subject. 'The vessel is aptly named, Mr Drinkwater,' he resumed his seat and continued. '*Falco tinnunculus* is characterised by its ability to hover, seeking out the exact location of its prey before it stoops. It lives upon mice, shrews and beetles, small fry, Mr Drinkwater, *bach*, but beetles can eat away an oak beam . . .' He paused to drain and refill his glass. 'Are you seeing the point of my allegory?'

'I, er, I think so, sir.' Griffiths refilled Drinkwater's glass.

'I mention these circumstances for two reasons. Lord Dungarth spoke highly of you, partly from your previous acquaintance and also on the recommendation of the Trinity House. I trust, therefore, that my own confidence in you will not prove misplaced. You will be responsible for our navigation. Remonstrations on lee shores are inimical to secret operations. Understand, do you?'

Drinkwater nodded, aware of the intended irony and continuing to warm to his new commander.

'Very well,' Griffiths continued. 'The second reason is less easy to confess and I tell you this, Mr Drinkwater, because there is a possibility of command devolving upon you, perhaps in adverse circumstances or at an inconvenient time . . .' Drinkwater frowned. This was more alarming than the previous half-expected revelations. 'Many years ago on the Gambian coast I contracted a fever. From time to time I am afflicted by seizures.'

'But if you are unwell, sir, a, er . . .'

'A replacement?' Griffiths raised an indignant eyebrow then waved aside Drinkwater's apology. 'Look you, I have lived ashore for less than two years in half a century. I am not likely to take root there now.' Drinkwater absorbed the fact as Griffiths's face became suddenly wistful, an old man lost in reminiscence. He finished his glass and stood up, leaving the commander sitting alone with his wine, and quietly left the cabin.

Overhead the white ensign cracked in the strong breeze as the big cutter drove to windward under a hard reefed mainsail. Her topsail yard was lowered to the cap and the lower yard cockbilled clear of the straining staysail. Halfway along her heavy bowsprit the spitfire jib was like a board, wet with spray and still gleaming faintly from the daylight fading behind inky rolls of cumulus to the westward. The wind drove against the ebb tide to whip up a short steep sea, grey-white in the dusk as it seethed alongside and tugged at the boat towing close astern. The cutter bucked her round bow and sent streaks of spray driving over the weather rail.

Acting Lieutenant Nathaniel Drinkwater huddled in his tarpaulin as the spume whipped aft, catching his face and agonising his cheek muscles in the wind-ache that followed.

He ran over the projected passage in his mind yet again, vaguely aware that an error now would blight any chances of his hoped-for promotion. Then he dismissed the thought to concentrate on the matter in hand. From Dover to their destination was sixty-five miles, parallel with the French coast, a coast made terrible by tales of bloody revolution. In the present conditions they would make their landfall at low water. That, Drinkwater had been impressed, was of the utmost importance. He was mystified by the insistence laid upon the point by Lieutenant Griffiths. Although the south-westerly wind allowed them to make good a direct course Griffiths had put her on the larboard tack an hour earlier to deceive any observers on Gris Nez. The cape was now disappearing astern into the murk of a wintry night.

Drinkwater shivered again, as much with apprehension as with cold; he walked over to the binnacle. In the yellow lamplight the gently oscillating card showed a mean heading of north-west by west. Allowing for the variation of the magnetic and true meridians that was a course of west by north. He nodded with satisfaction, ignoring the subdued sound of conversation and the chink of glasses coming up the companionway. The behaviour of his enigmatic commander and their equally mysterious 'passenger' failed to shake his self-confidence.

He walked back to the binnacle and called forward, summoning the hands to tack ship. A faint sound of laughter came up from below. After his interview, Griffiths had withdrawn, giving the minimum of orders, apparently watching his new subordinate. At first Drinkwater thought he was being snubbed, but swiftly realised it was simply characteristic of the lieutenant And the man who had boarded at Deal had not looked like a spy. Round, red faced and jolly he was clearly well-known to Griffiths and released from the Welshman an unexpected jocularity. Drinkwater could not imagine what they had to laugh about.

'Ready sir!'

From forward Jessup's cry was faintly condescending and Drinkwater smiled into the darkness.

'Down helm!' he called.

Kestrel came up into the wind, her mainsail thundering. Drinkwater felt her tremble when the jib flogged, vibrating the bowsprit. Then she spun as the wind filled the backed headsails, thrusting her round.

'Heads'l sheets!'

The jib and staysail cracked until tamed by the seamen sweating tight the lee sheets.

'Steadeeee . . . steer full and bye.'

'Full an' bye, sir.' The two helmsmen leaned on the big tiller as *Kestrel* drove on, the luff of her mainsail just trembling.

'How's her head?'

'Sou' by west, sir.'

That was south by east true, allowing two points for westerly variation. 'Very well, make it so.'

'Sou' by west it is, sir.'

The ebb ran fair down the coast here and the westing they had made beating offshore ought to put them up-tide and to windward of the landing place by the time they reached it, leaving them room to make the location even if the wind backed. Or so Drinkwater hoped, otherwise his commission would be as remote as ever.

Towards midnight the wind did back and eased a little. The reefs were shaken out and *Kestrel* drove southwards, her larboard rail awash. Drinkwater was tired now. He had been on deck for nine hours and Griffiths did not seem anxious to relieve him.

Kestrel was thrashing in for the shore. Drinkwater could sense rather than see the land somewhere in the darkness ahead. It must be very near low water now. Drinkwater bit his lip with mounting concern. With a backing wind they would get some lee from the cliffs that rose sheer between Le Tréport and Dieppe and it would be this that gave them the first inkling of their proximity. That and the smell perhaps.

In the darkness and at this speed *Kestrel* could be in among the breakers before there was time to go about. Anxiously he strode forward to hail the lookout at the crosstrees. 'Who's aloft?'

'Tregembo, zur.' The Cornishman's burr was reassuring. Tregembo had turned up like a bad penny, one of the draft of six men from the Nore guardship that had completed *Kestrel*'s complement. Drinkwater had known Tregembo on the frigate *Cyclops* where the man had been committed for smuggling. He was still serving out the sentence of a court that had hanged his father for offering revenue officers armed resistance. To mitigate the widow's grief her son was drafted into the navy. That he had appeared on the deck of *Kestrel* was another link in the chain of coincidences that Drinkwater found difficult to dismiss as merely random.

'Keep a damned good lookout, Tregembo!'

'Aye, aye, zur.'

Drinkwater went aft and luffed the cutter while a cast of the lead was taken. 'By the mark, five.' *Kestrel* filled and drove on. There was a tension on deck now and Drinkwater felt himself the centre of it. Jessup hovered solicitously close. Why the devil did Griffiths not come on deck? Five fathoms was shoal water, but it was shoal water hereabouts for miles. They might be anywhere off the Somme estuary. He suppressed a surge of panic and made up his mind. He would let her run for a mile or two and sound again.

'Breakers, zur! Fine on the lee bow!'

Drinkwater rushed forward and leapt into the sagging larboard shrouds. He stared ahead and could see nothing. Then he saw them, a patch of greyness, lighter than the surrounding sea. His heart beat violently as he cudgelled his memory. Then he had it, Les Ridins du Tréport, an isolated patch with little water over it at this state of the tide. He was beginning to see the logic of a landfall at low water. He made a minor adjustment to the course, judging the east-going stream already away close in with the coast. They had about three miles to go.

'Pass word for the captain.' He kept the relief from his voice.

The seas diminished a mile and a half offshore and almost immediately they could see the dark line of the land. Going forward again and peering through the Dollond glass he saw what he hardly dared hope. The cliffs on the left fell away to a narrow river valley, then rose steeply to the west to a height named Mont Jolibois. The faint scent of woodsmoke came to him from the village of Criel that sheltered behind the hill, astride the river crossing of the road from Tréport and Eu to Dieppe.

'*Da iawn*, Mr Drinkwater, well done.' Griffiths's voice was warm and congratulatory. Drinkwater relaxed with relief: it seemed he had passed a test. Griffiths quietly gave orders. The mainsail was scandalised and the staysail backed. The boat towing astern was hauled alongside and two men tumbled in to bale it out. Beside Drinkwater the cloaked figure of the British agent stood staring ashore.

'Your glass, sir, lend me your glass.' The tone was peremptory, commanding, all trace of jollity absent.

'Yes, yes, of course, sir.' He fished it out of his coat pocket and handed it to the man. After scrutinising the beach it was silently returned. Griffiths came up.

'Take the boat in, Mr Drinkwater, and land our guest.'

It took a second to realise his labours were not yet over. Men were piling into the gig alongside. There was the dull gleam of metal where Jessup issued sidearms. 'Pistol and cutlass, sir.' There was an encouraging warmth in Jessup's voice now. Drinkwater took the pistol and stuck it into his waistband. He refused the cutlass. Slipping below, screwing his eyes up against the lamplight from the cabin, he pushed into his own hutch. Behind the door he felt for the French *épée*. Buckling it on he hurried back on deck.

Mont Jolibois rose above them as the boat approached the shore. To the left Drinkwater could see a fringe of white water that surged around the hummocks of the Roches des Muron. He realised fully why Griffiths insisted they land at low water. As many dangers as possible were uncovered, providing some shelter and a margin of safety if they grounded. Forward the bowman was prodding over-side with his boathook.

'Bottom, sir!' he hissed, and a moment later the boat ran aground, lifted and grounded again. Without orders the oars came inboard with low thuds and, to Drinkwater's astonishment, his entire crew leapt overboard, holding the boat steady. Then, straining in a concerted effort that owed its perfection to long practice, they hove her off the sand and hauled her round head to sea. Drinkwater felt foolishly superfluous, sitting staring back the way they had come.

'Ready sir.' A voice behind him made him turn as his passenger rose and scrambled on to the seaman's back. The boat lifted to a small breaker and thumped back on to the bottom. The seaman waded ashore and Drinkwater, not to be outdone, kicked off his shoes and splashed after them with the agent's bag. Well up the beach the sailor lowered his burden and the agent settled his cloak.

'Standard procedure,' he said with just a trace of that humour he had earlier displayed. He held out his hand for the bag. 'Men with dried salt on their boots have a rather obvious origin.' He took the bag. 'Thank you; *bonsoir mon ami*.'

'Goodnight,' said Drinkwater to the figure retreating into the threatening darkness that was Revolutionary France. For a second Drinkwater stood staring after the man, and then trudged back to the boat.

There was a perceptible easing of tension as the men pulled back to the waiting cutter. As though the shadow of the guillotine and the horrors of the Terror that lay over the darkened land had touched them all. Wearily Drinkwater clambered on board and saluted Griffiths.

The lieutenant nodded. 'You had better get some sleep now,' he said. 'And Mr Drinkwater . . .'

'Sir?' said Drinkwater from the companionway.

'*Da iawn*, Mr Drinkwater, *da iawn*.'

'I'm sorry sir, I don't understand.' He wrestled with fatigue.

'Well done, Mr Drinkwater, well done. I am pleased to say I do not find my confidence misplaced.'

Chapter Two *December 1792*

First Blood

Not all their operations went as smoothly. There were nights that seemed endless when a rendezvous was missed, when the guttering blue lights shown at the waterline spat and sizzled interminably achieving nothing. There were hours of eye strain and physical weariness as the cutter was laboriously kept on a station to no purpose, hours of barely hidden bad temper, hunger and cold. Occasionally there was brief and unexpected excitement as when, in thick weather, *Kestrel* disturbed a mid-Channel rendezvous of another kind. The two boats that parted in confusion did so amid shouts in French and English; slatting lugsails jerked hurriedly into the wet air and the splash of what might have been kegs was visible in the widening gap between the two vessels. *Kestrel* had fired her bow chasers at the retreating smugglers to maintain the illusion of being the revenue cruiser she had been taken for.

Then there had been an occasion of dubious propriety on their own part. Griffiths sent two boats to creep for barricoes off St Valery while *Kestrel* luffed and filled in the offing, Griffiths handling her with patient dexterity. Sitting in one of the boats Drinkwater continually verified their position, his quadrant horizontal, the images of two spires and a windmill in alternating sequence as he made minute adjustments to the index. His voice cracked with shouting instructions to the other boat, his eyes streamed at the effort of adjusting to look for Jessup's wave before refocusing on the reflected images of his marks. The two boats trailed their grapnels up and down the sea bed for hours before they were successful. What was in the little barrels Drinkwater never discovered for certain. Griffiths merely smiled when he eventually reported their success. It crossed his mind it might, quite simply, be cognac; that Griffiths as a man entrusted with many secrets might have capitalised on the advantages his position offered. After all, thought Drinkwater, it was in the best traditions of naval peculation and there was the matter of a few loose gold coins he had himself acquired when he retook the *Algonquin* in the last war. Somehow it was reassuring to find Griffiths had some human failings beyond the obvious one of enjoying his liquor. Certainly *Kestrel* never lacked strong drink and Griffiths never stinted it, claiming with a mordant gleam in his eye, that a good bottle had more to offer a man than a good woman.

'A woman, look you, never lets you speak like a bottle does, boyo. She has the draining of you, not you her, but a bottle leaves your guts warm afterwards . . .' He finished on a long sigh.

Drinkwater smiled. In his half-century at sea poor Griffiths could only have experienced the fleeting affection of drabs. Hugging his own knowledge of Elizabeth to him Nathaniel had felt indulgent. But he had not refused the cognac that made its appearance after the day off St Valery.

Certainly Griffiths was unmoved by the presence of women which always sent a wave of lust through the cutter when they transferred fugitives from French fishing boats. The awkward bundles of women and children, many in bedraggled finery, who clambered clumsily over the stinking bulwarks into the boats to the accompanying grins of the Frenchmen, never failed to unsettle the exemplary order of the cutter. Griffiths remained aloof, almost disdainful, and obviously pleased when they had discharged their passengers. While their duties became this desperate business of strange encounters and remote landings Drinkwater patiently worked at his details. The tides, distances and the probabilities of unpredictable weather occupied him fully. Yet his curiosity and imagination were fed by these glimpses of fear and the glint of hatred that mingled with that of avarice in the fishermen's eyes as they handed over their live cargoes. 'We may stink of fish,' a giant Malouin had laughed as his lugger drew off, 'but you stink of fear . . .'

As time passed, by a gradual process of revelation, Drinkwater slowly acquired knowledge beyond the merely digital duty of his own part of the puppet's hand. From an apparently mindless juggling with the moon's phases and southing, with epacts and lunitidal intervals, a conspiratorially winking Jessup one day showed him a lobster pot containing pigeons. The bosun silently revealed the small brass cylinder strapped to a bird's leg. 'Ah, I see,' said Drinkwater, as pleased with the knowledge as the demonstration of trust bestowed by Jessup. Another link in the mysterious chain was added when he saw the pot hidden in the fishwell of a boat from Dieppe.

Greater confidence came from Griffiths on an afternoon of polar air and brilliant December sunshine when the gig landed them on the shingle strand below Walmer Castle. Within its encircling trees the round brick bastions embraced the more domestic later additions. Lord Dungarth was waiting for them with two strangers who talked together in French. He led them inside. Drinkwater spread the charts as he was bid and withdrew to a side table while Dungarth, Griffiths and the livelier of the two men bent over them.

Drinkwater turned to the second Frenchman. He was sitting bolt upright, his eyes curiously blank yet intense, as though they saw with perfect clarity not Drinkwater before him, but a mirrored image of his own memories. The sight of the man sent a chill of apprehension through Drinkwater. He restrained an impulse to shiver and turned to the window by way of distraction.

Outside the almost horizontal light of a winter afternoon threw the foreground into shadow; black cannon on the petal-shaped bastions below, the trees, the remains of the moat and the shingle. Out over the Downs sunlight danced in a million twinkling points off the sparkling sea, throwing into extraordinary clarity every detail of the shipping. Beyond the dull black hull and gleaming spars of *Kestrel* several Indiamen got under way, their topsails bellying, while a frigate and third-rate lay in Deal Road. A welter of small craft beat up against the northerly wind, carrying the flood into the Thames estuary. The sharp-peaked lugsails of the Deal punts and galleys showed where the local longshoremen plied their legal, daylight, trade. In the distance the cliffs of France were a white bar on the horizon.

Raised voices abruptly recalled Drinkwater's attention. The three men at the table had drawn upright. Griffiths was shaking his head, his eyes half closed. The stranger was eagerly imploring something. From the rear Drinkwater found the sudden froglike jerks of his arms amusing as the man burst into a torrent of French. But the atmosphere of the room extinguished this momentary lightening of his spirit. The silent man remained rigid.

Dungarth placated the Frenchman in his own tongue, then turned to Griffiths. The lieutenant was still shaking his head but Dungarth's look was sharply imperative. Drinkwater caught a glimpse of the old Devaux, not the ebullient first lieutenant, but a distillation of that old energy refined into urgent compulsion. Griffiths's glance wavered.

'Very well, my lord,' he growled, 'but only under protest and providing there is no swell.'

Dungarth nodded. 'Good, good.' The earl turned to the window. 'There will be no swell with the wind veering north-east. You must weigh this evening . . . Mr Drinkwater, how pleasant to see you again, come join us in a glass before you go. Madoc, pray allow Drinkwater here to send his mail up with yours, I'll have it franked gratis in the usual way, *messieurs* . . .' Dungarth addressed the Frenchmen, explaining the arrangements were concluded and Drinkwater noted a change in the seated man's expression, the merest acknowledgement. And this time he could not repress a shudder.

Neither the wine nor the facility of writing to Elizabeth eased his mind after he and Griffiths returned to *Kestrel*. The sparkling view, the shadowing castle, the frantic desperation of the Frenchman, the haunted aura of his companion and above all the misgivings of Griffiths had combined with a growing conviction that their luck must run out.

Kestrel must be known to the fanatical authorities in France and sooner or later they would meet opposition. Drinkwater had no need of Griffiths's injunction that as a British officer his presence on a French beach was illegal. An enquiry as to the fate of his predecessor had elicited a casual shrug from the lieutenant.

'He was careless, d'you see, he neglected elementary precautions. He died soon after we landed him.'

Drinkwater found his feeling of unease impossible to shake off as *Kestrel* carried the tide through the Alderney Race, the high land of Cap de la Hague on the weather quarter. The sea bubbled under her bow and hissed alongside as the steady north-easterly wind drove them south. The Bay of Vauville opened slowly to larboard and, as the night passed, the low promontory of Cap Flammanville drew abeam.

Judging by his presence on deck Griffiths shared his subordinate's uneasiness. Once he stood next to Drinkwater for several minutes as if about to speak. But he thought better of it and drew off. Drinkwater had heard little of the conversation at Walmer. All he really knew was that the night's work had some extra element of risk attached to it, though of what real danger he had no notion.

The night was dark and moonless, cold and crystal clear. The stars shone with a northern brilliance, hard and icy with blue fire. They would be abeam of the Bay of Sciotot now, its southern extremity marked by the Pointe du Rozel beyond which the low, dune-fringed beach extended six miles to Carteret. The wide expanse of sand was their rendezvous, south of the shoals of Surtainville and north of the Roches du Rit. 'On the parallel of Beaubigny,' Griffiths had said, naming the village that lay a mile inland behind the dunes. 'And I pray God there is no swell,' he added. Drinkwater shared his concern. To the westward lay the ever-restless Atlantic, its effect scarcely lessened by the Channel Islands and the surrounding reefs. There must almost always be a swell on the beach at Beaubigny, pounding its relentless breakers upon those two leagues of packed sand. Drinkwater fervently hoped that the week of northerlies had done their work, that there would be little swell making their landing possible.

He bent over the shielded lantern in the companionway. The last few sand grains ran the half hour out of the glass and he turned it, straightening up with the log slate he looked briefly at his calculations. They must have run their distance now. He turned to Griffiths.

'By my reckoning, sir, we're clear of the Surtainville Bank.'

'Very well, we'll stand inshore shortly. All hands if you please.'

'Aye, aye, sir.' Nathaniel turned forward.

'Mr Drinkwater . . . check the boats, now. I'll sway out the second gig when you leave. And Mr Drinkwater . . .'

'Sir?'

'Take two loaded scatter guns . . .' Griffiths left the sentence unfinished.

*

Drinkwater paced up and down the firm wet sand. In the starlight he could see the expanse of beach stretching away north and south. Inland a pale undulation showed where the dunes marked the beginning of France. Down here, betwixt high and low water, he walked a no-man's-land. Behind him, bumping gently in the shallows, lay the waiting gig. Mercifully there was no swell.

'Tide's making, zur.' It was Tregembo's voice. Anxious. Was he a victim of presentiment too?

It occurred to Drinkwater that there was something irrational, ludicrous even, in his standing here on a strip of French beach in the middle of the night not knowing why. He thought of Elizabeth to still his pounding heart. She would be asleep now little dreaming of where he was, cold and exposed and not a little frightened. He looked at the men. They were huddled in a group round the boat.

'Spread out and relax, it's too exposed for an ambush.' His logic fell on ears that learned only that he too was apprehensive. The men moved sullenly. As he watched he saw them stiffen, felt his own breath catch in his throat and his palms moisten.

The thudding of hooves and jingle of harness grew louder and resolved itself into vague movement to the south. Then suddenly, running in the wavelets that covered its tracks a small barouche was upon them. The discovery was mutual. The shrill neighing of the horses as they reared in surprise was matched by the cries of the seamen who flung themselves out of the way.

Drinkwater whirled to see the splintering of the boat's gunwale as a hoof crashed down upon it. The terrified horse stamped and pawed, desperately trying to extricate itself. With the flat of his hanger Drinkwater beat at it, at the same time grabbing a rein and tugging the horse's head round clear of the gig.

A man jumped down from the barouche. '*Êtes-vous anglais?*'

'Yes, *m'sieur*, where the hell have you been?'

'*Pardon?*'

'How many? *Combien d'hommes?*'

'*Trois hommes et une femme*, but I speak English.'

'Get into the boat. Are you being followed?'

'*Oui*, yes . . . the other man, he is, er, *blessé*' . . . he struggled with the English.

'Wounded?'

213

'That is right, by Jacobins in Carteret.'

Drinkwater cut him short, recognising reaction. The man was young, near collapse.

'Get in the boat,' he pointed towards the waiting seamen and gave orders. Two figures emerged from the barouche, a man and a woman. They stood uncertainly.

'The boat! Get in the boat . . .' They began to speak, the man turning back to the open door. Angry exasperation began to replace his fear and Drinkwater called to two seamen to drag the wounded man out of the carriage and pushed the dithering fugitive towards the gig. '*Le bateau, vite! Vite!*'

He scooped the woman up roughly, surprised at her lightness, ignoring the indrawn breath of outrage, the stiffening of her body at the enforced intimacy. He dumped her roughly into the boat. A waft of lavender brought with it a hint of resentment at his cavalier treatment. He turned to the men struggling with the wounded Frenchman. 'Hurry there!' and to the remainder, 'the rest of you keep this damned thing afloat.' They heaved as a larger breaker came ashore, tugging round their legs with a seething urgency.

'Damned swell coming in with the flood,' someone said.

'What about the baggage, *m'sieur*?' It was the man from the carriage who seemed to have recovered some of his wits.

'To hell with the baggage, sit down!'

'But the gold . . . and my papers, *mon Dieu*! My papers!' He began to clamber out of the boat. 'You have not got my papers!' But it was not the documents that had caught Drinkwater's imagination.

'Gold? What gold?'

'In the barouche, *m'sieur*,' said the man shoving past him.

Drinkwater swore. So that was behind this crazy mission, specie! A personal fortune? Royalist funds? Government money? What did it matter? Gold was gold and now this damned fool was running back to the carriage. Drinkwater followed. He pushed to the door and looked in. Two iron bound boxes lay on the floor, just visible in the gloom.

'Tregembo! Poll! Get this box! You *m'sieur, aidez-moi!*'

They staggered under the weight, the breath rasping in their throats as they heaved it aboard the gig. The boat was lifting now, thumping on hard sand as larger waves ran hissing up the beach.

Then from the direction of Carteret they heard shouts. The sand vibrated under the thunder of many horses' hooves; a troop of dragoons!

'Push the boat off! Push it off!' He ran back to the barouche, vaguely aware of the Frenchman struggling to get a canvas folio into the gig. Drinkwater stretched up and let off the brake. Running to the horses' heads he dragged them round then swiped the rump of the nearer with his hanger. There was a wet gleam of blood and a terrified neigh as the horse plunged forward. Drinkwater jumped clear as the carriage jerked into motion.

He ran splashing to the boat which was already pulling out, its bow parting a wave that curled ashore. The water sucked and gurgled round Drinkwater's thighs as he fell over the transom. A splinter drove into the palm of his hand and he remembered the plunging hoof as the nausea of pain shot through him. For a moment he lay gasping, vaguely aware of shouts and confusion where the barouche met its pursuers. Then a ball or two whined overhead and from seaward came a hail from the other boat asking if they required help. Drinkwater raised his head to refuse but a seaman stood and fired one of the blunderbusses beside his ear. Drinkwater twisted round and looked astern. Not ten yards away rearing among the breakers a horse threw its rider into the sea. Both were hit by the langridge in the gun.

'A steady pull now lads. We're all right now.' But a flash and roar contradicted him. The six-pounder ball ricochetted three yards away. Horse artillery!

'Pull you bastards! Pull!' They had no need of exhortation. The oar looms bent under the effort.

Another bang and a shower of splinters. Shouts, screams and the boat slewed to starboard, the woman standing and shrieking astern, her hands beating her sides in fury. They were firing canister and ball and the starboard oars had been hit. The boat was a shambles as she drifted back into the breakers.

Then from seaward there was an answering flash and the whine of shot passing low overhead as *Kestrel* opened fire. A minute later the other boat took them in tow.

Drinkwater threw his wet cloak into a corner of the main cabin. He was haggard with exhaustion and bad temper. His inadequacy for the task Griffiths had given him filled him with an exasperation brittle with reaction. Two dead and three wounded, plus the Frenchman now lying across the cabin table, was a steep price to pay for a handful of fugitives and two boxes of yellow metal.

'Get below and see to the wounded,' Griffiths had said, and then, in a final remark that cut short Drinkwater's protest, 'there's a case of surgical instruments in the starboard locker.'

Drinkwater dragged them out, took up a pair of tweezers and jerked the splinter from the palm of his hand. His anger evaporated as a wave of pain passed through him, leaving him shaking, gradually aware of the woman's eyes watching him from the shadows of her hood. Under her gaze he steadied, grateful for her influence yet simultaneously resentful of her presence, remembering that hint of enmity he had caught as he passed her into the gig. Two men stumbled into the cabin slopping hot water from basins. Drinkwater took off his coat and rolled up his shirt sleeves, taking a bottle of brandy from the rack.

Drinkwater braced himself The swinging lantern threw shadows and highlights wildly about as *Kestrel* made north on a long beat to windward. He bent over the Frenchman aware that the others were watching him, the woman standing, swaying slowly as they worked offshore, as if unwilling to accept the sanctuary of the cutter. The two men watched from the settee, slumped in attitudes of relieved exhaustion.

'Here, one of you, help me . . . *m'aidez!*'

Drinkwater found a glass and half filled it with cognac. He swallowed as the elder man came forward. Drinkwater held out the glass and the man took it eagerly.

'Get his clothes off. Use a knife . . . d'you understand?' The man nodded and began work. Drinkwater invoked the memory of Surgeon Appleby and tried to remember something of what he had been told, what he had seen a lifetime earlier in the stinking cockpit of *Cyclops*. It seemed little enough so he refilled the tumbler, catching the woman's eyes and the hostility in them. The fiery liquid made him shudder and he ignored the woman's hauteur.

He bent over the Frenchman. 'Who the devil is he?' he asked.

'His name, *m'sieur*,' said the elder Frenchman working busily at

216

the seam of the unconscious man's coat, 'is Le Comte de Tocqueville; I am Auguste Barrallier, late of the Brest Dockyard . . .' He pulled the sleeve off and ripped the shirt. 'The young man beside you is Etienne Montholon; *mam'selle* is his sister Hortense.' From the woman came an indrawn breath that might have been disapproval of his loquacity or horror as Barrallier revealed the count's shoulder, peeling the coat and shirt off the upper left breast. De Tocqueville groaned, raised his head and opened his eyes. Then his head lolled back. 'Lost a lot of blood,' said Drinkwater, thankful that the man was unconscious.

Barrallier discarded the soaked clothing. Drinkwater swabbed the wound clean and watched uncertainly as more blood oozed from the bruised, raw flesh.

'The Arabs use a method of washing with the wine *m'sieur,*' offered Barrallier gently, 'perhaps a little of the cognac might be spared, yes?' Drinkwater reached for the bottle.

'He was shot . . .' The young man, standing now next to Barrallier, spoke for the first time. He stated the obvious in that nervous way the uncertain have. Drinkwater looked up into a handsome face perhaps twenty years old.

Drinkwater slipped his hand beneath the count's shoulder. He could feel the ball under the skin. Roughly he scraped the wound to remove any pieces of clothing and poured a last measure of cognac over the mess. He searched among the apothecary's liniments and selected a pot of bluish ointment, smearing the contents over the wound, covering it with a pledget and then a pad made from the count's shirt.

' Hold that over the wound while we turn him over.' Drinkwater nodded to Barrallier who put out his bloody hands, then he looked at Montholon. 'Hold his legs, *m'sieur*, if you would. Cross them over, good. Now, together!'

Bracing themselves against *Kestrel*'s windward pitch they rolled De Tocqueville roughly over. Drinkwater was feeling more confident, the brandy was doing its work well. An over-active part of his brain was emerging from reaction to the events of the last hours, already curious about their passengers.

'Your escape was none too soon.' He said it absently, preoccupied as he rolled the tip of his forefinger over the blue lump that lay

217

alongside the count's scapula. He did not expect the gasp to come with such vehemence from the woman, cutting through the thick air of the cabin with an incongruous venom that distracted him into looking up.

She had thrown back the hood of her cloak and the swinging lantern caught copper gleams from the mass of auburn hair that fell about her shoulders. She appeared older than her brother with strong, even features heightened by the stress she was under. She stared at Drinkwater from level grey eyes and again he felt her hostility. Her lack of gratitude piqued him and he thought of the two dead and three wounded of *Kestrel*'s crew that had been the price of her escape.

Angry, he bent again over the count's shoulder, picking up the scalpel and feeling its blade rasp the scapula. A light-headed feeling swept over him as he encountered the ball.

'Hold the lantern closer,' he said through clenched teeth. And she obeyed.

The musket ball rolled bloodily on to the table.

Drinkwater grunted with satisfaction as he bound a second pledget and passed a linen strip round the count's shoulder. They strapped his arm to his side and heaved him on to the settee. Then they turned to the seamen with the splinter wounds.

Daylight was visible when Drinkwater staggered on deck soaked in perspiration. The chill hit him as he lurched to the rail and, shuddering, vomited the cognac out of his stomach. He laid his head on the rail. Hortense Montholon lay in his cot and he sank down beside the breeching of a four-pounder and fell asleep. Tregembo brought blankets and covered him.

Standing by the tiller Lieutenant Griffiths looked at the inert form. Although no expression passed over his face he was warm with approval. He had not misjudged the qualities of Nathaniel Drinkwater.

Chapter Three   *December 1792–February 1793*

A Curtain Rising

The incident at Beaubigny had ended *Kestrel*'s clandestine operations. Temporarily unemployed the cutter rolled in the swell that reached round Penlee Point to rock her at her anchor in Cawsand Bay.

Perspiring in his airless cabin Drinkwater sat twirling the cheap goosequill in his long fingers. Condensation hung from the deckhead, generated by the over-stoked stove in Griffiths's cabin next door. Drinkwater was fighting a losing battle against drowsiness. With an effort he forced himself to read over what he had written in his journal.

It was a matter of amazement to me that M. De Tocqueville survived my butchery. His debility was occasioned by loss of blood due to a severe grazing of the axillary artery which fortunately did not rupture entirely. The pectoral muscle was badly torn by the angle of entry of the ball but it seems we had the only chip of bone out of him. If it does not yet putrefy he will live.

He had been mildly interested in the medical details for it had been an old friend who had looked over his rudimentary surgery. Mr Appleby, appointed surgeon to the frigate *Diamond* then fitting in the Hamoaze, had been ordered aboard *Kestrel* to check the wounded. He had been complimentary about Nathaniel's unschooled suturing but had not let him escape without a lecture on the count's injuries.

Drinkwater smiled at the recollection. It had been an odd passage home. Of all the refugees *Kestrel* had brought out of France that last quartet had left an indelible impression. The feverish nobleman muttering incoherently in his delirium and the attentively ineffectual young Etienne Montholon were a contrast to their fellow travellers. The garrulous and enthusiastic Barrallier was a lively and amusing companion who let no detail of *Kestrel* escape his criticism or admiration. He seemed to cut himself off from the others, turning his back on France, as if desperate to be seen as anglophile in all things. Markedly different from the men, Hortense remained aloof; cold and contemptuous in the isolation of her sex. Her beauty caused a whispering, wondering admiration among the hands and a vague disquiet among the officers with whom she was briefly accommodated.

Drinkwater was not alone in his relief at their disembarkation at Plymouth with their specie and the folio of plans, but they left in their wake a sense of unease. Like many of his contemporaries who had served in the American War, Drinkwater found a wry amusement in the visitation of republican revolution on the French. Many of those who had served under Rochambeau and La Fayette, men who had drawn the iron ring around Cornwallis at Yorktown and professed admiration for liberty, now ran like rats before the Jacobin terriers.

But there was also a strand of sympathy for the revolution in Nathaniel's heart, born of a sympathy for the oppressed awakened years earlier on the stinking orlop of *Cyclops*. He could not entirely condemn the principles of revolution, though he baulked at the method. Despite the sanctuary given the émigrés, Englishmen of liberal principles and many naval officers of independent mind saw with eyes uncluttered by party interest. Drinkwater was no pocketed Whig nor heedless Tory adherent and he had precious little 'interest' to tie him to principles of dubious propriety.

He lay down his pen and snapped the cap on his inkwell, transferring himself to the cot. He picked up the creased newspaper that Griffiths had left him. The print danced in front of his eyes. In the light of recent events Mr Pitt's promises of peace and prosperity rang false. The letters marched like a thousand tiny black men: an army. He closed his eyes. War and the possibility of war were all that people talked of, paying scant attention to Mr Pitt's protestations.

It was odd that there had not been trouble over the Beaubigny affair since it seemed that only a pretext was wanted, a spark to fire the dry tinder of international relations. And it was not just the Jacobins who were eager for war. He had had dinner with Appleby and Richard White two nights earlier. White was already a lieutenant with five year's seniority and the air of a post-captain. His standing was high enough to command an appointment as second lieutenant on Sir Sydney* Smith's crack frigate *Diamond*. He had drunk to the prospects of 'glorious war' with a still boyish enthusiasm which had made Appleby curl his lip.

The dinner had been only a qualified success. Revived friendships had a quality of regret about them. White had become an urbane young man, possessed of disproportionate self-confidence so that Drinkwater had difficulty in recognising the frightened boy who had once sobbed in the blackness of *Cyclops*'s cockpit. Appleby too, had changed. The years had not been kind to him. The once portly surgeon had the loose flesh of penury, something of the old buoyancy was missing, eroded by years of loneliness and hard living, but beneath the ravages of time there were glimpses of the old Appleby, pedagoguish, prolix but astute as ever.

'Bound to be war,' he had said in answer to Drinkwater's worried questioning, while White eagerly agreed. 'And it will be a collision of mighty forces which England will be hard put to defeat. Oh, you can scoff, Mr White, but you siblings that thirst for glory chase moonbeams.'

'He's still a boy,' Appleby had muttered when the lieutenant had gone to relieve himself. 'But God help his men when he's made post, which will not be long if this war comes soon. I hope their lordships give him a tolerant, experienced and understanding first lieutenant.'

'He's certainly changed,' agreed Drinkwater, 'it seems he's been spoiled.'

'Promotion too rapid, cully. It works for a few, but not all.'

No, the dinner had not been a success.

Yet it was not entirely the bickering of his old friends that had failed to make it so. It was the approach of war that stirred unease in Nathaniel. The faint, inescapable thrill of coming excitement mixed with the fear he had already felt on the beach at Beaubigny caused his pulse to race, even now.

If war came was this tiny cutter the place to be? What chance had he of promotion? He must not think of competing with White, that was impossible. In any case *Kestrel* was a fine little ship.

*Nelson's spelling

Providence had brought him here and he must submit to his fate. It had not been entirely unkind to him so far. He contemplated the shelf of books, his own journals and the notebooks left him by Mr Blackmore, late sailing master of *Cyclops*. He had been touched by that bequest. The mahogany box containing his quadrant was lashed in a corner and his Dollond glass nestled in the pocket of his coat, hung on the door peg with the French sword. A collection of purchases, gifts and loot; the sum total of his possessions. Not much after thirty years of existence. Then his eye fell on the watercolour of the *Algonquin* off St Mawes, painted for him by his wife.

A knock at the door recalled him to the present. 'What is it?'

'Boat, zur.'

He threw his legs over the rim of the cot. 'Lieutenant Griffiths?'

'Aye zur.'

'Very well, I'll be up directly.' He slipped into his shoes and drew on the plain blue coat. Opening the door he jammed his hat on his head and leapt for the ladder, clearing the companionway with a bound and sucking gratefully at the raw, frosty air.

Griffiths brought orders from the port admiral. That afternoon *Kestrel* took the tide into the Barn Pool and warped alongside the mast hulk *Chichester*. The following morning the dockyard officials came aboard and consulted Griffiths. By the time the hands were piped to dinner *Kestrel*'s standing rigging had been sent down and by nightfall her lower mast had been drawn out of her by the hulk's sheers. Next day the carpenters were busy altering her carlings to take the new mast.

'We're to fit a longer topmast,' Griffiths explained, 'to set a square t'gallant above the topsail, see.' He swallowed the madeira and looked at Drinkwater. 'I don't think we'll be playing cat and mouse again, *bach*, not after that episode at Beaubigny. We're going to look a regular man o'war cutter when the artificers have finished, and become a bloody nursemaid to the fleet. Now, to other matters. The clerk of the cheque will see the men are paid before Christmas. But they're to have only half of their due until after, see. Give 'em the lot and they'll be leaving their brains in the gutters along with their guts and we'll have to beg the foot patrols for help. I want a crew aboard this cutter after Christmas.'

Drinkwater acknowledged the sense of Griffiths's draconian measures. His commander had somewhat anticipated the festive season, if his high colouring and desire to talk were anything to go by.

'And let the pawn shops know the people are being paid. That way their women might get to hear of it and it may not all go down the drain.' He paused to drink, then reached into his tail pocket. 'Here, this was given me at the port admiral's office.' He pulled out a crumpled letter and held it out. The superscription was in a familiar hand.

'Thank you, sir.' Drinkwater took the letter and turned it over, impatient for the privacy of his own cabin. Griffiths hoisted himself on to his settee and closed his eyes. Drinkwater made to leave.

'Oh, Mr Drinkwater,' an eye opened. 'The importunate ninny with an undeserved cockade who gave me that letter told me I ought to give you leave over Christmas.' Drinkwater paused, looking from the letter to Griffiths. 'I do not hold with such impertinence.' There was a long silence during which the eye slowly closed. Drinkwater stepped puzzled into the lobby.

'You can take leave when that t'gallant yard is crossed, Mr Drinkwater, and not a moment sooner.'

Half smiling Drinkwater closed the door and slipped into his own cubbyhole. He hastily slit the wafer and began to read.

My Darling Nathaniel,

I write in haste. Richd White called on me today on his way to see Sir S. Smith's prize agent at Portsmouth and promised to collect a letter for you on his return this evening. He is expectant of seeing you in Plymouth I understand. Thank you for yours of 29th. The news that you are likely to be idle at Plymouth combines with my great anxiety and apprehension I feel over the news of France and I worry greatly. Should it be true that war is likely as Richd is convinced, I cannot miss an opportunity to see my dearest. Please meet the London mail Christmas Eve. Until then, my love,

I remain, Ever your Devoted Wife,
Elizabeth

Drinkwater grinned to himself in anticipation. Perhaps his judgement of White had been a trifle premature. Only a friend would have thought of that. Warmed by his friend's solicitude and happy that he was soon to see Elizabeth he threw himself into the refitting of the cutter with enthusiasm. And for a time the shadow of war receded from his mind.

The topgallant yard was crossed, braced and the new sail sent up and bent on by the 23rd December. By the morning of Christmas Eve the rigging was set up. Drinkwater notified the clerk of the cheque and he sent a shrivelled little man with a bound chest, a marine guard and a book as big as a hatch-board to pay the cutter's people. By noon the harbour watch had been set and *Kestrel* was almost deserted, many of her crew of volunteers being residents of Plymouth. Free of duty, Drinkwater hurried below to shift his coat, ship his hanger and then made his way ashore. He was met by Tregembo who knuckled his forehead, ablaze in all the festive finery of a tar, despite the chill, with a beribboned hat and blue monkey jacket spangled with brass buttons, a black kerchief at his muscular neck, and feet shoved awkwardly into cheap pumps.

'I booked your room, zur, at Wilson's like you axed, zur, an' beggin' your pardon, zur, but the London mail's delayed.'

'Damn!' Drinkwater fished in his pocket for a coin, aware of Tregembo looking nervously over his shoulder. Behind him stood a girl of about twenty, square built and sturdy, slightly truculent in the presence of the officer, as though embarrassed for the station of her man. The red ribbon in her hair was carelessly worn, as though new purchased and tied with more ardour than art. 'Here,' he began to fish for another coin. Tregembo flushed.

'No, zur. It ain't that, er, zur, I was wondering if I could . . .' He hung his head.

'I expect you aboard by dawn on the 26th or I'll have every foot patrol in Plymouth out for a deserter.' Drinkwater saw the look of relief cross Tregembo's face.

'Thank 'ee, zur, and a merry Christmas to you an' Mrs Drinkwater.'

Elizabeth arrived at last, wearied by her journey and worried over the possibility of war. They greeted each other shyly and there was a reticence about them, as if their previous intimacies were not to be repeated until released from their present preoccupations. But the wine warmed them and their own company insulated them at last against the world outside, so that it was breakfast of Christmas morning before Elizabeth first spoke of what troubled her.

'Do you think war is likely, Nathaniel?'

Drinkwater regarded the face before him, the frown on the broad sweep of the brow, the swimmingly beautiful brown eyes and the lower lip of her wide mouth caught apprehensively in her teeth. He was melted with pity for her, aware that for him war might have its terrible compensations and grim opportunities, whereas for her it offered the corrosion of waiting. Perhaps for the remainder of her life. He wanted to lie to her, to tell her everything would be all right, to soothe her fears with platitudes. But that would be contemptible. Leaving her with a false half-hope would be worse than the truth.

He nodded. 'Everyone is of the opinion that if the French invade Holland it is most likely. For my own part, Bess, I promise you this, I shall be circumspect and take no unnecessary risks. Here,' he reached out for the coffee pot, 'let us drink a toast to ourselves and to our future. I shall try for my commission and at the present rate of progress, retire a half-pay commander, superannuated through old age to bore you with tales of my exploits . . .' He saw her lips twist. Elizabeth, bless her, was gently mocking him.

He grinned back. 'I shall not be foolhardy, Bess, I promise.'

'No, of course not,' she said taking the coffee cup from him. And as he withdrew his hand the mark of the splinter was still visible on his palm.

'*Hannibal*, sir, Captain Colpoys, just in from a cruise. Missed Christmas, poor devils.' Both men regarded the battleship anchoring across the Sound.

Griffiths nodded. 'The big boy-o's have all shaken the cobwebs from their topsails and are back to ground on their own chicken bones again. It's time we put to sea again Mr Drinkwater. This is a time for little birds with keen eyes; the elephants can wait a while longer. D'you have my gig ready in ten minutes.'

Waiting for Griffiths to return from the port admiral's, Drinkwater paced the deck. The hands were making preparation to

225

sail, skylarking until sent below by a fine drizzle, while he was oblivious of the grey pall that rolled up the Hamoaze.

Farewells, he concluded, were damnable.

Tregembo came aft and stood uncertainly next to him.

'What is it Tregembo?'

The seaman looked unhappily at his feet. 'I was wondering, zur . . .'

'Don't tell me you want leave of absence to see your doxy?'

Tregembo hung his head in assent.

'Damn it Tregembo, you'll get her with child or catch pox. I'm damned if I'll physic you!' Drinkwater instantly regretted the unkindness caused by his own misery.

'She ain't like that, zur . . . and I only want a quarter hour, zur.'

Drinkwater thought of Elizabeth. 'Damn it Tregembo, not a moment more then.'

'Thank 'ee, zur, thank 'ee.' Drinkwater watched him hurry off. Idly he wondered what the future held. The shots at Beaubigny might have formed a pretext for war, for *Kestrel*'s broadside had been an aggressive act. It was odd that the French had not made more of it, at least one of their men had been killed. But the advantages of peace were being protested by Pitt and such an insignificant cruiser as *Kestrel* could not be allowed to provide a *casus belli*. That, at least, had been the British position, and she had been kept refitting at Plymouth until the air cleared. All the same it was deuced odd that the French had failed to capitalise on the violation of their littoral.

He dismissed the thought. Now the cutter was ordered to join the growing number of brigs and sloops of war keeping the French coast under observation. Since Lord Hood had cruised with home-based frigates and guardships in the summer, the dockyard had been busy. Thanks to the Spanish and Russian crises of the preceding three years the fleet was in a reasonable state of preparedness. Across the Channel the Paris mob had massacred the Swiss guard and in September the French had invaded Savoy. It was known that Rear-Admiral Truguet had been ordered to sea with nine sail of the line. In November the Austrian Netherlands were overrun and the French seized control of the Scheldt. This made the whereabouts of all French naval squadrons crucial to the defence of Great Britain.

There were thirty-nine battleships at Brest, ten at Lorient and thirteen at Rochefort. As 1793 approached the Admiralty was taking a close look at them.

The grey overcast of Saturday 29th December 1792 seemed leaden, but the wind had backed into the north-west, the showers had ceased and the cloud was beginning to disperse. Griffiths and Drinkwater stood watching a brig-sloop running down the Sound for the open sea.

'*Childers*, Commander Robert Barlow,' muttered Drinkwater half to himself.

Griffiths nodded. 'Off to reconnoitre Brest Road,' he added confidentially.

On the last day of the old year, the wind veered northerly and blew from a clear sky. At noon a guard boat brought Griffiths the orders he had been expecting. By sunset *Kestrel* had left Smeaton's Eddystone lighthouse astern and was scudding south to the support of *Childers*.

During the night the wind freshened to a severe gale and *Kestrel* was hove to, her bowsprit reefed, her topmast and yards sent down and double breechings securing her guns. At first light a sail was seen to the westward and an exchange of signals revealed her as *Childers*. Taking the helm himself Griffiths steered *Kestrel* under the brig's lee and luffed. In his tarpaulin Barlow bellowed at them: 'Fired on by French batteries at St Matthew . . . honour of the flag, return to port . . . making for Fowey . . .' His words were ripped away by the gale.

'Probably of the opinion he's the first to be fired on, eh, Mr Drinkwater?' growled Griffiths, regarding his junior from beneath a wet and bushy white eyebrow.

'Aye, sir, and hastening home to make a noise of it if I'm not mistaken.'

Griffiths chuckled. Barlow's indignation was clear, even across the strip of white and foaming water. 'He'll be in a post-chaise before that brig's fetched an anchor, I'll warrant,' said Griffiths, heaving on the tiller and calling two men to relieve him.

The two little ships parted, plunging to windward with the spray shooting over them, the sea streaked pale by parallel lines of spume

227

that tore downwind. Here and there a fulmar banked and swooped on rigid, sabre-shaped wings, breaking the desolation of the view.

Three weeks later Louis XVI was guillotined and on the first day of February the French Naval Convention declared war on the Dutch Stadtholder and His Majesty King George III.

A Hunter Hunted

'Cap'n's compliments, sir, an' he'd be obliged if you'd attend him in the cabin.' Odd that a little cutter could produce a servant as diplomatic as Merrick. Drinkwater turned the deck over to Jessup and went below, crabbing down the companionway against the heel.

'Nothing in sight, sir,' he said removing his hat 'apart from *Flora*, that is.'

Griffiths nodded without looking up from his orders just received from the frigate. 'Sit down, Mr Drinkwater.'

Drinkwater eased himself on to the settee and stretched. Griffiths pushed a decanter across the table without a word, flicking a glance in Drinkwater's direction only to see that the latter had hold of it before he let go. Claret from their last capture, an unhandy little *bugalet* bound to the Seine from Bordeaux. Good wine too, and a tidy sum made from the sale. Drinkwater sipped appreciatively and watched his commander.

In the months since *Kestrel* had become a lookout cruiser and commerce raider, a gatherer of intelligence and a dealer of swift demoralising blows, Drinkwater and Griffiths had developed a close working relationship. The acting lieutenant had quickly realised that he shared with his commander a rare zeal for efficiency and a common love of driving their little ship for its own sake.

Griffiths folded the papers and looked up, reaching for the claret. 'Our orders, Mr Drinkwater, our orders. Another glass, is it . . .?' Drinkwater waited patiently.

Referring to the frigate's captain Griffiths said, 'Sir John Warren has sent a note to say that he's applied for us to join his flying squadron when it is formed.'

Drinkwater considered the news. Operating with frigates might be to his advantage. It all depended on how many young lieutenants were clamouring for patronage. Captains commanding Channel cruisers could have the pick of the list. So perhaps his chances were not very good. 'When will that be, sir?'

Griffiths shrugged. 'Who knows, *bach*. The mills of Admiralty grind as slow as those of God.'

Clearly Griffiths did not relish the loss of independence, but he looked up and added, 'In the meantime we have a little job to do. Rather like our old work. There's a mutual friend of ours who wishes to leave France.'

'Mutual friend, sir?'

'You know, Mr Drinkwater, fellow we landed at Criel. He goes under the name of Major Brown. His commission's in the Life Guards, though I doubt he's sat a horse on the King's Service. Made a reputation with the Iroquois in the last war, I remember. Been employed on "special service" ever since,' Griffiths said with heavy emphasis.

Drinkwater remembered the fat, jolly man they had landed on his first operation nearly a year ago. He did not appear typical of the officers of His Majesty's Life Guards.

Griffiths sensed his puzzlement. 'The Duke of York, Mr Drinkwater, reserves a few commissions for meritorious officers,' he smiled wryly. 'They have to *earn* the privilege and almost never see a stirrup iron.'

'I see, sir. Where do we pick him up? And when? Have we any choice?'

'Get the chart folio, *bach*, and we'll have a look.'

'God damn this weather to hell!' For the thousandth time during the forenoon Griffiths stared to the west, but the hoped-for lightening on the horizon failed to appear.

'We'll have to take another reef, sir, and shift the jib . . .' Drinkwater left the sentence unfinished as a sheet of spray whipped aft from the wave rolling inboard amidships, spilling over the rail and threatening to rend the two gigs from their chocks.

'But it's August, Mr Drinkwater, August,' his despairing appeal to the elements ended in a nod of assent, Drinkwater turned away.

'Mr Jessup! All hands! Rouse along the spitfire jib there!

Larbowlines forward and shift the jib. Starbowlines another reef in the mains'l!' Drinkwater watched with satisfaction as the men ran to their stations, up to their knees in water at the base of the mast.

'Ready, forrard!' came Jessup's hail.

Drinkwater noted Griffiths's nod and watched the sea. 'Down helm!'

As the cutter luffed further orders were superfluous. *Kestrel* was no lumbering battleship, her crew worked with the surefooted confidence of practice. With canvas shivering and slatting in a trembling that reached to her keel, the cutter's crew worked furiously. The peak and throat halliards were slackened and the mainsheet hove in to control the boom whilst the leech cringle was hauled down. By the mast the luff cringle was secured and the men spread along the length of the boom, bunching the hard, wet canvas and tying the reef points.

Forward men pulled in the traveller inhaul while Jessup eased the outhaul. By the mast the jib halliard was started and waist deep in water on the lee bow the flogging jib was pulled inboard. Within a minute the spitfire was shackled to the halliard, its tack hooked to the traveller and the outhaul manned. Even as the big iron ring jerked out along the spar the halliard tightened. The sail thundered, its luff curving away to leeward as *Kestrel* fell into the trough of the sea, then straightened as men tallied on and sweated it tight. 'Belay! Belay there!'

'Ready forrard!'

Drinkwater heard Jessup's hail, saw him standing in the eyes, his square-cut figure solid against the pitch of the horizon and the tarpaulin whipping about his legs, for all the world a scarecrow in a gale. Drinkwater resisted a boyish impulse to laugh. 'Aye, aye, Mr Jessup!'

He turned to the helmsman, 'Steady her now,' and a nod to Poll on the mainsheet. *Kestrel* gathered way across the wind, her mainsail peak jerking up again to its jaunty angle and filling with wind.

'Down helm!' She began to turn up into the wind again, spurred by that sudden impetus; again that juddering tremble as her flapping sails transmitted their frustrated energy to the fabric of the hull. 'Heads'l sheets!'

'Full an' bye, starboard tack.'

'Full an' bye, sir,' answered the forward of the two men leaning on the tiller.

'Is she easier now?'

'Aye sir, much,' he said shifting his quid neatly over his tongue in some odd sympathy with the ship.

Kestrel drove forward again, her motion easier, her speed undiminished.

'Shortened sail, sir,' Drinkwater reported.

'*Da iawn*, Mr Drinkwater.'

The wind eased a little as the sun set behind castellated banks of cloud whose summits remained rose coloured until late into the evening. In the last of the daylight Drinkwater had studied the southern horizon, noted the three nicks in its regularity and informed Griffiths.

'One might be an armed lugger, sir, it's difficult to be certain but he's standing west. Out of our way, sir.'

Griffiths rubbed his chin reflectively. 'Mmm. The damned beach'll be very dangerous, Mr Drinkwater, very dangerous indeed. The surf'll be high for a day or two.' He fell silent and Drinkwater was able to follow his train of thought. He knew most of Griffiths's secrets now and that *Flora*'s order had hinged on the word 'imperative'.

'It means,' explained Griffiths, 'that Brown has sent word to London that he is no longer able to stay in France or has something very important to acquaint HMG with,' he shrugged. 'It depends . . .'

Drinkwater remembered the pigeons.

'And if the weather is too bad to recover him, sir?'

Griffiths looked up. 'It mustn't be, see.' He paused. 'No, one develops a "nose" for such things. Brown has been there a long time on his own. In my opinion he's anxious to get out tonight.'

Drinkwater expelled his breath slowly, thinking about the state of the sea on the landing. He stared to the westward. The wind was still strong and under the windsea a westerly swell rolled up the Channel. He was abruptly recalled from his observations by the lieutenant. Griffiths was halfway out of the companionway.

'Come below, Mr Drinkwater, I've an idea to discuss with you.'

'Let go.' The order passed quietly forward from man to man and the cat stopper was cast off. *Kestrel*'s anchor dropped to the sandy bottom of the little bay as her head fell off to leeward and the seamen secured the sails, loosing the reefs in the mainsail and bending on the big jib. *Kestrel* had stood slowly in for the rendezvous immediately after dark. Now she bucked in the heavy swell as it gathered up in the shelving bay to fling itself into a white fury on the crescent of sand dimly perceptible below the cliffs that almost enclosed them.

'Hold on.' The cable slowed its thrumming rumble through the hawse as the single compressor nipped it against the bitts. The cutter jerked her head round into sea and swell as the anchor brought up. 'Brought to it,' came the word back from forward.

'Are you ready, Mr Drinkwater?' The acting lieutenant looked about him. His two volunteers grunted assent and Drinkwater found the sound of Tregembo's voice reassuring. The other man, Poll, was a pugnacious red-bearded fellow who enjoyed an aggressive reputation aboard *Kestrel*. 'Aye, sir, we're ready . . . Come lads.'

The three men moved aft where Jessup, judging his moment nicely, had dropped the little jolly boat into the sea as *Kestrel*'s bow rose. As her bottom smacked into the water the davit falls were let fly and unrove. The boat drifted astern until restrained by its painter, then it was pulled carefully alongside and Drinkwater, Tregembo and Poll jumped into it.

Forward Tregembo received the eye of four-inch hemp from the deck and secured it round the forward thwart. Amidships Poll secured the shaded lantern and loosed the oar lashings while Drinkwater saw that the coil of line aft was clear to run, as was the second of small rope attached to the grapnel. They would have to watch their feet in those two coils.

'Ready lads?' Tregembo and Poll answered in the affirmative and Drinkwater hailed the deck in a low voice, 'Let go the painter and veer away the four-inch.'

'Aye, aye, sir.' Drinkwater could see heads bobbing at the rail as Jessup eased the little boat downwind. 'Good luck, Mr Drinkwater,' came Griffiths's low voice.

Bucking astern Drinkwater raised his arm in acknowledgement and turned his attention to the beach. Tregembo touched his shoulder.

'Lantern's ready, zur.'

'Very well.' They were bobbing up and down now, the seas

233

shoving the craft shorewards, the hemp rope restraining it, jerking it head to sea then veering away again as they rolled into ever steepening seas. The moment he saw the waves begin to curl, gathering themselves before tumbling ashore as breakers, Drinkwater ordered the shaded lantern shown seaward. Almost immediately the boat came head to sea and remained there. Tregembo came aft.

'They're holding, zur.'

'Very well.' Drinkwater slipped off his shoes. He was already stripped to his shirt. As he stood up to fasten the light line about himself Tregembo said: 'I'll go zur, it ain't your place, zur, beggin' your pardon.'

Drinkwater grinned in the darkness. 'It *is* my place, Tregembo, do you tend the lines, on that I rely absolutely . . . now Poll, pass me the grapnel and I'll secure the stern.'

Thanking providence that it *was* August, Drinkwater slipped over the transom and kicked out shorewards, the small grapnel over his shoulder, shaking the lines free.

He felt himself caught in the turbulence of a breaking wave, then thrust forward, the thunder of the surf in his ears, his legs continually fouling the ropes. Desperately he turned on his side and kicked frantically with his free leg, thrashing with his unencumbered arm. The undertow dragged him back and he felt his hand drive into sand. Another wave thundered about him, forcing the breath out and turning him over so that the ropes caught. Again his hand encountered sand and he scrabbled at it, panic welling in his winded guts.

Then he was ashore, a raffle of rope and limbs, stretched out in the final surge of a few inches of water, grasping and frightened.

Another wave washed around him as he lay in the shallows, then another as he struggled to his feet. Recovering his breath by degrees he sorted out the tangle of ropes, knowing Tregembo and Poll had each an end over opposite quarters. The need to concentrate steadied him. He drove the grapnel into the sand and jerked the line hard. He felt it tighten and saw it rise dripping and straight. Wading out he could just see the grey shape of the boat bobbing above the white line of the breakers. He untied the line from his waist and belayed it slackly around one of the exposed grapnel flukes. Moored head and stern the boat seemed safe and Drinkwater settled down to wait. Presently, despite the season, he was shivering.

An hour later he was beginning to regret his insistence on making the landing. He was thoroughly cold and thought he detected the wind freshening again. He watched where *Kestrel* lay, watched for the lantern at the masthead that would signal his recall. But he knew Griffiths would wait until the last moment. Even now he guessed Jessup and the hands would be toiling to get a spring on the cable so that, when the time came, the cutter could be cast away from the wind and sail off her anchor. She was too close inshore to do anything else. He preoccupied himself as best he could and was oblivious of the first shots. When he did realise something was wrong he could already see the flashes of small arms on the cliff top and just below it, where a path dropped down to the beach. From his shelter he leapt out and raced for the grapnel, looking along the sand expectantly.

He saw the man break away from the shadow around the base of the cliff. Saw him stumble and recover, saw the spurts of sand where musket balls struck.

'Over here!' he yelled, reaching the grapnel.

He uncoiled the loop of light line and passed it around his waist in a bowline with a three fathom tail. The man blundered up gasping.

'Major Brown?'

'The same, the same . . .' The man heaved his breath in as Drinkwater passed the end of the line round his waist.

'A kestrel . . .'

'. . . for a knave.' Brown finished the countersign as Drinkwater grasped his arm and dragged him towards the sea. Already infantrymen were running down on to the beach. Resolutely Drinkwater turned seawards and shouted: 'Heave in!'

He saw Tregembo wave and felt the line jerk about his waist. The breath was driven out of him as he was hauled bodily through a tumbling wavecrest. He lost his grip on the spy. Bobbing to the surface he glimpsed the night sky arched impassively above his supine body as he relinquished it to Tregembo's hauling. He desperately gasped for breath as the next wave rolled over him. Then he was under the transom of the boat, feeling for the stirrup of rope Poll should have rigged. His right leg found it and he half turned for Major Brown who seemed waterlogged in his coat.

'Get him in first, Tregembo,' Drinkwater gasped, 'he's near collapse.'

Somehow they pulled him up to the transom and Drinkwater helped turn him round with his back to the boat. 'Get clear Mr Drinkwater!' It was Tregembo's voice and Drinkwater was vaguely aware of the two seamen, their hands on the shoulders of the Major, lifting him, lifting him, then suddenly plunging him down hard, down so that he disappeared then thrust to the surface where they waited to grab him and drag him ungainly into the boat. Drinkwater felt the tug on the line as Brown went inboard. He wearily replaced his foot in the stirrup and tried to heave himself over the transom but his chilled muscles cramped. Tregembo grabbed him and in a second he was in the bottom of the boat, on top of Brown and it no longer mattered about the coils of rope.

'Beg pardon, zur,' Tregembo heaved him aside with one hand and then his axe bit into the quarter knee cutting the grapnel line. Forward Poll showed the lantern and on board *Kestrel* all hands walked away with the hemp rope. Musket shot whistled round them and two or three struck splinters from the gunwales.

Wearily Drinkwater raised his head, eager to see the familiar loom of *Kestrel* over him. Ten yards to go, then safety. To seaward he thought he saw something else. It looked very like the angled peaks of a lugger's sails.

Even as he digested this they were alongside and arms were reaching down to help him out of the boat on to the deck. Roughly compassionate, Griffiths himself threw a boat cloak around Drinkwater while the latter stuttered out what he had seen.

'Lugger is it? Aye, *bach*, I've seen it already . . . are you all right?'

'Well enough,' stammered Drinkwater through chattering teeth.

'Get sail on her then. Mr Jessup! Larboard broadside, make ready . . .' Griffiths had given him the easy, mechanical job, Jessup's job, while he recovered himself. He felt a wave of gratitude for the old man's consideration and stumbled forward, gathering the men round the halliards at the fiferail. Staysail and throat halliards went away together, then the jib and peak halliards. The great gaff rose into the night and the sails slatted and cracked, the mast trembled and *Kestrel* fretted to be off.

There was a flash from seaward and the whine of a ball to

starboard, surprising the men who had not yet realised the danger from the sea but who assumed they were to fire a defiant parting broadside at the beach.

The halliards were belayed and Drinkwater went aft to Griffiths.

'*Da iawn*, sheet all home to starboard then stand by to cut that cable.'

'Aye, aye, sir.' Drinkwater felt better. From somewhere inside, fresh reserves of strength flowed through him. The exercise at the halliards had invigorated him. He called the carpenter to stand handy with his axe and found Johnson already at his station. The sails thundered less freely now the sheets were secured.

'Larbowlines, man your guns, stand by to fire at the lugger!' Griffiths's words were drowned as the lugger's gunfire rent the air. A row of spouts rose close to starboard. 'Short by heaven,' muttered Drinkwater to himself.

'Cut!'

The axe struck twice at the cable. It stranded, spinning out the fibres as the strain built up, then it parted. *Kestrel*'s bow fell off the wind.

'Meet her.' The stern was held by the spring, led from aft forward and frapped to the end of the severed cable. *Kestrel* spun, heeled to the wind and drove forward.

'Cut!'

At the after gunport Jessup sawed against the cavil and the spring parted. Leaving her jolly boat, two anchors and a hundred fathoms of assorted rope, *Kestrel* stood seaward on the larboard tack.

Drinkwater turned to look for the lugger and was suddenly aware of her, huge and menacing ahead of them. He could see her three oddly raked masts with their vast spread of high peaked sails athwart their hawse and he was staring into the muzzles of her larboard broadside.

'Oh my God! She'll rake, sir, she'll rake!' he screamed aft, panic obscuring the knowledge that they had to stand on to clear the bay.

'Lie down!' Griffiths's rich voice cut through the fear and the men dropped obediently to the deck. Drinkwater threw himself behind the windlass, aware that of all the cutter's people he was the most forward. When the broadside came it was ragged and badly aimed. The lugger was luffing and unsteady but her guns took their

237

toll. The wind from a passing ball felt like a punch in the chest but Drinkwater rose quickly from his prone position, adrenalin pouring into his bloodstream, aware that the worst had passed. Other shots had struck home. Amidships a man was down. The lee runner and two stays were shot through and the mainsail was peppered with holes made by canister and two ball. Daylight would reveal another ball in the hull and the topsides cut up by more canister.

Griffiths had the helm himself now, holding his course, the bowsprit stabbing at the overhanging stern of the lugger as she drew out on the beam at point blank range. Drinkwater saw the captain of number 2 gun lower his match and his eyes lifted to watch the result of the discharge. As they crossed the stern of the lugger the priming spurted and the four-pounder roared. Not twenty feet away from him Drinkwater stared into the eyes of a tall Frenchman who stood one foot on the rail, grasping the mizen shrouds. Even in the darkness Drinkwater detected the commanding presence of the man who did not flinch as the ball tore past him. The two little ships were tossing in the rough sea and most of *Kestrel*'s shot passed harmlessly over the lugger, but the flashes and roar of their cannon, firing as they bore, were gratifying to the cutter's crew.

Kestrel cleared the lugger's stern and Drinkwater walked slowly aft as Griffiths bore away. 'Get a couple of pairs of dead-eyes and lanyards into that lee rigging Mr Jessup,' he said passing the bosun who was securing the guns. He said it absently, his mind full of the sight of that immobile Frenchman.

'Do you think she'll chase, sir?' he wearily asked Griffiths.

He was relieved to hear Griffiths's reply took notice of reality.

'Bound to, boy-o, and we must run. Now slip below and shift that wet gear. Major Brown is opening my cognac. Help yourself and then we'll trice up a little more canvas and see what she'll do.'

She did very well. She was still being chased at daylight by which time they had rigged preventer backstays, had the squaresails drawing and stunsails set to leeward. At eight bells in the morning watch Drinkwater logged eleven knots as the cutter staggered, her bow wave a mass of foam driving ahead of her. Aft, by the weather running backstay, Griffiths hummed a tune, never once looking astern. By mid afternoon they could see the white cliffs of Dover and the lugger had abandoned them. Leaving the deck to Jessup they dined with Major Brown.

'That *chasse marée* was the *Citoyenne Janine*, French National Lugger,' said Brown, hungrily devouring a slice of ham. 'She's at the disposal of an audacious bastard called Santhonax . . . By heaven Madoc, I thought they had me that time; Santhonax had clearly got wind of my departure and intended to cut you off.' He munched steadily and swallowed, gulping half a glass of brandy. 'They were after me within an hour of my leaving Paris . . . but for the skill and enterprise of your young friend here they would have succeeded.'

Drinkwater muttered something and helped himself to the ham, suddenly very hungry.

'Mr Drinkwater has done well, Major. You may assume he has my full confidence.'

Brown nodded. 'Damned well ought to have. Shameful trick you played on him that night last November.' They all grinned at the release from tension and the bottle went round, jealously guarded from *Kestrel*'s urgent, hurrying list.

'Excuse me, sir,' said Drinkwater, 'But how did you know the identity of the lugger? Did you see her commander?'

'Santhonax? Yes. That fellow standing at her stern. He don't command the vessel, it runs at his convenience. The French Ministry of Marine have given him a roving commission, not unlike my own,' he paused and tossed off his glass. 'I'll lay even money on his being as familiar with the lanes of Kent as any damned hop picker.' He shrugged, 'But I've no proof. Yet. You could tell the lugger was the *Citoyenne Janine*. Even in the dark you could see the black swallowtail flag. For some reason Santhonax likes to fly it, some bit of damned Celtic nonsense. Sorry Madoc, no offence.'

Drinkwater had not seen the flag but he wondered at the recondite nature of Brown's knowledge. He did not yet appreciate the major's capacity for apparently trifling details.

'It's going to be a bloody long war, Madoc,' continued the major. 'I can tell you this, the god-damned Yankees are involved. We'll fight them again yet, you see. They've promised the Frogs vast quantities of grain. Place would starve without their help, and the revolutionaries'll make trouble in Ireland . . . that'll be no secret in a month or two.' He paused frowning, gathering words suitable to

239

convey the enormity of his news and Drinkwater was reminded of Appleby. 'They're going to carry their bloody flag right through Europe, mark my words . . .' He helped himself to another slice of ham. Drinkwater knew now why the man had appeared so jovial all those months ago. He himself felt the desire to chatter like Brown, as a reaction to the events of the night before. How much worse for Brown after that terrible isolation. Once ashore he would have to be circumspect but here, aboard *Kestrel*, he occupied neutral ground, was among friends. He emptied his glass for the fourth time and Griffiths refilled it.

'Did you get Barrallier out?' Brown asked settling back and addressing Drinkwater.

'Yes, sir, we picked him up at Beaubigny.'

'Beaubigny?' Brown looked startled and frowned. 'Where the devil's that? I arranged for Criel.' He looked at Griffiths who explained the location.

'I protested, Major, but two aristos had Dungarth's ear, see.'

Brown nodded, his eyes cold slits that in such a rubicund face seemed quite ugly.

'And one was a, er, misanthrope, eh?'

Griffiths and Drinkwater both nodded. 'And was De Tocqueville with Barrallier?'

'Yes,' said Griffiths, 'with a deal of specie too.' Brown nodded and relapsed into thought during which Drinkwater heard him say musingly 'Beaubigny . . .'

At last he looked up, a slightly puzzled expression on his face as though the answer was important. 'Was there a girl with them?' he asked, 'a girl with auburn hair?'

'That's correct, sir,' put in Drinkwater, 'with her brother, Etienne.'

Brown's eyebrows rose. 'So you know their names?'

'Aye, sir, they were called Montholon.' It seemed odd that Brown, a master of secrets should evince surprise at what was common gossip on Plymouth hard. 'Barrallier told us, sir,' continued Drinkwater, 'it did not seem a matter for secrecy.'

'Ha!' Brown threw back his head and laughed, a short, barking laugh like a fox. 'Good for Barrallier,' he said half for himself. 'No, 'tis no secret, but I am surprised at the girl leaving . . .' A silence fell over the three of them.

Brown ruminated upon the pieces of a puzzle that were beginning to fit. He had not known that it had been *Kestrel* that had caused the furore off Carteret, but he had been fortuitously close to the row that had erupted in Paris and well knew how close as a cause of war the incident had become. *Childers*'s comparatively innocent act had been just what the war hawks needed, having stayed their hands a month or so earlier.

The major closed his eyes, recalling some fascinating details. *Capitaine de frégate* Edouard Santhonax had been instrumental in checking the Convention's belligerence. And apart from the previous night, the last time Brown had seen Santhonax, the handsome captain had had Hortense Montholon gracing his arm. She had not seemed like a woman fleeing from revolution.

Lieutenant Griffiths watched his passenger, aware of mystery in the air and hunting back over the conversation to find its cause, while Drinkwater was disturbed by a vision of auburn hair and fine grey eyes.

Chapter Five

Incident off Ushant

In the weeks that followed Drinkwater almost forgot about the incident at Beaubigny, the rescue of Major Brown and the subsequent encounter with the *chasse marée*. Occasionally, on dark nights when the main cabin was lit by the swinging lantern, there appeared a ghost of disquieting beauty and auburn hair. And that half drowned sensation, as Tregembo hauled him through the breakers with the dead weight of the major threatening to drag them both to the bottom, emerged periodically to haunt half-awake hours trying to sleep. But they were mere shades, thrown off with full consciousness together with recollections of the swamps of Carolina and memories of Morris, the sodomite tyrant of *Cyclops*'s cockpit.

The spectre of the fugitives of Beaubigny appeared once in more positive form, revived by Griffiths. It was only a brief item in an already yellowing newspaper concerned with the death of a French nobleman in the gutters of St James's. Footpads were suspected as the gentleman's purse was missing and he was known to have been lucky at the tables that evening. But the man's name was De Tocqueville and Griffiths's raised eyebrow over the lowered paper communicated to Drinkwater a suspicion of assassination.

Such speculations were swept aside by duty. Already the Channel was full of French corsairs, from luggers to frigates, which commenced that war on trade at which they excelled. Into this mêlée of French commerce-raiders and British merchantmen, solitary British frigates dashed, noisily inadequate. Then on 18th June Pellew in *La Nymphe* took *Cleopâtre* off the Start and his knighthood sent a quiver of ambition down many an aspiring naval spine.

Kestrel, meanwhile, attended to more mundane matters, carrying despatches, fresh vegetables, mail and gossip to and from the detached cruisers, a maid of all work that fled from strong opposition and struck at weaker foes. Pellew took some men from her to supplement his crew of Cornish tin miners, despite Griffiths's protest, but they suffered only twice from this abuse. *Kestrel*'s people, mostly volunteers, were a superlative crew, worthy of a flagship under the most punctilious admiral.

'Better'n aught the Cumberland Fleet can offer,' Jessup claimed with pride, alluding to the Thames yachts that made a fetish of such niceties as sail drill. Griffiths too reserved an approbatory twinkle in his eye for a smart manoeuvre executed under the envious glare of a frigate captain still struggling with a crew of landsmen. He could imagine the remarks on a score of quarterdecks about the 'damned insolence of unrated buggers'.

Amid this activity Drinkwater was aware that he was part of a happy ship, that Griffiths rarely flogged, nor had need to, and that these were halcyon days.

Whatever his misgivings about his future they were hidden from the taut deck of the cutter and reserved for the solitude of his cabin. The demands of watch and watch, the tension of chase or flight and the modest profits on prizes were in part compensation for the lack of prospects on his own, personal horizon.

December found them off the low island of Ushant cruising in search of Warren with the news that the commodore's squadron, after many delays and dockyard prevarications, would assemble under his command at Falmouth in the New Year.

It was a day of easterly wind which washed the air clear of the damp westerlies that had dogged them through the fall. Depression had followed depression across the Atlantic, eight weeks in which *Kestrel* had sought her principals under the greatest difficulties, her people wet and miserable, her canvas sodden and hard, her galley stove mostly extinguished.

The bright sunlight lay like a benefice upon the little ship so that she seemed reborn, changing men's moods, the skylarking crew a different company. Damp clothing appeared in the weather rigging giving her a gipsy air.

The low island that marked the western extremity of France lay astern on the larboard quarter and from time to time Drinkwater took a bearing of the lighthouse on the rising ground of Cape Stiff. He was interrupted in one such operation by a hail from the masthead: 'Deck there! Sail to windward!'

'Pass the word for the captain.'

'Aye, aye, sir.'

Griffiths hurried on deck, took a look at the island and the masthead pendant streaming over the starboard quarter in the easterly wind. 'Up you go Mr Drinkwater.' Agilely Drinkwater ascended the mast, throwing a leg over the topgallant yard. He needed but a single glance to tell him it was not *Flora* and to confirm a suspicion he knew he shared with Griffiths consequent upon the easterly breeze. The great naval arsenal of Brest lay ahead of them. The sail he was looking at had slipped down the Goulet that morning. Beyond he could see another.

'Two frigates, sir,' he said reaching the deck, 'bearing down on us and making sail.'

Griffiths nodded. 'Mr Jessup!' He cast about for the boatswain who was hurrying on deck, struggling into his coat. 'Sir?'

'We'll put her before the wind, I want preventer backstays and every stitch she'll carry. Mr Drinkwater, a course clear of the Pierres Vertes to open the Fromveur Passage . . .' He issued more orders as the hands tumbled up but Drinkwater was already scrambling below to consult the chart.

The Île d'Ouessant, or Ushant to countless generations of British seamen, lies some thirteen miles west of the Brittany coast. Between the island and Point St Matthew a confused litter of rocks, islets and reefs existed, delineated within a pecked line on the cutter's chart as: 'numerous dangerous shoals, rocks, and Co wherein are unpredictable tide rips and overfalls.' Even in the mildest of weather the area is subject to Atlantic swells and the ceaseless run of the tide which at springs reaches a rate of seven and a half knots. When the wind and tide are in opposition they generate a high, vicious and dangerous sea. At best the tide rips and overfalls rendered the area impossible to navigation. So great were the dangers in the locality as a whole that a special treaty had been drawn up between England and France that provided for the latter country to maintain a lighthouse on Point Stiff 'in war as in peace, for the general benefit of

244

humanity'. This tower had been erected a century earlier to a design by Vauban on the highest point of the island.

Two passages run through the rocks between Ushant and the mainland. The Chenal du Four, a tortuous gut between St Matthew and Le Four rocks, while the Fromveur lies along the landward side of Ushant itself. It was the latter that Drinkwater now studied.

As he pored over the chart Drinkwater felt the sudden increase of speed that followed the clatter, shudder and heel of the gybe. *Kestrel* thrust through the water responsive to the urgency felt by her commander. Bracing himself he slipped into his own cabin and took from the bookshelf a stained notebook. It had once belonged to Mr Blackmore, sailing master of the frigate *Cyclops*. He riffled through the pages, finding what he was looking for, his brow frowning in concentration. He looked again at the chart, a copy of an early French survey. The litter of dangers worried him, yet the Fromveur itself looked straight and deep. He cursed the lack of Admiralty enterprise that relied on commanders purchasing their own charts. Even *Kestrel*, employed as she had been on special service, received no more than an allowance so that Griffiths could have only what he could purchase.

Drinkwater went on deck. Ushant was on the starboard bow now and a glance astern showed the nearer frigate closing them fast. The sooner they got into the Fromveur and out-performed her the better. Drinkwater recalled Barrallier's superior air, his confidence in the sailing qualities of French frigates and his astonishment at finding Griffiths navigating the French coast on obsolete charts: the old government of France had established a chart office more than seventy years earlier, he had said.

A feeling of urgency surged through him as he bent over the compass, rushing below to lay off the bearings. Already the Channel flood had swept them too far to the north, pushing them relentlessly towards the rocks and reefs to starboard. He hurried back on deck and was about to request Griffiths turn south when another hail reached the deck.

'Breakers on the starboard bow!'

Jessup started for the mainsheet. 'Stand by to gybe!' he shouted. By gybing again *Kestrel* could stem the tide and clear the rocks by making southing. The men were already at their stations, looking expectantly aft, awaiting the order from Griffiths.

'Belay that, Mr Jessup . . . Are they the Pierres Vertes, Mr Drinkwater?'

'Yes, sir.' Griffiths could see the surge of white water with an occasional glimpse of black, revealing the presence of the outcrops. To gain southing would allow the frigate to close.

'Steer nor' west . . . harden your sheets a trifle, Mr Jessup . . . Mr Drinkwater, I'm going inside . . .' His voice was calm, reassuring, as though there was no imminent decision to be taken. Drinkwater was diverted by the appearance of a shot hole in the topgallant, a ball smacked into the taffrail, sending splinters singing across the deck. A seaman was hit, a long sliver of pitch pine raising a terrible lancing wound. They had no surgeon to attend him.

To clear the reef the French frigate had altered to larboard, her course slightly diverging from that of the cutter so that a bow gun would bear. The smoke of her fire hung under her bow, driven by the following wind.

'Steer small, damn your eyes,' Griffiths growled at the helmsman. Drinkwater joined him in mental exercises in triangulation. They knew they must hold *Kestrel* close to the Pierres Vertes to avoid the tide setting them too far to the north on to the Roche du Loup, the Roche du Reynard and the reefs between; to avoid the temptation of running into clear water where the dangers were just submerged.

The Pierres Vertes were close now, under the bow. The surge and undertow of the sea could be felt as the tide eddied round them. *Kestrel* staggered in her onward progress then, suddenly, the rocks lay astern. A ragged cheer came from the men on deck who were aware that their ship had just survived a crisis.

The relief was short lived.

'Deck there! Sail to starboard, six points on the bow!' Drinkwater could see her clearly from the deck. A small frigate or corvette reaching down the Passage Du Fromveur, unnoticed in their preoccupation with the rocks but barring their escape.

'Take that lookout's name, Mr Drinkwater, I'll have the hide off him for negligence . . .'

Another hole aloft and several splashes alongside. One ball ricochetted off the side of a wave and thumped, half spent, into the hull. They were neatly trapped.

Drinkwater looked at Griffiths. The elderly Welshman bore a

countenance of almost stoic resignation in which Drinkwater perceived defeat. True, *Kestrel* might manoeuvre but it would only be out of form, out of respect for the flag. It was unlikely she would escape. Griffiths was an old man, he had run out of resolution; exhausted his share of good fortune. He seemed to know this as a beaten animal slinks away to die. To surrender a twelve-gun cutter to superior force would be no dishonour.

As if to emphasise their predicament the new jolly boat, stowed in the stem davits, disintegrated in an explosion of splinters, the transom boards of the cutter split inwards and a ball bounced off the breech of No 11 gun, dismounting it with an eerie clang and whined off distorted over the starboard rail.

'Starboard broadside make ready!' Griffiths braced himself. 'Mr Drinkwater, strike the colours after we've fired. Mr Jessup we'll luff up and d'you clew up the square sails . . .'

A mood of sullen resignation swept the deck like a blast of canister, visible in its impact. It irritated Drinkwater into a sudden fury. A long war Appleby had said, a long war pent up in a French hulk dreaming of Elizabeth. The thought was violently abhorrent to him. Griffiths might be exchanged under cartel but who was going to give a two-penny drum for an unknown master's mate? They would luff, fire to defend the honour of the flag and then strike to the big frigate foaming up astern.

Ironic that they would come on the wind to do so. Reaching the only point of sailing on which they might escape their pursuers. If, that is, the rocks were not there barring their way.

Then an idea struck him. So simple, yet so dangerous that he realised it had been bubbling just beneath conscious acceptance since he looked at the notebook of old Blackmore's. It was better than abject surrender.

'Mr Griffiths!' Griffiths turned.

'I told you to stand by the ensign halliards . . .'

'Mr Griffiths I believe we could escape through the rocks, sir. There's a passage between the two islands . . .' He pointed to the two islets on the starboard beam; the Îles de Bannec and de Balanec. Griffiths looked at them, uncertainty in his eyes. He glanced astern. Drinkwater pressed his advantage. 'The chart's old, sir. I've a more recent survey in a manuscript book . . .'

'Get it!' snapped Griffiths, suddenly shedding his mood with his age. Drinkwater needed no second bidding and rushed below, stumbling in his haste. He snatched up Blackmore's old, stained journal and clambered back on deck where a pale, tense hope was alive on the faces of the men, Jessup had the hands aloft and the squaresails were coming in. A party of men was busily lashing the dismounted four pounder. Griffiths, now indifferent to the two ships closing ahead and astern like the jaws of pincers, was examining the gap between the two islands.

'Here sir . . .' Drinkwater spread the book on the companionway top and for a minute he and Griffiths bent over it, Drinkwater's finger tracing a narrow gutway through the reefs. A muttering of Welsh escaped the old man and then Drinkwater made out: 'Men ar Reste . . . Carrec ar Morlean . . .' He pronounced it 'carreg' in the Welsh rather than the Breton, as he stared at the outlying rocks that strewed the passage Drinkwater was suggesting, like fangs waiting for the eager keel of *Kestrel*.

'Can you get her through?' he asked shortly.

'I'll try, sir. With bearings and a lookout at the cross trees.'

Griffiths made up his mind. 'Put her on the chart.' He called one of the seamen over to hold the book open and stand by it. Drinkwater bent over the compass, his heart pounding with excitement. Behind him a transformed Griffiths rapped out orders.

'Mr Jessup! I'm going through the rocks. D'you attend to the set of the sails to get the best out of her . . .'

'Aye, aye, sir.' Jessup bustled off and his action seemed to electrify the upper deck. Men jumped eagerly to belaying pins, stood expectantly beside sheets and runners, while the helmsmen watched their commander, ready at a word to fling their weight on the great curved ash tiller.

There was a crash amidships and the pump trunking flew apart, the wrought arm bending impossibly. Yet another ball thumped into the hull and a glance astern showed the frigate huge and menacing. No more than two miles ahead of them the corvette, her main topsail to the mast, lay in their track. Drinkwater straightened from his extempore chart table.

'East, nor'east, sir, upon the instant . . .'

Griffiths nodded. 'Down helm! Full and bye! Heads'l sheets there!

248

You there!' he pointed at Number 12 gun's crew, '. . . a knife to that preventer backstay.' *Kestrel* came on to the wind, spray bursting over the weather bow. Drinkwater looked into the compass bowl and nodded, then he ran forward. 'Tregembo! Aloft there and watch for rocks, tide rips and guns . . .' and then, remembering the man's smuggling past from a gleam of exhilaration in his eye, 'The tide's in our favour, under us . . . I need to know bloody fast . . .'

'Aye, aye, zur!' The windward shrouds were bar taut and Drinkwater followed halfway up. Though fresh, the wind had little fetch here and they ought to see tidal runs on the rocks. He bit his lip with anxiety. It was well after low water now and *Kestrel* was rushing north-eastwards on a young flood.

'Run, zur, fine to starboard . . .' Tregembo pointed. 'And another to larboard . . .' Drinkwater gained the deck and rushed aft to bend over the chart. Four and a half fathoms over the Basse Blanche to starboard and less than one over the Melbian to larboard.

'Can you lay her a little closer, sir?' Griffiths nodded, his mouth a tight line. Drinkwater went forward again and began to climb the rigging. As he hoisted himself alongside Tregembo, his legs dangling, a terrific roar filled the air. The glass, the Dollond glass which he had just taken from his pocket, was wrenched from his hand and his whole body was buffeted as it had been in the breakers the night they picked up Major Brown. He saw the glass twinkle once as the sunlight glanced off it, then he too pitched forward, helpless as a rag doll. He felt a strong hand clutch his upper arm. Tregembo hauled him back on the yard while below them both the little telescope bounced on a deadeye and disappeared into the white water sluicing past *Kestrel*'s trembling side.

Drinkwater drew breath. Looking aft he saw the big frigate turning south away from them, cheated of her prey, the smoke from her starboard broadside drifting away. Across her stern he could see the letters of her name: *Sirène*. She would give them the other before standing away to the south-south-eastward on the larboard tack.

Drinkwater turned to Tregembo. 'Thank you for your assistance,' he muttered, annoyed at the loss of his precious glass. He stared ahead, ignoring the corvette obscured by the peak of the straining mainsail and unaware of the final broadside from *Sirène*.

White water was all around them now, the two green-grey islets of Bannec and Balanec, rapidly opening on either bow. The surge and suck of the tide revealed rocks everywhere, the water foaming white around the reefs. Ahead of them he could see no gap, no passage.

Hard on the wind *Kestrel* plunged onwards, driven inexorably by the tide which was running swiftly now. Suddenly ahead he could see the hummock of a black rock: the Ar Veoe lay dead in their path. Patiently he forced himself to line it up with the forestay. If the rock drew left of the stay it would pass clear to larboard, if to the right they would clear it to starboard but run themselves into danger beyond. If it remained in transit they would strike it.

The dark bulk of the Men ar Reste drew abeam and passed astern. Ar Veoe remained in transit and on either hand the reefs surrounding the two islets closed in, relative motion lending them a locomotion of their own.

Twisting round Drinkwater hailed the deck: 'She's not weathering the Ar Veoe, sir!' He watched as Griffiths looked at the book. They *had* to pass to the east of that granite stump. They could not run to leeward or they would be cast on the Île de Bannec and irrevocably lost.

The gap was lessening and the bearing remained unaltered. They would have to tack. Reaching for a backstay Drinkwater slid to the deck. Ignoring the smarting of his hands he accosted Griffiths.

'She's getting to loo'ard. We must tack, sir, immediately . . . there is no option.' Griffiths did not acknowledge his subordinate but raised his head and bawled.

'Stand by to go about! Look lively there!'

The men, tuned now to the high pitch of their officers, obeyed with flattering alacrity. '*Myndiawl*, I hope you know what you're doing,' he growled at Drinkwater. 'Get back aloft and when we've sufficient offing wave your right arm . . .' His voice was mellow with controlled tension, all trace of defeat absent, replaced with a taut confidence in Drinkwater. Briefly their eyes met and each acknowledged in the other the rarefied excitement of their predicament, a balance of expertise and terror.

By the time Drinkwater reached the crosstrees what had been the weather rigging was slack. *Kestrel* had tacked smartly and now her bowsprit stabbed south-east as she crabbed across the channel, the tide still carrying her north-east. Drinkwater had hardly marshalled his senses when instinct screamed at him to wave his right arm. Obediently the helm went down and beneath him the yard trembled with the mast as the cutter passed through the wind again.

Kestrel had barely steadied on the starboard tack as the hummocked, fissured slab of the Ar Veoe rushed past. The white swirl of the tide tugged the weed at its base and a dozen cormorants, hitherto sunning their wings, flapped away low over the sea. On either side danger was clearly visible. The Carrec ar Morlean lay on the starboard quarter, the outcrops of the Île de Bannec to larboard. *Kestrel* rushed at the gap, her bowsprit plunging aggressively forward. The rocks drew abeam and Drinkwater slid to the deck to lay another position on the makeshift chart. Griffiths peered over his shoulder. They were almost through, a final gap had to be negotiated as the Gourgant Rocks opened up to starboard. Cannon shot had long since ceased and the hostile ships astern were forgotten as the beginnings of relief showed in their eyes. The Gourgants drew astern and merged with the seemingly impenetrable barrier of black rock and white water through which they had just passed.

'Deck there!' It was Tregembo, still aloft at his post. 'Rock dead ahead and close zur!' Griffiths's reaction was instinctive: 'Up helm!'

Drinkwater was halfway up the starboard shrouds when he saw it. *Kestrel* had eased off the wind a point but was far too close. Although her bowsprit swung away from the rock the run of the tide pushed her stern round so that a brief vision of rending timber and a rudderless hulk flashed across Drinkwater's imagination. He faced aft and screamed 'Down helm!'

For a split second he thought Griffiths was going to ignore him, that his insubordination was too great. Then, shaking with relief he saw the lieutenant lunge across the deck, pushing the tiller to larboard.

Kestrel began to turn as the half-submerged rock rushed at her. It was too late. Drinkwater was trembling uncontrollably now, a fly in a web of rigging. He watched fascinated, aware that in ten, fifteen seconds perhaps, the shrouds to which he clung would hang in slack festoons as the cutter's starboard side was stove, the mast snapped like celery and she rolled over, a broken wreck. Below him men rushed to the side to watch: then the tide took her. *Kestrel* trembled, her quarter lifting on the wave made against the up-tide side of the rock, then swooped into the down-tide trough as the sea cast her aside like a piece of driftwood. They could see bladder wrack and smell bird droppings and then they were past, spewed out to the northward. A few moments later the Basse Pengloch, northern post of the Île de Bannec, was behind them.

Shaking still, Drinkwater regained the deck. 'We're through sir.' Relief translated itself into a grin made foolish by blood trickling from a hard-bitten lip.

'Aye, Mr Drinkwater we're through, and I desire you to pass word to issue grog to all hands.'

'Deck there!' For a second they froze, apprehension on their faces, fearing another outcrop ahead of them; but Tregembo was pointing astern.

When he descended again to return the borrowed telescope to Griffiths, Drinkwater said, 'The two frigates and the corvette are still hull up, sir, but beyond them are a number of tops'ls. It looks as if we have just escaped from a fleet.'

Griffiths raised a white eyebrow. 'Indeed . . . in that case let us forget *Flora*, Mr Drinkwater, and take our intelligence home. Lay me a course for Plymouth.'

'Aye, aye, sir,' Drinkwater turned away. Already the excitement of the past two hours was fading, giving way to a peevish vexation at the loss of his Dollond glass.

Chapter Six

A Night Attack

What neither Griffiths nor Drinkwater knew was that the frigates from which they had escaped off Ushant had been part of Admiral Vanstabel's fleet. The admiral was on passage to America to re-inforce the French squadron sent thither to escort the grain convoy safely back to France. The importance of this convoy to the ruined economy of the Republic and the continued existence of its govern-ment had been brought to British notice by Major Brown.

Vanstabel eluded pursuit but as spring of 1794 approached the British Admiralty sent out the long awaited flying squadrons. That to which *Kestrel* was attached was under the command of Sir John Borlase Warren whose broad pendant flew in the 42-gun frigate *Flora*. Warren's frigates hunted in the approaches to the Channel, sometimes in a pack, sometimes detached. *Kestrel*'s duties were unimaginatively recorded in her log as 'vessel variously employed'. She might run orders from *Flora* to another frigate, returning with intelligence. She might be sent home to Falmouth with despatches, rejoining the squadron with mail, orders, a new officer, her boats full of cabbages and bags of potatoes, sacks of onions stowed between her guns.

It was a busy time for her company. Their constant visits to Falmouth reminded Drinkwater of Elizabeth whom he had first met there in 1780 and the view from Carrick Road was redolent of nos-talgia. But he enjoyed no respite for the chills of January precipitated Griffiths's malaria and while his commander lay uncomplaining in his cot, sweating and half-delirious, Drinkwater, by express instruc-tion, managed the cutter without informing his superiors.

Griffiths's recovery was slow, interspersed with relapses. Drinkwater assumed the virtual command of the cutter unopposed.

Jessup, like all her hands, had been impressed by the acting lieutenant's resource in the escape from Vanstabel's frigates. 'He'll do all right, will Mr Drinkwater,' was his report to Johnson, the carpenter. And Tregembo further enhanced Drinkwater's reputation with the story of the retaking of the *Algonquin* in the American War. The Cornishman's loyalty was as touching as it was infectious.

Unbeknown to Warren, Drinkwater had commanded *Kestrel* during the action of St George's Day. Fifteen miles west of the Roches Douvres Warren's squadron had engaged a similar French force under Commodore Desgareaux. At the time Warren had with him the yacht-like *Arethusa* commanded by Sir Edward Pellew, *Concorde* and *Melampus*, with the unspritely *Nymphe* in the offing and unable to come up in time.

During the battle *Kestrel* acted as Warren's repeating vessel, a duty requiring strict attention both to the handling of the cutter and the accuracy of her signals. That Drinkwater accomplished it shorthanded was not known to Warren. Indeed no mention was even made of *Kestrel*'s presence in the account published in the *Gazette*. But Warren did not diminish his own triumph. Commodore Desgareaux's *Engageante* had been taken, shattered beyond redemption, while the corvette *Babet* and the beautiful frigate *Pomone* were both purchased into the Royal Navy. Only the *Resolue* had escaped into Morlaix, outsailing a pursuit in which *Kestrel* had played a small part.

'No mention of us sir,' said Drinkwater dejectedly as he finished reading Warren's despatch from the *Gazette*.

'No way to earn a commission is it, eh?' Griffiths commiserated, reading Drinkwater's mind as they shared a bottle over the newspaper. He looked ruefully at his subordinate's set face.

'Never mind Mr Drinkwater. Your moment will yet come. I met Sir Sydney Smith in the dockyard. He at least had heard we tried to cut off the *Resolue*.' Griffiths sipped from his glass and added conversationally, '*Diamond* is at last joining the squadron, so we will have an eccentric brain to set beside the commodore's square one. What d'you think of that then?'

Drinkwater shrugged, miserable with the knowledge that Elizabeth was not far from their mooring at Haslar creek and that the addition of *Diamond* to the squadron opened opportunities for Richard White. 'I don't know, sir. What do you predict?'

'Stratagems,' said Griffiths in a richly imitated English that made Drinkwater smile, cracking the preoccupation with his own misfortune, 'stratagems, Sir Sydney is the very devil for audacity . . .'

'Well gentlemen?' Warren's strong features, thrown into bold relief by the lamplight, looked up from the chart. He was flanked by Pellew, Nagle of the *Artois* and the irrepressibly dominating Smith whose bright eyes darted restlessly over the lesser officers: *Flora*'s first lieutenant and sailing master, her lieutenant of marines and his own second lieutenant who was winking at a slightly older man, a man in the shadows, among his superiors on sufferance.

'Any questions?' Warren pursued the forms relentlessly. The three post captains shook their heads.

'Very well. Sir Ed'd, then, leads the attack . . . Captain Nagle joins me offshore: the only problem is *Kestrel* . . .' They all looked at the man in the shadows. He was not so young, thought Sir Sydney, the face was experienced. He felt an arm on his sleeve and bent his ear. Lieutenant Richard White whispered something and Sir Sydney again scrutinised the acting lieutenant in the plain blue coat. Warren went on: 'I think one of my own lieutenants should relieve Griffiths . . .' Smith watched the mouth of the man clamp in a hard line. He was reminded of a live shell.

'Come, come, Sir John, I am sure Mr Drinkwater is capable of executing his orders to perfection. I am informed he did very well in your action in April. Let's give him a chance, eh?' He missed the look of gratitude from the grey eyes. Warren swivelled sideways. 'What d'you think Ed'd?'

Pellew was well-known for promoting able men almost as much as practising shameless nepotism when it suited him. 'Oh give him some rope, John, then he can hang himself or fashion a pretty bowline for us all to admire.' Pellew turned to Drinkwater. 'How is the worthy Griffiths these days, mister?'

'Recovering, Sir Edward. Sir John was kind enough to have his surgeon repair his stock of quinine.'

Warren was not mollified by this piece of tact and continued to look at Drinkwater with a jaundiced eye. He was well aware that both Smith and Pellew had protégés of their own and suspected their support of a neutral was to block the advancement of his own candidate. At last he sighed. 'Very well.'

Sir John Warren's Western Squadron had been in almost continual action during that summer while Admiral Howe's desultory blockade conducted from the comfort of an anchorage at Spithead or Torbay found many critics. Nevertheless the advocates of the strategic advantages of close blockade could not fail to be impressed by the dash and spirit of the frigates, albeit with little effect on the progress of the war. There had been a fleet action too: the culmination of days of manoeuvring had come on the 'Glorious First of June' when, in mid-Atlantic, Earl Howe had beaten Villaret Joyeuse and carried away several prizes from the French line of battle. Despite this apparently dazzling success no naval officer aware of the facts could fail to acknowledge that the victory was a strategic defeat. The grain convoy that Villaret Joyeuse protected and that Vanstabel had succoured, arrived unmolested in France.

Alongside that the tactical successes in the Channel were of little importance, though they read well in the periodicals, full of flamboyant dash and enterprise. Corrosive twinges of envy settled round Drinkwater's heart as he read of his own squadron's activities. Lieutenant White had been mentioned twice, through the patronage of Smith, for Warren was notoriously parsimonious with praise. It was becoming increasingly clear to Drinkwater that, without similar patronage, his promotion to lieutenant, when it came, would be too late; that he would end up the superannuated relic he had jestingly suggested to Elizabeth.

Yet he was eager to take part in the operation proposed that evening aboard *Flora*, eager to seize any opportunity to distinguish himself and guiltily grateful to White whose prompting of Smith's intervention had clearly diverted Warren's purpose.

Six months after his defeat Villaret Joyeuse was known to be preparing to slip out of Brest once more. Cruising westward from St Malo *Diamond* had discovered a convoy of two storeships being escorted by a brig-corvette and a *chasse marée*, an armed lugger. Aware of the presence of Warren's squadron in the offing they made passage at night, sheltering under batteries at anchor during daylight.

The weather had been quiet, though the night of the attack was heavily overcast, the clouds seeming to clear the mastheads with difficulty like a waterlogged ceiling, bulging and imminent in their descent. The south-westerly wind was light but had a steadiness that foreshadowed a blow, while the slight sea rippled over a low, ominous swell that indicated a disturbance far to the west.

With Griffiths sick, Drinkwater and Jessup felt the want of more officers but for the descent on the convoy they had only to keep station on *Diamond*, Sir Sydney having left a single lantern burning in his cabin for the purpose. Just visible to the westward was the dark bulk of *Arethusa*.

Drinkwater went below. The air in the cabin was stale, smelling sweetly of heavy perspiration. Griffiths lay in his cot, propped up, one eye regarding Nathaniel as he bent over the chart. The acting lieutenant was scratching his scar, lost in thought. After a while their eyes met.

'Ah, sir, you are awake . . . a glass of water . . .' He poured a tumblerful and noted Griffiths's hands barely shook as he lifted it to his lips. 'Well Mr Drinkwater?'

'Well, sir, we're closing on a small convoy to attack a brig-corvette, two transports and a lugger . . . we're in company with *Arethusa* and *Diamond*.'

'And the plan?'

'Well sir, *Arethusa* is to engage the brig, *Diamond* will take the two transports – she has most of *Arethusa*'s marines for the purpose – and we will take the lugger.'

'Is she an armed lugger, a *chasse marée*?'

'I believe so sir, my friend Lieutenant White was of the opinion that she was. *Diamond* reconnoitred the enemy . . .' He tailed off, aware that Griffiths's opinion of White was distorted by understandable prejudice.

'The only opinion that young man had which was of the slightest value might more properly be attended by fashion-conscious young women . . .' Drinkwater smiled, disinclined to argue the point. Still, it was odd that a man of Griffiths's considerable wisdom could so misjudge. White was typical of his type, professionally competent, gauche and arrogant upon occasion but ruthless and brave.

Griffiths recalled him to the present. 'She'll be stuffed full of men,

Nathaniel, you be damned careful, the French overman to the extent we sail shorthanded . . . What have you in mind to attempt?' Griffiths struggled on to one elbow. 'It had better convince me, otherwise I'll not allow you to carry it out.'

Drinkwater swallowed. This was a damned inconvenient moment for a return of the old man's faculties. 'Well sir, Sir John has approved . . .'

'Damn Sir John, Nathaniel. Don't prevaricate. The question is do *I* approve it?'

Six paces forward, six paces aft. Up and down, up and down, *Diamond*'s bell chiming the half hours until it was several minutes overdue. 'Light's out in *Diamond*'s cabin, sir.' It was Nicholls, the poor lookout, sent aft to interrupt Drinkwater's train of thought.

Smith was to signal which side of *Diamond* the *Kestrel* was to pass as soon as his officers, from the loftier height of her foremast, made out the enemy dispositions. 'Call all hands, there, all hands to general quarters!'

Minutes passed, then: 'Two lights, sir!'

So it was to larboard, to the eastward that they were to go. He gave his orders. Course was altered and the sheets trimmed. They began to diverge and pass the frigate, shaking out the reef that had held them back while *Diamond* shortened sail. Giving the men a few moments to make their preparations Drinkwater slipped below.

'Enemy's in sight, sir . . .' Griffiths opened his eyes. His features were sunk, yellow in the lamplight, like old parchment. But the voice that came from him was still resonant. 'Be careful, boy-o,' he said with almost paternal affection, raising a wasted hand over the rim of the cot. Drinkwater shook it in an awkward, delicate way. 'Take my pistols there, on the settee . . .' Drinkwater checked the pans. 'They're all ready, Nathaniel, primed and ready,' the old man said behind him. He stuck them in his belt and left the cabin. On deck he buckled on his sword and went round the hands. The men were attentive, drawing aside as he approached, muttering 'good lucks' amongst themselves and assuring him they knew what to do. As he walked aft again a new mood swept over him. He no longer envied White. He was in a goodly company, knew these men well now, had been accepted by them as their leader. A tremendous feeling of exhilaration coursed through him so strongly that for a moment he remained staring aft, picking out the pale streak of their wake while he recovered himself. Then he thought of Elizabeth, her kiss and parting remark: 'Be careful, my love . . .' So like Griffiths's and tonight so enormously relevant. He was on the verge of breaking that old promise of circumspection and giving way to recklessness. Then, unhidden, a fragment of long past conversation rose like flotsam on the whirlpool of his brain. 'I have heard it said,' Appleby had averred, 'that a man who fails to feel fear when going into action is usually wounded . . . as though some nervous defence is destroyed by reckless passion which in itself presages misfortune . . .'

Drinkwater swallowed hard and walked forward. Mindful of his sword and the loaded pistols in his belt, he began to slowly ascend the rigging, staring ahead for a sight of the enemy.

'Make ready! Make ready there!' The word was passed in sibilantly urgent whispers. 'Aft there, steer two points to larboard! Larboard guns train as far forrard as you can!'

And then the need for silence was gone as, a mile west of them a ragged line of fire erupted into the night where one of the frigates loosed off her broadside. The rolling thunder of her discharge came downwind to them.

Drinkwater could see the lugger clearly now. He stood on the rail, one hand round the huge running backstay. She was beating up to cover a barque, presumably one of the storeships. He ordered the course altered a little more and noted where the sheets were trimmed.

At three hundred yards the lugger opened fire, revealing herself as a well-served *chasse marée* of about ten guns. Drinkwater held his fire.

'When your guns bear, open fire.' Men tensed in the darkness as he said: 'Luff her!'

Kestrel's sails shivered as she turned into the wind. The crash and recoiling rumble of the guns exploded down her larboard side. Forward a bosun's mate had the jib backed, forcing the cutter on to her former tack. As she closed the *chasse marée* Drinkwater studied his opponent for damage, wondering if the specially prepared broadside had done anything.

It was impossible to say for certain but he heard shouts and screams and already his own gun captains were reporting themselves ready. He waited for Jessup commanding the battery. 'All ready Mr Drinkwater!'

'Luff her!'

A hundred yards range now and a flash and crash, a scream and a flurry of bodies where the Frenchman's broadside struck, then *Kestrel* fired back and steadied for the final assault on the enemy. As the last few yards were eaten up Drinkwater was aware of a furious exchange of fire where *Arethusa* and the brig-corvette engaged; then he snapped: 'Boarders!'

The cutter was gathering way, heading straight for the lugger. The French commander was no sluggard and sought to rake her. A storm of shot swept *Kestrel*'s deck. Grape and langridge forced Drinkwater's eyes tight shut as the whine and wind of its passing whistled about him. Thumps, shouts and screams forced his eyes open again. Soon they must run on board of the lugger . . . would the distance never lessen?

He could hear shouts of alarm coming from the Frenchman then he felt the deck tremble under his feet as *Kestrel*'s bowsprit went over the lugger's rail with a twanging of the bobstay. Then the deck heeled as a rending crash told where her stem bit into the enemy's chains and *Kestrel* slewed round. The guns fired again as they bore and the two hulls jarred together.

'Boarders away!'

The noise that came from forward was of a different tenor now as the Kestrels left their guns and swept over the rail. Forward and aft lashings were caught round the lugger's rufftree rail and the two ships ground together in the swell.

Drinkwater leapt across the gap, stepped on the lugger's rail and landed on the deck. He was confronted by two men whose features were pale blurs. He remembered his own orders and screamed through clenched teeth. Behind him the two helmsmen came aboard, their faces blackened, like his own, by soot from the galley funnel.

Drinkwater fired his pistol at the nearer Frenchman and jabbed his hanger at the other. They vanished and a man in front thrust at him with a boarding pike. He parried awkwardly, sliding on the deck, taking the thrust through his coat sleeve and driving the muzzle of the discharged pistol into the man's exposed stomach. His victim doubled over and Drinkwater savagely struck at the nape of his neck with the pommel of his sword. Something gave beneath the ferocity of the blow and like a discarded doll the man dropped into the anonymous darkness of the bloody deck.

He moved on and three, then four men were in front of him. He slashed with the hanger, hurled the pistol at another then whipped the second from his belt. Pulling the trigger the priming flashed but it misfired and with a triumphant yell the man leapt forward. Drinkwater was through the red-rimmed barrier of fighting madness now. His brain worked with cool rapidity, emotionless. He began to crouch instinctively, to turn his head away in a foetal position, but his passive submission was deceptive; made terrible by the sword. Bringing the hilt down into his belly, the blade ran vertically upwards between his right ear and shoulder. He sensed the man slash at where he had been, felt him stumble on to the exposed sword-blade in the confusion. Drinkwater thrust with his legs, driving upwards with a cracking of back muscles. Supported by fists, belly and shoulder the disembowelling blade thrust deep into the man's guts, through his diaphragm and into his lungs. Half crouched, with the dying Frenchman collapsed about his shoulder, he felt the sword nick his own ear. The weight of the body sliding down his back dragged the hanger over his shoulder and he tore it clear with both hands as another man pointed a pistol at his exposed left flank. The blade came clear as the priming flashed. In a terrible swipe the steel scythed round as the pistol discharged.

Drinkwater never knew where the ball went. Maybe in the confusion the fellow had forgotten to load it or it had been badly wadded and rolled out. Nevertheless his face bore tiny blue spots where the grains of spent powder entered his flesh. His left eye was bruised from the shock wave and blinded by yellow light but he went on hacking at the man, desperately beating him to the deck.

Drinkwater reeled from the discharge of the pistol, his head spinning. The other men had disappeared, melted away. The faces round him were vaguely familiar and he no longer had the strength to raise his arm and strike at them. It had fallen silent. Oddly silent. Then Jessup appeared and Drinkwater was falling. Arms caught him and he heard the words 'Congratulations, sir, congratulations . . .' But it was all a long way off and oddly irrelevant and Elizabeth was giving him such an odd, quizzical look.

When he awoke he was aware that he was in the cabin of *Kestrel* and that pale daylight showed through the skylight. He was bruised in a score of places, stiff and with a raging headache. A pale shape fluttered round other men, prone like himself. One, on the cabin table all bloody and trembling, the pale form, ghostly in a dress of white bent over him. Drinkwater saw the body arch, heard a thin, high whimper which tailed to a gurgle and the body relaxed. For a second he expected Hortense Montholon to round on him, a grey-eyed Medusa, barbering in hell and he groaned in primaeval fear, but it was only Griffiths probing a wound who looked round, the front of his nightshirt stiff with blood. Drinkwater realised he could only see through one eye, that a crust of dried blood filled his right ear. He tried to sit up, feeling his head spin.

'Ah, Mr Drinkwater, you are with us again . . .' Drinkwater got himself into a sitting position. Griffiths nodded to the biscuit barrel on the locker. 'Take some biscuits and a little cognac . . . you will mend in an hour or so.' Drinkwater complied, avoiding too protracted a look at the several wounded lying gasping about the cabin.

'A big butcher's bill, Mr Drinkwater, *Diamond*'s surgeon is coming over . . . Eight killed and fifteen wounded badly . . .' A hint of reproach lay in Griffiths's eyes.

'But the lugger, sir?' Drinkwater found his voice a croak and remembered himself screaming like a male banshee.

'Rest easy, you took the lugger.' Griffiths finished bandaging a leg and signalled the messman to drag the inert body clear of the table. 'When you've recovered yourself I want you to take charge of her, Jessup's fitting things up at the moment. I've my own reasons for not wanting a frigate's mate sent over.'

On deck Drinkwater looked about him. It was quite light now and the wind was freshening. The squadron was hove to, the coast of France blue grey to the south of them. *Arethusa* and *Diamond* lay-to apparently unscathed, as were the two transports. But the French corvette, her tricolour fluttering beneath the British ensign, had lost a topmast, was festooned in loose rigging with a line of gunports opened into one enormous gash. Her bulwarks were cut up and she had about her an air of forlorn hopelessness.

Kestrel's own deck showed signs of enemy fire. A row of stiffened hammocks lay amidships, eight of them. Her bulwarks were jagged with splinters while aloft her topmast was wounded and her topsail yard hung down in two pieces which banged against the mast as she rolled. A party of men were lowering the spar to the deck.

Tregembo rolled up, a grin on his face. 'We did for 'em proper 'andsome, zur.' He nodded cheerfully to starboard where eighty yards distant the lugger lay a shambles. Her rails were almost entirely shot away. That first, double-shotted broadside had been well laid. With her rails had gone the chains and she had rolled her topmasts over the side. Tendrils of blood could still be seen running down her brown sides.

'Oh, my God,' whispered Drinkwater to himself.

'Ay, there'll be some widders in St Malo tonight I'm thinking, zur . . .'

'How many were killed aboard her, Tregembo, d'you know?' Drinkwater asked, knowing the mutual comprehension of the Cornish and Bretons.

'I heard she had ninety-four zouls on board, zur, an' we counted four dozen still on their legs. Mr Jezup's got his mate Short over there along of him, keeping order.' Tregembo smiled again. Short was the more ruthless of *Kestrel*'s two bosun's mates and on a bigger ship would have become a brutal bully. 'Until you'm ready to take over, zur.' Tregembo concluded with relish. Mr Drinkwater had been a veritable fury in last night's fight. He had been just the same in the last war, Tregembo had told his cronies, a terrible man once he got his dander up.

The boat bearing *Diamond*'s surgeon arrived and Appleby climbed wearily aboard. He stared at Drinkwater unblinking, shaking his head in detached disapproval as he looked about the bloody deck.

'Devil's work, Nathaniel, damned devil's work,' was all he said by way of greeting and Drinkwater was too tired to answer as Appleby had his bag passed up. He took passage in *Diamond*'s boat across to the lugger.

The shambles apparent from *Kestrel*'s deck was ten times worse upon that of the lugger. In an exhausted state Drinkwater stumbled round securing loose gear, assessing the damage and putting the *chasse marée* in a fit state to make sail. He avoided the sullen eyes of her captive crew and found himself staring at a small bundle of bunting. It was made fast to the main flag halyards and stirred something in his brain but he was interrupted by a boat from *Flora*. *Kestrel* was to escort the prizes to Portsmouth, among them the lugger. At noon the British frigates stood westward, the prizes north-north-east.

It was late afternoon before Drinkwater emerged from the brief but deep sleep of utter exhaustion. He was slumped in a chair and woke to surroundings unfamiliar enough to jar his brain into rapid recollection. As he emerged into full consciousness he was aware of a fact that needed urgent clarification. He rushed on deck, ignoring the startled look of the two helmsmen. He found what he was looking for amidships and pulled the black flag from where it had been shoved on lowering. He held it out and the wind caught it, fluttering the soft woollen material and arousing the attention of three of the Bretons exercising forward.

It was a black swallowtail flag.

'Mr Short!'

'Sir?' Short hurried up.

'What's the name of the lugger?'

Short scratched his head. 'Er *Cityee-en Jean*, I think sir.'

'*Citoyenne Janine*?'

'Yeah, that's it, sir.' The man nodded his curly head.

'Where's her commander? Who was in charge when we took her? Is Tregembo in the prize crew?'

Short recoiled at the rapid questioning. 'Well, sir, that blackguard there, sir.' He pointed at a man standing by the forward gun. 'As to Tregembo, sir, he ain't in the crew, sir . . .'

'Damn. Bring that man aft here . . .' Drinkwater unhitched the black flag as Short shoved the man aft. He wore a plain blue coat and while not very senior, was clearly an officer of sorts.

'*Ôu est vôtre capitaine*?' he asked in his barbarous French. The Frenchman frowned in incomprehension and shrugged.

'*Vôtre capitaine*?' Drinkwater almost shouted.

Understanding woke in the man, and also perhaps a little cunning, Drinkwater thought. '*Mon capitaine*?' he said with some dignity. '*M'sieur, je suis le capitaine.*'

Drinkwater held the flag under his nose. '*Qu'est-ce que c'est?*' He met the Frenchman's eyes and they looked at each other long enough for Drinkwater to know he was right. Even as the Frenchman shrugged again Drinkwater had turned aft.

He noticed the aftermost guns turned inboard, each with a seaman stationed with a lighted match ready to sweep the waist. Drinkwater did not remember turning any guns inboard but Short seemed in total control and relishing it. The presence of *Kestrel* on the weather beam was reassuring and Drinkwater called 'Carry on Mr Short,' over his shoulder as he slid down the companionway, leaving the startled Short gaping after him while the Frenchman turned forward, a worried frown on his face.

Below, Drinkwater began to ransack the cabin. It had two cots one of which was in use. He flung open a locker door and found some justification for his curiosity. Why did the skipper of a small lugger have a bullion-laden naval uniform, along with several other coats cut with the fashionable high collar?

With a sense of growing conviction Drinkwater pulled out drawers and ripped the mattress off the cot. His heart was beating with excitement and it was no surprise when he found the strong box, carefully hidden under canvas and spunyarn beneath the stern settee. Without hesitation he drew a pistol and shot off the lock. Before he could open it Short was in the doorway, panting and eager for a fight.

To Drinkwater he looked ridiculous but his presence was reassuring.

'Obliged to you Mr Short but there's nothing amiss. I'm just blowing locks off this fellow's cash box,' Short grinned. 'If there's anything in it, Mr Short, you'll get your just deserts.'

'Aye, aye, sir.' Short closed the door and Drinkwater expelled his breath. At least with such a maniac on board there was little chance of being surprised by the enemy attempting to retake their ship. He dismissed the memory of similar circumstances aboard *Algonquin*. When one sailed close to the wind the occasional luff was easily dismissed. Provided one avoided a dismasting.

He opened the box. There was money in it. English money. Sovereigns, guineas and coins of small denominations. There were also a number of charts rolled up and bound with tape. They were charts of the English coast, hand-done on linen-backed paper with the carefully inscribed legend of the French Ministry of Marine. A small signal book with a handwritten code was tied up with a bundle of letters. These Drinkwater gave only a cursory glance, for something else had caught his eye, something which he might almost have imagined himself to have been looking for had not the notion been so improbable.

It was a single letter, written in a female hand on rice paper and bound with a thin plait of hair. Human hair.

And the hair was an unmistakable auburn.

Chapter Seven   *December 1794–August 1795*

An Insignificant Cruiser

Villaret Joyeuse escaped from Brest at Christmas dogged by Warren and his frigates. In Portsmouth *Kestrel* lay in Haslar Creek alongside the *Citoyenne Janine* while they awaited the adjudication of the prize court. No decision was expected until the New Year and as the officers of the dockyard seemed little inclined to refit the cutter until then, *Kestrel*'s people were removed into the receiving guardship, the *Royal William*. Drinkwater took leave and spent Christmas with Elizabeth. They were visited by Madoc Griffiths. The old man's obvious discomfiture ashore was as amusing as it was sad, but by the evening he was quite at ease with Elizabeth.

At the end of the first week in January the prize court decided the two transports be sold off, the corvette purchased into the service and the lugger also brought into the navy. Griffiths was triumphant.

'Trumped their ace, by damn, Mr Drinkwater. Hoist 'em with their own petards . . .' He read the judgement from a Portsmouth newspaper then grinned across the table, over the remnants of a plum duff, tapping the wine-stained newsprint.

'I'm sorry, sir, I don't see how . . .'

'How I hoist 'em? Well the frigate captains had an agreement to pool all prize money so that they shared an equal benefit from any one individual on detached duty. I, being a mere lieutenant, and *Kestrel* being a mere cutter, was neither consulted nor included. As a consequence, apart from the commodore's share, we will have exclusive rights to the condemned value of the *Citoyenne Janine*. You should do quite handsomely, indeed you should.'

'Hence the insistence I took the prize over . . .?'

'Exactly so.' Griffiths looked at his subordinate. He found little of his own satisfaction mirrored there, riled that this rather isolated moment of triumph should be blemished. In his annoyance he ascribed Drinkwater's lack of enthusiasm to base motives.

'By damn, Mr Drinkwater, surely you're not suggesting that as I was sick you should receive the lion's share?' Griffiths's tone was angry and his face flushed. Drinkwater, preoccupied, was suddenly aware that he had unintentionally offended.

'What's that, sir? Good God, no! Upon my honour sir . . .' Drinkwater came out of his reverie. 'No sir, I was wondering what became of those papers and charts I brought off her.'

Griffiths frowned. 'I had them despatched to Lord Dungarth. Under the circumstances I ignored Warren. Why d'ye ask?'

Drinkwater sighed. 'Well, sir, at first it was only a suspicion. The evidence is very circumstantial . . .' he faltered, confused.

'Come on, *bach*, if there's something troubling you, you had better unburden yourself.'

'Well among the papers was a private letter. I didn't pass it to you, I know I should have done, sir, and I don't know why I didn't but there was something about it that made me suspicious . . .'

'In what way?' asked Griffiths in a quietly insistent voice.

'I found it with a lock of hair, sir, auburn hair, I, er . . .' He began to feel foolish, suddenly the whole thing seemed ridiculously far fetched. 'Damn it, sir, I happen to think that the man who used the lugger, the man we're convinced is some kind of a French agent, is also connected with the red-haired woman we took off at Beaubigny.'

'That Hortense Montholon is in some kind of league with this Santhonax?'

Drinkwater nodded.

'And the letter?'

Drinkwater coughed embarrassed. 'I have the letter here, sir. I took it home, my wife translated it. It was very much against her will, sir, but I insisted.'

'And did it tell you anything, this letter?'

'Only that the writer and this Santhonax are lovers.' Drinkwater swallowed as Griffiths raised an interrogative eyebrow. 'And that the letter had been written to inform the recipient that a certain mutual obstacle had died in London. The writer seemed anxious that the full implications of this were conveyed in the letter and that it, in some way, made a deal of difference . . .'

'Who is the writer?' Griffiths asked quietly.

Drinkwater scratched his scar. 'Just an initial, sir, "H.",' he concluded lamely.

'Did you say *are* lovers?'

Drinkwater frowned. 'Yes sir. The letter was dated quite recently, though not addressed.'

'So that if you are right and they were from this woman who is now resident in England she and Santhonax are maintaining a correspondence at the very least?'

'The letters suggested a closer relationship, sir.'

Griffiths suppressed a smile. Having met Elizabeth he could imagine her explaining the contents of the letter in such terms. 'I see,' he said thoughtfully. After a pause he asked, 'What makes you so sure that this Miss "H" is the young woman we took off at Beaubigny and what is the significance of this "mutual obstacle"?'

It was the question Drinkwater had been dreading but he was too far in now to retreat and he took encouragement from Griffiths's interest. 'I'm not sure, sir. It is a feeling I have had for some time . . . I mean, well as you know my French is poor, sir, limited to a few stock phrases, but at the back of my mind is the impression that she didn't want to come with us that night . . . that she was there on sufferance. I remember her standing up in the boat as we came off the beach and the French opened fire. She shouted something, something like "don't shoot, I'm your friend, I'm your friend!"' He tried to recall the events of the night. 'It ain't much to go on, sir, we were all very tired after Beaubigny.' He paused, searching Griffiths's face for some sign of contemptuous disbelief. The old man seemed sunk in reflection. 'As for the "obstacle",' Drinkwater plunged on, 'I just had this conviction that it was De Tocqueville . . .' He cleared his throat and in a firmer voice said, 'To be honest, sir, it's all very circumstantial and I apologise about the letter.' Drinkwater found his palms were damp but he felt the relief of the confessional.

Griffiths held his hand up. 'Don't apologise, *bach*, there may be something in what you say. When we mentioned the Montholons and Beaubigny to Major Brown something significant occurred to him. I don't know what it was but I am aware that this Captain Santhonax is not only an audacious officer but is highly placed enough to exert influence on French politics.' He paused. 'And I

269

have often wondered why no action was ever taken after our broadside at Beaubigny. One can only assume that the matter was hushed up.' Griffiths lifted an eyebrow. 'Yet the French were damned touchy with Barlow and *Childers* a few weeks later . . .'

'That thought had occurred to me, sir.'

'Then we are of one mind, Mr Drinkwater,' said Griffiths closing the subject with a smile. Drinkwater relaxed, remembering Dungarth's words all those months ago. He began to see why Griffiths was regarded as a remarkable man. He doubted he could have told anyone else but the Welshman. The old lieutenant sat for a moment in silence, staring at the wine rings on the table cloth. Then he looked up. 'Do you return the letter to me, Mr Drinkwater. I'll inform his lordship of this. It may bear investigation.'

Relieved, Drinkwater rose and went to his cabin, returning to pass the letter to Griffiths.

'Thank you,' said the lieutenant, looking curiously at the thin plait of auburn hair. 'Well, Mr Drinkwater, out of your prize money I think you should purchase a new coat, your starboard shoulder tingle is well enough for sea service but won't do otherwise,' Griffiths indicated the repair he had effected to his coat. Elizabeth had already chid him for it. 'Take yourself to Morgan's, opposite the Fountain at number 85. You'll get yourself anything there, even another Dollond glass to replace that precious bauble you lost off Ushant . . .' They both laughed and Griffiths shouted at the messman, Merrick, to come and clear the table.

Lieutenant Griffiths's expectations of stratagems from Sir Sydney's fertile brain were to have a drastic effect upon the fortunes of *Kestrel* though not in the manner the old man had had in mind. Sir Sydney had conceived the idea that a French-built lugger attached to the squadron would prove a great asset in deceiving the enemy, plundering coastal trade and gathering intelligence. Her commander would be his own nomination in the person of Lieutenant Richard White, and *Kestrel*, with her unmistakably English rig, would be free for other duties.

Auguste Barrallier, now employed in the Royal Dockyard, arrived to authenticate the lugger's repairs and was affable to Drinkwater, watching progress from the adjacent cutter. Nathaniel did his best to disguise his pique when White arrived from Falmouth with a crew of volunteers from Warren's frigates. White, to his credit, made no attempts to lord over his old friend. He brought letters from Appleby and an air of breezy confidence that only a frigate cruising under an enterprising officer could engender. Appleby, it appeared, did not see eye to eye with this captain and White dismissed the surgeon with something like contempt. But Drinkwater was pleased when the lugger dropped out of sight behind Fort Blockhouse.

Her replacement as Warren's despatch vessel left *Kestrel* languishing between the greenheart piles in Haslar Creek through the still, chill grey days of January when news came of war with the Dutch. February passed and then, almost immediately it seemed, the windy equinoctials of March were over. A start had been made on removing the scars of her late action. But it was half-hearted, desultory work, badly done and Griffiths despaired, falling sick and passing to the naval hospital. Jessup took to the bottle and even Drinkwater felt listless and dispirited, sympathising with the bosun and affecting to ignore his frequent lapses.

Drinkwater's lassitude was due in part to a spiritual exhaustion after the action off the Île Vierge which combined with a helplessness consequent upon his conviction that a link existed between the mysterious Santhonax and Hortense Montholon. In sharing this suspicion with Griffiths, Drinkwater had sought to unravel it, imagining the old sea-officer might have some alchemical formula for divining such things. But this had proved foolish, and now, with Griffiths sick ashore and the authorities lacking interest in the cutter, Drinkwater felt oppressed by his helplessness, aground in a backwater of naval affairs that seemed to have no incoming tide to refloat his enthusiasm.

To some extent Elizabeth was to blame. Their proximity to Drinkwater's home meant that he took what leave he could. With Griffiths ashore his presence aboard *Kestrel* two or three times a week was sufficient. And the seduction of almost uninterrupted domestic life was sweet indeed. To pay for this lack of vigilance *Kestrel* lost six men to desertion and Drinkwater longed for orders, torn between Elizabeth and the call of duty.

Then, one sharp, bright April morning when the sun cracked over the roofs of Portsea with an expectant brilliance, a post captain came aboard, clambering over the rail from a dockyard boat unannounced, anonymous in plain clothes. He had with him a fashionably dressed and eccentric looking man who seemed familiar with the cutter.

It was Tregembo who warned Drinkwater and he had only learned from the grinning crew of the dockyard skiff that the gentlemen were of some importance. Some considerable importance in fact. Suddenly guilty, and thanking providence that this morning he had happened to be on board, Drinkwater hurried on deck, but the strangers were nowhere to be seen. Then a seaman popped out of the hold.

'Hey, sir, some bleeders down 'ere are poking about the bottom of the ship. One of 'em's a bleeding Frog unless I'm a Sumatran strumpet, sir . . .'

Bursting with apologies Drinkwater flung himself below to make his introductions. The intruders were dimly visible peering into *Kestrel*'s bilge having prised up a section of the ceiling.

'Good morning, gentlemen, please accept my . . . good lord! M'sieur Barrallier is it not?'

'Ah! My young friend, 'ullo. I have not come to build you your frigate, alas, but this is Captain Schank, and we have come to, how you say – modify – your fine cutter.'

Drinkwater turned to the gentleman rising from his knees and brushing his breeches. Captain Schank waved aside his apologetic protestations and in five minutes repaired his morale and reinspired him.

Later that day in Haslar Hospital Drinkwater explained to Griffiths.

'What he does is this, sir. He reinforces the keel with cheeks, then he cuts slots like long mortices through which he drops these plates, centre plates he calls 'em. The idea's been used in America for some time, on a small scale, d'you see. Captain Schank saw them when he was master's mate but,' Drinkwater smiled ruefully, 'master's mates don't carry much weight in these matters.'

Griffiths's brow wrinkled in concentration. 'Sort of midships leeboards, is it?'

'Aye, sir, that's it exactly,' replied Drinkwater nodding enthusiastically. 'Apparently you point up better to windward, haul your wind closer and reduce leeway significantly.'

'Wait,' interrupted Griffiths pondering, 'I recollect the name now. He built *Trial* like that in ninety or ninety-one. She and *Kestrel* were on the same lines. Yes, that's the man. *Trial*'s fitted with three of these, er, centre plates . . .' They began discussing the advantages it would give *Kestrel* and then Griffiths asked 'If they are doing all this have you got wind of any likely orders for us?'

Drinkwater grinned. 'Well, sir, nothing official, sir, but scuttle-butt has it that we're for the North Sea station, Admiral MacBride's squadron.'

It seemed to Nathaniel as he left the hospital that the news might restore Griffiths's health more rapidly than the doctors' physic.

The drawings spread over the cabin table slid to the deck from where the master shipwright recovered them, an expression of pained forbearance on his face. Captain Schank he knew and could tolerate, his post-rank was sufficiently awe-inspiring, but this younker who was no more than a master's mate: God preserve patient and professional craftsmen from the meddling of half-baked theorists.

'But if, as you say, it is the depth that's effective, sir, and the cutter's to work in shallow water, then a vertically supported plate might be very dangerous.' Drinkwater's imagination was coping with a vision of *Kestrel*'s extended keel digging into a sandbank, oversetting her and possibly splitting her keel. 'But if you had a bolt forward here,' he pointed to the plan, 'then it would hinge and could rise up into the casing without endangering the cutter.' He looked at the captain.

'What d'you think Mr Atwood?' The master shipwright looked over the pencil marks, an expression of scepticism on his face.

Drinkwater sighed with exasperation. Dockyard officers were beginning to rile him. 'Barrallier could do it, sir,' he said in a low voice. He thought he detected a half smile twitch Schank's face. Atwood's back stiffened. After a second or two of real attention to the plan he straightened up. 'It could be done, sir,' he ignored Drinkwater, 'but I don't want that Froggie whoremonger with his dancing master ways messing about with it . . .'

273

A day later they were warped alongside the sheer hulk and the mast was removed. Then they were hauled out. The work went well and a week later Griffiths reappeared with a cheerful countenance and a lightness of step that betrayed neither his age nor his recent indisposition.

He advised Drinkwater to air his best uniform coat, the new acquisition from Mr Morgan's 'We are invited to dine with Lord Dungarth, Mr Drinkwater, at the George . . . hey Merrick! God I'm getting old, why do the damned artificers always leave a job half finished, dismantling the companionways and leaving rickety ladders? Ah, Merrick, pass along my best uniform coat and air Mr Drinkwater's. Polish his best shoes and get some sharkskin for that damned murderous French skewer he calls a sword,' he turned to Drinkwater, all traces of fever absent from his face. 'I've a feeling there's more to tonight's meal than mere manners . . .' Drinkwater nodded, aware that Griffiths's instinct was usually uncannily accurate and glad to have the old man on board again.

The George Inn at Portsmouth was traditionally the rendezvous of captains and admirals. Lieutenants like Griffiths patronised the Fountain, while master's mates and midshipmen made a bear pit of the Blue Posts, situated next to the coach office. There were, therefore, a number of raised eyes when, amidst an unseasonal swirl of rain and wind, Griffiths and Drinkwater entered the inn and the removal of their cloaks revealed them as an elderly lieutenant and what appeared to be a passed over mate.

Their presence was explained by the appearance of Lord Dungarth who greeted them cordially. 'Ah, there you are gentlemen, pray be seated. Flip or stingo on such a wretched night? Well Madoc, what is it like wiping the arses of frigate captains after your independence, eh?'

Griffiths smiled ruefully. 'Well enough, my lord,' he said diplomatically. An elderly captain at the next table turned a deep puce with more than a hint of approaching apoplexy in it and muttered that the service was 'Going to the dogs.'

Dungarth went on heedlessly, an old, familiar twinkle in his eye. 'And you Nathaniel, I heard you took that lugger single-handed. An exaggeration I suppose?'

'Aye my lord, a considerable one I'm afraid.'

Dungarth went on, 'I suppose the dockyard are prevaricating with your refit in the customary fashion, eh?'

Griffiths nodded. 'Yes, my lord. I believe they consider us too insignificant a cruiser to take note of,' he said, a bright gleam in his eye and noting Dungarth cast significant glances at other officers in the room, several of whom Drinkwater recognised as dockyard superintendents.

'Insignificant!' exclaimed his lordship. 'Indeed. Damned crowd of peculating jobbers, rotten to the core. The greatest treason is to be found in His Majesty's dockyards, from time to time they hang an arsonist to assure their lordships of their loyalty . . .' Dungarth distributed the glasses. 'Your health gentlemen. Yes, you remark me well, one day they will receive their just deserts. You remember the *Royal George*, Nathaniel, aye and you've good cause to . . . Well gentlemen if you feel recovered from this damnable weather I've a fine jugged hare and a saddle of mutton awaiting you.' They emptied their glasses and followed Dungarth to a private room. Drinkwater was aware that their exit appeared most welcome.

Conversation remained light. Dungarth had dismissed his servants and they attended to themselves. As they finished the hare he announced 'I am expecting another guest before the night is out, but let the business of the evening wait upon his arrival, it is a long time since I set a t'gallant stuns'l even over a meal . . .'

They were attacking the mutton when a knock at the door occurred.

'Ah Brown, come and sit down, you know the company.'

Major Brown, smoothing his hair and muttering that the night was foul and diabolical for early June, nodded to the two naval officers. 'Your servant, my lord, gentlemen.'

'Sit down, some of this excellent mutton? Madoc would you assist the major? Good . . .' Dungarth passed a plate. Drinkwater was aware that Griffiths's theory about the reason for their summons to dinner might be right. Major Brown had brought more than a waft of wet air into the room. Dungarth shed his familiar air and became crisply efficient. 'Well? D'ye find anything?'

Brown fixed Dungarth with a stare. 'Nothing of real significance. And you my lord?'

'No.' Dungarth looked at Griffiths and Drinkwater objectively, apparently forgetful that the last hour had been spent in genial conversation. He asked Nathaniel to pass another bottle from the sideboard then said: 'The information you forwarded, Madoc, that Nathaniel here found aboard the *chasse marée* confirms what we have for some time suspected, that Capitaine Santhonax is an agent of the French government with considerable contacts in this country. The later information that you submitted about Nathaniel's supposed link between him and the Montholon woman seems not to be so . . .' Drinkwater swallowed awkwardly.

'Hmm, the evidence was somewhat circumstantial my lord, I thought it my duty . . .'

'You did quite rightly. Do not reproach yourself. We took it seriously enough to send Brown here to ferret out the whereabouts of Miss Montholon since there had been other indications that your theory might not be as wild as it might first appear.' He paused and Drinkwater found his heart-beat had quickened. He waited patiently while Dungarth sipped his wine and dabbed his lips with a napkin.

'When De Tocqueville died in London it was given out that he had been robbed by footpads. He had been robbed all right, a considerable sum was found to be missing from his lodgings, not his person. They had also been ransacked. The count had been run through by a sword. Murdered; and in the subsequent search of his rooms, papers were discovered that indicated he had not only contracted a marriage with Miss Montholon but arranged for its solemnisation. The woman was therefore located living with the count's mother in Tunbridge Wells. Although there was an outpouring of grief it came, I believe, mainly from the mother . . . Major . . .'

Brown swallowed hastily and took up the tale. 'As I mentioned to you some time ago Santhonax was known to me as a *capitaine de frégate*, yet he has never held an independent command, always being on detached duty like myself. We know he is the head of naval intelligence for the Channel area and extensively employs *chasses marées*, like the one you captured, to make contact with his agents in this country. He is also bold enough to land, even, perhaps to spend some time in England . . .'

Brown chewed then swallowed a final mouthful and washed it

down in complete silence. He continued: 'We believe him responsible for the death of De Tocqueville and your suggestion that there might be a connection with Mlle Montholon was most interesting.' He shrugged with that peculiar Gallic gesture that seemed so out of place. 'Though the letter you captured might confirm a suspicion it does not prove a fact, and to date surveillance has failed to indicate anything other than that Mlle Montholon is the unfortunate affianced of the late count who, in her present extremity, is a companion to her late lover's mother, herself widowed by the guillotine. I am told that their mutual grief is touching . . .' Brown's ironic tone led Drinkwater to assume that his own suspicions were not yet satisfied.

'But is Santhonax likely to continue his activities after losing his papers?' asked Griffiths.

'I do not think a man of his calibre and resource will lightly be deterred,' answered Dungarth. 'Besides, it depends how incriminating he regards what he lost. We are all hostages to fortune in this business but the odds against someone finding and identifying the letter and its writer must be very long. After all I doubt the lugger was the only one in the Channel that night with charts of our coasts, nor money. The gentlemen devoted to free trade might conceivably be similarly equipped . . .'

'But the uniform, my lord,' put in Drinkwater. Dungarth shrugged. 'I'll warrant Santhonax will not abandon his little projects over that, though doubtless whoever ordered his lugger to assist that convoy is now regretting his action. No, we'll back Nathaniel's hunch a little longer with surveillance on the De Tocqueville *ménage*. As for you fellows,' the earl leaned forward and fished in his tail pocket, drawing out a sealed packet, 'here are your orders to cruise in the Channel – in theory, against the enemy's trade. In fact I want you to stop every lugger, punt, smack and galley 'twixt the North Foreland and the Owers and search 'em. Perhaps we'll apprehend this devil Santhonax before more mischief occurs . . . Now Nat pass that bottle or, here, Madoc you are partial to sercial, those damned slaving days, I suppose.' The atmosphere changed, lightened a little as a sense of self-satisfaction embraced them.

'My lord,' said Griffiths at last, 'I should like to solicit your interest in favour of a commission for Mr Drinkwater here. Is there no way you might induce their lordships to reward a deserving officer?'

Drinkwater thrust aside a haze that was not entirely due to the tobacco smoke out of which he had been conjuring images of the beautiful Hortense.

Dungarth was shaking his head, his speech slurring slightly. 'My dear Madoc I would like nothing better than to oblige by confirming Nathaniel's commission but, by an irony, I am out of favour with the present Board having criticised Earl Howe's failure to stop that deuced grain fleet. Brown's intelligence was laid before the Board and they had plenty of warning that it should be stopped at all costs. We might have destroyed France at a blow.' Dungarth was leaning forward, his voice sharp and a cold fire in his hazel eyes. Then he sat back, slumping into his chair and brushing a weary hand across his forehead. 'But the pack of poxed fools ignored me and Brown's sojourn at the peril of his life was wasted . . .'

Later, splashing through puddles as the rain gurgled in drainpipes and their white hose were spattered black; leaning together like sheer-legs, Griffiths and Drinkwater staggered back from the George. They had dined and drunk to excess and Griffiths kept muttering apologies that Dungarth had failed him in the matter of the commission while Nathaniel assured him with equal insistence that it did not matter. Drinkwater felt fortified against disappointment. The evening had brought him a kind of victory and in his drunken state his belief in providence was absolute. Providence had brought him to *Kestrel* and providence had had a hand in his presence at Beaubigny. Providence would see he had a lieutenant's cockade when it was due. And the ringing in his ears said the time was not yet.

It was only when they passed the momentary shelter of the dockyard gate and Griffiths roared the countersign at the sentry that it occurred to Nathaniel how foolish they must seem. And suddenly he wished he were in bed beside Elizabeth instead of lurching along in the wet and windy darkness supporting his increasingly heavy commander.

Chapter Eight   *September–December 1795*

The Black Pendant

The *Royal William*, receiving ship, was one of the oldest vessels in the British Navy. She had brought Wolfe's body home from Quebec and now played host to the bodies of unfortunate men waiting to be sent to ships. Like all such hulks she smelt, not the familiar living odour of a ship in commission but a stale, damp, rotting smell that spoke of stagnation, of neglect, idleness and despair. At the time of Drinkwater's visit she had nearly three hundred wretched men on board, from which *Kestrel* must replace her deserters. There were pressed men, Lord Mayor's men and quota men. There were even, God help them, volunteers, an isolated minority of social misfits with no other bolt hole to run to. There were disenchanted merchant sailors, home after long voyages and taken by the press or the patrolling frigates in The Soundings and sent into Portsmouth in the despatch boats. There were the pressed men, the pariahs, the drunks and the careless who had been caught by the officers of the Impress Service and brought by the tenders to be incarcerated on the *Royal William* until sent to ships. Here they were joined by village half-wits and petty thieves generously supplied by patriotic parish fathers as part of their quota. From London the debtors, felons, reprieved criminals and all the inadequate and pathetic flotsam of eighteenth-century society came fortnightly by the Tower tender. As a consequence the old ship groaned with misery, dirt, indiscipline and every form of vermin parasitic upon unwashed humanity. *Royal William* was little distinguishable from the prison hulks further up the harbour with her guard boats, gratings and sentries.

The regulating captain in charge of the Impress Service regarded Drinkwater with a jaundiced eye. For a moment or two Drinkwater could not understand the man's obvious hostility, then he recognised the apoplectic captain from the George the night they had dined with Dungarth.

'Six men! Six! Now where in the world d'you think I can find six men, God rot ye? And for what? A third rate? A frigate? No! But for some poxy little cutter whose officers spend their time ashore in ill-mannered abuse of their betters. No sir! You may think that because I have a deck full of hammocks I've men to spare. I don't doubt that suspicion had crossed your mind, but six men for an unrated cutter . . .' Drinkwater stood silently waiting for the man to finish blustering and cursing until, at last, he turned up a ledger, ran his finger down a column, shook his head and slammed the book shut.

'Scratch!' He shouted.

An obsequiously cowed clerk entered, dragging a misshapen foot behind him. 'Sir?'

'Present complement and dispositions please.'

'Ah, yes sir, er,' the man thought for a moment then rattled off, 'two hundred and ninety-one men on board sir. Sixty-two prime seamen, eighty-five with previous service, ninety-one mayor's men and fifty-three from the parishes. Er, three tailors among 'em, four blacksmiths, a locksmith, four cobblers, one apothecary under sentence for incest . . .' The man's eyes gleamed and Drinkwater was reminded of some carrion eater that subsisted on the dying bodies of ruined men.

'Yes, yes,' said the regulating captain testily, obviously considering his clerk was ruining his own case, 'now the dispositions.'

'Ah, yes, sir, well, most for Captain Troubridge on the *Culloden*, thirty-eight to go to Plymouth for *Engadine*, two dozen for *Pomone*, six to be discharged as unfit and the balance replacements for the Channel Fleet, sir, leaving a few odds and ends . . .'

'They will do us, sir,' suggested Drinkwater in an ill-timed remark that robbed the regulating captain of his triumph.

'Hold your damned tongue!' He snapped, nodding his thanks to the clerk. 'Now my young shaver, you perceive I do *not* have men to spare for your cutter. Tell your commander he can do his own recruiting. As far as I'm concerned the thing's impossible, quite impossible. My lieutenants are out scouring the country for the fleet, your damned cutter can go to the devil!' The regulating captain's face was belligerently red. He dismissed Drinkwater with a wave and the latter followed the sallow, misshapen little clerk in brown drab out of the cabin.

Furious Drinkwater made eagerly for the side, anxious to escape the stink of the ship when he felt a hand on his arm. 'Do not act so intemperately, young man, pray stay a moment.' The clerk's tone was all wheedling. 'For a consideration, sir,' he whined, 'I might be able to oblige a young gentleman . . .'

Drinkwater turned back, contempt rising in him like bile in the throat. Then he recalled the state of the cutter and the pressing need for those few extra men. He swallowed his dislike. Finding he had a couple of sovereigns on him he held one out to the clerk who took it in the palm of his hand and stared at it.

Drinkwater sighed and gave him the second coin. Like a gin-trap the man's hand closed on the gold and he spoke insolently. 'Now, young man, we can perhaps do a little business . . . your name?' The clerk opened his book on an upright desk and ran a finger down a column of names, muttering to himself. He drew up a list and handed it to Drinkwater. 'There, Mr Drinkwater, six men for your cutter . . .' he chuckled wickedly, 'you might find the apothecary useful . . .'

'Send a boat for 'em in the morning,' said Griffiths, removing his hat and sitting heavily. Merrick brought in a pot of coffee and a letter. Griffiths opened it and snorted. 'Huh! and about time too. It seems we are at last to be manned on the proper establishment,' his face dropped, 'oh . . .'

'What is it, sir?'

'You . . . you are to sail as master, your acting commission will be revoked. As we are no longer on special service only one commissioned officer is required.' Griffiths lowered the letter. 'I am very sorry.'

'But we are operating under Dungarth's orders,' said Drinkwater bitterly.

Griffiths shook his head, 'Nominally we're part of MacBride's squadron now, clerks, Mr Drinkwater, the bloody world is run by clerks.'

Drinkwater felt a terrible sense of disappointment. Just when

Kestrel's fortunes seemed to offer some promise after the long sojourn in the dockyard this news came.

'No matter, sir. What is to be our complement?' he asked hurriedly, eager for distraction.

'Er, myself, you as sailing master, two mates, Jessup, Johnson the carpenter, a warrant gunner named Traveller, a purser named Thompson and a surgeon named Appleby.'

'Appleby?'

'God, man, we're going to be damned cramped.'

The six men sent from the *Royal William* were a pathetic group. They were not, by any stretch of the imagination, seamen. Even after three days on board Short's starter and Jessup's rattan had failed to persuade them that they were in the navy. Above his head Drinkwater could hear the poor devils being roundly abused as he discussed the final stowing of the cutter's stores and powder with Jessup. Already he foresaw the course events would take. They would be bullied until one of them would be provoked into a breach of discipline. The flogging that would inevitably follow would brutalise them all. Drinkwater sighed, aware that these things had to be.

'Well, Mr Jessup, we'll have to conclude these arrangements in the gunner's absence. I just hope he's graced us with his presence by the time we're ready to sail.'

'Aye sir, he'll be here. I seen him last evening Gosport side but Jemmy Traveller is like to be last to join. His wife runs a pie shop near the ordnance yard. Jemmy's always busy counting shillings and making guineas.'

'So you know him?'

Jessup nodded. 'Aye with him in the *Edgar*. With Lord Rodney when we thrashed the Dons in eighty.'

'The Moonlight Action?'

'Aye, the same.'

'I remember . . .' But Drinkwater's reminiscences were abruptly curtailed by a shout on deck.

'Hey, sirrah! What in God's name d'you think you're about? Instruct the man, thrashing him is of no use.'

'What the devil?' Drinkwater leapt up and made for the companionway. He reached the deck as a portly man climbed awkwardly down from the rail. The familiar figure of Appleby stood scowling at Short.

'Ah, Nathaniel, I'm appointed surgeon to this, this,' he gestured extravagantly round him and gave up. Then he shot a black look at Short. 'Who's this damned lubber?'

The bosun's mate was furious at the intrusion. Veins stood out on his forehead as he contained his rage, the starter dangling from his wrist vibrated slightly from the effort it was costing Short.

'This is Short, Mr Appleby, bosun's mate and a first-class seaman.' Drinkwater took in the situation at a glance, aware that his reaction was crucial both to discipline and to those petty factions that always cankered in an over-crowded man o'war.

'Very well, Mr Short, if they cannot yet splice you must remember it takes time to make a real seaman of a landlubber.' He smiled at Short, who slowly perceived the compliment, and turned to the new hands who were beginning to realise Appleby might prove an ally. Drinkwater spoke sharply but not unkindly. 'You men had better realise your duty is plain and you're obliged to attend to it or take the consequences. These can be a deal more painful than Mr Short's starter or Mr Jessup's cane . . .' He left the sentence in mid air, hoping they would take heed of it. Comprehension began to spread across the face of one of them and Drinkwater grasped Appleby's elbow and propelled him aft. He felt the surgeon resist then succumb. Reaching the companionway Drinkwater called forward, 'Mr Short! Have those men get the surgeon's traps aboard, lively now!'

Appleby was slightly mollified by this piece of solicitude and his natural sociability gave way to Drinkwater's distracting barrage of questions.

'So what happened to *Diamond*? How's the squadron managing without us? How much prize money has Richard White made? What on earth are you doing here? I wondered if it was to be you when Griffiths mentioned the name, but I couldn't see you exchanging out of a frigate for our little ship.' Appleby felt himself shoved into a tiny box of a cabin and heard his young friend bawl for coffee. Drinkwater laughed as he saw the expression on the surgeon's face. Appleby was taking in his surroundings.

'I manage to fit,' grinned Drinkwater, 'but a gentleman of your ample build may find it something of a squeeze. This is my cabin, yours is across the lobby.' Drinkwater indicated the doorway through which the landsmen were just then lugging Appleby's gear. Appleby nodded, his chins doing a little rippling dance eloquent of disappointment. 'Better than that claustrophobic, blasted frigate,' he said rather unconvincingly. 'All that glitters is not, etcetera, etcetera,' he joked feebly.

Drinkwater raised his eyebrows. 'You surprise me. I thought Sir Sydney a most enterprising officer.'

'A damned eccentric crank, Nathaniel. The frigate was fine but Sir William festering Sydney had a lot of damned fool ideas about medicine. Thought he could physic the sick better than I . . . used to call me a barber, confounded insolence and me a warrant surgeon before he was a midshipmite. Ouch! This coffee's damned hot.'

Drinkwater laughed again. 'Ah, I recollect you don't like intruders, no more than we do here, Harry,' he said pointedly. For a minute Appleby looked darkly at his friend, stung by the implied rebuke. Then Drinkwater went on and he forgot his wounded pride. 'By the way, d'you remember that fellow we brought ashore wounded at Plymouth?'

Appleby frowned, 'Er, no . . . yes, a Frenchman wasn't he? You brought a whole gang of 'em out, including a woman if I recollect correctly.'

'That's right,' Drinkwater paused, but Appleby brushed aside the memory of Hortense.

'I take it from your self-conceit the patient survived?'

'Eh? Oh, yes, but he succumbed to assault in the streets of London.'

'Tch, tch, now you will appreciate my own despair when I exhaust myself patching you firebrands up, only to have you repeatedly skewering yourselves.'

They sipped their coffee companionably but it was not difficult to see that poor Appleby had become a most prickly shipmate.

'And what is our commander like?' growled Appleby.

'Excellent, Harry, truly excellent. I hope you like him.' Appleby grunted and Drinkwater went on wryly, 'It is only fair to warn you that he is quite capable of probing for a splinter or a ball.'

Appleby gave a sigh of resignation then wisely changed the subject.

284

'And you, I mean we, no longer poach virgins off the French coast, I assume? That seemed to be the opinion current in the squadron when this cutter cropped up in conversation.'

Drinkwater laughed again. 'Lord no! It'll be all routine stuff now. We're fleet tender to Admiral MacBride's North Sea Fleet. It'll be convoys and cabbages, messages, tittle-tattle and perhaps, if we're very lucky, a look into Boulogne or somewhere. All damned boring I shouldn't wonder.'

Appleby did not need to know about Dungarth's special instructions. After all he had only just joined. He was not yet one of the Kestrels.

'Your standing at Trinity House must be high, Mr Drinkwater,' said Griffiths, 'they have approved the issue of a warrant without recourse to further examination. The Navy Board have acted with uncommon speed too,' he added with a significant glance at Drinkwater implying *Kestrel* should not suffer further delay. 'Now Mr Appleby?'

'These new men are infested, sir,' complained the surgeon, referring to the draft received from the *Royal William*. Griffiths looked wearily back at the man.

'Aye, Mr Appleby and that won't be all they've got. What d'you suggest we do, send 'em back, is it?'

'No sir, we'll douse them in salt water, ditch their clothing and issue slops . . .' He trailed off.

'Now Mr Appleby, do you attend to your business and I'll attend to mine. Your sense of outrage does your conscience credit but is a disservice to your professional reputation.'

Drinkwater watched Appleby sag like a pricked balloon. No, he thought, he is not yet one of us.

The keen clean Channel breeze came over the bow as they stood down past the guardship at the Warner and on through the anchored warships at St Helen's, their ensign dipping in salute and the spray playing over the weather rail and hissing merrily off to leeward. Apart from an ache in his heart at leaving Elizabeth, Drinkwater was glad to have left Portsmouth, very glad.

'Very well, Mr Drinkwater . . .' It was Jeremiah Traveller, a mirror

285

image of Jessup, who, as gunner took a deck watch releasing Nathaniel from the repressive regime of four hours on deck and four below which he and Jessup had hitherto endured. They called the hands aft as eight bells struck and then, the watch changed, he slid below.

In his cabin he took out his journal, turning the pages of notes and sketches made in Portsmouth, a myriad of dockyard details, all carefully noted for future reference. He stared at his drawing of the centre plates. Beating out of Portsmouth they had already felt the benefit of those. Opening his inkwell he picked up the new steel pen that he had bought at Morgan's. *Kestrel* was already a different ship. With a cabin full of officers at meal times the old intimacy was gone. And Appleby had driven a wedge between Drinkwater and Griffiths, not intentionally, but his very presence seemed to turn Griffiths in upon himself and the greater number of officers increased the isolation of the commander.

Drinkwater sighed. The halcyon days were over and he regretted their passing.

Autumn gave way to the fogs of November and the first frosts, these periods of still weather were linked by a dreary succession of westerly gales that scudded up Channel to force them to reef hard and run for cover.

They had no luck with Dungarth's commission though they stopped and searched many coastal craft and chased others. Drinkwater began to doubt his earlier convictions as ridiculous imaginings. The wily Santhonax had disappeared, or so it seemed. From time to time Griffiths went ashore and although he shared fewer confidences with Nathaniel now, he did not omit to convey the news. A brief shake of the head was all that Drinkwater needed to know the quarry had gone to earth.

Then, during the tail of a blow from south-west, as the wind veered into the north-west and the sky cleared to patchy sunshine, as Drinkwater dozed the afternoon watch away in his cot, the cabin door flew open.

'Zur!' It was Tregembo.

'Eh? What is it?' he sat up blinking.

'Zur, cap'n compliments, an' we've a lugger in sight, zur. She's a big 'un an' Lieutenant Griffiths says to tell 'ee that if you're interested, zur, she's got a black swallowtail pendant at her masthead ...'

'The devil she has,' said Drinkwater throwing his legs over the cot and feeling for his shoes. Sleep left him instantly and he was aware of Tregembo grinning broadly.

The Star of the Devil

Drinkwater rushed on deck. Griffiths was standing by the starboard rail, white hair streaming in the wind, his face a hawk-like mask of concentration on the chase, the personification of the cutter's name. Bracing himself against the scend of the vessel Drinkwater levelled his glass to starboard.

Both lugger and cutter were running free with *Kestrel* cracking on sail in hot pursuit. Drinkwater watched the altering aspect of the lugger, saw her grow just perceptibly larger as *Kestrel* slowly ate up the yards that separated them. Almost without conscious thought his brain was resolving a succession of vectors while his feet, planted wide on the planking, felt *Kestrel*'s response to the straining canvas aloft.

Drinkwater could see a bustle on the stern of the lugger and was trying to make it out when Griffiths spoke from the corner of his mouth.

'D'you still have that black pendant on board?'

'Yes sir, it's in the flag locker.'

'Then hoist it . . .'

Drinkwater did as he was bid, mystified as to the significance of his actions and the importance of Brown's bit of 'Celtic nonsense'. But to Griffiths the black flag of the Breton held a challenge to his heart, it was he or Santhonax and he acknowledged the encounter in single combat.

There was a sound like tearing calico. A well-pointed ball passed close down the starboard side and Drinkwater could see the reason for the bustle aft. The lugger's people had a stern chaser pointing astern. Through his glass he could see her gun crew reloading and a tall man in a blue coat staring at them through a telescope. As he lowered the glass to address an officer next to him Drinkwater saw the face in profile. The dark, handsome features and the streaming curls, even at a distance, were unmistakably those of Santhonax.

Beside him Griffiths breathed a sigh of confirmation.

'Now Mr Traveller,' he said to the gunner, 'let us see whether having you on board improves our gunnery.'

Jeremiah Traveller rolled forward, his eyes agleam. The Kestrels had been at General Quarters since they sighted the lugger and every man was at taut as a weather backstay. Although her ports were closed to prevent water entering the muzzles, the gun crews were ready, their slow matches smouldering in the linstocks and the breeches charged with their lethal mixture of fine milled powder and the most perfect balls the gun captains could find in the racks. Now they watched Traveller elbow aside the captain of Number 1 gun and lower himself to sight along the barrel.

Drinkwater cast his eyes aloft. The huge mainsail was freed off to larboard, the square top and topgallant sails bowed their yards, widened by stunsails, and the weather clew of the running course was set. *Kestrel*, with a clean bottom, had rarely sailed better, tramping the waves underfoot and scending down their breaking crests.

A movement forward caught his attention and he watched Traveller straighten up, the linstock in his hand, waiting for the moment to fire. Swiftly Drinkwater clapped his glass to his eye. The stern of the lugger swung across the lens, her name gold on blue scrollwork: *Étoile du Diable*.

The report of the bow chaser rolled aft and Drinkwater saw a hole appear in the chase's mizen. Then her stern chaser fired and through his feet he felt the impact strike the hull.

'*Myndiawl!*' growled Griffiths beside him.

'We're overhauling him fast, sir,' said Drinkwater by way of reassurance. He felt a sense of unease emanating from the commander and began to divine the reason. Santhonax could haul his wind in a moment. *Kestrel*, with her squaresails set, would take much longer.

Traveller fired again and a cheer from forward told of success. The mizen yard sagged in two pieces, the sail collapsing and flogging. The triumph was illusory and Griffiths swore again. That loss of sail would the sooner compel Santhonax to turn to windward.

'Get the course and kites in Mr Drinkwater,' snapped Griffiths.

'In t'gallant stuns'ls . . .' Drinkwater began bawling orders. Men left each gun and swarmed aloft to handle the sails and rig in the booms. Short chivvied them up. A cluster gathered round the mast, tallying on to the ropes under Jessup's direction, a group on the downhauls and sheets, a couple to ease the tacks and halliards. Drinkwater saw Jessup's nod.

'Shorten sail!' Forward Traveller fired again but Drinkwater was watching the stunsails belly forward, lifting their booms.

'Steady there,' said Griffiths quietly to the helmsman. A broach now would be disastrous. The men on deck tramped away with the downhauls and sheets and the stunsails came down, flapping on to the deck like wounded gulls.

Vaguely aware of a second thump into the hull and a patch of blue sky through the topsail Drinkwater ordered in the topgallant.

'There she goes,' shouted Griffiths as *Étoile du Diable* swung to starboard, briefly exposing her stern. 'Fire as you bear!' he called to the gun captains, left by their charges as their crews shortened sail.

But as he turned Santhonax's stern chaser roared, double shotted. The ball skipped once on a wave top, smashed through *Kestrel*'s starboard rail and clove both helmsmen in two.

Griffiths leapt to the tiller and leant his weight against it.

'Leggo weather braces! Haul taut the lee! Man the sheets there!' He pushed down on the big tiller and brought *Kestrel* round in the wake of the lugger.

It was as well he did so for as he passed Santhonax fired his starboard broadside. Most of the shot plunged into the smooth green water, with the upwellings from her rudder, that trailed astern of *Kestrel*'s turning hull. But two balls struck the cutter, one demolishing four feet of cap and ruff tree rail, the other opened the muzzle of Number 11 gun like a grotesque iron flower.

Drinkwater had the topgallant in its buntlines and until he doused the topsail *Kestrel* would not point as close to the wind as the lugger. Already the alteration of course had increased the apparent wind speed over the deck. Spray was coming aboard now as *Kestrel* began to drop back from the chase, the angle between them widening.

It seemed an age before the squaresails were secured. Forward Traveller and the headmost gun captains were ganging away.

Johnson, the carpenter, was hovering at Griffiths's elbow. 'He's hulled us, sir, I'll get a man on the pump . . .' Griffiths nodded.

'Sail shortened, sir.'

'Harden right in, Mr Drinkwater, and lower those bloody centre plates.'

'Aye, aye, sir!'

Kestrel hauled her wind as close as possible, narrowing the angle with the lugger. The chase ran on for an hour in a westerly direction and pointing their pieces carefully the gunners of both ships continued their duel. The Kestrels cheered several times as splinters were struck from the rail of the lugger but their hearts were no longer in the fight.

Drinkwater had a sight of the deck of the *Étoile du Diable* as she heeled over to larboard, exposing the view. Even with all the quoins out they were having trouble pointing their guns while the Kestrels had all theirs rammed in to level their own cannon and the labour of hauling their carriages uphill against the list. Three men had gone below to Appleby nursing splinter wounds when a shot from the *Étoile du Diable*, fired below the horizontal, ricochetted off the face of a wave and hit *Kestrel*'s starboard chain-whale from below. The *lignum vitae* deadeye of the after mainmast stay was shattered and the lanyard parted. A second ball carried away the topmast stay and a sudden crack from aloft showed the topmast tottering slowly to larboard.

'Goddamn . . . cut that away!' But Drinkwater was already rushing forward, leaping into the weather rigging with an axe. The passage of a final ball winded him and left him clinging trembling to the lower shrouds, gasping for breath like a fly in a web. He felt the shrouds shudder as the topmast tore down the lee side, shaking the mast and carrying the yards with it. A stunsail boom end caught the mainsail and opened a small split which slowly enlarged itself. The wreckage fell half in the water, half on the larboard waist. *Kestrel* lost way.

She was beaten.

On the starboard bow *Étoile du Diable* drew ahead. Upon her quarter stood Santhonax with his plumed hat in his hand.

He waved it over his head. Then he jumped down amongst the gunners who had served the still smoking stern chaser.

'*Cythral*,' muttered Griffiths, his eyes glittering after the enemy. 'Let fly the sheets!' he shouted.

Drinkwater climbed down to the deck.

'Mr Drinkwater!'

'Sir?'

'Secure what you can of that gear overside.' Their eyes met in disappointment.

'"Pride cometh before a fall", Mr Drinkwater. See what you can do.'

'Aye, aye, sir.'

Drinkwater went forward again. Leaning over the side he surveyed the raffle of spars, canvas and cordage, of blocks and ironwork. And something else.

At the trailing masthead, one end of its halliard broken and dragging along the cutter's side, was the black swallowtail pendant, mocking them.

PART TWO

The North Sea

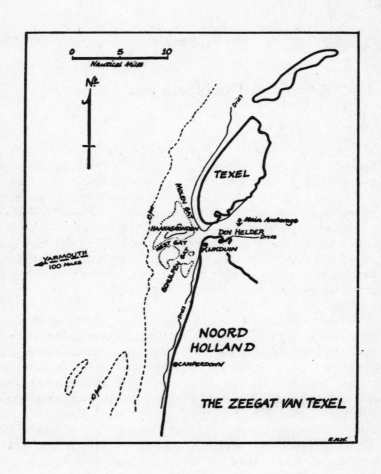

0   5   10
Nautical Miles

N°

Dries

TEXEL

Molen Gat

Main Anchorage

Haaks Gronden

Den Helder

West Gat

Dries

Zuider Hoek

Rijkduin

YARMOUTH
100 Miles

Dries

NOORD
HOLLAND

CAMPERDOWN

THE ZEEGAT VAN TEXEL

R.A.W.

Chapter Ten   *December 1795–November 1796*

The Apothecary

Short drew back his well-muscled arm then brought the cat down on the man's back. 'Seven!' called Jessup dispassionately.

The red weals that lay like angry cross hatching over the flesh were suppurating and blood began to ooze from the broken skin.

'Eight!'

Drinkwater could see the man's face in profile from where he stood by the starboard runner. Although he bit hard on the leather pad the victim's eyes glared forward, along the length of the gig across the transom of which he was spreadeagled.

'Nine!'

The inevitable had happened. The offender was the apothecary embarked from the *Royal William* and named Bolton. Bolton seemed unwilling or unable to make the best of his circumstances. He appeared to be a man penned up within a private hell that left him no rest. Appleby called him 'an human pustule, full of corrupt fluid and ripe for lancing'. He went about heedless of his surroundings to the point of apathy, tough enough to endure Short's abuse and starting without a word or apparent effect. What seemed to Short to be intransigence attracted all the bosun's mate's bullying fury. Short was unused to such stolid indifference and when violence failed he had recourse to crude innuendo. He found his barbs reached their mark. Ransacking every corner of his mind for human failings, he scoured the depths of every depravity, insensitive to the changing look of increasing desperation in Bolton's eyes. Pursued, Bolton ran until at last, flushed from cover, he turned at bay. Short had got there in the end over some clumsiness at gun drill, some trivial thing for which he had been waiting.

'Bolton! You crap-brained child-fucker . . .' And the rammer had swung round, driven into Short's guts with a screech of mortification from Bolton.

'Twelve!' Short was panting now, the bruise in his midriff paining him. Harris, the second bosun's mate, relieved him, taking the cat and running the tails through his left hand, squeezing out the blood and plasma. Harris spread his legs and drew back his arm.

'Thirteen!'

They were all on deck. Griffiths, Drinkwater and Traveller with their swords, the hands ranged in the waist, their faces dull, expressionless.

'Fourteen!'

Kestrel lay hove-to, her staysail aback. There had been no waiting for the punishment. They had only just secured the guns at which they had been exercising. In a cutter there were no bilboes and Griffiths ordered the flogging immediately.

'Fifteen!'

The sentence had been three dozen lashes. Already the man's back was a red and bloody mess. He was whimpering now. Broken. Drinkwater felt sickened. Although Griffiths was no tyrant and Nathaniel recognised the need to keep order, no amount of flogging would make a seaman out of Bolton. God alone knew what ailed the man, though Drinkwater had heard from the misshapen clerk on the receiving ship he had been sentenced for incest. But whatever madness or torment hounded him he had taken enough now. The punishment should be suspended and Drinkwater found himself staring at Griffiths, willing him to stop it.

'Sixteen!' A low, animal howl came from Bolton which Drinkwater knew would rise to a scream before the man lost consciousness. Whatever guilt lay on the man's soul he expiated it now, slowly succumbing to the rising pain of his opened back.

'Seventeen!'

'Belay there!' Griffiths's voice whipped out. A ripple of relief ran through the assembled people. 'That'll do, cut him down, pipe the watch below, Mr Jessup!'

Drinkwater saw Bolton stiffen as a bucket of sea water was thrown over his back. Then he fainted. Appleby came forward to attend him. Drinkwater turned away.

'Leggo weather staysail sheet, haul taut the lee!'

Was there a perceptible resentment in the way the order was obeyed? 'Lively now! 'Vast and belay!' He walked aft. Or was he too damned sensitive?

'Steer north by east.'

'Nor' by east it is, sir.'

Kestrel steadied on her course and made after the convoy.

She had not been a happy ship since she had left Portsmouth. Her officers were a discordant mixture of abrasive characters. Appleby's pompous superiority which suited the bantering atmosphere of a crack frigate's gunroom was out of place here. Even Drinkwater found him difficult at times, for age and bachelorhood had not moderated his tendency to moralise. Griffiths had withdrawn as Drinkwater had known he would and their former intimacy was in abeyance. Jessup and Traveller, old acquaintances of long standing and great experience, employed their combined talents to prick Appleby's self-esteem, while the two master's mates, Hill and Bulman, both promoted quartermasters, survived by laughing or scowling as occasion seemed to demand.

Drinkwater felt a sense of personal isolation and took refuge in his books and journal, maintaining a friendship with Appleby when the latter was amenable but quietly relieved that his tiny cabin allowed him an oasis of privacy. This disunity of the officers spilled forward to combine with a growing resentment among the men over lack of pay and for whom the small, wet cutter was a form of purgatory.

They had weathered the great gale of mid-November shortly after their arrival in the Downs and barely a fortnight later learned of the mutiny on the *Culloden*. There had been an exchange of knowing looks round *Kestrel*'s cabin when Appleby had read the newspaper report, but the unreported facts sent a shiver of resentment through the crew.

The news that the authorities had agreed to favour the mutineers' petition without punishment had been followed by information that the law had exacted its terrible penalty. Imagination conjured a picture of the jerking bodies, run aloft by their own shipmates in all the awful guilt-sharing ceremonial of a naval execution while the marine drummers played the *rafale* and the picket trained their levelled muskets on the seaman. In the atmosphere prevalent aboard the cutter it was an image that lingered unbidden.

Griffiths looked aft over the transom and jolly boat in its stern davits. Above his head the ensign drooped like a rag but the morning, though chill, was fresh. A mood of mild enthusiasm infused Madoc Griffiths and he wondered if it was the effect of the man beside him. Drinkwater spoke with an old lilt in his voice, a tone that had been absent for some time now.

'I've given the matter a deal of thought, sir, and I reckon that it ain't unreasonable to bring Bolton aft as an additional messman. The mess is damned crowded, Merrick could do with some assistance and Short is still plotting against Bolton . . . pending your approval, of course, sir . . .'

Griffiths nodded. 'Very well, Mr Drinkwater, see to it. Glad I am that you are mindful of the hands. It is not always possible for a commander since he has other things to concern him, but it should be the prime consideration of his second. 'Tis a pity more do not follow your example.'

Drinkwater coughed with embarrassment. He was simply determined to do whatever lay in his power to ameliorate the condition of Bolton, the most abused and useless of *Kestrel*'s company. Here the man might be induced to assist Appleby medicinally and give his mind something to work on beyond its own self-consuming preoccupation. And perhaps thereby Drinkwater might stem the rot that he instinctively felt was destroying the cohesion of them all.

'See to that at once, Mr Drinkwater, and when you have done so sway out both gigs, run the larboard broadside out and the starboard in as far as the breechings will permit. It's a grand day for scraping the weed from the waterline and there'll be no wind before nightfall.'

If the mood of his sailing master had lightened his heart Lieutenant Griffiths did not find that of his surgeon so enjoyable. He looked up at Appleby an hour later from a table split by sunny squares let in through the skylight while from overside the rasp of bass brushes attacked the weed.

'He's not yet fit to return to duty,' said Appleby cautiously.

'Who is not fit, Mr Appleby? Bolton is it?'

'Yes sir,' said Appleby, aware that Griffiths was being deliberately obtuse.

'The man I had flogged?'

'Yes sir. He took it badly. At least three of Short's stripes were low, one seems to have damaged the left kidney.' Griffiths's face was expressionless. 'There has been some internal haemorrhaging, passing out with the man's urine, he's weak and the fever persists.'

'So cosset him, doctor, until he's fit again.'

'Yes sir.' Appleby stood his ground.

'Is there something else?'

'Sir, I . . .' Perspiration stood like pearls on Appleby's forehead as he balanced himself against the increasing list induced by the gun trucks squealing overhead as they prepared to scrape the other side. 'I was sorry that you found it necessary to flog Bolton, sir, his state of mind concerns me. I had thought you a most humane officer . . .'

'Until now?' asked Griffiths sharply, his eyebrows knitting together in a ferocious expression made more terrifying by the colour mounting to his cheeks. Appleby's courage was tested and, though his chins quivered gently, he lowered his head in silent assent.

With an effort Griffiths mastered himself and rose slowly to his feet, expelling breath in a long, low whistle. He leaned forward resting himself on his hands.

'Mr Appleby, indiscipline is a most serious crime in a man of war, especially when striking a superior is concerned . . .' He held up a hand to stop Appleby's protest. 'Provocation is no mitigation. That too is in the nature of things. We live in a far from perfect world, Mr Appleby, a fact that you should by now have come to terms with. As commander I am not permitted the luxury of sympathising with the individual.' Griffiths looked significantly at Appleby. 'Even the well-intentioned may sometimes be misguided, Mr Appleby.' He paused, allowing the implication to sink in. The surgeon's mouth opened and then closed again, Griffiths went on.

'There is some deep unhappiness in Bolton. Ah, you are surprised I noticed, eh? Nevertheless I did,' Griffiths smiled wryly. 'And Short tripped the spring of some rare device in his brain. Well Short has a sore belly as a consequence, see, so some justice had been done. I appreciate your concern but, if Bolton is a rotten apple you must see *Kestrel* as little more than a barrel full of ripe ones.' Griffiths paused and, just as Appleby opened his mouth to speak, added 'I offer this explanation not to justify myself but out of respect for your intelligence.'

Appleby grunted. He knew Bolton's insubordination could not go unpunished but he felt the case justified a court-martial at a later date. Griffiths's summary justice had clashed with his professional opinion. By way of rebuke Griffiths added 'Mr Drinkwater has suggested that Bolton comes aft as an additional messman. I am sorry that the suggestion did not come from you.'

Griffiths watched Appleby leave the cabin. It was strange how two men could take alarm from the same cause and react so differently as a result. Or was it his own reactions that were so disparate? Prejudice and partiality played such a large part in the affairs of men it was impossible to say.

Christmas and the arrival of 1796 passed almost unnoticed by the crew of *Kestrel*. They had not been long left independent and a peremptory order to join Admiral MacBride in the Downs had put paid to their chasing in the Channel after the mauling they had received from the *Étoile du Diable*. Although they did not know it at the time the failure of Dungarth's department to locate the mysterious Capitaine Santhonax had brought him into worse odour with their Lordships than his remonstrances over Howe's failure to turn Brown's intelligence reports to good account in 1794. As a consequence *Kestrel* found herself employed on pedestrian duties. In company with the ship-sloop *Atropos* the cutter was assigned to convoy work. From the Thames to the Tyne and back again with two score or so of colliers, brigs and barques, all commanded by hard case Geordie masters with independent views was, as Nathaniel had predicted, boring work. It could be humiliating too. When *Kestrel* was ordered up to Leith Road to escort the crack passenger and mail smack to London with a cargo of gold, the packet master treated the occasion as a race. With a prime crew protected by press exemption and a reputation for smart passages, the smack proved a formidable opponent. She had a fuller hull than her escort and properly should have been beaten by the man o'war cutter. But *Kestrel* carried her mainsail away off Flamborough Head while the smack drove on and left her hull down astern of the packet. Had not the wind hauled to the south-east and *Kestrel* not been able to point harder by virtue of her new centre plates, they might never have seen their charge again. As it was they caught her by the Cockle Gatt and stormed through Yarmouth Roads neck and neck with the flood tide under them.

During the summer they had idled round the dispersed herring fleet in the North Sea on fishery protection. Sickened by a diet of herrings, all chance of action seemed to elude them. Only twice did they have to chase off marauders, both Dutch and neither very eager. The expected depredations of French corsairs never materialised and it was confidently asserted that a nation that subsisted on snails and frogs was unlikely to have the sense to favour herrings. In reality French privateers found richer pickings in the Channel.

The war was going badly for Britain. In January Admiral Christian's West Indies expedition was severely mauled by bad weather and dispersed. In February a Dutch squadron got out of the Texel and then, in late summer, Spain went over to the French camp in an uneasy alliance.

At the conclusion of the fishing season *Kestrel* was ordered to refit before the onset of winter, the weatherly cutters being better ships to keep the sea than larger, more vulnerable units of the fleet. Along with these orders came news that Sir Sydney Smith had been taken prisoner on a boat expedition.

It brought a measure of personal satisfaction to Harry Appleby.

Leaning on the rail Drinkwater stared across the muddy waters of the Medway, over the flat extreme of the Isle of Grain to the Nore lightvessel, a half smile on his face

'What the deuce are you grinning at, Nat?' Drinkwater's reverie was abruptly shattered by the portly bulk of Appleby.

'Nothing Harry, nothing.' He crackled the letter in his pocket.

'Thinking of Elizabeth no doubt.' Appleby looked sideways. 'Ah you are surprised our worthy commander is not the only person capable of divining others' thoughts,' he added with a trace of bitterness, 'and the symptoms of love have long been known. Oh, I know you think I'm good only for sawing off limbs and setting broken bones, but there's little enough of that to occupy me so that I am reduced to observing my fellows.'

'And what have you observed of late then?'

'Why, that you have received a letter from Elizabeth and will be looking for some furlough before we sail.'

'Is that all?' replied Drinkwater with mock disappointment. 'No my friend, I doubt there'll be time for leave, Griffiths is eager to be gone. Ah, but it's a beautiful morning ain't it?' he added, sniffing to windward.

'Nat.' Appleby was suddenly serious.

'Uh?' Drinkwater turned abstractedly, 'what is it?'

'I have also been observing Bolton. What d'ye make of him?'

'Bolton?' Drinkwater frowned. 'He seems well enough content since we brought him aft. Surely you're in a better position to answer your own question since he's been pounding pestle and mortar in your service.'

Appleby shook his head. 'No. I mean the inner man. What d'ye make of the inner man?'

Drinkwater's pleasant introspection following the arrival of Elizabeth's letter was gone beyond recall. He sighed, slightly resentfully.

'For heaven's sake, Harry, come to the point.'

'Do you know what passed between Bolton and Short the afternoon they had their altercation?'

Drinkwater hesitated. He had not mentioned Bolton's crime aboard *Kestrel*. The relish with which the twisted clerk had mentioned it had sickened Nathaniel. He had had no desire to promulgate such gossip. He shook his head. 'No. Do you?'

Appleby's chins quivered in negation. 'I gather it was some sort of an unpleasant accusation. The point is Nat, and recollect that I spend a great deal of time between decks and am party to much of the rumour that runs about any vessel, the point is that I'd say he was eating himself up.'

'What d'you mean?'

'His mind is close to the precipice of insanity. I've seen it before. He lives in his skull, Nat, a man with a bad conscience.'

Drinkwater considered what Appleby had said. A ship was no

place for a man with something on his mind. 'You reckon he's winding himself up, eh?'

Appleby nodded. 'Like a clock spring, Nat . . .'

Drinkwater stood on the Gun Wharf at Sheerness and shivered, watching the boats coming and going, searching for *Kestrel*'s gig among them. Beside him James Thompson, the purser, stood with the last of his stores. Merrick and Bolton were with him. Drinkwater was anxious to get back on board. The winter afternoon was well advanced and the westerly wind showed every sign of reaching gale force before too long.

Their refit was completed and they were under orders to join Vice-Admiral Duncan at Yarmouth.

'Here's the gig now,' said Thompson and turned to the two messmen, 'get that lot into the boat smartly now, you two.' Drinkwater watched the boat pull in, Mr Hill at the tiller. As soon as it was secure he passed a bundle of charts, the letters and newspapers to the master's mate. Then he stood back while a brace of partridges, some cheeses, cabbages, an exchanged cask of pork and some other odds and ends were lowered into the boat.

'Bulman completed watering this afternoon, Mr Drinkwater,' volunteered Hill.

Drinkwater nodded. Thompson looked at Drinkwater. 'That's it, then.'

'Very well, James, let's get on board before this lot breaks,' he nodded to the chaos of cloud speedily eclipsing the pale daylight to the west, behind the broken outlines of the old three-deckers that formed the dockyard workers' tenements.

'Come on you two, into the boat . . .' Merrick descended the steps. 'Come on Bolton!' The man hesitated at the top, then turned on his heel.

'Hey!'

Drinkwater looked at Thompson. 'He's running, James!'

'The devil he is!'

'Mr Hill, take charge! Come on James!'

At the top of the steps Drinkwater saw Bolton running towards the old battleships.

'Hey!'

The wind was sweeping the wharf clear and Bolton pushed between two lieutenants who spun, a swirl of boat cloaks and displaced tricornes. Drinkwater began to run, passing the astonished officers. Already Bolton had reached the shadows in the lane leading to what was called the Old Ships, traversing the dockyard wall and away from the fort at Garrison Point. He knew that Bolton could not pass the sentries at the gates or cross the ditches that surrounded the place. He was making for the Old Ships and a possible way to Blue Town, the growing collection of inns, tradesmen's dwellings and brick built houses that was accumulating outside the limits of the dockyard.

Abruptly he reached a ditch, James Thompson puffing up beside him. At the top of the low rampart a short glacis sloped down to the water. It was slightly overgrown now, elderberry bushes darker patches against the grey-green grass. The pale sky in the west silhouetted a movement: Bolton. Drinkwater began running again. Thompson came after him then tripped and fell, yelling obscenities as he discovered a patch of nettles.

Drinkwater ran on, disturbing a rabbit which bobbed, grey-tailed, ahead of him before turning aside into a burrow. Then he approached the first of the hulks, vaguely aware that behind him shouts indicated where someone had turned out a foot patrol.

The old battleship rose huge above him, its lines made jagged with additions: chimneys, privvies and steps. The rusting chains from her hawse pipes disappeared into the mud and men were trudging aboard, looking at him curiously as he panted past them. The smell of smoke and cooking assailed his dilating nostrils and he drew breath.

A shadow moved out from the far hulk, a running man stooped along the tideline and Drinkwater wished he had a pistol. Bolton was making for a ramshackle wooden bridge that lay over the fosse, an unofficial short cut from the Old Ships to Blue Town. It was getting quite dark now. He clattered across the black planking over mud and a silver thread of water. The violent tug of the rising wind at his cloak slowed him and the breath was rasping in his throat at the unaccustomed exercise. To his right the flat expanse of salt marsh gave way to the Medway, palely bending away to Blackstakes and Chatham. To the left the huddle that was Blue Town.

It was almost dark when he entered the first narrow street. He passed an inn and halted. Bolton had evaded him. He must draw breath and wait for that foot patrol to come up, then they must conduct a house-to-house search.

'Shit!' Exasperation exploded within him. They had been at Sheerness for weeks. Why had Bolton chosen now to desert? He turned to the inn to make a start in the search. In the violence of his temper he flung open the door and was utterly unprepared for the disturbingly familiar face that confronted him.

The two men gaped in mutual astonishment, each trying to identify the other. For Edouard Santhonax recognition and capture were instinctively things to avoid. His reaction was swift the instant he saw doubt cloud Drinkwater's eyes. For Nathaniel, breathless in pursuit of Bolton, the appearance of Santhonax was perplexing and unreal. As his brain reacted to the change of quarry Santhonax turned to escape through a rear exit.

He attempted to shout 'Stop! In the King's name', but the ineffective croak that he emitted was drowned in the buzz of conversation from the artisans and seamen in the taproom. He pushed past several men who seemed to want to delay him. Eventually he struggled outside where he ran into the foot patrol. A sergeant helped him up.

'This way,' wheezed Drinkwater, and they pounded down an alleyway, no one noticing Bolton crouched beneath a hand cart in the inn yard, his heart bursting with effort, the scarred and knotted muscles of his back paining him from the need to draw deep gulps of air into his heaving lungs.

The sergeant spread his men out and they began to search the surrounding buildings. Drinkwater paused to collect his thoughts, realising they were now hunting two men, though the soldiers did not yet know it. He thought Santhonax might have doubled on him. It was quite dark and Drinkwater was alone. He could hear the sergeant and his men calling to each other further down the lane. Then the rasp of a sword being drawn sounded behind him.

He spun round.

Santhonax stood in the alleyway, a grey shadowy figure with a faint gleam of steel barring the passage. Drinkwater hauled out his hanger.

They shuffled cautiously forward and Drinkwater felt the blades engage. He could hear a voice in his head urging him not to delay, to attack simply and immediately; that Santhonax was quite probably a most proficient swordsman. Now!

Barely beating the blade and lunging low, Drinkwater extended. But Santhonax was too quick and leapt back, riposting swiftly though off balance. Drinkwater's parry was clumsy but effective.

They re-engaged. Drinkwater was blown after his run. Already his hanger felt heavy on his arm. He felt Santhonax seize the initiative as his blade was beaten, then, with an infinite slowness, the rasp of steel on steel, he quailed before the extension. He clumsily fell back, half turning and losing his balance and falling against the wall. He felt the sharp prick of the point in his shoulder but the turn had saved him, he was aware of Santhonax's breath hot in his face, instinctively knew the man's belly was unguarded and turned his point.

'*Merde!*' spat the Frenchman leaping back and retracting his sword. Drinkwater's feeble counter attack expended his remaining energy on thin air. Then he was aware of the swish of the *molinello*, the downward scything of the slashing blade. He felt the white fire in his right shoulder and arm and knew he was beaten.

He had been precipitate. He had broken his promise of circumspection to Elizabeth. As he awkwardly sought to parry his death thrust, the hanger weighing a ton in his hand, he felt Santhonax hesitate; was aware of running feet pounding up the alleyway from his rear, of something warm and sticky trickling over his wrist. Then he was falling, falling while running, shouting men were passing over him and above them the wind howled in the alleyway and made a terrible rushing noise in his ears. He could run no more.

Chapter Eleven *December 1796–April 1797*

A Time of Trial

'Hold still!'

'Damn it Harry . . .' Drinkwater bit his lip as *Kestrel* slammed into a wave that sent a shudder through her fabric.

'There!' Appleby completed the dressing.

'Well?'

'Well what?'

'What effect is it going to have? My arm's damned stiff. Will I fence again?'

Appleby shrugged. 'The bicep was severely lacerated and will be stiff for some time, only constant exercise will prevent the fibres from knotting. The wound is healing well, though you will have a scar to add to your collection.' He indicated the thin line of pale tissue that ran down Nathaniel's cheek.

'And?'

'Oh, mayhap an ache or two from time to time,' he paused, 'but I'd say you will be butchering again soon.'

Drinkwater's relief turned to invective as *Kestrel* butted into another sea and sent him sprawling across Appleby's tiny cabin, one arm in and one arm out of his coat. In the lobby he struggled into his tarpaulin while Appleby heaved himself on to his cot, extended one leg to brace himself against the door jamb, and reached for his book. Drinkwater went on deck.

Eight bells struck as he cleared the companionway. The wind howled a high-pitched whine in the rigging, a cold, hard northerly wind that kicked up huge seas, grey monsters with curling crests which broke in rolling avalanches of white water that thundered down their advancing breasts with a noise like murder, flattening and dissipating in streaks of spindrift.

Spume filled the air and it was necessary to turn away from the wind to speak. As he relieved Jessup a monstrous wave towered over the cutter, its crest roaring over, marbled green and white, rolling down on them as *Kestrel* mounted the advancing sea.

'Hold hard there! Meet her!' Men grabbed hold-fasts and the relieving tackles on the tiller were bar taut. Drinkwater tugged the companionway cover over as the roar of water displaced the howl of wind and he winced with the pain of his arm as he clung on.

Kestrel staggered under the tremendous blow and then the sea was all about them, tearing at them, sucking at their legs and waists, driving in through wrist bands, down necks and up legs, striving to pluck them like autumn leaves from their stations. A man went past Drinkwater on his back, fetching up against number 10 gun with a crunch of ribs. Water poured off the cutter as she rode sluggishly over the next wave, her stout, buoyant hull straining at every strap and scarph. Men were securing coils of rope torn from belaying pins and relashing the gigs amidships. Shaking the water from his hair Drinkwater realised, with a pang of anger that fed on the ache in his bicep, that he would be cold and wet for the next four hours. And the pain in his arm was abominable.

The winter weather seemed to match some savage feeling in Drinkwater's guts. The encounter with Capitaine Santhonax had left a conviction that their fates were inextricably entwined. The ache of this wound added a personal motive to this feeling that lodged like an oyster's irritant somewhere in his soul. What had been a vague product of imagination following the affair off Beaubigny had coalesced into certainty after the encounter at Sheerness.

I cannot escape, Nathaniel wrote in his journal, *a growing sense of apprehension which is both irrational and defies the precepts of reason, but it is in accord with some basic instincts that are, I suppose, primaeval.* He laid his goosequill down. No one but himself had realised his assailant was not Bolton for they had found the wretch in the inn yard, cramped in the stable straw and he had been taken defending himself with a knife. The sergeant had drawn his own conclusions. Lugged unconscious aboard *Kestrel*, Drinkwater had been powerless to prevent the foot patrol from beating up Bolton before throwing him into a cell. In the confusion Santhonax had vanished.

Drinkwater sighed. Poor Bolton had been found hanged in his cell the next morning and Drinkwater regretted he had never cleared the man of his own wounding. But *Kestrel* was at sea when he recovered his senses and even then it was some time before the dreams of his delirium separated from the recollection of events.

Drinkwater kept the news of the presence of Santhonax to himself with the growing conviction that they would meet again. Santhonax's presence at Sheerness seemed part of some diabolical design made more sinister by the occurrence of an old dream which had confused the restless sleep of his recovery. The clanking nightmare of drowning beneath a white clad lady had been lent especial terror by the medusa head that stared down at his supine body. Her face had the malevolent joy of a jubilant Hortense Montholon, the auburn hair writhed to entangle him and his ears were assailed by the cursing voice of Edouard Santhonax. But now, when he awoke from the dream, there was no comforting clanking from *Cyclops*'s pumps to chide him for foolish imaginings. Instead he was left with the sense of foreboding.

His wound healed well, though the need to keep active caused many a spasm of pain as the weather continued bad. In a perverse way the prevailing gales were good for *Kestrel*, preventing any grievances becoming too great, submerging individual hatreds in the common misery of unremitting labour. The cold, wet and exhaustion that became part of their lives seemed to blur the edges of perception so that the common experience drove men together and all struggled for the survival of the ship. *Kestrel* was now on blockade duty, that stern and rigorous test of men and ships. Duncan's cutters were his eyes, stationed as close to the Texel as they dared, watching the Dutch naval arsenal of Den Helder just beyond the gap between Noord Holland to the south and the island of Texel to the north.

The channel that lay between the two land masses split into three as it opened into the North Sea, like a trident pointing west. To the north, exit from the haven was by the Molen Gat, due west by the West Gat and southwards, hugging the Holland shore past the fishing village, signal station and battery of Kijkduin, lay the Schulpen Gat.

These three channels pierced the immense danger of the Haak Sand, the Haakagronden that surfaced at low water and upon whose

309

windward edges a terrible surf beat in bad weather. Fierce tides surged through the gattways and, when wind opposed tide, a steep, vicious breaking sea ran in them.

Duncan's cutters lay off the Haakagronden in bad weather, working up the channels when it eased and occasionally entering the shaft of the trident, the Zeegat van Texel, to reconnoitre the enemy. Drinkwater's eyebrows were rimed with salt as he took cross bearings of the mills and church towers that lined the low, grass-fringed dunes of Noord Holland and Texel, a coastline that sometimes seemed to smoke as it seethed behind the spume of the breakers beating upon the pale yellow beach. It was a dreary, dismal coast, possessed of shallows and sandbanks, channels and false leads. The charts were useless and they came to rely on their own experience. Once again Drinkwater became immersed in his profession and, as a result of their situation, the old intimacy with Griffiths revived. Even the ship's company, still restless over their lack of pay, seemed more settled and Griffiths seemed justified in his suggestion that Bolton might have been a corrupting influence.

Even Appleby had ceased to be so abrasive and was more the jolly, easily pricked surgeon of former times. He and Nathaniel resumed their former relationship and if Griffiths still occasionally appeared remote in the worries of his command and harassed by senior officers safe at anchor in their line-of-battleships, the surgeon was more able to make allowances.

Drinkwater was surprised that in the foul weather and the staleness of the accommodation Griffiths did not succumb to his fever but the continuous demands made upon him did not affect his health.

'It is often the way,' pronounced Appleby when Drinkwater mentioned it. 'While the body is under stress it seems able to stand innumerable shocks, as witness men's behaviour in action. But when that stimulus is withdrawn, perhaps I should say eased, the tension in the system, being elastic and at its greatest extension, retracts, drawing in its wake the noxious humours and germs of disease.'

'You may be right, Harry,' said Drinkwater, amused at the pompous expression on the surgeon's face.

'May, sirrah? Of course I am right! I was right about Bolton, was I not? I questioned his mental stability and, poof! Suddenly he's off and then, when he's taken he becomes a suicide.' Appleby flicked his fingers.

Drinkwater nodded. 'Aye Harry, but even you doubted your own prognosis when he did not run earlier. He did leave it to the last minute, even you must admit that.'

'Nat, my boy,' gloated Appleby the gleam of intellectual triumph in his eyes, 'one always has to leave suicide until the last minute!'

'You're just good at guess-work, you damned rogue,' he said, wondering what Appleby would make of his own suspicions and convictions.

'Oh ho! Is that so?' said Appleby rolling his eyes in mock outrage, his chins quivering. 'Well my strutting bantam cock, listen to old Harry, there's more that I can tell you . . .' He was suddenly serious, with that comic pedagoguish expression that betokened, in Appleby, complete sincerity.

'I'll back my instinct over trouble in the fleet . . .' Drinkwater looked up sharply.

'Go on,' he said, content to let Appleby have his head for once.

'Look, Nat, this cutter's an exception, small ships usually are, but you are well aware to what I refer, the denial of liberty, the shameful arrears of pay, the refusal of many captains to sanction the purchase of fresh food even in port and the general abuses of a significant proportion of our brother officers, these can only have a most undesirable effect.

'Take the current rate of pay for an able seaman, Nathaniel. It is twenty-four shillings, twelve florins for risking scurvy, pox, typhus, gangrene, not to mention death itself at the hands of the enemy . . . d'you realise that sum was fixed in the days of the Commonwealth . . .' Appleby's indignation was justly righteous. To be truthful Drinkwater did not know that, but he had no time to acknowledge his ignorance before Appleby continued his grim catalogue of grievances.

'To this you must add the vast disparity of prize money, the short measure given by so many pursers that has added the purser's pound of fourteen ounces to the avoirdupois scale; you must add the abatement of pay when a man is sick or unfit for duty, even if the injury was sustained in the line of that duty; you must add deductions to pay for a chaplain when one is borne on the books, the

deductions for Greenwich Hospital and the Chatham Chest . . .'
Appleby was becoming more and more strident, counting the items off on his fingers, his chins quivering with passion.

'And if that were not enough when a man is gricomed by the whores that are the only women he is permitted to lie with, according to usage and custom, he must *pay me* to cure him whilst losing his pay through being unfit!

'The families of seamen starve in the gutters while their menfolk are incarcerated on board ship, frequently unpaid for years and when they do return home they are as like to be turned over to a ship newly commissioning as occasion demands.

'I tell you, Nathaniel, these are *not* facts that lie comfortably with the usual canting notions of English liberty and, mark me well, if this war is protracted there will be trouble in the fleet. You cannot fight a spirited enemy who is proclaiming Liberty, Equality and Fraternity with a navy manned by slaves.'

Drinkwater sighed. Appleby was right. There was worse too. As the prime seamen were pressed out of homeward merchant ships the Lord Mayor's men and the quota men filled the Press Tenders, bringing into the fleet not hardened seamen, but the misfits of society, men without luck but not without intelligence; demagogues, lower deck lawyers; men who saw in the example of France a way to power, to overturn vested interest in the stirring name of the people. With a pot so near the boil, was the purpose and presence of Capitaine Santhonax at Sheerness to stir it a little? The proximity of Sheerness to Tunbridge occurred to him. A feeling of alarm, of duty imperfectly performed, swept over him.

'Aye, Harry. Happen you are right, though I hope not. It might be a bloody business . . .'

'Of course, Nat! *When* it comes, not "if"! *When* it comes it could be most bloody, and the authorities behave with crass stupidity. See how they handled that *Culloden* business,' Drinkwater nodded at the recollection but Appleby was still in full flood.

'Half the admirals are blind. Look how they ridiculed John Clerk of Eldin because he was able to point out how to win battles. Now they all scrabble to fight on his principles. Look how the powdered physicians of the fleet ignored Lind's anti-scorbutic theories, how difficult it was for Douglas to get his cartridges taken seriously.

Remember Patrick Ferguson's rifle? Oh, the list of thinking men pointing out the obvious to the establishment is endless . . . what the deuce are you laughing at?'

'Your inconsistent consistency,' grinned Nathaniel

'What the devil d'you mean?'

'Well you are right, Harry, of course, these things are always the same, the prophet unrecognised in his own land.'

'So, I'm correct. I know that. What's so damned amusing?'

'But you yourself objected to Sir Sydney Smith meddling in your sick bay, and Sir Sydney has a reputation for an original mind. You are therefore inconsistent with your principles in your own behaviour, whilst being comfortingly consistent with the rest of us mortal men.'

'Why you damned impertinent puppy!'

Drinkwater dodged the empty tankard that sailed towards his head.

Thus it was that they rubbed along together while things went from bad to worse for British arms. Sir John Jervis evacuated the Mediterranean while Admiral Morard de Galles sailed from Brest with an army embarked for Ireland. That he was frustrated in landing General Hoche and his seasoned troops was a piece of luck undeserved by the British. The south-westerly gale that ruined the enterprise over Christmas 1796 seemed to the Irish patriot, Wolfe Tone, to deny the existence of a just God, while in the British fleet the gross mismanagement of Lord Bridport and Sir John Colpoys only reduced the morale of the officers and increased the disaffection of the men.

Again only the frigates had restored a little glitter to tarnished British laurels. And that at a heavy price. Pellew, now in the *razée* *Indefatigable*, in company with *Amazon* off Brest, sighted and chased the *Droits de l'Homme* returning from Ireland. In a gale on a lee shore Pellew forced the French battleship ashore where she was wrecked. *Indefatigable* only escaped by superlative seamanship while *Amazon* failed to claw off and was also wrecked.

In the North Sea, action of even this Pyrrhic kind was denied Admiral Duncan's squadron. Maintaining his headquarters in Yarmouth Roads, where he was in telegraphic communication with

London, Duncan kept his inshore frigates off the Texel and his cutters in the gattways through the Haakagronden, as close as his lieutenant-commanders dared be. Duncan's fleet was an exiguous collection of old ships, many of sixty-four guns and none larger than a third rate. The admiral flew his flag in the aptly named *Venerable*.

The Dutch, under Vice-Admiral de Winter, were an unknown force. Memories of Dutch ferocity from King Charles's day lingered still, forgotten the humiliation of losing their fleet to a brigade of French cavalry galloping over the ice in which they were frozen. For like the Spanish they were now the allies of France, but unlike them their country was a proclaimed republic. Republicanism had crossed the Rhine, as Drinkwater had predicted, and the combination of a Franco-Dutch fleet to make another attempt on Ireland was a frightening prospect, given the uneasy state of that unhappy country.

Then, as the wintry weather gave way to milder, springlike days, news of a different kind came. The victory of St Valentine's Day it was called at first, then later the Battle of Cape St Vincent. Jervis had been made an earl and the remarkable, erratic Captain Nelson, having left the line of battle to cut off the Spanish van from escape, had received a knighthood.

The air of triumph even permeated *Kestrel*'s crowded little cabin as Griffiths read aloud the creased copy of the *Gazette* that eventually reached the cutter on her station in the Schulpen Gat. Drinkwater received an unexpected letter.

My Dear Nathaniel, he read,

I expect you will have heard the news of Old Oak's action of St Valentine's Day but you will be surprised to hear your old friend was involved. We beat up the Dons thoroughly, though I saw very little, commanding a battery of 32's on Victory, into which ship I exchanged last November. You should have been here, Nat. Lord, but what a glorious thing is a fleet action. How I envied you Rodney's action here in '80 and how you must envy us ours! Our fellows were so cool and we raked Salvador del Mundo wickedly. The Dons fought better than I thought them capable of and it was tolerably warm work . . .

Drinkwater *was* envious. Envious and not a little amused in a

314

bitter kind of way at Richard White's mixture of boyish enthusiasm and sober naval formality. There was a good deal more of it, including the significant phrase *Sir John was pleased to take notice of my conduct.* Drinkwater checked himself. He was pleased for White, pleased too that his old friend, now clearly on the path to success, still considered the friendship of an obscure master's mate in an even more obscure cutter worth the trouble of an informative letter. So Drinkwater shared vicariously in the euphoria induced by the victory. The tide, it seemed, had turned in favour of British arms and the Royal Navy reminded her old antagonists that though the lion lay down, it was not yet dead.

Then one morning in April *Kestrel* rounded the Scroby Sands and stood into Yarmouth Road with the signal for despatches at her masthead. Coming to her anchor close to *Venerable* her chase guns saluted the blue flag at the flagship's main masthead. A moment or so later her boat pulled across the water with Lieutenant Griffiths in the stern.

When Griffiths returned from delivering his message from the frigates off the Texel he called all the cutter's officers into the cabin.

Drinkwater was the last to arrive, late from supervising the hoisting of the boat. He closed the lobby door behind him, aware of an air of tense expectancy. As he sat down he realised it was generated by the frigid gleam in Griffiths's eyes.

'Gentlemen,' he said in his deep, clear voice. 'Gentlemen, the Channel Fleet at Spithead is in a state of mutiny!'

A Flood of Mutiny

'Listen to the bastards!' said Jessup as *Kestrel*'s crew paused in their work to stare round the crowded anchorage. The cheering appeared to come from *Lion* and a ripple of excitement ran through the hands forward, several staring defiantly aft where Jessup, Drinkwater and Traveller stood.

Yarmouth Roads had been buzzing as news, rumour, claim and counter-claim sped between the ships anchored there. The red flag, it was said had been hoisted at the Nore and Duncan's ships vacillated between loyalty to their much respected admiral and their desire to support what were felt to be the just demands of the rest of the fleet.

The cheering was enough to bring others on deck. Amidships the cook emerged from his galley and the knot of officers was joined by Appleby and Thompson. 'Thank God we're anchored close to the flagship,' muttered the surgeon. His apprehensions of mutiny now having been confirmed, Appleby feared the possibility of being murdered in his bed.

Kestrel lay anchored a short cannon shot from *Venerable*. The battleship's guns were run out and the sudden boom of a cannon echoed flatly across the anchorage. A string of knotted bunting rose up her signal halliards to jerk out brightly in the light breeze of a May morning.

'Call away my gig, Mr Drinkwater,' growled Griffiths emerging from the companionway. Admiral Duncan was signalling for his captains and when Griffiths returned from the conference his expression was weary. 'Call the people aft!'

Jessup piped the hands into the waist and they swarmed eagerly over the remaining boat on the hatch. 'Gentlemen,' said Griffiths to his officers, 'take post behind me.'

The officers shuffled into a semi-circle as ordered, regarding the faces of the men. Some open, some curious, some defiant or truculent and all aware that unusual events were taking place.

'Now hark you all to this, do you understand that the fleets at Spithead and the Nore are in defiant mutiny of their officers . . .' He looked round at them, giving them no ground, despite his inner sympathy. 'But if any man disputes my right to command this cutter or proposes disobeying my orders or those of one of my officers,' he gestured behind him, 'let him speak now.'

Griffiths's powerful voice with its rich Welsh accent seemed to come from a pulpit. His powerful old body and sober features with their air of patriarchy exerted an almost tangible influence upon his men. He appeared to be reasoning with them like a firm father, opposing their fractiousness with the sure hand of experience. 'Look at me,' he seemed to say, 'you cannot rebel against me, whatever the rest of the fleet does.'

Drinkwater's palms were damp and beside him Appleby was shaking with apprehension. Then they saw resolution ebb as a sort of collective sigh came from the men. Griffiths sent them forward again.

'Get forrard and do your duty. Mr Jessup, man the windlass and inform me when the cable's up and down.'

It was the season for variable or easterly winds in the North Sea and Duncan's preoccupation was that the Dutch fleet would leave the Texel, taking advantage of the favourable winds and the state of the British squadrons. The meeting to which Griffiths had been summoned had been to determine the mood of the ships in Duncan's fleet. The small force still off the Texel was quite inadequate to contain De Winter if he chose to emerge and it was now even more important to keep him bottled up. There was a strong possibility that the mutinous ships at the Nore might attempt a defection and this was more likely to be to the protestant Dutch than the catholic French, for all the republican renunciation of formal religion. A demonstration by De Winter to cover the Nore Squadron's exit from the Thames would be all that was necessary to facilitate this and strengthen any wavering among the mutineers. It was already known at Yarmouth that most of the officers had been removed from the warships with the significant exception of the sailing masters. They were held aboard the *Sandwich*, the 'flagship' of the self-styled admiral, Richard Parker.

For a few days *Kestrel* remained at anchor while Duncan, who had personally remonstrated with the Admiralty for redress of many of the men's grievances and regarded the mutiny as a chastisement and warning to the Admiralty to mend its ways, waited on events.

The anonymous good sense that had characterised the affair at Spithead was largely responsible for its swift and satisfactory conclusion. Admiral Howe was given special powers to treat with the delegates who knew they had 'Black Dick's' sympathy. By mid-May, amid general rejoicing, fireworks and banquets the Channel Fleet, pardoned by the King, returned to duty.

There was no evidence that foreign sedition had had anything to do with it. The tars had had a case. Their cause had been just, their conduct exemplary, their self-administered justice impeccable. They had sent representatives to their brethren at the Nore and it would only be a matter of days before they too saw sense.

But it was not so. The Nore mutiny was an uglier business, its style aggressive and less reasonable. By blockading trade in the Thames its leaders rapidly lost the sympathy of the liberal middle-class traders of London and as the Government became intransigent, Parker's desperation increased. The tide in favour of the fleet turned, and as the supplies of food, fuel and merchandise to the capital dwindled, troops flooded in to Sheerness and the ships flying the red flag at the Nore felt a growing sense of isolation.

At the end of May there arrived in Yarmouth an Admiralty envoy in the person of Captain William Bligh, turned out of the *Director* by his crew and sent by the authorities to persuade Duncan to use his ships against Parker's. He also brought news that four delegates from the Nore had seized the cutter *Cygnet* and were on their way to Yarmouth to incite the seamen there to mutiny.

Duncan considered the intelligence together with the mooted possibility of Parker defecting with the entire fleet to Holland or France. In due course he ordered the frigate *Vestal*, the lugger *Hope* and the cutter *Rose* to cruise to the southward to intercept the visitors. If Parker sailed for the Texel or Dunquerque then, and only then, would the old admiral consider using his own ships against the mutineers. In the meantime he sent *Kestrel* south into the Thames to guard the channels to Holland and to learn immediately of any defection.

'By the mark five.'

Drinkwater discarded the idea of the sweeps. Despite the fog there was just sufficient wind to keep steerage on the cutter and every stitch of canvas that could be hoisted was responding to it.

'I'll go below for a little, Mr Drinkwater.'

'Aye, aye, sir.' Their passage from Yarmouth had been slow and Griffiths had not left the deck for fear the men would react, but they were too tired now and his own exhaustion was obvious. Grey and lined, his face wore the symptoms of the onset of his fever and it seemed that the elasticity of his constitution had reached its greatest extension. Drinkwater was glad to see him go below.

Since the news of the Spithead settlement the hands had been calmer, but orders to proceed into the Thames had revived the tension. In the way that these things happen, word had got out that their lordships were contemplating using the North Sea squadron against the mutineers at the Nore, and Bligh was too notorious a figure to temper speculation on the issue.

The chant of the leadsman was monotonous so that, distracted by larger events and the personal certainty that the Nore mutiny was made the more hideous by the presence of Capitaine Santhonax, Drinkwater had to force himself to concentrate upon the soundings. They were well into the estuary now and should fetch the Nubb buoy in about three hours as the ebb eased.

'By the deep four.'

'Sommat ahead, sir!' The sudden cry from the lookout forward.

'What is it?' He went forward, peering into the damp grey murk.

'Dunno sir . . . buoy?' If it was then their reckoning was way out.

'There sir! See it?'

'No . . . yes!' Almost right ahead, slightly to starboard. They would pass very close, close enough to identify it.

''s a boat, sir!'

It was a warship's launch, coming out of a dense mist a

319

bowsprit's length ahead of them. It had eight men in it and he heard quite distinctly a voice say, 'It's another bleeding buoy yacht . . .', and a contradictory: 'No, it's a man o'war cutter . . .'

Mutually surprised, the two craft passed. The launch's men lay on their oars, the blades so close to *Kestrel*'s side that the water drops from their ends fell into the rippling along the cutter's waterline. Curiously the Kestrels stared at the men in the boat who glared defiantly back. There was a sudden startled gasp, a quick movement, a flash and a bang. A pistol ball tore the hat from Drinkwater's head and made a neat hole in the mainsail. There was a howl of frustration and the mutineers were plying their oars as the launch vanished in the fog astern.

'God's bones!' roared Drinkwater suddenly spinning round. The men were still gaping at him and the vanished boat. 'Let go stuns'l halliards! Let go squares'l halliards! Down helm! Lively now! Lively God damn it!'

The men could not obey fast enough to satisfy Drinkwater's racing mind. He found himself beating his thighs with clenched fists as the cutter turned slowly.

'Come on you bitch, come *on*,' he muttered, and then he felt the deck move beneath him, ever so slightly upsetting his sense of balance, and another fact struck him.

He had run *Kestrel* aground.

Kestrel lay at an alarming angle and her sailing master was still writhing with mortification. Used as he had been to the estuary while in the buoy yachts of the Trinity House the situation was profoundly humiliating.

Lieutenant Griffiths had said nothing beyond wearily directing the securing of the cutter against an ingress of water when the tide made. It was fortunate that they had been running before what little wind there was and their centre plates had been housed. The consequences might have been more serious otherwise. An inspection revealed that *Kestrel* had suffered no damage beyond a dent in the pride of her navigator.

Below, Griffiths had regarded him in silence for some moments after listening to Drinkwater's explanation of events. As the colour mounted to Drinkwater's cheeks a tired smile curled Griffiths's lips.

'Come, come, Nathaniel, pass a bottle from the locker . . . it was no more than an error of judgement and the consequences are not terrible.' Griffiths threw off his fatigue with a visible effort. 'One error scarcely condemns you, *bach*.'

Drinkwater found himself shaking with relief as he thrust the sercial across the table. 'But shouldn't we have pursued sir? I mean it was Santhonax, sir. I'm damned sure of that.' In his insistence to make amends, not only for grounding the cutter but for his failure earlier to report the presence of the French agent, the present circumstances gave him his opportunity. For a second he recollected that Griffiths might ask him how he was so 'damned sure'. But the lieutenant was not concerned and pushed a full glass across the table. He shook his head.

'Putting a boat away in this fog would likely have embroiled us in a worse tangle. Who ambushes whom in this weather is largely a matter of who spots whom first,' he paused to sip the rich dark wine.

'The important thing is what the devil is Santhonax doing in a warship's launch going east on an ebb tide with a crew of British ne'er-do-wells?'

The two men sat in silence while about them *Kestrel* creaked as the first of the incoming tide began to lift her bilge. Was Santhonax a delegate from the Nore on his way to Yarmouth? If he was he would surely have used the Swin. Their own passage through the Prince's Channel had been ordered to stop up the gap not covered by *Vestal*, *Rose* or *Hope*. And it was most unlikely that a French agent would undertake such a task.

If Santhonax's task was to help suborn the British fleet he had already achieved his object by the open and defiant mutiny. So what was he doing in a boat? Escaping? Was the mutiny collapsing? Or was his passage east a deliberate choice? Of course! Santhonax had attempted to kill Drinkwater. Nathaniel was the only man whose observation of Santhonax might prejudice the Frenchman's plans!

'There would seem to be only one logical conclusion, sir . . .'

'Oh?' said Griffiths, 'and what might that be?'

'*Santhonax must be going to bring aid to the Nore mutineers*. . .' He outlined his reasons for presuming this and Griffiths nodded slowly.

'If he intends bringing a fleet to support the mutiny or to cover its defection does he make for France or Holland?'

'The Texel shelters the largest fleet in the area, sir. Given a fair wind from the east which they'd need to get up the Thames with a fair certainty of a westerly soon afterwards to get 'em all out together . . . yes, I'll put my money on the Texel, anything from Brest or the west'll have the Channel to contend with.'

'Yes, by damn!' snapped Griffiths suddenly, leaning urgently forward. 'And our fellows will co-operate with a fleet of protestant Dutch and welcome their republican comrades! By heaven Nathaniel, this Santhonax is a cunning devil! *Cythral*! I'll lay gold on the Texel . . .'

The two of them were half out of their chairs, leaning across the table like men in heated argument. Then Griffiths slumped down as *Kestrel* lurched a little nearer the upright.

'But our orders do not allow me discretion. Santhonax has escaped, in the meantime we must do our duty.' He paused, rubbing his chin while Drinkwater remained standing. 'But,' he said slowly, 'if we could discover the precise state of the mutiny . . . if, for instance there were signs that they were moving out from the Nore, then, by God, we'd know for sure.'

Drinkwater nodded. He was not certain how they could discover this without running their heads into a noose, but he could not now tell Griffiths of the encounter in Sheerness and the premonitions that were consuming him at that very moment. For the time being he must rest content.

Two hours later they were under way again. The breeze had come up, although the fog had become a mist and the warmth of the sun could be felt as *Kestrel* resumed her westward passage. It was late afternoon when a cry from forward caught the attention of all on deck.

'Sir!'

'What is it?' Drinkwater scrambled forward.

'Sort of smashing sound,' the man said, cocking one ear. They listened and Drinkwater heard a muffled bang followed by crashes and the splintering of timber. He frowned. 'Swivel gun?' He turned aft. 'Call all hands! Pass word for the captain! Clear for action!' He was damned if he was going to be caught a second time.

In a few moments the lashings were cast off the guns and the men were at their stations. Griffiths emerged from the companionway pale and drawn. Drinkwater launched into an explanation of what they had heard when suddenly the fog lifted, swept aside like a curtain, and bright sunshine dappled the water.

'What the devil . . .?' Griffiths pointed and Drinkwater turned sharply, then grinned with relief.

'It's all right, sir, I recognise her.'

Ahead of them, a cable distant, lay an ornate, cutter-rigged yacht, decorated aft like a first rate, with a beak head forward supporting a lion guardant. Alongside the yacht the painted bulk of the Nubb buoy was being systematically smashed by axes and one-pound swivel shot.

'Trinity Yacht ahoy!' Faces looked up and Drinkwater saw her master, Jonathan Poulter, direct men aft to where she carried carronades. He saw the gunports lift and the muzzles emerge.

'Hold your fire, damn your eyes! We're a King's cutter,' then in a lower voice as they closed the yacht, 'Heave to, Mr Drinkwater, while we speak him.'

The two cutters closed, their crews regarding each other curiously. 'Do you have news of the Nore fleet, is there any sign of them moving?'

A man in a blue coat stood beside Poulter and Drinkwater recognised Captain Calvert, an Elder Brother of Trinity House.

'No, sir,' Calvert called, 'and they'll find it impossible when we've finished. All the beacons are coming down and most of the buoys are already sunk. Another night's work will see the matter concluded . . . is that Mr Drinkwater alongside of you?'

Drinkwater stood on the rail. 'Aye sir, we had hopes that you might have news.'

'They had a frigate down at the Middle flying the red flag yesterday to mark the bank and the fear is they'll try treason . . . they've gone too far now for anything else . . . my guess is they'll try for France or Holland. Are you from Duncan?'

'Aye,' it was Griffiths who spoke now. 'Are you sure of your facts, sir?'

'Aye, sir. We left Broadstairs yesterday. The intelligence about the frigate we learned from the buoy yacht *Argus* from Harwich; I myself called on Admiral Buckner at Sheerness on my way from London.'

Griffiths reflected a moment. 'And you think they'll try and break out?'

'It's that or starve and swing.'

Griffiths eyed the pendant. 'Starboard tack, Mr Drinkwater,' then in a louder voice as *Kestrel* turned away, 'Much obliged to you, sir, God speed.'

The two cutters parted, *Kestrel* standing seawards again. Griffiths came aft to where Drinkwater was setting the new course.

'Black Deep, sir?'

'Aye if she'll hold the course.' Griffiths shivered and wiped the back of his hand across his forehead.

'She'll hold it, sir, with the centre plates down. I take it we're for Yarmouth?'

Griffiths nodded. 'Mr Drinkwater . . .' He jerked his head sideways and walked to the rail, staring astern to where, alongside the Trinity Yacht, the Nubb buoy was sinking. In a low voice he said, 'It seems we have our proof, Nathaniel . . .' His white eyebrows shot up in two arches.

'Aye sir. I'd come to pretty much the same conclusion.'

After *Kestrel* the admiral's cabin aboard *Venerable* seemed vast, but Admiral Duncan was a big man with a broad Scots face and, even seated, he dominated it. There was a story that he had subdued *Adamant*'s crew by picking up one of her more vociferous seamen and holding him, one armed, over the side with the sarcastic comments that the fellow dared deprive him of command of the fleet. The general laughter that followed this spectacle had ensured *Adamant*'s loyalty.

As Griffiths, unwell and sweating profusely, strove to explain the significance of their news, Drinkwater examined the other occupants of the cabin in whose august company he now found himself. There was Captain Fairfax, Duncan's flag-captain, and Captain William Bligh. Drinkwater regarded 'Bounty' Bligh with ill-concealed curiosity. The captain had a handsome head, with a blue jaw and firm chin. The forehead was high, the hairline balding and his grey hair drawn back into a queue. Bligh's eyes were penetrating and hazel, reminding Drinkwater of Dungarth's, the nose straight and flanked with fine nostrils. Only the mouth

324

showed anything in the face that was ignoble, a petulance confirmed by his voice which had a quality of almost continuous
exasperation. The remaining person was Major Brown, summoned
by telegraph from London and still eating the chicken leg offered
him on his arrival.

'Now I'm not quite clear about the significance of this Santhonax,'
frowned the admiral, 'if I'm losing my ships do I really have to
bother about one man?'

'If he's the man we think, sir,' put in Bligh in his high-toned voice,
'I consider him to be most dangerous. If he is the man said to have
been seen aboard several of the ships at the Nore as this gentleman,'
Bligh indicated Brown, 'seems to think, then I'd rate him as the most
seditious rascal among the clutch of gallowsbirds. They deserve to
swing, the whole festering nest of them.'

'Thank ye, captain,' said Duncan, with just a touch of irony.
'Major Brown?'

The major always seemed to be called on for explanations in the
middle of a mouthful, thought Drinkwater as he pricked up his ears
to hear what news Brown had brought.

'It seems certain, gentlemen, that this man was indeed Capitaine
Santhonax, a French agent whose current duty seems to be to suborn
the Nore fleet. There were reports of him in connection with the
Culloden affair. One of the sailing masters held aboard *Sandwich*
recognised him as a Frenchman and smuggled word ashore by a
bumboat. Apparently they had fought hand to hand off Trincomalee
in the last war,' he explained, 'and a number of other reports,' here
he paused and inclined his head slightly towards Drinkwater and
Griffiths, 'have led us to take an interest in him . . . it would appear
he has been the *eminence grise* behind Richard Parker.'

Bligh nodded sharply, 'And behind the removal of myself and my
officers from my ship!'

'But he has escaped us now,' soothed Duncan, 'so where's all this
leading us?'

Brown shrugged, 'Captain Fairfax tells me you captured the Nore
delegates on their way here.'

'Aye, Major, *Rose* took *Cygnet* off Orfordness so our friend is not
coming here.'

Drinkwater looked desperately round the circle of faces. Did none of them see what was obvious to him? He looked at Griffiths but the lieutenant had drifted into a doze.

'Excuse me sir.' Drinkwater could hold his tongue no longer.

'Yes, what is it Mr, er, Drinkwater?' Duncan looked up.

'With respect, sir, may I submit that I believe Santhonax was in the boat on passage to Holland . . .' he paused, faltering before the gold lace that appeared to take heed of him for the first time.

'Go on, Mr Drinkwater,' encouraged Brown, leaning forward a half-smile on his face.

'Well sir,' Drinkwater doggedly addressed the admiral, 'I believe from all the facts I know, including the news from the Trinity Yacht relative to the movements of the Nore ships, that a defection of the fleet was ripe. Santhonax was bound for Holland to bring out Dutch ships . . .'

'To cover the defection of the Nore squadron, by heaven!' Fairfax finished the sentence.

'Exactly, sir,' Drinkwater nodded.

'But that smacks of conspiracy, gentlemen, of collusion with a foreign power. Och, I don't believe it, man.' The admiral looked for support to Fairfax who, with the discretionary latitude of a flag-captain said gently, 'Your good-nature, sir, does you credit but I fear Mr Drinkwater may be right. Jack Tar is not always the easy-going lion the populace likes to imagine him . . .' They all looked at the old admiral until Brown's voice cut in.

'We have a woman in Maidstone Gaol that would support Mr Drinkwater's theory, sir.'

'A woman, sir! What in God's name has a woman to do with a fleet mutiny?'

Drinkwater's pulse had quickened as he realised Brown knew more than he had so far admitted. He was eager to ask the woman's identity but he already knew it.

'That, Admiral Duncan, is something we'd very much like to know.'

'Well has the woman told ye anything?'

Brown smiled. 'She is not the type to go in for confessions, sir.'

'But she is not beyond sustaining a conspiracy, sir,' put in Drinkwater with a sudden vehemence.

'So you ken the woman, Mr Drinkwater?' The admiral's brows

showed signs of anger. 'There seems to be a deal about this matter that is known to the masters of cutters and denied to commanders-in-chief. Now, sir,' he rounded on Brown, 'd'ye tell me exactly who and what this woman is, what her connection is with our French agent and what it's all to do with my fleet.'

'*Kestrel* brought Mlle Montholon, the woman now in custody, out of France, sir . . .' Brown went on to outline the incidents that had involved the cutter. Drinkwater only half listened. So Hortense was in prison now. His suspicions had been confirmed after all. He wondered if Santhonax knew and doubted it would have much effect on him if he did. Hortense would not have confessed, but he guessed her pride had made her defiant and she had let slip enough. He wondered how Brown's men had eventually taken her and was satisfied in his curiosity as the major concluded: '. . . and so it seemed necessary to examine the young woman more closely. A theft of jewellery was, er, traced to a footman attending the Dowager Comtesse De Tocqueville and in the resulting search of her house a number of interesting documents and a considerable sum of gold was discovered.' He paused to sip from a glass of wine and ended with that curiously Gallic shrug. 'And so we had her.'

When he had finished Duncan shook his head. 'It's all most remarkable, most remarkable. She must be a she-devil . . .'

Beside Drinkwater Griffiths stirred and growled in Welsh, '*Hwyl*, sir . . . she has *hwyl*, the power to stir men's bowels.'

'But it is not the woman that concerns us now, Admiral Duncan,' said Brown. 'The man Santhonax is the real danger. Mr Drinkwater is right and we are certain he intends to bring out the Dutch. He has been in close consultation with Parker and if the mutiny is wavering De Winter must come out at the first opportunity or be more securely shut up in the Texel. If, on the other hand, he emerges to cover the Thames and the Nore ships join him, I leave the consequences to your imagination. Such a force on the doorstep of London would draw the Channel fleet east uncovering Brest, leaving the road clear for Ireland, the West Indies, India. Whichever way you look at it to have the Dutch at sea, *mutiny or not*, would put us in a most dangerous situation. Add the complication of an undefended east coast and a force of republican mutineers in the Thames, then,' Brown spread his hands and shrugged again in that now familiar gesture that was a legacy of his sojourns amongst the Canadians and the French. But it was supremely eloquent for the occasion.

Duncan nodded. 'Those very facts have been my constant companions for the past weeks. I begin to perceive this Santhonax is something of a red hot shot.'

'What is the state of your own ships, Admiral?' asked Brown.

'That, Major, is a deuced canny question.'

Admiral Duncan's fleet deserted him piecemeal in the next few days. Off the Texel Captain Trollope in the *Russell*, 74, with a handful of cutters, luggers and a frigate or two, maintained the illusion of blockade. Five of his battleships left for the Nore.

On the 29th May Duncan threw out the signal to weigh. His remaining ships stood clear of Yarmouth Roads until, one by one, they turned south-west, towards the Thames. Three hours after sailing only *Venerable*, 74, *Adamant*, 50 and the smaller *Trent* and *Circe*, together with *Kestrel*, remained loyal to their admiral.

The passage across the North Sea was a dismal one. In a way Drinkwater was relieved they were returning to the Texel. Wearying though blockade duty was, he felt instinctively that that was where they should be, no matter to what straits they were reduced. Brown thought so too, for after sending a cipher by the telegraph to the Admiralty, he had joined the cutter with Lord Dungarth's blessing.

'I think, Mr Drinkwater,' he had said, 'that you may take the credit for having set a portfire to the train now and we must wait patiently upon events.'

And patiently they did wait, for the first days of June the wind was in the east. De Winter's fleet of fourteen sail of the line, eight frigates and seventy-three transports and storeships were kept in the Texel by the two British battleships, a few frigates and small fry who made constant signals to one another in a ruse to persuade the watching Dutch that a great fleet lay in the offing of which this was but the inshore squadron.

But would such a deception work?

Chapter Thirteen

No Glory but the Gale

The splash of a cannon shot showed briefly in the water off *Kestrel*'s starboard bow where she lay in the yeasty waters of the Schulpen Gat, close to the beach at Kijkduin.

'They have brought horse artillery today, Mr Drinkwater,' said Major Brown from the side of his mouth as both men stared through their telescopes.

Drinkwater could see the knot of officers watching them. One was dismounted and kneeling on the ground, a huge field glass on the shoulder of an orderly grovelling in front of him.

'That one in the brown coat, d'you know who he is?'

Drinkwater swung his glass. He could see a man in a brown drab coat, but it was not in the least familiar. 'No sir.'

'That,' said Brown with significant emphasis, 'is Wolfe Tone . . .'

Drinkwater looked again. There was nothing remarkable about the man portrayed as a traitor to his country. *Kestrel* bucked inshore and Drinkwater turned to order her laid off a point more. 'I'll give them the usual salute then.'

'Yes – no! Wait! Look at the man next but one to Tone.' Brown was excited and Drinkwater put up his glass again to see a tall figure emerge from behind a horse. Even at that distance Drinkwater knew the man was Santhonax, a Santhonax resplendent in the blue and gold of naval uniform, and it seemed to Drinkwater that across that tumbling quarter mile of breakers and sea-washed sand that Santhonax stared back at him. He lowered the glass and looked at Brown. 'Santhonax.' Brown nodded.

'You were right, Mr Drinkwater. Now give 'em the usual.'

Drinkwater waved forward and saw Traveller stand back from the gun. The four-pounder roared and the men cheered when the ball ricochetted amongst the officers. Their horses reared in fright and one fell screaming on broken legs.

'Stand by heads'l sheets there! Weather runner! Stand by to gybe! Mind your head, Major!' Drinkwater called to Brown who had hoisted himself on to Number 11 gun to witness the fall of shot. 'Up helm . . . mainsheet now, watch there! Watch!'

Kestrel turned away from the shore as the field-gun barked again. The shot ripped through the bulwarks on the quarter and passed between the two helmsmen. The wind of its passage sent them gasping to the deck and Drinkwater jumped for the big tiller. Then the cutter was stern to the beach and rolling over in a thunderous clatter of gybing spars and canvas. 'Larboard runner!' Men tramped aft with the fall of the big double burton and belayed it, the sheets were trimmed and *Kestrel* steadied on her course out of the Schulpen Gat to work her way round the Haakagronden to where Duncan awaited her report.

The admiral was on *Venerable*'s quarterdeck when Drinkwater went up the side. He saluted and made his report to Duncan. The admiral nodded and asked, 'And how is Lieutenant Griffiths today?'

Drinkwater shook his head. 'The surgeon's been up with him all night, sir, but there appears to be no improvement. This is the worst I've known him, sir.'

Duncan nodded. 'He's still adamant he doesn't want a relief?'

'Aye sir.'

'Very well, Mr Drinkwater. Return to your station.'

The strange situation that Duncan found himself in of an admiral almost without ships, compelled him to tread circumspectly. He did not wish to transfer officers or disrupt the delicate loyalties of his pitifully small squadron. Griffiths was known to him and had indicated the professional worth of *Kestrel*'s sailing master. The admiral, astute in the matter of personal evaluation, had formed his own favourable impression of Drinkwater's abilities.

As the week of easterly winds ended, when the period of greatest danger seemed to be over, Duncan received reinforcements. Sir Roger Curtis arrived with some units of the Channel Fleet. *Glatton*, the curious ex-Indiaman armed only with carronades, had mutinied, gone to the Downs and cooled her heels. There her people resolved not to desert their admiral and returned to station. Other odd ships arrived including a Russian squadron under Admiral Hanikov. Then, at the end of June, the Nore mutiny had collapsed and Duncan's ships returned to him. At full strength the North Sea squadron maintained the blockade through the next spell of easterly winds at the beginning of July.

Kestrel made her daily patrols while Griffiths lay sweating in his cot, Appleby a fretful shadow over him. They saw no more of Santhonax and still the Dutch did not come out. Major Brown became increasingly irritated by the turn of events. Santhonax had shot his bolt. The Nore mutiny had collapsed and the French captain had failed, just as he had failed on the *Culloden*. Now, if he was still at the Texel, Santhonax had failed to coerce De Winter.

'A man of action, Mr Drinkwater, cannot sit on his arse for long. This business of naval blockade is the very essence of tedium.'

Drinkwater smiled over his coffee. 'I doubt you would be of that opinion, sir, if the conduct of the ships were yours. For us it is a wearing occupation, requiring constant vigilance.'

'Oh I daresay,' put in Brown crossly, 'but I've a feeling that De Winter won't shift. When we next report to the admiral I shall transfer to the flagship and take the first despatch vessel to Yarmouth. No, Mr Drinkwater, that train of powder has gone out.'

'Well sir,' answered Drinkwater rising from the table and reaching for his hat, 'perhaps it was a little longer than you expected.'

Major Brown stared after the younger man, trying to decide if he had been the victim of impertinence or perception. Certainly he bridled at Drinkwater's apparent lack of respect for a major in His Majesty's Life Guards, but he knew Nathaniel was no fool, no fool at all. Brown remembered the dinner at the Fountain and Drinkwater's insistence that the presence of the uniforms, charts and money indicated the *Citoyenne Janine* held a secret. He also remembered that he had been less than frank about what he had discovered at Tunbridge Wells.

It was true, as he had said to Lord Dungarth, that he had not *found* anything. But where the wolf has slept the grass remains rank. That much he had learned from the Iroquois, and he was no longer in doubt that Santhonax lay frequently at Tunbridge, in enviable circumstances too. A refuge in Hortense's arms was typically Gallic, and if Santhonax had not persuaded her to flee from France in the first place he had turned that fortuitous exit to his own advantage.

But Brown could not admit as much to Dungarth before *Kestrel*'s officers. He had lain a trap and until Santhonax sprung it the hunter remained silent. He had learned that too from the painted men of the Six Nations.

Whether Dungarth had guessed as much when he had ordered surveillance of the Dowager Comtesse's household mattered little. Santhonax had eluded Brown just as Brown had escaped from Santhonax in Paris.

The major bit his lip over the recollection. Had the girl detected him? As he had seen her on the arm of her handsome naval lover in Paris, had she perhaps seen Brown himself some time during the negotiations with Barrallier and De Tocqueville? That would have revealed his true allegiance, and Etienne Montholon had been a party to the arrangements. He tried to recollect if she might have discovered him with Santhonax during his spell as a clerk in the Ministry of Marine. Then he shrugged, 'It's possible . . .'

Santhonax had reached the coast before him, had nearly cut off *Kestrel* but for Madoc's skill and young Drinkwater's timely rescue. It brought him full circle. Was Drinkwater right and Santhonax still trying to bully Jan De Winter into sailing? Brown knew Santhonax to be ruthless. He was certain the man had had De Tocqueville assassinated in London, the more so as it removed a threat to his occupancy of Hortense's bed. And the officer commanding the naval forces at Roscoff had been shot for his prudence in strengthening a convoy escort by the addition of the *Citoyenne Janine*. His mistake was in requisitioning Santhonax's own lugger. Brown's reflection that that meant one less Frenchman to worry about begged the pressing question. It pecked at his present frustration, counselling caution, caution.

Was Santhonax still at the Texel? Was Drinkwater right? Did the train of powder still sputter here, off the Haakagronden? Was De Winter under French pressure?

'It's possible,' he repeated to himself, 'and there is only one way to find out.'

And he shuddered, the old image of geese over a grave springing unbidden into his mind.

*

Drinkwater was very tired. The regular swing of the oarsmen had a soporific effect now that they had run into the smoother water of the Zeegat van Texel. Astern of them in the darkness the curve of sand dunes and marram grass curled round to Kijkduin and the Schulpen Gat, where *Kestrel* lay at anchor. It was late before full darkness had come and they had little time to execute their task. Drinkwater pulled the tiller slightly to larboard, following the coast round to the east. He steadied it again, feeling the bulk of the man next to him.

Major Brown, wrapped in a cloak under which he concealed a small bag of provisions, had insisted that he be landed. From his bunk Griffiths had been powerless to prevent what he felt to be a hopeless task. He did not doubt Brown's abilities but the gleaning of news of De Winter's intentions was a desperate throw. Griffiths had therefore instructed Drinkwater to land the agent himself. Johnson, the carpenter, had contrived a pair of clogs and they had been carefully scuffed and dirtied as Brown prepared himself in the seamen's cast-offs as a grubby and suitably malodorous fisherman.

Drinkwater turned the boat inshore and whispered 'Oars'. The men ceased pulling and a few moments later the bow of the gig grounded with a gentle lift. Brown shrugged off the cloak and scrambled forward between the pairs of oarsmen. Drinkwater followed him on to the beach and walked up it with him to discover a landmark by which they might both return to the spot. They found some fishing stakes which were sufficient to answer their purpose.

'I'll be off then, Mr Drinkwater.' Brown shouldered his bag and a dimly perceived hand was thrust uncertainly out in an uncharacteristic gesture. 'Until two days hence then. Wish me luck . . . I don't speak Dutch.'

As he turned away Drinkwater noticed the carriage of confidence was missing, the step unsure. Then he jeered at his qualms. Walking in clogs was bad enough. Doing it in soft sand damned near impossible.

On the afternoon of the day on which they were due to recover Major Brown, *Kestrel* sailed into the Schulpen Gat, taking the tide along the coast on her routine patrol. When the masts of the Dutch fleet had been counted over the intervening sand dunes and attempts made to divine whether De Winter had advanced his preparations to sail, which all except Drinkwater were now beginning to doubt, she would retire seawards until her midnight rendezvous with the agent.

As she stood inshore towards the battery at Kijkduin, Drinkwater scanned the beach. The usual officer and orderly were observing their progress. He slewed the telescope and caught in its dancing circle the rampart of the battery. Then he saw something that turned his blood cold.

A new structure had been erected above the gun embrasures, gaunt against the blue of heaven and terrifying in its sinister outline. And from the gibbet, unmistakable in the faded blue of *Kestrel*'s slops, swung the body of Major Brown.

Drinkwater lowered the glass and called for Jessup. The bosun came up immediately aware of the cold gleam in Drinkwater's grey eyes. 'Sir?'

'See if Lieutenant Griffiths is fit enough to come on deck.' Drinkwater's voice was strangely controlled, like a man compelled to speak when he would rather weep.

'Nat, what the deuce is this . . .?' Appleby came protesting out of the companionway.

"Vast that, Harry!' snapped Drinkwater, seeing Griffiths following the surgeon on deck, the flutter of his nightgown beneath his coat.

Without a word Drinkwater handed the telescope to Griffiths and pointed at the battery. Even as he watched the lieutenant for a sign of emotion Drinkwater heard the dull concussion of the first cannon shot roll over the sea. He did not see the fall of shot, only the whitening of the already pallid Welshman and when he lowered the glass Griffiths, too, spoke as though choking.

'Our friend Santhonax did that, Mr Drinkwater, put the vessel about upon the instant.' Griffiths paused. 'That devil's spawn is here then,' he muttered, turning aft.

Drinkwater gave orders and watched Griffiths stagger back to the companionway, a man who looked his years, sick and frail. The battery fired again, shot rained about them and they were hulled once. Running south with the wind free and his back to the gibbet, Drinkwater imagined he could hear the creaking of the contraption

334

and the laughter of the gunners as they toiled beneath their grim trophy.

The death of Major Brown had a desolating effect on *Kestrel*. The enigmatic army officer had become almost one of themselves and the cramped cabin was a sad place without him. For Madoc Griffiths the loss was more personal, their friendship one of long standing. In the twilit world of their professions strange and powerful bonds drew men together.

'Brown was not his real name,' Griffiths had muttered, and it was all the epitaph the Major ever had.

It seemed that his death extinguished the powder train whose extent he had been so eager to determine. Whatever Santhonax's achievements in the apprehension of spies it was apparent to the watching British that he had failed to persuade De Winter to sail.

Yet Duncan, and in a lesser way Nathaniel Drinkwater too, persisted in their belief that the Dutch might yet sally; or at least must be prevented from so doing. As the summer waned and turned to autumn the routine blockade wore down men and ships. Much of the time the line of battleships lay anchored, weighing and standing offshore, even sheltering in Yarmouth Road when the weather became too boisterous. Hovering on the western margins of the Haakagronden the inshore squadron, the frigates *Beaulieu* and *Circe* and the sloop *Martin*, maintained the visual link between the admiral and those in close contact with the enemy, the lieutenants in command of the little flotilla of cutters and luggers working inside the Haak Sand.

The cutters *Rose*, *King George*, *Diligent*, *Active* and *Kestrel* kept their stations through the long weeks, assisted by the luggers *Black Joke* and *Speculator*. The last two named provided endless witticisms as to predicting whether the Dutch would, or would not, emerge. When *Speculator* was on an advanced station the chances were said to be better than when the sardonically named *Black Joke* was inshore.

These small fry fell into a routine of patrolling the gatways, acting as fleet tenders and advice boats. It was exhausting work that seemed to be endless. Scouting through the approaches to the channels, counting the mastheads of the enemy, determining which had their topmasts up and yards across, constantly worrying about the shoals, the state of the tide and whether a change of wind might not bottle them up in range of a field-gun or battery.

Griffiths's health improved and he reassumed effective command of *Kestrel*. But the Dutch did not come out. As week succeeded week, expectancy turned to irritation and then to grumbling frustration. In the fleet, officers, still suspicious after the mutiny, watched for signs of further trouble as the quality of rations deteriorated with the passing of time. Imperceptibly at first, but with mounting emphasis, discipline was tightened and a return 'to the old days' feared on every lower deck. Among the men the triumph of the mutiny was lost in petty squabblings and resentments. Men remembered that executions had followed the suppression of the Nore affair, that they still had had no liberty, that the pursers were not noticeably more generous or their pay more readily available.

Then the weather worsened with the onset of September and the admiral, taking stock of the condition of his fleet, decided that he must return to Yarmouth to refit, replenish stores and land his sick. For scurvy had broken out and no admiral as considerate of his men as Adam Duncan could keep the sea under those circumstances. Yet, in the leaking cabin of *Venerable* he still fretted as to whether the Dutch, supine for so long, might not still take advantage of his absence.

Drinkwater peered into the screaming darkness, holding on to the weather shrouds and bracing himself against the force of the westerly gale. *Kestrel*, hard reefed with her centre plates down, stood north-west, beating out of the Molen Gat, clawing to windward for sea-room and safety. Somewhere to the south of her, across the roaring fury of the breakers on the Haakagronden, *Diligent* would be thrashing out of the Schulpen Gat while *Rose* should have quitted the West Gat long since.

Drinkwater rubbed his eyes, but the salt spray inflamed them and the fury of the wind made staring directly to windward impossible. He had hoped to see a lantern from *Circe* but he had difficulty seeing further than the next wave as it rose out of the darkness to larboard, its rolling crest already being torn to shreds by the violence of the wind.

Kestrel's bow thumped into it, the long line of her bowsprit disappearing. Water squirted inboard round the lips of her gunports and a line of white foam rose to her rail but she did not ship any green water. Drinkwater was seized with a sudden savage satisfaction in the noble way the cutter behaved. In the tense moments when they could do nothing but hang on, trusting to the art of the Wivenhoe shipwrights who had built her, she never failed them.

He turned and cautiously moved aft, his tarpaulin flapping round him. When he had checked the course, he secured himself by the larboard running backstay, passing a turn of its tail around his waist.

Tregembo approached, a pale blur in the darkness. 'You sent for me sir?'

'Aye, Tregembo. An occasional cast of the lead if you can manage it.' He sensed rather than saw the Cornishman grin.

They must not go aground tonight.

Drinkwater adjusted himself against the big stay's downhaul. He could feel the trembling of the top-hamper transmitted down to the hull as a gentle vibration that transferred itself to his body, so that he felt a part of the fabric of the cutter. It was a very satisfying feeling he concluded, a warm glow within him defying the hideous howl of the gale. For a time the image of Brown in his gibbet was dimmed.

Drinkwater noted the helm relieved, the two men leaving the tiller, flexing their arms with relief and seeking shelter beneath the lee gig. A sea crashed against the hull and foamed brutally over the rail, sluicing the deck white and breaking in eddies round the deck fittings. They would be clearing the Molen Gat now, leaving the comparative shelter of the Haakagronden.

Again he peered to windward seeking a light from the frigate. Nothing.

The Dutch would never come out in weather like this, thought Drinkwater. It was going to be a long, dirty night for the British blockaders and there was little glory in such a gale.

They reached the admiral at ten in the morning. The gale was at its height, a low scud drifting malignantly across the sky reducing the visibility to a monotonous circle of grey breaking waves, streaked with white spindrift that merged at its margins with the lowering clouds. In and out of this pall the pale squares of reefed topsails and the dark shapes of hulls streaming with water were all

337

that could be seen of the blockading battleships. Even the patches of the blue ensigns of Duncan's squadron seemed leeched to the surrounding drab.

Kestrel had come up under *Venerable*'s lee quarter like a leaping cork, or so it seemed to the officers on the flagship's quarterdeck, and the admiral had had his orders sealed in a keg and thrown into the sea.

With great skill Griffiths had manoeuvred in the flagship's wake to recover the keg. 'Orders for the fleet, Mr Drinkwater, excepting for *Russell*, *Adamant*, *Beaulieu*, *Circe*, *Martin* and two cutters, ah, and *Black Joke*, the fleet's for Yarmouth Road.'

'And we're to tell 'em?'

Griffiths nodded. 'Very good, sir, we'll bear away directly.'

Dipping her ensign in acknowledgement of her instructions *Kestrel* turned away.

As she steadied on her course Drinkwater returned to Griffiths's side. 'What about us, sir?'

'*Active* and *Diligent* to remain, the rest of us for Yarmouth.'

Drinkwater nodded. The nagging notion that they had unfinished business off the Texel caused him to catch Griffiths's eye. Griffiths held his gaze but said nothing. Both of them were thinking of the shrivelling body of their friend.

They were running downwind now, closing Vice-Admiral Onslow in the *Monarch*. Passing their message they reached down the line of Onslow's division, watching the lumbering third rates, *Powerful*, *Montagu* and *Russell*, the smaller sixty-fours *Veteran* and *Agincourt* with Bligh's *Director*. Next they passed word to the obsolete old *Adamant*, she that so gallantly supported Duncan's deception off the Texel. They found *Circe* and *Beaulieu* and both the luggers hanging on to the frigates like children round their mother's skirts. It was dark before they returned to *Venerable* and sent up a damply fizzing blue rocket as a signal to the admiral.

Drinkwater scrambled below, jamming himself into a corner of the cabin and gratefully accepted a bowl from Merrick. The skillygolee was all that could be heated on the galley stove but it tasted excellent laced with molasses and he wolfed it, aware that Appleby was hovering in the doorway.

'D'you want me, Harry?' Drinkwater asked, nodding to Traveller

338

who was groping his way into the cabin, bracing himself against the violence of the cutter's motion, also in search of something to eat.

Appleby nodded too. 'A word, Nat, if you've a moment . . .' He plucked at Drinkwater's sleeve and drew him towards his own cabin.

'By God, that skilly was good . . . Hey! Merrick! D'you have any more?' Fresh from the deck and very hungry Drinkwater found Appleby irritated him.

'Nat, for heaven's sake, a moment of your time. Listen, while you and Griffiths have been busy on deck I have been increasingly aware of unrest in the ship . . . nothing I can pin down, but this miserable blockade duty at a season of the year when no self-respecting Dutchman is going to emerge into the North Sea when he has a bed ashore, is playing the devil with the men. No, don't dismiss me as a meddling old fool. I have observed glances, mutterings, listened to remarks dropped near me. Damn it, Nat, you know the kind of thing . . .'

'Oh come now Harry, I doubt now that we're going back to Yarmouth that anything will materialise,' Drinkwater bit off a jibe at Appleby's increasing preoccupation with mutiny. Blockade duty in such a small vessel was playing on all their nerves, even those of the men, and it was doubtless this irritation had manifested itself to Appleby. 'What seaman doesn't grumble, Harry? You are worrying for nothing, forget it . . .'

There was a thumping crash and the bulkhead behind them trembled. From the lobby outside a torrent of Welsh oaths mixed with Anglo-Saxon expletives ended the conversation. Appleby threw open the door to reveal Lieutenant Griffiths lying awkwardly at the foot of the ladder. His face contorted with pain.

'My leg, doctor . . . By damn, I've broken my leg!'

Chapter Fourteen *5th–7th October 1797*

A Private Insurrection

'Can you manage the cutter, Mr Drinkwater?'

Drinkwater looked at the admiral. Duncan's eyes were tired from a multitude of responsibilities. He nodded. 'I believe so, sir.'

'Very well. I will have an acting commission made out immediately. You have been acting before, have you not?'

'Yes sir. Twice.'

Duncan nodded. 'Good. If you discharge your duty to my satisfaction I shall see that it is confirmed without further ado . . . now sit down a moment.' Duncan rang a bell and his servant entered the cabin. 'Sir?'

'My secretary, Knapton, and my compliments to Captain Fairfax and will he bring in his lordship,' he turned to Drinkwater. 'It'll not hurt you to know what's in the wind, Mr Drinkwater, as you are to occupy an advanced station. Were you not part of the prize crew that brought in *Santa Teresa* to Gibraltar in '80?'

'Yes sir. She was commanded by Lieutenant Devaux, Lord Dungarth as is now, sir.'

'Aye, I remember your name now, and here is his lordship,' Duncan rose stooping under the deckhead to motion Lord Dungarth and Captain Fairfax to chairs.

Drinkwater covered his astonishment at the earl's sudden appearance with a bow. He remained standing until the admiral motioned him to sit again.

'Now gentlemen, Mr Drinkwater is to remain. Under the circumstances he ought properly to be informed of our deliberations and can convey their substance to Trollope. I have given him an acting commission. Now, my Lord, what have you to tell us?'

'You could not have made a better choice, Admiral,' put in Dungarth, smiling at Drinkwater. 'Now when are you able to sail?'

The old admiral passed a hand over his face. 'I *must* have a few more days to recruit the fleet. Yes what is it?' Duncan paused at the knock on the door. A large man with a saturnine face entered. He was in admiral's uniform. 'Ah, Richard, come in, you know Fairfax of course, this is Lord Dungarth, from the Admiralty . . .' Onslow's eyebrows lifted, '. . . and this is Lieutenant Drinkwater of *Kestrel*.'

Drinkwater rose and bowed. 'Your servant, sir.'

'What happened to Griffiths?'

Duncan said, 'Broke his leg and I've promoted Drinkwater, he kens the crew and I'm not one to be fussing about with officers on other ships with the situation as delicate as it is now . . .' He looked significantly at Onslow who nodded his agreement. Drinkwater realised there were doubtless a score of passed midshipmen who might regard their claim on the first available commission as better than his own.

'Congratulations, Mr Drinkwater,' said Onslow. 'Are you familiar with Psalm 75? No? "Promotion cometh neither from the east, nor from the west, nor from the south, but God is the judge; he pulleth down one and setteth up another."'

The little group chuckled. Onslow was well-known for his Biblical references so that signals midshipmen had to keep a copy of the Bible alongside Kempenfelt's code.

'Most apposite. But to business. My Lord?'

'Well, gentlemen, since the regretted loss of Major Brown,' Dungarth paused and there was a deferential murmur as death passed his grim shadow across their council, 'I have learned from our people in Paris that Capitaine Santhonax has been seen there. However, his stay was not long and he was seen in The Hague last month. It is confidently expected that he is now back at the Texel breathing down De Winter's neck. We were under the impression that enthusiasm for another attempt upon Ireland has dwindled since the death of General Hoche. But Austria has reached an accommodation with this new General Bonaparte at Leoben and it seems likely that troops will be available for other enterprises.' He paused and accepted a glass of wine from Knapton who appeared with silent ease, bearing tall glasses on a silver salver.

'Most of you will know of the Director's raid last February on Fishguard. It was American led . . .' a murmur of anger went round the listeners. 'Although it was an ignominious failure the Directory learned that it was perfectly possible to land on our soil.

'Whether the target is Ireland or the mainland we do not know. However it seems certain that the Directory, in the person of Santhonax, will exert great pressure upon De Winter to sail. If he prevaricates he will be superseded and possibly more will be struck down than his flag. Jan De Winter is a convinced republican but a soldier by training. I think Santhonax is at his elbow to overcome his misgivings. So you see, gentlemen, De Winter *must come out* and you *must stop him*. A junction with the Brest squadrons would be disastrous for us on all fronts.'

There was an awkward shuffling of feet as Dungarth finished. The collection of ships that made up the North Sea squadron was far from the crack units of the Channel fleet, the Grand Fleet as it was commonly called.

'I must have a few more days,' said Duncan, looking anxiously at Onslow for support.

'I agree Adam. You'll have to inform Government, my Lord, we must have time, this squadron is cranky enough. Look, even its commander-in-chief has to endure this sort of thing . . .' Onslow pointed to the strategically located buckets in Duncan's cabin that had been placed to catch water from the leaks in the deckhead.

Drinkwater listened to the deliberations of his seniors with one ear and turned over Dungarth's news in his mind. So, his instinct had been right. They were not yet finished with the Texel. And he was not yet finished with Santhonax. He began to see that Ireland was probably the key. At least the paralysis of the British Fleet and combination of the republican navies for some expedition had been the mainspring of Santhonax's actions. And Brown had taken an interest in Wolfe Tone on the beach at Kijkduin. Yes, Santhonax's actions were clear now: the suborning of the British Fleet that had so nearly succeeded, the urgency to get Dutch support before the collapse of Parker's resolve. When that failed a last thrust from Brest with the combined fleets to force aside a Royal Navy weakened by mutiny, and then a descent on the naked coasts of Britain by a French army under this new general, said to be more brilliant than Hoche or Moreau, this General Bonaparte . . .

'Mr Drinkwater? . . . Mr Drinkwater!'

He came to with a start. 'I beg your pardon, sir. I, er, I was just digesting the implications of Lord Dungarth's . . .' he tailed off flushing scarlet.

'Yes, yes,' said Duncan testily, 'I will have written orders within the hour, please make yourself at home in the wardroom. You will convey my despatches to Trollope then station yourself as close to Kijkduin as ye can. I want to know the moment the Dutch move. D'ye understand, man?'

Drinkwater rose. 'Aye sir. Thank you for taking me into your confidence. Your servant gentlemen.' He bowed and made his way back on deck.

'You two are in collusion, damn you both,' Griffiths muttered, sweat standing out on his pale forehead, his pupils contracted by the opiate administered by Appleby.

'No sir,' said Drinkwater gently, 'that is really not the case at all. Admiral Duncan's orders, sir. If you will permit us we will have you ashore directly and into the hospital.' He motioned Short and a seaman into the cabin to lift Griffiths on to the stretcher. As they struggled through the door Appleby mopped his forehead.

'Phew! He took it from you like a lamb, Nat my boy. He's been tearing the seat out of my breeches this hour past.'

'Poor old fellow,' said Drinkwater, 'will his leg mend?'

Appleby nodded. 'Yes, if he keeps off it for a while, his constitution is remarkable considering the Gambia fever.'

'He'll miss his bottle in hospital.' They followed the stretcher up on deck where Jessup was preparing to lower the lieutenant into the waiting boat.

'Mr Drinkwater,' croaked Griffiths, trying to raise his head.

'Sir?' Drinkwater took the extended hand.

'Good luck to you Nathaniel *bach*, this may be your opportunity, see. Be vigilant and success will be within your grasp. Good luck now. Lower away you lubbers and handsomely, handsomely.'

Drinkwater saw the old man, wrapped in his wood and canvas shroud, pulled away from the cutter. He watched the gig curve away

343

for the shore and found his eyes misting. He dismissed sentiment from his mind and turned his attention inboard.

'Mr Jessup!'

'Sir?'

'Pipe the hands aft.'

His heart beat with a mixture of excitement and apprehension. His elevation to command might only be that of an officer 'acting', unsubstantive and very temporary, but for as long as it lasted he held power over the men who crowded round the remaining gig amidships, and was accountable for every movement of the cutter, the duty and mistakes of his subordinates. He reached into his pocket and withdrew the roll of paper.

When silence fell he began to read himself in.

At the conclusion of the solemnly formal words he added a sentence of his own. 'I trust you will do your duty for me as you did for Lieutenant Griffiths. Very well Mr Jessup, we will weigh directly the boat returns, you may heave short now.' Jessup shouted and the men turned away to make preparations. Drinkwater called to Hill. 'Mr Hill! Mr Hill, I am rating you master, do you take the first watch in my place.'

While the cutter's sails were cast loose he slipped below. Merrick, fussing like an old hen, was lugging the last of Drinkwater's gear out of the little cabin and settling it in the lieutenant commander's. It was a trifle larger than his own but in the rack for glass and carafe, Drinkwater wryly noted, the two objects were in place. As he hung the little watercolour he thought of Elizabeth. They had been separated for eighteen months now. It was a pity he had had no time to let her know of his promotion and Duncan's promise. A knock on the door interrupted his privacy. It was Appleby.

'Nat, er, sir,' Appleby rubbed a large, pudgy hand across his several chins.

'What is it?' asked Drinkwater, settling his books.

'I'm damned glad to see you promoted, Nat . . . sir . . . but believe me it is imperative you are circumspect with the men. They are still in an ugly mood. Orders for the Texel will do nothing to ameliorate that. It's nothing specific,' Appleby hurried on before Drinkwater could interrupt, 'but I anticipate that they will try you now Griffiths is gone, that's all . . .'

'You seem,' said Drinkwater passing a lashing round his quadrant box, 'to have let sedition, mutiny and all manner of lower deck bogeys infect your otherwise good sense, Harry.'

'For God's sake, Nat, damn it, sir, take my warning lightly and you do so at your peril.'

Drinkwater felt anger rising in him. To be thwarted now filled him with horror and Appleby's defeatism galled him. He mastered himself with difficulty.

'Look Harry, we have been weeks on this tedious blockading, we are all worn with it, sick of it, but it is our duty and now, more than ever, there exists a need for cruisers off the Texel. D'you cease this damned cant at once.'

'For God's sake man, this command nonsense has gone to your head!'

'Have a care Harry,' said Drinkwater with low and furious menace in his voice. He pushed past the surgeon in search of the fresh air of the deck.

Bulman met him at the companionway. 'Mr Hill's compliments, Mr Drinkwater, and the anchor's underfoot and the gig approaching.'

Drinkwater nodded and strode to the rail, grasping it with trembling hands. Damn Appleby and his pusillanimous soul. He wanted to clear his mind of such gloomy thoughts to concentrate on his duty.

They recovered the gig and weighed, heading south east for St Nicholas Gat and the passage south of the Scroby Sands.

Forward the last lashings were being passed over the gig, the last coils of the halliards turned on to their pins and the taut sheets belayed. Hill had the cat stoppers clapped on and was passing the shank painter to secure the anchor against its billboard. Already two men had buckets over the side and were sluicing the mud of Yarmouth Road off the planking. Traveller was walking round the guns, checking their breechings. All was reassuringly normal. He relaxed and checked the course. Ahead of him lay the challenge of the Texel.

At midnight Appleby's apprehensions were fulfilled. When Hill turned the deck over to Jessup the men demanded to be paid. It was an odd and impossible request but had ranked as a grievance for many months. It was now that those who influenced the grumblings of the fo'c's'le chose to make it manifest itself. *Kestrel's* complement had not been paid for over a twelvemonth. Their recent period at anchor had been marred by a refusal of further credit by James Thompson, the purser, largely because that gentleman had himself run out of ready cash. This denial had led to the men being unable to make purchases from the bumboats of Yarmouth. The consequent lack of small comforts exacerbated the already strong resentment of the hands. By an irony several bottles of liquor had found their way on board and the consumption of these in the first watch had led to the midnight revolt.

Drinkwater was called and sleepily tumbled from his cot. But his dreams were quickly displaced by anger at the news Jessup brought him. For a minute, as he dressed while Jessup spoke he fulminated against the men, but he forced himself to acknowledge their grievance and that his own anger was unlikely to get him anywhere. But to pay them was not merely out of the question, it was impossible.

'Who's behind this, then, Mr Jessup, come on, there must be a ring-leader?'

Jessup shrugged. 'Not that I know of . . . here I'll do one of those.' He took one of the pistols that Drinkwater had taken out of their case. They belonged to Griffiths and Drinkwater thought furiously as he slipped the little ramrod back into its socket. 'Can I count on you Mr Jessup?'

'O' course, sir,' said Jessup indignantly.

'Very well, you keep that pistol then. Where are the men now?'

'On deck waiting for you.'

'Call all the other officers.'

'I did that on my way to you, ah, here's Mr Appleby . . .'

Appleby pushed into the cabin. 'I told you, Nat, I warned you . . .' His face was grey with worry and his nightgown increased his girth where it protruded from hastily drawn on breeches.

'To the devil with your premonitions, Harry. Are you armed?'

'Of course,' he held up a brace of heavy pistols. 'I've had these loaded and ready for a month.'

'Have you checked the primings then,' snapped Jessup and Appleby withered him at a glance.

'Right gentlemen. Let's go!' Traveller joined them in the lobby and they went on deck.

It was a clear night with a quartering wind and sea driving them east at a spanking rate. Patches of cloud obscured the stars. As his eyes adjusted to the darkness he could see Bulman had the helm and a blur of faces amidships showed where the hands waited to see what he would make of their action. Drinkwater knew that he must act with resolution and he turned briefly to the officers behind him.

'I expect your support. To the utmost if need be.'

Then he turned forward until he was no more than a yard from the waiting men. A cold and desperate feeling had settled on him. He would not be diverted from his orders now, nor from the one chance providence had so parsimoniously offered him. Instinctively he felt no man would offer him bodily harm. He was less sure of his own restraint.

He drew his hanger with a rasping flourish and noted the involuntary rearward movement, heard the sharp intake of breath.

'Now my lads, I know your grievance but this is not the time to air it. We are on urgent service and you'll all do your duty.' He let the words sink in.

'Bollocks,' came a voice from the rear of the crowd and he saw grins in the darkness.

He whipped the pistol from his belt and held it suddenly and terribly against the skull of the nearest seaman.

'Mr Jessup! Mr Appleby! Your weapons here upon the instant!'

Again he felt the will of the men waver: resolution from the rear, weakening from those in front. 'I will shoot this man if you do not disperse at once. I beg you not to force me to this extremity . . .' The man's eyes were enlarged with fear, the whites clear in the gloom.

'Jesus mates,' he whispered.

'Get fucked, Mr Drinkwater, you can't bluff us, we want our money.' A murmur of supporting approval greeted this sentiment.

With a click Drinkwater pulled the pistol hammer back to full cock. 'I'm not bluffing.' He ranged his eyes over the men. Behind him Appleby spoke, 'Mr Drinkwater has a reputation for courage, lads, I most earnestly recommend you not to strain his patience . . .'

'Aye, lads, Mr Appleby's right, remember that Froggy lugger . . .'
It was Tregembo's voice and Drinkwater held his tongue, aware of

the deadly little melodrama being played out. He did not know of the grisly reputation he had acquired for hand to hand fighting, of how it was said that he cleared the deck of the *Citoyenne Janine*, of how, in the American War, Mr Drinkwater killed the French officer of *La Creole* and still carried the dead man's sword to prove it.

Drinkwater felt the tide turn. 'I will count to five. If the watch below isn't off the deck by then I'll shoot. Otherwise we'll let the matter drop and I'll personally apply to the admiral for your pay. One . . . two . . .' The man beside him was trembling uncontrollably. Drinkwater brought the muzzle up. 'Three.'

A rearward surge went through the men. 'Four.'

Murmuring to themselves they went forward.

Drinkwater lowered his pistol. 'Carry on,' he said quietly to the frightened man beside him who trembled with reaction.

The mutiny was over. It was just one bell in the middle watch.

'Time for bed, gentlemen,' said Drinkwater in a tone taken for coolness by those who heard, but redolent with relief to his beating heart.

'Four bells, sir.'

Drinkwater stirred, swimming upwards from the depths of sleep to find Merrick bent over him and the aroma of coffee in his nostrils. Swinging his legs over the edge of the cot he took the mug while Merrick put a glim to his lantern. Drinkwater shivered in the predawn chill and felt a dull ache in his right arm. The pain reminded him of the events of the night and he was suddenly wide awake.

Merrick turned from adjusting the lantern. 'Mr Traveller said to tell you 'e expects to sight the squadron at first light, sir.'

'Then why didn't you say so when you called me?' Drinkwater felt a peevish irritation rising in him, together with a flood of loneliness that combined with the bitter realisation that in addition to a heavy responsibility to Duncan, he had to contend with a disobedient crew. He did not listen to Merrick's mumbling excuse and experienced a mean delight when the man fled.

While he shaved he calmed himself, shaking off resentment as the coffee scoured his mouth and cleared his head. Duncan's task was not impossible. Griffiths had been right, this could be his opportunity and he was damned if he was going to lose it now. Wiping the lather from his face he completed dressing and went on deck.

Exchanging courtesies with Traveller he walked to the weather rail. The north westerly breeze had held during the night and the eastern horizon was becoming more clearly defined against the coming daylight. For a moment he drank in the cold air of the morning then called to Traveller.

'Mr Drinkwater?'

'All quiet?'

'Not a peep. Begging your pardon, Mr Drinkwater, but I'd say as how you'll have no more trouble with this lot.' Drinkwater looked at the gunner.

'Let us hope you are right, Mr Traveller,' he replied as coolly as he could.

'We should sight the squadron very soon, sir. She was making nine knots at four bells.'

Drinkwater nodded and walked forward as far as the boats. Surreptitiously he shot a glance at the two helmsmen. They were intent on the compass. He had cowed them, it seemed, and with an effort he stopped twisting his hands nervously behind his back. He set his mind to preparing what he would say to Trollope in an hour or two.

'Wind's dying,' Hill said. They were well up into the Schulpen Gat, the battery at Kijkduin broad on the bow, just out of cannon shot. Mercifully the gibbet was no longer there. Against the south going tide they were making no headway and Drinkwater gave the order to anchor. Already the sun was westering and the night's chill could be felt in the air. Drinkwater looked at the sky. The cloud was clearing, the dunes, mills and churches of the Dutch coast had a sharpness that owed more to a drying of the air than the sinking of the sun.

'A shift of wind to the east, I think, Mr Hill.'

'Aye sir, happen you are right.'

Drinkwater waited until the hands had the sails down and stowed. Then he ordered a spring clapped on the cable, the charges drawn and the guns reloaded. While the men bustled round he ascended the rigging to the hounds. Securing himself he levelled his glass to the eastward.

He recalled the words of William Burroughs, first lieutenant of *Russell*, who had entertained him while Trollope digested his orders. 'I envy you that cutter, so will a number more, I don't wonder, once they hear old Griffiths is laid up. At least you set eyes on the square-heads, all I've seen is a few mastheads over the dunes. Trying to make an intelligent guess at the number of ships they represent is like . . . is like,' Burroughs had searched for a simile and failed with a shrug. 'Well you know it's damned impossible. Yes, I do envy you that. It gets deuced boring out here week after week, it's not the Mediterranean, don't you know, no blue seas and snow-capped sierras to moon over, just acres and acres of dung coloured water and a lot of squareheaded Dutchmen sitting on their arses laughing at us, eh?' It was a sentiment commonly expressed in the fleet. But Burroughs's farewell had been less flippant. 'Good fortune, m'dear fellow, we will all be relying most heavily upon you.'

Well, he must do better than Burroughs. Wiping his eye on his sleeve he replaced the glass and concentrated.

The dreary coast extended far to the south in wave after wave of dunes and marram grass. Here and there the cluster of habitations huddled round the conspicuous spires of churches. Shreds of smoke rose into the tranquil air. In the circle of the glass he picked up a lone horseman riding along the tideline keeping an eye on them. He swung left to where the parapet of the battery fronted the cottages of Kijkduin. The Dutch tricolour hung limply above the dun coloured rampart and here too he could see men, the flash of light on a bayonet or telescope. Beyond Kijkduin the coast trended away into the anchorage where the black masts of ships could be seen. He felt his heart skip as he realised that most of the ships had their yards crossed. Preparations for sailing were well advanced. Lord Dungarth was right! He counted twenty ships at the least. He swept the glass to the north. On the far side of the Zeegat van Texel the island of Texel faded into the far distance. A Dutch yacht lay in the channel. De Winter's eyes, as he was Duncan's.

Northwards in the Molen Gat he could see a little dark shape that was *Diligent* while to the westwards the three masts of *Black Joke*, one time advice boat to Earl Howe, lay anchored in the West Gat.

Between them a flat expanse of sand, fringed with the curl of shallow breakers, the Haakagronden, covering as the tide rose. To the west the sun sank redly, the sea a jade green except where the sun laid a golden bar upon its rippled surface.

He returned to the deck, prepared the signal 'Enemy has yards crossed,' hoisted it and fired a gun. As the sun set *Black Joke* acknowledged it and Drinkwater could just see where she repeated it to Trollope's innermost ship, the sloop *Martin*. Drinkwater smiled to himself with self-satisfaction. Elizabeth would think him very pompous just at the moment.

'Did you see the way Mr Drinkwater smiled just now,' muttered Tregembo to another seaman leaning on the rail beside him, 'I reckons as how us'll be seeing some action afore long, my handsome.'

The light airs had died completely by midnight and a glassy calm fell on the black water; the rudder creaked and the tiller kicked gently in the tackles.

'Good tide running now, we'll get under way with the centre plates down and sweep her up to the north a little, Mr Jessup. Call the hands.'

Drinkwater had no desire to work the men unnecessarily but one mile to the north they would command a much better view of the Dutch fleet at anchor, still out of dangerous gunshot of the battery. The centre plates would give them ample warning of going around on such a quiet night and the labour at the sweeps would keep the men busy, giving them little time to reflect on their grievances, imagined or otherwise.

The steady clunk of pawls tripping on whelps told where the windlass was manned, while down the cutter's side the carpenter and his mate were knocking the poppets out of the sweep rowlocks. A muffled thudding in the darkness amidships indicated the hands were getting the ungainly lengths of the sweeps from their stowage between the gigs into position. Two men came aft and cast off the tiller lashings. They stood ready to execute Drinkwater's orders.

From forward came the low cry, 'Up and down,' and after a little, 'Anchor's aweigh.'

'Hard a-starboard.' The two men pushed the tiller over. 'Give way together, Mr Jessup.'

The sweeps came to life, swinging awkwardly across the deck, splashing alongside while the men got into their stride and Jessup belaboured them with rhythmic obscenities, curiously inflected with emphatic syllables so that they gradually came into unison. *Kestrel* gathered way, turning to bring the tide under her while Jessup intoned his meaningless invective in the ingenuous way of the British seaman. Drinkwater steadied the cutter on course and half an hour later they re-anchored.

'Get a spring on the cable, Mr Jessup, then send the watch below. We'll clear for action at dawn just in case that Dutch yacht has moved.'

'Aye, aye, sir.' Jessup moved off giving orders. Drinkwater was pleased with himself. The centre plates had not touched once. They should be in the position he wanted. Wrapping himself in his cloak and kicking off his shoes he threw himself on to his cot and was soon asleep.

He was called at six. Five minutes later he was on deck. The wind was sharp and from the east. At five bells he called all hands and the men tumbled up to draw and reload the guns. Alternate lashings were cast off the mainsail and the halliards prepared for rapid hoisting, their falls faked out along the deck in case daylight revealed them too close to the battery. Daylight came with a mist.

An hour later Drinkwater stood the men down and went below to shave and break his fast. The skillygolee and molasses warmed him and only his new found dignity as commander prevented him from chaffing Appleby who was making a half-hearted protest that the creaking of the sweeps had kept him awake. The fact that the wind was from the east had set Drinkwater in a state of tension that would not let him relax.

He returned to pacing the deck while he waited for the mist over the land to lift. If they had anchored in the wrong place they might have to cut and run before being caught in the cross fire of the yacht and the heavier guns at Kijkduin. He tried to calm himself, to stay the prickling sweat between his shoulder blades and forget the fine, fire-eating phrase that kept leaping unbidden into his mind: *morituri te salutant* . . .

'Mist's clearing, Mr Drinkwater.' It was Traveller, anxious to fire his precious guns.

'Thank you Mr Traveller.' Drinkwater went forward and began

climbing the mast. From his perch he could see the mast trucks of the Dutch fleet rising from the white shroud that enveloped the town of Den Helder. In the foreground the land was already clear and the solitary boom of a gun echoed seawards where the battery ranged them. The Dutch yacht still lay in the fairway, some eight cables away, and beyond her, now emerging dramatically from the evaporating vapour, lay the Dutch fleet.

Movement was clearly discernible. There were men aloft and he started to count as the ships began to warp themselves clear of the buoys. At noon *Black Joke*, beating skilfully up through the West Gat, came alongside. By agreement it was she that ran out to Trollope during the afternoon of the 7th October to inform him that the Dutch were on the move. There was every prospect that if the wind held east, Admiral De Winter would sail.

Late afternoon came and still the breeze was steady. Drinkwater kept the deck, not trusting himself to go below. The weary months of blockage duty had screwed him to a pitch that cried out for the release of action. What was true of him was true of all of *Kestrel*'s people. He looked round the deck. Men lingered half hoping, half dreading that the Dutch would come out. He looked away to the east. The yacht remained at her anchor, like a dog at the door of his master's hall, and beyond . . .

Drinkwater reached for his glass. One of the ships had sail set and a bone in her teeth. He hastened forward and levelled the glass, steadying it against a stay.

It was a frigate, coming down the fairway under topsails. Would she re-anchor or was she leading the fleet to sea? Drinkwater's mouth was dry, his back damp and his heart hammered. The frigate was still heading seawards. He stared at her for perhaps ten minutes then relaxed. He saw her topsails shiver and her hull lengthen as she turned into the wind to anchor. She was to act as guardship then, weighing first and sweeping the puny opposition outside from the path of De Winter's armada. Drinkwater found himself shaking with relief. He was about to turn aft when a movement beside the frigate caught his eye. A boat had put off from her side and was being pulled seawards, towards the yacht.

As the sun dropped *Kestrel* made the signal 'Enemy in an advanced state of preparation' to *Black Joke* five miles to the west.

They saw her repeat it and a few minutes later received a reply from Trollope. It was a distance signal of three square flags and a black ball and it meant 'I am unsupported.'

Duncan had not arrived.

Drinkwater turned east once more. They would have to run before the enemy then. The boat had left the yacht and was pulling back for the frigate. He wondered what orders the commander of the yacht had received. Positive sailing instructions, he concluded. And then he noticed something else. Something that made the muscles of his stomach contract and his whole body tense.

The Dutch yacht had hoisted a flag to her masthead.

A black, swallowtailed pendant.

Camperdown

Sleep eluded Nathaniel Drinkwater that night. When he heard four bells struck in the middle watch he rose and entered the cabin, opening the locker where Griffiths kept his liquor. His hands closed round the neck of the first bottle and he drew it out, pulling the cork and pouring cognac into his throat. The smell of it reminded him of the night off Beaubigny and the eyes of Hortense Montholon. He had a strong sensation of events coming full circle. 'This is witchery,' he muttered to himself, and drew again at the bottle, shuddering from the effect of the raw spirit. He shifted his mind to Elizabeth, deliberately invoking her image to replace that of Hortense as a man touching a talisman; as he had done years ago in the swamps of South Carolina. But Elizabeth was distant now, beyond the immense hurdle of the coming hours, obscured by the responsibilities of command. Somehow his old promise of circumspection to Elizabeth now seemed as pompously ridiculous as that of doing his duty to Duncan.

He hurled the bottle from him and it shivered to pieces against the far bulkhead.

'Damned witchery,' he repeated, heading for the companionway. Up and down he strode, between the taffrail and the gigs, the anchor watch withdrawing from his path. From time to time he paused to look in the direction of Kijkduin. Santhonax *had* to be at Kijkduin. Had to be, to feed the cold ruthlessness that was spreading through him. If his chance lay in the coming hours he must not lack the resolution to grasp it.

Vice-Admiral De Winter ordered his fleet to sail on the morning of 8th October. The frigate that Drinkwater had watched the previous afternoon stood seawards at first light, catching up the yacht in her wake. *Kestrel* weighed too, standing seawards down the West Gat, firing her chasers and flying the signal for an enemy to windward. *Black Joke* caught the alarm, wore round and stood in her grain, hoisting the same signal.

For an hour *Kestrel* ran ahead of the Dutch fleet as ship after ship rounded the battery at Kijkduin, turning south for the Schulpen Gat. The cutter, diverging towards Trollope, observed them, her commander making notes upon a tablet.

They rejoined the squadron at noon, closing the commodore for their orders.

'What d'you make of them?' Trollope called through his speaking trumpet.

'Twenty-one ships, sir, including some ship-sloops and frigates, say about fifteen of the line. There are also four brigs and two yachts . . . I'd say his whole force excepting the transports . . .'

'So Ireland's out.'

Drinkwater shook his head. 'No sir, they could come out next tide or wait until he's dealt with us, sir.' He saw Trollope nod.

'Take station on my lee beam. I'm forming line, continue to repeat my signals. Good luck!'

'And you sir.' He exchanged a wave with Burroughs, then turned to Hill.

'Mr Hill, our station is the commodore's lee beam. Do you see to it.'

'Aye, aye, sir.'

'You may adjust sail to maintain station and watch for any signals either general to the squadron for repeating, or particular to us.'

Drinkwater felt a great burden lifted from his shoulders. It was good to be in company again, good to see the huge bulk of *Russell* a cannon shot to windward. He suddenly felt very tired but there was one thing yet to do. 'Mr Jessup!'

'Sir?'

'Call the hands aft!'

'Now my lads,' began Drinkwater, leaping up on to the breech of one of the three pounders when they had assembled. 'I'm not one to bear a grudge, and neither are you. We are now in the presence of an enemy force and disobedience to an order carries the penalty of death. I therefore rely absolutely upon your loyalty. Give me that and I promise I will move heaven and earth to have you paid the instant we return to Sheerness.' He paused and was pleased to find a murmur of approval run through the men.

'Carry on, Mr Jessup, and pipe up spirits now . . .'

Drinkwater jumped down from the gun. 'Mr Hill, you have the deck. Call me if you need me.' He went gratefully below, passing through the cabin where light through the skylight had exorcised the spectres of the preceding night.

'Spirit ration, Mr Thompson,' said Jessup to the purser. James Thompson nodded and indicated the guns of *Russell* half a mile to windward. They were a dumb but powerful incentive to obedience.

'He chooses his moments for exhortatory speeches, don't he, Mr Jessup?'

Jessup had only the vaguest idea of what an exhortatory speech was, but the significance of *Russell*, surging along, sail set to the topgallants as she stood south to maintain station with De Winter, was not lost on him.

'Aye, Mr Thompson, he's a cool and calculating bastard,' muttered Jessup, unable to keep the admiration out of his voice.

Captain Trollope formed his squadron into line with the sloop *Martin* ahead and to larboard, keeping De Winter in sight as he edged south along the coast. Then, as the day wore on and his rear cleared the Schulpen Gat De Winter altered more to the west.

Trollope's main body consisted of the *Beaulieu*, a frigate of forty guns, following by the faithful fifty *Adamant* and his own *Russell*. In her wake came the smaller frigate *Circe* of twenty-eight guns. *Kestrel* and *Active*, cutters, lay to leeward of the line and *Black Joke* had long since been sent to Duncan to inform him the enemy was out.

Towards evening the wind fell away then backed round to the south-west. De Winter tacked in pursuit of Trollope who drew off, while the Dutch, unable to catch the British, stood south again, confirming Drinkwater's theory that they intended to force the Straits of Dover.

During the following two days the wind hauled more steadily into the west and De Winter's fleet began to beat to windward, closing the English coast in the vicinity of Lowestoft with Trollope just ahead, covering his communications with Yarmouth.

'What d'you make of it, Nat?' asked Appleby confidentially at dinner. 'D'you still hold to your idea that they're bound for Brest, then Ireland?'

Drinkwater nodded, wiping his mouth with the crumpled napkin. 'He's covering Duncan while the troopships and storeships get out of the Texel. They'll get south under the cover of the French coast and then De Winter'll follow 'em down Channel.'

Appleby nodded in uncharacteristic silence. 'It seems we've been wasting our time then,' he said.

On the morning of the 10th October Trollope despatched *Active* to find Duncan with the latest news of De Winter. At this time De Winter had learned from a Dutch merchant ship that Duncan had left Yarmouth and had been seen standing east. Alarmed for his rear De Winter turned away and, with the wind at north-west stood for the Dutch coast in the vicinity of Kampenduin.

Meanwhile Duncan, having left Yarmouth in great haste on seeing *Black Joke* making furious signals for an enemy at sea while still to seaward of the Scroby Sands, had indeed headed east for the Texel.

Trollope, though inferior in force, had hung on to the windward position chiefly because the shallow draughted Dutch ships were unable to weather him. He was still there on the morning of the 11th when officers in the Dutch fleet saw his ships throw out signals from which they rightly concluded Duncan was in sight of the main body of the British fleet. De Winter headed directly for the coast where he could collect his most leeward ships into line of battle and stand north for the Texel in the shallow water beloved by his own pilots. About twelve miles off the coast De Winter formed his line heading north under easy sail and awaited the British.

Admiral Duncan, having first reconnoitred the Texel and discovered the troop and storeships were still at their moorings, collected *Diligent* and turned south in search of his enemy. During the forenoon Trollope's detachment rejoined their admiral. Duncan's ships were indifferent sailors and he had neither time nor inclination to form line. De Winter's fleet was dropping to leeward into shoal water by the minute and the old admiral accepted their formal challenge with alacrity. Duncan hoisted the signal for 'general chase' and the British, grouped together into two loose divisions, Duncan's to the north and Onslow's slightly advanced to the south, bore down on the Dutch.

The increase in the westerly wind with its damp air had brought about a thickening of the atmosphere and the battle that was now inevitable seemed to be marred by disorder amongst the British ships. Just before noon Duncan signalled that his intention was to pass through the enemy line and engage from leeward, thus denying the Dutch escape and ensuring all the windward batteries of the British ships could be used. The signal was repeated by the frigates and cutters. At noon they hoisted that for close action.

Thirty minutes later Onslow's *Monarch* opened the action by cutting off De Winter's rear between the *Jupiter* and *Harlem*, ranging up alongside the former, raked by the heavy frigate *Monikendaam* and the brig *Atalanta* forming a secondary line to leeward of the Dutch battleships. Amid a thunder of guns the battle of Camperdown had begun.

Kestrel, in common with the other cutters as a repeating vessel, was not a target. Stray shot might hit her but in general the conventions of a fleet action were observed. The British cutters and Dutch yachts were expected to render assistance to the wounded where they could be found clinging to fallen spars and continue to repeat their admirals' signals. *Kestrel* had formed part of Onslow's division and Drinkwater found himself in a confusing world of screaming shot, choppy seas and a strong wind. Smoke and mist enveloped the combatants as gun flashes began to eclipse the dull daylight.

Within minutes Drinkwater had lost sight of *Monarch* behind the Dutch line and he altered to the north to maintain contact with *Russell*, but Trollope, too, cut through the line and *Kestrel* found herself passing under the stern of the Dutch seventy-four *Brutus*, bearing the flag of a rear-admiral at her mizen.

Through the rolling clouds of smoke a brig was seen to leeward and her commander did not extend the courtesy or disdain of his bigger consorts. Shot whistled about *Kestrel* and a shower of lancing splinters from the starboard rail sent one man hopping bloodily below in agony to where Appleby had his gruesome instruments laid out on the cabin table.

'Down helm!' roared Drinkwater, his eyes gleaming with concentration now the final, cathartic moment of action had arrived. 'Haul the sheets there!' the cutter bore away from her overlarge opponent and headed north, passing *Brutus* as the latter turned to assist De Winter ahead, now being pressed by several British ships tearing pell-mell into battle.

Suddenly ahead of them loomed a Dutch sixty-four, fallen out of line with her colours struck. For a moment Drinkwater contemplated putting a prize crew on board for it seemed unlikely that her antagonist, *Triumph*, engaged to larboard by a frigate and the seventy-four *Staten General*, had had the opportunity. But a sudden crash shook the cutter. One of the crew of Number 12 gun fell dead, cut clean in half by a ball that destroyed the jolly boat and the handsome taffrail. The brig which had fired on them had set her topgallants and was coming up fast in pursuit.

Drinkwater looked wildly round him. 'Down helm! Harden in those sheets there, put her on the wind, full and bye! Down centre plates! And throw that,' he indicated the faintly twitching lumps that a moment before had been a living man, 'overboard, for God's sake!'

Kestrel pointed up into the wind, escaping as she had done off Ushant, heeling to the hardening of her sails. Spray whipped over the rail and tore aft. Drinkwater looked astern.

'Well I'm damned,' he said aloud and beside him Hill whistled. The brig, unable to continue the chase so close to the wind, had come up with her consort, the surrendered sixty-four *Wassanaer*. Seeing her shameful plight the brig opened fire into her. In a few moments the Dutch tricolour jerked aloft again and snapped out in the wind.

'This ain't like fighting the Frogs, Mr Drinkwater. Look, there's hardly a mast down, these bloody squareheads know how to fight by Jesus . . . The bastards are hulling us. Christ! There'll be a butcher's bill after this lot . . .'

Russell loomed up ahead and *Kestrel* wore round in her wake.

'Ahead of you, sir,' Drinkwater bellowed through the speaking trumpet, 'a seventy-four. Yours for the taking . . .' He saw Trollope wave acknowledgement.

For a moment or two they kept pace with the battleship, huge, majestic and deadly, as she ran down her quarry. Her sides were already scarred by shot, several of which could be clearly seen embedded in her strakes. Seamen grinned at them from a jagged hole where adjacent gunports had been amalgamated. Thin streaks of blood ran down her sides.

'Spill some wind, Mr Hill. We'll drop astern.' *Russell* drew ahead, driving off the brig with one, apocalyptic broadside. *Wassanaer* surrendered again.

Kestrel crossed *Russell*'s wake. To larboard two or three ships lay rolling, locked in a death struggle. One was the *Staten General*.

Suddenly, from behind the hard-pressed Dutchman, leapt a small but familiar vessel. Her bowsprit stabbed at the sky as her helm was put over and her course steadied to intercept the British cutter. At her masthead flew the black swallowtail pendant.

Drinkwater had no idea how Santhonax had persuaded De Winter to allow him the use of the yacht. She flew the Dutch tricolour from her peak but there was no mistaking the significance of that sinister weft at the masthead. Drinkwater thought of the corpse of Major Brown, of the hanged mutineers of the *Culloden*, of the scapegoats of the Nore and of the collusion between Capitaine Santhonax and the red-haired witch now in Maidstone Gaol. He was filled with a cold and ruthless anger.

'Larboard battery make ready!'

The yacht was on the larboard bow, broad-reaching to the north-east and closing them. For a few minutes they both ran on, lessening the range.

'Ease her off a point,' then in a louder voice, 'fire when you bear, Mr Bulman!'

Almost immediately the first report came from forward and Number 2 gun recoiled inboard, its crew fussing about it reloading. A ragged cheer broke from the Kestrels as they opened a rolling fire. Holes appeared in the yacht's sails. She was trying to cross *Kestrel*'s bow to rake and Drinkwater had a sudden idea.

'Down helm! Headsail sheets! Hard on the wind!' *Kestrel* turned, presenting her bow for the raking broadside but at a time of her own choosing and too quickly for Santhonax to take full advantage. Only two balls from his broadside came near and they struck harmless splinters from the starboard gig. 'Starboard guns! Starboard guns!'

Traveller held his hand up in acknowledgement, as if coolly assuring his commander that no last minute manoeuvre would rob Jeremy Traveller of his moment. He had all the quoins out and the guns at full elevation as they made to cross the yacht's stern.

But Santhonax rose to the occasion. The yacht turned now, spinning to starboard so that the two vessels passed on opposite courses at a combined speed of nearly twenty knots. Doggedly they fired gun for gun, time permitting them one shot from each as they raced past. Drinkwater saw huge sections of the yacht's rail shivered into splinters. Jeremy Traveller had double shotted his guns.

Then the whine of shot, the impact, thumps and screams of the yacht's fire turned *Kestrel*'s deck into a shambles of wounded and dead men who fell back from their cannon. Aft, Drinkwater laid his pistol at a tall man near the yacht's tiller and squeezed the trigger. The ball missed its mark and the fellow coolly raised his hat and smiled. Drinkwater swore but he was cold as ice now, lifted on to a terrible, calculating plane that was beyond fear. He had surrendered to providence now, was a hostage to the capricious fortune of war and had long forgotten his earnest promises to Elizabeth. Elizabeth was of another world that had no part in this dull and terrible October afternoon. For this was not the Nathaniel known to Elizabeth, this was a man who had taken the French lugger and quelled incipient mutiny. This was an intelligent man butchering his fellows, and doing it with consummate ability.

'Up helm! Stand by to gybe!'

There was a scrambling about the decks as Jessup, aware of Drinkwater's intentions, whipped the shocked men to their stations. He had not yet felt the pain of the splinter in his own leg. *Kestrel* swung round in pursuit of the yacht, heeling violently as her huge boom, barely restrained by its sheet, flew across the deck. The unsecured guns of the starboard battery rolled inboard to the extent of their breechings and those of the larboard thumped against the rail, their outboard wheels in the water that drove in through the open gunports. They steadied after the yacht. Across her stern they could see her name: *Draaken*. Shot holes peppered her sails as they did their own, and frayed ropes' ends streamed to leeward from her masthead.

Drinkwater never removed his eyes from his quarry, gauging the distance. It was closing, the yacht with her leeboards sagging down to leeward as *Kestrel* came up on her larboard quarter. He was aware of, rather than saw, Jessup clapping a set of deadeyes on a weather shroud, wounded in the action, that had parted under the sudden strain of that impetuous gybe. And beneath his feet there was a sluggishness that told of water in the hold. Even as his subconscious mind identified it he heard too the clanking of the pumps where Johnson was attending to his duty.

'Mr Traveller!' There was no answer, then Jessup called 'Jem's bought it, sir . . .' There was a pause, eloquent of eulogy for a friend. 'I'll do duty if it's the starboard guns you'll be wanting . . .' There was a high, strained quality of exaggerated emphasis in Jessup's voice, also present in his own. He knew it for the voice of blood-lust, a quality that made men's words memorable at such moments of heightened perception.

'It's the starboard battery I want, right enough Mr Jessup,' he confirmed, and it seemed that a steadying influence ran along *Kestrel*'s deck. The wounded had been pulled clear of the guns from where Merrick and his bearers could drag the worst of them below, to Appleby.

The surrounding battle had ceased to exist for Drinkwater. His whole being was concentrated on overhauling the *Draaken*, attempting to divine Santhonax's next move. Jessup came up to him.

'I've loaded canister on top o'ball, sir, in the starboard guns, an' the larbowlines will be ready to board.'

With an effort Drinkwater directed his attention to the man beside him. There was the efficiency he had first noted about Jessup, paying dividends at last. He must remember that in his report. If he lived to write it.

'Thank you, Mr Jessup.' His eye ran past the boatswain. Forward he could see James Thompson checking the priming in a pistol and taking a cutlass from Short. Short, a kerchief round his grimy head, was lovingly caressing a boarding pike. By the companionway Tregembo was thumbing the edge of another pike and glancing anxiously aft at Drinkwater. All along the starboard side the starbowlines knelt by their guns as if at gun drill. He could see the red beard of Poll pointed at the enemy.

A wave of emotion seized Drinkwater for a terrible moment. It

363

seemed the cutter and all her people were in the grip of some coalescing of forces that stemmed from his own desire for vengeance. They could not have caught the same madness that led Drinkwater in hot pursuit of Santhonax, nor all be victims of the witchcraft of Hortense Montholon.

He shook his head to clear it of such disturbing thoughts. It was merely the result of discipline, he reassured himself. Then he cast all aside as ahead of them *Draaken* luffed.

Unable to escape, she would stand her ground while she had a lead, lie athwart *Kestrel*'s bow, rake her and run north, delivering a second broadside as she did so.

'Lie down!' Drinkwater commanded, lending his own weight to the tiller and turning *Kestrel* a quarter point to starboard, heading directly for the yacht.

The cutter staggered under the impact of *Draaken*'s broadside. The peak halliard was shot through and the mainsail sagged down. Splinters rose in showers from the forward rails and a resonating clang told where at least one ball had ricochetted off a bow chaser. Someone screamed and one of the helmsmen dropped into eternity without a sound, falling against Drinkwater's legs. Then *Draaken* completed her turn and began to pass the cutter on the opposite tack, no more than twenty yards to windward.

'Now Jessup! Now!' Scrambling up from their prone positions the men gathered round the starboard guns.

Draaken drew abeam. 'Fire!'

Drinkwater saw the bulwarks fly as smoke from the yacht's own fire rolled down over *Kestrel*. As it cleared he saw her sails flogging uncontrolled. Santhonax had let fly his sheets and *Draaken* was dropping to leeward. With her shallow draught she would drive down on top of the cutter as *Kestrel* lost way, her mainsail hanging in impotent folds, the gaffshot through and her jib blowing out of the bolt ropes through shot holes.

'Let fly all sheets! Boarders stand by!'

All along her side *Kestrel*'s gunners poured shot after shot into the yacht as fast as they were able. It was murder and the cracking sails added to the screams of wounded men and the roar of the cannon. Then, in the smoke and confusion, *Draaken* was on top of them, her mast level with *Kestrel*'s tiller.

364

'Boarders aft here!' Drinkwater roared, lugging a pistol from his belt and drawing his hanger. Through the smoke he saw Tregembo and Short and James Thompson and half a dozen other faces familiar as old friends.

Kestrel shook as *Draaken* ground into her and the Dutchmen passed lashings over anything prominent. The wind whipped the last shreds of smoke from the now silent guns and as it cleared they saw their enemy.

They were poised to board, round red faces hedged with the deadly spikes of cutlass, axe and pike. Drinkwater sought vainly for Santhonax and then forgot him as the Dutchmen poured over the rail. The Kestrels were flung back, swept from their own deck as far as the gigs in a slithering, sliding *mêlée* of hacking stabbing and murdering. Drinkwater thrust, twisted and thrust with Tregembo grunting and swearing on his right hand and James Thompson on his left. He felt himself step on a body that still writhed. He dared not look down as he parried a clumsy lunge from a blond boy with the desperate look of reckless terror in his eyes. The boy stabbed again, inaccurately but swiftly in short defensive reflexes. Drinkwater hacked savagely down at the too-extended forearm. The boy fell back, unarmed and whimpering.

Briefly Drinkwater paused. He sensed the Dutch attack falter as the British, buttressed by the solid transoms of the gigs, found their defence was effective.

'Come on the Kestrels!' Drinkwater's scream cracked into a croak but about him there was a hefting of pikes, a re-gripping of cutlasses and then they were surging forward, driving the Dutch before them. Over a larboard gun leapt Short, a maniacal laugh erupting from him as he pitched a man overboard then drove two more before him into the larboard quarter. They were disarmed and with his pike Short tossed them both over the shattered transom like stooks on to a rick.

Drinkwater swung himself left, across to the starboard quarter where the enemy were in retreat. 'Board the bastard, James, board the bastard!' he yelled, and next to him Thompson grinned.

'I'm with 'ee, Mr Drinkwater!' Tregembo's voice was still there and here was Hill, and Bulman with the chasers' crews, having fought their way down the starboard side. Then they were up on the rail and leaping down on to *Draaken*'s deck, their impetus carrying them forward, men made hard and ruthless by months of blockade carried with them a more vicious motivation than the Dutch, torn from comfortable moorings and doing the bidding of foreign masters.

Opposition fragmented, lost its edge and above it all Drinkwater could hear the furious oaths in a fairer tongue than the guttural grunts of dying Dutchmen.

With careless swathes of the hanger Drinkwater slashed aft. A Dutch officer came on guard in front of him and instinct made him pause and come into the same pose but he was passed by Short, his face a contorted mask of insane delight, his pike levelled at the officer. A pistol ball entered Short's eye and took the back of his skull off. Still the boatswain's mate lunged and the Dutch lieutenant crashed to the deck, pierced by the terrible weapon with Short's twitching corpse on top of him.

Drinkwater stepped aside and faced the man who had fired the pistol.

It was Edouard Santhonax.

The Frenchman dropped the pistol and swiped downwards with his sword in the *molinello* he had used at Sheerness. Drinkwater put up his hanger in a horizontal parry above his head and the blades crashed together. Then Tregembo was beside him his pike extended at Santhonax's exposed stomach.

'Alive, Tregembo! Take him alive!' and on the last word, with a final effort Drinkwater twisted his wrist, disengaged and drew his blade under Santhonax's uncovered forearm.

Santhonax, attacked by two men, took greater terror from the levelled pike and tried to push it aside even as Tregembo obeyed Drinkwater and brought it up. The vicious point entered the Frenchman's face and ripped his cheek in a bloody, disfiguring wound and he fell back, covered in blood.

Drinkwater turned to see the deck of *Draaken* like a butcher's shambles. Lolling on the yacht's companionway James Thompson was holding his entrails, staring with disbelief. Drinkwater turned away, appalled. A kind of hush fell on them all, the moaning of the wind rising above the groans of the wounded. Then Hill said, 'Flag's signalling, sir . . . Acts 27 verse 28 . . .'

'For Christ's sake . . .'

All along the line of ships the smoke had cleared away. Admiral De Winter had surrendered and those of Onslow's commanders still with men on their quarterdecks able to open bibles obeyed their chief. They sounded and found, not fifteen fathoms, but nine. In great peril the British fleet secured their prizes.

Among them, her decks cluttered with corpses, her gear wounded, her bulwarks riven by shot, plunged the King's cutter *Kestrel*.

Chapter Sixteen *October 1797*

Aftermath

'How is he, Mr Appleby?' In the swaying lamplight *Kestrel*'s cabin had the appearance of an abattoir and Appleby, grey-faced with exhaustion, was stained by blood, his apron stiff with it. They stared down at the shrunken body of James Thompson, the purser, his waist swathed in bloody bandages.

'Sinking fast, sir,' said the surgeon, his clipped formality proper in such grim circumstances. 'The livid colour of the lips, the contraction of the nostrils and eyebrows an indication of approaching death . . . besides he has lost much blood.'

'Yes.' Drinkwater felt light-headed, aware of a thousand calls on his time, unable to tear himself away from the groans and stench of the cabin as though by remaining there he could expiate himself for the murder they had been doing a few hours earlier. 'Yes,' he repeated, 'I am told he supported me most gallantly in boarding.'

Appleby ignored the remark.

'You are giving him an opiate?' Appleby lacked the energy to be indignant. He nodded.

'He is laced with laudanum, Mr Drinkwater, and will go to his maker in that state.' There was reproach in his voice.

Drinkwater left the cabin and returned on deck, passing the cabin, his own former hutch, where Santhonax lay, sutured and waxen, his hands bound. The rising wind had reached gale force and the British fleet clawed offshore, each ship fending for itself. In the howling blackness, lurching up and down the plunging deck, Drinkwater calmed himself before he could lie down and submit to the sleep his body demanded.

Rain came with the wind, driving over the wavecaps with a greater persistence than the sheets of spray that lashed the watch.

Out in the night an occasional lantern showed where one of the battleships struggled to windward and twice he heard Bulman caution the lookouts to exert themselves.

Drinkwater knew he had not escaped the brutalising of his spirit that had begun so many years ago in the cockpit of *Cyclops*, nor escaped the effects of the events in the swamps of Carolina. The savagery he displayed in battle was a primaeval quality that those events had dragged out of the primitive part of him. But such ferocity could not be sustained against the earlier influence of a gentle home and in reaction he veered towards sentiment, like so many of his contemporaries.

He took refuge in the satisfaction of a duty acquitted and an increased belief in providence. As fatigue tamed the feelings raging in him since the battle, numbing his recollections, he felt better able to trust himself to write his report.

. . . the vessels were laid board and board, Drinkwater wrote carefully, *and after a sharp engagement the Draaken, despatch vessel, was carried.*

I have to inform you that the enemy defended themselves with great gallantry and inflicted severe losses on the boarders. All of the latter, however, conducted themselves as befitted British seamen and in particular James Thompson, Purser, Edward Jessup, Boatswain, and Jeremiah Traveller, Gunner, who died in the action or of mortal wounds sustained therein.

He paused, reflecting on the stilted formality of the phraseology. One final piece of information needed to be included before this list of dead and wounded.

He began to write again. *Among those captured was a French naval officer, Capitaine de frégate Edouard Santhonax, known to your Honour to have been an agent of the French Government. Among his papers were found the enclosed documents relative to a proposed descent upon Ireland.* Drinkwater carefully inscribed his signature.

When he had appended the butcher's bill he went on deck. The frightful casualties inflicted on their number could not damp the morale of the crew. The Kestrels shared a common sense of relief at being spared, and a corporate pride in the possession of the *Draaken*, following astern under the command of Mr Hill, whose gashed arm seemed not to trouble him.

Drinkwater could not be offended at the mood of the crew. Of all the Kestrels he knew he and Appleby were alone in their sense of

369

moral oppression. It was not callousness the men displayed, only a wonderful appreciation of the transient nature of the world. Drinkwater found he envied them that, and he called them aft to thank them formally, for their conduct. It all sounded unbelievably pompous but the men listened with silent attention. It would have amused Elizabeth, he thought, as he watched the cautiously smiling seamen. He felt better for those smiles, better for thinking of Elizabeth again, aware that he had not dared contemplate a future since the Dutch showed signs of emerging from the Texel. The grey windy morning was suddenly less gloomy and the sight of *Adamant* out of the corner of his eye was strangely moving.

He completed his speech and a thin cheer ran through the men. Drinkwater turned to the grey bundles between the guns. There were thirteen of them.

He had murdered and harangued and now he must bury his dead in an apparently meaningless succession of contradictory rituals.

From the torn pocket of his grubby coat he took the leather prayer book that had once belonged to his father-in-law and began to read, 'I am the resurrection and the life, saith the Lord . . .' and overhead the bright bunting snapped in the wind.

Duncan's fleet anchored at the Nore to the Plaudits of Parliament and the gratitude of the nation. At first the strategic consequences of the battle were of secondary importance to the relief of ministers. Despite the mutiny the North Sea fleet was unimpaired in efficiency. The seamen had vindicated themselves and the Government had been justified in its intransigence. Vicarious glory was reflected on all parties, euphoria was the predominating emotion and honours were heaped upon the victors. Admiral Duncan's earlier ambition of quiet retirement with an Irish peerage was eclipsed by his being made a baron and viscount of Great Britain, Onslow was made a baronet, Trollope and Fairfax knights and all the first lieutenants of the line of battleships were promoted to commander. Medals were struck, swords presented and the thanks of both Houses of Parliament voted unanimously to the fleet. The latter was held to be, as Tregembo succinctly put it, of less use than his own nipples.

Before reporting to Duncan, Drinkwater interviewed Santhonax.

The Frenchman could only mutter with difficulty, his lacerated mouth painfully bruised round the crude join Appleby had made of his cheek. He had given his name after prompting, using English, but Drinkwater had troubled him little after that, too preoccupied with managing the damaged cutter with half his crew dead or wounded.

But on the morning they anchored at the Nore, Santhonax was a little better and asked to see Drinkwater.

'Who are you?' he asked, through clenched teeth but in an accent little disfigured by foreign intonation.

'My name, sir, is Drinkwater.'

Santhonax nodded and muttered 'Boireleau . . .' as if committing it to memory then, in a louder voice, 'you are not the commander of this vessel?'

'I am now.'

'And the old man . . . Griffiths?'

'You know him?' Drinkwater was surprised and lost his chill formality. Santhonax began to smile but broke off, wincing.

'The quarry always knows the hunter . . . your boat is well named, *La Crécerelle*.'

'Why did you hang Brown?'

'He was a spy, he knew too much . . . he was an enemy of the Revolution and of France.'

'And you?'

'I am a prisoner of war, M'sieur Boireleau . . .' This time Santhonax crinkled the skin about his eyes. Stung, Drinkwater retorted, 'We have evidence to hang you. We have Hortense Montholon in custody.'

Santhonax's sneer was cut short. He looked like a man unexpectedly whipped. What colour he had, drained from his face.

'Take him away,' snapped Drinkwater to Hill, standing edgily behind the prisoner, 'and then have my gig made ready.'

'Drinkwater, good to see you, my word but what a drubbing we gave 'em and what a thundering good fight they put up, eh?' Burroughs met him at *Venerable*'s entry port, bubbling with good spirits and new rank. He gestured round the fleet, 'hardly a spark knocked down among the lot of us but hulls like colanders . . . by

371

heaven but I'm glad we did for 'em, damned if I'd like another taste of that . . . not a single prize that's worth taking into service . . . except perhaps yours, eh?'

'Aye, sir, but it's already cost a lot.'

Burroughs became serious. 'Aye, indeed. Our losses were fearful, over a thousand killed and wounded . . . but come, the admiral wants a word with you, I was about to send a midshipman to fetch you.'

Drinkwater followed Burroughs under the poop and was swept past the marine sentry. 'Mr Drinkwater, my Lord.' Burroughs winked at him and left. Drinkwater advanced to where Duncan was writing at his desk, its baize cloth lost under sheaves of paper.

'Sit down,' said the admiral wearily, without looking up, and Drinkwater gingerly lowered himself on to an upright chair, still stiff from the bruises and cuts of Camperdown. He felt the chair had suffered the repose of many backsides in the last twenty-four hours.

At last Duncan raised his head. 'Ah, Mr Drinkwater, I believe we have some unfinished business to attend to, eh?'

Drinkwater's heart missed a beat. He felt suddenly that he had made some terrible mistake, failed to execute his orders, to repeat signals. He swallowed and held out a packet. 'My report, my Lord . . .'

Duncan took it and slit the seal. Rubbing tired eyes he read while Drinkwater sat silently listening to the pounding of his own heart. The white paintwork of the great cabin was cracked and flaking where Dutch shot had impacted the *Venerable*'s side and in one area planks had been hastily nailed in place. A chill draught ran through the cabin and a faint residual stain on the scrubbed deck showed where one of *Venerable*'s men had bled.

He heard Duncan sigh. 'So you've taken a prisoner, Mr Drinkwater?'

'Yes, my Lord.'

'You'd better have him transferred over here immediately. I'll have a marine detachment sent back with you.'

'Thank you, my Lord.'

'The conduct of Captain Trollope's squadron, of which you were a part, was most gratifying and I have here a paper for you.' He held out a document and Drinkwater stood to take it. It was a commission as lieutenant.

'Thank you, my Lord, thank you very much.'

Duncan had already bent to his papers again and he said, without looking up, 'It's no more than you deserve, Mr Drinkwater.'

Drinkwater had his hand on the door handle when he recollected something. He turned. Duncan was immersed in the details of his fleet. There was talk of a court-martial on Williams of the *Agincourt*. Drinkwater coughed.

'My Lord?'

'Uh?' Duncan continued writing.

'My people are long overdue for their pay, my Lord, might I ask you for an order to that effect?'

Duncan laid his pen down and looked up. The admiral was too experienced a sea-officer not to know something lay behind the request. He smiled faintly at the earnest young man. 'See my clerk, Mr Drinkwater, see my clerk,' and the old admiral bent once again to his work.

Kestrel lay a week in Saltpan Reach while they did what they could to patch her up. Drinkwater was confirmed in command until they decommissioned for extensive repairs and he gave a dinner for those of his officers still alive. It was a modest affair at which they were served by Merrick and Tregembo who volunteered for the task and accomplished it with surprising adroitness. Afterwards he sought out Drinkwater.

'Begging your pardon, zur,' he began awkwardly, shuffling from one foot to the other and finally swallowing his diffidence. 'Ar damnation, zur, I ain't one for beating about, zur, but seeing as how you're promoted I'd like to volunteer for your cox'n, zur.'

Drinkwater smiled at the Cornishman. 'I'm only promoted lieutenant, Tregembo, that ain't quite post-captain, you know.'

'We've been shipmates a year or two now, zur . . .'

Drinkwater nodded, he felt very flattered. 'Look Tregembo, I can pay you nought beyond your naval pay and certainly not enough to support you and your future wife . . .' he got no further.

'tis enough, zur, your prize money'll buy you a handsome house, zur an' my Susan can cook, zur.' He grinned triumphantly. 'Thank 'ee, zur, thank 'ee . . .'

Taken aback Drinkwater could only mutter 'Well I'm damned,' and stare after the retreating seaman. He remembered Tregembo's Susan as a compact, determined woman and guessed she might have some part in it.

He had better write to Elizabeth and tell her he had a commission and she, it appeared, had a cook.

Chapter Seventeen   *November 1797*

The Puppet Master

'Orders, sir.' Hill passed the oiled packet that the guard boat had just delivered. Drinkwater pushed the last bottle of Griffiths's sercial across to Appleby and opened the bundle on the table.

As he read the frown on his brow deepened. Silently Appleby and Hill searched their commander's face for some indication of their fate. Eventually Drinkwater looked up.

'Mr Hill, we drop down to the Nore with the ebb this afternoon and I will require a boat to take me to the Gun Wharf at five of the clock . . .' He looked down again at the papers.

Hill acknowledged his instructions and left the cabin. 'What is it?' enquired Appleby.

Drinkwater looked up again. 'Confidential I'm afraid, Mr Appleby,' he said with chilly formality. But it was not Appleby's curiosity that had set Drinkwater on edge. It was the signatory of his orders. They had not come from Admiral Duncan but from Lord Dungarth.

It was the earl who descended first from the carriage that swung to a halt on the windy quay. Drinkwater advanced to greet him as he turned to assist the second occupant out of the carriage. The hooded figure was obscured in the gathering dusk, but there was something about the newcomer that was vaguely familiar.

'So,' she said, looking about her, 'you are going to deport me, no? Not shoot me after all?'

Drinkwater recognised Hortense Montholon as Dungarth replied 'Aye ma'am against both my judgement and inclination, I do assure you.' He turned to Drinkwater. 'Good evening, Lieutenant.' Dungarth gave a thin smile of congratulation.

'Good evening, my Lord.'

Lord Dungarth turned to the woman and removed a pair of handcuffs from his coat pockets. 'Be so kind as to hold out your right wrist.'

'Must you practice this barbarity,' she said frowning and shooting Drinkwater a look full of pathetic helplessness. He avoided her gaze.

'We are men, not saints sweet lady,' quoted his lordship as he handcuffed himself to the prisoner then led her towards the waiting boat.

Kestrel weighed and carried a favourable westerly breeze out of the Thames. Drinkwater came below at midnight to find Lord Dungarth sitting in the lamplit cabin with Hortense Montholon asleep on the leeward settee.

Silently Drinkwater brought out a bottle. He poured two glasses and passed one to Dungarth. The wheel had come full circle now, the cutter's cabin that had been the scene of its beginning witnessed its end. Dungarth raised his glass.

'To your cockade, Nathaniel, you have earned it.'

'Thank you, my Lord.' His eyes strayed to the woman. The auburn hair tumbled about her shoulders and a slight emaciation of her face due to her incarceration lent her a saintly, martyr-like quality. Something of her effect on Drinkwater was visible on his face.

'She is as dangerous as poison,' said Dungarth in a low voice and Drinkwater turned guiltily away.

'What is to be done with her?'

Dungarth shrugged. 'Were she a man we would have shot her, were she an English woman in France the regicides would have guillotined her. As it is she is allowed her freedom.' The cynical way in which Dungarth made his remarks clearly indicated he did not approve of the decision.

'Her brother has some influence in emigré circles and pressure was brought to bear upon Government,' he sighed. 'Would that poor Brown had had such an advocate.'

'Aye my Lord . . .' Drinkwater thought of the gibbet hanging over the battery at Kijkduin. 'And what of Santhonax?'

'Ah,' Dungarth grunted with greater relish, a cruel smile crossing his mouth. 'We have *him* mewed up close, very close. You ruined his looks Nathaniel, tch, tch.' Drinkwater passed the bottle as *Kestrel* lurched into a wave trough. Dungarth waved it towards the sleeping woman. 'She does not yet know of his apprehension. It is going to be something of a disappointment to her when she arrives home.' He smiled and sipped his wine.

Drinkwater looked at Hortense again. She stirred as *Kestrel* butted another wave and her eyes opened. She sat up puzzled, then shivered and drew the cloak round her in a curiously childish way. Then her eyes recognised the company and her circumstances and an expression close to satisfaction settled upon her face.

'Watch her well, Nathaniel,' said Dungarth, 'she is an old deceiver, a veritable Eve. It was a pity Jacobin sentiment, undiscriminating though it is, had not been a little more zealously employed at Carteret and saved us the trouble of rescuing such a viper.'

'Can you believe such a face could betray her betrothed, eh?'

Drinkwater saw Hortense frown, uncomprehending. He remembered poor De Tocqueville and his unrequited passion.

'What do you mean?' she asked, 'betray . . .'

'Do not mock me ma'am, your lover Santhonax had De Tocqueville cut down in the gutters of London and well you know it.'

'No, no . . . I knew nothing of that.' For a moment she digested the news then held up her head. 'I do not believe you. You lie . . . you lie to protect yourself, you are fools, already your navy is crippled by the brave republicans, soon the Dutch will come to help and then all the ships will join those of France and the greatest navy in the world will be at our command . . .' Her eyes blazed with the conviction of one who had sustained herself in prison with such thoughts. 'Even now you have spared me to use me in your plight.'

Beside him Drinkwater heard Dungarth begin to laugh. Quietly Nathaniel said, 'The mutiny in our navy is over, ma'am. The Dutch are not coming, their fleet is destroyed.'

'You see,' put in Dungarth, 'your plan has gravely misfired. Command of the Channel is ours and Ireland is safe.'

'Ireland is never safe,' snapped Hortense, a gleam of rekindled fire in her eyes which died abruptly as Dungarth replied, 'Neither is Santhonax.'

Hortense caught her breath in alarm, looking from one to another

377

and finding no comfort in the expressions of her captors. 'He is in France,' she said uncertainly.

'He *was* in Holland, madam, but Mr Drinkwater here took him prisoner in the recent battle with the Dutch fleet.'

She opened her mouth to protest they were bluffing but read the truth in their eyes. Drinkwater had not baited her, Drinkwater did not deal in words and intrigue. She recollected him probing De Tocqueville's wound here, in this very cabin, an age ago. He was a man of deeds and she knew Santhonax had been taken, immured like herself by these barbarian English.

'And I believe his face was much disfigured by a pike,' Dungarth said abstractedly.

Both Dungarth and Drinkwater went ashore in the gig. Above them the height of Mont Jolibois rose into the night, its summit shrouded in a light mist that the breeze rolled off the land. The sea was smooth under the mighty arch of the sky.

Between the two of them the hooded figure remained obscured from the oarsmen. The gig was run on to the beach and Drinkwater lifted Hortense into his arms, splashing ashore and setting her down on the sand.

'There madam,' said Dungarth pointedly, 'I hope we never meet again.'

Hortense caught Drinkwater's eyes in the gloom. Hers were openly hostile that this nondescript Englishman had taken her lover and disfigured his beauty. Then she turned and made off over the sand. Drinkwater watched her go, oblivious of Dungarth beside him until the pistol flashed.

'My Lord!' He stared after Hortense, feeling Dungarth's hand restraining him from rushing forward. She stumbled and then they saw her running, fading into the night.

He stood staring with Dungarth beside him. Behind them he heard the boat's crew murmuring.

'It wasn't loaded,' said Dungarth, 'but she'll run the faster.'

He smiled at Drinkwater. 'Come, come, Nathaniel, surely you are not shocked. She had even half-seduced you.' He chuckled to himself. 'Why sometimes even a puppet master may pull a wrong string.'

They turned and walked in silence back to the boat.

A Brig of War

For Christine

Contents

Author's Note

Detractors of Napoleon have insinuated that his Indian project was a fantasy of St Helena. There is evidence, however, to suggest there was a possibility that he contemplated such an expedition in 1798 or 1799. Certainly Nelson regarded it seriously enough to send Lieutenant Duval overland to Bombay *after* his victory at the Nile, and as late as November 1798 the dissembling Talleyrand suggested it.

The British attack on Kosseir is rather obscure. Even that most partial of historians, William James, admits that *Daedalus* and *Fox* shot off three quarters of their ammunition to little effect. He finds it less easy to explain how about a hundred diseased French soldiers, the remnants of two companies of the 21st Demi-brigade under Donzelot, could drive off a British squadron of overwhelming power. Perhaps this is why he makes no mention of *Hellebore*'s presence, since Captain Ball did not do so in his report, thus saving a little credit for the British.

The senior officers who appear in these pages actually existed. Rear Admiral Blankett commanded the Red Sea squadron at this time, though his character is my own invention. So too is Mr Wrinch, though a British 'agent' appears to have resided at Mocha at about this period.

The part played by Edouard Santhonax is not verified by history, but the consequences of his daring are the only testimony we have to Nathaniel Drinkwater's part in this small campaign. Napoleon later complained that the British had a ship wherever there was water to float one. The brig *Hellebore* was one such ship.

As to sources of other parts of the story, the mutiny on the *Mistress Shore* is based on the near contemporary uprising on the transport *Lady Shore*, while the presence of women on British men-of-war was not unknown.

For proof of drunkenness and homosexuality in the navy of this time I refer the curious to the contemporary evidence of Hall, Gardner and Beaufort amongst others. Much may also be inferred from other diarists.

'I shall believe that they are going on with their scheme of possessing Alexandria, and getting troops into India – a plan concerted with Tipoo Sahib, by no means so difficult as might at first be imagined.

NELSON, 1798

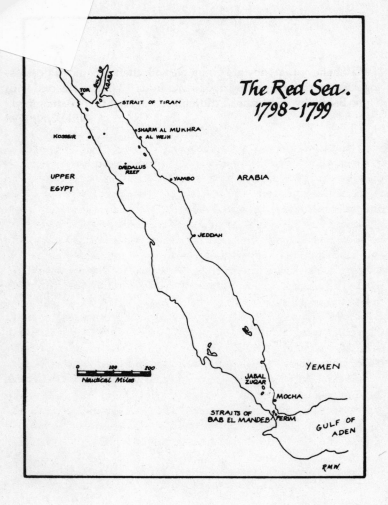

The Red Sea.
1798~1799

GULF OF AQABA

TOR

STRAIT OF TIRAN

SHARM AL MUKHRA
AL WEJH

KOSSEIR

DAEDALUS
REEF

UPPER
EGYPT

YAMBO

ARABIA

JEDDAH

100   200
Nautical Miles

YEMEN

JABAL
ZUQAR

MOCHA

STRAITS OF
BAB EL MANDEB   PERIM

GULF OF
ADEN

R.M.N.

Paris

Rain beat upon the rattling window and beyond the courtyard the naval captain watched the tricolour stiff with wind, bright against the grey scud sweeping over Paris. In his mind's eye he conjured the effect of the gale upon the green waters of the Channel and the dismal, rain-sodden shore of the English coast beyond.

Behind him the two secretaries bent over their desks. The rustle of papers was reverently hushed. An air of expectancy filled the room, emphasised by the open door. Presently rapid footsteps sounded in the corridor and the secretaries bent with more diligence over their work. The naval officer half turned from the window, then resumed his survey of the sky.

The footsteps sounded louder and into the room swept a short, thin, pale young man whose long hair fell over the high collar of his over-large general's coat. He was accompanied by an hussar, whose elaborate pelisse dangled negligently from his left shoulder.

'Ah, Bourienne!' said the general abruptly in a voice that reflected the same energy as the restless pacing he had fallen into. 'Have you the dispatches for Generals Dommartin and Cafarelli, eh? Good, good.' He took the papers and glanced at them, nodding with satisfaction. 'You see Androche,' he remarked to the hussar, 'it goes well, very well and the project of England is dead.' He turned towards the window. 'Whom have we here, Bourienne?'

'This is Capitaine de Frégate Santhonax, General Bonaparte.'

'Ah!'

Hearing his name the naval officer turned from the window. He was much taller than the general, his handsome features severely disfigured by a recent scar that ran upwards from the corner of his mouth into his left cheek. He made a slight bow and met General Bonaparte's appraising grey eyes.

'So, Captain, you contrived to escape from the English, eh?'

'Yes Citizen General, I arrived in Paris three weeks ago.'

'And have already married, eh?' Santhonax nodded, aware that the Corsican knew all about him. The general resumed his pacing, head sunk in thought. 'I have just come from an inspection of the Channel Ports and the arrangements in hand for an invasion of England . . .' he stopped abruptly in front of Santhonax. 'What are your views of the practicality of such an enterprise?'

'Impossible without complete command of the Channel: any attempt without local superiority would be doomed, Citizen General. Conditions in the Channel can change rapidly, we should have to hold it for a week at least. The British fleet, if it cannot be overwhelmed, *must* be dissipated by ruse and threat . . .'

'Exactly! That is what I have informed the Directory . . . but do we have the capability to achieve such a local superiority?'

'No, Citizen General.' Santhonax lowered his eyes before the penetrating stare of Bonaparte. While this young man had been trouncing the Austrians out of Italy he had been working to achieve such a combination by bringing the Dutch fleet to Brest. The attempt had been shattered by the British at Camperdown four months earlier.

'Huh!' exclaimed Bonaparte, 'then we agree at all points, Captain. That is excellent, excellent. The Army of England is to have employment in a different quarter, eh Androche?' He turned to the hussar, 'This is Androche Junot, Captain, an old friend of the Bonapartes.' The two men bowed. 'But the Army of England will lay the axe to the root of England's wealth. What is your opinion of the English, Captain?'

Santhonax sighed. 'They are the implacable enemies of the Revolution, General Bonaparte, and of France. They possess qualities of great doggedness and should not be underestimated.'

Bonaparte sniffed in disagreement. 'Yet you escaped from them, no? How did you accomplish that, eh?'

'Following my capture I was taken to Maidstone Gaol. After a few weeks I was transferred to the hulks at Portsmouth. However my uniform was so damaged in the action off Camperdown that I managed to secure a civilian coat from my gaolers. When the equipage in which I was travelling changed horses at a place called Guildford, I made my escape.'

'And?'

Santhonax shrugged. 'I turned into an adjacent alleyway and then the first tavern where I took a corner seat. I speak English without an accent, Citizen General.'

'And this?' Bonaparte pointed to his own cheek.

'The escort were looking for a man with a bandage. I removed it and occupied an obscure corner. I was not discovered.' He paused, then added, 'I am used to subterfuge.'

'Yes, yes, Captain, I know of your services to the Republic, you have a reputation for intrepidity and audacity. Admiral Bruix speaks highly of you and as you are not at present quite persona grata with the Directory,' Bonaparte paused while Santhonax flushed at the illusion to his failure, 'he recommends you to this especial command.' The general stopped again in front of Santhonax and looked directly up at him. 'You are appointed to a frigate I understand, Captain?'

'The *Antigone*, Citizen General, now preparing for a distant cruise at Rochefort. I am also to have the corvettes *La Torride* and *Annette* with me. I am directed to take command as commodore on receipt of your final orders.'

'Good, very good.' Bonaparte held out his hand to Bourienne and the secretary handed him a sealed packet. 'The British have a small squadron in the Red Sea. They should cause you no fear. As you have been told, the Army under my command is bound for Egypt. When my veterans reach the shores of the Red Sea I anticipate you will have secured a sufficiency of transport, local craft of course, and a port of embarkation for a division. You will convey it to India, Captain Santhonax. You are familiar with those waters?'

'I served under Suffren, Citizen General. So we are to harrass the British in India.' Santhonax's eyes glowed with a new enthusiasm.

'You will carry but the advance guard. Paris burns the soles of my feet, Captain. In India may be found the empire left by Alexander. There greatness awaits us.' It was not the speech of a fanatic, Santhonax had heard enough of them during the Revolution. But Bonaparte's enthusiasm was infectious. After the defeat of

Camperdown and his capture, Santhonax's ambition had seemed exhausted. But now, in a few words, this dynamic little Corsican had swept the past aside, like the Revolution itself. New visions of glory were opened to the imagination by a man to whom all things seemed possible.

Abruptly Bonaparte held out the sealed packet to Santhonax. Junot bent forward to whisper in his ear. 'Ah! Yes, Androche reminds me that your wife is a celebrated beauty. Good, good. Marriage is what binds a man to his country and beauty is the inspiration of ambition, eh? You shall bring Madame Santhonax to the Rue Victoire this evening, Captain, my wife is holding a soirée. You may proceed to Rochefort tomorrow. That is all Captain.'

As Santhonax left the room General Bonaparte was already dictating to his secretaries.

Chapter One

The Convoy Escort

A low mist hung in the valley of the Meon where the pale winter sunshine had yet to reach. Beneath the dripping branches of the apple trees Lieutenant Nathaniel Drinkwater paced slowly up and down, shivering slightly in the frosty air. He had not slept well, waking from a dream that had been full of fitful images of faces he had done with now that he had come home. The nocturnal silence of the cottage was still disturbingly unfamiliar even after two months leave of absence from the creaking hull of the cutter *Kestrel*. It compelled him to rise early lest his restlessness woke his wife beside him. Now, pacing the path of the tiny garden, the chill made the wound in his right arm ache, bringing his mind full circle to where the dream had dislodged it from repose.

It had been Edouard Santhonax who had inflicted the wound and of whom he had dreamed. But as he came to his senses he recollected that Santhonax was now safely mewed up, a prisoner. As for his paramour, the bewitching Hortense Montholon, she was in France begging for her bread, devil take her! He felt the sun penetrate the mist, warm upon his back, finally dispelling the fears of the night. The recent gales had gone, giving way to sharp frosty mornings of bright sunshine. The click of a door latch reminded him he was in happier circumstances.

The dark hair fell about Elizabeth's face and her brown eyes were full of concern. 'Are you not well, my dear?' she asked gently, putting a hand on his arm. 'Did you not hear the knock at the street door?'

'I am quite well, Bess. Who was at the door?'

'Mr Jackson at the Post Office sent young Will up from Petersfield with letters for you. They are on the table.'

'I am indebted to Mr Jackson's kindness.' He moved to pass inside the cottage but she stopped him. 'Nathaniel, what troubles you?' Then, in a lower voice, 'You have not been disappointed in me?'

He caught her up and kissed her, then they went in to read the letters. He broke the one with the Admiralty seal first: *Sir, you are required and directed that upon receipt of these instructions you proceed . . .* He was appointed first lieutenant of the brig-sloop *Hellebore* under Commander Griffiths. In silence he handed the letter to Elizabeth who caught her lower lip in her teeth as she read. Drinkwater picked up the second letter, recognising the shaky but still bravely flowing script.

My Dear Nathaniel,

You will doubtless be in receipt of their L'dships' Instructions to join the Brig under my Command. She is a new Vessel and lying at Deptford. Do not hasten. I am already on board and doing duty for you, the end of the month will suffice. Our Complement is almost augmented as I was able to draft the Kestrels entire. We sail upon Convoy duty. Convey my felicitations to your wife,

I remain, etc
Madoc Griffiths

P.S. I received News but yesterday that M. Santhonax Escaped Custody and has been at Liberty for a month now.

Drinkwater stood stunned, the oppression of the night returned to him. Elizabeth was watching, her eyes large with tears. 'So soon, my darling . . .'

He smiled ruefully at her. 'Madoc has extended my leave a little.' He passed the second letter over. 'Dear Madoc,' she said, brushing her eyes.

'Aye, he does duty for me now. He has nowhere else to go.' He slipped his arm around her waist and they kissed again.

'Come we have time to complete the purchase of the house at Petersfield and your cook should arrive by the end of the week. You will be quite the *grande dame*.'

'Will you take Tregembo with you?'

He laughed. 'I doubt that I have the power to stop him.'

They fell silent, Elizabeth thinking of the coming months of lone-liness, Drinkwater disloyally of the new brig. 'Hellebore,' he said aloud, 'ain't that a flower or something? Elizabeth? What the devil are you laughing at?'

Lieutenant Richard White had the morning watch aboard *Victory*. Flying the flag of Earl St Vincent the great three decker stood north west under easy sail, the rest of the blockading squadron in line ahead and astern of her. To the east the mole and lighthouse of Cadiz were pale in the sunshine but White's glass was trained ahead to where a cutter was flying the signal for sails in sight to the north.

A small midshipman ran up to him. 'Looks like the convoy, sir.'

'Thank you, Mr Lee. Have the kindness to inform His Lordship and the Captain.' Mr Lee was ten years old and had endeared him-self to Lieutenant White by being the only officer aboard *Victory* shorter than himself. Instinctively White looked round the deck, checking that every rope was in its place, every man at his station and every sail drawing to perfection before St Vincent's eagle eye drew his attention to it.

'Good morning, my lord,' said White, vacating the windward side of the deck and doffing his hat as the admiral ascended to the poop for a better view of the newcomers. 'Good morning sir,' responded the admiral with the unfailing courtesy that made his blasts of admonition the more terrible.

Captain Grey and Sir Robert Calder, Captain of the Fleet also came on deck, followed by *Victory*'s first lieutenant and several other officers, for any arrival from England brought news; letters and gossip to break the tedium of blockade.

They could see the convoy now, six storeships under the escort of a brig from whose masthead a string of bunting broke out. In White's ear Mr Lee squeaked the numerals followed by a pause while he hunted in the lists. 'Brig-sloop *Hellebore*, sir, but newly com-missioned under Commander Griffiths.'

'Thank you, Mr Lee. Brig *Hellebore*, Captain Griffiths, my lord, with convoy.'

'Thank you, Mr White, have the goodness to desire him to send a boat with an officer.'

'Aye, aye, my lord.' He turned to Lee who was already chalking the signal on his slate and calling the flag numbers to his yeoman.

White, who had given the commander his courtesy title when addressing the punctilious St Vincent, was wondering where he had heard the name before. It was not long before he had his answer.

When the brig's boat hooked on to *Victory*'s chains he recognised the figure who came in at the entry.

'Nathaniel! My dear fellow, so you're still with Griffiths, eh? How capital to see you! And you've been made.' White indicated the gilt-buttoned lieutenant's cuff that he was vigorously pumping up and down in welcome. 'Damn me but I'm delighted, delighted, but come, St Vincent will not tolerate our gossiping.'

Drinkwater followed his old friend apprehensively. It was many years since he had 'trod such a flagship's deck and the ordered precision of *Victory* combined with her size to show Admiral Duncan's smaller, weathered and worn-out *Venerable* in a poor light. Drinkwater uncovered and made a small and, he hoped, elegant bow as White introduced him to the earl. He felt himself under the keenest scrutiny by a pair of shrewd old eyes that shone from a face that any moment might slip from approbation to castigation. Lord St Vincent studied the man before him. Drinkwater's intelligent gaze met that of the admiral. He was thirty-four, lean and of middle height. His face was weathered and creased about the grey eyes and mouth, with the thin line of an old scar puckering down the left cheek. There were some small blue powder burns about the eyes, like random inkspots. Drinkwater's hair, uncovered by the doffed hat, was still a rich brown, clubbed in a long queue behind the head. Not, the admiral concluded, a flagship officer, but well enough, judging by the firm, full mouth and steady eyes. The mouth was not unlike Nelson's, St Vincent thought with wry affection, and Nelson had been a damned pain until he had hoisted his own flag.

'Are you married sir?' St Vincent asked sharply.

'Er, yes, my lord,' replied Drinkwater, taken aback.

'A pity, sir, a pity. A married officer is frequently lost to the service. Come let us descend to my cabin and arrange for the disposition of your convoy. Sir Robert, a moment of your time . . .'

When the business of the fleet had been attended to Drinkwater had a few minutes for an exchange of news with White while *Victory* backed her maintopsail and summoned *Hellebore*'s boat.

'How is Elizabeth, my dear fellow?'

'She goes along famously, Richard, and would have asked to be remembered to you had she known we might meet.'

'When were you gazetted, Nat?'

'After Camperdown.'

'Ah, so you were there. Damn! That still gives you the advantage of one fleet action to boast of ahead of me,' he grinned. 'D'you have many other old Kestrels besides Griffiths on your brig?'

'Aye, Tregembo you remember, and old Appleby . . .'

'What? That old windbag Harry Appleby? Well I'm damned. She looks a long-legged little ship, Nat,' he nodded at the brig.

'She's well enough, but you still have the important advantages,' replied Drinkwater, a sweep of his hand including *Victory*, the puissant personages upon her deck and alluding to White's rapid rise by comparison with his own. 'Convoy work ain't quite the way to be made post.'

'No, Nat, but my bet is you're ordered up the Mediterranean, eh?' Drinkwater nodded and White went on, 'that's where Nelson is, before Toulon, Nat, and wherever Nelson is there's action and glory.' White's eyes gleamed. 'D'you know St Vincent sent him back into the Med after we evacuated it last year and a month ago he reinforced Nelson with Troubridge's inshore squadron. Sent the whole lot of 'em off from the harbour mouth before Curtis's reinforcements had come up with the fleet. And the blasted Dons didn't even know the inshore squadron had been changed! What d'you think of that, eh? No,' he patted Drinkwater's arm condescendingly, 'the Med's the place, Nat there's bound to be action with Nelson.'

'I'm only escorting a convoy in a brig, Richard,' said Drinkwater deprecatingly.

White laughed again and held out his hand. 'Good fortune then Nat, for we're all hostage to it, d'you know.'

They shook hands and Drinkwater descended to the boat where Mr Quilhampton, two years older than Mr Lee, but with a fraction of the latter's experience, overawed by the mass of *Victory* lumbering alongside his cockleshell cutter, made a hash of getting off the battleship's side

393

'Steady now, Mr Q. Bear off forward, put the helm over and *then* lower your oars. 'Tis the only way, d'you see,' Drinkwater said patiently, looking back at *Victory*. Already her main topsail was filled and White's grin was clearly visible. Drinkwater looked ahead towards the tiny, fragile *Hellebore*. The cutter rose over the long, low Atlantic swells, the sea danced blue and gold in the sunshine where the light westerly wind rippled its surface. He felt the warmth in the muscles of his right arm.

'*Hecuba* and *Molly* to accompany us into the Med, sir, to Nelson, off Toulon. We're to proceed as soon as possible.' Drinkwater looked at Griffiths who lent heavily against the rail, gazing at the stately line of the British fleet to the eastward. '*Prydferth, bach,* beautiful,' he muttered. Drinkwater stared astern at the convoy, their topsails aback in an untidy gaggle as they waited to hear their fate. Boats were bobbing towards the brig. 'I've sent for their masters,' Griffiths explained.

'How's the leg today, sir?' Drinkwater asked while they waited for the boats to arrive. The old, white-haired Welshman looked with disgust at the twisted and puffy limb stretched stiffly out on the gun carriage before him.

'Ah, devil take it, it's a damned nuisance. And now Appleby tells me it's gouty. And before you raise the matter of my bottle,' he hurried on with mock severity, 'I'll have you know that without it I'd be intolerable, see.' They grinned at each other, their relationship a stark contrast with the formality of *Victory*'s quarterdeck. They had sailed together for six years, first in the twelve-gun cutter *Kestrel*, and their intimacy was established upon a mutually understood basis of friendship and professional distance. For Griffiths was an infirm man, subject to recurring malarial fevers, whose command had been bestowed for services rendered to British intelligence. Without *Hellebore* Griffiths would have rotted ashore, a lonely and embittered bachelor in anonymous lodgings. He had requested Drinkwater as his first lieutenant partly out of gratitude, partly out of friendship. And if Griffiths sought to protect his own career by delegating with perfect confidence to Drinkwater, he could console himself with the thought that he did the younger man a service.

394

'You forget, Mr Drinkwater, that if I had not broke my leg last year you'd not have been in command of *Kestrel* at Camperdown.'

Drinkwater agreed, but any further rejoinder was cut short by the arrival of the storeship commanders.

To starboard the dun-coloured foothills of the Atlas Mountains shone rose-red in the sunset. To larboard the hills of southern Spain fell to the low promontory of Tarifa. Far ahead of her elongated shadow the Mediterranean opened before the bowsprit of the brig. From her deck the horizontal light threw into sharp relief every detail of her fabric: the taut lines of her rigging, the beads of her blocks, her reddened canvas and an unnatural brilliance in her paintwork. Astern on either quarter, in dark silhouette, *Hecuba* and *Molly* followed them. Drinkwater ceased pacing as the skinny midshipman barred his way.

'Yes, Mr Q?' The gunroom officers of H.M. Brig *Hellebore* had long since ceased to wrap their tongues round Quilhampton. It was far too grand a name for an animal as insignificant as a volunteer. Once again Drinkwater experienced that curious reminder of Elizabeth that the boy engendered, for Drinkwater had obtained a place for him on the supplication of his wife. Mrs Quilhampton was a pretty widow who occasionally assisted Elizabeth with her school, and Drinkwater had been both flattered and amused that anyone should consider him a person of sufficient influence from whom to solicit 'interest'. And there was sufficient resemblance to his own introduction to naval life to arouse his natural sympathy. He had acquiesced with only a show of misgivings and been rewarded by a quite shameless embrace from the boy's mother. Now the son's eager-to-please expression irritated him with its power to awaken memories.

'Well,' he snapped, 'come, come, what the devil d'you want?'

'Begging your pardon, sir, but Mr Appleby's compliments and where are we bound, sir?'

'Don't you know, Mr Q?' said Drinkwater mellowing.

'N . . . no, sir.'

'Come now, what d'you see to starboard?'

'To starboard, sir? Why that's land, sir.'

'And to larboard?'

'That's land too, sir.'

'Aye, Mr Q. To starboard is Africa, to larboard is Europe. Now what d'you suppose lies between eh? What did Mrs Drinkwater instruct you in the matter, eh?'

'Be it the M . . . Mediterranean, sir?'

'It be indeed, Mr Q,' replied Drinkwater with a smile, 'and d'you know who commands in the Mediterranean?'

'Why sir, I know that. Sir Horatio Nelson, K.B., sir,' said the boy eagerly.

'Very well, Mr Q. Now do you repair directly to the surgeon and acquaint him with those facts and tell him that we are directed by Earl St Vincent to deliver the contents of those two hoys astern to Rear Admiral Nelson off Toulon.'

'Aye, aye, sir.'

'And Mr Q . . .'

'Sir?'

'Do you also direct Mr Appleby to have a tankard of blackstrap ready for me when I come below at eight bells.'

Drinkwater watched the excited Quilhampton race below. Like the midshipman he was curious about Nelson, a man whose name was known to every schoolboy in England since his daring manoeuvre at the battle of Cape St Vincent. Not that his conduct had been put at risk by the enemy so much as by those in high places at the Admiralty. Drinkwater knew there were those who considered he would be shot for disobedience before long, just as there were those who complained he was no seaman. Certainly he did not possess the abilities of a Pellew or a Keats, and although he enjoyed the confidence of St Vincent he had been involved in the fiasco at Santa Cruz. Perhaps, thought Drinkwater, he was a man like the restless Smith, with whom he had served briefly in the Channel, a man of dynamic force whose deficiencies could be forgiven in a kind of emulative love. But, he concluded, pacing the deck in the gathering darkness, whatever White said on the subject, it did not alter the fact that *Hellebore* was but a brig and fitted for little more than her present duties.

Nelson

'She hasn't acknowledged, sir. Shall I fire a gun to loo'ard?'

Griffiths stared astern to where *Hecuba*, her jury rigged foremast a mute testimony to the violence of the weather, was struggling into the bay.

'No, Mr Drinkwater. Don't forget she's a merchantman with a quarter of our complement and right now, *bach*, every man-jack aboard her will be busy.'

Drinkwater felt irritated by the mild rebuke, but he held his tongue. The week of anxiety must surely soon be over. South of Minorca, beating up for Toulon the northerly mistral had hit the little convoy with unusual violence. *Hecuba*'s foremast had gone by the board and they had been obliged to run off to the eastward and the shelter of Corsica. Drinkwater stared ahead at the looming coastline of the island, the sharp peaked mountains reaching up dark against the glow of dawn. To larboard Cape Morsetta slowly extended its shelter as they limped eastward into Crovani Bay.

'Deck there! Sail dead ahead, sir!'

The cry from the masthead brought the glasses of the two men up simultaneously. In the shadows of the shoreline lay a three-masted vessel, her spars bare of canvas as she lay wind-rode at anchor.

'A polaccra,' muttered Griffiths. 'We'll investigate her when we've brought this lame duck to her anchor,' he jerked his head over his shoulder.

The convoy stood on into the bay. Soon they were able to discern the individual pine trees that grew straight and tall enough to furnish fine masts.

'Bring the ship to the wind Mr Lestock,' Griffiths addressed the master, a small, fussy little man with a permanent air of being put upon. 'You may fire your gun when we let the bower go, Mr Drinkwater.'

'Aye, aye, sir.' Lestock was shouting through the speaking trumpet as men ran to the braces, thankful to be in the lee of land where *Hellebore*'s deck approximated the horizontal. The main topsail slapped back against the mast and redistributed its thrust through the standing rigging to the hull below. *Hellebore* lost forward motion and began to gather sternway.

'Let go!'

The carpenter's topmaul swung once, then the brig's bow kicked slightly as the bower anchor's weight was released. The splash was lost in the bark of the six pounder. While Lestock and his mates had the canvas taken off the ship, Drinkwater swung his glass round the bay. *Molly* was making sternway and he saw the splash under her bluff, north-country bow where her anchor was let go. But *Hecuba* still stood inshore while her hands struggled to clew up her forecourse. Unable to manoeuvre under her topsails due to her damaged foremast, her master had been obliged to hold on to the big sail until the last moment, now something had fouled.

'Why don't he back the damned thing,' Drinkwater muttered to himself while beside him Lestock roared 'Aloft and stow!' through the speaking trumpet. The Hellebores eagerly leapt into the rigging to pummel the brig's topsails into the gaskets, anxious to get secured, the galley stove relit and some steaming skillygolee and molasses into their empty, contracted bellies.

Then he saw *Hecuba* begin her turn into the wind, saw the big course gather itself into folds like a washerwoman tucking up her skirts, the main topsail flatten itself against the top and the splash from her bow where the anchor was let go.

'Convoy's anchored, sir,' he reported to Griffiths.

The commander nodded. 'Looks like your gun had another effect.' Griffiths pointed his glass at the polaccra anchored inshore of them. Drinkwater studied the unfamiliar colours that had been hoisted to her masthead.

'Ragusan ensign, Mr Drinkwater, and I'll warrant you didn't know 'em from the Grand Turk's.'

Drinkwater felt the tension ebbing from him. 'You'd be right, sir.'

Lestock touched his hat to Griffiths. 'She's brought up, sir, and secured.'

'Very well, Mr Lestock, pipe the hands to breakfast after which I want a working party under Mr Rogers ready to assist the re-rigging of *Hecuba*. Send both your mates over. Oh, and Mr Dalziell can go too, I'd very much like to know if that young man is to be of any service to us.'

'Aye, aye, sir. What about Mr Quilhampton, sir? He is also inexperienced.'

Griffiths eyed Lestock with something approaching distaste.

'Mr Quilhampton can take a working party ashore with the carpenter. I think a couple of those pines would come in useful, eh? What d'you think Mr Drinkwater?'

'A good idea, sir. And the Ragusan?'

'Mr Q's first task will be to desire her master to wait upon me. Now, Mr Drinkwater, you have been up all night, will you take breakfast with me before you turn in?'

Half an hour later, his belly full, Drinkwater stretched luxuriously, too comfortable to make his way to his cabin. Griffiths dabbed his mouth with a stained napkin.

'I think Rogers can take care of that business aboard *Hecuba*.'

'I hope so sir,' yawned Drinkwater, 'he's not backward in forwarding opinions as to his own merit.'

'Or of criticising others, Nathaniel,' said Griffiths solemnly. Drinkwater nodded. The second lieutenant was a trifle overconfident and it was impossible to pull the wool over the eyes of an officer as experienced and shrewd as Griffiths. 'That's no bad thing,' continued the commander in his deep, mellifluous Welsh voice, 'if there's substance beneath the façade.' Drinkwater agreed sleepily, his lids closing of their own accord.

'But I'm less happy about Mr Dalziell.'

Drinkwater forced himself awake. 'No sir, it's nothing one can lay one's finger upon but . . .' he trailed off, his brain refusing to work any further.

'Pass word for my servant,' Griffiths called, and Merrick came into the tiny cubby hole that served the brig's officers for a common mess. 'Assist Mr Drinkwater to his cot, Merrick.'

'I'm all right, sir.' Drinkwater rose slowly to his feet and made for the door of his own cabin, cannoning into the portly figure of the surgeon.

Griffiths smiled to himself as he watched the two manoeuvre round one another, the one sleepily indignant, the other wakefully apologetic. Appleby seated himself at the table. 'Morning sir, dreadful night . . .' The surgeon fell to a dissertation about the movement of brigs as opposed to ships of the line, to whether or not their respective motions had an adverse effect on the human frame, and to what degree in each case. Griffiths had long since learned to disregard the surgeon's ramblings which increased with age. Griffiths remembered the mutual animosity that had characterised their early relationship. But that had all changed. After Griffiths had been left ashore at Great Yarmouth in the autumn of the previous year it had been Appleby who had come in search of him when the *Kestrel* decommissioned. It had been Appleby too who had not merely sworn at the incompetence of the physicians there, but who had nearly fought a duel with a certain Dr Spriggs over the manner in which the latter had set Griffiths's femur. Appleby had wished to break and reset it, but was prevailed upon to desist by Griffiths himself, who had felt that matters were passing a little out of his own control.

Still raging inwardly Appleby had written off to Lord Dungarth to remind the earl of the invaluable services performed by Griffiths during his tenure of command of the cutter *Kestrel*. Thus the half-pay commander with the game leg had found himself commissioning the new brig-sloop *Hellebore*. Appleby's appointment to surgeon of the ship was the least Griffiths could do in return and they had become close in the succeeding weeks.

Lord Dungarth had pleaded his own cause and requested that a Mr Dalziell be found a place as midshipman. It was soon apparent why the earl had not sent the youth to a crack frigate, whatever the obligation he owed the Dalziell family. Griffiths sighed; Mr Dalziell was fortunately small beer and unlikely to cause him great loss of sleep, but he could not escape a sense of exasperation at having been saddled with such a make-weight. He poured more coffee as Appleby drew to his conclusion.

'And so you see, sir, I am persuaded that the lively motion of such a vessel as this, though the buffetting one receives below decks is apt to give one a greater number of minor contusions than enough, is, however, likely to exercise more muscles in the body and invigorate the humours more than the leisurely motion of, say, a first rate. In the latter case the somnolent rhythms may induce a langour, and when coupled to the likelihood of the vessel being employed on blockade, hove to and so forth, actually contribute to that malaise and boredom that are the inevitable concomitants of that unenviable employment. Do you not agree sir?'

'Eh? Oh, undoubtedly you are right, Mr Appleby. But frankly I am driven to wonder to what purpose you men of science address your speculations.'

Appleby expelled his breath in an eloquent sigh. 'Ah well, sir, 'tis no great matter . . . how long d'you intend to stay here?'

'Just as long as it takes Mr Rogers to assist the people of *Hecuba* to get up a new foremast. Under the circumstances they did a wonderful job themselves, for in that sea there was no question of them securing a tow.'

'Ah! I was thinking about that, sir. Nathaniel was talking about using a rocket to convey a line. Now, if we could but . . .' Appleby broke off as Mr Q popped his head round the door.

'Beg pardon sir, but the captain of the Ra . . . Rag . . .'

'Ragusan,' prompted Griffiths.

'Yes, sir . . . well he's here sir.'

'Then show him in, boy, show him in.'

Griffiths summoned Drinkwater from sleep at noon. The tiny cabin that accommodated the brig's commander was strewn with charts and Lestock was in fussy attendance.

'Ah, Mr Drinkwater, please help yourself to a glass.' Griffiths indicated the decanter which contained his favourite *sercial*. As the lieutenant poured, Griffiths outlined the events of the morning.

'This mistral that prevented our getting up to Toulon has been a blessing in disguise . . .' Drinkwater saw Lestock nodding in sage agreement with his captain. 'The fact that we have had to run for shelter has likely saved us from falling into the hands of the French.'

Still tired, Drinkwater frowned with incomprehension. Nelson was blockading Toulon; what the devil was Griffiths driving at?

'The French are out, somewhere it is believed in the eastern

Mediterranean. That polaccra spoke with Admiral Nelson off Cape Passaro on June the twenty-second . . . two weeks ago. He's bound to Barcelona and was quizzed by the admiral about the whereabouts of the French armada.'

'Armada, sir? You mean an invasion force?'

Griffiths nodded. 'I do indeed, *bach. Myndiawl*, they've given Nelson the slip, see.'

'And did this Ragusan offer Sir Horatio any intelligence?'

'Indeed he did. The polaccra passed the entire force, heading east . . .'

'East? And Nelson's gone in pursuit?'

'Yes indeed. And we must follow.' Drinkwater digested the news, trying to make sense of it. East? All his professional life the Royal Navy had guarded against a combination of naval forces in the Channel. His entire service aboard *Kestrel* had been devoted to that end. Indeed his motives for entering the service in the first place had had their inspiration in the Franco-Spanish attempt of 1779 which, to the shame of the navy, had so nearly succeeded. East? It did not make sense unless it was an elaborate feint, the French buying time to exercise in the eastern Mediterranean. If that were the case they might draw Nelson after them – such an impetuous officer would not hold back – and then they might turn west, slip through the Straits, clear St Vincent from before Cadiz and join forces with the Spanish fleet.

'Did our informant say who commanded them, sir?' he asked.

'No less a person than Bonaparte,' said Lestock solemnly.

'Bonaparte? But we read in the newspapers that Bonaparte commanded the Army of England . . . I remember Appleby jesting that the English Army had long wanted a general officer of his talent.'

'Mr Appleby's joke seems to have curdled, Mr Drinkwater,' said Lestock without a smile. Drinkwater turned to Griffiths.

'You say you'll follow Nelson, sir, to what rendezvous?'

'What do you suggest, Mr Drinkwater? Mr Lestock?'

Lestock fidgetted. 'Well, sir, I er, I think that in the absence of a rendezvous with the admiral we ought to proceed to, er . . .'

'Malta, sir,' said Drinkwater abruptly, 'then if the French double for the Atlantic we might be placed there with advantage, on the other hand there will doubtless be some general orders for us there.'

'No, Mr Drinkwater. Your reasoning is sound but the Ragusan also told us that Malta had fallen to the French.' Griffiths put down his glass and bent over the charts, picking up the dividers to point with.

'We will proceed south and run through the Bonifacio Strait for Naples, there will likely be news there, or here at Messina, or here, at Syracuse.'

There was no news at Naples beyond that of Nelson's fleet having stopped there on 17th June, intelligence older than that from the polaccra. Griffiths would not anchor and all hands eyed the legendary port wistfully. The ochre colours of its palazzi and its tenements were lent a common and ethereal appeal by distance, and the onshore breeze enhanced a view given a haunting beauty beyond the blue waters of the bay by the backdrop of Vesuvius.

'God, but I'd dearly love a night of sport there,' mused Rogers, who had acquitted himself in re-rigging the *Hecuba* and now seemed of the opinion that he had earned at least one night of debauchery in the Neapolitan stews. Appleby, standing within earshot and aware of the three seamen grinning close by said, 'Then thank the lord you've a sane man to command your instincts, Mr Rogers. The Neapolitan pox is a virulent disease well-known for its intractability.'

Rogers paled at the sally and the three men coiled the falls of the royal halliards with uncommon haste.

Hellebore worked her way slowly south, past the islands of the Tyrrhenian Sea and through the narrow Straits of Messina; but there was no further news of Nelson or the French.

On 16th July the convoy stood into the Bay of Syracuse to wood and water and to find a welcome for British ships. Through the good offices of the British Ambassador to the Court of the Two Sicilies, Sir William Hamilton, facilities were available to expedite the reprovisioning of units of the Royal Navy.

'It seems,' Griffiths said to his assembled officers, 'that Sir Horatio has considered the possibility of using Syracuse as a base. We must simply wait.'

They waited three days. Shortly before noon on the 19th the British fleet was in the offing and with the *Leander* in the van, came into Syracuse Harbour. By three minutes past three in the afternoon the fourteen ships of the line under the command of Rear Admiral Sir Horatio Nelson had anchored. Within an hour their boats swarmed over the blue waters of the bay, their crews carrying off wood and water, their pursers haggling in the market place for vegetables and beef.

Hellebore's boat pulled steadily through the throng of craft, augmented by local bumboats which traded hopefully with the fleet. Officers' servants were buying chickens for their masters' tables while a surreptitious trade in rot-gut liquor was being conducted through lower deck ports. The apparent confusion and bustle had an air of charged purpose about it and Drinkwater suppressed a feeling of almost childish excitement. Beside him Griffiths wore a stony expression, his leathery old face hanging in sad folds, the wisps of white hair escaping untidily from below the new, glazed cocked hat. Drinkwater felt a wave of sympathy for the old man with his one glittering epaulette. Griffiths had been at sea half a century; he had served in slavers as a mate before being pressed as a naval seaman. He was old enough, experienced enough and able enough to have commanded this entire fleet, reflected Nathaniel, but the man who did so was only a few years older than Drinkwater himself.

'You had better attend on me,' Griffiths had said, giving his first lieutenant permission to accompany him aboard *Vanguard*, 'seeing that you are so damned eager to clap eyes on this Admiral Nelson.'

Drinkwater looked at Quilhampton who shared his curiosity. Mr Q's hand rested nervously on the boat's tiller. The boy was concentrating, not daring to look round at the splendours of British naval might surrounding him. Drinkwater approved of his single-mindedness; Mr Q was developing into an asset.

'Boat ahoy!' The hail came from the flagship looming ahead of them, her spars and rigging black against the brilliant sky, the blue rear-admiral's flag at her mizen masthead. Drinkwater was about to prompt Quilhampton but the boy rose, cleared his throat and in a resonant treble called out *'Hellebore!'* The indication of his commander's presence thus conveyed to *Vanguard*, Quilhampton felt with pleasure the half smile bestowed on him by Mr Drinkwater.

At the entry port four white gloved side-boys and a bosun's mate greeted *Hellebore's* captain and his lieutenant. The officer of the watch left them briefly on the quarterdeck while he reported their arrival to the demi-god who resided beneath the poop. Curiously Drinkwater looked round. *Vanguard* was smaller than *Victory*, a mere 74-gun two decker, but there was that same neatness about her, mixed with something else. He sensed it intuitively from the way her people went about their business. From the seamen amidships, rolling empty water casks to the gangway and from a quarter gunner changing the flints in the after carronades emanated a sense of single-minded purpose. He was always to remember this drive that superimposed their efforts as the 'Nelson touch', far more than the much publicised manoeuvre at Trafalgar that brought Nelson his apotheosis seven years later.

'Sir Horatio will see you now sir,' said the lieutenant re-emerging. Drinkwater followed Griffiths, ignoring the gesture of restraint from the duty officer. They passed under the row of ciphered leather fire-buckets into the shade of the poop, passing the master's cabin and the rigid marine sentry. Uncovering, Drinkwater followed his commander into the admiral's cabin.

Sir Horatio Nelson rose from his desk as Griffiths presented Drinkwater and the latter bowed. Nelson's smallness of stature was at first a disappointment to Nathaniel who expected something altogether different. Disappointing too were the worn uniform coat and the untidy mop of greying hair, but Drinkwater began to lose his sense of anti-climax as the admiral quizzed Griffiths about the stores contained in *Hecuba* and *Molly*. There was in his address an absence of formality, an eager confidence which was at once infectious. There was a delicacy about the little man. He looked far older than his thirty-nine years, his skin fine drawn, almost transparent over the bones. His large nose and wide, mobile mouth were at odd variance with his body size. But the one good blue eye was sharply attentive, a window on some inner motivation, and the empty sleeve bore witness to his reckless courage.

'Do you know the whereabouts of my frigates, Captain?' he asked Griffiths, 'I am driven desperate for want of frigates. The French have escaped me, sir, and I have one brig at my disposal to reconnoitre for a fleet.'

Drinkwater sensed the consuming frustration felt by this most diligent of flag officers, sensed his mortification at being deprived of his eyes in the gale that had dismasted *Vanguard*. Yet *Vanguard* had been refitted without delay and the battle line was impressive enough to strike terror in the French if only this one-armed dynamo could catch them.

'There is *Hellebore*, Sir Horatio,' volunteered Griffiths.

'Yes, Captain. Would that the whereabouts of the French squadron was my only consideration. But I know that their fleet, besides sail of the line, frigates, bomb vessels and so forth, also comprises three hundred troop transports; an armada that left Sicily with a fair wind from the west. It is clear their destination is to the eastward. I think their object is to possess themselves of some port in Egypt, to fix themselves at the head of the Red Sea in order to get a formidable army into India, to act in concert with Tipoo Sahib. No, Captain, I may not permit myself the luxury of retaining *Hellebore* . . .' The admiral paused and Drinkwater felt apprehensive. Nelson made up his mind. 'I must sacrifice perhaps my reputation but that must always subordinate itself to my zeal for the King's service which demands I acquaint the officer on the station of the danger he may be in. I have already written to Mr Baldwin, our consul at Alexandria, to determine whether the French have any vessels prepared in the Red Sea. As yet I have had no reply. Therefore, my dear Griffiths, I desire that you wood and water without delay and send a boat for your written orders the instant you are ready to proceed to the Red Sea.'

Drinkwater felt his mouth go dry. The Red Sea meant a year's voyage at the least. And Elizabeth had given him expectation of a child in the summer.

Chapter Three

A Brig of War

Lieutenant Drinkwater stared astern watching the seas run up under the brig's larboard quarter, lifting her stern and impelling her forward, adding a trifle to her speed until they passed ahead of her and she dragged, slowly, into the succeeding trough. *Hellebore* carried sail to her topgallants as she raced south west before the trade wind, the coast of Mauretania twenty-five leagues to the east.

Drinkwater had been watching Mr Quilhampton heave the log and had acknowledged the boy's report, prompted by the quartermaster, that they were running at seven knots. Something would not let him turn forward again but kept him watching the wake as it bubbled green-white under the stern and trailed away behind them in an irregular ribbon, twisted by the yaw of the ship and the oncoming waves. Here and there a following seabird dipped into its disturbance.

He had felt wretched as they passed the Straits of Gibraltar and took their departure from Cape Espartel, for he had been unable to send letters back to Elizabeth, so swift had been *Hellebore*'s passage from Syracuse, so explicit the admiral's orders. Now it was certain he would be separated from her until after the birth of their child, he regretted his inability to soften the blow of his apparent desertion.

He was aware of someone at his elbow and resented the intrusion upon his private thoughts.

'Beg pardon, zur.' It was Tregembo. Ten years older than Drinkwater the able seaman had long ago attached himself to him with a touching and unsolicited loyalty. He had cemented the relationship by supplying Elizabeth with a cook in the person of his wife Susan, certain that service with the Drinkwaters represented security. The personal link between them both gratified and, at that moment, annoyed Drinkwater. He snapped irritably, 'What is it?'

'Your sword, zur, 'tis now but half a glass before quarters, zur.'

Drinkwater looked guiltily at the half-hour sand-glass in the little binnacle and took his sword. Since they left the Mediterranean Griffiths had adopted the three watch system. It was kinder on the men and more suited to the long passage ahead of them. There were no dog watches now but at five hours after noon, ship's time, they went to general quarters to remind them all of the serious nature of their business.

Drinkwater turned forward and looked along the deck of the *Hellebore*. She was a trim ship, one of a new class of brig-sloop designed for general duties, a maid of all work, tender, dispatch vessel, convoy escort and commerce raider. He stood on a tiny raised poop which protected the head of the rudder stock and tiller. Immediately forward of the poop the tiller lines ran through blocks to the wheel with its binnacle, forward of which were the skylight and companionway to the officer's accommodation. Beneath the skylight lay the lobby which served her two lieutenants, master, surgeon, gunner and purser as a gunroom, their cabins leading off it. Griffiths messed there too, unless he dined alone in his cabin, set right aft and entered via the gunroom. Forward of the companionway to this accommodation rose the mainmast, surrounded by its pin rails and coils of manila rigging, its pump handles and trunks. Between the main and foremast, gratings covered the waist, giving poor ventilation to the berth space below, covered by tarpaulins at the first sign of bad weather. Here too was the capstan. Just beyond the foremast the galley chimney rose from the deck next to the companionway that led below to the berth space where the hundred men of *Hellebore*'s company swung their hammocks in an overcrowded fug. The remaining warrant officers and their stores were tucked under the triangular foredeck. A tiny raised platform served as a fo'c's'le, providing just enough foothold to handle the headsail sheets and tend the catheads.

She was pierced with twenty gunports but so cluttered did she become in the eyes that the foremost were unoccupied. The remaining eighteen each sported an iron six-pounder. These guns were still a subject of frequent debate amongst her officers. Many vessels of similar size carried the snub barrelled carronades, short-ranged but devastating weapons that gave a small sloop a weight of metal heavy enough at close quarters to rival frigates of the sixth rate. But *Hellebore* had been armed by a traditionalist, retaining long guns each with its little canvas covered flintlock firing device. The only carronade she carried was her twelve-pounder boat guns which lay lashed under the fo'c's'le.

Drinkwater descended from the poop as Griffiths came on deck. The glass was turned and the people piped to general quarters. The hands tumbled up willingly enough, the bosun's mates flicking the occasional backside with their starters more for form than necessity. But Drinkwater was not watching that; he was seeing his laboriously drawn up quarter-bill come to life. The gun crews ran to their pieces to slip the breechings and lower the muzzles off the lintels of the gunports. The port lids were lifted as the coloured tompions were knocked out and the men threw their weight on the train tackles. Irregularly, but not unpleasantly discordant, the trucks rumbled over the deck. One by one the gun captains raised their right arms as their crews knelt at the ready position. It was not quite like a frigate. There were no bulkheads to come down since *Hellebore* carried her artillery on her upper deck, there was no marine drummer to beat the *rafale*; not many officers to go round once the gunner had disappeared into his magazine and Lestock and Drinkwater had come aft to the quarterdeck. There was a quarter gunner to each section and a master's mate at either battery. Second Lieutenant Rogers was in overall command of the engaged side with Mr Quilhampton (nominally a 'servant' on the ship's books, but fulfilling the function of a midshipman) as his messenger. Dalziell, the only midshipman officially allowed the brig, commanded the firemen, two men from each gun who assisted each other to extinguish any fires started by an enemy. Drinkwater himself commanded the boarders while Lestock attended to the sails. Under the first lieutenant's command were the men in the tops, sail trimming topmen and a detail of sharpshooters, seamen picked from a competition held weeks earlier in the Downs, and mostly landsmen whose past included either service in the sea fencibles, the volunteers or in a longer feud with their local gamekeepers.

Drinkwater glanced aloft to where Tregembo as captain of the maintop touched his forehead and a man named Kellet acknowledged his section alert in the foretop. He uncovered to Griffiths. 'Main battery made ready, sir. I'll check below.'

'Very good.'

It was only a formality. Below her upper deck *Hellebore's* accommodation, stores and hold consisted of 'platforms' set at various levels according to the breadth of the hull available at each given point. Her berth space, above the main hold, was no more than five feet deep. In the gloom of the hammock space he found the carpenter with his two mates, their tools and a bag of shot plus. 'All correct Mr Johnson?' The man grinned. His creased features and his Liverpool accent reminded Drinkwater of *Kestrel* and the same Johnson hacking the anchor warp as they beat off the French coast one desperate night two years earlier. 'All correct, Mr Drinkwater.'

He passed on, descending a further ladder to where, whistling quietly to himself Mr Appleby presided over his opened case of gruesome instruments, the lantern light gleaming dully on his crowbills, saws, daviers and demi-lunes. His two mates sat on the upturned tubs provided for the amputated limbs honing surgical knives. A casual air prevailed that annoyed Drinkwater when compared to the deck above. He raised an eyebrow at Appleby who nodded curtly back conveying all his professional hostility to the rival profession of arms that made his presence in the septic stink of the hold necessary. Drinkwater proceeded aft, beneath the officers' quarters where, in less than four feet of headroom, lay the magazine. Trussel's face peered at him through the slit in the felt curtain.

'Ready Mr Trussel?'

'Aye, sir, ready when you are.' His ugly face was illuminated by fiercely gleaming yellow eyes that caught the light from the protected lanterns and Drinkwater was reminded of a remark of Appleby's when he was dissecting the physiognomy of his messmates. 'Yon's arse spends so much time six inches from powdered eternity that it's bound to have an effect on the features.' The gunner's bizarre head, disembodied by the felt, was reflected in the awesome apprehension of the quartet of powder monkeys, boys of eight or nine who crouched ready to bear the cartridges, hot-potato like, to the guns above.

Drinkwater returned to the hammock space, passing the cook

and his assistant in the galley standing amid the steam generated by the extinguishing of the fire and the purser at his post by the washdeck pump. He blinked at the brightness of the daylight after the gloom of the brig's nether regions.

'Ship cleared for action, sir,' he reported.

'Very well. Mr Rogers, larboard broadside, run in and load. Three rounds rapid fire, single ball.'

'Aye, aye, sir.'

Drinkwater watched Rogers draw his sword with a flourish watched little Quilhampton run to the after grating and call for powder. In a small ship on such a long passage Griffiths refused to keep his guns loaded, considering the morning discharge practised on so many ships to rid the guns of damp powder as a quite unnecessary extravagance. The two powder monkeys serving the larboard battery emerged to scamper across to the nine six-pounders trundled inboard. The charges, wads and balls were rammed home and the gun captains inserted their priming quills as Rogers barked out the ordered steps. 'Cock your locks!' The crews moved back from the guns as the captains stretched their lanyards. Each raised his free hand.

'Larboard battery made ready, sir!' reported Rogers.

'You may open fire,' ordered Griffiths.

'Fire!'

The rolling roar that erupted in a line of flame and smoke along the brig's side was matched inboard by the recoil of the squealing trucks. Daily practice had made of the broadside a thing of near unanimity.

'Fire as you will!'

For the next two minutes the larbowlines, watched critically by the idlers on the starboard side, sponged and rammed and hauled up their pieces in a frenzy of activity.

'Numbers two and eight are good, sir,' shouted Drinkwater above the din.

'Let's wait until we are becalmed and try them at a target Mr Drinkwater, then I'll be looking for accuracy not speed.'

Number eight gun was already secured, its crew kneeling smartly rigid but for the panting of their bare torsos.

There was a scream from forward. In their haste not to be last

411

Number Four gun had been fired too early. The recoiling truck had run over the foot of the after train tackle man. He lay whimpering on the deck, blood running from his bitten tongue his right foot a bloody mess. Drinkwater ran forward.

'Mr Q, warn the surgeon to make ready, you there, Stokeley bear a hand there.' They dragged the injured man clear of the gun and Drinkwater whipped his headband off, twisting it swiftly round his ankle. He had fainted by the time the stretcher bearers came up.

'Secure all guns! Secure there!' Rogers was bawling, turning the men back to their task. As Drinkwater saw the casualty carried below, the guns were fully elevated and run up with their muzzles hard against the port lintels. The lids were shut and the breechings passed.

'Both batteries secured, sir,' reported Rogers, 'bloody fool had his damned foot in the way . . .'

'That will do, Mr Rogers,' snapped Griffiths, colour mounting to his cheeks and his bushy white eyebrows coming together in imperious menace across the bridge of his big nose.

'Secure from general quarters, Mr Drinkwater.' The commander turned angrily below and Rogers looked ruefully at Drinkwater for consolation.

'Stupid old bastard,' he said.

Drinkwater regarded the young lieutenant and for the first time realised he did not like him. 'Carry on Mr Rogers,' he said coldly, 'I have the deck.' Drinkwater walked forward and Rogers turned aft to where Midshipman Dalziell was gathering up his signal book and slate. 'I have the deck,' mimicked Rogers and found Dalziell smiling conspiratorially at him.

The sun went down in a blaze of glory. As it set Drinkwater had the deck watch check the two boats that hung in the new-fangled davits on either quarter in case they were needed during the night. They also checked the lashings on the four long pine trunks that were secured outboard between the channels, as there was no stowage elsewhere. Briefly he recalled the depression he had suffered earlier and found its weight had lightened. He tried to divine the source of the relief. Guiltily he concluded that the injured man and Rogers' lack of compassion had awoken him to his duty. He recalled the words of Earl St Vincent: 'A married officer is frequently lost to the service . . .'

That must not be the case with himself. He had a duty to the ship, to Griffiths and the men, and especially to Elizabeth and the child growing within her. That duty would best be served by anticipation and diligence. They had a long way to go, and even further to come back.

At eight bells Drinkwater went below to where Appleby, fresh washed but still smelling of gore, ate his biscuit and sipped his wine.

'How is the patient?' asked Drinkwater hanging his coat and hat in his cabin and joining the surgeon in the gunroom. 'It was Tyson, wasn't it?'

'Yes. He's well enough,' spluttered Appleby, crumbs exploding from his lips, 'as we were not in action I was able to take my time.' He paused, emptied his glass and dabbed at his mouth with a stained napkin. 'I saved the heel, if it does not rot he will walk on his own leg though he'll limp and find balance a trouble.'

'The devil you did! Well done, Harry, well done.' Appleby looked pleased at his friend's approval and his puffy cheeks flushed.

'I must amend my books,' said Drinkwater reaching to the shelf that contained the half-dozen manuscript ledgers without which the conduct of no King's ship, irrespective of size, could be regulated.

He opened the appropriate volume and turned up his carefully worked muster list. 'Damn it, the man's a boarder . . . when will he be fit again?'

Appleby shrugged. 'Given that he avoids gangrene, say a month, but the sooner he has something to occupy his mind the better.'

'I wonder if he can write?'

'I doubt it but I'll ask.'

Mr Trussel came in for his glass of madeira. I hear the captain is not stopping at the Canaries, is that so, sir?'

'We stop only of necessity for water, Mr Trussel, otherwise Admiral Nelson's orders were explicit,' explained Drinkwater, 'and we are to limit ourselves to one glass each of wine per evening to conserve stocks.'

Trussel made a face. 'Did you not know that powder draws the moisture from a man, Mr Drinkwater?'

'I don't doubt it, Mr Trussel, but needs must when the devil drives, eh?'

'I shall savour the single glass the more then,' answered the old gunner wryly.

Drinkwater bent over his ledger and re-wrote the watch and quarter bills, pulling his chair sideways as Lestock joined them from the deck to stow his quadrant and books.

'I can't make it out, can't make it out,' he was muttering. Drinkwater snapped the inkwell closed. 'What can't you make out, Mr Lestock?'

'Our longitude, Mr Drinkwater, it seems that if our departure from Espartel was truly three leagues west . . .' Drinkwater listened to Lestock's long exposition on the longitude problem. *Hellebore* carried no chronometer, did not need to for the coastal convoy work to which she had been assigned. Recent events however, revealed the need for them to know their longitude as they traversed the vast wastes of the Atlantic. Lestock had been dallying with lunar observations, a long and complicated matter involving several sets of near simultaneous sights and upon which the navigational abilities of many officers, including not a few sailing masters, foundered. The method was theoretically simple. But on the plunging deck of the brig, with the horizon frequently interrupted by a wave crest and the sky by rigging and sails, the matter assumed a complexity which was clearly beyond the abilities of Lestock.

As he listened Drinkwater appreciated the fussy man's problems. He knew he could do little better but he kicked himself for not having thought of the problem in Syracuse. With a chronometer the matter would have been different and Nelson had offered them whatever they wanted from the fleet. He had had to. In the matter of charts alone *Hellebore* was deficient south of the Canaries. They had scraped together the bare minimum, but the chart of the Red Sea was so sparse of detail that its very appearance sent a shudder of apprehension down Lestock's none too confident spine.

'. . . And if the captain does not intend to stop we'll have further difficulties,' he concluded.

'We will be able to observe the longitude of known capes and islands,' said Drinkwater, 'we should manage. Ah, and that reminds me, during the morning watch tomorrow I'll have a jackstay rigged over the waist and spread and furl a spare topsail on it to use as an awning and catchwater . . . keep two casks on deck during your watch, Mr Lestock, and fill 'em if you get the opportunity. Captain Griffiths intends only to stop if it becomes necessary, otherwise we'll by-pass the Cape of Good Hope to avoid the Agulhas current and take wood and water somewhere on the Madagascan coast. In the meantime direct your attention to the catchwater if you please.' Lestock returned to the deck, the worried look still on his face.

'It would seem that an excess of salt spray also draws the moisture from a man,' observed Appleby archly.

'Aye, Mr Appleby, and over-early pickles the brain,' retorted Trussel.

Day succeeded day as the trades blew and the internal life of the brig followed its routine as well as its daily variations. Daily, after quarters, the hands skylarked for an hour before the hammocks were piped down. The flying fish leapt from their track and fanned out on either bow. Breakfasts were often spiced by their flesh, fried trout-like and delicious. During the day dolphins played under the bowsprit defying efforts to catch them. The sea at night was phosphorescent and mysterious, the dolphins' tracks sub-aqueous rocket trails of pale fire, the brig's wake a magical bubbling of light. They reeled off the knots, hoisting royals and studding sails when the wind fell light. Even as they reached the latitude of the Cape Verdes and the trades left them, the fluky wind kept a chuckle of water under the forefoot.

It was utterly delightful. Drinkwater threw off the last of his depression and wallowed in the satisfying comfort of naval routine. There was always enough to occupy a sea-officer, yet there was time to read and write his journal, and the problems that came inevitably to a first lieutenant were all sweetly soluble. But he knew it could not last, it never did. The very fact of their passage through the trade-wind belt was an indication of that. At last the winds died away and the rain fell. They filled their water casks while Griffiths had the sweeps out for two hours a daylight watch and *Hellebore* was hauled manually across the ocean in search of wind.

'*Duw*, I cannot abide a calm hereabouts,' Griffiths growled at Drinkwater, staring eastward to where, unseen below the horizon, the Gambia coast lay.

'I remember the smell, *bach*. Terrible, terrible.' For a second Drinkwater could not understand, then he remembered Griffiths's slaving past. 'The Gambia, sir?' he asked quietly.

'Indeed yes . . . the rivers, green and slow, and the stockades full of them; the chiefs and half-breed traders and the Arabs . . . and us,' he ended on a lower note. 'Christ, but it was terrible . . .' It was the first time he had ever disclosed more than the slightest detail of that time of his life. They had often discussed the technicalities of slaving ships, their speed and their distant loveliness, but though there was a growing revulsion to the trade in Britain neither he nor Griffiths had ever voiced the matter as a moral problem. He was tempted to wonder why Griffiths had remained to become chief mate of a slaver when the old man answered his unasked question.

'And yet I stayed to become mate. You are asking yourself that now, aren't you?' He did not wait for a reply but plunged on, like a man in the confessional, too far to regret his repentance. 'But I was young, *duw*, I was young. There was money there, money and private trading and women, *bach*, such women the like of which you'd never dream of, coal black and lissom, pliant and young, opening like green leaves in spring,' he sighed, 'they would do anything to get out of that stinking 'tween deck . . . anything.'

Drinkwater left the old man to his silence and his memories. He was still at the rail when Lestock came on deck at eight bells.

In the morning a breeze had sprung up.

Chapter Four

September 1798

Shadows of Clouds

'I want him flogged, Drinkwater!'

Drinkwater looked up from his breakfast of burgoo at the angry face of Lieutenant Rogers. 'It is not for you to decide the punishment,' he said coldly.

'I know Tregembo's your damned toady, Drinkwater, and that you and the captain are close, but damn it, I threatened him with a flogging and a flogging he shall have!'

'I shall present the facts to the captain and . . .'

'Oh, devil take the facts man, and devil take your sanctimonious cant . . .'

'Have a care what you say, *Mr* Rogers.' Drinkwater stressed the title and resisted the impulse to stand and swing his hand across Roger's choleric face. The restraint was not appreciated.

'Flog him, Drinkwater, or by Christ I'll bring charges against you for failure to maintain good order . . .'

'You'll do no such damned thing, sir,' snapped Drinkwater. 'You will sit down and be silent while we examine precisely what happened. And, by God, you'll address me as *mister*.'

'You fail to intimidate me *Mister* Drinkwater. Your commission predates mine by two weeks. That ain't seniority enough to cut much ice in the right quarters . . .'

Drinkwater sprang to his feet and leaned across the intervening table. 'Another word, sir, and I'll clap you in irons upon the instant, d'you hear? By God you've gone too far! Two weeks is sufficient to hang you!'

Their faces were inches apart and for a long moment they remained so; then Rogers subsided, answering Drinkwater's questions in resentful monosyllables.

417

It appeared that during the middle watch Midshipman Dalziell, proceeding forward on routine rounds had stumbled over the feet of Tregembo. The Cornishman had been sleeping on deck. With the three watch system in operation and the brig in the tropics the berth space became intolerable and a number of men slept on deck. There had been an exchange between the midshipman and the able seaman which had resulted in Dalziell bringing Tregembo aft to Rogers. From what Drinkwater had seen of Dalziell he was not surprised at Tregembo's reaction. Drinkwater did not entirely support Earl St Vincent's contention that the men should be made to respect a midshipman's coat. He qualified it by requiring that the midshipman within was at least partially deserving of that respect. He doubted that Mr Dalziell answered the case at all. Besides Drinkwater was damned if Tregembo, or anyone else for that matter, was going to have his back laid open for such a trivial matter.

'Thank you, Mr Rogers.'

'I want the whoreson flogged, d'you hear?' Rogers flung over his shoulder as he withdrew to his cabin. Drinkwater sat in the gunroom alone, sunlight from the skylight sliding in six parallelograms back and forth across the table. He knew Griffiths would not hesitate to flog if necessary. Insolence was not to be tolerated. But had Tregembo been insolent? Drinkwater was by no means certain and he had seen the man flogged before. Griffiths, who had slung his hammock above the guns on the lower deck of a seventy-four understood the mentality of the men. There were always those who would challenge authority if they thought they could get away with it, and he knew many seamen who approved of flogging. Life below decks was foul enough without suffering the molestations of the petty thieves, the queers, the cheats and liars, never mind the drunks who could knock you from a yard in the middle of the night. No, swift retribution was welcomed by both sides.

But only if it was just.

'Mr Lestock, Mr Appleby, you are sitting on a tribunal to determine the precise nature of an incident occurring in the middle watch last night during which the captain of the main top, Able Seaman Tregembo, is alleged to have used abuse against Mr Midshipman Dalziell.'

The two warrant officers nodded, Lestock fidgetting since he had had to be relieved on deck by Trussel and was anxious about observing the meridian altitude of the sun at noon. Appleby was splendidly portentous but, for the moment, silent.

'Lieutenant Rogers,' Drinkwater inclined his head to the second lieutenant sitting opposite with one leg dangling over the arm of his chair, contemptuously examining his nails, 'is in the nature of the accusing officer.' He raised his voice, 'Mr Q!'

The door opened. 'Sir?'

'Pass word for Mr Dalziell and then have Tregembo wait outside to be called.'

'Aye, aye, sir,' replied the boy casting a frightened look round the interior of the gunroom which had changed its normal prefectural atmosphere to one of chilly formality. Dalziell knocked and entered. He had not had the sense to put on full uniform.

'Now Mr Dalziell, this is an inquiry to establish the facts of the incident that occurred this morning . . .' Drinkwater went laboriously through the formal process and listened to Dalziell's carefully stated account.

He had gone forward on the rounds that were performed by either a master's mate or a midshipman at hourly intervals. He had found the man Tregembo asleep under the fo'c's'le with his legs obstructing the ladder and had stumbled over them. The man had woken and there had been an exchange. As a consequence Dalziell had ordered him below. There had been a further exchange after which Dalziell had brought Tregembo aft to the officer of the watch. 'And Lieutenant Rogers said he would see the man flogged for his insolence, sir.' It was all very plausible, almost too plausible, and the malice in that last sentence set a query against the whole.

They called Tregembo. 'What did you say to Mr Dalziell when he stumbled against you?' asked Drinkwater, careful to keep his voice and expression rigidly formal.

Tregembo shrugged. 'I'd been awakened zur, I thought it was one of my mates,' he growled.

'Were you abusive?' butted in Lestock, 'come man, we want the truth.'

Tregembo shot a glance at Drinkwater. 'Happen I was short with

419

him, zur,' he conceded but repeated, 'I thought it was one of my mates, zur . . . I didn't know it was Mr Dalziell, zur.'

'A storm in a tea cup,' muttered Appleby and Rogers flushed. Drinkwater was tempted to leave the matter there, but Lestock persisted to fuss.

'What *exactly* did you say, man?' he asked testily.

Drinkwater sighed, both Rogers and Dalziell were only holding their peace with difficulty. 'Come Tregembo,' he said resignedly, 'what did you say?'

Tregembo frowned. He knew Drinkwater could not protect him and his head came forward belligerently. 'Why zur, what I'd say to a messmate, that he was a clumsy fucker . . . zur.'

Drinkwater stifled a grin and he saw both Dalziell and Rogers relax, as though their case was proved.

'That seems to be clear abuse,' said Lestock and Drinkwater suddenly felt angry about the whole stupid business. Without Lestock's tactless interjections he might have ended it then and there, but he now had to take the offensive.

'Now think carefully, Tregembo. What was then said to you? Remember we want the truth, as Mr Lestock says.' Tregembo looked at Dalziell, opening his mouth then closing it again before he caught the intense expression in Drinkwater's eyes. He had known the lieutenant long enough to take encouragement from it.

'He called me an insolent whoreson bastard, zur, and told me to get my pox-ridden arse below decks where it belonged.'

Drinkwater swung his glance swiftly to Dalziell. There was no denial from the midshipman, only a slight flushing of the cheeks. Dalziell blurted. 'And he called me a cocky puppy, damn it!'

'Silence, Mister!' snapped Drinkwater. 'Tregembo, do you mind your tongue in future when you address an officer.' The two exchanged glances and Drinkwater dismissed him. He turned to his two colleagues, suddenly aware that he had closed the case without consultation. 'I am sure you agree with me, gentlemen, that Tregembo's initial remarks were made by mistake under the false assumption that another hand had tripped over him. The manner of Mr Dalziell's subsequent ordering of him below was of such a nature as to disqualify him from receiving the manner of address expected from an able seaman to a midshipman.' There was a sharp indrawn breath from Rogers but Drinkwater was undeterred. 'The midshipmen aboard any ship of which I am first lieutenant will be obliged to behave properly. I will not tolerate the apeing of bloods out whoring which seems the current fashion. It would not be in the interests of the ship to flog Tregembo.'

'Damn you, Drinkwater, damn you to hell.' Rogers leapt from the chair.

'Be silent, sir!' stormed Drinkwater, suddenly furious at Rogers. Then, in a quieter tone he turned to the master and surgeon. 'Well gentlemen, d'you agree?'

'Of course, Nathaniel, damned stupid business if you ask me.' Appleby eyed Rogers disapprovingly.

'Is my character to be disputed by an apology for a pox-doctor . . .?' he got no further. Emerging from his cabin Commander Griffiths appeared. The five men in the gunroom rose to their feet. He had clearly heard every word through the flimsy bulkhead.

'I approve of your decision, Mr Drinkwater, just as I disapprove of your conduct, Mr Rogers.' Griffiths spoke slowly then paused turning his lugubrious face on Dalziell. His bushy white eyebrows drew together. 'As for you, sir, I can think of only one place where your presence will not infect us all. Proceed to the fore t'gallant masthead.'

The commander passed between Rogers and the scarlet midshipman with ponderous contempt and made for the upper deck.

They had rolled Polaris and the constellations of the far north below the horizon without ceremony. To the south blazed Canopus, Rigel Kentaurus and the Southern Cross, whilst Orion wheeled overhead, astride the equinoctial. They had picked up the south-east Trades in five degrees south latitude and romped southwards. The matter of Dalziell faded from Drinkwater's mind almost as soon as the boy had descended from the mastheading. Ruling all their lives, burying their petty quarrels with its stern and soothing rhythm, the routine of a King's ship proceeded remorselessly. They had avoided all ships in case any were French cruisers. It was unlikely, but only a single mischance could disrupt the delicate strategy of empire. Even a ship of equal force might jeopardise their mission and it was likely that a French cruiser in the South Atlantic would be one of their fast, well-found frigates.

On a morning of alternating sunshine and shadow as an endless stream of fair-weather cumulus scudded before the fresh wind and the large dark petrels and bizarre red-footed boobies swooped about the ship, the matter of Dalziell was revived.

Appearing to take his meridian altitude Mr Quilhampton was found to possess a black eye.

'Where the deuce did you get that from, young shaver?' asked Drinkwater who had of late made a practice of joining Lestock on the tiny poop to help determine the brig's latitude.

'Oh, I banged into my cabin door, sir.' The boy was nearly sobbing and the excuse was clearly fabricated. He failed to catch the sun successfully and it was Dalziell's smirking 'I made my altitude seventy degrees fifty-four minutes, Mr Lestock,' that formed the suspicion in Drinkwater's mind that he might be the cause of Mr Quilhampton's misery. It seemed confirmed by the muffled grunt from the young midshipman as the first lieutenant agreed his own altitude within a minute of Dalziell's. Lestock pursed his lips in disapproval when Quilhampton announced his failure.

'Mr Q has a contused eye, Mr Lestock. Cut along to the surgeon, cully, and get him to look at it.' He watched the boy move away and turned to Mr Dalziell. 'Now what d'you make our latitude?' He knew he was displacing Lestock but noted that Dalziell was suddenly less confident. The sun was chasing them south, would cross the equator in a day or so and the calculation was elementary. A mere matter of addition and subtraction but Dalziell baulked at it. Drinkwater suspected he cribbed frequently from the younger boy who showed a certain aptitude for the mysteries of astronomical navigation.

'Er, sixteen degrees, er . . . about sixteen degrees south, sir, er . . .' he frowned over his slate while Lestock tut-tutted and nodded agreement at Drinkwater's figures.

'Perhaps you would do better studying Robinson, Mr Dalziell, than thrashing your messmate.'

Dalziell's open-mouthed stare as he descended the ladder made him chuckle inwardly. He remembered wondering as a midshipman how the first lieutenant always seemed so omniscient. Experience was a wonderful teacher and there was little new under the sun. The reference to the late object of their observations further amused him and he was in a high good humour as he returned his quadrant to its carefully lashed mahogany box. It was only on straightening up from the task that his eye was caught by the little watercolour of the American privateer *Algonquin*, wearing British over Yankee colours. She had been his first command. It was a trifle stained by damp now and had been done for him by Elizabeth before they were married. The thought of Elizabeth scudded like one of those cumulus clouds over his good humour. In the oddly circuitous way the mind works it made him think of Quilhampton and the misery that could be a midshipman's lot. He called the messman. 'Pass word for Mr Quilhampton, Merrick.'

When the boy came he had clearly been crying. He was fortunate, Drinkwater thought. The brig had no cockpit and the two midshipmen each had a tiny cabin, mere hutches set on the ship's plans as accommodation for stewards. At least they did not have to live in the festering stink of the orlop as he had had to aboard *Cyclops*. But the atmosphere of Quilhampton's environment was a relative thing. It might be easier than Drinkwater's had been, but it was no less unpleasant for the boy.

'Come now, Mr Q, dry those eyes and tell me what happened.'

'Nothing, sir.'

'Come, sir, do not make honour a sticking point, what happened?'

'N . . . nothing, sir.'

Drinkwater sighed. 'Mr Q. If I were to instruct you to lead a party of boarders on to the deck of a French frigate, would you obey?'

'Of course, sir!' A spark of indignant spirit was rekindled in the boy.

'Then come, Mr Q. Do not, I beg you, disobey me now.'

The muscles along Quilhampton's jaw hardened. 'Mr Dalziell, sir, struck me, sir. It was in a fair fight, sir,' he added hurriedly.

'Fights are seldom fair, Mr Q. What was this over?'

'Nothing, sir.'

'Mr Quilhampton,' Drinkwater said sharply, 'I shall not remind you again that you are in the King's service, not the schoolroom.'

'Well, sir, he was insulting you, sir . . . said something about you and the captain, sir . . . something not proper, sir.'

Drinkwater frowned. 'Go on.'

'I er, I thought it unjust, sir, and I er, demurred, sir . . .' The boy's powers of self-expression had improved immeasurably but the thought of what the boy was implying sickened Drinkwater.

'Did he suggest that the captain and I enjoyed a certain intimacy, Mr Q?' he asked softly. Relief was written large on the boy's face.

'Yes sir.'

'Very well, Mr Q. Thank you. Now then, for fighting and for not obeying my order promptly I require from you a dissertation on the origin of the brig-sloop, written during your watch below this afternoon and brought to me when you report on deck at eight bells.'

The boy left the cabin happier in spite of his task. But for Drinkwater a cloud had come permanently over the day and a dark suspicion was forming in his mind.

He spoke to Dalziell when he relieved Rogers at the conclusion of the afternoon watch. Quilhampton had delivered into his hand an ink-spattered paper which he folded carefully and held behind his back.

'For fighting, Mr Dalziell, I require an essay on the brig-sloop. I desire that you submit it to me when I am relieved this evening. '

Dalziell muttered his acknowledgement and turned away. Drinkwater recalled him.

'Tell me, Mr Dalziell, what is the nature of your acquaintanceship with Lord Dungarth?' Dalziell's face relaxed into a half-concealed smirk. Drinkwater hoped the midshipman thought him a trifle scared of too flagrantly punishing an earl's élève. That feline look seemed to indicate that he was right.

'I am related to his late wife . . . sir.'

'I see. What was the nature of your kinship?'

'I was second cousin to the countess.' He preened himself, as if being second cousin to a dead countess absolved him from the formalities of naval courtesy. Drinkwater did not labour the point; Mr Dalziell did not need to know that Lord Dungarth had been the director of the clandestine operations of the cutter *Kestrel*. 'You are most fortunate in your connections, Mr Dalziell,' he said as the boy smirked again.

He was about to turn away and give his attention to the ship when Dalziell volunteered, 'I have a cousin on my mother's side who knows you, Mr Drinkwater.'

'Really?' said Drinkwater without interest, aware that Rogers had neglected to overhaul the topgallant buntlines which were taut and probably chafing. 'And who might that be?'

'Lieutenant Morris.'

Drinkwater froze. Slowly he turned and fixed Dalziell with a frigid stare.

'And what of that, Mr Dalziell?'

Suddenly it occurred to Dalziell that he might be mistaken in securing an advantage over the first lieutenant so soon after the tribunal. He realised Mr Drinkwater would not cringe from mere innuendo, nor could he employ the crudities that had upset Quilhampton. 'Oh, n . . . nothing sir.'

'Then get below and compose your essay.' Drinkwater turned away and fell to pacing the deck, forgetting about the topgallant buntlines. He hated the precocity of Dalziell and his ilk. The day was ruined for him, the whole voyage of the *Hellebore* poisoned by Dalziell, a living reminder of the horrors of the frigate *Cyclops* and Morris, the sodomite tyrant of the midshipman's mess. Many years before, during the American war, Drinkwater had been instrumental in having Morris turned out of the frigate. Morris was lucky to have escaped with his life: an Article of War punished his crime with the noose. Now a drunken threat, uttered by Morris before he left the frigate, was recalled to mind. It seemed Morris had kept in touch with his career, might have been behind Dungarth's request that Dalziell be found a place, though it was certain the earl knew nothing of it. Something about Dalziell's demeanour seemed to confirm this suspicion. For half an hour Drinkwater paced furiously from the poop ladder to the mainmast and back. His mind was filled with dark and irrational fears, fears for Elizabeth and her unborn child far behind in England, for long ago Morris had discovered his love for her and had threatened her. Gradually he calmed himself, forced his mind into a more logical track. Despite the influence he once appeared to wield at the Admiralty through the carnal talents of his sister, he had risen no further than lieutenant and many years had passed since that encounter in New York. Perhaps, whatever Dalziell knew of the events aboard *Cyclops*, it would be no more than that he and Morris were enemies. Surely Morris would have concealed the reason for their enmity. Strange

425

that he had planted in the midshipman's mind the notion that Drinkwater indulged in the practices that had come close to breaking Morris himself. Or perhaps it was not so strange. Evil was rightly represented as a serpent and the twists of the human mind to justify its most outrageous conduct were, when viewed objectively, almost past belief.

Nevertheless, two hours passed before Drinkwater remembered the topgallant buntlines. He found Mr Quilhampton had already attended to them.

Chapter Five   *September–October 1798*

The *Mistress Shore*

The following morning Drinkwater found a moment to study the literary efforts of the two midshipmen. It was clear that Mr Dalziell's essay had suffered from being written after that by Mr Quilhampton. True the penmanship was neater and better formed than the awkward, blotchy script of Mr Q, but the information contained in the composition was a crib from Falconer's *Marine Dictionary* with a few embellishments in what Mr Dalziell clearly considered was literary style.

. . . *And so the Brig-Sloop, so named to indicate that she was commanded by a Commander or Sloop-Captain, as opposed to a Gun-Brig, merely the command of a Lieutenant, arrived to take its place in the lists of the Fleet and perform the duties of a small Cruiser to the no small satisfaction of Admiralty* . . . Was there a sneer within the lengthy sentence? Or was Drinkwater unduly prejudiced? Certainly there was little information.

By contrast Mr Quilhampton's erratic, speckled contribution, untidy though it was, demonstrated his enthusiasm.

. . . *The naval Brig was developed from the merchant Snow and Brig, both two-masted vessels. In the former the mainmast carried both a square course and a fore and aft spanker which was usually loose footed. Its luff was secured to a small mast, or horse, set close abaft the lower mainmast. The merchant Brig did not carry the maincourse, the maintopsail sheeting to a lower yard of smaller dimensions, not unlike the cross-jack yard. The mainsail was usually designated to be the fore and aft spanker which was larger than that of the snow and furnished with a boom, extending its parts well aft and making it an effective driver for a vessel on the wind* . . .

Drinkwater nodded, well satisfied with the clarity of Mr Quilhampton's drift, but the boy was in full flood now and did not baulk at attempting to untangle that other piece of etymological and naval confusion.

The naval brig is divided into two classes, the gun-vessel, usually of shallow draft and commanded by a Lieutenant, and the brig-sloop, under a Commander. The term 'sloop' in this context (as with the ship-sloop, or corvette) indicates its status as the command of Captain or Commander, the ship-sloop of twenty guns being the smallest vessel commanded by a Post-Captain. The Captain of a brig-sloop, (sometimes known, more particularly in foreign navies, as a brig-corvette) is always addressed as 'Captain' by courtesy but is in reality called Master and Commander since at one time no master was carried to attend to the vessel's navigation. The term 'sloop' used in these contexts, should not be confused with the one-masted vessel that has the superficial [there were several attempts to spell this word] *appearance of a cutter. These type of sloops are rarely used now in naval service, having been replaced by the faster cutter. They differ from the cutter in having less sail area, a standing bowsprit and a beakhead . . .*

Drinkwater lowered this formidable document in admiration. Young Mr Q had hit upon some interesting points, particularly that of Masters and Commanders. He knew that many young and ambitious lieutenants had objected to submitting themselves for the navigational examination at the Trinity House to give them the full claim to the title, and that the many promotions on foreign stations that answered the exigencies of war had made the system impracticable. The regulation of having a midshipman pass for master's mate before he could be sent away in a prize was also one observed more in the breach than otherwise. As a result the Admiralty had seen fit to appoint masters or acting masters to most brigs to avoid losses by faulty navigation. In Mr Lestock's case Drinkwater was apt to think the appointment more of a burden to the ship than a safeguard.

Quilhampton's essay echoed the gunroom debate as to the armament of brigs, repeating the carronade versus long gun argument and concluding in didactic vein, . . . *whatever the main armament of the deck, the eighteen-gun brig-of-war is, under the regulation of 1795, the smallest class of vessel to carry a boat carronade.*

Drinkwater was folding the papers away when a cry sent him hurrying on deck.

'Deck there! Sail on the weather bow!'

He drew back from the ladder to allow Griffiths, limping painfully but in obvious haste, to precede him up the ladder. As the two men emerged on deck the pipes were shrieking at the hatch-ways. Lestock jumped down from the weather rail and offered his glass to Griffiths. 'French cruiser, by my judgement.'

Griffiths swore while Drinkwater reached in his pocket for his own glass. It was a frigate beyond doubt and a fast one judging by the speed with which her image grew. She was certainly French built and here, south of Ascension Island in the path of homecoming Indiamen, probably still in French hands.

'All hands have been called, sir,' said Lestock primly.

'Mr Drinkwater, have the mast wedges knocked out and I want preventer backstays rigged to t'gallant mastcaps!'

'Aye, aye, sir!' Lestock was already bawling orders through the speaking trumpet and the topmen were racing aloft to rig out the stunsail booms. Drinkwater slipped forward to where Johnson, the carpenter, was tending the headsails, hoisting a flying jib and tending its sheet to catch any wind left in the lee of the foresails as their yards were braced square across the hull.

'Mr Johnson, get your mates and knock the mast wedges out, give the masts some play: we want every fraction of a knot out of her. Then have the bilges pumped dry and kept dry for as long as this goes on.' Drinkwater jerked his head astern.

Johnson acknowledged the order and sung out for his two mates in inimitable crudity. Drinkwater turned away and sought out Grey, the bosun.

'Mr Grey, I want two four-inch ropes rigged as preventer back-stays. Use the cable springs out of an after port. Get 'em up to the t'gallant mastcaps and secured. We'll bowse 'em tight with a gun tackle at the rail.'

'Aye, aye, sir.'

'And Mr Grey . . .'

'Sir?'

'I don't want any chafing at the port. See to it if you please.' It was stating the obvious to an experienced man, but in the excitement of the moment it was no good relying on experience that could be lost in distraction.

As he went aft again Drinkwater was aware of the lessening of the wind noise in the rigging. Running free cut it to a minimum, while the hull sat more upright in the sea and it was necessary to look to the horizon to see the wave-caps still tumbling before the strong breeze to convince oneself that the weather had not suddenly moderated. Already the stunsails were being hoisted from their stowage in the tops, billowing forward and bowing their thin booms. Lestock was bawling abuse at the foretopmen who had failed in the delicate business of seeing one of them clear of the spider's web of ropes between the top and its upper and lower booms. A man was scrambling out along the topgallant yard and leaning outwards at the peril of his life to clear the tangle.

Lestock's voice rose to a shrill squeal and Drinkwater knew that on many ships men would be flogged for such clumsiness. Lestock's vitriolic diatribe vexed him.

'Belay that, Mr Lestock, you'll only fluster the man, 'twill not set the sail a whit faster.'

Lestock turned, white with anger. 'I'll trouble you to hold your tongue, damn it, I still have the deck and that whoreson captain of the foretop'll have a checked shirt at the gangway, by God!'

Drinkwater ignored the master. The distraction had silenced Lestock for long enough to ensure the stunsail was set and he was far too eager to get aft and study the chase.

He joined Griffiths by the taffrail, saying nothing but levelling his glass.

'He's gaining on us, *bach*. I dare not sacrifice water, nor guns . . . not yet . . .'

'We could haul the forward guns aft, sir. Lift her bow a little, she's burying it at the moment . . .' Both men spoke without removing the glasses from their eyes.

'Indeed, yes. See to it, and drop the sterns of the quarterboats to catch a little wind.' Drinkwater snapped the glass shut and caught Quilhampton's eye.

'Mr Q, do you see to lowering the after falls on each of the quarterboats. Not far enough to scoop up water but to act as sails.' He left Quilhampton in puzzled acknowledgement and noted with satisfaction the speed with which Grey's party had hauled the four inch manila hemp springs aloft. The gun tackles were already rigged and being sweated tight.

'Mr Rogers!'

'Yes? What is it?'

Drinkwater explained about the guns. 'We'll start with the forward two and get a log reading at intervals of half an hour to check her best performance.'

Rogers nodded. 'She's gaining is she?'

'Yes.'

'D'you think the old bastard's lost his nerve,' he paused then saw the anger in Drinkwater's face. 'I mean she might be British . . .'

'And she might not! You may wish to rot in a French fortress but I do not. I suggest we attend to our order.'

Drinkwater turned away from Rogers, contempt flooding through him that a man could allow himself the liberty of such petty considerations. Although the stranger was still well out of gunshot it would need only one lucky ball to halt their flight. And the fortress of Bitche waited impassively for them. Drinkwater stopped his mind from wandering and began to organise the hauling aft of the forward guns.

In the waist the noise of the sea hissing alongside was soon augmented by the orchestrated grunts of men laying on tackles and gingerly hauling the brig's unwieldy artillery aft. Two heavy sets of blocks led forward and two aft, to control the progress of the guns as the ship moved under them. From time to time Grey's party of men with handspikes eased the awkward carriage wheels over a ringbolt. After four hours of labour they had four guns abaft the mainmast and successive streaming of the log indicated an increase of speed of one and a half knots. But that movement of guns aft had not only deprived *Hellebore* of four of her teeth, it had seriously impeded the working of her after cannon since the forward guns now occupied their recoil space.

When the fourth gun had been lashed the two lieutenants straightened up from their exertions. Drinkwater had long forgotten Rogers's earlier attitude.

'I hope the bastard does not catch us now or it'll be abject bloody surrender, superior goddam force or not,' Rogers muttered morosely.

'Stow it, Rogers, it's well past noon, we might yet hang on until dark.'

'You're a bloody optimist, Drinkwater.'

'I've little choice; besides faith is said to move mountains.'

'Shit!'

Drinkwater shrugged and went aft again. Despite the work of the past hours it was as if he had left Griffiths a few moments earlier. The old Welshman appeared not to have moved, to have shrunk in on himself, almost half-asleep until one saw those hawkish eyes, staring relentlessly astern.

There was no doubt that they were losing the race. The big frigate was clearly visible, hull-up from the deck and already trying ranging shots. As yet these fell harmlessly astern. Drinkwater expressed surprise as a white plume showed in their wake eight cables away.

'He's been doing that for the past half hour,' said Griffiths. 'I think we have about two hours before we will feel the spray of those fountains upon our face and perhaps a further hour before they are striking splinters from the rail. His hands clenched the taffrail tighter as if they could protect the timber from the inevitable .

'We could swing one of the bow chasers directly astern, sir,' volunteered Drinkwater. Griffiths nodded.

'Like that *cythral* Santhonax did the day he shot *Kestrel*'s topmast out of her, is it?'

'Aye.'

'We'll see. It will be no use for a while. Did Lestock in his zeal douse the galley fire?'

'I've really no idea, sir.' At the mention of the galley Drinkwater was suddenly reminded of how hungry he was.

'Well see what you can do, *bach*. Get some dinner into the hands. Whatever the outcome it will be the better faced on full bellies.'

Half an hour later Drinkwater was wolfing a bowl of bungoo. There was an unreal atmosphere prevailing in the gunroom where he, Lestock and Appleby were having a makeshift meal. Throughout the ship men moved with a quiet expectancy, both fearful of capture and hopeful of escape. To what degree they inclined to the one or to the other depended greatly upon temperament, and there were those lugubrious souls who had already given up all hope of the latter.

Drinkwater could not allow himself to dwell over much on defeat. Both his private fears and his professional pride demanded that he appeared confident of ultimate salvation.

'I tell you, Appleby, if those blackguards had not fouled up the starboard fore t'gallant stunsail we'd have been half a mile ahead of ourselves,' spluttered Lestock through the porridge, his nerves showing badly.

'That's rubbish, Mr Lestock,' Drinkwater said soothingly, unwilling to revive the matter. 'On occasions like this small things frequently go wrong, if it had not been the stunsail it would likely have been some other matter. Perhaps something has gone wrong on the chase to delay him a minute or two. Either way 'tis no good fretting over it.'

'It could be the horseshoe nail, nevertheless, Nat, eh?' put in Appleby, further irritating Drinkwater.

'What are you driving at?'

'On account of which the battle was lost, I paraphrase . . .'

'I'm well acquainted with the nursery rhyme . . .'

'And so you should be, my dear fellow, you are closer to 'em than I myself . . .'

'Oh, for heaven's sake, Harry, don't you start. There's Mr Lestock here like Job on a dung heap, Rogers on deck with a face as long as the galley funnel . . .'

'Then what do we do, dear boy?'

'Hope we can hold on until darkness,' said Drinkwater rising.

'Ah,' Appleby raised his hands in a gesture of mock revelation, 'the crepuscular hour . . .'

'And have a little faith in Madoc Griffiths, for God's sake,' snapped Drinkwater angrily.

'Ah, the Welsh wizard.'

Drinkwater left the gunroom with Lestock's jittery cackling in his ears. There were moments when Harry Appleby was infuriatingly facetious. Drinkwater knew it stemmed from Appleby's inherent disapproval of bloodshed and the illusions of glory. But at the moment he felt no tolerance for the surgeon's high-flown sentiments and realised that he shared with Rogers an abhorrence of abject surrender.

He returned to the deck to find the chasing frigate perceptibly nearer. He swore under his breath and approached Griffiths.

'Have you eaten, sir?'

'I've no stomach for food, *bach*.' Griffiths swivelled round, a look

433

of pain crossing his face as the movement restored circulation to his limbs. His gouty foot struck the deck harder than he intended as he caught his balance and a torrent of Welsh invective flowed from him. Drinkwater lent him some support.

'I'm all right. *Duw*, but 'tis a dreadful thing, old age. Take the deck for a while, I've need to clasp the neck of a little green friend.'

He was on deck ten minutes later, smelling of sercial but with more colour in his cheeks. He cast a critical eye over the sails and nodded his satisfaction.

'It may be that the wind will drop towards sunset. That could confer a slight advantage upon us.'

It could, thought Drinkwater, but it was by no means certain. An hour later they could feel the spray upon their faces from the ranging shots that plummetted in their wake.

And the wind showed no sign of dropping.

Appleby's crepuscular hour approached at last and with it the first sign that perhaps all was not yet lost. Sunset was accompanied by rolls of cloud from the west that promised to shorten the twilight period and foretold a worsening of the weather. The brig still raced on under a press of canvas and Lestock, earlier so anxious to hoist the stunsails was now worried about furling them, rightly concluding that such an operation carried out in the dark was fraught with dreadful possibilities. The fouling of ropes at such a moment could spell disaster and Lestock voiced his misgivings to Griffiths.

'I agree with you, Mr Lestock, but I'm not concerned with stunsails.' Griffiths called Drinkwater and Rogers to him. The two lieutenants and the master joined him in staring astern.

'He will see us against the afterglow of sunset for a while yet. He'll also be expecting us to do something. I'm going back on him . . .' He paused, letting the import sink in. Rogers whistled quietly, Drinkwater smiled, partly out of relief that the hours of passivity were over and partly at the look of horror just visible on Lestock's face.

'Mr Lestock is quite correct about the stunsails. With the preventer backstays I've no fear for the masts. If the booms part or the sails blow out, to the devil with them, at least we've all our water and all our guns . . . As to the latter, Mr Rogers, I want whatever waist guns we can work double shotted at maximum elevation. You will not fire without my order upon pain of death. That will be only, I repeat only, if I suspect we have been seen. Mr Drinkwater, I want absolute silence throughout the ship. I shall flog any man who so much as breaks wind. And the topmen are to have their knives handy to cut loose anything that goes adrift or fouls aloft. Is that understood, gentlemen?'

The three officers muttered their acknowledgement. A ball struck the quarter and sent up a shower of splinters. 'Very well,' said Griffiths impassively, 'let us hope that in forty minutes he will not be able to see us. Make your preparations, please.'

'Down helm!'

The brig began to turn to larboard, the yards swinging round as she came on the wind. The strength of the wind was immediately apparent and sheets of stinging spray began to whip over the weather bow as she drove to windward.

'Full an' bye, larboard tack, sir,' Lestock reported, steadying himself in the darkness as *Hellebore* lay over under a press of canvas.

Drinkwater joined Griffiths at the rail, staring into the darkness broad on the larboard bow where the frigate must soon be visible.

'There she is, sir,' he hissed after a moment's pause, 'and by God she's turning . . .'

'*Myndiawl!*' Drinkwater was aware of the electric tension in the commander as Griffiths peered into the gloom. 'She's coming on to the wind too; d'you think she's tumbled us?'

Drinkwater did not answer. It was impossible to tell, though it seemed likely that the stranger had anticipated Griffiths's manoeuvre even if he was unable to see them.

'He must see us . . .'

The two vessels surged along some nine cables apart, running on near parallel courses. Drinkwater was studying the enemy, for he was now convinced the frigate was a Frenchman. Two things were apparent from the inverted image in the night glass. *Hellebore* had the advantage in speed, for the other was taking in his stunsails. The confusion inherent in the operation had, for the moment, slowed her. She was also growing larger, indicating she did not lie as close to the wind as her quarry. If *Hellebore* could cross her bow she might yet escape and such a course seemed to indicate the French captain was cautious. And then several ideas occurred to Drinkwater simultaneously. He could imagine the scene on the French cruiser's deck. The stunsails would be handled with care, men's attention would be inboard for perhaps ten minutes. And the Frenchman was going to reach across the wind and reduce sail until daylight, reckoning that whatever *Hellebore* did she would still be visible at daylight with hours to complete what had been started today.

He muttered his conclusions to Griffiths who pondered them for what seemed an age. 'If that is the case we would do best to wear round his stern . . .'

'But that means we might still encounter him tomorrow since we will be making northing,' added Drinkwater, 'whereas if we hold on we might slip to windward of him and escape.'

He heard Griffiths exhale. 'Very well,' he said at last.

There was half a mile between the two ships and still the distance lessened. At any moment they *must* be observed. Drinkwater looked anxiously aloft and he caught sight of a white blur that was Lestock's face. Nearby stood Dalziell and Mr Q.

Hellebore's mainmast was drawing ahead of the frigate's stem and Drinkwater could see her topgallants bunching up where the sheets were started and the buntlines gathered them up prior to furling. He was certain that his assumption was correct. But another thought struck him: one of the topmen out on those yards could not fail to see the brig close to leeward of them.

A minute later the cry of alarm was clearly heard across the three hundred yards of water that separated the two ships. Drinkwater tried to see if her lee ports were open and waited with beating heart for a wild broadside. He doubted that any of their own guns would bear. He could see Rogers looking aft, itching to give the order to fire. Lestock's fidgetting was growing unbearable while all along the deck the hands peered silently at the ghostly black and grey shape that was the enemy.

There were several shouts from the stranger and they were unmistakably French. A low murmur ran along *Hellebore*'s deck.

'Silence there!' Drinkwater called in a low voice, trusting in their leeward position not to carry his words to the frigate. 'Mr Q. See to the hoisting of a Dutch ensign.'

A hail came over the water followed by a gunshot that whistled overhead, putting a hole in the leeward lower stunsail. A second later it tore and blew out of the bolt ropes.

The horizontal stripes of the Dutch colour caused a small delay, a moment of indecision on the enemy quarterdeck but it was not for long. The unmistakable vertical bands of the French tricolour jerked to her peak and her forward guns barked from her starboard bow. Three of the balls struck home, tearing into the hull beneath the quarterdeck making a shambles of Rogers's cabin, but not one was hit and then the brig had driven too far ahead so the enemy guns no longer bore. Eighty yards on the beam *Hellebore* drove past the cruiser's bowsprit.

'He's luffing, sir . . .'

'To give us a broadside, the bastard.' Griffiths looked along his own deck. 'Keep her full and bye Mr Lestock, I'll not lose a fathom, see.'

Drinkwater watched the French ship turn towards the wind and saw the ragged line of flashes where she fired her starboard battery. Above his head ropes parted and holes appeared in several sails, but not a spar had been hit.

'Ha!' roared Griffiths in jubilation, 'look at him, by damn!'

Drinkwater turned his attention from the fabric of *Hellebore* to the frigate. He could hear faint cries of alarm or anger as she luffed too far and lost way, saw her sails shiver and the flashes of a second broadside. They never remarked the fall of shot. Griffiths was grinning broadly at Drinkwater.

'Keep those stunsails aloft, mister, even if they are all blown to hell by dawn, we'll not have another chance like this.'

'Indeed not, sir. May I secure the guns and send the watch below?'

Griffiths nodded and Drinkwater heard him muttering 'Lucky by damn,' to himself.

'Mr Rogers! Secure the guns and pipe the watch below. Mr Lestock, relieve the wheel and lookout, keep her full and bye until further orders.'

Lestock acknowledged the order and Drinkwater could not resist baiting the man.

'It seems, Mr Lestock, that our opponent appeared to be the one with the lack of horseshoe nails.'

'A matter of luck, Drinkwater, nothing more.'

Drinkwater laughed, catching Rogers's eye as he came from securing his guns. 'Or of faith moving mountains, eh Samuel?'

When he looked astern again two miles separated the two ships. The French ship was again in pursuit but five minutes later she had disappeared in the first rain shower.

Daylight found them alone on an empty ocean and as the hours passed it became apparent that they had eluded their pursuer. They resumed their course, dragged the cannon back to their positions and continued their voyage. The stunsail gear needed overhauling for three booms had sprung during that night and several of the sails needed attention. A week later the even tenor of their routine had all but effaced the memory of the chase.

And then the South Atlantic surprised them a second time. At four bells in the forenoon eight days after their escape from the French cruiser a cry from the masthead summoned Drinkwater on deck.

'Deck there! Boat, sir, broad on the weather bow!'

He joined Lestock by the rail, steadying his glass against a shroud. A minute later Griffiths limped over to them.

'Well?' he growled, 'can you see it?' Both officers answered in the negative.

Patiently they scanned the tumbling waves until suddenly something held briefly in clear silhouette against the sky. It was undoubtedly a boat and for the smallest fraction of a second they could see the jagged outline of waving arms and a strip of red held up in the wind.

'On the beam, sir, there! Passing fast!' The boat was no more than half a mile from them and had already disappeared in the trough of a wave.

'Watch to wear ship, Mr Lestock. Call all hands.'

The cry was taken up as Lestock turned to pass orders through the speaking trumpet. 'I'll get up and keep an eye on 'em sir.' Without waiting for acknowledgement Drinkwater leapt into the main rigging and raced for the top. The sudden excitement lent energy to his muscles and he climbed as eagerly as any midshipman. Over on his back he went, scrambling outboard over the futtocks and up the topmast shrouds to cock his leg over the doublings at the topmasthead. Below him, her spanker brailed, *Hellebore* had begun her turn to starboard, the watch squaring the yards until she had the wind aft. Drinkwater looked out on the starboard beam. At first he could see nothing. The occupants of the boat might have subsided in despair and he could think of no greater agony than being passed so close by a vessel that did not sight them. Then he saw the flicker of red. Despair had turned to joy as the castaways watched the brig manoeuvre. *Hellebore* was still turning, the red patch nearly ahead now. Around him the yards groaned slightly in their parrels as the braces kept them trimmed.

'Keep her off the wind, sir, they are fine on the weather bow,' he yelled down.

Hellebore steadied with the wind on her beam. The watches below, summoned for whatever eventuality that might arise, were crowding excitedly forward. Drinkwater saw an arm outstretched, someone down there had spotted the boat. Mindful of his dignity he descended to the deck.

'Afterguard! Main braces! Leggo and haul!' *Hellebore* was hove to as the main topsail and topgallant cracked back against the mast, reining her onward rush and laying her quiet on the starboard tack some eighty yards from the boat.

They could see it clearly now as its occupants got out a couple of oars and awkwardly pulled the boat to leeward.

''Ere, there's bleeding women in it!' came a shout from forward as the Hellebores crowded the starboard rail. A number of whistles came from the men, accompanied by excited grins and the occasional obscene gesture. 'Cor ain't we lucky bastards.'

'Don't count yer luck too early, one of 'em's pulling an oar.'

'An 'hore on an oar, eh lads?'

'If them's whores the officers'll 'ave 'em!' The ribald jests were cut short by Drinkwater's 'Silence! Silence there! Belay that nonsense forward!'

He and Griffiths exchanged knowing glances. Griffiths had refused to sanction celebrations on the equator for a good reason. 'They'll dress them powder monkeys up like trollops, Nathaniel, and all manner of ideas will take root . . . forget it.' They had forgotten it then but now they were confronted with a worse problem.

There seemed to be three women in the boat, one of whom was a large creature whose broad back lay on an oar like a regular lighter-man on his sweep. She had a wisp of scarlet stuff about her shoulders and it was the waving of this that had saved their lives. Exciting less interest there were also six scarecrows of men in the boat which bumped alongside the *Hellebore*. The brig's people crowded into the chains and reached down to assist. There was much eager heaving and good natured chaffing as the unfortunate survivors were hoisted aboard. ''Ere, there's a wounded hofficer 'ere.' A topman jumped down into the boat and the limp body of a red-coated infantry captain was dragged over the rail.

Appleby was called and immediately took charge of the uncon-scious man; in the meantime the other nine persons were lined up awkwardly on deck. They drank avidly from the beakers brought from the scuttlebutt by the solicitous seamen. The six bedraggled men consisted of two seamen and four private soldiers. The sol-diers' red coats were faded by exposure to the sun and they wore no cross-belts. They were blear-eyed, the skin of their faces raw and peeled. The two seamen were in slightly better shape, their already tanned skins saving them the worst of the burning. But it was the women who received the attention of the Hellebores.

The big woman was in her forties, red-faced and tough, with forearms like hams and a tangled mass of black hair about her shoul-ders. She tossed her head and planted her bare feet wide on the planking. Next to her was a strikingly similar younger version, a stocky well-made girl whose ample figure was revealed by rents in the remains of a cotton dress. Her face was burnt about the bridge of her nose and slightly pockmarked.

Beside him Drinkwater heard Griffiths relieve himself of a long sigh. 'Convicts,' he muttered, and for the first time Drinkwater noted the fetter marks on their ankles. The third woman was a sharp faced shrew whose features fell away from a prominent nose. She was about thirty-five and already her dark eyes were roving over the admiring circle of men.

'Which of our men is the tailor, Mr Drinkwater?'

'Hobson, sir.'

'Then get him to cobble something up this very day to cover their nakedness; he can use flag bunting if there's nothing else, but if I see more than an ankle or a bare neck tomorrow I'll have the hide off him.'

'Aye, aye, sir.'

'And turn the two midshipmen out of their cabins. They can sling their hammocks in the gunroom. I want the women accommodated in their cabins,' he raised his voice, 'now you have had something to drink which of you will speak? Who are you and whence do you come from?'

'We come from His Majesty's Transport *Mistress Shore*, captain,' replied the big woman, clearing her throat by spitting on the spotless deck. The officers started at this act of gross impropriety for which a seaman would have had three dozen lashes. Griffiths merely raised his voice to send the off-duty watches below and to get the gobbet swabbed off His Majesty's planking.

'Do not do that again,' he said quietly, 'or I'll flog you. Now why were you adrift?'

'Ask the sojers, captain, they're the blackguards who . . .'

'Shut your mouth woman,' snapped one of the soldiers appearing to come out of a trance. Drinkwater guessed the poor devils had been sick as dogs in the boat while the indomitable spirit of this big woman had kept them all alive. The woman shrugged and the soldier took up the tale, shambling to a position of attention.

'Beggin' your honour's pardon, sir, but I'm Anton, sir, private soldier in the New South Wales Corps. Forming part of a detachment drafted to Botany Bay, sir. The officer wot's wounded is Captain Torrington, sir. We was aboard the *Mistress Shore*, sir, twenty men under the Cap'n. The main guard consisted of French emigré soldiers and some pardoned prisoners of war, sir, who had volunteered for service with the colours,' Anton turned his head to express his disapproval of such an improvident arrangement and caught himself from spitting contemptuously at the last moment. He wiped the back of his hand across his mouth.

'Beg pardon, sir . . . these dogs rose one night and under a French gent called Minchin they overpowered the guard, murdered the officers of the ship and took her over.'

'You mean they overpowered the whole crew?'

'It were a surprise, sir,' Anton said defensively, 'they put twenty-

441

nine off in the longboat and twelve of us away in the cutter . . . two of 'em died, sir.'

'How many days were you adrift?'

'Well, sir, I don't rightly . . .'

'Twenty-two, Captain,' said the big woman, 'with a small bag of biscuit and a small keg o' water.'

Griffiths turned to Drinkwater. 'Have the men berthed with the people, the soldiers to be quartered in the tops, the two seamen into the gun crews. As to the women I'll decide what to do with them tomorrow when they are presentable. In the meantime, Mr Lestock, we will now be compelled to call at the Cape.'

Drinkwater and Lestock touched their hats and moved away to attend their orders.

Manifold and strange are the duties that may befall a lieutenant in His Majesty's service, Drinkwater wrote in the long letter he was preparing for Elizabeth and that he could send now from the Cape of Good Hope. It was two days after the rescue of the survivors of the *Mistress Shore*. Already they had been absorbed in the routine of the ship. Drinkwater had learned something of their history. The big woman and her daughter were being transported for receiving stolen goods, offenders against the public morality who had yet thought their own virtue sacrosanct enough to have denied it to the treacherous Frenchmen. So spirited had been their resistance that Monsieur Minchin had wisely had them consigned to a boat before they tore his new found liberty to pieces. The woman was known as Big Meg and her daughter's name was Mary. They were decked out in bizarre costume by Hobson since when Big Meg was also known as 'Number Four', the greater part of her costume having been made from the black and yellow of the numeral flag.

Both Meg and her daughter adapted cheerfully to the tasks that Drinkwater gave them to keep them occupied. They chaffed cheerfully with the men and appeared to maintain their independence from any casual liaisons as Griffiths intended. This the men took in good part. There were women aboard big ships of the line, legitimate wives borne on the ship's books and of inestimable use in tending the sick. They became mothers to the men, confessors but not lovers, and stood to receive a flogging if they transgressed the iron rules that prevailed between decks. But on *Hellebore* a more delicate situation existed. While the women might be thought to be everybody's without actually being anybody's, while they were willing to banter with the men, their effect was salutary. Even, despite the roughness of their condition, the nature of their convictions and their intended destinations, improving both the manners and the language of the officers. Rogers paid a distant court to Miss Mary who was much improved by some crimson stuff Hobson had laid his hands on which had been tastefully piped with sunbleached codline. Opinion was apt to be kind to them: there were, after all, kindred spirits on the lower deck. If they were guilty in law there was in them no trace of flagitiousness.

Big Meg and her daughter picked oakum and scrubbed canvas, scoured mess kids, mended and washed clothes, while the third woman assisted Appleby. Her crimes were less easy to discover. A sinister air lay about her and it was darkly hinted by her companions that abortion or murder might have been at the root of her sentence of seven years transportation, rather than the procuring commonly held to be her offence. Certainly she claimed to have been a midwife and Appleby was compelled to report she had a certain aptitude in the medical field.

Knowing Appleby's distrust of the sex in general, Drinkwater was amused at his initial discomfiture at having Catherine Best as his assistant. His mates found their unenviable work lightened considerably and that in the almost constant presence of a woman. Catherine Best made sure that her presence was indispensible and whatever her lack of beauty she had a figure good enough to taunt the two men, to play one off against the other and secure for herself the attentions of both. But this was not known to the inhabitants of the gunroom.

'Ha, Harry, it is time you damned quacks had a little inconvenience in your lives,' laughed Drinkwater as he directed a thunderstruck Appleby to find employment for the woman.

'I emphatically refuse to have a damned jade among my business . . . if it's true she's a midwife then I don't want her on several accounts.'

'Why the devil not?'

'Perceive, my dear Nathaniel,' began Appleby as though explaining rainfall to a child, 'midwives know very little, but that little knowledge being of a fundamental nature, they are apt to regard it as a cornerstone of science and themselves as the high priestesses of arcane knowledge. Being women, and part of that great freemasonry that seeks to exclude all men from more than a passing knowledge of their privy parts, they dislike the sex for the labour they are put to on their behalf and can never tolerate a man evincing the slightest interest in the subject without prejudice .'

Drinkwater failed to follow Appleby's argument but sensed that within its reasoning lay the cause of his misogyny. He was thinking of Elizabeth and her imminent accouchement. He did not relish the thought of Elizabeth in the hands of someone like Catherine Best and hoped Mrs Quilhampton would prove a good friend to his wife when her time came. But he could not allow such private thoughts to intrude upon his duty. He was impotent to alter their fates and must surrender the outcome to Providence. For her part the woman Catherine Best attended to Captain Torrington and earned from Appleby a grudging approval.

The men who had been rescued were soon indistinguishable from *Hellebore*'s crew, the soldiers as marines under Anton, hastily promoted to corporal. Captain Torrington emerged from his fever after a week. He had been thrust twice with a sword, in the arm and thigh. By great good fortune the hasty binding of his wounds in their own gore had saved them from putrefaction, despite the loss of blood he had suffered.

The sun continued to chase the brig into southerly latitudes so that they enjoyed an October of spring sunshine. The beautiful and unfamiliar albatrosses joined them, like giant fulmars, elegant and graceful on their huge wings. Here too they found the shearwaters last seen in the Channel, and the black and white Pintada petrels the seamen called 'Cape pigeons'.

They sighted land on the second Sunday in October, Griffiths's sonorous reading of Divine Service being rent by the cry from the masthead. At noon Lestock wrote on the slate for later transfer to his log: *Fresh gales and cloudy, in second reefs, saw the Table land of the Cape of Good Hope. East and half North eight or nine leagues distant.* In the afternoon they knocked the plugs out of the hawse holes and dragged the cables through to bend them on to the anchors. The following morning they closed the land, sounding as they approached, but it was the next afternoon before they let go the bowers and finally fetched an open moor in twenty-two fathoms with a sandy bottom. To the north of them reared the spectacular flat-topped massif of Table Mountain. Beneath it the white huddle of the Dutch-built township. Drinkwater reported the brig secure. The captain's leg was obviously giving him great pain.

'Very good, Mr Drinkwater. Tomorrow we will purchase what fresh vegetables we may and water ship. If any citrus fruits are available we will take them too. Do you let the purser know. As for our guests we will land them all except the seamen. They will stay. I wish the gig to be ready for me tomorrow at eight of the clock. I will call upon the Governor then; in the meantime do you direct Rogers to salute the fort.'

'Aye, aye, sir.' He turned away.

'Mr Drinkwater.'

'Sir?' Griffiths was lowering himself on to his chair, his leg stiffly extended before him. An ominous perspiration stood out on his forehead and his flesh had a greyish pallor.

'There are Indiamen inshore there, three of them. I am sure one of them will carry our mails to England.'

'Yes, sir. Thank you.'

As he sat to finish the long letter to Elizabeth the first report of the salute boomed out overhead.

445

Chapter Six

The Cape of Storms

Drinkwater woke with a start, instantly alert. He stared into the inky blackness while his ears strained to hear the sound that had woken him. The ship creaked and groaned as the following sea rolled up astern and passed under her. It had been blowing a near gale from the south-west when he had come below two hours earlier and now something had woken him from the deepest sleep. Whatever the cause of his disturbance it had not alerted those on deck, for there were no shouts of alarm, no strident bellows of 'All Hands!' He thought of the ten cannon they had struck down into the hold before leaving the Cape a week ago. There had been barely room for them and they were too well lashed and tommed to move. It might have been the boats. They had both been taken out of the davits and turned keels up either side of the capstan, partially sheltering the canvas covered grating amidships, in the room made by the absent six-pounders. He doubted they would have sent such a tremble through the hull as he was now persuading himself he had felt.

Then it came again, a slight jar that nevertheless seemed to pass through the entire hull. It had a remorseless quality that fully alarmed Drinkwater. He swung his legs over his cot and reached for his breeches and boots. The source of that judder was not below decks but above. Something had carried away aloft. In the howling blackness of the night with the roar and hiss of the sea and the wind piping in the rigging, those on deck would not be aware of it. He pulled on his tarpaulin and turned the lengths of spunyarn round his wrists. The bump came again, more insistent now but Drinkwater was almost ready. Jamming his hat on his head he left the cabin.

He was doubly anxious, for effective command of the brig was his. Griffiths had been afflicted with malarial fever, contracted long ago in the Gambia, which returned to incapacitate him from time to time. He had been free of it for over a year but as *Hellebore* reached into the great Southern Ocean, down to forty south to avoid the Agulhas current, and made to double the Cape before the favourable westerlies, it had laid him delirious in his cot.

The wind hit Drinkwater as he emerged on deck and pulled the companionway cover over after him. Holding his hat on he cast his eyes aloft, staggered over to the foot of the mainmast and placed his hand upon it. He could feel the natural tremble of the mast but nothing more.

A figure loomed alongside. 'Is that you, Mr Drinkwater?'

'Yes, Mr Lestock,' he shouted back, 'there's something loose somewhere, but I'm damned if I know where.' He turned forward as a sea foamed up alongside and sluiced over the rail. The first dousing after a dry spell was always the worst. Drinkwater shuddered under the sudden chilling deluge. He was cursing foully as he reached the foremast and looked up. The topgallant masts had been sent down and he saw the topmast sway against the sky. The racing scud made it impossible to determine details but the pale rectangle of the triple-reefed topsail was plain. The instant he put his hand upon the mast he felt the impact, a mighty tremble that shook the spar silently, transmitting a quiver to the keelson below. He looked up again, spray stinging his eyes. It crossed his mind that Lestock had furled the forecourse since the change of watch. Drinkwater would have doused the topsail to keep the centre of effort low. Lestock seemed to do things by some kind of rote, an old-fashioned, ill-schooled officer. He felt the shudder again and then he saw its cause.

Above him the bunt of the fore topsail lifted curiously, the foot forming a sharp hyperbola rather than an elliptical arc. The foreyard below it looked odd, not straight but bending upwards.

'Mr Lestock!' Drinkwater turned aft. Somewhere in the vicinity of the jeers the big yard had broken, only the forecourse furled along it was preventing it from breaking loose. 'Mr Lestock!' Drinkwater struggled aft again, tripping over the watch huddling abaft the boats.

'I think the foreyard has carried away near the slings. One end

447

seems to be fast under the jeers but t'other is loose and butting the mast. You can feel it below. We must get the fore topsail off her. Don't for God's sake start the braces; the whole thing will be down round our ears. Let the ship run off dead before the wind under the fore topmast staysail and rouse up all hands.' He was shouting in Lestock's ear but someone heard the cry for all hands and in a second the duty bosun's mate was bellowing down the companionway Drinkwater grabbed one of the seamen.

'Ah, Stokeley, get everybody mustered abaft the boats, if that lot comes down it'll likely take someone with it. Who's on the fo'c's'le?'

'Davies, sir.'

'Right, Mr Lestock, Mr Lestock!'

'What is it?'

'Pass me the speaking trumpet.' He took the trumpet and held it up. 'Fo'c's'le there! Davies! Come aft here at once!' The wind carried his voice and the man came aft. Drinkwater left the explanations to Stokeley and joined the men assembling at the mainmast.

'Listen carefully, my lads. The foreyard has broken. We must start the sheets and clew up the topsail as quickly as possible. Then I want four volunteers to come aloft with me and pass a rope round the broken end of the yard, to lash it against the top until daylight.'

The men moved forward. Rogers emerged from the after companionway, he could see the two midshipmen. 'Be ready to tail on as required.' He gave his orders to have the men stationed to take in the topsail but as soon as they eased the sheets he could see it would not work. The eagerness with which the men sought to quell the flogging topsail by heaving on the clew and buntlines only added to the weight of wind in the sail, forcing it upwards like washing on a clothesline. The topsail sheets tugged the fore-yardarms upwards, twisting the furled course below. Perhaps the broken wood severed the first gasket that restrained the huge sail but suddenly three or four gaskets parted and the forecourse blew out in a vast pale billow. There was a crack like a gun and it disintegrated into a thousand streaming ribbons fluttering along the broken yard. The sail had blown clean out of the bolt ropes and the extent of the wounded yard could now be seen. It was a view that all contemplated for a split second. Then with a juddering crash the whole starboard half of the yard came down, the topsail stretched flat before splitting and tearing loose then blew off to leeward in an instant. The larboard half of the yard trailed its outboard extremity in the water, crashing downwards parting lifts, halliards and buntlines which fell in entangling coils, snaking across the deck to be torn overside by the wind then dragged aft past *Hellebore*'s onrushing hull. What Drinkwater had intended to be the ordered application of manpower turned into a confused bedlam of shouts, curses and orders.

Drinkwater swore deeply and began to shout. At all costs those spars should be saved, not for their own sake but for the iron fittings that they would be unable to replace. 'Mr Lestock! Keep the ship off before the wind! Mr Rogers! A party to secure that starboard yardarm before we lose it!'

Rogers gathered men about him. He was not argumentative thought Nathaniel, terrible circumstances and the assertion of discipline drove the men in their common necessity. Drinkwater turned forward with his volunteers.

Gathering up a long length of manila hemp that had previously been part of the yard lifts he dragged it into the rigging, the men assisting. The inner broken end of the larboard half of the yard had come up under the forward edge of the top, the wooden platform round the join of the lower and topmasts. Beneath the top the jeers, a big tackle that held the yard aloft by its slings, was chafed as the whole thing twisted and turned, its splintered end grinding and splitting the top so that the structure bucked under the forces playing on it.

The outboard edges of the top supported the shrouds of the topmast. If it was weakened the whole topmast was in jeopardy and at present the only thing that kept *Hellebore* manageable was the foretopmast staysail below them, its stay secured round the mast just above the damaged jeers. That too was in imminent danger of parting under the relentless grinding of the broken yard.

Drinkwater leant over the forward edge of the top, his tarpaulin blowing up over his head. The men crouched close by awaiting his orders. Beneath his belly he could feel the heavy timbers of the platform bucking and straining. The kick of the butt end of the yard was enormous, close to. Even in the dark he could see the chafe in the jeers and his extended fingers confirmed his worst fears.

He wriggled round and looked at the men. Tregembo was there, and Stokeley and Kellet. Mr Quilhampton too, his small face a blur with two dark patches where his eyes were wide with the wild excitement of the night. It crossed Drinkwater's mind inconsequentially to wonder if the boy knew the danger they were in: that to broach in such a sea meant death for them all. Mr Quilhampton had a very pretty mother, Drinkwater remembered, she would weep for the loss of her son. He shook his head clear of such irrelevant thoughts, aware that they were a symptom of his indecision.

'Mr Q!'

'Sir?'

'Descend to the deck and have Mr Lestock get a turn of something strong round the yard in the vicinity of the rail, get one of the loose gun tackles on it and bowse it tight. Then lash it to the chess tree. Tell him to let me know when he's done it and that the yard must come down to the deck but the jeers are enfeebled. Do you understand?'

Quilhampton repeated the instruction. 'Good. Off you go.'

'D'you wish me to return to the top, sir?'

'No.' He could do that much for a pretty widow. The midshipman's acknowledgement was crestfallen. 'Oh damn it, yes. But hurry; and find out how Mr Rogers is doing.' Quilhampton disappeared over the futtocks and Drinkwater turned his attention to the yard.

'We will have to pass the bight of this rope,' he indicated the manila, 'round the yard so that it will render. Tregembo, get that lead block up there,' he pointed to one of the blocks, vacated by the broken lift, banging against the upper ironwork of the doubling. Pulling his spike out Tregembo scrambled up to loosen the shackle .

'Stokeley, cut off a couple of fathoms and make up a strop.'

'Aye, aye, sir.'

Drinkwater looked over the forward edge of the top as he waited for the men to finish their tasks. The chafing was worse. They had very little time before the heavy yard crashed below. He looked down. Rogers's party was a confused huddle of men pulling, cutting and struggling but he could see the dull line of the starboard yardarm. He wondered what damage it had done in its descent, at least it was the smaller section and devoid of the heavy gear attached to the slings.

'Here, sir,' Stokeley had the strop and Tregembo the block. Drinkwater began to ease himself over the rim of the platform. 'Here zur, I'll do that,' said Tregembo indignantly. Drinkwater ignored him. It was his job. Maybe if he had joined the ship weeks before she sailed, as a good first lieutenant should, he would have spotted the defect in the spar. It had not been fair to suppose that Griffiths could do the work as efficiently as himself. Tonight he would pay Providence the debt he owed for that extra time with Elizabeth.

He lowered his weight gently on to the moving spar, gradually transferring his grip. He had hold of the lower jeers block and the movement of the whole thing was alarming now that his life depended on it. Reaching up he took the end of the strop and began to crouch, easing himself down until he was astride the yard, his legs wrapped round it. He let go of the jeers block to have both hands for the strop. His whole body was now transferred to the yard at its alarmingly cockbilled angle. Now the movement was exaggerated, swinging him from side to side with a twitch at the end of each oscillation that threatened to throw him off.

It gave a sudden violent jerk. Drinkwater flung his arms about the spar, retaining sufficient presence of mind not to let go of the strop. For a second the absence of further movement convinced him he was in wild descent.

Then from the deck came a hail: 'End's secure, sir!' The jerk had been Lestock's men bowsing the lower end down, unable to see their first lieutenant clinging to its upper extremity. Drinkwater passed the strop round the spar, pulled it tight through its own part and held it up. Stokeley grabbed it and, as Drinkwater scrambled back into the top, secured the block to it. Tregembo had rove the rope through the block and secured one end round the topmast. All that remained to do was to reeve the hauling part through another vacant block. Tregembo had brought a buntline block and shackled it to give a clear lead to the deck and it was the work of only a few minutes to prepare their extempore double whip.

Mr Quilhampton reappeared. 'Mr Rogers has secured the starboard piece, sir.'

'Right. All go below. I'll remain here. Have Mr Lestock man the jeers and beg to lower handsomely on them. Desire him to take the weight on this manila inch. Make sure he has caught a turn with it.'

'Aye, aye, sir.'

Drinkwater watched them go, leaning back against the topmast doubling, feeling hot and mad as the gale howled about him. His mouth was dry and he knew he would start shaking from the reaction of his exertions. Thank God they had a good man at the helm, the ship had not slewed from her course once. He must remember to find out who it was; the fellow was deserving of praise.

'Ready masthead there!' came the shout from below.

'Set tight the whip!' he bawled back, lowering himself on to his belly to watch progress. The strop drew tight.

'Ee-ease the jeers!'

The platform beneath him trembled. As *Hellebore* pitched forward and scended the yard moved down a foot, forward six inches. As the wave passed under her the bowsprit stabbed at the sky and the spar swung aft, hitting the mast with a judder. Damn! He should have thought of that! They needed a downhaul.

'Belay there! 'Vast lowering!' He peered down while the yard swung forward and back. Again the jarring shot through his body. Then he had it. He reached down. One of the clew garnet lead blocks had a trailing rope through it. If he could just reach it . . .

His fingers missed it by an inch. He thought of getting the hands to haul upon the whip but that might put too great a load on it. He wriggled over the top, turning so that his legs dangled over the edge. With one leg he hooked a trailing end of the line over his foot, bent his leg and, reaching down with one hand grabbed it, heaving himself back into the top. Quickly he fashioned a figure of eight knot in its end and let it go.

'Mr Lestock! Get the starboard clew garnet, it's trailing round the fiferail, pull it tight and lead it forward to the cathead. Use it as a downhaul to keep the yard off the mast!'

'Aye, aye!'

There was an interminable pause while Lestock sorted out the tangle of ropes. Then a shout that all was ready. Drinkwater peered once more over the edge of the top. His knot had drawn tight against the block and the rope led downwards.

'Lower away handsomely and keep the downhaul tight!'

The yard began its descent. The jeers parted, whirling to leeward in a cloud of dust causing confusion as the men on deck, suddenly relieved of the weight, fell over. The oscillations of the yard grew greater as it was lowered but the clew garnet, stretched like a thread, prevented its contact with the mast. As the yard's angle lessened the men at the chess tree slackened their lashings and there was a dull thud as the broken yard's second part finally lay across the deck. As if angry with a wild beast the men leapt upon it and threw lashings round it. Drinkwater climbed wearily down. Scrambling aft he joined the master. 'Well done Mr Lestock. Whom did you have on the wheel?'

'Gregory, sir.'

'Give him my compliments for keeping the ship so steady. When all the gear is secure you may send the watches below. What time is it?'

'Two bells in the middle watch.'

'Good God, I'd no idea . . .'

Their exertions had taken three hours. If he had been asked Drinkwater would have imagined no more than an hour had elapsed. Wearily he went below to find Appleby sitting in the gunroom, a baleful look upon his face and a jug of blackstrap before him.

'Couldn't you sleep, Harry? Did we poor jacks make too much noise banging about aloft?' His tone was ironic for he was too tired for sarcasm. 'If that's blackstrap for God's sake give me some. Harry? What's the matter?'

Appleby looked up at Drinkwater as though seeing him for the first time.

'Women,' he said in a low voice. 'We've got a festering bitch of a woman on board.'

Chapter Seven

Vanderdecken's Curse

Closing his mind to one problem Drinkwater was unwilling to face another. He was very tired and the implications of Appleby's remark took several seconds to penetrate his brain. The blackstrap coiled round his belly and radiated its warmth through him so that stiff muscles relaxed. But it stimulated his mind and he turned to Appleby. 'Woman? What the devil d'you mean? We landed 'em all at the Cape.'

Appleby shook his head, his jowls flapping lugubriously. 'You thought you did.'

Drinkwater swung his legs round and put both elbows on the table. 'Look man, I saw the bloody boat away from the ship's side. Big Meg actually smiled at me and I footed a bow at Miss Mary. Your wench was already in the boat when I reached the rail. '

'Exactly! Did she look up?'

'No. Why should she? She wasn't exactly undergoing a pleasure cruise. I daresay they put gyves on 'em as soon as they got ashore.'

'I don't doubt it, cully, but that is not the point. Who wrote out the receipt?'

'I did,' said Drinkwater rising to reach down the ship's letter book. He flicked over the pages. 'There!' He spun the book to face Appleby. The pasted in receipt bore the words 'Three convicts, ex *Mistress Shore*, Government Transport, female.'

'So?'

'Oh, for God's sake Harry, quit hazing me. If you've a woman on board let's see her.' But Appleby, angry and dismayed by the turn of events would not yet produce his evidence.

'That proves nothing, any fool can squiggle a signature and pretend it's that of a garrison subaltern. All one does is draw up a second one and throw it overboard on the way back to the ship.'

'But that indicates a conspiracy. Damn it, Griffiths would have reported three female convicts to the Governor; Torrington or his men knew there were three of 'em. Come on bring the woman in, I'm tired of fencing with words.' He swallowed the blackstrap.

'Look, Nat, I don't suppose Torrington gave it a second thought and I daresay the soldiers were a party to it. As for the Governor, who knows what our captain said to him? The Old Man was already feverish and we know His Excellency was annoyed that Griffiths had not called immediately upon arrival . . . who knows what either of them remembered to say during or after their interview? I daresay H.E. was obsessed with Griffiths's lack of protocol before worrying about whether he had reported two or three convicts. We sailed the following day . . . but one last question. Who took the boat ashore to see those trollops off?'

Drinkwater's argument was merely a symptom of his fatigue. Both of them knew Appleby was not lying but Drinkwater was trying to delay the inevitable with logic. It was a spurious argument. 'Rogers,' he said resignedly.

'Huh! Now, to reward your exemplary patience I will produce the evidence.' Appleby rose and left the gunroom. Drinkwater emptied the jug of blackstrap into his mug. The door opened and Appleby returned. Drinkwater looked up. Leaning against the closed door was Catherine Best. Her pinched face was almost attractive, half shadowed in the swaying lantern light. An insolent half-smile curled her mouth while a provocative hip was thrust out in allurement.

Drinkwater closed his mouth, aware that he had flushed. He was aware too that she knew well the hold she had over them all. It was not difficult to imagine a conspiracy among the hands, an easy woman amongst them would seem like the answer to a seaman's prayer.

'Where have you been living?'

'She's been in the cable tier,' volunteered Appleby.

'That is Lestock's province.'

'He delegates his rounds of the hold to one of his mates.'

'But I myself was there yesterday . . . no, no, the day before . . .'

'Efficient though you are, Nathaniel, you are an officer of regular habits. It is easy enough to give warning of your coming.'

Drinkwater nodded. It was all too true, a dreadful nightmare. He looked at the woman and was suddenly furious. 'I shall have you flogged!' he snapped vindictively. 'Turn Dalziell out of his cabin again and lock this trollop in for the night!' Appleby turned to take the woman out. She remained for a moment resisting the hand upon her arm, looked fixedly at Drinkwater. He felt again the colour mounting to his cheeks.

'Get out, damn you!' he roared, angry at his own weakness. As usual Drinkwater had the morning watch, from four until eight a.m. He woke with the realisation that something was very wrong and the bare two hours sleep that he had enjoyed left him in a foul temper when he reached the deck and realised the nature of his problems. Quilhampton brought him coffee but it did nothing to lighten his mood. The men avoided him, all knowing the mad scheme to carry their own doxy had been discovered by the surgeon and Mr Drinkwater.

Whilst the watch below melted away and the unhappy culprits in Mr Drinkwater's watch busied themselves about the decks, the first lieutenant paced up and down. An hour passed before he realised that daylight was upon them, that the sun was above the horizon, revealing a grey-white sea, furrowed and torn by the ferocity of the gale the night before. The wave crests, half a mile apart were already losing their anger as the gale abated, to turn them slowly from breaking seas to crested swells.

He swept his glance over the shambles of the deck. Luck had been with them again last night. Later he hoped he would find Griffiths surfacing for a lucid moment and could tell him what they had been through. But then he would also have to tell him about the woman Catherine Best, and he was not looking forward to that. He swore to himself. He could not flog the woman alone since all were guilty, all these sheepish seamen who crept round the deck pretending to check the lashings on the pieces of yard. Tregembo passed him and Drinkwater was struck by a feeling of abandonment.

'Tregembo!'

'Zur?'

'Did you know about this woman?' he asked in a low voice.

'Aye zur.'

'And you didn't tell me?'

Tregembo looked up agonised. 'I couldn't zur, couldn't welsh on my mates . . . besides, zur, there was officers involved.'

Drinkwater bit his lip. Tregembo could no more pass tittle-tattle than he could have favoured Tregembo over the ridiculous flogging business. Nevertheless the apparent disloyalty hurt. 'Have you lain with her?'

'No, zur!' Tregembo answered indignantly. 'I've my Susan, zur.'

'Of course . . . I'm sorry.'

'It's all right, zur . . . you've a right to be angry, zur, if you'll pardon me for so saying.' He made to move away. Drinkwater detailed him.

'Just tell me by whom I was deceived?'

'Zur?'

'Who dressed as the jade in the boat at the Cape?'

'Why Mr Dalziell, zur.'

Drinkwater closed his gaping mouth. 'How very interesting,' he said at last in an icy tone that brought an inner joy to Tregembo. 'Thank you Tregembo, you may carry on.'

Tregembo touched his forehead and moved aft, passing the wheel.

'What was he asking you?' growled the quartermaster apprehensively.

'Only who was tarted up like the woman at the Cape, Josh. And I reckon the buggers'll see the sparks fly now. He's got his dander up.'

Drinkwater took two more turns up and down the deck then he spun on his heel. 'Mr Quilhampton! Pipe all hands!'

That would do for a start. The middle watch would be deeply asleep now, damn them, and the members of the first watch had been a-bed too long. If they thought they could pull the wool over the eyes of Nathaniel Drinkwater they were going to have to learn a lesson; and if he could not flog them all then he would work them until sunset.

The men emerged sleepily. Lestock came up, followed by Rogers. 'Ah, Mr Lestock, I do not require your presence, thank you.' The elderly man turned away muttering. 'Mr Rogers I desire that you take command of the hands and unrig the broken yard, clear that raffle away and then get one of those Corsican pines inboard and rig it as a jury yard to reset the spare topsail without delay. Wind's easing all the time. When you have completed that bring in a second tree and get a party of men under the direction of Mr Johnson to start work with draw knives in shaping up a new yard, better Johnson choose the spars. We'll transfer the iron work after that and paint the whole thing before swaying it aloft. Your experience on *Hecuba* should stand you in good stead.'

Still fuddled with sleep Rogers could not at first understand what was happening. It dawned on him that it was not much past five a.m. and that he had had hardly any sleep. It was doubtful if he yet knew of Drinkwater's discovery of Mistress Best or of his part in the conspiracy. 'Look, damn you Drinkwater, if you think . . .'

Drinkwater took a step quickly and thrust his face close to Rogers's. 'It used to be said that every debt was paid when the main topsail halliards were belayed, Rogers, but it ain't so. Newton's third law states that every action has an equal and opposite reaction. Now you are about to have that demonstrated to you. You have had your pleasure, you poisonous blackguard, and by God, sir, now you are going to pay for it! Carry on!' Drinkwater turned contemptuously away and called Mr Quilhampton to his side.

'Fetch my quadrant and the time-keeper from my cabin, take your time, Mr Q. Make two trips. If you drop that chronometer it will be the worse for you.'

The boy hurried off. Drinkwater was beginning, just beginning, to feel better. He would take a series of sun altitudes in a while and calculate their longitude by chronometer. He was very proud of the chronometer. The convalescing Captain Torrington had been landed with his men at the Cape. The army officer had been most grateful to the commander and gunroom officers of the *Hellebore* and asked if there was any service he could perform for them. By chance his brother, a civil officer in the service of the East India Company was taking passage home in one of the Indiamen in Table Bay and Torrington intended to return with him to England. His brother had advanced the Captain a considerable sum of money to defray his expenses whilst the Indiamen were at the Cape and he was willing to do his best to purchase some comforts for his benefactors.

Drinkwater, having missed the opportunity to obtain a timekeeper at Syracuse, knew that John Company's ships carried them. 'Sir, if I

458

could prevail upon you to beg a chronometer from the commander of one of the Indiamen we should be eternally obliged to you. You are aware of the nature of our mission and that we were sent on it somewhat precipitately; a chronometer would be of great use.'

'I should regard myself an ingrate if I were not to purchase you one my dear Drinkwater, a few wounds and a clock are a small price to pay to avoid Botany Bay.' They had laughed heartily at the noble captain as they lowered him into the boat.

'You know I used to deplore the sale of army commissions but when you have a generous and wealthy fellow like that to deal with it don't seem so bad a system,' Griffiths had said ironically.

The following morning the instrument arrived in an exotically smelling teak case. Drinkwater had taken it in charge, not trusting Lestock to wind it daily at the appointed hour. He had confirmed the longitude of Table Bay to within seven minutes of arc and this morning would be the first time they had seen the sun since leaving to run their easting down in the Roaring Forties. The result would make a nice matter for debate when Lestock came below for dinner.

After Lestock relieved him at eight bells and Drinkwater permitted the hands to cease their labour for half an hour to break their fasts, the first lieutenant sent for the woman. He sat himself down at the gunroom table and made her sit opposite while Appleby passed through into Griffiths's cabin to tend the commander.

The door had hardly closed on the surgeon when Drinkwater felt his calf receive a gentle and seductive caress from her leg. Last night, tired and a little drunk he had been in danger of succumbing. The lure of even Catherine's used body had sent a yearning through him. But this morning was different. His position would not tolerate such licence as the men toiled in expiation above his head. Besides, despite his fatigue, his spirit was repaired and his body no longer craved the solace of poor, plain and desperate Catherine. Daylight did not help her case.

'Last night I threatened to have you flogged. I have decided against that, but if you attempt the seduction of me or a single one of the men I will visit the cat upon your back.' He saw the initiative fade from her eyes. 'Have you ever seen a flogging, Catherine?' he asked coldly.

She nodded. Drinkwater opened the ship's muster book, snapped open the inkwell and took up his pen. 'I am entering you on the ship's books as a surgeon's assistant. You will be fed and clothed. If you prove by adhering to the regulations of the ship, that you can carry out your duties I will use my best endeavours to have your sentence remitted by whatever time you serve aboard this ship. I have a little influence through a peer of the realm and it may prove possible, if your services are of a sufficiently meritorious nature, that the remission of the whole of your sentence is not beyond the bounds of possibility.'

He did not know if such a course was remotely possible but it kindled hope in Catherine's eyes. She was a creature of the jungle, an opportunist, amoral rather than immoral and yet possessed of sufficient character to have hazed a whole ship's company. That showed a certain laudable determination, Drinkwater thought. His plan might just work. 'Will you agree to my conditions? The alternative is to be put in irons indefinitely.'

'Yes, yer honour.' She lowered her face.

'Look at me Catherine. You must understand that *any* infringement of the ship's rules will destroy our agreement.' She looked up at him then at Appleby who had come from Griffiths's cabin shaking his head over the captain's condition. 'Mr Appleby here will witness your undertaking.'

'I understand yer honour, but . . .'

'But what?'

'Well sir, she said ingenuously, 'it's Mr Jeavons and Mr Davey, sir.'

'The surgeon's mates?' She nodded.

'They're my regulars, like, sir, they've come to expect . . . you know . . .' She looked down again while Drinkwater looked at an Appleby empurpling with rage. 'Why the damned, festering . . .' Drinkwater held his hand up.

'I will deal with them Catherine. They will not trouble you again.' He turned the book round and held the pen out. 'Make your mark there,' he pointed to the place but she said indignantly 'I know, sir, I can read and write.'

She signed her name with some confidence. 'Very well, Catherine, now while I read out the men's names do you tell me with whom you have slept.' He began to read. She did not know all their names but the percentage of the crew who had visited her was large. But neither was it surprising. It was even possible that this bedraggled creature possessed a gentleness absent from the lives of the seamen and that it was for more than lust that they came to her.

'It must stop now, Catherine.' She nodded, while Appleby, with a hideous implication said, 'I will look into this matter.'

Drinkwater dismissed Catherine and sent for Appleby's mates. It was certain that they had been instrumental in suggesting Catherine dupe the brig's officers to their own advantage. Their plan had misfired when they discovered that many more of the hands would have to be a party to it and that those men would soon come calling for their share of the trophy. Besides, Catherine had to be found employment under supervision. Appleby was the only trustworthy person who did not have to keep a watch, and as the woman showed an aptitude for medical work she would be best employed with him.

It was the work of a moment to disrate the surgeon's mates. They protested they held their warrants from the College of Surgeons, that they were gentlemen unused to the labour of seamen. But being alone in the Southern Ocean had its advantages. There was neither court of appeal nor College of Surgeons south of the equator and they were soon turned to on deck where the starters of the bosun's mates were stinging their backsides with a venom spurred by a gradual realisation that the hands were being worked like dogs because of a certain lady of easy morals between decks. That her two pimps had been turned among them was a matter of some satisfaction.

Drinkwater concluded his morning's work by also appointing Tyson surgeon's assistant. He too could write, they had discovered, and Drinkwater was amused to find Appleby growling over the radical alterations to his department. 'My dear fellow,' said Drinkwater summoning Merrick from the pantry with some blackstrap, 'you have always fancied your chances as a philosopher, now you have the most literate department in the ship. You will be able to plead the benefit of clergy for all of 'em. Now do be a good fellow and allow me to compute this longitude before Lestock comes below.'

*

461

At noon Drinkwater called the hands aft. His announcement to them was brief and to the point. The woman, Catherine Best, he told them, had been apprehended. The deception against the Regulations for the Good Order of His Majesty's Navy on board His Britannic Majesty's Brig of War *Hellebore* was at an end. Although it verged upon the mutinous by virtue of its very nature as 'a combination', in the effective absence of the captain, he had decided that he could not flog the woman without inflicting the penalty upon them all. He held them all culpable, however, and would punish all of them by a stoppage of grog, to be indefinite against their good behaviour. The groan that met this announcement convinced Drinkwater that it was the correct measure. The deprivation of jack's grog was a punishment incomprehensible to landsmen. As for the woman, he continued, she was now part of the ship's company. Any man found lying with her would receive the same punishment as that prescribed by the Articles of War for that unnatural act whereby one man had knowledge of another. He did not need to remind them that the punishment for sodomy was death.

When he had finished he sent them to their dinner. 'By heaven, Nathaniel, that was a rare device,' muttered Appleby admiringly, 'what a splendid pettifogging notion. Worthy of Lincoln's Inn.'

Drinkwater smiled thinly. He was thinking how far they had yet to travel and how little of their task they had yet accomplished.

'What d'you intend to do about Dalziell and Rogers?'

'Let them stew a little, Harry, let them stew.'

In longitude forty-five east they hauled to the northward, the wind quartering them until it gradually eased and died away from the west. They entered the great belt of variables south of Madagascar and worked north by frequent yard trimming. Twice they sighted sails but on both occasions they did not seek to close the other. The men began to mutter. The deprivation of their grog continued days after they had toiled to get first the jury foreyard up, then its permanent replacement. The lack of it was beginning to rankle. As the weather continued to improve Drinkwater had sent up the topgallant masts. On their first day of light winds they had hoisted the boats out and hauled them up to the davit heads on either quarter. Griffiths had recovered sufficiently to be told of the events of the fortnight. He had been so choleric that Appleby feared for a recurrence of his fever, but the old man had subsided to order that Drinkwater continue the ban on grog just at the point when Drinkwater was considering reinstating it.

'No indeed! The weather is improving, the men do not need it to drive them aloft, see; let them feel the want of it a little longer. '

Catherine Best appeared a reformed character and Appleby was the butt of jokes about the reclamation of fallen women. Although he resisted at first, Griffiths had finally allowed her to attend him. Reporting to the commander one morning Drinkwater had commented on her as she left the cabin. 'There is a little good in the worst of us,' Griffiths quoted with more than a trace of Welsh piety, Drinkwater thought wryly. '*Duw*, but she's a sight better than those gin-soaked mountains of lard at Haslar . . . or for that matter the herring gutters they had in the hospital at Yarmouth . . .' Griffiths was beginning to enjoy his convalescence and if the men thought their commander had adopted their bawd then let them, he thought. They would be of that opinion anyway and Drinkwater was at last able to wring the issue of grog from Griffiths.

It was whilst observing Venus after sunset that he first heard the rumour. Beneath the poop two men sat in the gloom of dusk while *Hellebore* ran north-east under easy sail.

'We be a cursed ship with a woman on board,' said one voice.

'Ah, bull's piss. They Indiamen carry women *and* chaplains, they seem to manage. Anyway you tried hard enough to have her.'

'No I didn't.'

'You bloody well did, you said yerself that if you'd been below before that slimy rat Jenkins you'd'ave slipped her what she had coming to her. I heard you.'

'We still be accursed. You heard o'the Flying Dutchman? Him what inhabits these waters? You heard of him then?'

Drinkwater brought the planet down to the fast fading horizon, twisting the quadrant gently and smoothly. Satisfied he rocked it slightly from side to side so that the gleaming disc just cut the horizon, all the time adjusting the index to follow the planet's setting. 'Now!' he called to Quilhampton who was taking the time on the chronometer. He paid no more attention to the rubbish he had overheard. Lestock came up shortly afterwards to relieve him and looked suspiciously at the longitude Quilhampton had chalked on the slate.

'Come, come, Mr Lestock, the Board of Longitude thought the problem worth twenty thousand sterling. All I ask is that you have a little faith in their investment.' But he did not wish to get involved in an argument and he went on, 'It's high time we had those guns out of the hold. We're coming up with Île de France, even you latitude sailors must know that, and it's time we mounted a full broadside before we meet a Frenchman. If it is calm tomorrow we'll hoist 'em out. In the meantime she's full and bye, nor'nor'east, all plain sail and nothing reported. Logged six knots five fathoms at one bell, wheel and lookouts relieved. Good night, Mr Lestock.'

'Good night, Mr Drinkwater.'

As he broke his fast the following morning, when a dying wind held every prospect of their being able to remount the guns, he heard again the words 'Flying Dutchman'. He called Merrick from the pantry. 'Come now what's all this about?'

Merrick was shamefaced but clearly confused. He told how a tale was going round the brig about them being condemned to everlasting drifting about, like the Flying Dutchman. It was all on account of the woman. 'It's nothing but scuttlebutt, sir, but . . . well I . . .' Drinkwater smiled. It sounded ridiculous but he knew the grip a superstition could have over the minds of these men. It was not that they were simple but that their understanding was circumscribed. They had no idea where they were, they endured hours of remorseless labour to no apparent purpose. The best of them was paid twenty-nine shillings and sixpence gross, less deductions for the Chatham Chest, medical treatment, slops and whatever remaining delights, like tobacco, the purser sold them. Their lives were forfeit if they broke the iron-bound rules of conduct, and ruled by an arbitrary authority which was a yoke, no matter how enlightened. Recent events had conspired to make it the more irksome and there would be those among them with sufficient theology to assure their more credulous messmates that they were being punished for their carnal misdemeanours. It was not surprising therefore that their minds should react to a story as vivid as that of Vanderdecken, the legendary Flying Dutchman. The question was who had started its circulation?

'Where did you first hear the story, Merrick?'

The man pondered. 'It was here in the gunroom, sir. Begging your pardon sir, I wasn't listening deliberately, sir but I heard . . .'

'Well who was telling it, man?' said Drinkwater impatiently, well knowing Merrick eavesdropped and passed the conversation of the officers to the cook who, from his centrally situated galley where all came during the day, fed out to the hands the gossip he saw fit.

'I think it were Mr Quilhampton, sir.'

'Mr Q, eh? Thank you, Merrick. By the way you did not concern yourself over such things on *Kestrel* did you?'

'Lord love you no, sir. But we was never far from home, sir. Ushant, Texel, them's home for British jacks sir, but up there now,' he pointed to the deckhead, 'why nobody knows the stars, sir, even the bleeding sun's north of us at noon, sir. One of the men says there's islands of ice not many leagues to the south. It just don't seem right sir, kind of alarming . . .'

Drinkwater sent for Mr Quilhampton. 'Merrick tells me he heard you spinning the yarn of the Flying Dutchman, is this true?'

'Well no, sir. Actually I was listening. I mean I had heard it before, but I didn't like to say so, sir.'

'Who was telling the tale then?'

'Oh it was just by way of entertainment, sir. I was listening with Dalziell.'

'But who was telling it?'

'Why Mr Rogers, sir.'

'No wind, Mr Lestock.'

'None, Mr Drinkwater.'

'Very well, clew up all sails and square the yards. A tackle at each of the lower yardarms, one on the main topmast stay and a bull rope to the capstan. The watch can rig those then turn up all hands.'

He fell to pondering the problem. Since the discovery of Catherine Best, Rogers had been very quiet. Whether or not he had had a relationship with the woman Drinkwater did not know. Neither did he care. Appleby told him the woman believed herself barren and there seemed no evidence of other complications. Nevertheless Rogers had been a party to the conspiracy. More, Drinkwater hoped, out of a misplaced, schoolboy prankishness than a calculated act. But Drinkwater was not sure. Rogers might have been evening the score, proving himself smarter than the first lieutenant. But that did not ring quite true. Rogers was an impetuous, fiery officer, spirited if low in moral character, certainly able and probably brave. The service was full of his type; they were indispensible in action. But Rogers was not a dissembler. His weakness lay in his impetuous temper. When Dalziell had brought Tregembo for a flogging Rogers had acted without a second thought. So was Dalziell behind this silly rumour? There was an inescapable logic about it. Not that the yarn was, in itself sinister, but the persistence of its power to unsettle and subvert was real; very real. The sooner they had the guns remounted the better. Now that they were in temperate latitudes once again they could resume their routine of general quarters, suspended since the Cape in the heavy weather of the Roaring Forties. Drinkwater knew it was not sufficient to read the Articles of War once a month to keep the people on their toes. Only the satisfying roar and thunder of their brutish artillery could do that.

'All ready, Mr Drinkwater. Hands at the tackles, the hatches off and the toms off the guns.'

'Very well, Mr Lestock, then let us turn to.'

The first to emerge was the foremost starboard waist gun. The tackles of the starboard fore and main yardarms were overhauled and married to the big stay tackle. The three purchases thus joined were lowered into the hold. There they were hooked on to the gun, ready slung by a strop around its trunnions.

A bosun's mate commanded the hauling part of each tackle and at the gratings the bosun, Mr Grey, his silver chained whistle suspended about his neck, stood poised.

'Set tight all!' The slack in the three tackles was taken up.

'Stay tackle heave! Handsomely there now . . . yard tackles up slack!'

The black doubled hemp of the main topmast stay assumed a shallow angle and the mainmast creaked gently. The six pounder weighed eighteen hundredweights. Below in the hold six men tallied on a bull-rope round the gun's cascabel, steadying the black barrel. The next order came as the gun rose level with the deck: 'Yard tackles heave!' The men grunted away in concerted effort. There were no merchant ship's shanties but a rhythmic grunt as fifty men, barefoot and sweating in the sunshine, strained at their work. 'Walk back the stay tackle handsomely!'

The gun, suspended now from all three tackles, began to move horizontally across the deck. The bull-rope trailed slack and was pulled onto the deck by one of the topmen who ran forward to reeve it through a train tackle block.

"Vast heaving main yard!' As the stay tackle party lowered slowly back and the mainyard party ceased work, the gun slewed forward under the pull of the foreyard tackle. It began to move across the deck diagonally.

'Capstan party heave tight!' Twenty men walked round the capstan and tightened the bull-rope. Theirs was a job of adjustment, as was that of the gunner's party that stood by the waiting gun carriage.

'Walk back the mainyard!' The gun moved forward now, almost over the carriage.

"Vast all!'

'Walk back handsomely!' Slowly, almost imperceptibly, the gun began to descend. Trussel made some furious signals while Mr Grey held first the foreyard party, then the main. The gun stopped while Trussel's men shoved the carriage a little. A minute later the gun rested on its trunnions. The cap-squares were shut. The carriage was slewed into position and run up against its port lintel, then the breechings were passed.

'Overhaul all . . .' The three tackles were passed down into the hold for the second gun.

They finished by mid-afternoon and were piped to dinner after which they were piped up again and went to general quarters. The broadsides were ragged and from his cot Griffiths expressed his disappointment.

'Tell the people,' he muttered crossly, 'that if that is the best they can do I will stop their grog again.'

It was not an order Drinkwater made haste to obey. The mood of the ship was too delicate and Appleby had told him the fever had aggravated Griffiths's leg and he was likely to be irritable and a semi-invalid for some time.

'God knows what will become of him,' the surgeon said

worriedly, 'but his powers of recovery are greatly diminished since last year's attack.'

The silence of exhaustion fell upon the brig as the sun set. It was mixed with discontent for, despite reprovisioning at the Cape, some of the salt junk had been found bad and there had been no more that day to replace it. 'It is likely to be a long voyage,' Drinkwater had reluctantly told the purser, 'we must adhere to the rationing.'

He came below at eight p.m. his shirt sticking to his back, too tired for sleep. Not that sleep was to be had in the airless cabin. In the gunroom Appleby dozed over his madeira. Drinkwater slumped in a chair as the door to Griffiths's cabin opened and Catherine Best emerged. She held a finger to her lips, the very picture of solicitude.

As she passed Drinkwater she gave a little curtsey. He could scarcely believe his eyes and his mind was just forming a quite unjustified suspicion that she must have ulterior motives when a piercing cry of alarm came from the deck.

A silence followed, brief but oppressive with the most awful horror. Then, in that stunned hiatus, clearly heard through the open skylights and companionways: 'It's him, boys! It's the Dutchman!'

So potent had been the cry that the senses seemed devoid of reason. Drinkwater felt his intelligence replaced by fear, then with a curse he rose and rushed on deck. He ran forward to where Kellet, captain of the foretop, his arm outstretched was open mouthed in terror.

Others arrived and they too pointed, muttering fearfully, a papist or two crossing themselves, a good protestant on his knees confessing his sins direct to his maker. 'Oh God forgive me that I did indeed have carnal knowledge of Mistress Best when that vessel of uncleanness was a greater whore than all the . . .' Next to him Drinkwater saw Dalziell. The midshipman was shaking as though palsied.

Drinkwater stared ahead at the dull, greenish glow. The night had become cloudy and dark, there was just a breath of wind and the glow grew larger. If his theory about Dalziell having initiated the silly rumours was correct the youth was paying for it now in a paroxysm of fear.

'Whisht, listen boys! Listen!' The hubbub faded and they could hear the screams, the screams of souls in torment. 'Holy Mary, Mother of God, blessed is the fruit of thy womb . . .'

'Jesus Christ, what the hell is it?'

"Tis the Dutchman, boys . . . the Dutchman . . .'

Drinkwater pushed his way aft, unceremoniously grabbing Lestock's glass from the master's paralysed hand. He swung himself into the mainchains.

It was the hull of a galleon all right, with a high poop. But the vessel had been dismasted. He thought he could see movement, pale shapes flitting about on it. The hair on the nape of his neck crawled. He dismissed the superstition with an effort. But perhaps an old wreck, like those supposedly trapped in the weed of the Sargasso . . .?

No, there was something familiar about those screams. 'Mr Lestock!'

'Eh? What?'

'Do we have steerage way?'

'Steerage way? Eh, oh, er we did, sir, just. Come you lubbers back to the wheel, damn it, what d'ye think this is?'

'A point to starboard if you please.'

A gasp of incredulity greeted this order. Cries of supplication and threats floated aft. 'The devil may take you, Mr Drinkwater, but not us, hold your course mates.'

'Belay that forward! What's the matter my bully boys? Have you lost your stomachs? Come now, I don't believe it. A point to starboard there . . .'

'What the deuce is it Drinkwater?' muttered Rogers below him, 'lend me the glass.' Drinkwater handed it down. 'Let me see after you,' said Appleby. 'Damn your eyes, it's my bloody glass.' Lestock snatched it peevishly from Rogers's eye.

'You can see for yourself, Harry,' said Drinkwater suppressing laughter.

They were closing the apparition fast now. The supposition that it was a galleon had made a fantasy of distance. In fact it was quite close and as they passed it there was a surge backwards from the rails, cries of revulsion as the stink of the dead whale assailed their noses.

'Well it stinks like hell for sure!' There was the laughter of relief up and down the deck as they realised what huge fools they had been.

The decomposing whale had swelled up and glowed from the millions of tiny organisms that fed upon it. Shrieking and screaming above it a thousand seabirds enjoyed the funeral feast of the enormous mammal while the water about it was thrashed to a frenzy by a score of sharks.

They watched it fade astern. Laughing at themselves the men drifted below. It seemed the atmosphere about the ship had been washed clean by that appalling smell. Drinkwater wished his companions good night when a party was seen coming from forward. Four men were carrying the inert white-shirted and breeched body of a midshipman. 'Is that Mr Q?'

'Lord no, sir. I'm here.'

'It's Mr Dalziell, zur,' said Tregembo, lowering the midshipman. 'Fainted he did, zur, in a swoon.'

'Well, well, well,' said Drinkwater ironically, 'it seems that vengeance is still the Lord's.'

Chapter Eight   *November–December 1798*

A John Company Man

Drinkwater was bent over his books, alarmed at the high expenditure of cordage due to the loss of the foreyard, when he heard the cry from the masthead.

'Deck there! Sail ho! A point of starboard!' He gratefully accepted the excuse to rush on deck, feeling the welcome breeze ruffling his open shirt. They had sighted the high land of Ras Hafun three days earlier and doubled Cape Guardafui under the strong katabatic winds that blew down from the Somali plateau. Now they romped westward into the Gulf of Aden carrying sail to the mastheads. It was the forenoon and the watches below were preparing for dinner so that at the cry most of her hands crowded *Hellebore*'s waist. They were eagerly awaiting a sight of the stranger from the deck. Drinkwater saw Quilhampton at the rail.

'Up you go, Mr Q, and see what you make of her.' The boy grabbed a glass and leapt into the rigging. The sight of anything would be welcome. They had seen several dhows inshore of them as they closed the coast but the stranger might be a square-rigged ship, a friend or, just possibly, an enemy.

Hellebore had had her fill of the wonders of the Indian Ocean. Flying fish, whales and dolphins had been seen in abundance, turtles and birds of many descriptions, petrels, long-tailed tropic birds and the brown boobies that reminded them of the immature gannets of Europe. Little sketches filled the margins of Drinkwater's journal together with a description of a milk sea, an eruption of foaming phosphorescence of ethereal beauty. This phenomenon had prompted Quilhampton to essay his hand at poetry. The scorn of Mr Dalziell ended the endeavour, though Mr Quilhampton was quick to refute the assertion that poets were milksops by pointing out they were not the only persons to be sent into a swoon at the sight of the world's natural wonders. But none of these observations thrilled them as much as the two white topgallants that were soon visible from the deck.

'She's a brig sir, like us . . . or she might be a snow, sir,' reported Quilhampton with uncertain precision.

'Colours?'

'Not showing 'em, sir,' he answered, unconsciously aping Mr Drinkwater's abbreviated style.

'No colours, eh?' said Griffiths hobbling up on his swollen foot.

'No, sir.'

'Waiting for us to declare ourselves, eh? Clear for action Mr Drinkwater, Mr Lestock! Take the t'gallants off her, square away to intercept this fellow.'

The pipes squealed at the hatchways and the men lost their dinner as the cook doused his stove. All was hurrying urgency. They had improved their gunnery coming up from the south, shot at casks with the 'great guns' and shattered bottles at the yardarms from the tops. Their grog had long ago been reinstated and Catherine Best had assumed the demeanour of a nun. Never was a meal more cheerfully forgotten. This was no lurking French cruiser of overwhelming force. The sun was shining, the breeze was blowing and the shadows of the sails and rigging were sharp across the deck as it was sprinkled with sand.

'Cleared for action, sir.'

The two ships were three miles apart when the chase freed off, altering to the north so that she presented her broadside to them. 'She's a snow,' muttered Quilhampton pacing up and down the starboard battery in the wake of Lieutenant Rogers.

'She's an odd looking craft,' said Drinkwater. She was like a small sloop but with a long poop, painted green with enormous gun ports in it.

'Hoist the colours!'

'Or the god-damned topgallants, you bloody old goat,' muttered Rogers who thought the chase would escape his eager gunners.

Hellebore's ensign snapped out and jerked to the spanker peak, streaming out on the starboard beam. Griffiths watched the snow respond, heaving to with her main topsail against the mast. At her peak flew the horizontally striped ensign of the Honourable East India Company.

'A John Company ship,' said Griffiths relaxing. *Hellebore* foamed up to the stranger and came to the wind as the snow lowered a boat.

'He's all for co-operation,' said Griffiths to Drinkwater.

'Well, I'm damned . . . those ain't gunports, they're slatted blinds.'

'Jalousies, Mr Drinkwater, she's a dispatch vessel for the Company, a country ship they use for conveying their officials about and carrying dispatches. I'll wager it's that he wishes to see us about.'

Griffiths proved right. While the Hellebores, relaxing from action stations and eagerly salving what remained of their lukewarm dinner, chaffed incomprehensibly with the grinning lascars in the boat, a handsome sun-bronzed officer in the crisp well-laundered uniform of the Company's Bombay Marine told them the news.

'Lieutenant Lawrence, gentlemen, at your service.' They exchanged formal greetings and withdrew to Griffiths's cabin.

'Lieutenant Thomas Duval of His Majesty's ship *Zealous* arrived at Bombay on 21st October, sir, with the news from Admiral Nelson.' Griffiths and Drinkwater exchanged glances. *Hellebore* had been at the Cape then. 'Please go on, Lieutenant.'

'It seems that on 1st August last the British fleet under Rear-Admiral Nelson annihilated the French at Aboukir Bay. The attack was made at sunset while the French fleet lay at anchor. I understand that, despite the shoaling of the bay and the grounding of *Culloden*, the British engaged the French on both sides and the victory was a most complete one. The flagship, *L'Orient*, blew up.' He finished with a smile as though the disintegration of a thousand humans was a matter for personal satisfaction.

'Do you have sercial in Bombay, Lieutenant?' asked Griffiths ironically, motioning Drinkwater to open a bottle. He called through into the pantry for Merrick to bring in some glasses.

'We do not want for much in Bombay,' said Lawrence, 'but I have not tasted such excellent Madeira for a good while.' From his appearance Lawrence wanted for absolutely nothing. They toasted the victory.

'And where are you from now, Lieutenant, what is your purpose?'

'I am from Mocha, sir, where we left dispatches for Commodore Blankett. Captain Ball of *Daedalus* was daily expected. The Red Sea Squadron uses Mocha as a watering place, sir. Mr Wrinch is the agent there,' he paused, then added, 'a man of considerable parts, sir, you would find calling upon him most profitable.' Lawrence's eyes fell to Griffiths's gouty foot, then he rattled on, 'unfortunately we could not delay as the north-east monsoon in the Arabian Sea makes a lengthy passage for us back to Bombay.'

'And your dispatches conveyed the news of the victory at Aboukir to Blankett I assume?'

Lawrence nodded over the rim of his glass.

'And was there mention of a French army in those dispatches? Of a force landed in Egypt?'

'Oh that! Yes sir, there are indications of such a thing. Duval suggested that they might attempt a descent on India but the idea is quite preposterous: their force in the Red Sea is totally inadequate. It gave us a nasty shock, though,' he laughed faily, 'quite unexpected!'

'What?' snapped Griffiths, 'd'you mean there are already French ships in the Red Sea?'

'Oh yes, one of them, a smart little sloop, call 'em corvettes I recollect, attempted to chase us off Perim two days ago. We led him a merry dance through the reefs and soon shook him off.'

'*Myndiawl*,' growled Griffiths while Drinkwater asked, 'How many ships have the French got out there, sir?'

'I've really no idea, sir, two or three. The Arabs don't view their arrival with much enthusiasm since they seem to be taking dhows. God knows what for. It might be the will of Allah but the faithful don't take too kindly to it.'

'A true corsair by the sound of him,' said Griffiths pondering. 'Tell me sir, could you oblige us with a modern chart of the Red Sea? Ours is most fearfully wanting in detail.' Drinkwater pulled the appropriate chart from the drawer beneath the settee. He showed Lawrence. The lieutenant laughed. 'Good God, gentlemen, I believe Noah had a better. Yes, I am sure I can furnish your wants there, send a midshipman back with me.'

'There's a further thing,' said Griffiths, 'we've a woman on board and I want her given passage to Bombay.'

Lawrence's face clouded. 'Who is she?'

'Oh, some convict scum we found floating in a ship's boat in the South Atlantic. She got amongst the men with her damned fornicating.'

Lawrence was indignant: 'I'm sorry sir, but I cannot help you with convicts.'

'Damn it man, I order you to, I hold a commission in the King's Service . . .'

'You say you picked her up in the South Atlantic?' temporised Lawrence.

'Yes.'

'But you come from the Cape. Could you not have landed her there?' Lawrence frowned. He supposed these naval officers had tired of the jade and now wished to be rid of her. 'You must understand, sir, that I have a crew of lascars: their notion of Englishwomen is not such that they would readily comprehend the nature of a whore and a convict.' He picked up his hat and bowed. 'But the chart you shall have with pleasure. Good morning gentlemen, my thanks for your hospitality . . .'

'Wait, Mr Lawrence,' snapped Griffiths. The man's refusal to take Mistress Best had not surprised him. Other things were crowding the mind of Madoc Griffiths. 'A moment more. I desire you to inform the Governor at Bombay and the General Officer commanding the Company's troops that there *is* substantial risk of the French descending upon India. It is most important that you carry Admiral Nelson's apprehensions upon this matter with more conviction than did Lieutenant Duval. To this end I shall have the matter in writing . . .' The commander turned to his desk. Lawrence's face was a picture of scepticism; he seemed unable to take such a threat seriously. Drinkwater was not surprised; he had heard that prolonged service in India induced a euphoria in Europeans that was a consequence of their exalted position. Lawrence's lofty dismissal of Catherine Best amply demonstrated this attitude.

'See Mr Lawrence over the side, Mr Drinkwater,' Griffiths handed the Company officer a letter. Lawrence bowed, took the packet and left the cabin. As the two men climbed into the brilliant sunshine of the deck Drinkwater called Quilhampton to accompany the officer to his ship.

'I'll send my boat back with him, sir,' smiled Lawrence, 'lest it be said that I refused a woman but took a boy, eh?'

Drinkwater found the jest distasteful and dismissed Lawrence as a sybarite. But he managed a thin smile out of courtesy.

'You be careful of those Frogs,' Lawrence said lightly, 'you don't have the local knowledge that we do and even my chart is not a great deal of use above Jabal Zuqar; but it'll get you to Mocha. Good day, sir.'

'Good day, and thank you. I suppose you know no more of the French force?'

Lawrence shrugged. 'A frigate and one or two corvettes . . . commodore's name was unusual,' he paused with one elegant calf over the rail. 'I remember Tom Duval sounded more Frog than this villain. Something like Santon . . . Santa . . .'

'Santhonax?'

'You have it exactly sir, Santhonax. Good day, sir.'

'God's bones!' Nathaniel turned swiftly away and scrambled below while Lawrence returned to his ship. Drinkwater burst in upon Griffiths. 'I just asked that popinjay who commanded the French squadron, sir!'

Griffiths looked up: 'Well?'

'Santhonax!'

For a second Griffiths sat silent, then a torrent of Welsh oaths rolled from him in a spate of invective that terminated in the pouring of two further glasses of sercial. Both men sat staring before them. Both thought of the long duel they had fought with Santhonax in the Channel and the North Sea. They had put an end to his depredations by capture at Camperdown. Now, by some twist of fate, Santhonax had beaten them, arrived ahead of them in the Red Sea.

'It is not coincidence, Nathaniel, if that is what you are thinking. *Duw*, it is Providence . . . *myndiawl*, it is more than that, it is *proof* of Providence!'

'There is one thing, sir.'

'Eh? And what is that?' asked Griffiths pouring a third glass of the wine.

'He does not know it is us that are in pursuit.'

'Huh! That is something like cold comfort, indeed it is.'

The bump of a boat alongside told where Quilhampton had been

476

returned. A minute later the boy knocked and came in. He handed Drinkwater the rolled chart. 'Beg pardon, sir, but it *was* a snow, sir, name of *Dart*, sir and . . .'

'Mr Quilhampton!' snapped Griffiths.

'Sir?' said the boy blushing.

'Do you tell the master that I desire him to brace up and lay a course for the Straits of Bab el Mandeb.'

'B . . . Bab el . . .'

'Mandeb.'

'Aye aye, sir.'

Chapter Nine

December 1798–May 1799

Mocha Road

Lieutenant Drinkwater slowly paced *Hellebore*'s tiny quarterdeck. The almost constant southerly wind that blew hot from the Horn of Africa tended to ease at nightfall and Drinkwater, in breeches and shirt, had come to regard his sunset walks as an indispensible highlight to the tedium of these weeks. Now, as the sun sank blood-red and huge, its reflection glowing on the sea, he felt a bitter-sweet sadness familiar to seamen at the close of the day when far from home. He turned aft and strode evenly, measuring the deck. His eyes were caught by the rose-coloured walls and towers of Mocha to the east, a mile distant. The mud brick of the town's buildings also reflected the setting glory of the sun. The slender minaret pointed skywards like a sliver of gold and beside it the dome of the mosque blazed. Behind the town the Tihamah plain stretched eastward, already shadowing and cooling until, like a fantastic backcloth it merged with the crags and fissures of the Yemeni mountains that rose into a sky velvet with approaching night. It was not the first time that the beauty of a tropical night had moved him, provoking thoughts of home and Elizabeth and the worry of her accouchement. Then he chid himself for a fool, reminding himself that although he knew a good deal about the ship beneath his feet he knew precious little about the fundamentals of human life. Elizabeth would have been long since brought to bed. He wondered whether the child had lived and tore his mind from the prospect of having lost Elizabeth.

Mr Brundell approached him and reported the sighting of the captain's boat. Drinkwater hurried below for his coat and hat, then met Griffiths at the entry.

After the exchange of routine remarks Griffiths beckoned Drinkwater into the cabin; throwing his hat on to the settee he indicated the first lieutenant should pour them both a glass of wine. Flinging himself on to his chair the commander covered his face with his hands.

'No news, sir?' enquired Drinkwater pushing the wine across the table.

'Aye, *bach*, but of a negative kind, damn it. It *is* Santhonax. Wrinch is certain of it,' Griffiths's frequent visits ashore to the delightful residence of Mr Strangford Wrinch had almost assumed the character of a holiday, so regular a thing had they become in the last month. But it was not pleasure that drove Griffiths to the table of the British 'resident'.

Wrinch was a coffee merchant with consular powers, an 'agent' for British interests, not all of them commercial. Drinkwater had dined with him several times and formed the impression that he was one of those strange expatriate Britons who inhabit remote parts of the world, exercising almost imperial powers and writing the pages of history anonymously. It had become apparent to Griffiths and Drinkwater that the man sat spider-like at the centre of a web that strung its invisible threads beside the old caravan routes of Arabia, extended to the ancient Yemeni dependencies in the Sudan and the uncharted tracks of the dhows that traded and plundered upon the Red Sea.

Griffiths had long been involved with the gleaning of intelligence, had spent the latter part of his life working for greater men whose names history would record as the conductors of foreign policy. Yet it was a war within war that occupied Griffiths and Wrinch, a personal involvement which gave them both their motivation. And for Griffiths the personal element had reached an apogee of urgency. Santhonax had been their old adversary in the Channel and the North Sea in the anxious months before Camperdown. Santhonax had been responsible for the barbaric execution of Major Brown, a fact that stirred all Griffiths's latent Celtic hatred. Griffiths was an old, infirm man. Santhonax's presence in the Red Sea mocked him as a task unfinished.

So Griffiths sat patiently in the cool, whitewashed courtyard, brushing off the flies that plagued the town, and waited for news of

Santhonax. What Drinkwater did not share with his commander was the latter's patience.

In the weeks they had swung at anchor Drinkwater had concluded that Admiral Nelson had sent them on a wild goose chase; that Lieutenant Duval's overland journey to Bombay was sufficient. They had strained every sinew to reach the Red Sea only to find Admiral Blankett was not at Mocha, that he had gone in search of the French squadron and might have by now destroyed Santhonax. The admiral had been told by Wrinch that a French force was loose in the area. Wrinch affirmed the accuracy of his intelligence without moving from his rug where he would sit in his *galabiya* and *fadhl* with his fellow merchants, with the Emirs el Hadj that led the caravans, with commanders of dhows who swapped news for gold, pearls or hashish, or fondled the pretty boys Wrinch was said to prefer to women.

Whatever the truth about himself Wrinch was shrewd enough to know when an Arab invoked the one true God to verify his lies, and when he reported facts. And Griffiths was not interested in the moral qualities of his sources; for him the world was as it was.

Blankett too, had taken alarm. Red-faced and damning Wrinch roundly he had set off north while the season of southerly winds lasted. After his departure Lawrence had arrived, only to be chased by one of Santhonax's ships, appearing mysteriously in Blankett's rear. Despite this intelligence Wrinch urged Griffiths not to cruise in search of either party. He should simply wait. For Wrinch, waiting and 'fadhling' were part of the charm of Arab life. For Griffiths they were a tolerable way of passing the time, enduring the heat and sharpening his appetite for revenge. For Drinkwater the delay was intolerable.

'So we continue to wait, sir?'

Griffiths nodded. 'I know, *bach*, idleness is bad for the people forrard but, *duw*, we have no choice. Wrinch is right,' Griffiths soothed, brushing the flies away from his face. 'Damned flies have the impertinence of Arabs . . . No, Mocha Road is the rendezvous.' His white-haired head sank in thought. 'Hmmm, *Yr Aifft* . . .'

'Sir?'

'Egypt, Nathaniel, Egypt. There is great activity in Egypt. Bonaparte has made himself master of Cairo. A general named

480

Desaix is blazing a trail through Upper Egypt with the assistance of a Copt called Moallem Jacob.' He paused. 'I think Nelson may be right and with that devil Santhonax to reckon with . . .' He raised his white eyebrows and clamped his mouth tight shut. Then he blew out his cheeks. 'I wish to God you'd shot him.'

Inaction, like the heat, seemed to have settled permanently upon the brig. The pitch bubbled in the seams and Drinkwater had the duty watch keep the decks wet during daylight. They listed the ship with the guns and scrubbed the waterline, they overhauled the rigging and painted ship. Griffiths forbade exercising the guns with powder and a silent ritual was meaningless to the men. To divert them Drinkwater sent Lestock, his mates and the midshipman off in the boats to survey the road. Although this stimulated a competitiveness among the junior officers and promoted a certain amount of professional interest, once again high-lighting Mr Quilhampton's potential talents, it was limited in its appeal to the hands and soon became unpopular as the boats roamed further afield. Lethargy began to spread its tentacles through the brig, bearing out Appleby's maxim that war was mostly a waste of time, a waste of money and a waste of energy.

As week succeeded week Drinkwater's frustration mounted. He was tormented by worry over Elizabeth, worry that could not easily be set aside in favour of more pressing duties because there were none to demand his attention beyond the routine of daily life at anchor. The myriad flies that visited them drove them to distraction and the lack of shore leave for the hands exacerbated their own cramped lives.

Strangford Wrinch passed them alarming intelligence, gathered from a certain Hadji Yusuf ben Ibrahim, commander of a *sambuk*. In December of the old year a French division under General Bon had occupied Suez. Bonaparte himself had accepted tribute from the Arabs of Tor in Sinai and reached an accommodation with the monks of the mysterious monastery of St Catherine at the southern extremity of that peninsula. General Desaix was scattering the mamelukes to the four winds in an energetic sweep up the Nile Valley. Egypt had become a province of France and it was clear that, despite Nelson's victory at Aboukir and the subsequent blockade of the Mediterranean coast under Sir Samuel Hood, the French were far from beaten. They might yet move further east and in the absence of Blankett *Hellebore* would be no more than a straw under the hooves of the conqueror.

At the end of January Griffiths ordered them to sea. For a fortnight they cruised between Perim and Jabal Zugar, exercising the guns and sails. Then they returned to Mocha Road and the shallow bight of its bay, to the heat and flies and the deceptive, fairy-tale wonder of its minaret. Again Griffiths departed daily, smilingly ordering them to submit to the will of Allah, to learn to *keyf*, to sit in suspended animation after the manner of the Arabs.

'Holy Jesus Christ,' blasphemed the intemperate Rogers in sweating exasperation, 'the stupid old bastard has gone senile.' 'Mr Drinkwater!' The knocking at the door was violently urgent. The face of Quilhampton peered round it, white with worry. 'Mr Drinkwater!'

Drinkwater swam stickily into consciousness. 'Eh? What is it?'

'Two ships standing in from the south, sir!'

Drinkwater was instantly awake. 'Inform the captain! General Quarters and clear for action!'

The midshipman fled and Drinkwater heard the brig come alive, heard the boy's treble taken up by the duty bosun's mate piping at the hatchways. He reached for his breeches, buckled on his sword and snatched up the loaded pistol he habitually kept ready. He rushed on deck.

It was just light and the waist was all confusion with the slap of two hundred bare feet and the whispered exertions of five score of sleep-befuddled seamen driven by training and fear to their stations.

Drinkwater picked up the night glass from its box and did the required mental gymnastics with its inverted image. He swept the horizon and steadied it on the two shapes standing into the road. The larger vessel might be a frigate. Some of the new French frigates were big vessels, yet she seemed too high and not long enough to be a French thoroughbred. The smaller ship was clearly a brig of their own size.

Griffiths appeared. 'Hoist the private signal, Mr Drinkwater!'

Rogers reported the batteries cleared for action. 'Very well, Mr

Rogers. Man the starboard. Mr Drinkwater, set tight the spring. Traverse three points to larboard!'

'Aye, aye, sir.' Drinkwater cast a final glance at Quilhampton's party hoisting the private signal to the lee foretopsail yardarm where the wind spread it for the approaching ships to see. 'Mr Grey, waisters to the capstan!'

Hellebore trembled slightly as the spring came tight and she turned off the wind, bringing her starboard broadside to bear upon the strangers. Drinkwater watched apprehensively. There was no reply to the private signal.

'Starboard battery made ready, sir,' Rogers reported. All activity had ceased now, the gun crews squatting expectantly around their pieces, the captains kneeling off to one side of the recoil tracks, the lanyards tight in their hands.

Hellebore was a sitting duck, silhouetted against the sunrise while the newcomers approached out of the night shadows.

'Mr Rogers! Fire Number One gun astern of her if you please.'

Drinkwater raised his glass and watched the bigger of the two ships. Forward the gun barked. Daylight grew rapidly, distinct rays from the rising sun fanned out from behind the crags of the Yemeni mountains. As the Muezzin called the faithful to prayer from the distant minaret of Mocha, Drinkwater saw the British ensign hoisted to the peak of the approaching ships and an answering puff of smoke from the off-bow of the bigger one.

'British ensign, sir.'

'Then answer at the dip.'

An hour later he was anxiously waiting for Griffiths to return from the fifty-gun *Centurion*, commanded by Captain Rainier.

Drinkwater ran a surreptitious finger round the inside of his stock. He could not understand why, in the heat of the Red Sea, the Royal Navy could not relax its formality sufficiently to allow officers to remove their broadcloth coats when dining with their seniors. After all, this moment, when the humidor of cheroots followed the decanter of port round the table, was tacitly licensed for informality.

They were listening to an anecdote concerning the social life of Bombay told by *Centurion*'s first lieutenant. It was an irreverent story and concerned a general officer in the East India Company's service whose appetite for women was preserved within strictly formal bounds: '. . . and then, sir, when the nautch-girl threw her legs round him and displayed a certain amount of enthusiasm for the old boy, d'you see, he ceased his exertions and glared down at her; "any more of this familiarity," the old bastard said, "and this coupling's off"'!'

The easy laughter of *Centurion*'s officers was joined by that of the young commander of the eighteen-gun brig *Albatross*, a man more than ten years Drinkwater's junior. It seemed that all these officers from the India station led a life of voluptuous ease and licence. It suddenly rankled Nathaniel that their partners with Duncan in the grey North Sea, with St Vincent off Cadiz and with Nelson in the Mediterranean led a different life. He thought of the rock off Ushant and of the storm-lashed squadron that kept a ceaseless watch on Brest and, in the smoky heat of Captain Rainier's cabin, had a sudden poignant urge to be part of that windy scene, where the rain squalls swept like curtains across the sky, obscuring the reefs that waited impassively to leeward of the lumbering divisions of British watchdogs. This effete bunch of well-laundered, red-faced hedonists made Drinkwater feel uncomfortable, offended his puritan sensibilities. It was as if over-long exposure to the heady tropical beauty of Indian nights had affected them with moon-madness.

Neither had Griffiths forgotten his duty, as the slight edge of sarcasm in his voice implied.

'*Duw*, sir, 'tis a wonder you sallied so far from home with such delights to keep you at Bombay. May one enquire of your intentions?'

'Of course, Captain,' said Rainier, a large fleshy man with an expansive manner who appeared like an Indian Buddha surrounded by blue cheroot smoke. 'The news we had from Nelson, both from Duval and yourself, is what brings me to carry out the present reconnaissance of the Red Sea.'

'And effecting a junction with Admiral Blankett, sir?'

The captain shrugged. He did not seem eager to combine his force with Blankett's. Yet if he did the Red Sea squadron would almost certainly be sufficient to bottle up the Straits of Bab el Mandeb, locate and destroy whatever ship Santhonax had at his command.

'Blankett's whereabouts are somewhat unknown. My own instructions are clear. I am to determine the extent of French military action in Egypt relative to a descent upon India. That is all.' It was clear to Drinkwater that the nautch-girls of Bombay sang a sweeter song than the sirens lurking on the imperfectly known reefs of the Red Sea.

Rainier exhaled elaborately, indolently watching the three concentric smoke rings waft slowly towards the deckhead with obvious satisfaction.

'Oh bravo, sir,' breathed Adams sycophantically, giving Drinkwater a clue to his early promotion. Rainier raised his fingers in a gesture of unconcern that seemed not to warrant a shrug of the shoulders. 'I think the matter of little moment, 'tis but in the nature of an excursion.' He caught sight of Griffiths's frown. 'Oh, I know, Captain Griffiths, you come panting from the battlefields of Europe, lathered with the sweat of your own efforts, your energy is not the plague, you know. It is not contagious. We have our own way of attending to the King's business out here. We are not unaware that Tippoo Sahib, the Sultan of Mysore,' he added for the benefit of the new arrivals from England, 'is raising rebellion against us. We even have information that Bonaparte himself has been in contact with him. But I am not of the opinion any great risk attends the matter.'

Rainier drew heavily upon the cheroot and a comfortable little ripple of self-satisfaction went round the table amongst the officers of the two ships.

'I wish I shared your confidence, sir,' Griffiths said.

'Oh, come, sir,' put in Adams, 'the French are not here in force. Why, how many ships does Blankett have, eh?' Adams turned to the only non-uniformed figure at the table, strange in civilian clothing a decade out of fashion.

'He has three sixty-fours,' said Wrinch, '*America*, *Stately* and *Ruby*. The two first named were due home, the third on a cruise. He has two frigates, *Daedalus* and *Fox* with the sloop *Echo*. She too is due home.'

'You see, Griffiths,' said Adams, 'that is a sizeable squadron.'

'If it is all together,' growled Griffiths unconvinced.

Rainier seemed to want to terminate the argument.

'Come Griffiths, it is not as though we are up against Suffren, is

485

it?' The captain muttered through his fist as he picked at a sliver of mutton lodged irritatingly in his molars. 'Eh?'

'The French commander is a pupil of Suffren, sir. He is well-known to my first lieutenant and myself, sir. A true corsair, cunning as a fox, dangerous and resourceful. Not a man to underestimate.' Griffith's voice was low and penetrating.

'How come that you know him, sir?' enquired *Centurion*'s captain of marines.

Griffiths outlined the tasks assigned to the twelve-gun cutter *Kestrel* during her special service on the coasts of France and Holland. He spoke of how they had come into conflict with the machinations of Capitaine Edouard Santhonax, how they had tracked him from the coves of France to the sandy beaches of Noord Holland and how Drinkwater had finally captured him during the bloody afternoon of Camperdown. He told them of the brutal murder of the British agent, Major Brown, taken in civilian clothing and strung up on a gibbet above the battery at Kijkduin in full view of the blockading squadron. As his voice rose and fell, assembling the sentences of his account he compelled them all to listen, straightening the supercilious mouth of Commander Charles Adams. '. . . And so gentlemen, Santhonax contrived to escape, devil take him, by what means I do not know, and if this French army in Egypt is as powerful and as dangerous as Admiral Nelson seemed to think, then *myndiawl*, you should be cautioned against this man.' A silence followed broken at last by Rainier.

'That was bardic, captain, truly bardic,' said Rainier dismissively, taking snuff.

'Captain Griffiths is right, sir,' put in Wrinch at a moment when Drinkwater sensed Rainier wished to conclude matters. 'Santhonax is taking native craft, perhaps to use as transports to India, perhaps to prevent the transfer of the faithful from the Hejaz across the Red Sea to Kosseir. These "Meccan" reinforcements have been told that they have but to shake a Frenchman to dislodge the gold dust from his clothes. They are flocking to join Murad Bey by way of the caravan route to Qena. Murad,' he added with the same condescension as had been used to explain Tippoo Sahib to the uninitiated, 'is a Circassian who commands the Mameluke forces in Upper Egypt. Now, although Desaix has beaten him and scattered his forces,

Murad is, in reality, undefeated. To bring him to his knees Desaix must strangle his reinforcements from Arabia either by taking the dhows at sea, or by taking Kosseir. If this is done then additional tariffs will be levied on trade from Arabia, as Bon is already doing at Suez on the trade from Yambo and Jeddah. Bonaparte's government in Cairo is already said to be much pressed for cash and driven to all manner of expedients to raise it.'

'And do you think Santhonax and Desaix could concert their actions to the necessary degree?' asked Rainier at last, disquieted despite himself by the turn the conversation had taken.

'Indeed, sir. Men have done such things. Egypt is ungovernable, of course. It may well be that the French will push on to India. That would be more prestigious for them than ultimate retreat.'

'Do you think prestige would outweigh military sense?' sneered Adams.

'In France,' retorted Wrinch coolly, 'they have just undergone a revolution caused by inferiors revolting that they may be equal. Equals, like Bonaparte and Desaix, Captain Adams, revolt in order that they may be superior. Such is the state of mind that creates, and is created by, revolutions.'

'That is sophistry, sir,' bridled the commander flushing.

'That is Aristotle, sir,' replied Wrinch icily.

An uncomfortable silence fell on the table. Then Wrinch went on.

'By June the wind in the Red Sea will be predominantly from the north. Often this northerly wind reaches as far south as Perim and lasts until August. A *sambuk* goes excellent well down wind, a *baghala* could carry a battery of horse artillery or three companies of infantry. In the Arabian Sea from May to September the monsoon is favourable for a fast passage, if an uncomfortable one.'

'Ah,' interjected Adams, at last able to put a technical obstacle in front of Wrinch, 'but you cannot land at Bombay or on the Malabar coast during the south-west monsoon.'

Wrinch raised an eyebrow. 'Even a Frenchman may round Cape Comorin, Captain. They may still have friends in Pondicherry and it is not many miles from there to Mysore.'

Rainier had had enough. He rose. 'We sail in two days, gentlemen.'

'Am I to join you, sir?' asked Griffiths.

'No, Griffiths. Do you stay here and wait for Blankett. You are possessed of all the facts and can best acquaint the admiral of 'em. Your orders from Nelson were explicit. You have managed to convince me that perhaps I must look a little further into the matter, damn you.'

So *Hellebore* continued to wait. Having, as Appleby put it, sped with the wings of Hermes half way round the world, they had now to acquire the patience of Job. Griffiths spent less time ashore, apparently happier now that Rainier had gone north. But it was not only this that had relaxed the man. The true reason was revealed one night over a more frugal and less formal meal than that enjoyed aboard *Centurion*. In the cabin of *Hellebore* the brig's officers dined off mutton, of which there was a good supply in Mocha, and drank their madeira with dark coffee and sweet dates, listening to the reason for Griffiths's change.

'To be without pain, gentlemen, is like a rebirth. Mr Strangford Wrinch is a man of many parts. You have seen only one side of him; that of a gossiping coffee merchant who keeps a kind of court in Mocha. In fact he is much more than that. He has journeyed into the interior and tells of mysterious cities long deserted by their inhabitants. He is a hadji who has twice been where it is not permitted for an infidel to go. He has fought in three Arab wars, is an expert in mathematics, astronomy and Arab literature, writes verses in Arabic and keeps a flight of sakers worthy of a prince . . .' He paused and Drinkwater heard Rogers mutter a reference to boys. If Griffiths heard it he ignored it, fixing Appleby with a stare. 'And he has some medical knowledge.'

As if on cue Appleby snorted. 'You are going to tell me he knows a few nostrums, sir,' the surgeon said archly.

'Indeed not. I am going to tell you he knows a great deal. That he can cauterize a wound with hot oil, or sear the back with hot irons to cure rheumatism. Furthermore for open wounds an application of rancid butter or cow dung . . .'

'Cow dung?' Appleby's head shot up in disbelief, his chins quivering. Rogers was laughing silently as if this revelation proved his private theory that Griffiths was mad. Griffiths ignored him, obviously enjoying Appleby's scepticism.

'Just so, Mr Appleby. An application of cow dung, see, possesses certain properties which enable a wound to heal cleanly.'

Behind his hand Rogers muttered, 'No wonder there are so many flies . . . god-damned cow shit, for Christ's sake.' Mr Dalziell began to giggle and even the loyal Quilhampton found it impossible to resist. The sniggers spread to uncontrollable open laughter to which Appleby succumbed.

Drinkwater coughed loudly, mindful of a first lieutenant's duty. 'And this cure for your pain, sir, was that one of these, h'hm extreme and, er . . . h'hm unusual remedies?'

Griffiths turned towards Drinkwater, a mildly benevolent smile on his face. He shook his head, his eyes twinkling beneath their bushy eyebrows. 'For the gout, Mr Drinkwater, an affliction long considered by the best *English* brains as incurable, Mr Wrinch prescribed crocus bulbs and seeds . . .'

'Crocus bulbs . . .!' guffawed Rogers whose mirth was past rational control. The tears streamed down the faces of the midshipmen and even Appleby was too stunned to offer resistance to this challenge to *English* medicine.

'And you are quite without pain?' asked Drinkwater, controlling himself with difficulty.

'Quite, my dear Nathaniel. Fit enough to finish the task that brought us here.'

At the beginning of May Blankett arrived at Mocha having exchanged his flag into the *Leopard*, newly arrived from England. He had with him *Daedalus* and *Fox*. They had swept the Red Sea and the Gulf of Aden without discovering Santhonax. Off Guardafui Blankett had transferred into *Leopard* and sent the fourth-rates home. He was disinclined to listen to the dire warnings of Griffiths, not admitting the argument that he had not only failed to find the French but had missed Rainier. Annoyed, Griffiths returned to *Hellebore* and fumed like Achilles in his tent. Then, a week later Rainier returned. He had penetrated as far as Suez and bombarded the place. Although the French army was there no ships were to be seen and it was said that *Centurion* was the first ship of force seen before the town.

'That,' said Appleby, 'is a piece of conceit I mislike. I dare say Egyptian ships of force were off Suez while Rainier's ancestors were farting in caves.'

'Ah, but not with eighteen-pounders in their batteries,' said Drinkwater laughing, 'cannon are a powerful argument to revise history.'

'Pah! A matter of mere comparisons.'

'Like the ingredients of medicines, eh?' grinned Drinkwater at the surgeon.

Convinced that the French threat was illusory Rainier departed for India, leaving *Hellebore* to the mercies of Blankett. After his exertions the rear-admiral was not inclined to cruise further. He took himself to Wrinch's house to *keyf* and dally with a seraglio of houris while his squadron settled down to wait. Though for what, no-one seemed quite certain.

'Boat approaching, sir. Looks like that fellow Sinbad.' Quilhampton interrupted the first lieutenant who had had the carpenter make a small portable desk for him on deck where, beneath the quarter-deck awning, the breeze ruffled his shirt and made the intolerable paperwork that was part of his duty a trifle more bearable.

'Sinbad?'

'That damned Arab Yusef ben Ibrahim, sir!' Drinkwater looked up. It was a great pity that idleness was affecting Mr Quilhampton. The contempt the meanest of *Hellebore*'s people felt for the local population struck Drinkwater as quite incomprehensible. Perhaps it was a result of their being cooped up on board, but there was little contemptible about Yusef ben Ibrahim. A striking figure with the hawk-like good looks of his race who could handle his rakish *sambuk* with a skill that compelled admiration.

'Go and inform the captain, Mr Q.' Ben Ibrahim had assumed the duty of chief messenger between Wrinch and Griffiths now that Blankett's residence precluded Griffiths's presence. The Arab clambered over the rail. He salaamed at Drinkwater and handed over a sealed letter. Drinkwater bowed as he took it straightening up to see three men turning sheepishly back to their work while Mr Dalziell insolently essayed a bow himself.

'Bosun's mate,' Drinkwater called sharply, 'I desire you to keep those men at their duty or I will be obliged to teach 'em better manners. Mr Dalziell you will be mastheaded until sunset.' He turned away and went below. Griffiths read the letter then handed it back to

Drinkwater. 'Read it,' he said transferring his attention to the chart before him.

My Dear Madoc, [Drinkwater read] *I am writing to you as I doubt that blockhead Blankett will take alarm from what I have learned. It occurs to me that since you have no written instructions from the admiral you might still consider yourself under Nelson's orders. Although my official powers are limited, my influence is not. I can offer a considerable measure of protection in case of trouble with your superior.*

I have received news from Upper Egypt that Desaix is everywhere and Murad's force is scattered. This is confusing. What is certain is that General Belliard has occupied Kosseir and Murad's reinforcements from the Hejaz are choked. Also the bearer, Ben Ibrahim, has sighted French ships in the Gulf of Aqaba and at Kosseir. I am certain our quarry is accumulating dhows at Kosseir for Bonaparte or Desaix to proceed against India.

I shall exert pressure upon the admiral but, I beg you my dear Madoc, to go and cruise northwards with your brig. Even now Blankett snores upon my divan but I propose to wake him to his duty. I know his ships have yet still to water and anticipate he will yet delay. If you regard this Santhonax as dangerous, now is the time to locate him.

[The letter was signed] Strangford W.

Drinkwater looked up at Griffiths. 'I warned them both, damn them.' Griffiths beckoned Drinkwater over to the chart. The long sleeve of the Red Sea ran almost north to south. At its head in a gesture of vulgar contempt as if refusing to link up with the Mediterranean at the last minute, the two fingers of the Gulfs of Aqaba and Suez were divided by the mountains of Sinai.

Griffiths moved his finger up to the Gulf of Aqaba. 'These two numbskulls scoured the Egyptian coast while Santhonax hid round the corner and snapped up potential transports like a fox does chickens. *Duw bach*, what fools these Englishmen are . . .'

Drinkwater smiled ruefully. 'Not quite all, sir. Nelson's an Englishman, he could see clearly enough.'

Drinkwater put down the letter, seeing the postscript.

Take Yusuf and his dhow with you. I have instructed him to go as your eyes and ears. Though he does not speak English he understands the situation.

'Send that Arab down and pass word to get the spring off the cable. We'll slip an hour after dark. Send Lestock to me and have the water casks topped off.'

'With the greatest of pleasure, sir.' Drinkwater left the cabin eagerly.

Winging the Eagle

The favourable southerly breeze left them in the region of sixteen degrees north and they worked patiently through the belt of variables for a hundred miles before picking up the northern wind. Their passage became a long beat to windward with Yusuf ben Ibrahim laughing at their clumsy progress from his graceful and weatherly *sambuk*. But the wind, though foul, was fresh and cooling while the spray that swept over the weather bow sparkled in the sunshine and gave the occasion a yachting atmosphere. North of Jeddah they encountered several large dhows which Yusuf investigated, shepherding them alongside the brig. They were seen to be full of green-turbanned 'Meccans' who waved enthusiastically, having proclaimed a *jihad* against the infidel army of Desaix and Moallem Jacob.

'They say,' said Griffiths watching them through his glass, 'that Murad Bey deploys them in front of his Mameluke cavalry as a breastwork. Have the men give the poor devils three cheers.'

Sheepishly the Hellebores on deck raised a cheer for their expendable allies. The warlike enthusiasm of the 'Meccans' left an indelible impression of great events taking place over the horizon to the west; of the strength of Islam that could summon up such zealous cannon fodder and of the energy of French republicanism that it could raise such a ferment in this remote corner of the world.

They beat on to the north, passing the reef discovered for the Royal Navy by the frigate *Daedalus*, but they saw no sign of the tricolour of France. Griffiths declined to put into Kosseir until their southward passage, assuming Santhonax and his frigate might be there in overwhelming force.

'No, Mr Drinkwater, first we will reconnoitre the Gulf of Aqaba then cross from Ras Muhammad to the west coast and pass Kosseir with a favourable wind. I have no desire to meet our friend at anything but an advantage.'

Both of them wondered what would be the outcome if Santhonax was elsewhere.

Two days later they were off Ras Muhammad at the southern extremity of the Sinai peninsula. The land closed in upon them, the dun coloured landscape rising in row upon row of peaks that lay impassive under the blue skies and sunshine of noon and were transferred at sunrise and sunset into ruddy spines and deep purple gullies. Between this forbidding barrier the Gulf opened up, a deep blue channel of white-capped sea over which the wind funnelled with gale force.

Regarding this cradle of religions, Appleby observed wonderingly. 'You can imagine Moses striking those rocks and Almighty God handing down the commandments from such a place . . .' Robbed of his usual pomposity Appleby seemed reduced to a state of awe.

But if this grim landscape failed to impress the majority of *Hellebore*'s people, daylight the following morning had a different impact. From the masthead the news of several ships to windward included the intelligence that one was the square sail of a European vessel. There was no doubt that there was a French warship in the offing, though of what force they had yet to discover.

'Get aloft Nathaniel,' growled Griffiths anxiously and Drinkwater went forward and swung himself into the foremast shrouds. Around him *Hellebore*'s deck swarmed with activity as the men prepared for action.

At the topgallant doubling the wind was distinctly chilly. Stokeley was the lookout and he pointed the newcomers out. Settling himself against the exaggerated motion of the brig Drinkwater levelled his glass to larboard and caught the image of a dhow in the lens. There were five such craft being convoyed south by the warship. He searched the latter for details to determine her size. He counted her mastheads: there were three. A ship rigged corvette or a frigate? He transferred his attention to the hull. At this angle it was difficult to say as the enemy approached them, yawing slightly, a bone of white water in her teeth, but there was simplicity about her bow that inclined Drinkwater to dismiss his worst fears. He descended to the deck.

'I believe her to be a ship-sloop, sir, say about twenty guns.'

'Very well.' Griffiths paused and studied the approaching dhows. 'D'you think they're fitted with teeth or are they under convoy for Kosseir or Suez?' He did not wait for an answer, glancing astern at the supporting *sambuk* of Ben Ibrahim. 'We'll engage, Mr Drinkwater, take the topgallants off her and hoist French colours.' Drinkwater acknowledged the order and turned away while Griffiths bellowed forward for all to hear. 'Mr Rogers! Load canister on ball, run your larboard guns to the sills and secure them! Keep your ports closed and all the larbowlines to cheer as we pass the Frenchman, all except the gun captains who are to lay their pieces at the horizon and fire on command.' He lowered his voice. 'Mr Lestock, have a quartermaster ready to hoist British colours the moment I say, and men at the braces below the bulwarks. I shall wear to starboard then cross his stern.' Griffiths stood beside the men at the wheel. Drinkwater returned from amidships, casting his eyes aloft where the topgallants flogged impotently in their bunt-lines. The topmen were spreading out along the yards. Already *Hellebore* began her deception, peacefully clewing up her topgallants as she waited for her 'friend' to approach. '*Duw*', Nathaniel, tell them not to be so damned fast aloft.'

Drinkwater grinned and raised the speaking trumpet.

'Fore t'gallant there, take your time, you are supposed to be Frenchmen!' He could see from the attitudes of the men aloft who shouted remarks to their mates on the main topgallant that the business amused them. The obvious high spirits and exaggerated pantomime that followed this order spoke of a soaring morale amongst the hands at the prospect of action. Battle, conducted in such a spirit in such a breeze and in such brilliant sunshine could not fail to be exhilarating.

'That's better,' nodded Griffiths approvingly. 'Take station on the poop, Mr Drinkwater, when he is abeam I shall open fire then wear downwind. It means exposing the stern but I doubt he'll take advantage of it. Wave your hat as we pass, *bach*, do your best to look French.'

Rogers came aft and reported the larboard battery ready as directed.

Drinkwater wondered if the French squadron included a brig like themselves. If not then they were going to look decidedly foolish in a quarter of an hour. Astern of them Yusuf ben Ibrahim was dropping into *Hellebore*'s wake. He would be mystified as to their intentions unless he guessed from the tricolour now snapping out over the quarter. Yusuf might ruin their deception but then he might also enhance it, appearing to the approaching Frenchman like his own captured dhows. Drinkwater shivered slightly in his shirt-sleeves. He waited impatiently for the order to open fire. Drinkwater motioned to the men at the after starboard guns. 'Stand by to brail in the spanker there!'

He saw them grin, glad of something to do while their mates in the larboard battery went into action.

The dhows ahead had dropped back while the French corvette came on suspiciously, a private signal flying from her foremast. Drinkwater saw Mr Quilhampton instructed to hoist a string of meaningless bunting. As the enemy signal flew almost directly towards them a little confusion might be permitted. The two vessels were a mile apart now, the Frenchman broad on *Hellebore*'s larboard bow. The brig had slowed without her topgallants and she lay in wait for her opponent, her guns still hidden and several of the larbowlines hanging casually in the rigging waving.

To the Frenchman the brig lay off his bow, supinely furling her upper sails, men congregating about her decks while he came down before the wind to pass close under the stranger's stern where he could take her if she ultimately proved to be an enemy. But no enemy, least of all a British captain, would lay so passively before a windward foe. It was a deception lent piquancy by the remoteness of their location, and the belief, briefly true, that Egypt was a possession of France.

Drinkwater saw the corvette take in her own topgallants, as if about to round to and hail her 'compatriot'. His heart was thumping with excitement. He knew in a moment the weeks of waiting, of struggling off the Cape, of listening to the sweaty moanings of the members of the gunroom, of solving the problem of the hands, of Dalziell and of Catherine Best, would all dissolve in the drug-like excitement of action. There was also the possibility that they might find a permanent solution in death. He felt dreadfully exposed as fear and exhilaration fought for possession of him. He remembered an old promise to Elizabeth that he would be circumspect and run no needless risk. The recollection brought a rueful smile to his face.

The gun crew waiting at the mainmast fiferails for his order nudged one another and grinned too, taking encouragement from Drinkwater's apparent eagerness, seeing in his introspection their own relief at imminent action. For them action meant an interruption of the endless round of drudgery, of hauling and pumping that was their life, an opportunity to throw off the fear of the lash, to swear and kill to their heart's content.

'Brail in the spanker!' Drinkwater nodded to the men watching him. The outhaul was started and the huge sail billowed, flapped and was drawn to the mast, by the helm, Griffiths corrected the rudder for that loss of pressure aft. Drinkwater took off his hat and waved it with assumed Gallic enthusiasm about his head.

'Dip the ensign,' he ordered and the quartermaster at the peak halliards lowered the tricolour a fathom. Perhaps, by such a refinement, if the enemy captain did not expect to see a French brig hereabouts, he might be fooled into thinking it was a new arrival paying her respects to an old Red Sea hand.

The enemy ship was very close now. Men could be seen on her topgallant yards looking curiously across at them and Drinkwater heard a thin cry of 'Bonjour mes enfants.'

From the main topgallant he heard the ever resourceful Tregembo yell back 'Vive la République!'

The cheer that erupted from the enemy was echoed by the Hellebores whose joy at achieving such a complete deception lent their mad excitement a true imitation of revolutionary fervour.

'Braces there,' growled Griffiths in a low and penetrating voice. Drinkwater saw a French officer on the quarter-rail bowing. He swept his own hat across his chest in response. 'Bonne chance!' he yelled across the diminishing gap between them. An angle of sixty degrees lay between the ships, with every one of Hellebore's guns levelled at that crowded rail.

'Colours!'

Griffiths threw aside the mask.

Above their heads Old Glory replaced the half lowered tricolour. The gunports snapped open.

'Fire!'

The gun captains jerked their lanyards as the crews leapt back to the deck and grabbed rammers, swabs and buckets. The charring of the port lintels was quickly extinguished as the men toiled to reload.

'Up helm! Braces there! Wear ship!'

Hellebore turned, pointing her vulnerable stern at the Frenchman but avoiding the ignominious possibility of failing to tack. Griffiths had gambled on his plan working and, had it not done so, he had only to stand on and carry himself swiftly out of range. But a single glance astern told the ruse had been complete. Details were obscure but amidships the corvette's rail was a splintered and jagged shambles. The human wreckage behind that smashed timber could be imagined.

'Aloft there, let fall! Let fall!' Tregembo and his mates slipped the topgallant gaskets and the sails fell in folds.

'Leggo bunt and clewlines there! Sheet home!'

Hellebore was before the wind and still turning, bringing the wind first astern and then round, broad on the starboard quarter. Drinkwater descended from the tiny poop. 'The advantage of surprise, sir,' he said.

Griffiths nodded, his mouth suppressing a grim smile of self-congratulation. 'Do unto others, Mr Drinkwater, before they do unto you . . . clew up the foresail, I intend to rake.'

'Aye, aye, sir. D'you intend boarding?' Griffiths shook his head.

'Too great a risk of heavy casualties. Flesh wounds'll be the very devil to heal in this climate. No, we'll stand off and pound him.' Griffiths nodded to the distant Ben Ibrahim. 'He's playing a waiting game.'

They clewed up the forecourse as they made to cut across the corvette's stern. She was still running before the wind though many ropes had been severed at the pin rails on deck. Smoke appeared from her guns now as she attempted to halt the Nemesis that bore relentlessly down upon her. Then they were suddenly very close to her, surging across her stern, masking her from the wind. Rogers was shouting and running aft, commanding each gun to fire as it bore into the corvette's stern. Drinkwater read *La Torride* a split second before it was blown to atoms, saw the crown glass windows of her cabin shatter and the neat carvings about her quarters disintegrate into splinters. A row of men with pistols and muskets fired at the British ship as she rushed past and the hat that he had so insouciantly waved but a few moments ago was torn from his head. He aimed his own pistols, his mouth pulled back in a grimace. Then Griffiths was putting *Hellebore* on a parallel course with the Frenchman.

'Starbowlines to larboard!' Drinkwater roared. As if eagerly awaiting the call the frustrated men from the starboard guns hopped nimbly across the deck to fling their weight on the tackles of the larboard six pounders.

La Torride fired her starboard battery as the brig overtook and a storm of shot poured across *Hellebore*'s deck. Men were flung back clutching their heads and bellies. One stood staring at a vacant arm socket and from aloft a body fell on the deck with an obscene impact.

But the surprise of *Hellebore*'s manoeuvre had robbed the French of their greater weight of metal. The sudden appearance of a British cruiser had utterly surprised them, the more particularly as they had known Blankett's squadron did not include a brig. To this psychological advantage the British had added that first devastating broadside. The lethal spray of canister combined with the round shot to produce an appalling effect. The destructive power of the shot was augmented by the splinters it caused while the range concentrated its effect. French resistance was robbed of its edge. Half of *La Torride*'s gun crews were already dead or wounded, her wheel was shot away, her rudder stock split and her commander mortally wounded in the space of a few minutes.

Hellebore ran past her adversary as *La Torride* swung to starboard, broaching into the trough of the sea, out of control. *Hellebore* also swung to avoid being raked and came round to starboard, tacking through the wind and, once on the larboard tack, running back on to her victim. As the yards were secured there was a mad rush across the deck where the starbowlines returned to their guns.

'Maximum elevation there!' yelled Drinkwater, judging the angle of heel as the brig lay over to the wind. 'Cripple her, Rogers!' roared Griffiths and Drinkwater leapt at the after guns to pull out the quoins. Spinning round he grabbed a tiny powder monkey. 'Boy! Get Mr Trussel to send up some bar shot.'

But *La Torride* had recovered slightly, her men were not yet finished. Under her first lieutenant she had had the time to prepare another broadside for the British.

'Heel's too much, sir,' shouted Drinkwater straightening up from sighting along a gun barrel. 'Leggo t'gallant sheets!'

The pressure at her mastheads eased slightly and the brig came nearer the vertical as she sped past *La Torride*. Both ships fired their broadsides simultaneously. Amidships a gun was dismounted at the moment of discharge with a huge crash. Men fell back and blood spurted from the a dozen wounds while splinters of wood flew about. Griffiths was spun round by a musket ball that left his single epaulette hanging drunkenly from his shoulder. Drinkwater was hit by a splinter which lanced across his face, missing his eye and cheek and nicking his right ear. Then *Hellebore* was past and preparing to tack again. In the temporary respite Drinkwater supervised clearing the deck of wounded, while Lestock hauled the yards. He was aware of a large number of casualties, of blood staining the sanded planks in the waist but also of an unshaken band of men who toiled to make their lethal and brutish artillery ready for another broadside.

La Torride had had enough. A cheer from first one gun's crew then another spread along *Hellbore*'s deck. Looking up Drinkwater saw the tricolour that lay over the corvette's shattered rail. Her foremast had gone by the board.

'Take possession, Mr Drinkwater; Mr Lestock, heave to.' Drinkwater went to inspect the boats and found the cutter serviceable. Griffiths came up to him.

'I want neither prisoners nor prize, Nathaniel. Toss her guns overboard and order an officer aboard her as hostage against her good conduct. They may proceed to Suez if they are able.'

'Aye, aye, sir.'

'I think we have winged the eagle, Nathaniel,' he added confidentially. Drinkwater grinned back. 'Indeed sir, I believe you are right.'

Drinkwater threw a leg over the rail to descend to the cutter bobbing alongside.

'Knocked the bollocks of that Froggie, eh, Drinkwater?' said Rogers, smiling broadly, his tendency to criticise temporarily quiescent.

'Then perhaps you will consider our commander less senile than you are wont to assert.'

Drinkwater and his party scrambled over the side of the corvette to the disquieting crackle of musketry and the shouts and screams of intense fighting. The sight that met their eyes was astonishing. Amid the ruin of her upper deck, covered as it was by the wreckage of her foremast, broken spars and torn sails, amid the tangled festoons of rope, amid the bodies of her dead and the writhing tortures of her wounded *La Torride*'s survivors fought a furious hand to hand action with Yusuf ben Ibrahim and his men. The Arab's *sambuk* had held off, awaiting the outcome, but was now alongside the defeated corvette her men boarding in search of loot. Catching sight of the British a young *aspirant* waved frantically at the folds of the tricolour lying over the stern.

'M'sieur . . . J'implore . . . m'aidez . . .' The boy looked wildly round, seeing Drinkwater's bare sword blade, drawn in self defence at what he might find aboard the prize. The young officer had fallen at his feet in terror and Drinkwater put a calming hand upon his shoulder, but even so it was several minutes before the combined bullying of Drinkwater and his men had beaten off the fury of the Arabs.

Yusuf himself seemed angry at Drinkwater's refusal to allow his men to butcher the French. 'In'sh Allah,' he said shrugging, his eyes wild with the effects of hashish: 'It is the will of Allah.'

Drinkwater shook his head 'Bism' Allah,' he said in the only Arabic he knew, 'In the name of God, Emir Yusuf, the dhows . . .' he conveyed the gift of the captured dhows with dramatic gestures, knowing Griffiths was not interested in prizes so far from home. God knew there were enough Frenchmen aboard them to satisfy Yusuf's bloodlust without putting the corvette's crew to the sword. 'You,' he said pointing at Yusuf's chest, 'take dhows. This,' he said stabbing a finger at the deck of *La Torride* and to the French cadet, 'this belongs to me . . .' he waved his arm in a circular motion ending up pointing at his own chest.

To Drinkwater's surprise Yusuf rocked back on his heels and roared with laughter. Several members of his crew that had come menacingly to his support during the argument joined the laughter, after Yusuf had addressed a stream of Arabic at them. Yusuf made an aggressively sexual gesture with his forearm, tousled the cadet's hair and slapped the amazed Drinkwater upon the back. Then, still laughing, he took himself off, followed by his men who made a series of good naturedly obscene gestures in Drinkwater's direction.

Beneath his tan Nathaniel flushed at the implication. 'Dirty bastards, zur,' muttered Tregembo loyally but Drinkwater was not to escape so lightly. To his further embarrassment the young Frenchman, who was trying to smile while tears made furrows through the powder grime upon his face, embraced him.

Drinkwater shook the youth off. '*Vôtre capitaine? Où est vôtre capitaine?*' he asked. The reply was a torrent of French, incomprehensible to Drinkwater but containing what he took to be names, each succeeded by the word *mort*, from which he deduced that most of *La Torride*'s officers were either dead or dying. Certainly no other uniformed figure appeared. Leaving the *aspirant* to muster his crew and draw up a list of the casualties Drinkwater made a brief inspection of the ship before returning to *Hellebore*.

'She's the ship corvette *La Torride* of the Rochefort squadron, sir, hulled in several places and unmanageable with her steering destroyed . . .' He went on to outline the shambles he had found. When he had finished Griffiths pursed his lips and thought for a moment.

'If we can get a dhow back from Ben Ibrahim we'll let them go, *bach*, on parole for Suez. Take out of her powder, any useful shot, stores, water and rope, I recollect you want rope. In fact ransack her, though no man is to touch an item of personal belongings, we'll leave looting to our Arab friends. Go on, get back to her, quick now. I'll send Rogers and the other boat to requisition a dhow if that pirate has already grabbed them all. Bring back the cadet, he may be more forthcoming than a recalcitrant officer with ideas of his honour.'

There followed a day of back-breaking endeavour in which Drinkwater, with an enthusiasm engendered in first lieutenants when storehouses are thrown open to them, replenished almost every want of the *Hellebore*. On the basis that there were no officers surviving to lay claim to her cabin stores, he judiciously appropriated a quantity of wine which brought a gleam to Trussel's eye comparable to that bestowed on the French powder. Trussel begged

502

Drinkwater for a pair of fine brass chase guns but the condition of the boats and the state of the sea prevented their removal. The operation was carried out despite the sharks that were congregating astern, round the flotilla.

By nightfall, when Drinkwater's weary party finally returned to *Hellebore*, *La Torride* was stripped of useful moveables, an empty shell with smoke issuing from her hatchways and sufficient powder left aboard to dismember her. She blew up and sank an hour later but by then *Hellebore* with her attendant dhows was five miles to the southward, standing towards the Strait of Tiran and the Red Sea.

Leaving the deck to Lestock, Drinkwater stumbled wearily below, called for Merrick to pour him a glass of grog. He was relaxing as Dalziell entered, thrusting the French cadet before him with a vicious shove. He seemed slightly discomfited to find Drinkwater in the gunroom.

'Er, Mr Rogers's orders sir, the captain wants to interview him.' He jerked his head at the dishevelled French youth who looked terrified.

'You may leave him here, Mr Dalziell, and on your return to the deck acquaint Mr Rogers with my desire that he draws up a list of our casualties and brings it to me on completion.'

Dalziell took the muster book from Drinkwater's outstretched hand. Drinkwater motioned the French cadet to a seat and poured him some grog. He saw the boy gag on the spirit then swallow more. Gradually a little colour came to his cheeks.

'*Nom, m'sieur?*' asked Drinkwater in his barbarous French as kindly as he could manage.

'*Je m'appelle Gaston, m'sieur, Gaston Bruilhac, Aspirant de la première classe.*'

'*Comprenez-vous anglais, Gaston?*'

Bruilhac shook his head. Drinkwater grunted, finished the grog and made up his mind. He leaned across the table. '*Mon Capitaine, Gaston, il est très intrépide, n'est pas?*'

Bruilhac nodded. Drinkwater went on, '*Bon. Mon Capitaine . . .*' he struggled, failing to find the words for what he wished to convey. He picked up the pistol he had removed earlier from his belt and pulled back the hammer. Taking Bruilhac's hand he placed it palm down on the table and spread the fingers. 'Bang!' he said suddenly, pointing the weapon at the index finger. He repeated the melodrama for the other three. The colour drained from Bruilhac's face and Drinkwater refilled his grog. '*Courage, mon brave*,' he said, then, as the boy stared wide-eyed over the shaking rim of the beaker, '*Ecoutez-moi, Gaston: vous parlez, eh? Vous parlez beaucoup.*'

As if on cue Griffiths entered with Rogers behind him, bearing the muster book. Drinkwater stood up and snapped 'Attention!' Bruilhac sprang to his feet, rigidly obedient. 'I think he'll talk, sir,' said Drinkwater, quietly handing the pistol to Griffiths. 'Rum will loosen his tongue and I said you'd shoot each of his fingers off in turn if he did not speak.'

Griffiths's white eyebrows shot upwards and a wicked twinkle appeared in his eyes as he turned to the cadet, and the swinging lantern light caught his seamed face. To Bruilhac he seemed the very personification of Drinkwater's imminent threats.

Drinkwater motioned the boy to follow Griffiths into the after cabin. As he closed the door he heard Griffiths begin the interrogation. Words began to pour from the hapless boy. Drinkwater smiled; sometimes it was necessary to be cruel to be kind. He turned to Rogers.

'Well Rogers, what kind of a butcher's bill do we have?'

'Oh, not too bad, bloody shame we blew the prize up. I'd have made a comfortable purse from her.'

Drinkwater withheld a lecture on the impracticability of such a task as getting *La Torride* in order, and contented himself with saying, 'She was a wreck. Now, how many did we lose?'

'Only eleven dead.'

Drinkwater whistled. 'Only? For the love of God . . . what about the wounded?'

'Eighteen slight: flesh wounds, splinters, the usual. I caught a splinter in the cheek.' He turned so that the light caught the ugly jagged line, half bruise, half laceration, that was scabbing in a thick crust. 'You escaped unscathed, I see.'

Drinkwater looked Rogers full in the face, feeling again a strong dislike for the man. He found himself rubbing at a rough congealed mess in his right ear. 'Almost,' he said quietly, 'I was lucky. What about the serious cases?'

Rogers looked down at the muster book. 'Seven, six seamen and Quilhampton.'

'Quilhampton?' asked Drinkwater, a vision of the boy's pretty mother swimming accusingly into his mind's eye. 'What's the matter with him?'

'Oh, a ball took off his hand . . . hey, what's the matter?'

Drinkwater scrambled below to where Appleby had his cockpit at the after end of the hold. Already the stench was noisome. To the creak of the hull and the turbid swirl of bilgewater were added the groans of the wounded and the ramblings of delirium. But it was not only this that made Drinkwater wish to void his stomach. There seemed some sickness in his fate that Providence could pull such an appalling jest upon him.

He paused to allow his eyes to become adjusted to the gloom. He could see the pale figure of Catherine Best straighten up, a beaker in her hand. She came aft, catching sight of the first lieutenant. 'Mr Drinkwater?' she said softly, and in the guttering lamplight her face was once again transfigured. But it was not a beauty that stirred him. He saw for the first time that whatever life had done to this woman, her eyes showed a quality of compassion caused by her suffering.

'Where is Mr Q?' he asked hoarsely. Catherine led him past Tyson who was bent over a man Drinkwater recognised as Gregory, the helmsman who had held the brig before the wind the night they struggled with the broken foreyard. Tyson was easing a tourniquet with a regretful shake of his head. The woman stepped delicately over the bodies that lay grotesquely about the small, low space.

Quilhampton lay on his cloak, his head pillowed on his broad-cloth coat. His breeches stained dark with blood and urine. His left arm extended nine inches below his elbow and termined in a clumsy swathe of bloodstained bandages. His eyelids fluttered and he moved his head distressingly in a shallow delirium. Catherine Best bent to feel the pale sweating forehead. Drinkwater knelt beside the boy and put his hand on the maimed stump. It was very hot. He looked across the twitching body. Catherine's eyes were large with accusation.

Drinkwater rose and stumbled aft, suddenly desperate for the fresh air of the deck. At the ladder he ran into Appleby. The surgeon's apron was stiff with congealed blood. He was wiping his hands on a rag and he reeked of rum. He was quite sober.

'Another glorious victory for His Majesty's arms . . . you will have been to see Quilhampton?' Drinkwater nodded dumbly. 'I think he will live, if it does not rot.' Appleby spat the last word out, as if the words 'putrefy' or 'mortify' were too sophisticated to waste on a butcher like Drinkwater.

Nathaniel made to push past but Appleby stood his ground. 'Send two men to remove that . . . sir,' he said, pointing. Drinkwater turned. A large wooden tub lay in the shadows at the bottom of the ladder. Within it Drinkwater could see the mangled stumps and limbs amputated from Appleby's patients.

'Very well, Mr Appleby, I will attend to the matter.'

Appleby expelled his breath slowly. 'There's a bottle in the gun-room, I'll join you in a moment.' Drinkwater nodded and ascended the ladder.

Griffiths sat in the gunroom, while Rogers poured for both of them. 'The teat of consolation, *annwyl*,' said Griffiths gently, seeing the look in Drinkwater's eyes. 'Santhonax is at Kosseir.'

'Ah,' Drinkwater replied listlessly. The rum reached his belly, uncoiling the tension in him. He stretched his legs and felt them encounter something soft. Looking under the table he saw Bruilhac curled like a puppy and fast asleep.

'He still has all his fingers.'

Drinkwater looked at Griffiths and wondered if the commander knew in what appalling taste his jest was. Griffiths could not yet have seen the casualty list.

'He's lucky,' was all he said in reply.

Kosseir Bay

On the afternoon of 10th August it seemed that Santhonax had surprised them. Anxious glasses trained astern at the two ships foaming
up from the southward while *Hellebore* staggered under a press of
canvas in a desperate claw to windward and safety. The leading
pursuer was indisputably a frigate. Optimists claimed it was *Fox*, the
more cautious Griffiths assumed the worst. Bruilhac had told them
of a third ship in Santhonax's squadron, for whom *Hellebore* had
been taken by the officers of *La Torride*. He was not to be caught by
the same ruse. 'Let the wrecks of others be your seamarks, Mr
Drinkwater,' he said without removing his eye from the long glass.

'She's tacking.' They watched the leading ship come up into the
wind, saw her foresails flatten and the swing of the mainyards. As
she paid off, the foreyards followed suit and the bright spots of
bunting showed from her mastheads.

'British colours and Admiral Blankett's private signal, sir,'
reported Rogers. Her exposed side revealed her as *Fox*.

'It seems you were right, Mr Drinkwater,' said Griffiths drily.
Keeping his men at quarters the commander put *Hellebore* before
the wind and ran down towards his pursuers. They proved to be *Fox*
and *Daedalus*, sent north by Rear-Admiral Blankett who had taken
sufficient alarm from Strangford Wrinch to dispatch Captains Stuart
and Ball without seeing the necessity to come himself and thus forgo
the carnal delights of Mr Wrinch's hospitality.

Griffiths was summoned on board for a council of war, the outcome of which was to attack Kosseir, destroy Santhonax and open
the port to traffic from the Hejaz. French defeat would not only
result in an improvement to the Meccans able to join Murad Bey, but
would enable the British to pre-empt any French attempt upon India

the following year. Returning from the meeting Griffiths also brought back personal news.

A replacement for *Echo* had joined the squadron. The ship-sloop *Hotspur* had brought out mail, news and orders. The latter included a tersely worded instruction that *Hellebore* was to be returned at once to England. Nelson, the author of her present predicament was, it seemed, in disgrace. His euphoric languishing at Naples after Aboukir had been tarnished by the Caraccioli affair and followed by a leisurely return home by way of a circuitous route through Europe during which his conduct with the wife of the British Ambassador to the court of the Two Sicilies was scandalous.

Drinkwater paid scant attention to this gossip, depressed by the realisation that *Hotspur* had brought no letters from Elizabeth. Then Griffiths swiftly recalled him to the present.

'Oh, by the way, Nathaniel, *Hotspur* brought two lieutenants to the station. One is appointed to *Daedalus* and he wished to be remembered to you. He was insistent I convey his felicitations to you.'

An image of the ruddy and diminutive White formed in his mind. Perhaps White had news of Elizabeth! But he checked this sudden hope on the recollection that White would not exchange the quarterdeck of *Victory* for an obscure frigate in an even more obscure corner of the world without an epaulette on his shoulder.

'The gentleman's name, sir?'

'A Welsh one, *bach*. Morris if I recollect right.'

A strong presentiment swept over Drinkwater. From the moment he had jestingly suggested shooting off Bruilhac's fingers and found Quilhampton handless, Providence seemed to have deserted him. The strain of weary months of service manifested itself in this feeling. His worries for Elizabeth stirred his own loneliness. It was a disease endemic among seamen and fate lent it a further twist when he recalled the words Morris had uttered to him years earlier.

Drinkwater had been instrumental in having Mr Midshipman Morris turned out of the frigate *Cyclops* where he had dominated a coterie of bullying sodomites. Morris had threatened revenge even at the earth's extremities. Suddenly Drinkwater seemed engulfed in a web from which he could not escape. The revelation that Dalziell was related to Morris made months earlier seemed now to preface his present apprehension.

On the morning of 14th August 1799 in light airs the brig of war *Hellebore* led Captain Henry Lidgbird Ball's squadron slowly into Kosseir Bay. The indentation of the coast was formed by a headland, a small fort and a mole which protected a large number of native craft gathered inside. More dhows lay anchored in the inner roadstead. Above the fort the tricolour floated listlessly. Of the frigate of Edouard Santhonax there was no sign.

Griffiths swore as he paced up and down the quarterdeck, one ear cocked to hear the leadsman's chant from the chains. Whilst the taking of the dhows and fort were of importance to Ball, only the destruction of Santhonax would satisfy Griffiths.

The men waited round the guns, the sail-trimmers at their stations. Lestock fussed over a rudimentary chart he had copied from *Fox's* as *Hellebore* picked her way slowly inshore. Drinkwater stared at the town through his glass. It was past noon with the sun burning down on them from almost overhead. Drinkwater indicated the dhows.

'Santhonax's fleet of transports, I believe sir.' He handed the glass to Griffiths. The commander swept the yellow shoreline shimmering under the glare. He nodded. 'But that *cythral* Santhonax is nowhere to be seen.' Griffiths cast a glance about him. 'Strike number five the instant the leadsman finds six fathoms, the closer in we get the greater the risk of coral outcrops.'

As if to justify Griffiths's concern *Hellebore* trembled slightly. Griffiths and Drinkwater exchanged glances but even the jittery Lestock seemed not to have noticed the tremor. The leadsman allayed their fears: 'By the mark seven . . . by the deep eight . . . a quarter less eight!'

Hellebore crept onward. 'By the deep six!'

'Strike number five! Braces there! Main topsail to the mast!' The red and white chequered numeral flag fluttered to the deck and the brig lost way as the main yards braced round to back their sails. She ceased her forward motion.

'Let go!' The anchor dropped with a splash as the first gun boomed out from the fort. Unhurriedly the three British ships clapped springs on their cables and traversed to bring their full broadsides on the wretched town. The fire from the fort ceased, as though the gunners, having tried the range, paused to see what the British would do.

Aboard *Hellebore* they waited for Ball's signal to open fire, their own capstan catching a final turn on the spring to align the guns to Griffiths's satisfaction. Drinkwater listened to the stage whispers of the gun crew nearest him.

'Why don't the bastards open fire at us, Jim?'

"Cos they're shit-scared, laddy. Froggies is all the same.'

'Don't be bleeding stupid. They want to save their sodding powder until the brass have stopped pissing about and decide where to station us sitting ducks.'

'It's only a piddling little fort, mates. Bugger all to worry about.'

'But you still save your powder an' bleeding shot, Tosher, you stupid sod.'

'How the hell d'you know?'

'Look if you had to carry the fucking stuff over them mountains behind this dunghill you wouldn't throw the stuff away, now would you, my old cock?'

This debate was interrupted by *Daedalus* opening fire. Her consorts followed suit. The bombardment of Kosseir had begun.

For an hour the men toiled at the guns under a burning sun. The constant concussions killed the wind and when Ball hoisted the signal to cease fire the men slumped exhausted at their pieces or scrabbled for the chained ladle at the scuttlebutt. They tore off their headbands and shook their heads to clear the ringing from their ears, wiping the grimy sweat from their foreheads. In his berth two feet below the now silent cannon, Midshipman Quilhampton writhed, tortured by heat, inflammation and fever. From time to time Catherine Best wiped the heavy perspiration from his brow and desultorily fanned his naked body. Appleby waited for casualties in the cockpit, cooling himself with rum and ignoring the groans of the wounded that had survived their earlier action and now twisted in the stifling, stinking heat of *Hellebore*'s bowels.

Stripped to his shirt sleeves Drinkwater scanned the dun-coloured shore, watching for a response to the flag of truce now at *Daedalus*'s foremasthead. But although the fort's guns had fallen

510

silent the tricolour still hung limply from its staff. No movement could be discerned in the town after a first terrified evacuation of the dhows in the harbour. Drinkwater felt a strong sense of anti-climax. The fort seemed weak, no more than half-a-dozen cannon.

'Old guns installed by the Turks,' observed Lestock.

'Place looks like a heap of camel-shit,' muttered Rogers. They all suffered from a sense of being engaged in an unworthy activity, not least Griffiths.

'A most inglorious proceeding indeed,' he said, disgust filling his dry mouth. And Drinkwater knew the old man considered this a side-show compared with the task of destroying Santhonax himself.

'Commodore's signalling for an officer, sir.' Dalziell reported.

'*Duw* . . . see to it Mr Drinkwater.'

Clambering in at the entry of *Daedalus* Drinkwater was escorted by a cool-looking midshipman to the quarterdeck. He found a lieutenant from *Fox* already there, together with a figure he knew well.

Time had not been kind to Augustus Morris. The years had ravaged his body, the skin drawn over prematurely withered flesh, his stance flaccid, listless in a manner that could not entirely be attributed to the heat. His face bore the marks of a heavy drinker, a tic twitching beneath his right eye. But although time might be remarked in his person and emphasised by his long worn lieutenant's uniform, his eyes, beneath their heavy lids, glittered with a potent malevolence.

There was no time for formalities. Captain Ball turned from a consultation with his sailing master and addressed the three lieutenants.

'Gentlemen, I propose in an hour to hoist the Union at the foremasthead. Upon that signal I require you to take the boats from your ships and attack the native craft exposed in the outer roadstead. You should direct your respective boats to the nearest craft and thereafter concert your efforts as seems best to you. That is all.' Ball turned away dismissively.

'What's the date of your commission, Drinkwater?' asked Hetherington of *Fox*, a small, pinch-faced man with prominent ears.

'October '97.'

'That makes you senior, Morris.'

'It does indeed,' said Morris with relish, never taking his eyes off

511

Drinkwater. 'Mr Drinkwater once outranked me, Hetherington. A temporary matter, d'you know. It is only just that I should have the whip hand now.'

'Well what are we going to do?' enquired the anxious Hetherington who was not much interested in Morris's autobiography.

Morris took his eyes reluctantly off his old enemy and fixed Hetherington with an opaque look that Drinkwater remembered from twenty years earlier. 'Why, just what we have been told, Hetherington. Take the dhows of course. Mr Drinkwater will lead the attack . . .' Drinkwater met his gaze again, reading Morris's intentions quite clearly. Morris turned to Hetherington. 'You may return to your ship.' His hand shot out and restrained Drinkwater who had thought to leave.

'Not you, my dear Nathaniel,' said Morris with heavy sarcasm, his hand gripping viciously upon Drinkwater's right upper arm, twisting the muscle maimed two years earlier by Edouard Santhonax, 'we have an old acquaintance to revive.'

'I think not, Morris,' said Drinkwater coolly as the other dropped his hand.

'Ah, but I order you to stay, there is so much to discuss. Your wife for instance . . .'

Drinkwater froze, suddenly anxious and searching Morris's face for the truth.

'Oh, yes, I have seen her, Nathaniel. Heavy with child too. You have overcome your prudery I see. Unless it was another.' Morris broke out into low laughter as Drinkwater's hand reached for his hanger. Morris shook his head. 'That would be most imprudent.' Drinkwater clenched his fist impotently. 'She looked unwell.'

Drinkwater saw in Morris's expression a cruel delight, such as Yusuf ben Ibrahim had worn as he butchered the Frenchmen of *La Torride*.

Drinkwater opened his mouth to reply but the words were lost in the sudden roar of *Daedalus*'s guns. Ball had hauled down the flag of truce and resumed the bombardment. Spinning on his heel Drinkwater returned to his boat and *Hellebore*.

'Bear off forrard! Give way together!' Drinkwater took the tiller and swung the cutter away under *Hellebore*'s stern. Passing across *Daedalus*'s bow he steadied for the nearest dhow. Looking to starboard he saw Hetherington's boat shoot ahead of *Fox*, then Morris came out from the shelter of *Daedalus*.

'Pull, you lubbers. Let's get this business finished quickly!' The boat's crew were already grimed and sweat-seamed from working the guns in relays, but they lay back on their oars willingly enough. Over their heads shot whined through the sullen air. Drinkwater looked ahead at Kosseir. The town was passing into shadow, purple and umber as the sun westered behind the mountains of the Sharqiya.

They reached the first vessel, a large *baghala*, deserted by her crew. Drinkwater led his men aboard and it was the work of only a few minutes to set her on fire. As they tumbled back into the cutter *Daedalus*'s boat came alongside, a midshipman in charge of her.

'Mr Morris orders you to attack yon dhow, sir.' The youth pointed to a vessel anchored just off the ramshackle mole. Drinkwater swung round to look at the dhow next astern of them. He could see Morris on its deck. No smoke as yet issued from her, though their own target was well ablaze. A dark suspicion crossed Drinkwater's mind as he nodded to the midshipman. 'Very well.'

'Give way . . .' Rounding the burning *baghala*'s bow Drinkwater headed for the mole. They were no more than two hundred yards from the decaying breakwater, their new victim lying midway between.

'Is that match all right?' The gunner's mate in charge of the combustibles blew on the slow match and nodded. 'Aye, sir.'

'Pull, damn you!' growled Drinkwater, seeing for the first time men in blue uniforms running out along the mole and dropping to their knees. They were French sharpshooters, the trailleurs of the 21st Demi-Brigade. The oar looms bent under redoubled effort.

The cutter ran alongside the dhow and the seamen jumped aboard. At the instant they stood on the deck the sharpshooters opened fire. It was long musket range but Drinkwater immediately felt a searing pain across his thigh and looked down to see where a ball had galled him, reddening his breeches. Beside him a man was bowled over as though dead but sat up a few moments later, nursing bruised ribs from a spent musket ball. Drinkwater and his men

513

crawled about the deck, assembling enough combustibles to ignite the dhow, wriggling backwards with the small keg of black powder leaving a trail across the deck. Drinkwater nodded and the gunner's mate blew on his match and touched it to the powder train. The flame sputtered and tracked across the deck, over the coaming and below. Smoke began to writhe out of the dhow's hold.

'Back to the boat!' he called sharply over his shoulder, venturing one last look at the crumbling mud brick of Kosseir's pitiful defences. Overhead the whirr of cannon shot told where the squadron were thundering away, while puffs of dust and little settling disturbances of masonry showed the process of reduction. He scanned the beach that curved away to the left of the town. A few small fishing boats were drawn up on it and the dull green of vegetation showed where a hardy and pitiful cultivation was carried on. Some taller palms grew in a clump by a waterhole. As he ducked again and was about to crawl back to the boat Drinkwater noticed something else, something that brought him to his feet in a wild leap for the cutter. Round the end of the mole a boat was pulling vigorously towards them.

The cutter was shoved off from the burning dhow and pulled clear of its shelter. Shot dropped round them and a brief glance astern showed the enemy boat no more than thirty yards astern.

'She's closin' on us, sir,' muttered the man at stroke oak nodding astern. Drinkwater's back felt vulnerable. He looked over his shoulder and stared down the muzzle of a swivel gun. The puff of smoke that followed made his heart skip and he felt the ball hit the transom. Drinkwater looked down to see the dark swirl of water beneath him.

Twilight was increasing by the minute and they had no hope of reaching the brig before being overtaken or sinking. They had a single chance.

'Hold water all! Oars and cutlasses!'

The enemy boat came on and Drinkwater pulled a pistol from his belt. He laid the weapon on one of the gunners and saw the man stagger, a hand to his shoulder. A second later the two boats ground together.

Lent coolness by desperation, Drinkwater grabbed the gunwhale of the enemy boat. Beneath his feet *Hellebore*'s cutter felt sluggish and low as behind him the crew stumbled aft. Swiping upwards with his hanger Drinkwater leapt aboard the French boat. Manning the swivel were three artillerymen from Desaix's army. Their eyes were pus-filled from ophthalmia and one already clasped a wounded shoulder. A second had recovered from Drinkwater's sword swipe as he straightened up. Drinkwater lunged his shoulder into the man, knocking him backwards and banging the pommel of his sword into the side of the man's head.

The impetus of the approaching French boat had slewed the cutter round so that her crew could leap the easier from their sinking craft. Drinkwater was aware of a stumbling, swearing mêlée of men to his right as, over the fork of the swivel gun, the third gunner faced him, a heavy sword bayonet in his hand.

Drinkwater saw the matter in his eyes, and the mouth set hard beneath the black moustache. He stumbled as the boat rocked violently under the assault. A man, thrown overboard in the scuffle, screamed as the first shark, attracted by the blood, found him. His frenzied cries lent a sudden fury to them all.

The artilleryman struck down at Drinkwater as he recovered. Desperately Nathaniel caught the impact of the heavy blade on the forte of his sword and twisted upwards, carrying the big bayonet with him. Then, in a clumsy manoeuvre, he executed a bind, riding over the blade and forcing it across to the right. He made the movement in instinctive desperation, with every ounce of his strength. In this he had the advantage. The gunner, weakened by disease and malnutrition, only half able to see and unused to boats, lost his balance as he tried to avoid the Englishman's much longer blade. Drinkwater felt the pressure stop and saw, with a curious mixture of relief and pity, a pair of tattered bootsoles as the man fell overboard.

This emotion was swiftly replaced by a savage gratification as he swung half right to plunge amongst the fighting still ranging in the boat. Then it was all over, suddenly the boat was theirs and men were grabbing oars and tossing Frenchmen callously overboard. In perhaps three minutes the British had destroyed their pursuers and had begun to pull the boat offshore to where the three British warships still cannonaded the town. It was almost dark. The gun flashes of the squadron were reflected on the oily surface of the sea, the burning dhows flamed like torches. There were only four of them; so neither Morris nor Hetherington had burned more than one dhow and two still remained unscathed. It was clear to Nathaniel that he had run more than the gauntlet of death from the French. The events of less than an hour seemed at that moment to have lasted a lifetime. He felt very tired.

After reporting to Griffiths, Drinkwater went in search of rest. The British remained at quarters during the night, snatching what sleep they could beside their cannon as the chill of the desert night cooled them. From time to time a gun was discharged to intimidate the French. Rolling himself in his boat cloak Drinkwater settled down under the little poop to sleep. He had barely closed his eyes when someone shook him.

'Zur,' Tregembo whispered softly, 'Mr Drinkwater, zur.'

'Eh? What is it, Tregembo?'

'Did you know that bugger Morris was aboard *Daed'lus*, zur?'

'Of course I did. He commanded her boat in the raid.' A sudden desire to communicate his fears seized him. There was between the two of them a bond that stretched beyond the bulwarks of the brig to the small Hampshire town of Petersfield. This bond underran the social barriers that divided them. 'I think he tried to kill me this evening.'

Drinkwater heard Tregembo whistle. 'That explains it, zur. We saw *Fox*'s boat pull towards you when you was attacked. As it passed *Daed'lus*'s cutter it were turned back. Then the signal for recall was hoisted I heard say, zur. I also heard Mr Dalziell mention he knew the lieutenant just joined *Daed'lus,* and when I heard him tell Mr Lestock it was a Mr Morris . . . well I guessed, zur.'

Drinkwater's mind flew back to a day twenty years earlier when this same man had given a nervous midshipman the courage to challenge Morris.

'If anything happens to you, zur, I'll swing for the bastard.'

'No Tregembo,' said Drinkwater sharply. 'If anything happens to me do you get yourself home to your Susan and tell Lord Dungarth. Appleby'll help you. That's an order man.'

Tregembo hesitated. 'Damn it, Tregembo, I'll rest easier if I thought he'd died by due process of law.'

Tregembo sighed. Such niceties were the penalty he paid for his contacts with 'the quality'. 'Aye, zur. I will. And I'll keep a weather eye out for your lady.'

A wave of pure fear swept over Drinkwater but he suppressed it beneath a rough gratitude for Tregembo's loyalty. 'Aye, you do that Tregembo. My thanks to you. The sooner we are away out of this accursed bay the better. We have orders for England once . . .' he checked himself. He had been about to say 'once the captain has rid himself of his present obsession.' But that was too much of a confidence even for Tregembo. The recollection steadied him and Tregembo left, silently swearing to himself that Lieutenant Drinkwater need have no fear if it was left to him.

But sleep would not now come to Drinkwater. He rose and went below. The scratches of his wounds throbbed and in the gunroom he cleaned them with the remains of a bottle of rum. Above his head a guntruck squealed and the boom of the six-pounder split the night. Mr Rogers was clearly going to let the French know that he was on deck, middle watch or no. Drinkwater went forward to look at Quilhampton.

The apparently indefatigable Catherine Best still ministered to him, washing the small white body with wine and water so that evaporation might cool the boy.

'How is he?'

'A little cooler, but still fevered. You have been wounded, sir?'

'It is nothing at all.'

'But it will mortify in this climate.'

'No. I have washed it with rum. I shall survive.' He took the rag off her and gently pushed her aside. 'Get some rest. I shall sit with him a while.'

He eased himself down beside the midshipman and sniffed the bandages on the stump. Thank God there was no offensive taint to it, as yet. Presently his head dropped forward and he slept.

At five o'clock in the morning the three British cruisers reopened their cannonade on Kosseir. It was to last seven hours.

At noon when the bombardment halted, anxious gunners reported the serious depletion of their stocks of ammunition and Ball summoned his fellow captains. At four in the afternoon the boats of *Daedalus* succeeded in burning the two dhows that remained anchored in the inner roadstead.

As the day drew to a close a swell rolled into Kosseir Bay, setting the boats of the squadron bobbing and grinding one another as they assembled alongside *Hellebore*. The brig was the most southerly of the three British ships and a convenient starting place for the next phase of Captain Ball's questionable strategy. All the boats had their carronades mounted, those in the frigate's launches of eighteen pound calibre. The expedition was to land south of the town. Its object was to destroy the wells used by the French, located in the miserable oasis observed by Drinkwater earlier. About eighty seamen and marines were mustered for this purpose under the command of Captain Stuart of *Fox*. Seconding him were Lieutenants Morris, Hetherington and Drinkwater.

'Watch this swell upon the beach, *bach*,' said Griffiths at parting and Drinkwater nodded. Service in *Kestrel* and the buoy yachts of Trinity House had rendered him acutely conscious of sea state.

Night was again falling as they pulled away from the brig. Stuart's boat led, the others following. At the last moment Drinkwater had ordered Tregembo back on board with a message for Lestock. As soon as the Cornishman had disappeared Drinkwater pushed off.

Already the sun was touching the distant peaks of the Sharqiya, but in the gathering shadows troops could be seen hurrying along the road to the oasis. Drinkwater turned his boat, that captured from the French when the cutter had been lost, in the wake of Stuart's launch. As they approached the beach they could feel the swell humping up beneath them, see it rolling ahead of them to break in a heavy surf.

'Mr Brundell!' Drinkwater hailed the master's mate commanding the gig next astern. 'There's a surf. Do you use your anchor from forward, let go abreast of me!'

He saw Brundell wave acknowledgement. The gig did not mount a gun, was too light for the six-pounders lent to the boats that had no carronades. Thankful that there were old Kestrels in *Hellebore*'s company who would appreciate the technique, Drinkwater watched with misgiving where, ahead of them he saw Stuart's boat anchor by the stern.

'Forrard there!' He stood up to command attention. The gunner's mate looked astern. 'Sir?'

'You will have time for only a single discharge. Make sure you fire on the upward pitch. Make ready!'

Drinkwater could see the beach, becoming monochromatic in the dusk. Troops were deploying on it, well back from the water's edge. Drinkwater put the tiller over and cast a single glance astern. The build up of the breakers was very noticeable. He straightened the boat for the beach. 'Oars!' The men ceased rowing. 'Fire!' The carronade barked. 'Hold water starboard!' The boat slewed. 'Let go!' The anchor splashed overboard and the boat drifted broadside. 'Backwater starboard! Backwater all!' The boat turned and from the corner of his eye he saw Brundell bring the gig round.

'Drinkwater! What the hell d'you think you're playing at?' Morris's voice cut across the roar of the breakers. Drinkwater ignored it. 'Check her forrard!' A twitch on the anchor warp told the anchor held. 'Backwater all!' Drinkwater repeated, his back to the beach, watching the boat's head rise to the surf which increased in sharpness as they drove into shallow water. They were surrounded by tumbling wave crests. He cast a single glance astern. 'Hold on! Boat oars!'

He nodded to the corporal of the marine detachment from *Fox*. Together the two men led the boat's crew over the transom. For a minute they floundered, found their footing and scrambled ashore. Drinkwater cast a single glance back at the boat to see the boat-keepers at their stations.

To right and left the British were coming ashore. Stuart's men were already deploying, the marine in the centre, but his boat was in trouble, her forefoot pounding on the hard sand, her flat transom presenting a greater impediment to the breakers than the sharp bows of the *Hellebore*'s.

The marines had opened fire, a rolling volley designed to pin down any interference from the town while the seamen attacked the wells. The party began to advance up the beach as the last boats came in. Two had followed Drinkwater's example, the remainder had anchored by the stern, their carronades or borrowed long guns theoretically covering the landing. In the event the violence of the surf prevented more than an occasional lucky shot, while the gunners were bounced and shaken by the motion.

Drinkwater waved his detachment up on the flank of the marines. The men ran forward, their bare feet slapping on the sand, the cutlasses gleaming dully in their brawny hands.

The buzz of a thousand bees halted them. A company of French infantry occupied low scrub ahead of them, galling them with a furious musket fire. The seamen were in soft sand now. Several fired pistols while the officers cheered them forward. They could hardly see the enemy's dark uniform blending with the thorn scrub, the flashes of their muskets too brief to lay a pistol on. Men were falling and the forward rush was checked.

Then the French charged and a stumbling fight ensued, the seamen hacking with their clumsy weapons, glad of the proximity of their enemy, shaken by the earlier fire they had received on the open beach. Drinkwater thought they had a chance. He looked round hoping to find Morris's men coming up behind them. Morris and his men had halted seventy yards away. To his left Stuart was equally hard pressed. Hetherington's men seemed to be in support of the marines. Drinkwater's eye was caught by a movement at the water's edge. The stern line of one of the boats had parted. He saw her broach and roll over in the surf, saw her split like a melon. The moment's inattention was paid for as a Frenchman drove his musket butt into Drinkwater's guts. He gasped and retched, vaguely aware that Brundell's pistol butt caught the man's face, then he was on his knees fighting for breath.

He did not hear Stuart's order to retreat. A kind of obscurity was clouding his mind. He was not even aware that he was half crouched in a kind of stumbling run, with Brundell on one side of him and a seaman on the other. He did not feel the seaman fall, a musket ball in his heart, did not feel another's arm bear him up, nor hear the shouted instruction from Morris.

'I have him, Mister, he's an old friend. You take charge of the brig's detachment now.'

'Aye, aye, sir,' Brundell turned uncertainly away. There was nasty gossip in the squadron about Lieutenant Morris.

Everywhere men ran to the boats, the seamen first to man the oars and haul in the anchors. In a wavering line the marines retreated, holding the advancing French just far enough to permit the embarkation of the British.

It was as well the French garrison was both sickly and small. The commandant, Adjutant Donzelot, could not afford to lose men. To drive the British back to their boats and to preserve his wells was enough. Desert war had taught him not to attempt the impossible.

In the dark confusion of the embarkation Morris found it a matter of ease to spin the semi-conscious Drinkwater round as they waded into the water, to bring his knee up into Drinkwater's groin and to drop him as though shot. Morris spared a single glance at his enemy. In falling Drinkwater had cut his leg upon the blade of the sword that had all the while dangled on its martingale from his wrist.

Morris was smiling as he scrambled over the bow of his boat. In the final surge of the sea as it washed the beach of Kosseir Bay lay the body of Nathaniel Drinkwater.

Chapter Twelve August 1799

A Stink of Fish

Adjutant Donzelot's caution did not prevent him allowing his men to bayonet the wounded and dying British. Those that did not die during the night would be killed the following morning by Arabs and eaten by the yellow-necked vultures that wheeled above the town. That Drinkwater was not one of these unfortunates was the merest whim of fortune. He was washed all a-tumble among the wreckage of the smashed boat, one more black hummock upon the pale sand beneath the stars. Those of Donzelot's men who ventured to the edge of the sea were content to find the groaning body of an eighteen-year-old boy, an ordinary seaman from *Fox* whose task of tending the launch's anchor warp had resulted in his being rolled on by the heavy boat. The bayonets of the infantrymen only added to the perforations in the boy's lungs.

Drinkwater knew nothing of this. He came to long after the French had returned to their billets, long after the young seaman was dead. He was already missed by Griffiths and Appleby, already being revenged in the mind of Tregembo. And while Brundell puzzled over his disappearance, Morris was already half-drunk over it. Even aboard *Hellebore* it had its element of satisfaction. To Lestock it justified a certain mean pleasure that 'Mr Drinkwater was too clever for his own good,' while Rogers's career could only benefit from Nathaniel's death.

Whatever agency ensured his survival, be it fortune, the Providence he believed in, or the prayer Elizabeth daily offered for his preservation, it was pain, not life that he was first aware of.

Waves of it spread upwards from the bruises in his lower abdomen where his legs terminated in huge, unnatural swellings. It was an hour before the pain had subsided sufficiently for him to command his faculties. An hour before his mind, registering facts from casual observation, gave them the meaning of cause and effect. It penetrated his mind that it was the hog of a boat that blotted out his vision of the stars, that he lay on sand shivering and soaking wet, an occasional wave still washing up around him. Fear of a terrible loneliness slowly replaced that of death. And that comparative condition was the first awakening of his mental will to live. He became aware that he was sheltered from observation by the boat's wreckage, that he could not move his right arm only because its wrist was fast to the martingale of the sword upon which the inert weight of his body lay. He moved, this time by conscious effort, fighting the pain from his swollen testicles. The pain in his gut he could account for, that in his loins was a mystery.

He muttered a string of meaningless filth as he drew his knees up and tried to rise. Just as the distraction of the smashing boat had caused his incapacity yet saved his body, now the cold numbed him and revived him to make an effort. The North Sea had taught him the dangers of succumbing to cold. Cold was an enemy and the thought of it brought him unsteadily to his feet.

As he stood panting with shallow respirations, waiting for the nausea to wane, the necessity of a plan presented itself to him. He remembered where he was. Slowly he turned his head. The occasional flame and thump from seaward showed where the squadron fired its minute guns as it had the night before. Less than two miles away was all he held sacred. His career, the talisman of his love, his duty; the brig *Hellebore*. Like a vision of the Holy City beckoning Pilgrim on, that gunfire cauterised his despair.

Aware that the moving chiaroscuro of the sea's edge facilitated his own movement he began to crawl north, along the curve of the bay towards Kosseir itself.

At first it was easy. He developed a simian lope that accommodated his hurt, but as he approached the town his senses urged caution and progress slowed. He had no idea where the French posted their vedettes. They *must* have someone watching the beach. He rested in the protection of a small fishing boat drawn up above the high water line. The sharp stink of fish assailed him and from its offensive odour he had an idea. Wriggling round the boat he discovered a net lying nearby. Carefully, trying to prevent the slightest

523

gleam of starlight on its blade, he used the hanger to cut off a section the size of a blanket, pulling it round his shoulders like a cloak. If a sentry should challenge him he could pull it round him, humping his body so that in the darkness he might look like an old pile of net such as may be found on any beach in the world used by fishermen.

Encouraged he continued his painful and patient advance towards the little harbour that lay behind the mole. He could not risk swimming to the squadron. The presence of sharks made that a suicidal choice. But he could steal a boat. He came to the first building and heard the dull clink of accoutrements. Upon the flat roof a sentry yawned, the smell of his tobacco mingling with the stink that filled Drinkwater's offended nostrils as he struggled beneath his net.

It was after midnight when the prospect of the harbour was exposed to him. He was warm with exertion and his pain had subsided to inhabit only those parts of him that were worst affected. Hope had given him the courage to make the journey, now success this far spurred him on. He sat and caught his breath. The occasional crash told where the balls from the British guns landed. Once he heard a scream and shouts. The scream was a woman's and the shouts unmistakably French oaths.

The harbour presented a fantastic sight. It was crammed with native craft of all sizes. In the centre the large hulls of a group of *baghalas* were to be dimly perceived, rising above the lower decks of *sambuks* and fishing dhows. It was a testimony to the energy of Edouard Santhonax. But it was also a testimony to British seapower. For though it seemed to observers on board the squadron off-shore that Kosseir was capable of absorbing an infinity of round-shot, Drinkwater's seaman's eye saw immediately the irregularities in that close-packed wedge of ships. The broken masts, the jagged lines of their rails, the dark holes in their decks and the lower ones, already resting on the bottom, spoke of the results of cannon fire.

Drinkwater moved forward, sure that somewhere a dinghy or small boat existed to carry him back to *Hellebore*.

That hope was nearly his undoing. From nowhere a dog appeared. Both parties shared surprise but the dog barked, not once, but with the persistent yapping of the pariah. Above him Drinkwater heard an oath and curled like a woodlouse. The dog snuffled round him, its hunger almost audible. Then it began to bark again. The stone hit the ground an inch from his head and the dog yelped and ran off. Drinkwater froze, imagining the sentry looking down. Had he scanned the ground earlier? Would the presence of an old net excite his suspicion? For as long as his nerves could stand it Drinkwater remained immobile. Then he began to move forward, eager to reach a downward slope on to the crumbling quay that ran along the inside of the harbour. He made it without mishap, moving swiftly across the open quay when he heard a fortuitous disturbance within the town.

He knew it instinctively for what it was, an argument that would engage the interest of any sentries in the vicinity. A woman's shrill voice screamed outrage at some demand made on her by one of the 'moustaches', the man bellowed back. Thus did a Frenchman's passion cover his escape. Once on the first craft the shadows and fittings provided cover. All the craft were deserted and he moved across them cautiously, anxiously searching for a small boat. He found several but none could be moved to the outer limit of the moored craft and the open sea. He lay panting and cursing after a protracted and final attempt to dislodge one for his use.

He must have dozed, for he sensed the passage of time when he next had a conscious thought. If no boat were available he might, just might, be able to attract attention at dawn from the extremity of the mole. He knew Griffiths scanned the town at first light and he remembered loose stonework at the end where he might remain unobserved from the town. He reached the mole half an hour later and found himself a hiding place among a pile of nets and pots. He fell asleep.

He woke at dawn but it was not daylight that startled him. The pounding of feet was accompanied by the crackle of musketry, shouts and orders. He recognised Stuart's voice and peered out to see a file of marines trot past him. Then Stuart appeared, leading a band of armed seamen ashore. He saw Mr Brundell and the gig's crew from *Hellebore* and it was if he had been absent a hundred years. 'Mr Drinkwater!' He stood unsteadily and bowed at Brundell's smile, aware that he still clasped the fishnet about his shoulders.

'Have the goodness to direct a boat to convey me back to the ship, Mr Blundell.'

525

'Of course. Here you! Support the first lieutenant back to the gig. And go handsomely with him.'

Drinkwater accepted the rough arm, aware that a face appeared in front of him that was aghast with astonishment.

'Morning Morris,' he said, stumbling past as *Daedalus*'s landing party stormed the mole.

'How are you, sir?'

'Eh?' Drinkwater stared round him in the darkness. The stink of the orlop finally identified his whereabouts. He turned. Quilhampton lay next to him, a Quilhampton sitting up on his good elbow. 'I believe I am quite well,' he sat up and stopped abruptly. His bruises, severe at the outset, had been strained by the exertions of the night and the cut on his leg had gone septic from contact with the filthy fishnet.

'I am exceedingly glad to see you sir, notwithstanding the stink of fish hereabouts.' Safety and the impertinent cheek of the youngster blew the shadows of fear from Drinkwater's spirit. He was no longer alone.

'I am glad to hear it, Mr Q. I apologise for my malodorous condition.'

'That is all right, sir. The captain and Mr Appleby were glad you survived.'

'I am glad to hear that too,' observed Drinkwater drily.

'I wish the same could be said of Lieutenant Rogers.'

'Ahhh.' Drinkwater could imagine Rogers's rapid assumption of his own duties. 'You should not gossip, Mr Q. I understand Mr Rogers's motives as you will do one day. I trust he was the only one.'

'The only one I know of, sir. Except of course Gaston.'

'Gaston? Oh, yes, I recollect. The French boy. What of him? How have I offended to warrant such a return?'

'For some reason that I cannot fathom, sir, he is of the opinion that either the captain or yourself shot off my hand. Leastways that is what I think he meant, unless I mistook his sense.' The boy shrugged and smiled with a puzzled expression.

'It's damned good to see you smiling, Mr Q. One day I'll tell you the whole story.'

526

As if from nowhere Catherine Best appeared, a bowl of water in her hands. Simultaneously the concussion of *Hellebore*'s broadside roared overhead.

'What has happened?' Drinkwater asked making to get up and suddenly guiltily aware that the silence had driven all thoughts of duty from his mind.

He felt Catherine's hand firm on his breast. 'Lie back, sir. Mr Appleby's orders are that you are not to move, that your cut leg needs cleaning or you may yet lose it.'

He lay back while the vibration of the brig's cannon reached down through the hull. He closed his eyes, the dull throbbing in his lower parts reasserting itself.

'The attack on the town has been beaten off, sir.' Catherine's voice seemed to come from a great way off. So, the fight for Kosseir was over.

And Catherine's hands were unbelievably cool on his burning flesh.

Chapter Thirteen

Y Môr Coch

'How much, damn it?'

'Three feet, sir,' replied Johnson, screwing up his eyes against the glare of the newly risen sun.

'God's bones!' Drinkwater cursed with quiet venom, suddenly remembering something. 'Take a look forrard, larboard bow, low down.' He dismissed the carpenter who turned away with a puzzled look. The lieutenant fell to a limping pacing of the deck, his left leg still stiff from Appleby's ruthless cauterisation, his abdomen and loins still bruised and sore. But his mind no longer dwelt upon these matters. He thrashed over a score of problems that fluttered round in his head like so many bats seeking anchorage. He was aware of being bad tempered, for the gnawing presence of Augustus Morris on board clouded every issue. Morris was amongst the squadron's wounded, all bundled aboard *Hellebore* after Ball's withdrawal from Kosseir.

Morris had been wounded in the attack on the mole, a stone chipping driving into his shoulder, breaking his collar bone.

''Tis to disencumber himself of the evidence of defeat more than from compassion,' Appleby had said, referring to Captain Ball with a bitterness born of the prospect of additional duty as the two officers watched the silent procession out of the boats.

In compliance with the orders brought from England, Ball was sending *Hellebore* south, to call at Mocha and land the sick or carry them homewards at the behest of Rear-Admiral Blankett. And the admiral was not pleased with *Hellebore*'s unsanctioned departure from Mocha, a fact that had led Ball to take fifteen of her crew as replacements for losses sustained by the frigates. That loss was only one of the consequences of the sorry affair at Kosseir. Now the matter of the leak demanded Drinkwater's attention. He remembered the slight tremble *Hellebore* had given when standing into Kosseir Bay. She had probably caught a coral head and torn her copper sheathing. The damage was undoubtedly slight and had produced no significant inflow of water while they sat and pounded Kosseir. A few hours of working in a seaway would have torn off loose copper and strained any sprung planks.

Drinkwater swore again as the first of the wounded emerged on deck for their morning airing. The watch were just completing the ritual of washdeck routine and he noticed one or two of them wrinkle their noses. He realised that a faintly repulsive smell had been pervading the ship since the night before, overlaying the indigent stink of bilge and crowded humanity. He knew what it was: gangrene.

For a moment he worried that it might be Quilhampton, simultaneously wishing it were Morris and that Providence might twist a little in his favour. But Appleby's features were no more animated than usual as he appeared on deck and touched his hat to Drinkwater. 'Morning.'

'Mornin' Harry. Who's succumbed to gangrene?'

'Gregory. I cannot amputate again, the shock will kill him. They will be bringing him up now.'

Even with a following wind the stench was offensive, causing an involuntary contraction of the nostrils. The men lifting Gregory on deck performed the duty with a mixture of peremptory haste and rough solicitude. Appleby strode forward to direct a hammock slung on the fo'c's'le, where the unfortunate man was hastily suspended. He came aft again, tired and old, Drinkwater thought, but a sudden surprising light spread across the surgeon's features as Catherine Best emerged on deck, wiping a lock of greasy hair off her forehead and clearly as weary as Appleby himself.

Drinkwater smiled as the surgeon made to step forward then, as if recollecting himself, drew back. 'Mistress Best has surprised us all, eh Harry?' he said quietly. Catching his eye Appleby blushed and Drinkwater smiled again. Something was stirring old Harry Appleby and it was not his usual outrage at the bloody waste of action or the follies of mankind.

'How is Mr Quilhampton today, Catherine?' Drinkwater asked in a louder voice.

She refocussed tired eyes upon the first lieutenant, dragging them away from a distant horizon. 'He's on his feet this morning, Mr Drinkwater, I believe he is breaking his fast in the gunroom.' She looked shyly at Appleby. 'I think Mr Appleby intends to try the ligatures this morning . . .'

Appleby nodded. 'He's a healthy boy and healing well, thanks to Catherine's ministrations. Would that all my patients could have such treatment.'

'It's not your fault . . .' began the woman, breaking off with a look at Drinkwater. It was clear even to Nathaniel's preoccupied mind that there was an intimacy here, professional and ripeningly personal. It was curiously touching and he felt oddly embarrassed and strode across to the wheel where the helmsmen were half a point off course. Catherine Best influenced them all he reflected, suddenly irritable again.

'Quartermaster, you're half a point off your course. I'll have the hide off you for neglect if you don't pay more attention.'

'Aye, aye, sir.' Drinkwater strode forward and cast his eyes aloft at the foremast, spun on his heel and surveyed the mainmast. 'It'll be t'gallant buntlines next, my cockers,' muttered the quartermaster to his helmsmen, shifting a quid surreptitiously over his tongue.

'Mr Brundell!'

'Sir?' The master's mate came aft.

'D'you not know your damned business, sir? Those t'gallant buntlines are in need of overhauling. Get about it on the instant!' He missed Brundell's wounded look.

Drinkwater came aft again, scowling at the men at the wheel whose downcast eyes were attentively following the lubber's line.

The pale form of Lieutenant Morris emerged from the companionway. Morris wore his uniform coat over his shoulders and his left arm was slung across his chest. Mild fever sharpened the malevolent glitter in his curiously hooded eyes and Drinkwater was once again disturbed by the almost tangible menace of the man.

'Good morning, my dear Drinkwater,' he hissed, little agglomerations of spittle in the corners of his mouth.

'Mornin' Morris,' Drinkwater managed out of courtesy and passed aft.

Drinkwater judged the sun high enough to take an observation for longitude, ignoring Morris leaning negligently on the companionway, never taking his eyes off Drinkwater. In the middle of the calculation, hurriedly tabulated on a slate, a worried looking carpenter returned to the quarterdeck.

'Well, Mr Johnson?' said Drinkwater as he flicked the table of versines over.

'You was right, sir. Shifted two tiers of barricoes under the sail locker to larboard o' the cables an' found a bleeding split, sir. Reckon the copper's off outside.'

'H'm, can you do anything with it?'

Johnson rubbed his chin which was blue with a fast growing stubble. 'Reckon if I shift a few more o' the casks I can tingle it from the inside, temp'r'y like, sir.'

Drinkwater nodded. 'See to it after breakfast, Mr Johnson. I'll have Mr Rogers send the mate of the day below at eight bells to shift the casks for you.'

He bent again to his figures.

'Beg pardon, sir?'

'Yes, what is it?'

'How did you know it was the larboard bow?'

Drinkwater smiled. 'I thought she touched when we were entering Kosseir Bay, Mr Johnson. Probably hit a coral head and broke it off.'

Johnson nodded. 'Reckon that's the size of it, sir.'

Drinkwater watched him waddle off, saw him hop up on to the fo'c's'le and look into Gregory's hammock, then turn away shaking his head.

'Still a deuced clever and knowing dog are you not, my dear Drinkwater,' insinuated Morris. Drinkwater flicked a glance at the helmsmen. Their fixed expressions showed they had heard and Drinkwater was filled with a sudden anger.

'Don't presume upon our *friendship*, Morris, and mind your tongue upon *my* deck.'

But Morris did not react, merely smiled with his mouth, then turned away below. Drinkwater stared ahead. Mocha was eight hundred miles to the southward and the brig could not fly over the distance fast enough.

'Mr Brundell!'

'Sir?'

'At eight bells have both watches hoist studdin' sails.'

'Aye, aye, sir.'

He waited impatiently for the quadruple double ring and the arrival of Mr Lestock to relieve him.

The gunroom was crowded when he went below. Cots had been constructed in each of the two after corners, one for Dalziell, displaced by Catherine Best from his own cabin, the other, a hasty addition, for Morris. Gaston Bruilhac still slept beneath the table. Appleby was just emerging from the after cabin when Drinkwater sat for his bowl of burgoo.

The surgeon jerked his head over his shoulder as he caught Drinkwater's interrogative eye. 'Taken to his bed,' explained Appleby, 'the Gambia trouble again.'

Drinkwater sighed. Griffiths had taken the Kosseir débâcle very badly. He was never prodigal with the lives of his men, many of whom were old Kestrels, volunteers from the almost forgotten days of peace. The butcher's bill for the action with *La Torride* and the attack on Kosseir had been excessive. With the thunder of the silent guns ringing in his ears as they withdrew from before the battered but defiant town, Griffiths had succumbed to an onslaught of his malaria.

Finishing his breakfast Drinkwater went into the after cabin. The sweet smell of perspiration filled the stuffy space. Griffiths lay in his cot, his eyes closed, but he opened them as Drinkwater leaned over the twisted sheets.

'How are you sir?'

'Bad, Nathaniel, *bach . . . duw*, but get me a drink, get me a drink . . .'

Drinkwater found a bottle and poured the wine.

'Watch them all, Nathaniel, watch them all. You were the only one I ever trusted.' There was a frantic quality about him, a desperation that Drinkwater suddenly found frightening, reminding him of Griffiths's fragile mortality. The idea of being left without him was unthinkable. As if divining Drinkwater's sense of abandonment Griffiths suddenly asked, 'Where are we? What the devil's our position?'

'Latitude . . .'

'No *where*? *Where* for God's sake?' Griffiths had half sat up and was clawing at Drinkwater's sleeve, like a man who had laid down to sleep in a strange place and, on waking, is unable to recall his whereabouts.

'The Red Sea, sir,' Drinkwater soothed.

Griffiths lay back as though satisfied. 'Ah, *Y Môr Coch, Y Môr Coch* is it . . .' His voice trailed off in a murmur of incomprehensible Welsh. For a while Drinkwater sat with him as he seemed to drift off into sleep.

Then Griffiths struggled up, an abrupt frown seaming his gleaming forehead. 'The Red Sea, d'you say? Yes, yes, of course . . . and we head south, eh?'

'Aye sir.'

'Don't forget the sun's ahead of you, neglect the lookout at your peril . . .' He fell back from this vehement warning. Drinkwater left the cabin and went to find Johnson and his party in the forehold.

Griffiths's warning was timely. The central part of the Red Sea ran deep but the approach to Mocha was made dangerous by many coral reefs. Sailing north they had always had the sun behind them, facilitating the spotting of reefs from the foremasthead. Now the reverse was true and the force of a favourable wind lent a southerly course the quality of impetuosity. Drinkwater remembered his order to hoist the studding sails with a pang of cautionary misgivings, then allayed his fears with the reflection that this portion of the Red Sea was free of reefs except for the low islet of Daedalus Shoal some sixty leagues south-east of them.

He found Johnson busy crouched in the darkness between two timbers, the gleam of incoming water lit by lanterns held by ship's boys, burning weakly in the bad air. Johnson had a pad of picked oakum pressed against the leak to batten over with timber and tarred canvas. Drinkwater looked round him in the gloom.

'The devil's task moving the casks, eh, Mr Johnson?'

'Aye, sir. I reckon Josh Kirby's ruptured himself, like, beggin' your pardon.'

Drinkwater sighed. Another customer for one of Appleby's trusses. The hard physical labour of working His Majesty's ships of war resulted in frequent hernias, a debilitating condition for any man, let alone a seaman. Drinkwater knew of many officers who

533

suffered from them too, and next to addiction to alcohol it was the commonest form of affliction suffered by seamen of all stations.

Returning aft he called on Mr Quilhampton. Opening the flimsy cabin door he found the boy sitting in a chair, reading aloud from *Falconer's Marine Dictionary*. Drinkwater was aware of a sudden thrusting movement as Gaston Bruilhac shoved past him in apparent panic.

'Good mornin', Mr Q. What the deuce has that puppy been up to to look so damned guilty?'

'Morning sir.' Quilhampton frowned. 'Damned if I know, sir. It's rather queer, but despite my assurances to the contrary he's still terrified of all the officers sir, especially the captain, you and your friend Mr Morris.'

Drinkwater snorted. 'Mr Morris, Mr Q, is an old "Admiralty acquaintance" with whom I never saw eye to eye. You may disabuse yourself of ideas of intimacy.'

Quilhampton appeared pleased.

'What are you reading?' asked Drinkwater, aware that he should not discuss even Morris with a midshipman. 'Are you communicating with the French boy?'

'Yes, sir,' said Quilhampton enthusiastically, 'Falconer has a French lexicon appended to his dictionary, as you know, sir, and we're making some progress. If only he wasn't so damned nervous.'

'Well I'm glad to see you so cheerful, Mr Q.' He forebore mentioning the ligatures. If Appleby was premature in drawing them Quilhampton would suffer agony. That was the surgeon's province.

At noon Drinkwater and Lestock observed their latitude. Both expressed their surprise that the brig was not more to the south but their ponderings were interrupted by a strange cry from the masthead.

'Deck there! Red Sea ahead!'

Such an unusual hail brought all on deck to the rail. The sea had lost its brilliant blue and white appearance and at first seemed the colour of mud, then suddenly *Hellebore* was ploughing her way through vermillion waves. This strange novelty caused expressions of naïve wonder to cross the faces of the men and Drinkwater remembered Griffiths's muttered '*Y Môr Coch*'. They dropped a bucket over and brought up a sample. It was, in detail, a disappointing phenomena, a reddish dust lay upon the water, the corpses of millions of tiny organisms which, in dying, turned a brilliant hue. In less than an hour they had passed out of the area and the men went laughing to their dinners.

The sight, the subject of a long entry in Drinkwater's journal, drove all thoughts of the suspect latitude from their minds.

When he came on deck again at eight bells in the afternoon he based his longitude observation on the latitude observed at noon. He was not to know that refraction of the horizon made nonsense of the day's calculations. They were well to the south and east of their assumed position and for some it was to be a fatal error.

But it was Lieutenant Rogers whose greater mistake spelled disaster for the brig. They had experienced the magically disturbing phenomena of a 'milk sea' many times since that first eruption of phosphorescence in the southern Indian Ocean. Conversations with officers at Mocha, experienced in the navigation of the eastern seas, had led them to remit their instinctive fear of shoaling which was often occasioned by this circumstance. They had heard from Blankett's men how captains and all hands had been called and precious anchors lost on several occasions when an officer apprehended the immediate loss of the ship on a shoal in the middle of the night. Subsequent soundings had shown a depth greater than the leadline could determine and the 'foaming breakers' were discovered to be no more than the phosphorescent tumbling of the open sea.

But such arcane knowledge bestowed on a man of Rogers's temperament was apt to blunt his natural fears and he disallowed the report from the masthead with a contemptuous sneer.

And so, at ten minutes after three on the morning of the 19th August 1799 His Britannic Majesty's Brig of War *Hellebore* ran hard ashore on the outlying spurs of Abu al Kizan, ironically known to the Royal Navy as Daedalus Reef.

Chapter Fourteen   *August 1799*

The Will of Allah

Drinkwater was flung from his cot by the impact. In the darkness he was aware of shouts, curses and screams. The entire hull seemed to flex once as a loud crack was followed by the crash of falling spars and blocks, the muffling slump of canvas and the peculiar whirring slap of ropes falling slack across the deck. In his drawers he pushed his way through the confused press of men making for the upper deck. As he emerged he was aware that the lofty spread of the brig's masts, rigging and sails were gone, that the mighty arch of the heavens spread overhead uninterrupted. Lieutenant Rogers stood open-mouthed in shock, refusing to believe the evidence of his eyes.

Drinkwater leapt for the rail and in an instant saw the fringe of white water breaking round the low islet to larboard, lifeless patches of blackness in the night marked the presence of rock outcrops. All around *Hellebore* the surge and welter of water breaking over shallows confirmed what his nerves were already telling him. Beneath his feet the brig's hull was dead.

He turned to Rogers. It was pointless remonstrating with the man. Rogers would be needed in the coming hours and in any case Drinkwater's acute sense of responsibility was already aware that he himself was not without blame. The reef was undoubtedly Daedalus Reef; their assumed position had been woefully in error and, although he did not yet know why, his conscience nagged him.

'Well sir,' he said to Rogers in as steady a voice as he could muster, 'it seems that *we* have wrecked the ship . . . and for God's sake close your mouth.'

Drinkwater was suddenly aware of many faces in the night, all clamouring for attention. There was fear too, revealed by panicky movements to and from the rails. He saw Catherine Best, her face white, a shawl made of sennit-work round her shoulders. Undercurrents of disorder swept the deck.

'Silence there!' bawled Drinkwater, leaping on to a gun breech forgetful of his near-nakedness. 'We ain't going to sink, damn it, come away from those boats. Mr Rogers! A roll call if you please. Mr Lestock! Sound round the hull; Mr Johnson the well. Mr Trussel examine the extent of damage to the hull . . . take parties with you . . .' His voice trailed away. Rising from the companionway like an apparition, a tall nightcap falling to one side of his face, the wind whipping a voluminous nightshirt about him, came Commander Griffiths. Men fell silent and drew aside from his path.

'*Myndiawl*! What in the name of Almighty God have you done to my ship?'

Griffiths's mighty voice rolled in anguish across the shambles of the deck which had the appearance of a scene from hell. The jagged ends of the masts stuck upwards, their remains grinding alongside, worked by the surge of the sea. Forward of the galley funnel the ship was buried under spars, rigging and canvas which lifted like the obscene death-throes of a gigantic bird. By some fluke the main-mast had tottered over to larboard, leaving a clear patch of deck amidships which seethed with the brig's people.

Drinkwater felt a sharp contraction in his guts, a sudden sense, awful in its intensity, that he had betrayed Griffiths. His nakedness seemed at once shameful and penitent. He was robbed of speech before Griffiths's agony, then a brief anger spurred him to denounce Rogers. But his own underlying sense of culpability checked such a mean outburst. He looked at Griffiths whose eyes glittered with tears and fever then slipped sideways to another face, staring at him out of the gloom with amused satisfaction. Drinkwater's nakedness was reflected in Morris's expression. Real anger came to his aid; he found his voice.

'Carry on with my orders, gentlemen. Mr Grey . . .' The boatswain pushed forward, 'get a party to start raising provisions out of the storerooms. Master's mate, do you put a guard on the spirit room and if I find a man the worse for liquor I'll have him at the gratings calling for his mother before the sun's up.' He turned to Griffiths. 'Sir . . . I . . . we are lost, sir . . . Daedalus Reef . . . our reckoning was out sir, I, er . . .' He felt close to tears himself, a weak desire to capitulate to the overwhelming feelings of frustration that laid siege to his spirit. But then Griffiths tottered forward and Drinkwater caught him. Already the period of shocked lucidity had passed, the ague had reclaimed him and he muttered deliriously to himself in his native tongue. The sudden urgent need to get the captain below reassured Drinkwater. All round them the men were bustling to their new tasks. Catherine Best's hair brushed his face. 'Get him below, hey, you there, lend a hand . . .'

'Sir, can I . . .?' It was Mr Quilhampton, his stump across his chest, his right hand held protectively over it. Appleby had tried the ligatures without success. Mr Quilhampton had not flinched. 'Get the surgeon! And round up some men to carry the captain below.' Then he added in a lower voice, 'look after him Catherine, we have great need of him now.' Two seamen arrived to relieve them of their burden. The woman straightened up. In the darkness he could see her smile of reassurance.

'I will sir,' she said, and her hand closed for a second on his. Then Appleby appeared and Drinkwater turned to attend to Johnson.

'Five feet o' water in the well, sir, but the line's short. I think we've lost the bottom, sir.' Lestock arrived. 'Two fathoms aft barely one forrard, both masts gone by the board . . .'

'Twenty barrels of powder spoiled and we've lost some water. Deal of the dry stores spoiled and judging by the top tier of casks in the hold we've stove in the bottom . . .' Trussel reported.

Drinkwater forced his mind to assimilate the details. Already a plan for their immediate survival was forming in his mind. He already knew there was no chance of saving the ship.

'Well, Mr Rogers?'

Rogers had recovered his composure. 'Three men killed, sir. Gregory, the foremast fell across his hammock; Stock, foremast lookout, killed when the mast fell, and Jeavons, he was forrard and was struck by a block. There are quite a number of injuries . . .'

'Right,' Drinkwater cut him short, 'all the unfit to go below. Is that all?'

'Two missing,' added Rogers.

Drinkwater could imagine that, men on duty swept overboard in the chaos of falling gear. He thought for a moment.

'We must get the galley stove lit and all hands fed well at

daylight. Use broached stores to conserve stocks. I've put the master's mates in charge of the spirit store until we get things sorted out. Keep a watch for drunkenness, Rogers, if this lot get out of hand there will be the devil to pay.'

'And then what d'you propose?' a voice sneered. Lieutenant Morris intruded into the little group.

'We wait until daylight Morris,' replied Drinkwater coolly, 'unless you have any better suggestions, then we will move the wounded to the reef and salvage what we can. The boats, Mr Grey, must be preserved at all costs. About your duties gentlemen.' The officers dispersed and Drinkwater was left alone with Morris. He was again uncomfortably aware of his lack of clothing.

'I think, my *dear* Nathaniel, that this time even you have bitten off more than you can chew.'

Drinkwater moved towards the companionway to find a shirt and his breeches. He turned sharply towards his enemy and retraced his steps. For one delicious moment he wished he had had his sword for he would have had no compunction in thrusting it deep into Morris's belly. The satisfaction, like that of lancing a boil, would have been cathartic. Instead he was reduced to a venomous retort.

'Go to the devil!'

'Careful Nathaniel, remember that old Welsh goat is a sick man and I am far senior to you . . .' The insinuation was plain enough and it choked Drinkwater with his own rising bile.

'Go to hell, Morris!'

'Witness that remark, Mr Dalziell,' snapped Morris in a sudden change of tone as the midshipman hurried up. Drinkwater turned away in search of his breeches.

It was late afternoon before Drinkwater paused to take stock of their situation on the tiny island. In the hours that succeeded the brush with Morris he had worked ceaselessly. It was only as he stood staring westwards that he realised why the brig had been lost. As the sun sank the mountain peaks of Upper Egypt were clear on the horizon. Drinkwater knew they were sixty to seventy miles away, far over the sea horizon. It had been the unusual refraction of that very horizon that had caused their errors and he walked tiredly over to Lestock to point it out. But Mr Lestock, who had long ago been

539

prejudiced against Mr Drinkwater's methods of navigation, especially that of determining longitude by chronometer, merely curled his lip.

'Perhaps, Mr Drinkwater, it would have been more prudent to have observed the phenomena before the loss of the ship . . .' Lestock rose and cut him, leaving Drinkwater isolated as he stared after the retreating back of the retrospectively wise master whose fussing indecision seemed justified.

Mr Quilhampton appeared at his elbow. 'Beg pardon, sir, Miss Best says you are to drink this and take some rest, sir.' He took the tankard of blackstrap and felt it ease the tension from him. 'I'm keeping the log going, sir, and the ship's name, sir.' Drinkwater looked at the boy. 'Eh? Oh, oh, yes, quite, Mr Q, very well.'

Drinkwater looked at the sandy, scrub-covered island upon the flat top of which a dozen crude tents had been erected. Piles of casks of pork, powder and water were under guard of the master's mates. So too were those of spirits and biscuit.

They had toiled to heave as much of the ship's stores ashore as were available, rigging a stay from the stump of the mainmast to an anchorage ashore upon which rode a block to convey load after load. They had rigged shelter from spars and remnants of *Hellebore*'s sails; they had constructed a galley; they had tended the wounded and buried the dead; they had got the boats safely away from the wreck and into a small inlet that made a passable boat harbour on the lee side of the islet, and Drinkwater was pleased with their efforts and achievement. Perhaps he ought to be more charitable towards Lestock.

'It is a little like Petersfield market, ain't it Mr Q?' he said, managing a grin. The boy smiled back. 'Aye sir. A little.'

'How's your arm, Mr Q?'

'Oh, well enough, sir. I can write, sir,' he added eagerly, 'so I'm keeping the logs, sir, and I saw the chronometer ashore safe, together with your quadrant and your books.'

'You're a capital fellow, Mr Q, I had not thought of them at all.'

'Tregembo got your sword and uniforms.' Drinkwater realised that he was surrounded by good fellows. Lestock could go hang. 'Thank you, Mr Q.'

'They're all in the gunroom tent, sir.'

540

Drinkwater suppressed a smile. It was inconceivable that it should be otherwise, but every space on the islet already had its nautical name. The hold was where the stores were stowed, the gun-room tent where the officers were quartered, the berth deck where the forecourse was draped over its yard to accommodate the hands.

Drinkwater drained the blackstrap and handed the empty tankard back to Quilhampton. 'I had better do as Mistress Best directed me,' he said wrily.

'Very well, sir. She's a most remarkable woman,' the boy added precociously.

'She is indeed, Mr Q, she is indeed.'

In the two days that followed they added a quarterdeck to His Majesty's stone sloop *Hellebore*, hoisting the ensign from a topgallant yard set and stayed vertically. They blasted a few coral heads out of the boat channel and surveyed another haven for the boats in case the wind changed. They tore the brig's rails to pieces to provide firewood for cooking and built a beacon on the low summit of the reef to ignite if any passing ship was sighted, and they built a look-out tower from where a proper watch was maintained, with an officer, mate and petty officer in continual attendance. They dragged three guns ashore with plans to construct a proper battery in due course, for Drinkwater realised that the men must be kept busy, although he was equally worried about drinking water and the demand on their stocks that such a policy would entail. But morale was good, for *Daedalus* and *Fox* were expected south within the month. Drinkwater's greatest worry was for Griffiths. The com-mander had suffered a severe shock over the loss of the brig. His malarial attack was, as he himself had predicted, a bad one, exacer-bated by the wrecking. Appleby worried over him, but consoled Drinkwater, aware that the lieutenant had other things to worry about. That the old man was very ill was obvious, and the indis-posed presence of Lieutenant Morris, who refused to exert himself beyond the self-preservation of his person and belongings, had all the appearance of a vulture waiting for his prey to die.

On the morning of the fourth day they saw a large dhow. The vessel sailed slowly in towards the reef, clearly curious as to the islet's new inhabitants. But despite the firing of a gun and the friendly waves of a hundred arms it stood off to the eastwards. Spirits remained reasonably high, however, since it was confidently asserted that neither *Fox* nor *Daedalus* would miss them.

Then, at dawn, twelve days later, away to the south-east the square topsails of two frigates were discerned. Summoned from his bedroom Drinkwater ordered the beacon lit and climbed the lookout post. At the top he levelled his glass. He was looking at the after sides of mizzen topsails: *Daedalus* and *Fox* had passed them in the night.

For twenty-eight hours the Hellebores and their guests from the two now far distant frigates wallowed in the depths of despair. Even Drinkwater seemed exhausted of ideas but he eventually determined to fit out the Arab boat they had captured at Kosseir for a passage. The boat, too large to hoist aboard *Hellebore*, had been towing astern of the brig when she grounded. Although damaged she was repairable and the following morning Drinkwater had her beached and over-turned for repairs. The wrecked hull of *Hellebore* was once again resorted to for materials and by mid-afternoon a detectable lightening of spirits swept the camp.

As the men went to their evening meal a dhow was seen to the eastward. The beacon was lit and the dhow was still in sight as the sun set. At dawn the next day it stood purposefully inshore and Drinkwater put off in *Hellebore*'s gig. An hour later Mr Strangford Wrinch stood upon the sandy soil of Abu al Kizan.

He looked curiously about him, resplendant in yellow boots, a green *galabiya* and white head-dress. He smiled. 'I learned of the presence of infidels upon this reef from a dhow that sighted you a fortnight ago. They spoke of many men waving and the wreck of a ship close by.' He paused, his face more hawk-like than ever. 'I also learned of another ship. A French ship . . .'

'Santhonax?' asked Drinkwater eagerly. Wrinch nodded.

'*In'sh Allah*, my dear fellow, it is the will of Allah.'

Santhonax

Drinkwater moved forward on the heeling deck of the *sambuk* cursing the restrictions of the *galabiya*. The head-dress he found even less easy to handle as it masked his vision. He resolved to dispense with it the instant he could and turned his attention to the men cleaning small arms and sharpening cutlasses. Yusuf ben Ibrahim's Arab crew watched them with interest, shaking their heads over the crudity of the naval pattern sword.

The *sambuk* sliced across the sea, heading east with the wind on the larboard quarter, the great curved yards of the lateen sails straining to drag the slender hull along, as if as impatient as Drinkwater to put the present matter to the test. Strangford Wrinch came on deck, his green robe fluttering in the wind. He nodded to Drinkwater, then opened his hand in invitation as he squatted down on a square of carpet. Drinkwater joined him.

'Relax, Nathaniel,' said Wrinch, his dark eyes fixed on the face of the lieutenant and it occurred to Drinkwater that this strange man was not much older than himself. They fell to discussing the events of the previous weeks that had brought Wrinch so timely to their rescue.

A day or two after Blankett had sent *Daedalus* and *Fox* to follow *Hellebore* north, a report had reached Wrinch that a mysterious ship had appeared off the coast of the Hejaz. It was soon identified as the frigate commanded by Santhonax who had apparently left off molesting the native craft. On the contrary the captain was now known to have distributed large sums of *baksheesh* for assistance in piloting his ship through the reefs off Rayikhah and Umm Uruma islands. When Wrinch had passed this information to Blankett the rear-admiral had waved Wrinch's apprehensions aside, assuring the agent that if the 'poxed frog' were dangerous Ball and Stuart would 'trounce him'. In the meantime his escape from the Red Sea was sealed off by *Leopard*'s blockade of the Straits of Bab el Mandeb. Blankett did not apparently see the anomaly in this assertion, seeing that *Leopard* was comfortably anchored off Mocha and His Excellency was ashore seeking to board nothing more belligerent than a small seraglio of willing houris.

Wrinch, however, did not suffer from the admiral's lethargy. He had in any event been supine for too long and set out north with a small entourage. After an overland journey of six hundred miles which he passed off with an inconsequential shrug, Wrinch and his *mehari* camels reached Jeddah. Here he found Yusuf ben Ibrahim, luxuriating after the sale of the prizes taken for him by the *Hellebore* in the action with *La Torride*. Wrinch kicked him out of bed and in the *sambuk* both men sailed north to Al Wejh, where positive news awaited them of a great French ship, lying a few leagues to the northward in a *sharm*, with her guns ashore. Santhonax was careening his ship, preparing her for the next stage of his campaign.

'But what I don't comprehend, Strangford, is why a careenage on the Hejaz? Surely the Egyptian coast was more sensible, where he could contact Desaix.'

'Ah, my dear fellow,' said Wrinch putting an intimate hand briefly upon Drinkwater's knee, 'You profess to know the man without quite comprehending the depths of his cunning. Certainly the Egyptian coast would appear the best, but he would be harried continuously by mamelukes. Murad Bey would never suffer him to be left in peace for long enough to cast a timenoguy over a bobstay or whatever he does,' concluded Wrinch in mock ignorance.

'But Kosseir was held by the French. He could have done it there.'

'Not so. You yourself went a-looking for him there. Certainly he could have defended himself at Kosseir but not left his ship defenceless while he carried out the necessary maintenance. No, Santhonax needed the last place you'd look, so he found an isolated careenage on the Arabian side. The *sharms* of the Hejaz are ideal for the purpose being the flooded ends of *wadis*, dry river beds that run into these shallow bays, often well protected by coral and intricate approaches to foil a surprise attack and break up the sea. The usual

544

small village can provide some comforts for his men and the local headmen may be bribed with ease. Santhonax could lie for a month before taking alarm.' He paused, reaching for a paper beneath his *galabiya*. 'Now, this is my intention.'

Drinkwater bent over the sketch-map. He listened to Wrinch's words, feeling excitement coiling inside him, remembering the drawn-out council of war that had been held in the gunroom tent of 'HM sloop *Hellebore'*, a rocky islet in the middle of the Red Sea. Most he remembered its dramatic termination.

Griffiths had been there, half conscious and lying in his cot. The worst of the fever was over and he had slept peacefully for some hours. Wrinch had presided with Drinkwater, Rogers, Lestock and Appleby in attendance. Morris had also insinuated his presence.

Lestock was against the venture from the beginning. He was unable to see the strategic consequences of allowing Santhonax to refit and escape from his careenage. Appleby would embrace almost any expedient that got his precious patients to Mocha, a point that he made at considerable length, urging that the *sambuk* would more properly be employed in chasing Ball and Stuart and recalling them to attack the French frigate. 'For,' concluded the surgeon, 'it is patently obvious to even a non-combatant like myself that the presence of two frigates is decidedly superior to one.'

'They were of damn-all use at Kosseir, Appleby,' said Rogers with a trace of recurring impatience.

Drinkwater agreed. 'Besides,' he added cogently, 'virtually any delay will almost inevitably result in our losing this elusive Frenchman. And I for one, have not come all this way to lose the game to Edouard Santhonax.'

'Bravo, Nathaniel,' said Wrinch. 'I think we may accommodate the dissenters,' he said urbanely. 'If, gentlemen, after say seven days we have not made our reappearance you could send Mr Lestock off in the boat you were preparing on my arrival. I will leave you a man capable of seeing you into Mocha.'

Rogers accepted the idea of an attack on Santhonax with enthusiasm, while Lestock shook his head and mumbled his misgivings to Appleby. Morris remained silent, fitter than hitherto, but still with that predatory look of a man biding his time. Then, as they fell into groups and discussed the matter Griffiths sat up, fully conscious for the first time in days. He looked haggard and old beyond his years, the flesh hanging loosely about his face. But his eyes were bright with intelligence, like those of a child, instantly awake after a refreshing nap.

'Wrinch? Good God man, is it you? What . . . where the devil are we? Nathaniel? Where the deuce . . .' Drinkwater detached himself and came over to the commander while Appleby called for water. He knelt down beside Griffiths and patiently began the long explanation. The questions Griffiths shot at him from time to time made it plain that the old man's senses had returned to him and at the end of Nathaniel's speech he threw off his sheets and rose unsteadily to his feet. 'Gentlemen, this is no longer a matter for debate. Make preparations at once. I shall command you myself, Nathaniel, pick forty able men, Mr Rogers prepare small arms . . . Mr Lestock, you may take charge in our absence. Mr Appleby will second you.' He swayed a trifle but, by an effort held himself upright.

'Perhaps I might remind you, Commander Griffiths, that I am now fit enough to take command in your absence.' Morris spoke for the first time. Drinkwater opened his mouth to protest but Morris quickly added, 'After yourself I'm the senior officer.' His eyes met those of Drinkwater and the latter read the satisfaction of a small scoring over his enemy.

'Oh, very well, Mr Morris, you may command the invalids and cripples. The rest of us will prepare ourselves to catch Reynard in his den.'

Drinkwater did not let his mind dwell on the possible consequences of leaving Morris in charge of the island. He already had the amusing company of Dalziell, now perhaps he would exert his influence upon the scared rabbit Bruilhac or worse, the convalescing Quilhampton. There were also the ship's boys and, for added diversion, Catherine Best. Through her he might gain an advantage over Appleby, also a party to his former disgrace. Foreboding clouded Drinkwater's mind as he fought to concentrate on Wrinch's words. There had been a strange quiescence in Dalziell since Mr Morris came aboard. Drinkwater watched Wrinch's face, aware that he shared some of Morris's tastes, though to a less perverse degree. But what he found offensive in one, Nathaniel scarcely thought of in the other, associating Wrinch's peccadillo with his way of life.

'So you see, Nathaniel, we shall observe the three basic principles of warfare. First simplicity of purpose, second detail in preparations, hence the *galabiya* with which I perceive you are not yet familiar, and thirdly the advantage of surprise in execution.'

They reached Al Wejh after nightfall and anchored. A small boat was hauled over the side and Wrinch and Yusuf slipped ashore. Yusuf's men sat in a huddle and smoked hashish while Drinkwater briefed the Hellebores, explaining in detail what was to happen. Among the forty men selected for the enterprise were Tregembo and Kellett, together with most of the topmen, Mr Trussel and a party of the best gun captains. Mr Rogers was also there. Quilhampton had begged to come but Drinkwater had forbidden it. Instead he had entrusted a bundle of letters to the midshipman, 'in case of contingencies not, at this moment, envisaged.'

He went below and found Griffiths sleeping quietly in a hammock. At the moment of the final attack he hoped Griffiths would remain aboard the *sambuk* for he would be little use for anything else, weakened by the fever as he was. In the interim Drinkwater was glad to see him sleeping so peacefully. He returned to the deck and lay down. But he was restless and sat up, leaning against the bulwarks while the stars wheeled slowly overhead, aware that the smells of Al Wejh were unrelievedly noxious. He thought of Elizabeth and her child, curiously he could not think of it as his until he had seen it. He wondered if it were a boy or a girl and what Elizabeth had called it. In the darkness he whispered her name, very low, but loud enough to give it substance, to convince himself that somewhere a lady of this murmured name actually lived, and that reality was not Nathaniel Drinkwater sitting on the deck of a dhow dressed like an Arab horsethief, but a brown-haired woman with a child at her breast. Thinking thus he dozed.

He woke at the sound of a boat bumping alongside. Wrinch had returned and they weighed anchor. In the calm of the night four sweeps propelled the dhow closer inshore and soon they secured alongside a stone pier. Striking the hold open they swung the great lateen yards round and laboured to gingerly lift each of the three six-pounders out of the hold and on to the waiting carts. It was dawn before the last gun had gone, followed by Mr Trussel and his gunners who departed with their powder and shot on a fourth cart.

Wrinch came to say his farewells. He addressed Griffiths who was still in his huge nightshirt. 'It is all arranged Madoc. I had sufficient gold. Your artillery was a powerful persuader. Nathaniel is fully aware of the precise nature of my intentions. As for yourself, Madoc, I entreat you not to be quixotic. That you have come is sufficient. Let Nathaniel here lead the attack.'

'I am a naval officer, not a mawkish schoolgirl to be cozened,' growled Griffiths. In a milder tone he added, 'be off with you. Give us your blue light when y're ready and you'll not find us wanting.' He held out his hand.

'Let us hope that we may toast our success in this Santhonax's cabin stores before long.' Wrinch extended his hand to Drinkwater.

'Good luck, Strangford. I hope Allah wills our little enterprise.'

Wrinch had hardly disappeared before the Hellebores were bundled below and Yusuf ben Ibrahim called his drugged crew to order. With no apparent ill effects the *sambuk* slipped seawards and two hours after sunrise was beating northwards through sparkling seas. Aware that for the moment he was a passenger Drinkwater slept like a child.

By mid-morning they had left Rayikhah Island well astern and turned north-east to raise Ras Murabit. They began to fish as they closed the shore again and by the afternoon were in company with two other native craft similarly employed. At about four o'clock with the mountains of the Hejaz well defined against a sky of perfect blue and the low, paler dun-coloured coastal plain still shimmering in the heat, they made out the frigate, tiny at first, but growing larger as they sailed closer, in company with the other boats returning after their day's fishing to the *sharm* Al Nukhra. As they approached they could see the vessel was upright and lying head to wind with her yards crossed. They must have completed their maintenance work, for the ship had all the appearance of being ready for sea.

As the wind died towards evening their pace slackened. Once again the Hellebores were sent below, only the officers with Arab dress being permitted to keep the deck. Looking pale and drawn Commander Griffiths remained, his eyes fixed upon the enemy frigate.

The French ship lay in a *sharm* which formed a spoon-shaped indentation in the coastline. A few scrubby mangroves were visible on the foreshore and the square shapes of low, mud-brick houses squatted among palms. At the head of the *sharm* the dried up watercourse wound inland, the *wadi* that Wrinch would use to cover his own approach.

Boldly, and with the setting sun silhouetting them, the *sambuk* of Yusuf ben Ibrahim accompanied the boats from Al Mukhra, his crew exchanging shouted comments about the paucity of fish off Rayikhah and blaming it upon the anger of Allah that the infidel had overrun Egypt. The men from Al Mukhra were clearly of the same opinion. They pointed to the French frigate and made obscene gestures. Their women, they said, were being contaminated by the heathen French who had been anchored too long and were hornier than goats with their drunkenness and their lusting. Indeed Allah must have turned his face from the faithful of Al Mukhra who were among the most wretched of men. All this was perfectly comprehensible to Drinkwater, accompanied as it was by universally accepted gestures. It was clear that though Santhonax might have bought the local headmen with gifts and gold, the humbler people who dwelt here had no love for the French.

Drinkwater tried to concentrate on the approach to the *sharm* storing up knowledge for later use but it seemed to be well chosen, for the approach was wide and deep and clearly Santhonax relied upon the fear of reefs more than their actual presence. Drinkwater found himself thinking more of Santhonax himself and knew intuitively that that was what preoccupied Griffiths. The tall, handsome Frenchman with the livid scar, whom they had chased the length and breadth of the English Channel and pursued along the sandy coast of Holland, seemed drawn towards them by a curious fate. Drinkwater thought of the extraordinary circumstances that had led them to the grey afternoon off Camperdown when, in a Dutch yacht, they had taken him prisoner. And there had been his mistress too, the beautiful auburn-haired Hortense, who had fooled the British authorities for months, living as an émigrée in England. He wondered what had become of her, whether Santhonax knew that he, Drinkwater, had released her, turned her loose on a French beach like an unwanted bitch.

He shook his head and drew his glass from under his robe. Careful not to catch the sun upon its lens he levelled it at the French frigate. Half an hour later they anchored off the beach and settled to wait for nightfall.

The fish-hold of the *sambuk* presented a bizarre spectacle. Crammed into its odoriferous space the Hellebores, faces blackened with soot, prepared for battle. The two lieutenants checked the men and struggled aft to where Griffiths waited, sitting on a coil of rope. He had hardly spoken since they had left Daedalus Reef.

'We are prepared sir. I am almost certain that she is not fully armed yet, her draft is too light and there is still a large encampment ashore. A boat came off just after we anchored but pulled ashore again. The land breeze is already stirring and we will need only a little sail to cover the two cables 'twixt us and the enemy.'

'*Da iawn*, Mr Drinkwater, well done. You will want to be leaving soon, is it?'

'Aye, sir, in a moment or two.'

'Did you observe our friend at all?'

'Santhonax? No sir.'

Griffiths grunted. 'Very well, good luck. I hope Wrinch told this blackamoor not to move till he saw the signal.'

'Yes sir. I do not think Yusuf will move without a fair chance of victory. He is not the kind to embark on forlorn hopes.'

'Off you go then, *bach*, and be careful.'

Drinkwater went on deck. The small dinghy was bobbing alongside and Rogers waited to see him off. Yusuf ben Ibrahim was also on deck, smoking hashish with his wild-eyed crew. The moon was up, a slender crescent, an omen of singular aptness thought Drinkwater pointing it out to the Arab. Yusuf grinned comprehendingly. '*In'sh Allah*' he breathed fervently, drawing a wickedly curved sabre that gleamed dully in the starlight.

'Good luck, Drinkwater,' said Rogers offering his hand. ''Tis a damned desperate measure but if it don't succeed . . .' he left the sentence unfinished.

'If it don't succeed, Samuel, we can all kiss farewell to a prosperous future.' Nathaniel took the man's hand, searching for the blackened face in the night. Rogers was much chastened since wrecking the brig and Drinkwater found himself liking the man for the first time since leaving home. 'Good luck, Samuel.'

He descended into the little boat. Drinkwater squatted aft and saw where Kellett and Tregembo each took an oar. The third topman, named Barnes, settled himself in the bow. Drinkwater struggled out of his *galabiya* as they pulled away from the dhow and made a wide detour round the stern of the frigate as she pointed landwards, head to the offshore breeze. When they had worked round to a position on her starboard bow they began to pull quietly in towards her and, three quarters of an hour after leaving, Barnes caught the boat's painter round the heavy hemp cable of the frigate. Kellett and Tregembo brought their oars inboard and all four men sat in silence under the stem and figurehead of the ship. They had achieved total surprise. Perfection of the plan now depended upon Wrinch.

Faint sounds came to them; the myriad creaks of a ship at rest, a whistled snatch of the *Ça Ira* ended in mid-phrase. A muted burst of laughter and the low tone of conversation indicated where the watch on deck spun yarns and played cards. Once the coarse noise of hawking and a loud expectoration was followed by a plop in the water close to them.

The minutes dragged by and a man came forward to use the heads. The four men maintained a stoic silence beneath the arc of urine that pattered down beside them accompanied by the quiet humming of a man on his own.

As the man returned inboard Mr Trussel's rocket soared into the night and burst over Al Mukhra with a baleful blue light.

For what seemed an age total silence greeted the appearance of this spectral flare then above their heads the fo'c's'le of the frigate was crowded with men. They jabbered together and pointed ashore while Drinkwater made a motion of his hand to Barnes. They eased the dinghy further under the round bow of the frigate, slackening the long painter until level with the tack bumpkin. Now they would have to wait for Griffiths and the *sambuk* to divert the attention of the men above.

Drinkwater turned his attention ashore. A flash and bang told where Mr Trussel's six-pounders on their improvised carriages were going into action. The concussions increased the speculation and excitement on the deck above them and now the noise of whooping

Arab horsemen could be heard, mingling with the shouts of surprised Frenchmen and the commands of officers. Flickering movements around the fires told their own story and on the fo'c's'le above them someone was giving orders too.

A terrific explosion shook the air, making Drinkwater's ears ring. The wave of reeking powder smoke that engulfed them a second later told that those on board had at least one gun mounted, a long bow chaser fired more for effect than anything, for no one could say where the fall of shot was. Two minutes later it boomed out again and Drinkwater wished he had a kerchief to wrap around his ears like the seamen were doing. But then there came another cry. A sharp '*Qui vive?*' of alarm from amidships and suddenly the fo'c's'le was empty as the Frenchmen streamed away to repel the threat from the approaching dhow.

'Now lads!' Caution did not matter any more. With an effort Drinkwater swung himself upwards at the bumpkin, dangled a moment then felt Tregembo heave him upwards. The dinghy bobbed dangerously beneath the topman but Drinkwater scrambled upwards reaching the stinking gratings of the heads and covering himself with more filth. He wiped his hands on the gammoning of the bowsprit as his men joined him then they went over the bow on to the now deserted fo'c's'le.

'Is the boat all right?'

'Aye zur,' answered Tregembo's offended tone. Tregembo had been offended since the evening Drinkwater had left him behind at Kosseir, but that was of little moment now.

Coming round the foremast they could see the whole of the waist filling with men from the lower deck. The masts of the *sambuk* were visible alongside and already Drinkwater could see several Hellebores on the rail. Lieutenant Rogers was there, hacking downwards, one hand grasping a mainmast shroud. He saw the squat shapes of quarterdeck carronades then there were more figures on the rail, British and Arab. Drinkwater recognised Yusuf and his wicked scimitar.

'Up we go!' he called to the men behind him and flung himself in the larboard foremast rigging. He felt Tregembo beside him; Barnes and Kellet made for the opposite side. Drinkwater looked down once. The *sambuk* could be seen now, its deck empty. The waist of the frigate was a mass of heaving bodies, of dully flashing blades and the yellow spurts of pistol fire. Then, as he swung back downwards into the futtocks, he heard above the grunting, swearing, shouting men below the thunder of cannon and the blood curdling screams of Arab horsemen as they decimated the French camp at the head of the *sharm*.

Drinkwater reached the foretopsail yard and moved out along the footrope. He felt for the seaman's knife on its lanyard and began to slit the ties. At the bunt, having done the same thing, Tregembo was busy severing the bunt and clew lines. In heavy folds, flopping downwards by degrees the huge topsail fell from its stowed position and flattened itself against the mast, all aback.

Out on the other yardarm Kellett and Barnes completed their half of the task. In a few minutes they were in the top. Kellett and Tregembo ran out along the foreyard, whipping yarns from their belts and seizing the topsails clews to the sheet blocks. The sail secured, the four men scrambled to the deck. Amidships the struggle raged with unabated fury.

'Below lads!' he snapped pushing them towards the forward companionway. They descended to the gundeck. It was deserted and in the glimmering light of the lantern at the after companionway sixty feet astern of them, they could see the six guns that had been mounted. The empty gun carriages at the remaining gunports along the deck and the untidy raffle of ropes, blocks, tackles, spikes and ropeyarns bespoke a busy day tomorrow. 'Untidy bastards,' volunteered Barnes as he followed Drinkwater to where the lieutenant had already begun work on the cable.

'Not too much, Barnes,' Drinkwater said, 'there will be a fair weight on it with that topsail aback. It musn't part before we're ready.' Drinkwater ran aft with Tregembo and Kellett in his wake. It was obvious now why the boarding nettings were down. The encumbrance caused by them when hoisting in the guns would have combined with Santhonax's feeling of security to persuade him that they were unnecessary. Besides a further day's labour and the frigate would be ready for sea, ready to challenge any other vessel on the Red Sea. They had arrived only just in time. Above their heads the fight for the deck went on, a scuffing, stamping, shouting mêlée of men. The legs and waists of several Frenchmen below the level of the deck were temptingly exposed but the three men trotted past their undefended posteriors. Drinkwater swung below into the berth deck.

There was a whimpering and stifled cry from the dense shadows and Drinkwater picked up the single lantern allowed near the companionway after dark. Holding it before him he continued aft. They found the rudder and tiller lines abaft the cadet's cockpit. Sudden reminders of the hell-hole aboard *Cyclops* flooded his mind. He dreaded finding the tiller lines unrove but no, Santhonax had obligingly rigged new ones.

They cut them by the lead blocks to the deck above and hauled the tiller across to starboard, forcing the rudder over to port. 'You two remain here!' Leaving the lantern with Kellett and Tregembo, Drinkwater ran forward and up on to the gun deck, finally reaching Barnes after pushing through a number of wounded Frenchmen who stumbled about the gundeck tripping over their own breechings.

'Cut the bloody thing, Barnes!'

'Aye, aye, sir!' Drinkwater reached the upper deck via the forward companionway only to blunder into more Frenchmen. He drew his hanger and yelled, slashing wildly out to right and left. Like butter they parted before him and he was aware of the last remnants of French resistance crumbling. Against Griffiths, Rogers and their two score men the French had had an anchor watch of thirty-six under a lieutenant. The officer lay mortally wounded, having surrendered his sword to Commander Griffiths. Griffiths stood panting with his exertions, his white hair plastered to his skull by sweat, his sword blade dark. Behind Griffiths stood Yusuf ben Ibrahim, arms akimbo like a harem guard, his men about him daring the surprised Frenchmen to lift a further finger against their conquerors while their frigate was raped.

Barnes yelled triumphantly as the cable parted.

'Foretopsail halliards!' shouted Drinkwater, 'Forebraces there!' The special details of men ran to the pinrails.

The sheeted topsail rose into the night, its bunt pressed against the foremast. He looked over the side. The frigate was gathering sternway.

'Mr Rogers, secure the prisoners!' Griffiths ordered.

'We've the tiller lines cut and men manning it, sir. As soon as this lot is under control I'll splice 'em, in the meantime we've sternway on and men at the forrard braces,' Drinkwater reported.

'*Da iawn*. Foredeck there! Heave larboard braces!' The frigate's head swung slowly to starboard as she gathered sternway. The foreyards came round against the catharpings and she increased the speed of her swing. Already the noise and flames of the battle ashore were on the beam. The weather leech of the foretopsail was a-flutter.

'Leggo and haul!' shouted Griffiths and then, turning to Drinkwater and in a quieter voice. 'Very well, put your helm over and restore steering to the wheel.'

Drinkwater dashed below and ordered Tregembo and Kellett to haul the huge tiller hard across to the other extremity, then he directed the shortening and resecuring of the tiller lines. In the meantime he stationed several men in a chain for passing orders. With the foretopsail yard braced square the frigate stood seawards.

'D'you have the blue light, Mr Rogers?'

After a search the rocket was found, still in the *sumbuk* bobbing and grinding alongside. It was leaned against the taffrail and, after more delays, finally ignited. It whooshed skywards and burst in a blue light over the *sharm* and was answered by a second that soared up from the hand of Mr Trussel somewhere ashore.

'So that's why they call the gunner "Old Blue Lights",' quipped Rogers flippantly and Drinkwater chuckled, moving over to the compass to watch the steering. It had all gone very smoothly, very smoothly indeed. He saw the Frenchmen had been herded forward and one of the quarterdeck carronades spiked round to cover them. Topman Barnes sat negligently on its breech, a slow match in one hand while the other was employed to pick his nose. Tregembo also stood guard, watching Yusuf ben Ibrahim with patent distrust.

Drinkwater wiped his sword and sheathed it, walking aft to stand by Griffiths.

'Congratulations, sir.'

'Thank you, Nathaniel. Your party played their part to perfection.'

'Thank you, sir . . .' He was about to say more but took sudden alarm from the expression on Griffiths's face. 'Behind you, *bach*!'

Spinning round he saw a man standing on the rail, some six feet from him. As the pistol he held flashed Drinkwater saw who it was. The light from the priming pan flared momentarily on the disfigured features of Edouard Santhonax, contorted with fury and recognition.

The Price of Admiralty

It was supremely ironic that it should have been Santhonax's astute intelligence that saved Drinkwater's life. For that brilliant officer, so swift in resource and quick in perception, instantly recognised Nathaniel Drinkwater, even in the dark. And that second of distraction from the purpose of discharging his pistol made him miss his aim. Even as the priming sparked, Drinkwater threw up his left arm to cover his face and the ball passed his ribs with an inch to spare.

'*Vous!*' howled the Frenchman in exasperated fury, flinging the pistol from him and leaping to the deck to draw his sword. Drinkwater's épée rasped from its scabbard. Other figures came over the rail behind Santhonax. Forward there was an ugly movement as the huddle of Frenchmen recognised their commander. Drinkwater heard Griffiths's voice steady the men on the tiller ropes as he and Santhonax circled each other warily.

Suddenly the carronade roared as the captured French seamen surged aft. Barnes had applied his match and as several of them fell screaming to the deck Drinkwater felt the jar of steel on steel. Yusuf ben Ibrahim was alongside him, advancing on the three officers and half dozen armed seamen that had boarded with Santhonax. He was aware of a white-haired figure on his other flank, a pistol extended towards Santhonax. Then Drinkwater was savagely parrying Santhonax's cut, lunging and riposting as Yusuf's whirring scimitar swung pitilessly to his right. He did not know what happened, but suddenly Santhonax was falling back against the rail, his sword hanging uselessly by its martingale, his left arm clutching his shoulder. Drinkwater turned in time to see Griffiths too falling, a dark stain on his breast. Six feet from him a French officer stood with the pistol still smoking in his hand. Cheated of Santhonax and in the full fury of his cold battle lust, Drinkwater swung half left, the French sword singing in his hand. The blade bit down on the officer's shoulder, bumping over clavicle and ribs, opening a huge bloody wound across the chest. Drinkwater pressed the blade savagely, all around him men were closing on Santhonax's party: battle was to become massacre for already in his heart he knew Griffiths was dying. But in that moment this knowledge was refined into a mere lunge, an increase of pressure on the sword-blade that reached the lower limits of the officer's ribs and, slashing through the muscles of his stomach, eviscerated him.

Drinkwater turned from his act of vengeance to see Yusuf ben Ibrahim stretched on the planking, his head and chest laid open by the blades of three Frenchmen, men who had soon succumbed to the overwhelming numbers of Ben Ibrahim's supporters. The whole incident had taken perhaps five minutes, five minutes in which the slashed tiller lines had been temporarily repaired and the frigate drew offshore, steered from her wheel.

'*Attendez votre capitaine!*' snapped Drinkwater to one of the cowering Frenchmen and turned away to discover the extent of Griffiths's injuries.

Tregembo had already loosened the commander's shirt and they found the hole above the heart. Blood issued darkly from the old man's mouth and breathing was accomplished only with an immense effort. Struggling, they propped him up against the breech of a carronade. Rogers came up.

'Is he bad?' Drinkwater nodded.

'What course d'you want, Nathaniel?'

'West, steer due west. Get the main topsail on her and then the foretopmast staysail . . . and for God's sake get those bloody Frogs mewed up below.'

'There aren't many left after Barnes blew them to hell.' Rogers hurried off and checked the course then bellowed for the hands to gather at the foot of the mainmast. Drinkwater turned back to Griffiths. The old man's eyes were wide open and his lips formed the name 'Santhonax?'

Drinkwater flicked a glance in the direction of the French captain He was still slumped in a faint against the bulwarks. Drinkwater jerked his head in the wounded man's direction.

Tregembo, make arrangements to secure yonder fellow when he comes round.'

'Does I recognise him as that cap'n we took before, zur?'

Drinkwater nodded wearily. 'You do, Tregembo.' He called for water but Griffiths only choked on it, feebly waving it aside.

'No good, *annwyl*,' he whispered with an effort, 'too late for all that . . . done my duty . . .' One of the seamen approached him with a boat cloak found below and they made Griffiths comfortable, but as they moved him he choked on more blood. His eyes were closed again now and the sweat poured from him like water wrung from a sponge.

Nathaniel put an arm round him, hauling him upright to ease the strain on his chest muscles. He felt the final paroxysm as Griffiths choked, drowning on his own blood, felt the will to live finally wither. Griffiths opened his eyes once more. In the darkness they were black holes in the pallor of his face, black holes that gradually lost their intensity and at the end were no more than marks in the gloom.

They recovered Mr Trussel and his party off Al Wejh that afternoon. By the time Wrinch rejoined them the frigate was well in hand. The Frenchmen had been turned-to securing the gun deck and stowing the loose gear, while the slashed rigging was made good aloft. Trussel cast his eyes about the frigate with gnomish amusement.

'This *is* an improvement, Mr Drinkwater.'

'Indeed, Mr Trussel,' said Drinkwater gravely. 'We have paid a heavy price for it by losing the captain.'

'I beg your pardon, sir, I had no idea . . .'

'No matter, Mr Trussel. What about your guns?'

The cloud on the wrinkled face further deepened. 'All gone sir, all of my beauties gone, but surely we have some replacements here?'

'No, we are only armed *en flûte*, Mr Trussel, these carronades and half a dozen main deck guns below. The Frogs had 'em all ashore. But yours, what happened to *Hellebore*'s sixes?'

'Those damned Arab carts fell apart after half a dozen discharges, though we moved 'em up like regular flying artillery.' He checked his flight of fancy, remembering the circumstances of his report. 'Left my black beauties in the desert, sir, and damned sorry I am for it.'

'Very well, Mr Trussel,' Drinkwater lowered his voice, 'you will find a bottle of claret in the great cabin. Use it sparingly.'

Trussel's eyes gleamed with anticipation. Drinkwater turned his attention to Wrinch. 'A moment, Mr Wrinch, if you please. Forrard there! Hands to the braces! Hard a-starboard, steer nor'west by west!'

'Nor'west by west, aye, aye, sir.'

They braced the yards and set more sail, hoisting the topgallants and lowering the forecourse. The frigate slipped through the water with increasing speed. It ought to have given Drinkwater the feeling of keenest triumph. He turned to Wrinch.

'I went to report to Griffiths . . . I'm sorry. What happened?'

'He took a pistol ball in the lungs. He was trying to save me from Santhonax.'

'You took this Frenchman then?'

Drinkwater nodded. 'Yes, Griffiths shot him and shattered his shoulder. He's very weak but still alive. He chased us in a boat. Boarded us after we had taken the ship. Ben Ibrahim was killed in the scuffle.'

'I know, his men told me.'

'But what of your part? The plan worked to perfection.'

Wrinch managed a wry little laugh. 'Well almost, the guns were more terrifying to us than to the enemy in fact, though their reports in the dark confused then. The two sheiks whose horsemen I led had a blood feud with the very man whom Santhonax had brought to protect his immunity at Al Mukhra. When I offered gold, guns and the distraction of yourselves it was more tempting than a pair of thoroughbreds. Although those damned guns cost us a deal of labour, we had them in position without the French knowing. The ride had strained the carts and they flew to pieces, but I doubt, despite Mr Trussel's excellently contrived lashings, they would have managed much more. My cavalry, however, were superb. You have never seen Arab horsemen, eh? They are fluid, restless as sand itself. The enemy rushed from their miserable tents and the hovels in which they were quartered and we chased them through the thorn scrub . . .' he paused, apparently forgetful of their dead friend, reliving the moment of pure excitement as a man reflecting on a passionate memory. Drinkwater remembered the feeling of panic that had engulfed the men of *Cyclops* when caught on land by enemy cavalry.

'We lost four men, Nathaniel, four men that walk now with Allah in paradise. We killed God knows how many. There will not be a Frenchman alive in the Wadi Al Mukhra.'

There was an alien, pitiless gleam in Wrinch's eye as he described the murder of a defeated enemy as a scouring of the sacred earth of the Hejaz after the defiling of the infidel. It occurred to Drinkwater that Wrinch was a believer in the one true faith. It was Islam and patriotism that kept this curious man in self-imposed exile among the wild horsemen and their strangely civilised brand of barbarity. And as he listened, it occurred to him that his own life was beset by paradoxes and anomalies; brutality and honour, death and duty. As if to emphasise these disturbing contradictions Wrinch ended on a note of compassion: 'Do you wish me to attend this Santhonax?'

Drinkwater nodded. 'If you please. Would that your skills had arrived early enough to have been of use to Griffiths.'

'Death, my dear Nathaniel,' said Wrinch, putting his hand familiarly upon Drinkwater's shoulder, 'is the price of Admiralty.'

A Conspiracy of Circumstances

Drinkwater stared astern to where Daedalus Reef formed a small blemish on the horizon. He felt empty and emotionless over the loss of Griffiths, aware that the impact would be felt later. They had buried him among the roots of the scrubby grass on the islet, a few yards from the burnt out shell of his brig. During the brief interment several of the hands had wept openly. An odd circumstance that, Drinkwater thought, considering that he himself, who of all the brig's company had been closest to the commander, could feel nothing. Catherine Best had cried too, and it had been Harry Appleby's shoulder that supported her.

Drinkwater sighed. The blemish on the horizon had gone. Griffiths and *Hellebore* had slipped from the present into the past. Such change, abrupt and cruel as it was, nevertheless formed a part of the sea-life. The Lord gave and took away as surely as day followed night, mused Drinkwater as he turned forward and paced the frigate's spacious deck. The wind shifted and you hauled your braces; that was the way of it and now, in the wake of Griffiths came Morris.

It had taken two days to get the stores off Daedalus Reef, two days of hard labour and relentless driving of the hands, of standing the big unfamiliar frigate on and offshore while they rowed the boats, splashed out with casks and bundles and hauled them aboard. The paucity of numbers had been acutely felt and officers had doffed coats and turned-to with the hands.

Morris had taken command by virtue of his seniority. It was an incontravertible fact. Drinkwater did not resent it, though he cursed his ill-luck. It happened to sea-officers daily, but he dearly hoped that at Mocha Morris would return to his own ship.

Drinkwater took consolation in his profession, for there was much to do. As he paced up and down, the sinking sun lit the frigate's starboard side, setting the bright-work gleaming. She was a beautiful ship whose name they had at last discovered to be *Antigone*. She was identical to the *Pomone*, taken by Sir John Warren's frigate squadron in the St George's Day action of 1794. Although she had only six of her big maindeck guns mounted, her fo'c's'le and quarterdeck carronades were in place, as were a number of swivels mounted along her gangways. With the remnants of the brig's crew it would be as much as they could manage.

Drinkwater clasped his hands behind his back, stretched his shoulders and looked aloft at the pyramids of sail reddening in the sunset. She would undoubtedly be purchased into the service. All they had to do was get her home in one piece. Inevitably his mind slid sideways to the subject of prize money. He should do well from the sale of such a splendid ship. Griffiths would . . . he caught himself. Griffiths was dead. As the sun disappeared and the green flash showed briefly upon the horizon Drinkwater suddenly missed Madoc Griffiths.

That passage to Mocha in the strange ship, so large after the *Hellebore*, had a curious flavour to it. As though the tight-knit community that had so perfectly fitted and worked the brig now rattled in too large a space, subject too suddenly to new influences. The change of command, with the nature of Morris's character common knowledge, served to undermine discipline. Men obeyed their new commander's orders with a perceptible lack of alacrity, displaying for Drinkwater a partiality that was obvious. The presence on board of Santhonax and Bruilhac was also unsettling, although the one was still weak from his wound and the other too terrified to pose a threat.

But it was Morris who exerted the most sinister influence upon them, as was his new prerogative. Two days after leaving the reef the wind had freshened and Rogers had the topgallants taken off. Morris had gone on deck. During the evolution a clew line had snagged in a block, the result of carelessness, of few men doing a heavy job in a hurry. Rogers had roared abuse at the master's mate in the top while the sail flogged, whipping the yard and setting the mainmast a-trembling.

'Take that man's name, Mr Rogers, by God, I'll have him scream-ing for his mother yet damn it!' Morris came forward shaking with rage, the stink of rum upon him. 'Where's the first lieutenant? Pass word for the first lieutenant!'

A smirking Dalziell brought Drinkwater hurriedly on deck to where Morris was fuming. The rope had been cleared and the topmen were already working out along the yard, securing the sail.

'Sir?' said Drinkwater, touching his hat to the acting commander.

'What the hell have you been doing with these men, Mr Drinkwater? Eh? The damned lubbers cannot furl a God-damned t'gallant without fouling the gear!'

Morris stared at him. 'What d'you say, sir? What d'you say?'

Drinkwater looked at Rogers and then aloft. 'I expect they are still unfamiliar with the gear sir, I . . .' He faltered at the gleam of triumph in Morris's eye.

'In that case, Mr Drinkwater, you may call all hands and exercise them. Aloft there! Let fall! Let fall!' He turned to Rogers. 'There sir, set 'em again, sheet 'em home properly then furl 'em again. And this time do it properly, damn your eyes!'

Morris stumped off below and Rogers met Drinkwater's eyes. Rogers too had a temper and was clearly containing himself with difficulty.

'Steady Samuel,' said Drinkwater in a low voice. 'He *is* the senior lieutenant . . .'

Rogers expelled his breath. 'And two weeks bloody seniority is enough to hang a man . . . I know,' he turned away and roared at the waisters, 'A touch more on that lee t'garn brace you damned lubbers, or you'll all feel the cat scratching . . .'

It was only a trivial thing that happened daily on many ships but it had its sequel below when Drinkwater was summoned to the large cabin lately occupied by Edouard Santhonax. It was now filled with the reek of rum and the person of Morris slumped in a chair, his shirt undone, a glass in his hand.

'I will have everything done properly, Drinkwater. Now I com-mand, and by God, I've waited a long time for it, been cheated out of it by you and your ilk too many times to let go now, and I'll not tol-erate one inch of slip-shod seamanship. Try and prejudice my chances of confirmation at Mocha, Drinkwater, and I'll ruin you . . .'

'Sir, if you think I deliberately . . .'

'Shut your mouth and obey orders. Don't try to be clever or to play the innocent for by God you will not thwart me now. If you so much as cross me I'll take a pretty revenge upon you. Now get out!'

Drinkwater left and shunned the company of Appleby and Wrinch that evening while he thought over their circumstances.

'Well, well, my dear Wrinch, a most brilliant little affair by all accounts and the loss of the *Hellebore* more than compensated by the acquisition of so fine a frigate as the *Antigone*. Pity *Daedalus* and *Fox* knocked the brig *Annette* about so much that she's not worth burning for her damned fastenings, eh?' Blankett sniffed, referring to the capture made by the two frigates on their way south of the third vessel in Santhonax's squadron.

'I think the frigate the better bargain, Your Excellency,' said Wrinch drily. Admiral Blankett dabbed at his lips then belched discreetly behind the napkin. 'A rather ironic outcome, don't you know, considering the *Hellebore* ain't under my command. I suppose I may represent that in this affair she was operating under my orders even though you exceeded your damned authority in sending her.'

Wrinch merely smiled while the admiral weighed Wrinch's impertinence against the gains to be made upon the fulcrum of his own dignity. He appeared to make up his mind.

'Well her damned commander's dead and so it seems I owe that popinjay Nelson a favour after all, eh?'

Wrinch nodded. 'French power is no longer a factor in the Red Sea, sir.'

'What did you make of that damned cove Santhonax?' asked the admiral recollecting his duty together with the fact that Wrinch had interrogated the French officer.

'He was quite frank. Had no option as we had captured his papers entire. He was to have carried a division to India this year, then Bonaparte invaded Syria and Murad Bey tied down Desaix in Upper Egypt and he was ordered to wait. He decided to careen on the coast of the Hejaz, as we know, and was in the process of collecting his squadron before seeking out Your Excellency. Had we arrived two days later he might have achieved his aim. After all he *had* secured Kosseir and Ball's attempt to dislodge his men failed somewhat abysmally, I believe . . .' Wrinch went no further, aware that the admiral had had the Kosseir affair represented in a somewhat more flattering light.

'Ha h'm. Well we have a handsome prize to show for our labours, eh Strangford?' Wrinch smiled again. The admiral would make a tidy amount in prize money, despite the loss of *Annette*. He would receive one-eighth of the *Antigone*'s value if she were purchased into the Royal Navy.

'We had better get *Antigone* home without delay, eh?' Wrinch inclined his head in agreement. 'And we'll disburse a little more than you claim to those Arabs, they're well-known for their rapacity.' The admiral grinned boyishly, 'you and I split the difference, what d'you say, eh?'

Wrinch shrugged as though helpless. 'Whatever you say, Your Excellency.'

'Good.' Blankett looked pleased and Wrinch reflected he had good reason. Without stirring from his anchorage at Mocha he had enriched himself considerably by the capture of the *Antigone* and the embezzlement of public money that would be officially disbursed to contingent expenses. Furthermore his subordinates had removed all threat of French expansion to India and, at least from Captain Lidgbird Ball's account of it, his squadron had taken part in a highly creditable bombardment of Kosseir. That this had been rendered significant more by the capture of Santhonax and his ship than the six thousand rounds of shot picked up by the French upon the foreshore was of no consequence to the admiral. While all this excitement had been going on he had been enjoying the voluptuous pleasure of two willing women. All in all Blankett's circumstances were most satisfactory.

'Whom will you appoint to command the prize home, sir?' enquired Wrinch.

The admiral screwed his face up. 'Well there's young what's his name on the Bombay station to be given a step in rank, but I think one of my own officers . . . er, Grace, the commander of *Hotspur* could be posted into the ship; but ain't she only *en flûte*?'

Wrinch nodded, 'Only six main-deck guns mounted, sir.'

'Hmmm, I doubt Grace'd thank me if I posted him into a sitting duck for a Frog cruiser . . .' Blankett rubbed his chin which rasped in the still, hot air. 'No, we'll give a deserving lieutenant a step to commander. If he loses the prize on the way home then there's one less indigent on the navy list. Now let me see . . .'

'Surely the honour should go to the officer whose exertions secured the prize? Isn't that the tradition?'

Blankett waved the assumption aside. 'Well 'tis tradition, to be sure, but sometimes a little done for one's friends . . . you know well enough, Strangford.'

'True sir, but I thought *myself*,' Wrinch laid a little emphasis on the pronoun to indicate his was a position of some influence, 'that the officer most deserving was Drinkwater. His efforts have been indefatigable.' Wrinch met the eyes of the admiral. 'I am sure you agree with me, sir, now that Griffiths is dead, that you will see eye to eye in the matter.' Wrinch's voice had an edge to it which changed abruptly to a tone of complicit bonhomie, 'As of course we have over so much lately: your accommodation at my house with its attendant comforts, the matter of the disbursement to my Arab friends at Al Wejh . . .' he trailed off, allowing the significance of his meaning to sink in.

But Blankett was unabashed and shrugged urbanely. 'Perhaps, Strangford, but Mr Morris is a pressing candidate, he has some clout with their Lordships though why he is only a lieutenant I cannot guess. I shall consult Ball upon the matter. At all events I am obliged to hold an enquiry into the loss of the *Hellebore*, the more now that their Lordships are screaming out for her speedy return home.'

The court was convened aboard *Leopard* on 1st October 1799 under the chairmanship of the rear-admiral. The members of the court were Captain Surridge of the *Leopard*, Ball and Stuart of *Daedalus* and *Fox*, and Commander Grace of the *Hotspur*, the sloop that had brought Morris out from England.

In his capacity as British consular agent Strangford Wrinch, having some formal knowledge of the law, sat as judge advocate. He wore European clothes for the purpose.

In the absence of her commander, Drinkwater was called first. His deposition as to the brig's loss was read out. In it he outlined his own misgivings about the accuracy of their assumed position. It was followed by that of Mr Lestock, a cautiously worded and prolix document which said a great deal about Mr Lestock's character and little in favour of his abilities. It called forth a *sotto voce* comment from the admiral that the master seemed very like his 'damned namesake', referring to an Admiral Lestock who had failed to support his principal in battle half a century earlier.

Rogers's statement was then read out to the court who were by this time finding the heat in *Leopard*'s cabin excessive, packed as it was by so many officers in blue broadcloth coats. Rogers was called to the stand.

'Well, Mr, er . . .'

'Rogers, sir.'

'. . . Rogers,' said the admiral whose wig was awry above his florid face, 'this ain't a hanging offence but it does seem that you presumed a great deal, eh?' On either side of him three post-captains and the commander nodded sagely, as if men of their eminence never made errors of judgement.

'It was hardly "a misfortune" that breakers turned out to be over a reef, sir, is it, eh? Stap me, where else d'you expect to find 'em? Had you hove-to and found two hundred fathoms and made yourself the laughing stock of the whole damned squadron you could hardly have been blamed. It would certainly have made more sense.'

Drinkwater watched the colour mount to Rogers's face and felt sorry for him. He knew the loss of the brig had been acutely felt by Rogers. It had tempered his fiery self-conceit into an altogether different metal. Blankett whispered to the officers on either side of him. Drinkwater noted Commander Grace seemed to be making a point and looking in his direction. Blankett passed a napkin across his streaming face and addressed the court.

'Very well gentlemen, I see there are mitigating factors. Captain Grace reminds me of Mr Drinkwater's observations about refraction and adds he has been making a study of the phenomena. In the circumstances the court take cognizance of these factors, though these do not relate directly to Mr, er, er the lieutenant's conduct on the night in question.' He looked round at his fellow judges and they each nodded agreement.

'It is the opinion of this court of enquiry that the loss of His Britannic Majesty's Brig-of-War *Hellebore* upon the night of 19th

568

August last was due to circumstances of misadventure. But it wishes to record a motion of censure upon Lieutenant . . .'

'Rogers,' put in Wrinch helpfully.

'Rogers, as to the degree of care he employs while in charge of a watch aboard one of His Majesty's ships of war.' The sweat was pouring down Blankett's face and he wiped it solemnly. 'That I think concludes our business.'

The admiral rose heavily and withdrew as the court broke up. Drinkwater found himself approached by Grace who wished to see his figures on refraction while Rogers hovered uncomfortably. When Grace had been satisfied Drinkwater turned to Rogers. 'Well Sam, 'twasn't too bad, eh?'

'Is that it? Does that mean there will be no formal court-martial?'

'I think not. Griffiths is dead and the navigation of the Red Sea intricate enough to mollify this court. By the time the admiral's secretary has dressed up the minutes of these proceedings for the consumption of a London quill-pusher, and by the time it takes for the mills of Admiralty to grind, I wager you'll not hear another word about it.'

They went out into the blinding sunshine of the quarterdeck to bid Wrinch farewell.

'I doubt we will meet again, Nathaniel,' said Wrinch extending his hand which emerged from an over lavish profusion of cuff extending from a sober black sleeve. 'Now that the matter of the brig's loss is concluded Blankett will be anxious to have you on your way. I have done you a little service. I think by sunset you will have an epaulette.' Wrinch smiled while Drinkwater stammered his thanks. 'Do not mention it, my dear fellow. God go with you and do you mind that sot Morris, there's no love for him in the squadron and I think he'll accompany you home.'

They watched him descend into the admiral's barge and were on the point of calling their own boat when a midshipman approached Drinkwater.

'The admiral desires that you attend him in the cabin, sir.'

Drinkwater returned to the admiral's presence. The green baize covered table was swept clear of papers and a bottle and glass had replaced them. The admiral sat in his shirt-sleeves with his stock loosened.

'Ah, Mr er, Mr . . .'

'Drinkwater, sir.'

'Ah, yes, quite so. Prefer wine myself,' chuckled the admiral pouring himself a glass. He swallowed half of it and looked up. 'The matter of the *Antigone*. I have it in mind to promote you, subject of course to their lordships' ratification. You will receive your commission and your orders to proceed without delay to Spithead. You will also carry my dispatches. Have the goodness to send an officer an hour before sunset. I understand the frigate is adequately supplied?'

Drinkwater expressed his gratitude. 'As to provisions, sir, she was wanting only her guns when we took her. The French had salted a quantity of mutton looted from the Arabs and we were able to salvage much from the *Hellebore*.'

'Good, good. Now Mr, er, Mr Drinkwater, as to the conduct of the prize, I understand that Commander Griffiths had no prize money arrangement with Stuart or Ball, is that so?' Blankett's voice was suddenly confidential.

'I believe that to be the case, sir.'

'Good. Well you stand to profit from the venture if you bring her home in one piece.' The admiral fixed Drinkwater with a steely eye.

'I think your eighth will be safe, sir,' he volunteered, forming the shrewd and accurate suspicion that the rear-admiral had some designs on Griffiths's share of the head money on the action with *La Torride* as well as his portion of the condemned value of the *Antigone*. Blankett scratched his head beneath his wig.

'You will need an additional officer; best keep that fellow Morris with you. Ball don't want him aboard *Daedalus*. Damned fellow's got some petticoat influence but Ball says he's a sodomite. I'll send the bugger home before I have to hang him.'

Drinkwater's mouth fell open. It was clear Blankett would not want Morris left on his hands, even that he knew all about him to the point of remembering his name.

'That will do, Mr, er . . . yes that will do, now be damned sure you look after that frigate. Use caution in the Soundings, I don't want my prize money ending up as firewood in some poxy Cornish wrecker's hovel.'

Drinkwater withdrew, mixed feelings raging within him. He stopped outside the admiral's cabin to trim his hat. 'Commander

Nathaniel Drinkwater,' he muttered experimentally beneath his breath. Then he flushed as the rigid marine sentry, bull-necked and bright red in the heat, coughed discreetly. He strode out on to *Leopard*'s quarterdeck.

'Nothing serious I hope?' asked Rogers anxiously, still smarting over the censuring of the court. Drinkwater smiled.

'Depends on your point of view, Samuel.'

'I'm sorry, I don't follow.'

'That venal old reprobate,' Drinkwater checked his wild exuberance at having his step in rank at last, 'His Excellency Rear-Admiral John Blankett has had the goodness to promote me to commander.'

'Well I'm damned! I mean, damn it, congratulations, Mr Drinkwater.'

'That's very decent of you, Samuel. But don't let us count our chickens just yet. This news will poison Morris.'

'Isn't he to return to *Daedalus* . . . sir?'

'No, I regret he is not. By a wonderful irony he is to be my first lieutenant. I'm sorry it ain't you, Samuel, but there we are.'

They hailed their boat, resolving to remain silent upon the matter until Drinkwater had the commission in his hand and could read himself in.

He waited impatiently for the interminable afternoon to draw to a close. At two bells in the first dog watch he quietly desired Rogers to send a boat to *Leopard* for their orders. Rogers sent Mr Dalziell.

Drinkwater sat in his cabin and took out his journal and began to write. *It was with great satisfaction that I attended the R.Ad this morning and was acquainted with the fact that I am to be made Master and Commander. This in my thirty-sixth year, after twenty years' sea service. This step in rank removes many apprehensions and vain imaginings from my mind.* He paused then added: *I thank God for it.*

It was both pious and pompous but he felt his moment of vanity, though it might earn a rebuke from Elizabeth, could be allowed expression in the privacy of his journal. He fell into a brown study dreaming of home.

Aboard *Leopard* Mr Dalziell waited in the admiral's secretary's cabin while that worthy, a man named Wishart, inscribed with painful slowness upon a packet.

'There are your orders.' He carefully handed over a sealed bundle and being a proper man insisted Dalziell signed the receipt before receiving a second. 'And there are the admiral's dispatches. See that your commander puts them in a secure place.' Again they performed the ritual of signature and exchange. And now,' said Mr Wishart drawing a paper towards him, 'the admiral has a dreadful memory for names, what is the name of your senior lieutenant, eh?'

He dipped his pen and held it expectantly. 'Morris, sir, Mr Augustus Morris, related by marriage to the Earl of Dungarth not unknown to the Earl of Sandwich sir,' Dalziell wheedled ingratiatingly.

'Is that so? In that case,' said Mr Wishart, sprinkling sand over the recipient's name, 'he seems admirably fitted to sail so fine a frigate home. Here is Mr Morris's commission as Commander.'

Morris

Drinkwater was not listening to the garbled words of divine service
as Morris mumbled his way through them. Morris's voice had not
the resonant conviction of Griffiths's splendid diction and
Drinkwater's loathing of Morris's too-obvious feet of clay made
parody of the Book of Common Prayer. Instead Drinkwater looked
forward, beyond the semi-circle of commissioned and warrant officers in full uniform with their left hands upon their sword hilts and
cocked hats beneath their elbows, at the hands massed in the waist.
There were about eighty men left to take the big frigate home, not
many to work her, not enough to fight her.

But it was not the quality of the number that concerned
Drinkwater. His acute senses were tuned to their mood, and in the
present calm as the Indian Ocean lay quiet waiting for the first
breath of the north-east monsoon, there was an ugliness about it. It
was as though the expectant oiliness of the sea exerted some influence upon the minds of the men like that of the moon upon the sea
itself.

Drinkwater discarded the over-ripe metaphor, aware that his own
chronic disappointment was souring him. Their hurried departure
from Mocha, the stunned disbelief as he had stood as he did now
and listened to Morris confidently reading his commission to the
ship's company had triggered his depression and sent him miserable
to his cabin, to grieve over his own ill-fortune and, at last, the loss of
Griffiths.

In reality that onset of depression had saved him from rashness.
Later Rogers had accosted him over the matter, only to reveal that he
had himself sent Mr Dalziell to obtain the commission. Now Rogers,
already shaken in his confidence over the loss of the brig and the

censure of the admiral, had retreated into his own resentment. With the two lieutenants nursing their private grievances Morris had triumphed and *Antigone* was out of the Gulf of Aden before Drinkwater cast aside his 'blue devils' and resolved to make the best of things.

But he knew it was already too late. While the officers had sulked the men had been scourged. Morris flogged savagely for every small offence that was brought to his notice by his toadies. Among these was a man name Rattray, Morris's servant sent over from *Daedalus*, a thin seedy man who padded silently about the ship and swiftly became known, predictably, as 'the Rat'. There was Dalziell, of course, promoted acting lieutenant by Morris, who terrorised the hands to Drinkwater's fury; and there was Lestock, whose fussing temperament seemed seduced by Morris's brand of command by terror. It was these men who formed the Praetorian Guard round their new commander, a little coterie of self-seekers and survivors who wielded enormous influence and filled the punishment book with trivial entries.

Drinkwater's mouth set in a hard line as he thought of the increased number of times he had had to make entries in that book. The binding no longer cracked as it had done when Griffiths commanded them. Of course the entries read well. Insolence for a man laughing too loudly when the captain was on deck; Defiling the Deck for a man who spilled his mess kit by accident; Improper Conduct when a rope was untidily belayed on the fife-rails, all trivial matters ending up with the culprit being seized to the gratings.

Morris closed the Prayer Book with a snap, recalling Drinkwater to his duty.

'On hats!' Routinely Drinkwater touched his hat brim as Morris went below.

'Bosun! Pipe the hands to dinner!' he turned away to find Rattray alongside him, as though he had been there all the time, silently listening to Drinkwater's thoughts.

'Cap'n's compliments, sir, and he'd be obleeged if you'd join him for dinner at four bells.'

Drinkwater searched the man's face for some reason for this unexpected courtesy. He found nothing except a pair of shifty eyes and replied. 'Very well. My thanks to the captain.'

He looked forward again to see Appleby and Catherine Best crossing the deck. They had become very close since Morris took command and Drinkwater thought that the presence of the woman even exerted some restraining influence upon Morris himself. Drinkwater uncovered to her. 'Mornin' Mistress Best. I see Mr Wrinch's promise of something more suitable to wear was no vain boast.'

Catherine smiled at him, a shy kind of happiness lighting her eyes while her right hand swirled the skirt of Arab cotton in a small coquettish movement.

'Indeed, Mr Drinkwater, it was not.' Drinkwater looked at Appleby, who was blushing furiously. He smiled, touched his hat again and turned to the quartermaster.

'Well bless my soul,' he muttered to himself, then, in a louder tone, 'call me if there's any wind.' The quartermaster acknowledged the first lieutenant and Drinkwater went below to change his shirt.

The meal, at which no others were present, was conducted in silence. Rattray padded behind their chairs and even with the after sashes lowered the air in the large cabin was stale and hot. When the dishes were cleared away a bottle of port was decanted in Santhonax's personal crystal and, Drinkwater noticed, circulation was slow. The decanter did duty at Morris's glass three times before being shoved reluctantly in his direction. Drinkwater drank sparingly, aware that Morris's appetite was gross.

'Have you seen that?' Morris pointed to where, half hidden behind the cabin door a woman's portrait hung on the white bulkhead. Already his voice was slurred. 'I presume it to be the Frog's whore.' Drinkwater found the portrait amazing. Hortense's grey eyes stared out of the canvas, her long neck bared and her flaming hair piled up above her head, wound with pearls. A wisp of gauze covered the swell of her breasts. He remembered the woman in the cabin of *Kestrel* and stumbling on the beach at Criel where they had let her go free. He found the portrait disquieting and turned back to Morris. The man was watching him from beneath his hooded eyelids.

'She's his wife,' said Drinkwater, returning Morris's stare.

'And what of Appleby's whore, Nathaniel? Is she what I am told she is, a convict?'

It was pointless to deny it, but then it was unnecessary to confirm it. 'I believe she has redeemed herself by her services to the ship. As to her status, I think you are mistaken.'

Morris waved aside Drinkwater's compassion, to him the pompous assertion of a liberal. 'Pah! She is Appleby's whore,' repeated Morris, slumping back into his chair.

Drinkwater shrugged, aware that Morris was wary, beating about the bush of his intention in asking Drinkwater to dine. He wished they might reach a truce, unaware that Morris had left him upon the beach at Kosseir. Their enmity aboard *Cyclops* was long past, they were grown men now. Whatever Morris's private desires were, they were not overt.

'You are wondering why I have asked you to dine with me, eh? You, who crossed me years ago, who saw to it that I was dismissed out of *Cyclops* . . .'

'I did no such thing, sir.'

'Don't haze me, damn you!' Morris restrained himself and Drinkwater was increasingly worried about the reason for this cosy chat. Drinkwater had played a small part in Morris's disgrace, which had largely been accomplished by his own character. The captain of the frigate was long dead; the first lieutenant, now Lord Dungarth, beyond Morris's vengeance. But Drinkwater was again at his mercy and Morris had intended his ruin, for he had nursed a longing for revenge for twenty years; twenty years that had twisted rejected desire into an obsession.

The pure, vindictive hatred that had made Morris drop the fainting Drinkwater on the beach at Kosseir had been thwarted in the latter's survival, but was now complicated by his reliance on the man he had tried to kill.

'I have my own command now, Drinkwater,' he said, his mouth slack, his chin on his chest, a sinister cartoon by Rowlandson. 'Do anything to prejudice me again and I'll see you in hell . . .'

'I shall do my duty, sir,' said Drinkwater cautiously, but too primly for Morris's liking.

'Aye by God you will!' Spittle shot from Morris's mouth.

'Then why should you suppose . . .'

'Because there is a damned rumour persisting in this ship that I have the swab,' he gestured at the damaged epaulette on his shoulders that he had rifled from Griffiths's belongings, 'that should have gone to you.' It was not the only reason but one on which Morris might draw a reaction from Drinkwater whom he now watched closely, his mind concentrated by alcohol on the focus of his obsession.

But Drinkwater did not perceive this, merely saw the matter as something to be raised between them, another ghost to be laid. 'I *was* given to understand Admiral Blankett desired I should command the prize, certainly. Whatever made him change his mind is no longer any concern of mine.' He paused, sitting up, hoping to terminate the interview. 'But in the meantime I shall do my duty as first lieutenant as I did for Commander Griffiths, sir.' Then he added, irritated at being catechised: 'Unless you have a notion to promote Mr Dalziell over my head.'

'What the hell d'you mean by that?' flared Morris, and Drinkwater sensed he had touched a nerve. Dalziell. The relative, quiescent of late. A catamite? Drinkwater looked sharply at Morris. The commander's glare was unchanged but a sheen of sweat had erupted across his face.

All was suddenly clear to Drinkwater. Morris had obtained his command at last. Unable to earn it by his own merits, a twist of fate had delivered it unexpectedly into his lap. A further helix in that turn of circumstances had made Drinkwater both his unwitting benefactor and first lieutenant on whose abilities he must rely to take advantage of this new opportunity. He would not sacrifice the possibility of a post-captaincy even for revenge on Drinkwater, but Drinkwater knew of his past and might know of his present. Morris, long driven by vengeance, could not imagine another dismissing such an opportunity with contempt. Even a sanctimonious liberal like Drinkwater. And Morris was guilty of unnatural crimes specifically proscribed by the Articles of War.

But this potential nemesis was of small apparent consolation to Nathaniel. He merely found it odd that that usurped tangle of gold wire could tame so disturbed a spirit as Augustus Morris's.

'It was a poor jest, sir. I am sure you will know how to keep Mr Dalziell in his proper place.' Drinkwater rose. It had not been a deliberate innuendo but Morris continued to stare suspiciously at him. 'Thank you for the courtesy of your invitation.' He turned for the door, his eye falling on the picture of Hortense. 'By the way sir, the surgeon tells me Santhonax would benefit from some fresh air. May I have permission to exercise him on deck tomorrow?'

'Solicitude for prisoners, eh?' slurred Morris, his eyes clouding, turning inwards. 'Do as you see fit . . .' He dismissed Drinkwater with a flick of his wrist, then reached for the decanter. Alone, he saw, with the perception of the drunk the pair of level grey eyes staring at him from the bulkhead. They seemed to accuse him with the whole mess of his life. Viciously his hand found a fork left on the table by the careless Rattray. With sudden venom he flung it at the canvas. The tines vibrated in the creamy shoulder, reminding Morris of the past, good old days when the senior midshipmen drove a fork into a deck beam as a signal to send their juniors to bed while they 'sported'. The euphemism covered many sins. Things had changed in His Majesty's navy since the mutinies of 1797. Now canting bastards like Drinkwater with their liberal ideas were ruining the Service, God damn them. He flung his head back and roared 'Rattray!'

'Sir?'

'Pass word for Mr Dalziell.'

Drinkwater drew the air into his lungs. After the calm the strengthening north-easter was like champagne. Above his head the watch had just taken in the royals and were descending via the backstays. Those to windward were taut and harping gently as a patter of spray came over the windward rail. He walked over to the binnacle. 'Steer small now, a good course will bring us home the sooner.'

He resumed his pacing, free of the effects of his bruising and the cauterised cut on his leg that would not even leave a scar worth mentioning. He passed along the squat black breeches of the quarterdeck carronades, as near content as his circumstances would permit. After the dinner with Morris he sensed an easing of tension between them, aware that his own duties preoccupied him while Morris, isolated in command, would brood in his cabin. Despite the promotion of Dalziell to acting lieutenant, Drinkwater had not relinquished his watch. He might have availed himself of big-ship tradition, had not the notion with so small a crew been a piece of conceit that ran contrary to his nature. In Dalziell's abilities he had no

578

confidence whatsoever, regarding his elevation as a shameful abuse of the system, a blatant piece of influence that he thought unlikely to last long after their return home. For himself he kept the privacy of his morning and evening watches while the poor devils forward were compelled to work watch and watch. It could not be helped. It was the way of the world and the naval service in particular.

Unfamiliar figures emerged on deck and Drinkwater remembered his own orders. Gaston Bruilhac assisted the tall figure of Edouard Santhonax whose arm was still slung beneath his coat. The hands idled curiously as Santhonax cast his eyes aloft, noting the set of the sails.

'Good mornin', sir.' Drinkwater touched his hat out of formal courtesy. Long enmity had bred a respect for the Frenchman and Drinkwater hoped his presence as a prisoner satisfied the shade of Madoc Griffiths.

'Good morning, Boireleau . . .' He winced, adjusting himself against the motion of the ship. 'Perhaps I should call you Drinkwater, now the ship is yours.'

'I should be honoured, sir. She is a fine ship.'

'That is a compliment, yes?'

'It was intended so, sir, and the only one I can offer, under the circumstances.'

Santhonax narrowed his eyes. 'You do not have many men to work her.'

'Sufficient, sir.'

'You are pleased with your success, *hein*?' He bit his lip as a wave of pain swept over him, 'pleased that I am your prisoner?'

'*C'est la guerre*, sir, the fortune of war. I would rather Griffiths lived, you have the advantage over him there.'

'He saved your life.' Santhonax looked down at his shoulder.

'But you are not dead, Capitaine.'

Santhonax smiled. 'He intended to kill me.'

'He was intent upon revenge.'

'Revenge? *Pourquoi*?'

'Major Brown,' Drinkwater said icily, 'rotting on a gibbet over the guns of Kijkduin.'

Santhonax frowned. 'Ah, the English spy we caught . . .' Drinkwater remembered the jolly brevet-major Santhonax had captured in Holland. He and Griffiths had been friends, brothers-in-arms.

Santhonax shrugged. 'Most assuredly, Lieutenant, we are all of us mortal. My wife has not yet forgiven you this . . .' His finger reached up and indicated the disfigurement of his face. 'I doubt she ever will.'

For a moment it occurred to Drinkwater to roll up his sleeve and reveal the twisted flesh of his own right arm, but the childishness of such an action suddenly struck him. He remained silent.

'You are bound for England, yes?' Santhonax went on. Drinkwater nodded. 'It is a long way yet, eh?' Santhonax turned and began to pace the deck, leaning on Bruilhac's shoulder.

'Mr Drinkwater!' Morris's voice cut across the quarterdeck as he emerged from the companionway.

'Mornin' sir,' Drinkwater uncovered again.

'Mr Drinkwater, hands are to witness punishment at four bells.'

'Punishment, sir? Nothing has been reported to me . . .'

'Insolence, Mr Drinkwater, insolence was reported to me at six bells in the first watch, Mr Dalziell's watch.'

'And the offender sir?'

'Your lackey, Drinkwater,' said Morris with evident pleasure, 'Tregembo.'

Drinkwater forced himself to watch Tregembo's face. The eyes were tight shut and the teeth bit into the leather pad that prevented the Cornishman from biting through his own tongue as each stroke of the cat made him flinch. At the twelfth stripe the bosun's mates changed. The second man ran the bloody tails of cat through his hand as he braced his feet. He hesitated.

'Lay on there, damn you!' Morris snapped and Drinkwater sensed the wave of resentment that ran through the people assembled in the waist. Tregembo's 'insolence', Drinkwater had learned in the roundabout way that a good first lieutenant might determine the true course of events, had consisted of no more than being last back on deck after working aloft during Dalziell's watch. When accused of idleness Tregembo had mumbled that one must always be last on deck and it was usually the first aloft who had been working on the yardarm.

For this piece of logic Tregembo was now being flayed. The bosun's mates changed again. Drinkwater recollected Dalziell's earlier attempt to have Tregembo flogged and the smirk on the young man's face fully confirmed his present satisfaction. Morris too had a reason for flogging Tregembo. The Cornishman had been a witness to his disgrace aboard *Cyclops*, indeed Tregembo had had a hand in the disappearance one night of one of Morris's cabal.

Drinkwater was pleased to note that Lieutenant Rogers appeared most unhappy over an issue that previously might have pleased him, while Quilhampton, Appleby and the rest stood mutely averting their eyes. At the conclusion of the third dozen Tregembo was cut down. Drinkwater dismissed the hands in a dispassionate voice.

That evening it fell calm again, the sea smooth on its surface with the ship rolling on a lazy swell. The sun had set blood-red, leaving an after glow of scarlet reaching almost to the zenith, through which the cold pin-pricks of stars were beginning to break. Venus blazed above Africa eighty leagues to the west. Drinkwater paced the deck, an hour and a half of his watch to go. His uniform coat stuck to his back, a prickling example of Morris's tyranny, for the commander had refused to allow his officers to appear on the quarterdeck in their shirt-sleeves as they had done under Griffiths.

Already shadows were deepening about the deck. The second dog-watch idled about restlessly. Drinkwater picked up the quadrant Quilhampton had brought up.

'Ready, Mr Q?'

'All ready, sir,' replied the midshipman, squatting down on the deck next to the chronometer box and jamming the slate between his crossed knees in the position he had found most suitable, minus one hand, for jotting down the first lieutenant's observations. Drinkwater smiled at the small, crouched figure. The boy frowned in concentration as he watched the second hand jerk round, the slate pencil poised in his only fist.

'Very well then, Venus first.' Drinkwater set the index to zero and caught the planet in the mirrors, twisting his wrist and rotating the instrument about its index. His long fingers twiddled the vernier screw and he settled the planet's disc precisely on the horizon, his fingers turning slowly as he followed the mensurable descent of it, rocking the whole so that the disc oscillated on the tangent of the horizon. 'On!'

Quilhampton noted the time as Drinkwater read the altitude off the arc and called the figures to the midshipman. Quilhampton dutifully repeated them.

Drinkwater took a second observation of Venus then crossed the deck. 'Canopus next!'

'Get up, brat!' Drinkwater turned at the intrusion. Morris stood over the midshipman who, in his concentration had not seen the commander arrive on the quarterdeck. 'Have you never been taught respect, you damned whoreson?'

Quilhampton put out his left arm to push himself to his feet, forgetting he had no hand. The still soft stump gave under him and he slipped on to his knees, the colour draining from his face. 'I, I'm sorry sir, I was watching the chronometer . . .' Morris's foot came back and sent the chronometer box spinning across the deck. It caught against a ring bolt, tipped and the glass shattered.

Drinkwater swiftly crossed the deck. 'Turn a glass,' he snapped at the quartermaster by the binnacle. Perhaps there was not too much damage and any stopping of the timepiece might be allowed for, 'then go below and get the precise time from Mr Appleby's hunter.' Morris had begun to rail at the terrified midshipman. It was clear that he was drunk.

'I think, sir,' intervened Drinkwater, 'that you are mistaken in supposing Mr Quilhampton intended any disrespect. The loss of his hand necessitates that he . . .'

'Be silent, Mr Drinkwater,' slurred Morris, 'and have this scum at the foremasthead at once.'

Drinkwater took one look at the swaying figure of Morris. 'Up you go, Mr Q,' he said quietly, lowering the quadrant into its case. Quilhampton's eyes were filling with tears. Drinkwater jerked his head imperceptibly and the boy turned forward. Drinkwater bent over the chronometer case.

'Mr Drinkwater! I am addressing you!' Drinkwater picked up the case.

'Sir?' he was looking down at the bent gimbals. The second hand no longer moved. 'I don't expect that sort of disrespect on my quarterdeck . . .' Morris was very drunk. It was clear that he had not yet realised what it was he had kicked across the deck.

'I doubt that it will occur again, sir,' said Drinkwater looking down at the ruined chronometer.

'It had better bloody not.' Suddenly Morris heaved, swallowed and staggered below. Darkness stole over the ship. The time to take stellar observations had passed. Drinkwater did not know precisely where they were and, in truth, he did not greatly care.

'Don't worry, Mr Drinkwater,' said Lestock, apparently pleased at the destruction of the timepiece. 'Your theoretical navigation lost us a brig and the captain has had the sense to deprive you of your toy before you cause more damage.'

'Go to the devil, you addle-brained old fool!' snapped Drinkwater.

They got Quilhampton down at dawn, calling the surgeon to roll him in warmed blankets and chafe him with spirits. The inside of his left elbow was raw from where the laborious climb had caused him to use it as a hook. At the conclusion of his watch Drinkwater sought out the surgeon and found him still attending the boy in the company of Catherine Best.

'How is he?'

'He'll live, but he's chilled to the marrow and cramped.'

'Aye the damned wind got up during the middle watch and it's already half a gale. This is the monsoon all right.'

'Damn your monsoon, Nat, have we to put up with that vicious bastard aft all the way home? Oh, don't worry about Catherine,' he added seeing Drinkwater's covert glance at the woman, 'she well knows all my sentiments on Mister festering Morris.'

'You know the answer to your own question, Harry.'

'So it's shorten canvas and ride out the gale even if it lasts another three or four months, eh?'

'Your metaphor is good enough.'

'Pity he can't be ill like poor old Griffiths, then he could let you run the blasted ship.'

'I doubt he would allow that,' smiled Drinkwater resignedly.

'Well if he goes on swilling rum at the present rate he'll either destroy his intestines or drink us out of the damned stuff and be raving from delirium tremens!' Appleby stood up as Quilhampton opened his eyes. 'Then you would have to take over, eh?'

'That talk from another I would take as sedition, Harry,' said Drinkwater seriously. 'I beg you do not be so free with your opinions.'

'Bah!' said Appleby contemptuously while Catherine Best gave both the men an odd look.

Chapter Nineteen *October–November 1799*

A Woman's Touch

Appleby regarded his new patient with distaste. Commander Morris lay exhausted in his cot, the sweat pouring from him, the seat lid of his cabin commode lifted and a bucket swilling with vomit by his side. Appleby moved nearer the open stern window for some fresh air. *Antigone* slipped south, her clean hull slicing the blue waters of the Indian Ocean, her towering pyramids of canvas expanding laterally as studding sails increased her speed. Beneath her elegant bowsprit and white figurehead the bottle-nosed dolphins leapt and cavorted, effortlessly outstripping the ship as she threw up scores of flying fish on either hand. October was passing to November and the high summer of the southern hemisphere .

The hiss of the sea, upwelling green and white from under the frigate's plunging stern, the creak of the rudder chains and tiller ropes a deck below and the chasing seas seemed a cleansing antidote to the stink of the cabin. Appleby turned back into it.

'The diaphoresis is very severe, sir, and the flux abnormal. How many times did you purge yourself during the night?'

'Don't bandy your medical quackery here Appleby, I was up shitting most of the night and when I was not doing that I was puking my guts into that bucket. I tell you someone is poisoning me !'

'Come, come, sir. Don't be ridiculous. These are not the symptoms of poison. Where would one obtain poison on a ship? My chest is locked and I wear the keys, here,' he jingled the bunch on his fob.

'Appleby, you damned fool, you can poison a man . . .'

'Sir,' cut in Appleby sharply, 'I assure you that you are *not* being poisoned. Such a notion is preposterous. You are exhibiting symptoms of chronic gastritis. Your dependence upon alcohol has ulcerated the mucous membrane of the stomach as a result of which you are unable to retain nourishment in your belly. The natural reaction of the body is to void itself. If you do not trust my diagnosis sir, I would be only too happy to transfer to another ship at the Cape. In the meantime I shall send Tyson in to attend you and clean up some of this mess. Good morning.'

Appleby left the commander to attend to Santhonax. His wound was healing badly, a continuing process of exfoliation preventing the tissues from knitting properly. An easy familiarity had developed between the Frenchman and the surgeon as commonly exists between a man and his physician.

'Where did you learn to speak English, sir?' asked Appleby removing the dressing.

'I was the son of a half-English mother, Mr Appleby, the daughter of a wild-goose Englishman who supported King James III.'

'Ah, the Old Pretender, eh?' said Appleby wryly, 'but you are not so partial to kings since the Revolution?'

'They are not noted for their gratitude to even their most loyal adherents.'

'We notice that in King George's navy.'

'Treason, Mr Appleby?'

'Truth, Captain Santhonax.'

'You would make a most excellent revolutionary.'

'Perhaps, if the material was worth the saving, but I doubt even your brand will materially alter this tired old world. Were you not yourself about to enslave the Hindoos?'

Santhonax smiled, a bleak, wolfish smile. 'Had that damned combination of Drinkwater and Griffiths not been at my tail I might have succeeded.'

'You forget, captain, I too was on *Kestrel* . . .'

'*Diable*, I had forgot . . . yes it was you sutured my face. It is a strange coincidence is it not, that we should find ourselves fighting a private war?'

Appleby finished binding the new dressing over a clean pledget. 'Griffiths called it proof of Providence, Captain. What would your new religion of Reason call it?'

'Much the same, Mr Appleby . . . thank you.'

'You will be well enough soon. I think the exfoliation almost complete. It will be a whole man we return to the hulks at Portsmouth.'

'You have yet to get your stolen vessel past Île de France, Appleby. Perhaps it may yet be me who will be visiting you.'

'Well what *is* the matter with him?' asked Drinkwater, straightening up from the chart spread on the gunroom table, 'he tells me he is of the opinion that he is being poisoned. Damn it, I think he half thought I might have instigated it! What Morris surmises he believes, God help us all, and if there is a shred of truth behind such an apparently monstrous allegation . . .'

'Oh for the love of heaven don't you start, Nat. Permit me the luxury of knowing my own business yet. You would take exception to my advice upon the reduction of altitudes. I tell you the man is suffering from alcohol induced gastritis.'

'Very well, Harry, I trust your judgement.' Drinkwater cut short the long dissertation that he knew would follow once Appleby was allowed to start expanding on Morris's symptoms.

Rattray scratched at the gunroom door. 'Cap'n's compliments, Mr Drinkwater, and would you join him in the cabin.' Drinkwater cast a significant glance at the surgeon, picked up his hat and followed 'the Rat'.

Drinkwater bridled at the stench in the cabin. Morris looked ghastly, weak and pale, his face covered with perspiration, his cot sheets twisted. He spoke with the economy of effort.

'Would you poison me, Drinkwater?' The man was clearly desperate.

'Certainly not!' Drinkwater's outrage was unfeigned. He recollected himself. Whatever Morris was, he was a sick man now. 'Please rest assured that the surgeon is quite confident that you are suffering from a gastric disorder, sir. I have no doubt that if you modify your diet, sir . . .'

'Get out, Drinkwater, get out . . . Rattray! Where the devil is that blagskite?'

As he left Drinkwater noticed the tear in the portrait of Hortense.

The bottle Rattray brought to Drinkwater's cabin that evening for him to take with his biscuits in the gunroom was a surprise. Drinkwater removed the cork and sniffed suspiciously. He was alone in the room, Rogers having turned in and Appleby gone to change Santhonax's dressing. He poured the Oporto that had arrived, uncharacteristically, with the captain's compliments and held the glass against the light of the lantern. He sniffed it then, shrugging, he sipped.

If it was supposed that this was poisoned wine, Drinkwater mused, then it was indeed nonsense and Morris's generosity was but a manifestation of his phobia. He finished the glass and felt nothing more than a comfortable warmth radiating in his guts. Dismissing the matter he sat down, pulled his stores ledger towards him and unsnapped the ink-well. Merrick brought him a new quill from his cabin and he dismissed the messman for the night and stretched his legs.

The water biscuits were in quite good condition, he thought, picking up a third. He settled to his work. And poured a second glass of wine.

Dawn found Nathaniel Drinkwater violently sick, a pale sheen of perspiration upon his face. He sent for Appleby who came on deck expecting he had been summoned to attend the captain.

'What is it, Nat?' Drinkwater beckoned the surgeon to windward, out of earshot of the helmsmen and the quartermaster at the con.

'What d'you make of my complexion, Harry?'

'Eh?' Appleby paused then peered at the lieutenant. 'Why a mild diaphoresis.'

'And I've been violently sick for an hour past. Also I purged myself during the middle watch . . .'

Appleby frowned. 'But that's not possible . . . no, I mean . . .'

'It means that Morris may indeed be being poisoned, man. Last night he sent me a bottle of Oporto . . . he must have meant me to try it, to see if it had any effect upon me! I drank it entire!'

'For God's sake, Nat, of course he's being poisoned. Rum and fortified wines addle the brain, corrode the guts. Try cleaning brass with them.' Appleby's exasperation was total. Then he calmed, looking again at his friend. 'Forgive me, that was unpardonable. Your own condition I would ascribe to a tainted bottle. Maybe Morris had been consuming a case of bad wine. That would produce such symptoms and aggravate the peptic ulcer I am certain he suffers from.'

'But the wine tasted well, seemed not to be bad.'

Appleby was not listening. Even in the vehemence of his diagnostic defence a tiny doubt had crept into his mind. The symptoms were those produced by sudorifics, used by himself to promote the sweating agues that eased Griffiths's malaria. And though the key to his dispensary never left his side he was wondering who possessed the knowledge enough to incapacitate Morris.

'. . . 'tis commonly supposed a woman's weapon,' he muttered to himself.

'I beg your pardon?'

Appleby shook his head. ''Tis nothing,' he turned away then came back, having thought of something. 'Nat, would you oblige me by concealing your indisposition . . . at least for the time being.'

Puzzled, Drinkwater nodded wanly. 'As you wish, Harry.' He fought down a spasm of nausea and stared seawards. Whatever the cause it was not lethal. Just bloody uncomfortable.

'Deck there!' The hail broke from the masthead: 'Ship on the lee beam!'

'God's bones!' swore Drinkwater beneath his breath, fishing in his tail pocket for his Dollond glass.

Chapter Twenty

The Fortune of War

In the mizen top Drinkwater fought down a bout of nausea with the feeling that the effect of the bad wine was weakening. In reality the bluish square on the horizon distracted him. He levelled the glass, crouched and trimmed it against a topmast shroud. It was difficult to see at this angle, although the sail was dark against the dawn, but it appeared to be a ship on the wind like themselves. Not that there was a great deal of wind, and the day promised little better. He wiped his eye, looked again and then, still uncertain, he determined to do what any prudent officer could do in a ship as ill-armed as *Antigone*: assume the worst.

Descending to the deck he addressed Quilhampton. 'You have the deck, Mr Q.' Such an errand as he was bound on was not to be left to a midshipman. Mr Quilhampton's astonishment changed to pride and then to determination.

'Aye, aye, sir!' Despite his preoccupation Drinkwater could not resist a smile. Quilhampton had turned into a real asset, competent and with a touch of loyalty that marked him for a good subordinate. Drinkwater recollected how it had been Mr Q that had brought his effects off Abu al Kizan. It had been touching to discover his books and journals neatly shelved, his quadrant box lashed and the little watercolour done for him by Elizabeth all in place in the cabin aboard *Antigone*. That had been a long time ago. There were more pressing matters now.

Drinkwater knocked perfunctorily and entered Morris's stateroom. Automatically his eyes flicked over the portrait of Hortense Santhonax.

'What the hell d'you want? What brings you from the deck?'

'An enemy, sir. To loo'ard,' Drinkwater fought back the desire to vomit. He had forgotten his own sickness and retched on the stink of Morris's. 'I believe her to be a French cruiser out of Île de France.'

Morris absorbed the news. He swallowed, then frowned. 'But, I . . . a French cruiser d'you say? What makes you so sure?'

'Does it matter, sir? If she's British and we run there's nothing lost, if she's French and we don't we may be.'

'May be what?' Morris frowned again, his obtuseness a symptom of his feeble state. Drinkwater was suddenly sorry for him.

'May be lost, sir. I recommend we make our escape, sir, put the ship on the wind another half point and see what she will do.' He paused. 'We are without a main battery, sir,' he reminded Morris.

The responsibility of command stirred something in Morris. He nodded. 'Very well.'

Drinkwater made for the door.

'Drinkwater!'

Nathaniel paused and peered back into the cabin. Dragging his soiled bedding behind him Morris was straining to see the enemy through the stern windows. 'Yes, sir?' Morris turned, his face grey and fleshless beneath the skin.

'I . . . nothing, damn it.' Morris looked hideously alone. And frightened.

'Truly sir, you will be better if you abstain from all strong and spirituous liquors.' He hurried off, almost glad to fasten his mind on the problem of escape.

'Hands to the braces!' The cry was taken up.

'All hands sir?' Quilhampton asked eagerly, 'Beat to quarters?'

'Not yet, Mr Q,' said Drinkwater looking aloft, 'we have no marine drummer to do the honours. Besides, one runs away with less ceremony.' It occurred to Drinkwater that he had said something shaming to the boy, as if, occasionally even British tars may not run when probably outgunned and certainly outnumbered. 'Trice her up a little, there! Half a point to windward, damn you!' He looked aloft as the watch hauled the yards against the catharpings, each successively higher yard braced at a slightly more acute angle to the wind.

'Royals, sir?'

'Royals, Mr Q.'

The chase wore on into the afternoon and the wind became

591

increasingly fluky. The quality of drama was absent from the desperate business with such a light breeze but it was replaced by a sense of the sinister. Drinkwater kept the deck, amazed at the dark looks of outrage cast by Acting Lieutenant Dalziell. Morris made several appearances on deck, borrowing Drinkwater's glass and mumbling approval at his conduct before slipping below to continue his debilitating flux.

Drinkwater wondered what Appleby had done with the news that he too had been sick, then realised that he was no longer so, merely hungry and that there was another matter to occupy his brain.

'Mr Dalziell, be so kind as to fetch my quadrant from my cabin.'

'Mr Drinkwater, may I remind you that I hold an acting . . .'

'You may stand upon the quarterdeck, devil take you, but not upon your festerin' dignity! Go sir, at once!' Dalziell fled. For the next half hour he carefully measured the angle subtended by the enemy's uppermost yard and the horizon. In that time it increased by some twelve minutes of arc.

'I do not know if I might do that, sir.' He heard Quilhampton's voice and looked up to see the midshipman clasping the watch glass behind his back. He was withholding it from the outstretched hand of Capitaine Santhonax.

'Do you allow the captain the loan of your glass, Mr Q. Perhaps he will be courteous enough to oblige us with his opinion.' Santhonax grinned his predatory smile over Mr Quilhampton's head. 'Ah, Drinkwater, you would not neglect any opportunity to gain information, eh?'

'Your opinion, sir.' Santhonax took the glass and hoisted himself carefully into the lee mizen rigging. His wound had much improved in recent days and Drinkwater saw from the set of his mouth that his own fears were confirmed. Santhonax regained the deck. 'It is a French vessel, is it not captain?'

Santhonax favoured Drinkwater with a long penetrating look. 'Yes,' he said quietly, 'she is French. And from Île de France.'

Drinkwater nodded. 'Thank you, sir. Mr Quilhampton, pass word for the gunner.' He turned to Santhonax. 'Captain I regret the necessity that compels me to confine you but . . .' he shrugged.

'You will revoke my parole, please?'

Drinkwater nodded as the gunner arrived. 'Mr Trussel, Captain Santhonax and Cadet Bruilhac are to be confined in irons . . .'

'Merde!'

'My pardon, sir, but your character is too well-known,' he spun on his heel, 'pipe all hands, Mr Dalziell, and take the deck while I confer with the captain.'

Morris listened to what Drinkwater had to say, aware that he was powerless. A man who had never been troubled by moral constraints, who had managed his profession by a bullying authoritarianism and sought to excuse his failures upon others, found it easy to delegate to Drinkwater's competence. Although a bitter irony filled his mind it was not caused by the chance that Drinkwater might steal his thunder and fight a brilliant action. Whatever happened, a victory would be attributed to him as commander. What wormed in Morris's mind was that Drinkwater might botch it, perhaps deliberately.

'If you desert me, or disgrace me, as God is my witness I shall shoot you.'

There was no dissembling in Drinkwater's reply, uttered as it was over his shoulder. 'I should never do that, not in the face of the enemy.'

Drinkwater ran back on deck. One glance to leeward confirmed his worst fears. He could see the enemy hull now. *Antigone* was losing the race. He began to shout orders.

The burst of activity on deck was barely audible in the orlop. Inside the tiny dispensary, by the light of a guttering candle end Appleby looked from book to pot and back again. At last he sat back and stared at the jar, its glass greenish and clouded, and holding something given apparent life by the flame that flickered uncertainly in the foetid air.

He pulled the stopper from the jar and poured a trickle of white crystals into the palm of his hand. The potassium antimonyl tartrate twinkled dully from the candle flame.

Appleby poured them back. A few adhered to his perspiring skin. He sighed. 'Tartar emetic,' he muttered to himself, replacing the jar in its rack, 'a sudorific promoting diaphoresis.' He sighed.

The sudden glare of a lantern through the louvred door made his hand shoot out and nip the candlewick. In the sudden close darkness he almost prayed that he might be mistaken, but he heard her indrawn and alarmed breath as she discovered the padlock hanging unlocked in the staple and the hasp free. She paused and he knew she was wondering whether anyone was within. Making up her mind she drew back the door and thrust her lantern into the tiny hutch.

He sat immobile, the trembling lantern throwing his face into sharp relief, its smooth rotundities lit, the shadows of his falling cheeks and dewlap etched black. She drew back a hand at her throat.

'Oh! Mr Appleby! Sir, how you did frighten me, sitting in the dark like that . . .'

'Come in and close the door.'

He watched her with such an intensity that she thought it was lust, not displeasure. Indeed she began to compose herself for his first embrace as he stood, stooped under the deckhead beams.

'What in the name of heaven are you up to?' Appleby's breath was hot with the passion of anger. She drew back. He picked up the lantern from where she had placed it on the bench and held it over the jar of Tartar Emetic.

'You are giving this to the captain,' he said it slowly, as a matter of fact.

'You know then . . .'

'I do. In his wine, though I have not yet discovered how you do it.'

For a long moment she said nothing. Appleby put the lantern down and sat again. He looked up at her. 'I am disappointed . . . I had hoped . . .'

She knelt at his knees and took his hands, her huge eyes staring up at him.

'I did not . . . I wished only to make him indisposed, too ill to command. You yourself suggested it in conversation with Mr Drinkwater . . .'

'I . . .?'

'Yes sir,' she had sown the seed of doubt now, caught him between her suppliant posture and her rapid city-bred quick wittedness. 'You see what he has done to the men, how he has flogged them without mercy or reason. Why look at the way he sent poor little Mr Q to the top of the mast, and him with one hand miss-

594

ing . . .' She appealed to his inherent kindness and felt him relax. 'We all know what Mr Rogers said about what happened at Mocha, how Mr Drinkwater should've been in command.'

'That is no reason to . . .'

'And the kind of man he is, sir . . .' But Appleby rallied.

'That is not for you to say,' he said vehemently, a trace of misogyny emerging, 'it does not justify poisoning . . .'

'But I gave him only a little, sir, enough to purge himself with a flux. Why 'twas little more than you gave the old Captain for his ague, sir. 'Twas not a lethal dose.'

Appleby knitted his brows in concentration. His professional sense warred with his curious regard for this woman kneeling in the stinking darkness. He would not call it love for he thought of himself as too old, too ugly and too much a man of science to be moved by love. This wish to defend her was aided by his dislike of Morris. He found he was no longer angry with her. He could understand her motives much as one does a child who misbehaves. It did not condone the crime.

'You poisoned Mr Drinkwater, Catherine,' he said, unknowingly reproving her most effectively.

'Mr Drinkwater, my God! How?'

'Morris sent him in a bottle last night.'

'Oh!' It was Catherine's turn to deflate. She had not meant to harm any other person, especially he who offered her almost her only chance of avoiding a convict transport. 'H . . . how is he?'

'He will be all right.' He paused. 'Are you sorry?'

She could read him now. She had won. Flipping open the lantern she blew it out. And sealed her advantage.

On the gun deck every man who could be spared was at work. Drinkwater had relinquished the upper deck to Dalziell with an admonition to the quartermaster that if he was a degree off the wind more than was necessary he would be flayed. The man grinned cheerfully and the first lieutenant went below to orchestrate the idea that was already causing a buzz of comment, much of it unfavourable.

'Belay that damned Dover court and take heed of what I have to say . . .'

The wind eased by the minute but it continued to blow down to leeward, conferring an advantage on the pursuer. She could be plainly seen from the deck now but Drinkwater no longer fretted over her approach. Instead he sweated and swore, admonished and encouraged, belaboured and bullied the tired Hellebores as they lugged the six larboard eighteen-pounders across the deck to assemble a battery of twelve in the vacant gunports on the starboard side.

The deck was criss-crossed with tackles, bull ropes and preventers. After several hours employed in hauling first one and then another, of casting stoppers on and off, of wracking seizings and heaving on handspikes, Rogers, stripped to his shirt and mopping his florid face with a handkerchief, fought his way over the network of lines.

'Christ alive, Drinkwater, this is a confounded risky trick, ain't it. Damn me if I can see the logic of putting all your eggs in one basket.' There was a murmur of agreement from several of the men.

'Why, Mr Rogers,' said Drinkwater cheerfully, suddenly realising that his flux and nausea had vanished, and pitching his voice loud enough for all to hear, 'the easier to hurl 'em at the French!'

'So's they can make bleeding hommelettes . . .'

'To go with their fucking frog's legs . . .' A burst of laughter greeted this sally while Mr Lestock, peering down from the deck, tut-tutted and went aft.

'The captain is aware of our doin's, Mr Lestock,' called Drinkwater and another burst of laughter came from the men. It might be a dangerous indication of indiscipline but what the hell? They might all be dead in the coming hours. Or exchanging places with Santhonax. 'Right; a touch more on that tackle, Mr Brundell, if you please.'

'Come then, lads,' roared the master's mate. The men spat on their hands and lay back. They broke out into the spontaneous cry they had evolved for concerted effort: 'Hellee-ee-bores . . . Bellee-ee-whores . . .!' The eighteen-pounder moved across the deck and Drinkwater thought Griffiths would have approved of that cry.

Night found them almost becalmed but the whisper of wind remained constant in direction and Drinkwater held to his belief that they must not throw away their position to windward, that to attempt to run down past their enemy and escape only put the French between them and the Cape. But dawn found them to leeward, the wind backing and rising as, in growing daylight they were able to see the wind fill the enemy's sails before their own.

But Drinkwater's chagrin was swiftly replaced by hope an hour after dawn. Without warning the wind chopped round to the southwest again and began to freshen, both ships leaned to it, *Antigone* less than usual since she carried all her artillery on her starboard, windward side.

But the fluky quality of the wind had overnight brought their opponent almost within gunshot. At last Drinkwater was compelled to order his men to quarters.

He had not done so earlier to preserve their energy but, hardly had he taken the decision and the watch below came tumbling sleepily on deck, than the first shot fell short upon their larboard quarter.

The four-score Hellebores ran to their stations. Rogers came aft and received his instructions. When Drinkwater explained what he intended to do Rogers held out his hand.

'I've misjudged you in the past, Nathaniel, and I'm sorry for it. I only hope my new-found confidence is not misplaced.'

'Amen to that, Samuel,' replied Drinkwater, smiling ruefully. Appleby came on deck.

'D'you have your saws and daviers at the ready, Harry?' jested Drinkwater hollowly, shuddering at the thought of being rendered limbless by such instruments.

'Aye, Nat, and God help me,' he added with a significant stare at Drinkwater, 'Kate Best assists me.' He disappeared below, followed by Rogers en route to command the battery of eighteen-pounders. Lestock coughed beside him, affecting to study the enemy and remarking upon his shooting as the French bow chaser barked away at them. The tricolour could be seen trailing astern from her peak and mainmasthead. As yet no colours flew from *Antigone*'s spars. Mr Dalziell strutted nervously along the line of larboard quarterdeck carronades. To starboard Mr Quilhampton was quietly pacing up and down, his stump behind his back, doing his best to ape Mr Drinkwater. At the mainmast Mr Brundell commanded the waisters to board or trim sail as the need arose while, legs apart on the fo'c's'le Mr Grey, his silver whistle about his neck commanded the head party.

The person of Rattray appeared carrying a chair. He placed it upon the quarterdeck and Morris, pale and shaking, slumped into it. Drinkwater approached him.

'I am glad to see you sir, your presence will encourage the hands.' Under the circumstances he could say no more. Morris's courage had surely been misjudged, perhaps the responsibility of command could yet temper the man just as culpability had changed Rogers.

Morris stared up at Drinkwater and moved his hand from beneath the blanket. The lock of a pistol was visible in his lap.

'Stuff your sanctimonious cant, Drinkwater. Fight my bloody ship or I'll blow you to hell.'

Drinkwater opened his mouth in astonishment. Then he closed it as a thump hit the ship and a spatter of splinters flew from the larboard quarter rail. The action had begun.

All on deck stared astern. In the full daylight the frigate foaming up looked glorious, her hull a rich brown, her gunstrake cream. She was a point upon their larboard quarter. Thank God for a strengthening wind, thought Drinkwater as he spoke to Lestock. 'Mr Lestock! Do you let her fall off a little, contrive it to look a trifle careless.'

'D'you give away weather gauge, Mr Drinkwater?' contradicted Lestock with a look in Morris's direction.

'Do as you are told, sir!' The quartermaster eased the helm up a couple of spokes and *Antigone* paid off the wind a few degrees. The gunfire ceased. Relative motion showed the Frenchman slowly crossing *Antigone*'s stern. For the moment his bow chasers would not bear.

'British colours, Mr Q.' Old Glory snapped out over their heads and almost immediately the enemy's larboard bow chaser opened fire. She had crossed their stern. Drinkwater had surrendered the weather gauge and still the *Antigone* had not fired a shot.

Drinkwater walked forward and gripped the rail. 'Mr Brundell! Ease your foremast lee sheets a little!' A tiny tremble could be felt through the palms of his damp hands as he clasped the rail tightly. *Antigone* was losing power through those trembling foresails. He hoped the enemy could not see those fluttering clews behind the sails of the mainmast. The French ship began to draw ahead, overtaking them on their starboard side, a fine big ship, almost, now,

598

they could see her in profile, identical to themselves. 'Are you ready, Mr Rogers?' Drinkwater hailed and the word was passed back that Samuel Rogers was ready. To vindicate his honour, Drinkwater guessed.

'I hope you know what you are about Mr Drinkwater.' Morris's voice sounded stronger. 'So do I, sir,' replied Drinkwater swept by a sudden mood of exhilaration. If only the Frog would hold his broadside until all his guns would bear.

'Stand by mizen braces, Mr Brundell,' he called in a sharp, clear voice.

'What the bloody hell . . .?'

'For what we are about to receive . . .'

'Holy Mary, Mother of God . . .'

A puff of smoke erupted from the forward larboard gun of the French frigate. They were her lee guns, pointing downwards on a deck sloping towards the enemy. So much for the weather gauge once the manoeuvring was over.

But it was not over: 'Mizen braces! Mr Rogers!'

The lee mizen braces were flung from their pins, a man at each to see them free, with orders to cut them if a single turn jammed in a block. The faked ropes ran true as the weather braces were hauled under the vociferous direction of Brundell. All along the starboard side the smoke and flame of the main-deck battery opened fire, the twelve eighteen-pounders rumbling back on their trucks to be sponged and reloaded. Drinkwater did not think they would manage more than a single shot at their adversary as, under the thundering backing of the mizen sails, *Antigone* slowed in the water, appeared to stop dead as the enemy stormed past, suddenly firing ahead of the British prize. Quilhampton was hauling the carronade slides round to get off a second shot, screaming at his gun crews like a regular Tarpaulin officer.

'Come you sons of whores, move it up, lively with that sponge, God damn you . . .'

Drinkwater looked for the fall of shot. At maximum elevation with the ship heeling *away* from the enemy they must have done some damage. Christ, they had hurled all the damned bar shot and chain shot they could cram in the guns, all the French dis-masting projectiles to give the Frogs a taste of their own medicine.

And they had missed her. Mortified, Drinkwater's ever obser-
vant eye could already read the name of the passing frigate: *Romaine*.
And now, by heaven, they *must* run.

A cheer was breaking out on the fo'c's'le and he looked again. The
enemy's maintopmast was tottering to leeward. It formed a graceful
curve then fell in a splintering of spars and erratic descent as stays
arrested it and parted under the weight.

Relief flooded Drinkwater. There was cheering all along the
upper deck and from down below. Rogers had come up and was
pumping his hand. Even Lestock's face wore a sickly, condescending
grin.

'Sir! Sir!' Quilhampton was pointing.

'God's bones!'

The wreckage was slewing the *Romaine* sharply to larboard,
across *Antigone*'s bow. In the perfect position to rake. And men were
working furiously at the wreckage with axes. Forward a man
screamed as his leg flew off. It was Mr Brundell. 'Mr Grey! Back the
yards on the foremast!' He turned, 'Mr Dalziell, back the yards on
the main, lively now.'

He waited impatiently. *Antigone* had hove herself to. Now they
must make a stern board, to get out of trouble before . . .

The raking broadside hit them, the balls whirling the length of the
deck. Mr Quilhampton fell and beside Drinkwater Lestock went
'Urgh!' and a gout of blood appeared all over Drinkwater's breeches.
Drinkwater stood stock still. On the fo'c's'le, legs still apart, stood
Mr Grey. The two men stood numbed, one hundred feet apart,
regarding each other over a human shambles. As if by magic figures
stood up and the main yards groaned round in their parrels. They
were followed by those on the foremast. *Antigone* began to gather
sternway. The next broadside roared out. It had been fired on an
upward roll. *Antigone*'s foretopgallant mast went overboard.

'Helm a weather! Hard a-starboard!' But Drinkwater's order was
too late. The frigate was already paying off, her bows coming up into
the wind, across the wind, until finally she wallowed with her
unarmed larboard side facing the enemy.

'Lee forebrace!' If he could trim the yards to the larboard tack they
might yet escape. The third broadside brought the main topmast
down, the mizen topgallant with it. No one stood alive at the wheel.

Drinkwater looked at the *Romaine*. French cruisers, he knew, carried large crews. Now the advantages thus conferred upon them became apparent. Already the wreckage was cleared away and she was under control, setting down towards them.

'Mr Dalziell, prepare your larboard carronades. Mr Grey! Larboard fo'c's'le carronades.' Bitterly Drinkwater strode forward and jerked one of the brass gangway swivels. He lined it up on the approaching frigate.

'Mr Drinkwater!' He turned to find Morris pointing the pistol at him. 'You failed, Drinkwater . . .'

'Not yet, by God, Morris, not yet!'

'What else can you do, dog's turd, your cleverness has destroyed you.' Drinkwater's brain bridled at Morris's suggestion. True, a second earlier he himself had been on the verge of despair but the human mind trips and locks onto odd things under stress. It did not occur at that moment that Morris's action in pointing the gun at him was irrational; that Morris's apparent delight at his failure would also result in Morris's own capture. It was that old cockpit epithet that sparked his brain to greater endeavours.

'No, sir. By God there's one card yet to play!' he shouted below for Mr Rogers even as Dalziell approached with a coloured bundle in his arms.

'What the hell is that?' screamed Drinkwater.

'I was ordered to strike,' said Dalziell.

Chapter Twenty-One

A Matter of Luck

Drinkwater snatched the ensign from Dalziell's grasp. The red bunting spilled onto the deck. He turned to Morris, the question unasked on his lips. Morris inclined his head, implying his authority lay behind the surrender.

The belief that he was dying had taken so sharp a hold upon his mind that he was sure surrender offered him survival. The enemy cruiser was from Île de France. As commander of such a well-fought prize he would be treated with respect, and removed from the source of his poisoning he would recover. Into Morris's mind came another reason, adding its own weight in favour of surrender. While he enjoyed an easy house arrest at Port Louis his officers would be incarcerated. Drinkwater would be mewed up for the duration of the war. It would finish the work he had failed to do at Kosseir.

In the electric atmosphere that charged the quarterdeck all this was plain to them both. Their mutual antipathy had reached its crisis.

'The French are sending a boat, sir,' said Dalziell, eyes darting from one to the other. Drinkwater turned and shoved the ensign back at Dalziell.

'That is *Hellebore*'s ensign, by God! I'll not see it struck yet!'

Rogers arrived on the quarterdeck. He saw the ensign. 'Surely we haven't . . .?'

'No, by Christ, we have not!' Dalziell was pushed towards the halliards as Drinkwater snapped to Rogers. 'Get Santhonax up here, and Bruilhac! Quick!'

Drinkwater looked at the approaching boat, a launch packed with men, a cable from them.

'I command, damn you!' Morris hissed furiously. Drinkwater turned and looked down the barrel of the pistol.

He crossed the deck in two strides and wrenched the gun from his grasp. 'You may rot, Morris, but I am not through yet . . . get that ensign up, Dalziell, you lubber . . .'

Drinkwater was aware that he was holding the pistol at the young man. Dalziell threw a final, failing glance at Morris then did as he was bid. He belayed the halliards as Santhonax came on deck. The Frenchman looked curiously about him, took in the fallen spars, the broken bodies and blood spattered across the deck. He saw too the ensign being belayed and his quick mind understood. A glance to windward showed him his countrymen, the gunports of *Romaine*, and the boat, almost alongside.

'Get 'em up on the rail, Rogers, that Frog won't fire on his own boat.'

But a gun did fire, the ball whistling overhead, a single discharge to recall the British to the etiquette of war.

Drinkwater pointed the pistol at Santhonax. 'Captain, tell that boat to pull off. This ship has not surrendered. The ensign halliards were shot through. If the officer in the boat pulls off I will not open fire until he has regained his ship, otherwise I shall destroy him,' he paused, 'and you also, Captain.'

The French boat was ten yards off, the officer standing in the stern, looking up in astonishment at the apparition of a Republican naval officer standing beneath the British ensign like Hector on the walls of Troy.

Santhonax looked at Drinkwater. 'No,' he said simply. 'I leave it to the desperation of your plight and your conscience to shoot me.'

Drinkwater's heart was thumping painfully and he could feel the sweat pouring out of him. He sensed Morris awaiting events. He swore beneath his breath.

'Get up, Bruilhac!' The terrified boy climbed trembling on the rail as Drinkwater jerked his head at Rogers to pull Santhonax off the rail. Rogers leapt forward, together with Tregembo. But they were too late.

Drinkwater was about to threaten Bruilhac with instant death if he did not do his bidding but he was spared this cruel necessity. A sudden eruption of cannon fire to the east of them swung the focus of attention abruptly away from the wretched little drama on *Antigone*'s rails. At first is seemed *Romaine* had fired a final shattering broadside to compel *Antigone* to strike. In their boat the French thought the same. There was a simultaneous ducking of heads. Bruilhac fainted through sheer terror while a similar reflex caused Santhonax to dive outboard.

Even as Drinkwater registered Santhonax's escape and heard the howl of rage from Morris he had noticed there was no flame from *Romaine*'s larboard broadside. The sun beat down through the clearing smoke of their earlier discharges as the wind shredded the last of it to leeward and there, in the bright path laid by the sun upon the sea, they saw the newcomer.

'A British frigate, by all that's wonderful!' shouted Rogers, suddenly releasing them all from their suspended animation. Tregembo picked up two round-shot from the carronade garlands and tried to lob them into the French boat. The Frenchmen suddenly laid on their oars and spun her round just as Captain Santhonax's hand reached up for help. Drinkwater had a brief glimpse of his face, disfigured and distorted by the pain in his shoulder, his left arm trailing, his long legs kicking powerfully.

Another thundering broadside, this time from *Romaine*, caused a second's pause. There was no fall of shot near *Antigone*; *Romaine* was bracing her yards round to fill her sails with wind.

Drinkwater leapt to the deck. 'Rogers! Tregembo!'

He picked up a cartridge and rammed it into the nearest carronade. Tregembo rolled a shot into the muzzle and joined Rogers on the tackles. Drinkwater spun the screw and watched the blunt barrel depress. He leant against the slide and felt it slew on its heavy caster. 'Secure!'

Through the gunport he could see the boat, see the officer and a man hauling Santhonax over the transom. Rogers drove the priming quill into the touch-hole and blew powder into the groove. Still sighting along the barrel Drinkwater's right hand cocked the lock and his long fingers wound round the lanyard. The boat traversed the back-sight.

It occurred to him that it was easier to kill at a distance, removed from the confrontation from which Santhonax had just escaped. He had only to jerk the lanyard and Santhonax would die. He thought of the grey eyes staring from the portrait below, and of how he and Dungarth had let her go. From Hortense he thought of Elizabeth. The boat's transom crossed the end of the barrel. He jerked the lanyard.

The carronade roared back on its slide. Drinkwater leapt up to mark the fall of shot. He saw the spout of water a foot off the boat's quarter. He was surprised at the relief he felt.

'Let's try for a frigate,' Drinkwater spun the elevating screw again, bringing the retreating *Romaine* into his sights as, with crippled masts she moved sluggishly away. The wind was falling light, the concussion of their guns having killed it. They fired six shots before giving up. *Romaine* was out of range.

They craned their necks to see what was happening. They saw their rescuer begin to turn, trying to work across *Romaine*'s stern to rake. The French captain put his helm over and followed the British ship so they circled one another like dogs, nose to tail. A shattering broadside crashed from *Romaine*, a slighter response from the other. Another came from the Britisher. The *Romaine* began to draw off to the south-east. The stranger wore in pursuit, her mizen topmast going by the board as she did so.

'*Telemachus*,' Drinkwater spelled out, peering through his glass. The two ships moved slowly away, leaving *Antigone* rolling easily. The boat had vanished.

Drinkwater turned inboard. He and Morris exchanged a glance. Beneath his hooded lids Morris bore a whipped look. He went below.

Without any feeling of triumph Drinkwater's eyes fell upon the body of Quilhampton. Tregembo joined him.

'There's not a mark on him. Hold, he's not gone . . . Mr Q! Mr Q! D'you hear me?' Drinkwater began to chafe the boy's wrists. His eyes fluttered and opened. Rogers bent over them. 'Winded by a passing shot. He'll live,' said Rogers.

It took three days to re-rig the frigate, three days of strenuous labour during which the much depleted crew struggled and cursed, ate and slept between the guns. But although they swore they laboured willingly. They were not Antigones but Hellebores and the big frigate was their prize, the concrete proof of their corporate endeavours. She was also the source of prize money, and their shrinking numbers increased each individual's share.

By dint of their efforts they sent up new or improvised topmasts and could cross courses and topsails on all three masts. Later, Drinkwater thought, after they had carried out some additional modifications to the salvaged broken spars they might manage a main topgallant.

For Drinkwater the need to bring the frigate under command over-rode everything else. Morris retired to his cabin from whence came the news that he was keeping food down at last. From the cockpit came the hammock-shrouded corpses that failed to survive Appleby's surgery, the bravely smiling wounded and the empty rum bottles that sustained Appleby during the long hours he spent attending his grim profession.

Johnson reported they had been struck in the hull by twenty-one shot, but only two low enough to cause serious leakage.

The pumps clanked regularly even as the remaining men toiled to slew those half-dozen eighteen-pounders back into their larboard ports. They had lost sixteen men killed and twenty wounded in the action. Rank had almost ceased to exist as Drinkwater urged them on, officers tailing on to ropes and leading by example. Mr Lestock shook his head disapprovingly and Drinkwater left the deck watch to him and his precious sense of honour, deriving great comfort from the loyal support of Tregembo and even poor, handless, Mr Quilhampton who did what he could. Samuel Rogers emerged as a man who, given a task to do, performed it with that intemperate energy that so characterised him.

Late in the afternoon of the third day after the action with *Romaine* a sail was seen to leeward. Nervously glasses were trained on her, lest she proved the re-rigged *Romaine* come to finish off her late adversary. The last anyone aboard *Antigone* had seen of the two ships had been the *Telemachus* in pursuit of the *Romaine*. There had been no sign of Santhonax and the French boat and it was supposed that she had made the shelter of *Romaine*.

Drinkwater put *Antigone* on the wind and informed Morris. He was favoured with a grunt of acknowledgement.

'I think she's the *Telemachus*, sir,' Quilhampton informed Drinkwater when he returned to the deck.

'Hoist the interrogative, Mr Q. Mr Rogers! General quarters if you please!'

The pipes squealed at the hatchways and the pitifully small crew tumbled up, augmenting the watch on deck. The stranger was coming up fast, pointing much higher than the wounded frigate. The recognition signal streamed from her foremasthead. 'She's British, then,' said Lestock unnecessarily.

Drinkwater kept the men at their stations as the ship closed them. At a mile distance she fired a gun to leeward and hoisted the signal to heave to.

Drinkwater gave the order to back the main topsail. In her present state *Antigone* could neither outsail nor outfight the ship to leeward.

'Sending a boat, sir,' Quilhampton reported.

Drinkwater went below to inform Morris. He found the commander watching the newcomer from the larboard quarter gallery.

'A twenty-eight, eh? A post ship. D'you know who commands her?'

'No, sir.'

'I'll come up.'

The boat bobbed over the wave-crests between them. 'There's a midshipman in her, sir,' reported Mr Quilhampton, his eyes bright with excitement. It occurred to Drinkwater that Mr Q was suddenly proud of his lost hand. It was little enough compensation, he thought. 'Do you meet the young gentleman, Mr Q.'

The men were peering curiously at the approaching boat, those at the guns through the ports. 'Let 'em,' said Drinkwater to himself. They had earned a little tolerance.

His uniform awry Morris came on deck, holding out his hand for a glass. Lestock beat Dalziell in the matter. The midshipman swung himself over the side. There were catcalls from the lower gunports and Rogers's voice snapped 'Silence there!' The boat's crew were tricked out in blue and white striped shirts and trousers of white jean. They wore glazed hats with ribbons of blue and white and their oars were picked out in the same colours. Such a display amused the Hellebores and led Drinkwater to the conclusion that her captain was a wealthy man. An officer with interest of the 'Parliamentary' kind, probably young and probably half his own age. He was almost right.

Quilhampton approached the quarterdeck, saw Morris and diverted his approach from Drinkwater to the commander. 'Mr Mole, sir.'

The midshipman bowed. His tall gangling fair haired appearance was in marked contrast with his name. His accent was rural Norfolk, though mannered.

'My respect, sir, Commander Morris, I believe.' Morris stiffened.

'Captain to you, you damned brat. Who commands your vessel, eh?'

The lad was not abashed. 'Captain White, sir, Captain Richard White, he desires me to offer whatever services you require, though I perceive,' he swept his hand aloft, 'that you have little need of them. My congratulations.'

Drinkwater smiled grimly. The young gentleman's affront could only be but admired, particularly as he appeared impervious to Morris's forbidding aspect.

Morris's mouth fell open. He closed it and turned contemptuously away, crossing the deck towards the companionway. 'Mr Drinkwater, I expect the nob who commands yonder will want us to obey his orders. Tell this dog's turd what we want, then kick his perfumed arse off my ship.' He disappeared below.

'Aye, aye, sir.' Drinkwater regarded the midshipman. 'Well, Mr Mole, are you commonly addressing senior officers in that vein?'

The boy blinked and Drinkwater went on, 'Your captain; is that Richard White from Norfolk, a small man with fair hair?'

'Captain White is of small stature, sir,' Mole said primly.

'Very well, Mr Mole, I desire you to inform Captain White that we are short of men but able to make the Cape. We carry dispatches from Admiral Blankett and are armed *en flûte*. We are the prize of a brig and most damnably grateful for your arrival the other day.'

Mole smirked as though he had been personally responsible for the timely arrival of *Telemachus*.

'Oh, and Mr Mole, I desire that you inform him that the captain's name is Augustus Morris and my name is Drinkwater. I urge that you give him those particulars.'

Mole repeated the names. 'By the way, Mr Mole, what became of the Frenchman?'

'He slipped us in the night, sir.'

'Tut tut,' said Drinkwater catching Quilhampton's eye. 'That would never have happened to us, eh, Mr Q?'

'No, sir,' grinned Quilhampton.

'See what happened to Mr Quilhampton the last time we had an engagement . . .'

Quilhampton held up his stump. 'Mr Quilhampton stopped the enemy from running by taking hold of her bowsprit . . .' Laughter echoed round *Antigone*'s scarred quarterdeck and Mole, aware that the joke was on him, touched his forehead and fled.

'Boat ahoy!' Lestock hailed the returning boat.

'*Telemachus*!' That hail confirmed that she bore the frigate's captain.

'How d'you propose we man the side, Mr Drinkwater?' Lestock asked sarcastically. Drinkwater lowered his glass, having recognised the little figure in the stern.

'Oh, I'd say that you and Mr Dalziell will do for decoration, Mr Grey with his mates for sideboys. This ain't the time for punctiliousness. Mr Q!'

'Sir?'

'Inform the captain that Captain White is coming aboard.'

'Aye, aye, sir.' Drinkwater went forward to join the side party. Lestock was furious.

Grey's pipe twittered and Drinkwater swept his battered hat from his head.

'Strap me, but it *is* you!' Richard White, gold lace about his sleeve and upon his shoulder, held out his hand in informal greeting, 'Deuced glad to see you, Nat . . .' he looked round the deck expectantly. 'What's it that imp of Satan Mole said about . . .?' he paused and Drinkwater turned to see Morris emerging on deck.

'Well damn my eyes, if it isn't that bugger Morris!'

Chapter Twenty-Two   *November 1799–January 1800*

The Cape of Good Hope

Captain Richard White had many years earlier suffered from the sadistic bullying of Morris when he and Drinkwater served on the frigate *Cyclops* as midshipmen. Since that time, when the frightened White had been protected by Drinkwater, service under the punctilious St Vincent followed by absolute command of his own ship had turned White into an irascible, forthright character. Beneath this exterior his friends might perceive the boyish charm and occasional uncertainty of a still young man, but the accustomed authority that he was now used to, combined with an irresistible urge to thus publicly humiliate his former tormentor.

There was for a moment a silence between the three men that was pregnant with suppressed emotions. Drinkwater, caught like a shuttlecock between two seniors, prudently waited, watching Morris's reaction, aware that White had committed a gross impropriety. Unaccountably Drinkwater felt a momentary sympathy for Morris. If the commander called for satisfaction at the Cape he would have been justified, whatever the naval regulations said about duelling. For his own part White was belligerently unrepentant, weeks of adolescent misery springing into his mind as he confronted his old tormentor.

Morris stood stock still, colour draining from his face as the insult on his own quarterdeck outraged him. Brought up in the old school of naval viciousness, protected by petticoat influence from the consequences of his vice, his brutal nature protected by the privileges of rank for so long, Morris now found himself confronted by a moral superiority undeterred by the baser motives of naval intrigue. White's impetuous candour had disarmed him.

Morris shot White a look of pure venom, but his new-found

accession to command caused him to hold his tongue. He turned and made for the companionway below, half jostling Drinkwater as he did so, his mouth twisted with rage and humiliation.

White ignored Drinkwater's embarrassed glance after the retreating figure of Morris. 'Well, Nat, I'm darned sorry we lost the Frog, gave me the slip during the night. Blasted wind fell light under a threatening overcast. Black as the Earl of Hell's riding boots, by God. A damned shame.' He cast his eyes over *Antigone*'s spars and rigging. By comparison with when he had last seen them they had all the hallmarks of Drinkwater's diligence. 'You've been busy I perceive. But come, tell me what the deuce became of that brig I last saw you on, heard you'd been sent to the Red Sea. St Vincent was damned annoyed. I do believe if Nelson had not blown Brueys to hell at Aboukir he might have been called to account.' White grinned his boyish smile. 'I wrote to Elizabeth and told her. Didn't think you'd get word off until you reached the Cape . . .' Drinkwater tried to express his thanks but White rattled on, all the while pacing the deck and staring curiously about him. 'By the devil but you've a fine frigate here, and no mistake. Mole said you were *en flûte*.'

'Aye, sir. Twelve eighteens on the main deck.'

'And you fought the *Romaine* with a broadside of six, eh?'

'Not quite. We had 'em all mounted to starboard.' White's eyebrows went up and then came down with comprehension. 'So your larboard battery was empty?'

'Yes, sir.'

'Well stap me. You're becoming as unorthodox as Nelson. But we thought you'd struck.'

'Ensign halliards shot through,' Drinkwater said obscurely.

'Ahhh.' White gave Drinkwater a quizzical look. 'We had been looking for a French cruiser ever since *Jupiter* was mauled by *Preneuse* in October. We thought *Romaine* was the *Preneuse*, damn it.' He rubbed his hands. 'Still, we will see you to the Cape, eh? Table Bay for orders, you may tell Morris that. What d'you say to dinner on the *Telemachus*, eh?'

Drinkwater cast a rueful glance at the cabin skylight. 'I shall be honoured to accept, sir. And I am indebted to you for writing to Elizabeth. She was with child d'you see.'

White made a deprecating gesture with his hand, pregnant

women being outside his experience. He had caught the significance of Drinkwater's concern for the smouldering Morris beneath them. 'Haven't made it too hard for you, have I? Between you and Morris, I mean?'

'It couldn't be much worse, sir.'

White cocked a shrewd eye at Drinkwater. 'Had you struck?' 'I hadn't sir.' Drinkwater returned the stare and emphasised the personal pronoun.

'I'll see you at the Cape, Nat.' Drinkwater watched White's gig pull smartly away. The Cape of Good Hope was still a thousand miles distant and seamen called it the Cape of Storms. It had been that on the outward voyage, he hoped it might live up to its other name on the homeward. Drinkwater put his hat on.

'Brace her sharp up, Mr Lestock. A course of south-west if she'll take it.'

He went below to confront Morris.

The commander sat bolt upright in his chair, his hands gripping the arms. He was paralysed by the judicial implications of White's remark and fear of the noose warred with a sense of outrage at being humiliated on his own quarterdeck. The timid White had become a choleric, devil-may-care captain, a coming man and recognisably dangerous to Morris's low cunning.

Drinkwater had the distinct impression that Morris would spring at his throat even while he sat rigid with shock. Perhaps Nathaniel saw in his mind's eye the intent of Morris's spirit.

'I am sorry for Captain White's remark sir, I was not a party to . . .'

'God damn you, Drinkwater! God damn you to hell!' Morris spat the words from between clenched teeth, but so great was his fury as it burst through his self-restraint that his words became an incomprehensible torrent of filth and invective.

Drinkwater spun on his heel. Later Rattray came in search of Dalziell.

Two weeks passed during which Morris made no appearance on deck. Appleby paid him daily visits, announcing that though there was some improvement in his condition it was not as rapid as he himself had hoped. He did not amplify the remark but it was made with a significant gravity that was not lost on Drinkwater.

They were not to come to the shelter of Table Bay without leave of the sea. *Antigone* carried the favourable current round the southern tip of Africa ignorant of the fact that somewhere off the Agulhas Bank, where the continental shelf declines into the depths of the Southern Ocean, a combination of the prevailing westerlies opposing the force of the current produces some of the most monstrous seas encountered by man.

As the frigate beat laboriously to windward, her small crew wet through, tired and hungry, the westerly gales blew furiously. Even the bad jokes about the southern summer faded, giving way to hissed oaths as men struggled to haul the third earings out to the topsail yardarms.

In the screaming madness of an early morning Lieutenant Drinkwater clung onto a mizen backstay. The decks were shiny with water, pools of it still running out through the lee ports from the last inundation. Every rope ran with water, the sails were stiff with it. To windward *Telemachus* butted into the seas.

Amidships he heard a cry and saw the seaman's pointing arm.

'Oh, my God,' whispered Drinkwater, his voice filled with awe. He reached for the speaking trumpet: 'Hold fast! Hold fast there !'

At the cry Mr Quilhampton looked up from the coil of log line in its basket. His gaze fell stupidly on his left arm. He had a hook there now, cunningly fashioned from a cannon worm by Mr Trussel. He flung himself down behind the aftermost carronade slide and hooked its point round a slewing eye, throwing a bight of the train tackle round his waist and catching a turn on the gun's cascabel. It was his very vulnerability that saved him.

At the main deck companionway Dalziell emerged on deck unbidden, dismissed by Morris in the dawn. The wave was three-quarters of a mile away when they had seen it, looming huge over the crests before it, a combination of forces far beyond the imagination. Its crest was reaching that critical state of instability that would induce its collapse in a rolling avalanche of water.

The frigate fell into the trough and her sails cracked from loss of wind. Even in the depths of her hull, where Appleby was doing his morning rounds this momentary hiatus was felt. Then the mass of solid water thundered over the ship.

Drinkwater was mashed to his knees and swept along the deck

613

like flotsam. He was washed beneath a gun, the air squeezed from his lungs as his mind filled with a red and roaring struggle for breath. Mr Quilhampton too, lay gasping as the seemingly endless mass of water poured green across the deck. Forward a tremble and a shudder told where the frigate's long jib-boom detached itself from the bowsprit. A body bumped past Drinkwater and then *Antigone* began to rise, the water sluicing from her decks. The succeeding waves were much lower, giving men time to catch their breath. They staggered to their feet, stumbling among the shot, dislodged from the garlands and rolling menacingly from side to side, ready to trip or cripple the unwary.

Drinkwater coughed the last of the sea water from him and helped Mr Quilhampton to his feet. 'Get below, see Merrick for a flask of rum!' He raised his voice.

'Quartermaster! Up helm! East the ship before the wind.' He picked up the speaking trumpet rolling fortuitously past him across a deck that was still inches deep in water. 'Mr Grey! Have your men at the braces! Rise foretacks and sheets, get the ship before the wind! Have Johnson sound the well!'

Already the ship was turning, gathering way from her broached position, supine in the huge wave troughs and rolling abominably, sluggish from the water washing about below.

'Spanker brails there! Douse the spanker, Mr Q!' He grabbed the flask from the midshipman and drew on its contents.

He looked forward as the spirit warmed him. They might have lost the jib-boom but they could still set a fore topmast staysail. He would get everything off her in a minute, leaving only the clews of the forecourse to goosewing her before the wind while they sorted out the shambles and pumped her dry. They must not run off too much easting for they would have to claw every inch back again.

Slowly they fought the ship before the wind, cutting away the raffle forward, unjamming the blocks aloft where parted ropes had fouled, and laboriously pumping the Southern Ocean from their bilges. It was four hours before they brought ship to the wind again. *Telemachus* had disappeared.

It was only then they found Dalziell was missing.

'Permission to make the signal, sir?' Drinkwater requested. Morris did not turn, merely nodded. Drinkwater looked up at the peak of the gaff. Old Glory, the British red ensign they had salvaged from *Hellebore* and that had fluttered briefly over a tiny islet in the Red Sea, now cracked, tattered, in the sharp breeze blowing into Table Bay. Beneath it flew the much larger ensign of France, its brilliant scarlet fly snapping viciously, as though resenting its inferior position.

'Hoist away, Mr Q.' The little bundles rose to break out in the sunshine and stream colourfully to leeward. Mr Quilhampton looked aloft with evident pride.

'Beg pardon, zur,' said Tregembo belaying the halliards, 'but what do it say?'

'It says, Tregembo,' explained Quilhampton expansively 'that this ship is the prize of the brig-sloop *Hellebore*.'

Not one of the most memorable of signals, Drinkwater concluded, levelling his glass at the fifty-gun two-decker *Jupiter* with a broad pendant at her masthead. But given the limitations of the code an apt description of *Antigone*. He wished it was old Griffiths who occupied the weather side of her quarterdeck.

Morris turned, as if aware of Drinkwater's thoughts. There was a calmness about the commander that had come with returning health. It pleased Appleby but worried Drinkwater. There was a triumph in those hooded eyes.

'Have the ship brought to the wind, Mr Lestock,' ordered Morris. There was a new authority about Morris too, a confidence which disturbed Drinkwater. The sailing master obeyed the order with obsequious alacrity. Morris had exploited the dislike between his master and first lieutenant to make Lestock a creature of his own. Lestock now wore a permanently prim expression, anticipating Drinkwater's imminent downfall. It occurred to Drinkwater as he observed this new and unholy alliance that Dalziell had gone unmourned.

Drinkwater touched the letter in his pocket. If he could have it delivered to White all might yet be set right, provided it did not fall into the wrong hands or was misconstrued. That thought set doubts whirling in his brain and to steady himself he raised his glass again.

Antigone was turning into the wind, her sails backing. At an order from the quarterdeck Johnson let the anchor go. The splash was followed by the rumble of the cable snaking up from the tiers.

'Topsail halliards!'

'Aloft and stow! Aloft and stow!'

'Commence the salute, Mr Rogers!'

Drinkwater could see six vessels in the anchorage. Three flew the blue pendant of the Transport Board and partially obscured what appeared to be two frigates and a sloop. He stared hard, satisfying himself that one of the frigates was *Telemachus*. White had beaten them to the Cape after their separation in the gale. He felt a sensation of relief at the sight of the distant frigate.

'Hoist the boat out.' Morris addressed the perfunctory order to Drinkwater who ignored the implied discourtesy. They had repaired a single boat for use at the Cape and Drinkwater watched it swung up from the waist and over the side by the yardarm tackles. The crew tumbled down into it. A sight of the land had cheered the hands at least, he mused, wondering if he dared dispatch the letter in the boat.

He decided against it and joined the side party waiting to see Commander Morris ashore. He knew Morris would keep them all waiting. Rogers joined him, having secured his signal guns.

'I suppose we must wait for that dropsical pig like a pair of whores at a wedding, eh?' Rogers muttered into Drinkwater's ear. Drinkwater found himself oddly sympathetic to Rogers's crude wit. From a positive dislike of each other the two men had formed a mutual respect, acknowledging their individual virtues. In the difficulties they had shared since the loss of the brig and assumption of command by Morris this had ripened to friendship. Drinkwater grinned his agreement.

Morris emerged at last in full dress. He paused in front of Drinkwater, swaying slightly, the stink of rum on his breath.

'And now,' said Morris with quiet purpose, 'we will see about you.'

As he stared into Morris's eyes Drinkwater understood. The death of Dalziell removed substantial evidence of any possible case against Morris. Dalziell was a used vessel, the breaking of which liberated Morris from his past. The action which *Antigone* had fought with *Romaine* had been creditable and, as commander, Morris would benefit from that credit. A feeling almost of reform animated Morris, consonant with his new opportunities and encouraged by his reinvigoration after his illness. The huge irony that Morris had obtained his step in rank thanks to Drinkwater's efforts was enlarged by the reflection that he might yet found a professional reputation based on his lieutenant's handling of the *Antigone* during the action with the *Romaine*. All these facts were suddenly clear to Nathaniel as he returned Morris's drunken stare.

He took his hat off as Morris turned to the rail. Another thought struck him. To succeed in his manipulation of events Morris must now utterly discredit Drinkwater. And Nathaniel had no doubt that was what he was about to do.

The problem of conveying the letter to *Telemachus* solved itself an hour later when Drinkwater renewed his acquaintance with Mr Mole. Drinkwater had viewed the approaching boat with some misgivings but was relieved when Mole's mission was revealed to be the bearing of an invitation to the promised dinner aboard White's frigate.

'Would you oblige me, Mr Mole,' Drinkwater had said after accepting the kindness and privately hoping he was still at liberty to enjoy it, 'by delivering this note to Captain White when you return to your ship. It is somewhat urgent.'

'Captain White attends the commodore aboard *Jupiter*, sir.'

Drinkwater thought for a second. 'Be so kind to see he receives it there, Mr Mole, if you please.' The departure of Mr Mole sent Drinkwater into an anxious pacing during which Appleby tried to interrupt him. But Appleby was snubbed. Drinkwater knew of the surgeon's apprehensions, knew he was worried about the possible discovery of Catherine Best's activities and guessed that the future of Harry Appleby himself figured largely in those fears. But Drinkwater's anxiety excluded the worries of others. That pendant at the masthead of *Jupiter* meant the formal and sometimes summary justice of naval regulation. The Cape might be an outpost, a salient held in the Crown's fist at the tip of Africa but it was within the boundaries of Admiralty. Nathaniel shivered.

When nemesis appeared a little later it was in the person of a midshipman even more supercilious than Mr Mole. Mr Pierce was conducted to Drinkwater by Quilhampton.

'The commodore, desires, sah, that you be so kind as to accompany me to the *Jupiter* without unnecessary delay, sah,' he drawled. Pierce's manner was so exaggerated that it struck Drinkwater that all these spriggish midshipmen must see him as an old tarpaulin lieutenant, every hair a rope-yarn, every finger a marline spike. The thought steadied him, sent him below for his sword with something approaching dignity. When he emerged in his best coat, now threadbare and shiny, the battered French hanger at his side and his hat fresh glazed with some preparation concocted by Merrick from God knew what, only the violent beating of his heart betrayed him.

'Very well, Mr Pierce, let us be off.'

Watching from forward Tregembo muttered his 'good luck', aware that his own future was allied to Drinkwater's. Further aft Mr Quilhampton saw him go. The midshipman had watched the furious pacing of the last hour, knew the *Antigone*'s open secret and shared his shipmates' hatred of their commander. He had also once taken a most ungentlemanly look at Mr Drinkwater's journals. He too muttered his good wishes which mingled with a quixotic vision of shooting Morris dead in a duel if anything happened to Mr Drinkwater.

Captain George Losack, commodore of the naval forces then at the Cape, leaned back in his chair and looked up at Captain White. The cabin of *Jupiter* had an air of relief in it, as though something unpleasant had just occurred and both men wished to re-establish normality as quickly as possible; to divert their minds from contemplating the recently vacated chair and the papers surrounding it. Commander Morris's hat still lay on the side table where he had laid it earlier.

'Well, by God, what d'you make of that?'

'He did not want me here, sir,' replied White, 'it was clear he considered I prejudiced his case.'

'Because you are an acquaintance of this fellow Drinkwater?'

'That sir, and the fact that the baser side of his nature is known to me . . .'

Losack looked up sharply. 'Be advised and drop that, Richard. A court-martial under that Article would be politically risky for us both. Though Jemmy Twitcher no longer rules the Admiralty and addresses blasphemous sermons to a congregation of cats he is still powerful. To antagonise the brother of his lordship's mistress would not only move the earl's malice it might invite the enmity of his whore.'

White shut his mouth. He did not subscribe to the older man's fear of the Earl of Sandwich. Petticoat interference in the affairs of the navy had affected men of his generation deeply. The disasters of the American War could in part be attributed to this form of malign influence. 'Nevertheless,' he said, 'Morris terrorised the cockpit and lower deck of the *Cyclops* in the last war. Sometimes a man is called to account for that.'

'Rarely,' replied Losack drily, ringing the bell on his deck 'though 'tis a fine, pious thought.' His man appeared. 'Wine, Jacklin, directly if you please.'

White watched Losack as the commodore once again scanned the papers before him. The allegations that Morris had made against Drinkwater looked serious for the lieutenant. But the circumstances that had followed White's own questions had thrown a doubt over the whole and Losack was too diligent an officer to take refuge in his isolation from London and dismiss the affair. And the matter of Morris's influence could not be ignored. It behove Losack to tread carefully. He had seen something of one party. What of the other?

'You say Drinkwater had a commission years ago?'

'He had a commission as acting lieutenant back in eighty-one. He passed over Morris.'

'Ah. Then Morris was appointed over him at Mocha, eh? The first action turns his head, the second overturns his senses. The consequence is bad blood . . .' Losack paused as the wine arrived. Jacklin placed the salver and decanters. He turned to White.

'Mr Mole's compliments sir, and I was to give you this at once.' White took the letter Losack went on: 'There would be a case to answer if I was sure . . .' he stopped indecisively, worried about Morris's wild allegations.

'I do not think Drinkwater was greatly disappointed in eighty-one, sir. His commission dates from ninety-seven . . .'

'Well what manner of man is he, White?' snapped Losack exasperated. 'You seem damned eager to befriend him.'

'Damn it, sir,' said White flushing with anger, "tis a devilish difficult business serving under a . . . a . . .' he recovered himself. 'Drinkwater, sir, is a thoroughly professional officer. He commands little or no influence. I doubt he gave Morris grounds for his allegations beyond an excess of zeal and surely it has not come to an officer suffering for that?'

Losack stood and turned to stare through the cabin windows, his hands clasped behind his back. He found his command at the Cape a tiresome business. His force was inadequate to police the converging trade routes that made this post so important and such a rich hunting ground for French corsairs. The parochial problems of passing ships were a confounded nuisance. The present one was no exception; bad feeling between the officers of a prize, a woman convict mixed up in some unholy cabal. He felt irritated by the demands of his rank, envying White who sat on the table edge, his leg swinging while he read the letter Jacklin had brought in.

'It was the remark you made about the striking of the flag that caused our late visitor to fly into a passion. What was behind that, eh?'

White looked up from the letter. 'May I suggest you ask Drinkwater, sir. I have here a letter from him. It would appear that at Mocha some error was committed. Morris's commission should have gone to him!'

'Good God!' Losack looked up sharply. 'An excess of zeal, d'you say? By God, it looks to me more like bloody-minded madness! "Quos deus vult perdere, prius dementat".'

'I do not think for a moment that he is mad, sir. Overwrought, perhaps. Angry even. As Horace has it, "Ira furor brevis est".'

'Hmmm. Let us send for this friend of yours.'

Appleby too had been summoned. He sat on a bench in the bare anteroom of the hospital and looked down at the chequered Dutch floor tiles. Despite the cool of the room he was sweating profusely, his mind a confusion of counteracting thoughts in which his professional detachment was knocked all awry by the depth of his feeling for Catherine Best. 'They have sent for me,' he had told her shakily. 'I am too old to dissemble, Catherine, I am fearful there may be consequences . . .'

She had been silent, having said all she had to say days before.

Now her opportunist nature waited upon events. She was not a maker of circumstances, simply a manipulator of their outcome. But she kissed him as he left, puffing up the ladders, fat, ungainly, ageing and kind. Now he sweated like a man under sentence .

'You seem to be suffering from diaphoresis yourself, Mr Appleby,' said the physician, surprising him. Appleby rose to his feet. 'Shall we take a turn in the garden, my dear sir?'

Mr Macphadden was a dry, bent little Scot who exuded an air of erudition; the garden was a cloistered square of trimmed lawn suitable for the exchange of medical confidences. 'From the message that ran ahead of the patient I fully expected to find I had a derangement on my hands. Indeed I had effected the precaution of preparing a jacket for the fellow. But I was misinformed. The ravings were no more than those of a drunk far gone in his cups and overcome by an exaggeration of the choleric humour, so my anticipation was a little out of kilter with the facts.' The doctor chuckled wheezily to himself while Appleby held his breath. 'The effects of rum are well-known. I don't doubt but that you know Haslar is full of men for whom rum has been a consolation, men for whom responsibility is too great, whose expectations have been disappointed, whose abilities are inadequate. Why the chemical effect of rum upon the brain itself . . .'

'But his sickness, doctor. The diaphoresis, the purging and vomiting . . .' Appleby could restrain himself no longer, though he checked himself sufficiently to adopt a tone of deference, not daring to suggest a diagnosis lest such presumption invited contradiction.

'Oh, you are worried about his wild allegations about being poisoned, eh? Well he is, in a manner of speaking, but I think we may consider that he is effecting his own ruin. No, he has chronic gastric inflammation, undoubtedly due to a peptic ulcer of some inveteracy. You see, my dear sir, his temperament seems to vacillate between the choleric and the melancholic humours. The man who depends upon drink hides both an acknowledged weakness and an inability to accept his own culpability for self-destruction. The consequence of such a vicious spiral can have but one result. That of the unhappy man now lying in his bed yonder.'

Macphadden turned and they began pacing back to the white walled hospital. A flood of relief began to wash over Appleby and he nodded at the physician's words: 'I doubt you will want a commanding officer in the throes of a delirium tremens.'

Drinkwater returned to *Antigone* after the frustrations of an hour-long interview with Losack. It was clear from the manner of the commodore's questions that the contents of his letter to White had been made known. A sense of betrayal that the information had been made available to Losack was heightened by White's silence during Drinkwater's ordeal. The letter had been a private document between friends. Now it seemed a court-martial might be pending against him.

The knock at his cabin door announced the arrival of Appleby for whom he had sent as soon as the surgeon arrived from the shore.

'Things have turned out well, Nat. A didactic Scot named Macphadden has diagnosed gastritis . . .'

'Things are *not* well, Harry . . .'

'What the devil is it?'

'Catherine, Harry. She is known to be a convict. She is to be transported. I did my best,' he paused at the unintended pun, 'my uttermost, but Morris has revealed her real status to Losack.'

The colour drained from Appleby's face. 'Why the uncharitable whoreson bastard!'

'Calm yourself. There is nothing either of us can do here. Perhaps when we reach home . . .' It was a straw held out to a drowning man. It was doubtful if he would reach home with a reputation untarnished enough to secure a convict's pardon, no matter how meritorious her services.

'But Nat, I cannot let her go.'

'She is to take passage in the *Lord Moira* without delay. I am so very sorry.'

In silence Appleby left the cabin. Opening his desk Drinkwater took out inkwell and pen and began to write the report Losack had requested.

Drinkwater sat in silence while Losack read his report, occasionally referring to the corroborative evidence of the deck and signal logs and what remained of Griffiths's papers. At last the commodore looked up and removed his spectacles. For a moment he regarded the man sitting anxiously before him.

'Mr Drinkwater,' he said after this pause, 'it seems that I have been unnecessarily suspicious of you.' He waved the spectacles over the books and papers spread out upon the table. 'I am persuaded that your services merit some recognition, but you will understand it is a difficult matter to resolve. I am not empowered to restitute your commission and it may be some consolation to you that in any event it would have required their Lordships' ratification. There the matter must rest.'

Drinkwater inclined his head. 'I understand, sir.'

Losack smiled. 'The only reparation I can offer you is command of the prize home. Do you attend to her refit. A convoy sails in some three weeks. You should be ready to join it. Your devoted friend Captain White will command the escort.'

'Thank you, sir. And Commander Morris?'

'Is sick, Mr Drinkwater. A peptic ulcer, I understand.' Losack closed the subject.

Drinkwater rose and Losack tossed a bundle across the table. 'My secretary recognised your name, this letter has been here for months waiting for you.'

With a beating heart he picked up Elizabeth's letter.

The air of the quarterdeck of the *Jupiter* was undeniably sweet and in an unoccupied corner he tore open the packet, catching the enclosure for Quilhampton and stuffing it in his pocket. Impatiently he began to read.

My Dearest Nathaniel,

At long last I have received news of you, that you were sent round Africa in accordance with some notion of Ad. Nelson's. I write in great anxiety about you and pray nightly for your well-being and that, if God wills it, you will return whole and safe.

But you will not wish to hear of me now that another claims your affections, my dearest. Your daughter Charlotte Amelia is past a twelve-month now and has her father's nose poor lamb . . .'

Drinkwater handed the letter with the thin feminine superscription to Quilhampton. 'Pass word for Tregembo, Mr Q.' When the boy had gone he peered into the mirror let into the lid of his cabin chest. What the devil was the matter with his nose?

Tregembo coughed respectfully at the open door and Drinkwater started, aware that for several minutes he had been staring vacantly at his reflection contemplating his new role as a father.

'Ah, Tregembo. Your Susan is quite well. Mrs Drinkwater writes to tell me the news. She had a little quinsy some months past but was in good spirits. The letter is some months old I am afraid.'

'An' your baby, zur?'

'A daughter, Tregembo.'

'Ahhh.' The awkward, almost embarrassed monosyllable was full of hidden pleasure. Tregembo flushed and Drinkwater swallowed. 'And the commission, zur?'

'No commission, not yet.'

''Tis nought but a matter of time, zur.'

Drinkwater smiled as Tregembo resumed his duties. It occurred to him that he was smiling a lot this morning. He turned again to the letter and re-read it.

Appleby burst in upon him. 'Nat, a word, do I hear correctly that you command the ship home?'

Drinkwater looked up. The surgeon was agitated, his hands fluttering, his jowls wobbling. 'Yes I do.'

'Then I beg you will permit me to leave the ship.'

'What the devil d'you mean?'

'The *Lord Moira* has a vacancy for a surgeon's assistant. I have made enquiries, there are precious few surgeons in the colony . . . I have taken the vacancy for the passage.' Appleby swallowed hard. He had crossed his Rubicon.

'Harry, you sly dog, do you purpose to become an emigrant?'

Appleby ran a finger round his collar. 'She'd hardly be fit company for me at Bath, would she?'

Drinkwater began to laugh but was interrupted by Appleby. 'Come Nat, I pray your attention for a moment, I have little time. Here are some papers giving you powers to act on my behalf in the matter of prize money. I beg you consent and purchase for me the quantities of medicines here listed. Any apothecary will comprehend these zodiacal signs. I am also in need of a few instruments, doubtless I will need become a man-midwife and I am without forceps . . .'

Drinkwater nodded at Appleby's instructions, taking the bundle of papers, thinking of Catherine Best, of Elizabeth and of Charlotte Amelia and the power of the hand that rocks the cradle.

Drinkwater returned the decanter to White and leaned forward to light the cheroot from the candle flame. 'I think now that the others have left we might forget the divisions of rank, eh?' White chuckled. 'Young Quilhampton is something of an imp of Satan, is he not? Did you hear his assertion that young Bruilhac considers you eat human limbs? No, don't protest, my dear fellow, I heard quite clearly.'

'Mr Quilhampton is given to exaggeration, I regret to say,' said Drinkwater with some affection. Then he frowned. 'There's something I want to ask you Richard. Something I don't understand. What exactly happened the other day when Morris reported to Losack? You *were* there, were you not?'

White puffed out his florid cheeks. 'Yes, I was there and my presence seemed to infuriate Morris. I suppose he thought I was going to mention his unpleasant habits. He began to complain about you. Minor matters; the way you did not always refer to him when shortening sail, you know the sort of thing. He kept looking at me as if I might contradict him. I could smell rum on his breath and could see he was enunciating his words with care. He began some cock and bull allegations that you were poisoning him. I didn't like the sound of that! I could tell Losack was taking an interest and I asked Morris why he struck to the *Romaine*.' White laughed.

'By heaven, that threw him flat aback! He looked at me with his jaw hanging like a scandalised gaff. Then he began a stream of meaningless abuse, interspersed with occasional reference to you and poison. He was beside himself and in the middle of this outburst he had what I took at first to be a fit. In fact I understand it to have been a gastric spasm.'

White paused, refilled his glass and continued. 'Although it was obvious that Morris was ill, or drunk, or both, Losack fretted over the allegations of poisoning. I'm certain he had it in mind to put the matter to a court-martial, he had sufficient ships here to convene one. While I thought Morris had gone off his head he thought you were mad.'

'Me?'

'Aye, you. I showed him the letter in which you claimed the commission granted Morris had been intended for you.'

'Oh, my God . . . I thought you had. But that was a private letter, Richard, I had no idea . . .'

'I know, I know, my dear fellow, but it did the trick. Losack wanted to see you, and once he had the doctor's diagnosis and had studied your report he knew the truth as well as I did. But for a while I thought he would have you examined! He quoted Euripides at me. Er, "Whom God destroys he first makes mad".'

'That might more readily be applied to Morris.'

'To which,' White pressed on, not to be deterred, 'I managed to reply with a snippet of Horace, to wit *"Ira furor brevis est"*.'

'I'm sorry, you have the advantage of me.'

'"Anger is a brief madness".'

'Ahhh.' Drinkwater leaned back in his chair. He had had a narrow escape from a dangerous vindictiveness. 'I am greatly indebted to you, Richard.'

White waved his thanks aside. 'I owed you for your support on the *Cyclops* against the unsavoury rakehell.'

'Well the score is even now,' said Drinkwater. 'I suppose I had better see Morris. Try to make my peace with him before we leave.'

White looked at him sharply. 'See Morris? What the devil for? Let the bastard rot.'

'But he is ill, Richard . . .'

'Strap me, Nat, you are a soft-hearted fool. But 'tis why we love you, Bruilhac's limbs notwithstanding. Besides, Morris would not thank you for it. He would misconstrue your motives, assume you had come to gloat. There is no point in seeing Morris. Ever again.' The remark seemed final and White tossed off his glass. Refilling it, he too eased back in his chair. The cabin filled with a companionable silence, broken only by the creak of the hull, the groaning of the rudder chains and the occasional muffled noise from the people forward. Drinkwater felt a massive weight lift from him. White's explanation had cleared the air of lingering doubts, images of Elizabeth and the yet unseen Charlotte Amelia floated in the blue cheroot smoke. He felt a great contentment spread through him.

'I recollect another piece of Horace that is perhaps more apposite to the case,' said White at last. '"*Caelum non animum mutant qui trans mare currunt*". Which rendered into English is, "They change their skies but not their souls who run across the sea".'

And looking across the table at his flushed friend Drinkwater nodded his agreement.

BENEATH THE AURORA

Richard Woodman

'This author has quietly stolen the weather-gauge from
most of his rivals in the Hornblower stakes'
Observer

The year 1813. As the Grand Army of Napoleon faces
defeat on the battlefields of Germany, Captain Nathaniel
Drinkwater succeeds Lord Dungarth as head of the Royal
Navy's Secret Department. Before long he is caught up in
a vast intrigue which leads him into the most desperate
mission of his career among the forbidding fiords of
Norway. In a compelling narrative the author links the fate
of one of Napoleon's most charismatic marshals with
American privateers, escaped prisoners, the Danish navy
and a violent confrontation set beneath the aurora.

'Packed with exciting incident, worthy of wide appeal to
those who love thrilling nautical encounters and the sea'
Nautical Magazine

THE SHADOW OF
THE EAGLE

Richard Woodman

'This author has quietly stolen the weather-gauge from
most of his rivals in the Hornblower stakes'
Observer

It is 1814. Napoleon has abdicated and the 'Great War' is
at an end. As King Louis XVIII is escorted back to France
by an Allied squadron, and Europe prepares to celebrate
the return of legitimate monarchy, tensions remain. The
Tsar of Russia has grand designs of his own, while, from
the ashes of defeat, Bonapartists plot to restore the eagle
whose shadow still lies across the continent. Attending
King Louis, Captain Nathaniel Drinkwater receives secret
intelligence of an imminent threat to peace, and seizing an
opportunity only he can exploit, risks his life and
reputation to prevent disaster befalling his country . . .

'Packed with exciting incident, worthy of wide appeal to
those who love thrilling nautical encounters and the sea'
Nautical Magazine

EBB TIDE

Richard Woodman

'This author has quietly stolen the weather-gauge from most of his rivals in the Hornblower stakes'
Observer

It is 1843, and Captain Sir Nathaniel Drinkwater embarks on the paddle-steamer *Vestal* for an inspection of lighthouses on the west coast of England. Bowed with age and honours, the old sea-officer has been drawn out of retirement on half-pay to fulfil his public duty. The following day, however, tragedy strikes, and Drinkwater, the punctilious seaman and sympathetic libertarian, is suddenly confronted with the spectre of his past life: the sins and follies, valour and heroics, triumphs and disasters.

'Packed with exciting incident, worthy of wide appeal to those who love thrilling nautical encounters and the sea'
Nautical Magazine

WATERFRONT

Richard Woodman

Brought up amid the twin certainties of church and state in Edwardian Britain, young James Dunbar goes to sea in search of romantic adventure. Even when he falls in love with a waterfront prostitute named Conchita, he continues to believe that the purity of his emotion can rescue her from the Hotel Paradiso, the notorious brothel of Puerto San Martin.

But Puerto San Martin is a place of commercial trafficking and commerce – and no place for the innocent or the romantic. What Dunbar learns about his shipmates and the local inhabitants has a profound effect upon him. His meeting with the mysteriously veiled owner of the Hotel Paradiso reveals an event of terrifying brutality and makes him the agent of retribution; his encounter with the brothel's Madame confronts him with the demands of his own lust and these events not only alter his perception of life, but lead him to discover in himself a powerful artistic talent.

'It is the human angle that Richard Woodman conveys so well, but he also makes a considerable contribution to marine history'
Lloyds List

Time Warner Paperback titles available by post:

☐	A Private Revenge	Richard Woodman	£5.99
☐	Under False Colours	Richard Woodman	£5.99
☐	The Flying Squadron	Richard Woodman	£5.99
☐	Beneath The Aurora	Richard Woodman	£6.99
☐	The Shadow of the Eagle	Richard Woodman	£5.99
☐	Ebb Tide	Richard Woodman	£6.99
☐	Waterfront	Richard Woodman	£6.99

The prices shown above are correct at time of going to press. However, the publishers reserve the right to increase prices on covers from those previously advertised without prior notice.

TIME WARNER PAPERBACKS
P.O. Box 121, Kettering, Northants NN14 4ZQ
Tel: 01832 737525, Fax: 01832 733076
Email: aspenhouse@FSBDial.co.uk

POST AND PACKING:
Payments can be made as follows: cheque, postal order (payable to Time Warner Books) or by credit cards. Do not send cash or currency.

All U.K. Orders	**FREE OF CHARGE**
E.E.C. & Overseas	25% of order value

Name (Block Letters) _____

Address_____

_____

Post/zip code:_____

☐ Please keep me in touch with future Time Warner publications

☐ I enclose my remittance £_____

☐ I wish to pay by Visa/Access/Mastercard/Eurocard

Card Expiry Date

_____